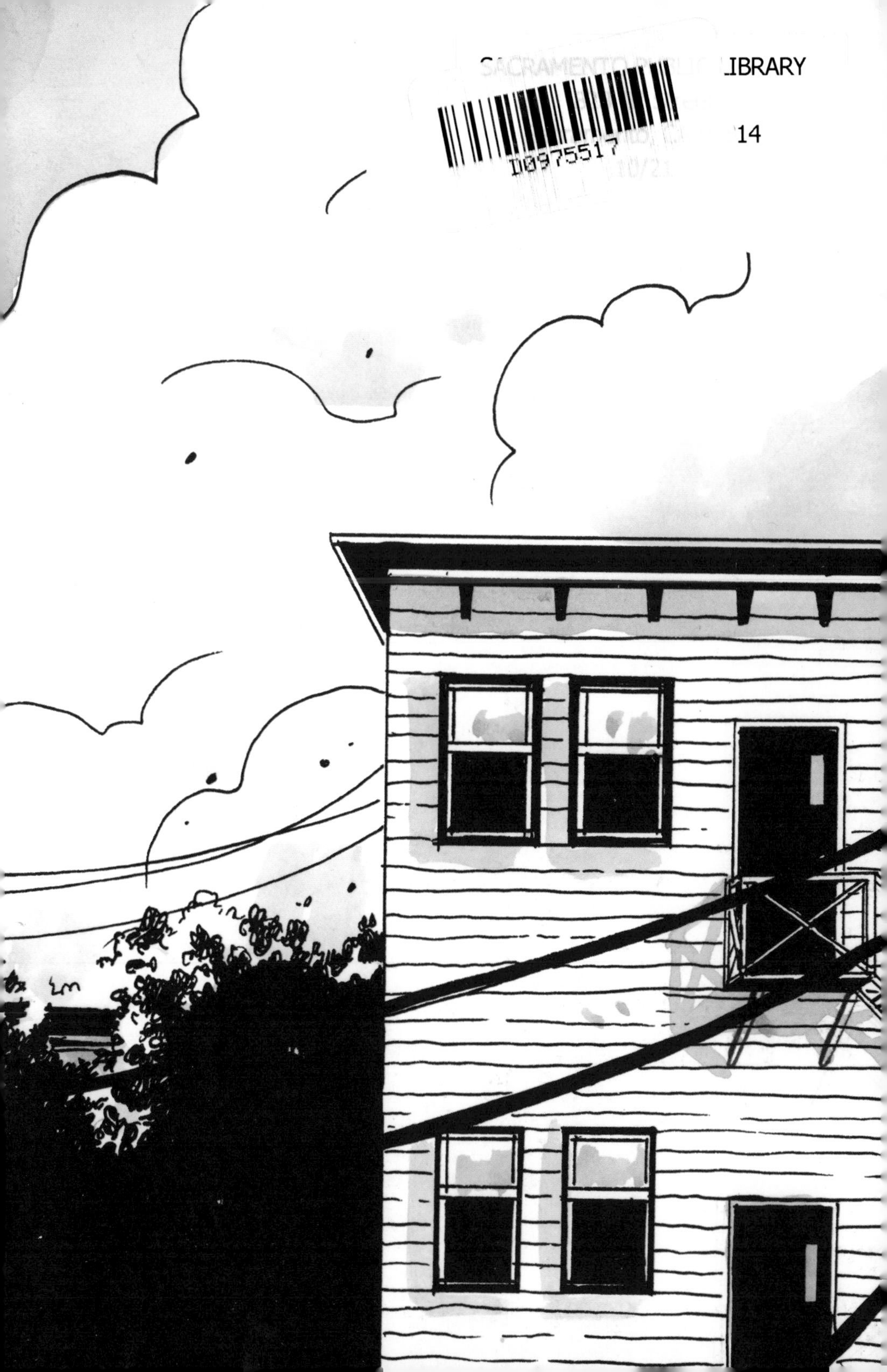

Published by Avery Hill Publishing, 2021

10 9 8 7 6 5 4 3 2 1

First published in the UK in 2021 by Avery Hill Publishing
Unit 8
5 Durham Yard
London
E2 6QF
Printed in Malta

A CIP record for this book is available from the British Library

ISBN: 978-1-910395-58-5

This book is for Ricky Miller, who started my career by noticing a
retweet of one of my silly high school drawings and sending me an email.
Cheers to all the years we've had together, Ricky, and all the years to come.

Tillie Walden
www.tilliewalden.com

Avery Hill Publishing
www.averyhillpublishing.com

ALONE IN SPACE

a collection

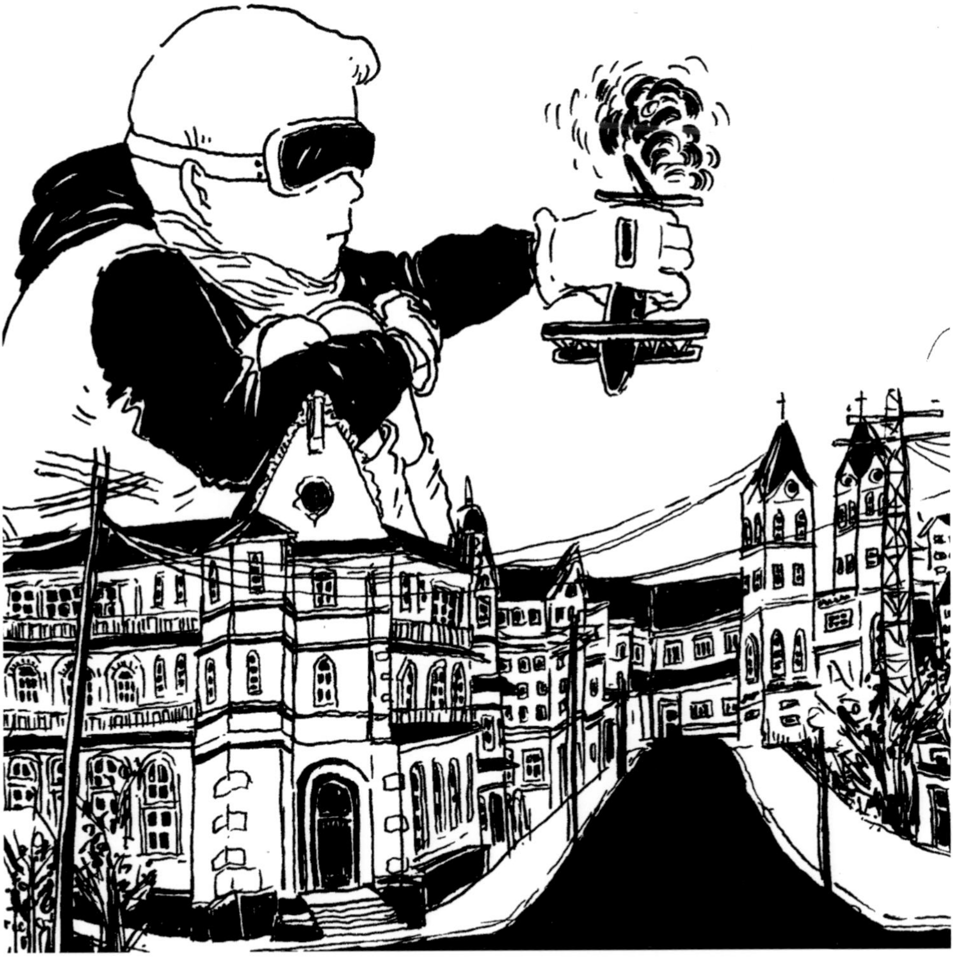

CONTENTS

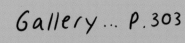

Introduction by Warren Bernard

Go grab your fav reading beverage, find that special place where you like to relax and get ready for a journey through the amazing, talented mind of Tillie Walden.

Let us cast aside her talents in music (she plays the cello), athletics (she is a great ice skater) and dance (she competed in synchronized ice skating). As *Alone in Space* is a compendium of her early works, let us delve into a very specific area of Tillie's synapses and neurons to look at her prodigious talents in the visual world of comics.

At the tender age of six or so, Tillie's very cool Dad would give her manga and other comics to spur her interest. One of the books was a collection of *Little Nemo in Slumberland* Sunday pages by the famous cartoonist Winsor McCay that were published from 1905-1912. The books were big enough that she sat on the book as she read them, allowing her to absorb all of McCay's fantastic visualizations. She once said about McCay's comics:

"I think I knew from that very young age that space and geography and people and relationships could all be played with, there was nothing that had to exist exactly like reality."

When you read *I Love This Part*, you will see that Tillie had indeed totally absorbed The Winsor McCay School of Art, placing the story within her soaring McCay-sian influenced fantasy perspectives and architectural details. Showing the strength of her amazing visual memory, when she wrote and drew *I Love This Part*, she had not looked at Winsor McCay's work since she sat on those books when she was six. Though maybe, just maybe, she most probably did look back at least once, as her short comic, *Slumberland*, is laid out exactly like the Little Nemo strip from December 5, 1905, bibliographically speaking.

Tillie's amazing memory coupled with her innate synthesis of experience strikes again in *The End of Summer*. That very first panel you see is actually Tillie's remembrance from a trip with her school orchestra to Washington, D.C. Tillie became separated from her troupe (and yes, got very lost) because she was gazing intently at the walls and ceilings of The Great Hall in the Jefferson Building at the Library of Congress, one of the great Beaux Arts architectural masterpieces in the world. This memory sat in her brain until she fused it and her childhood memory of McCay's fantasies as the basis for the soaring home in the story.

By the way, it is no coincidence that the cat's name is Nemo.

Comics, art and architecture are not the only foods Tillie eats to feed her multi-faceted visual interests. She does love movies and you can see that with the cinematic approach she takes with her stories as to where she places her camera's 'eye.' You can see that 'eye' as she runs through the forest in *Lost Trees*. Or the changing visual perspective of the conversation between the two protagonists in *Glare*. Film Noir, German Expressionism, Alfred Hitchcock, Orson Welles; Tillie has them all.

The film director that clearly influences her the most is Hayao Miyazaki and the works he put out from Studio Ghibli. Miyazaki and McCay share many qualities; fantastic beasts, giant perspectives and the sense of a self-contained fantasy world that one could easily find themselves in. *Princess Mononoke* and *Spirited Away* in particular leave their mark on Tillie's work.

Tillie said she carries these visual influences inside her because she has an emotional attachment to them. They spark something inside of her that causes that amazing brain to retain those images she has read and experienced until she subconsciously retrieves them when they are synthesized into the panel defined tableaus that comes forth from her ink-laden pen. These tableaus establish a very real sense of place in her comics, one can feel the forest that is hiked, the streets that are strolled, the rooms that are being lived in and the cityscapes that are being walked over.

But what good is all that emotionally attached visual stimulation without stories? Well, no need to worry about that, because that incredible noggin that sits atop Tillie's shoulders has plenty to say about love, relationships, death, alienation and her sexuality, all told against those amazing visuals. Emotion not only rules her visual memory, it also rules her storytelling. Whether protagonists are in love, breaking up, having an argument or just experiencing a day together, there is a real, palpable emotional connection between the people in her stories. Emotion also pervades the turmoil her and her characters find themselves in, whether lost in the forest or trying to fit into expected sexual societal norms.

Tillie's great brain pulled together for us the visuals, the storytelling and the emotions of the works in *Alone In Space*. So sit back in that special place where you like to relax, sip on that beverage and read these stories to get some visual and emotional connections of your own.

Warren is a comics historian and author who has twice been nominated for a prestigious Eisner Award. He has contributed to over two dozen books and a number of exhibits on comics history, as well as curating retrospective exhibitions. He has lectured on comics at the Center for Cartoon Studies, Parsons School of Design and other centers of higher learning. Warren has established two institutional collections dedicated to the preservation of indie comics at the United States Library of Congress. Warren is also the Executive Director of Small Press Expo, one of the most influential indie comics festivals in the world.

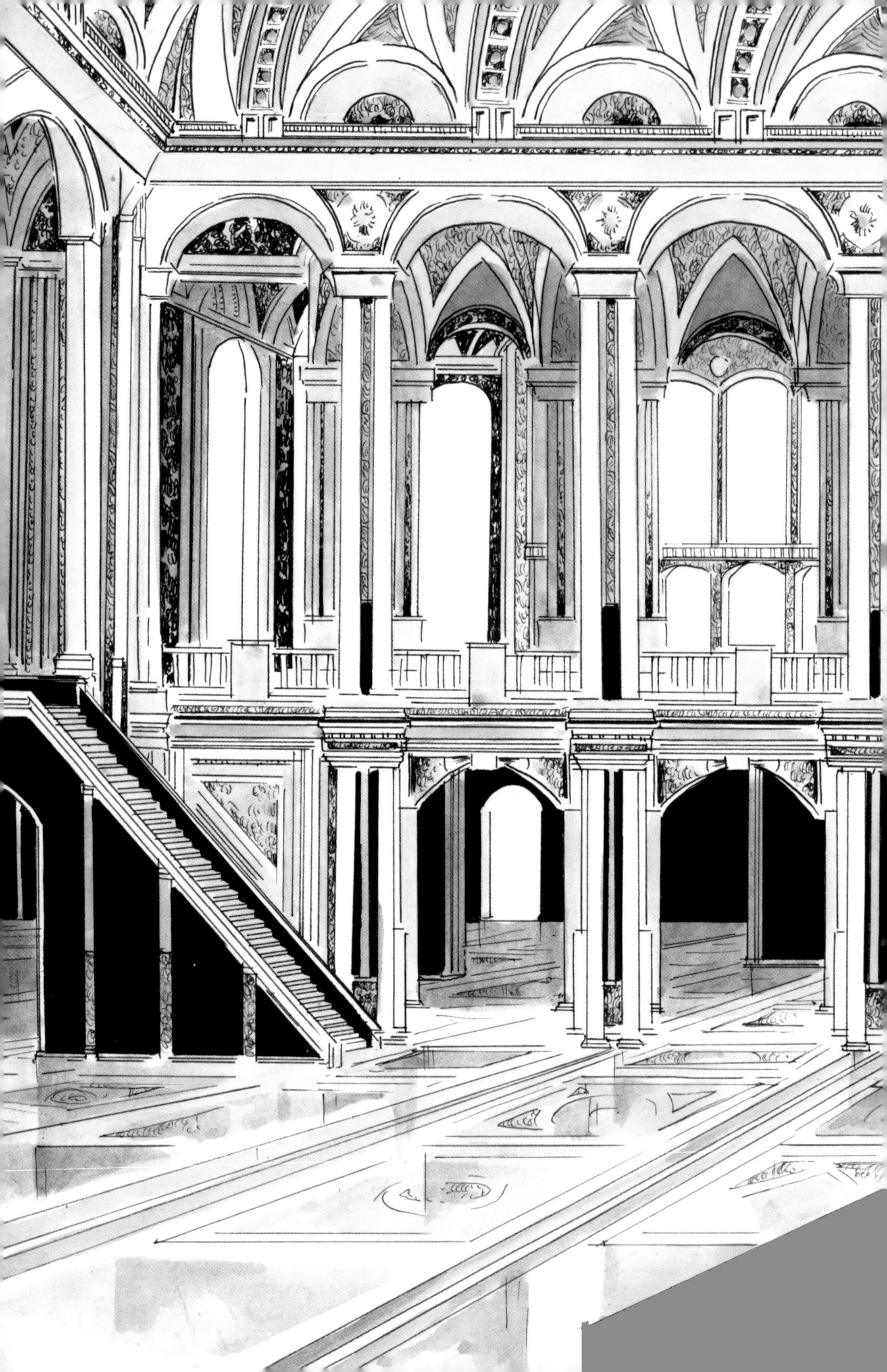

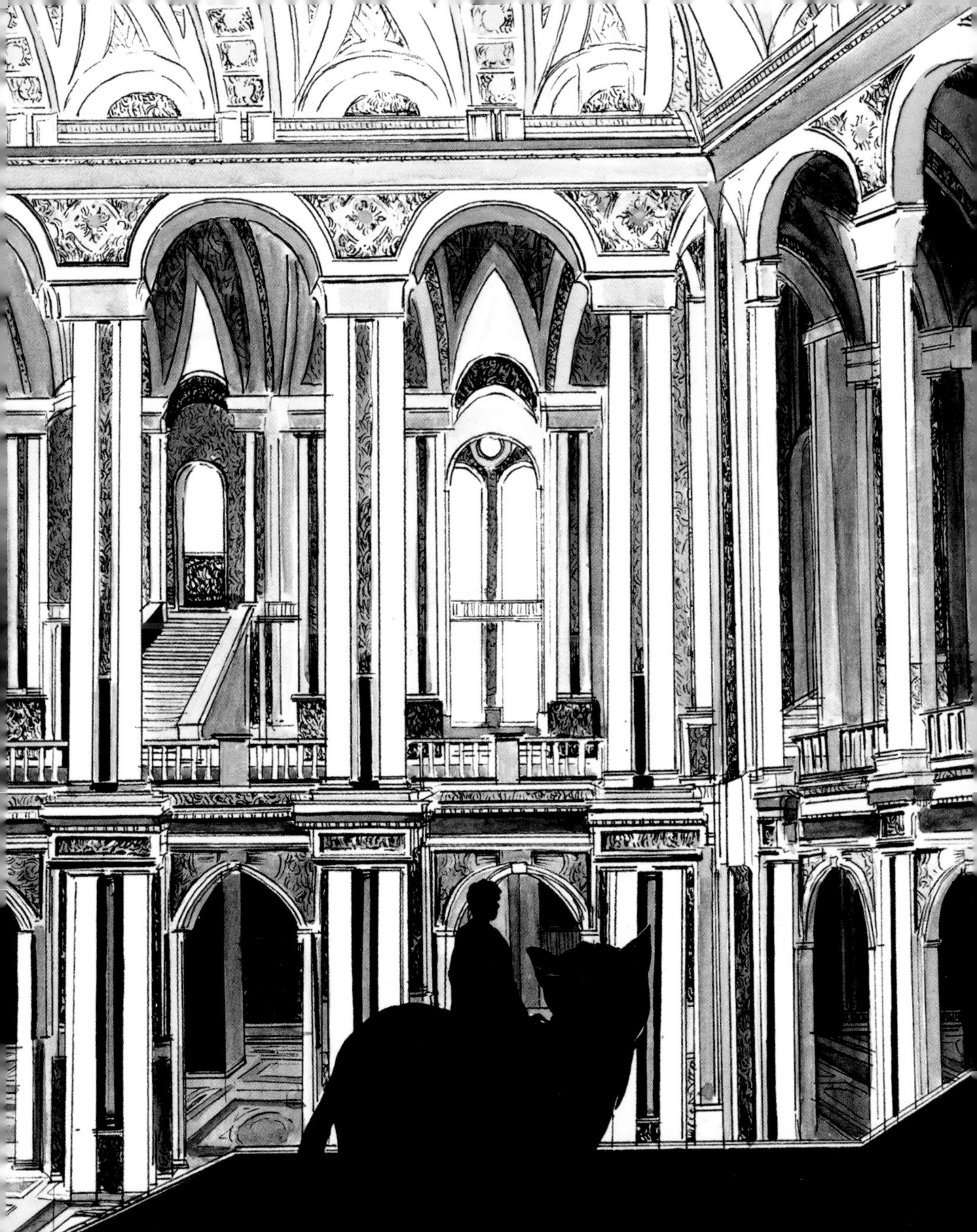

THE END OF SUMMER

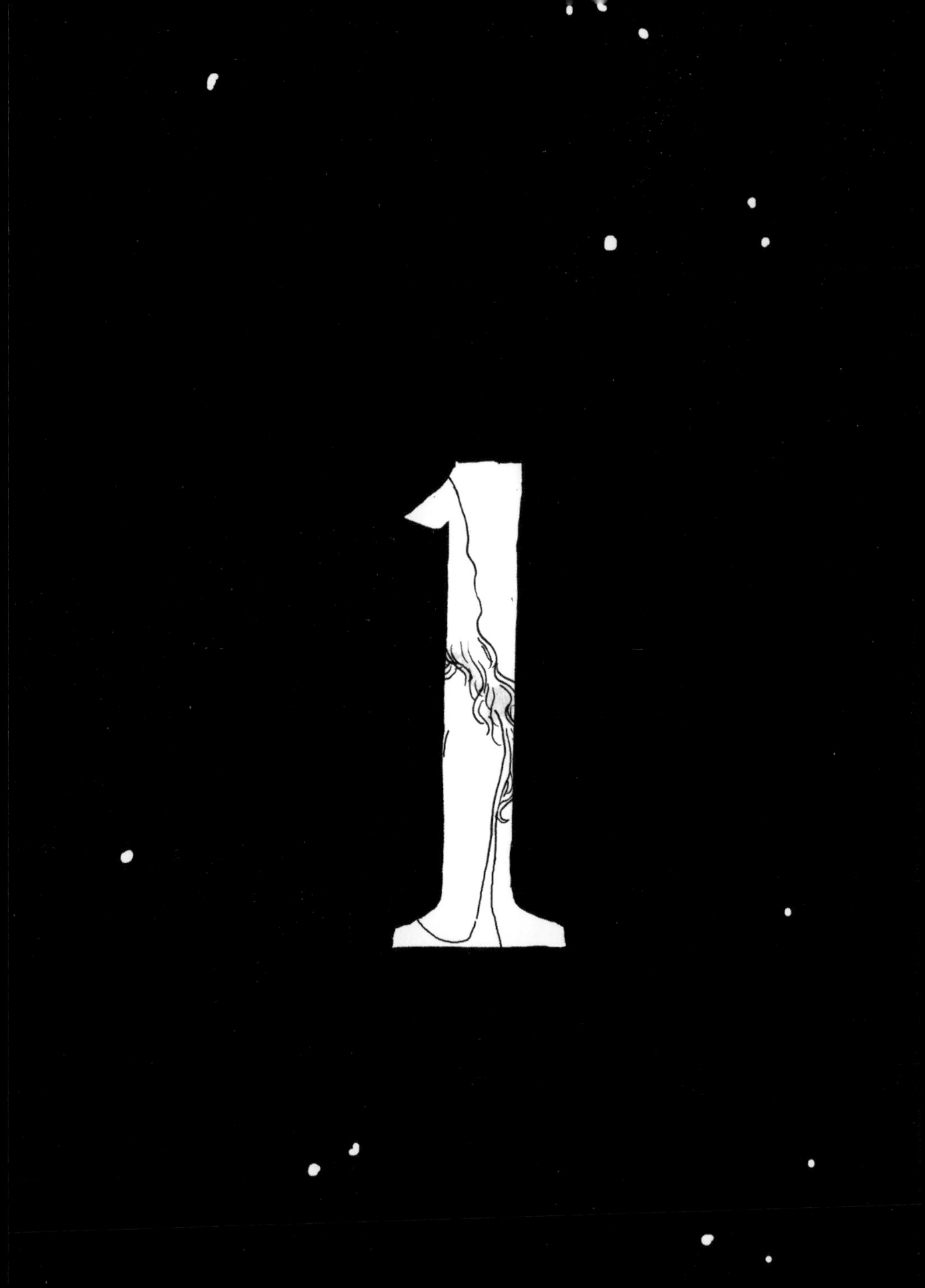
1

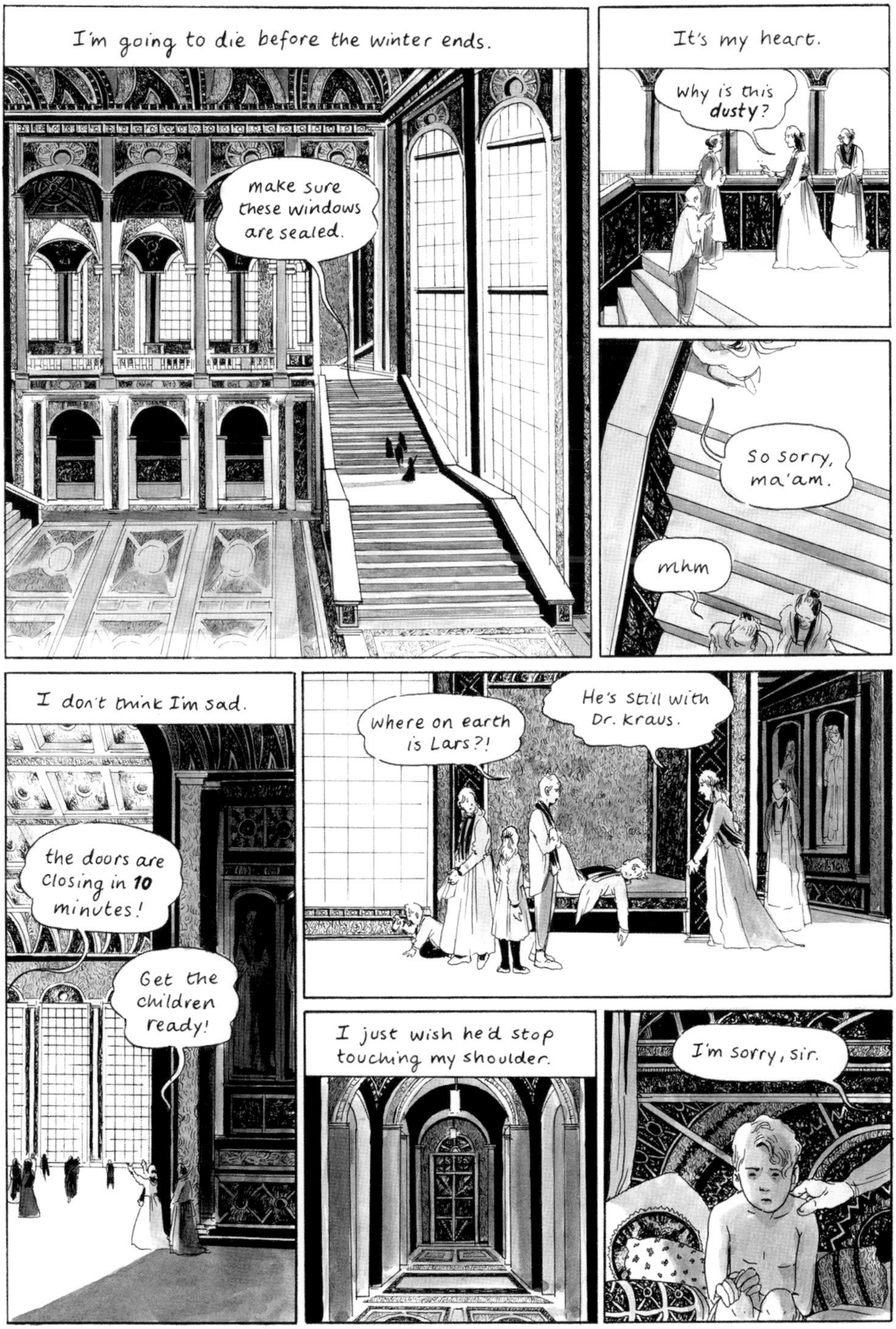
I'm going to die before the winter ends.
make sure these windows are sealed.
It's my heart.
Why is this **dusty**?
So sorry, ma'am.
mhm
I don't think I'm sad.
the doors are closing in **10** minutes!
Get the children ready!
Where on earth is Lars?!
He's still with Dr. Kraus.
I just wish he'd stop touching my shoulder.
I'm sorry, sir.

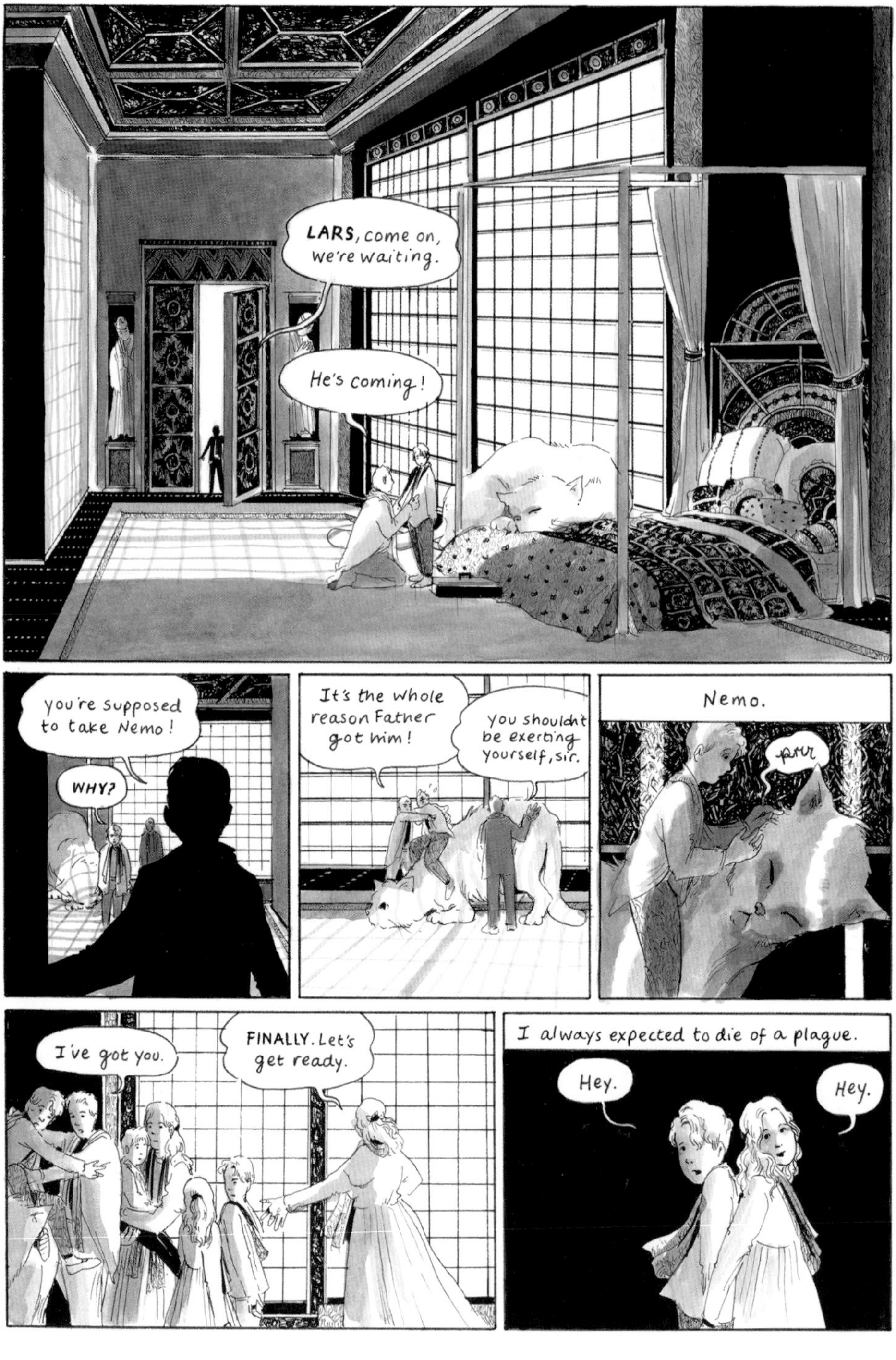
LARS, come on, we're waiting.
He's coming!
you're supposed to take Nemo!
WHY?
It's the whole reason Father got him!
You shouldn't be exerting yourself, sir.
Nemo.
prrr
I've got you.
FINALLY. Let's get ready.
I always expected to die of a plague.
Hey.
Hey.

My skin would rot, I'd vomit blood.

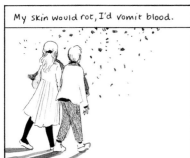

These doors are to be opened again in three years time. May we take this winter in stride as we did the last.

We ask the Gods that we may have warmth in this time of cold.

And I always imagined dying on a cloudy day. Like the world couldn't handle sunshine because it would be losing me.

But I don't think I'm interesting enough for the weather to mourn me.

Thank you!

Thank y

Maybe... I should read more.

Lars?

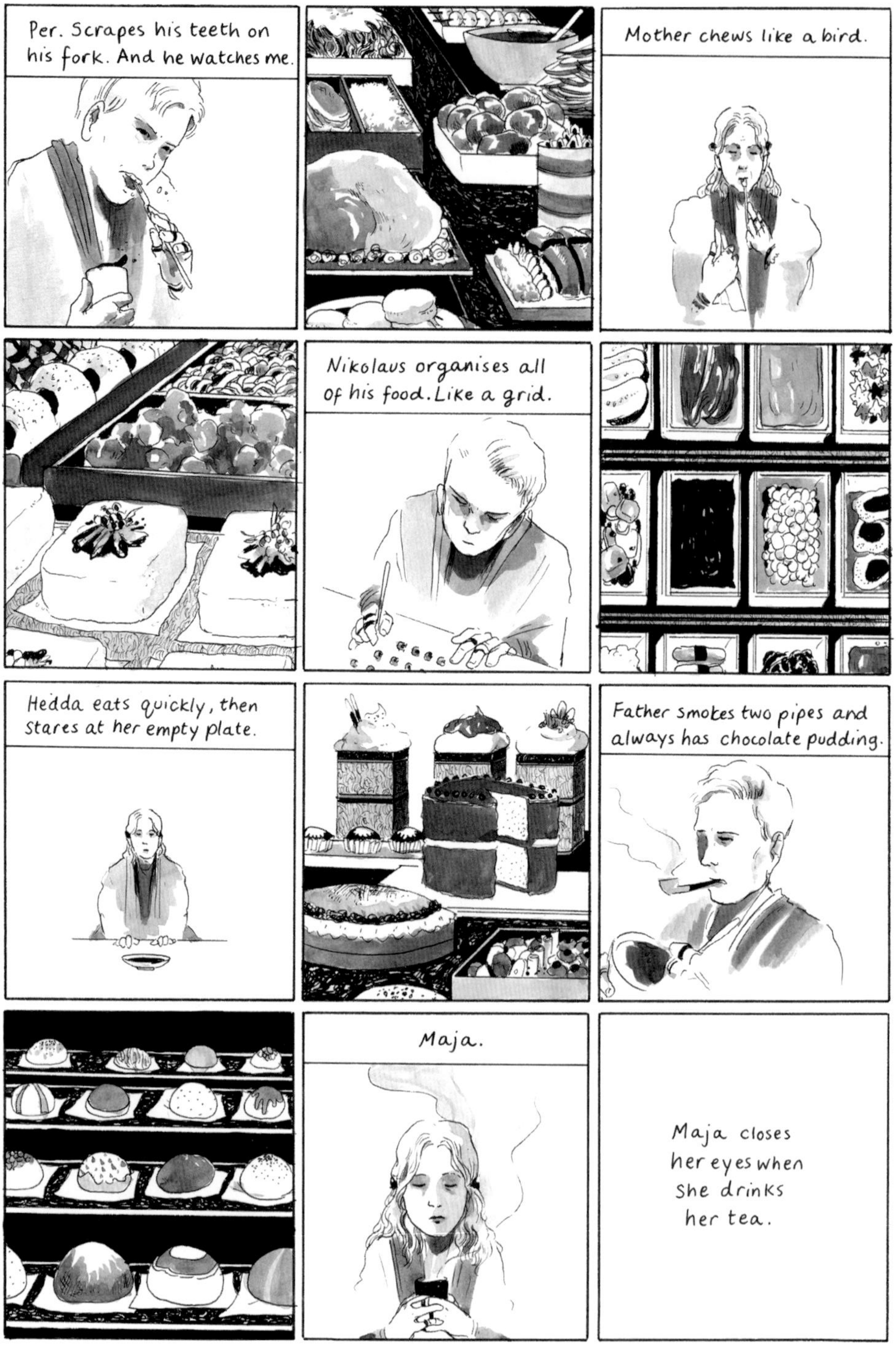
Per. Scrapes his teeth on his fork. And he watches me.
Mother chews like a bird.
Nikolaus organises all of his food. Like a grid.
Hedda eats quickly, then stares at her empty plate.
Father smokes two pipes and always has chocolate pudding.
Maja.
Maja closes her eyes when she drinks her tea.

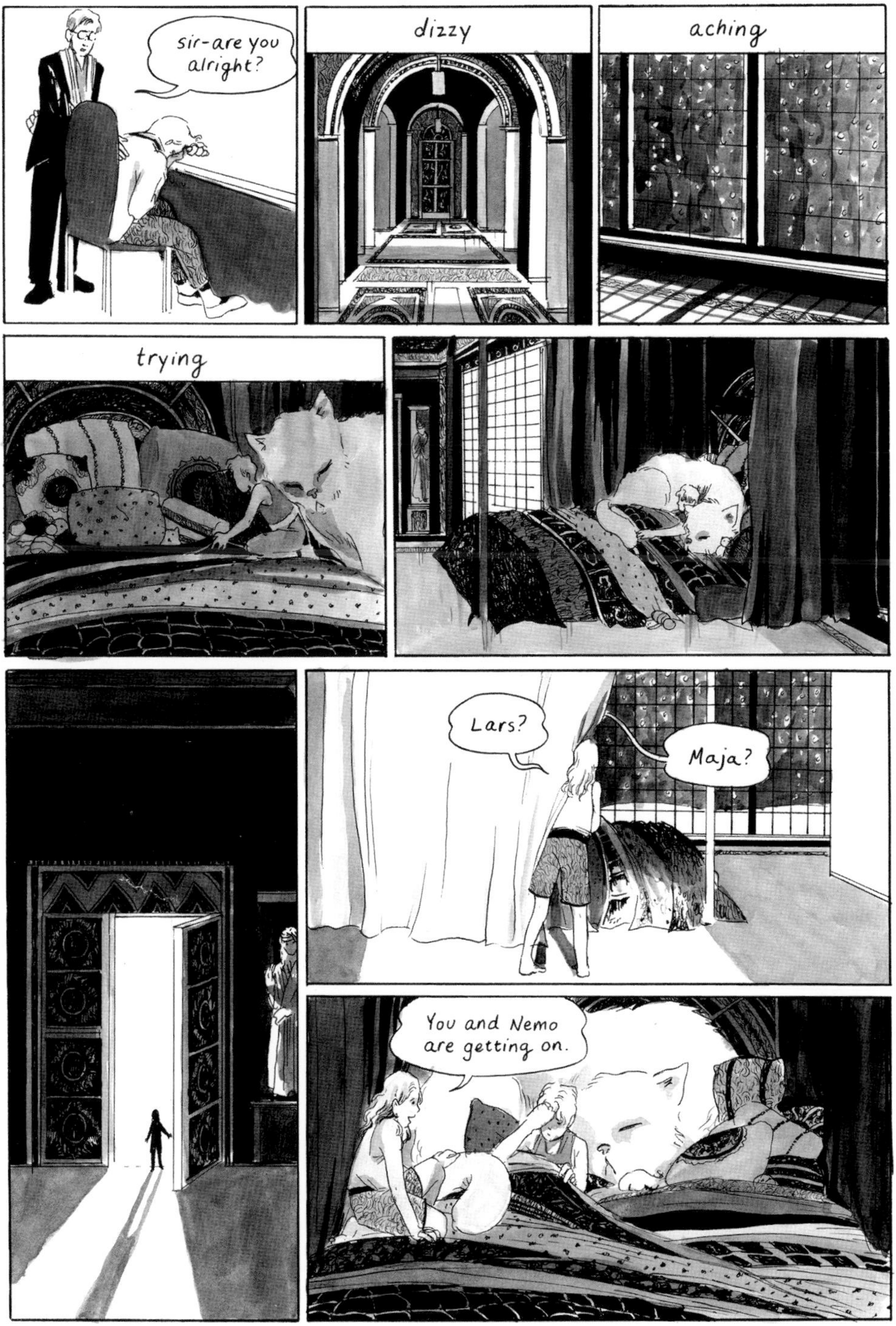
sir-are you alright?
dizzy
aching
trying
Lars?
Maja?
You and Nemo are getting on.

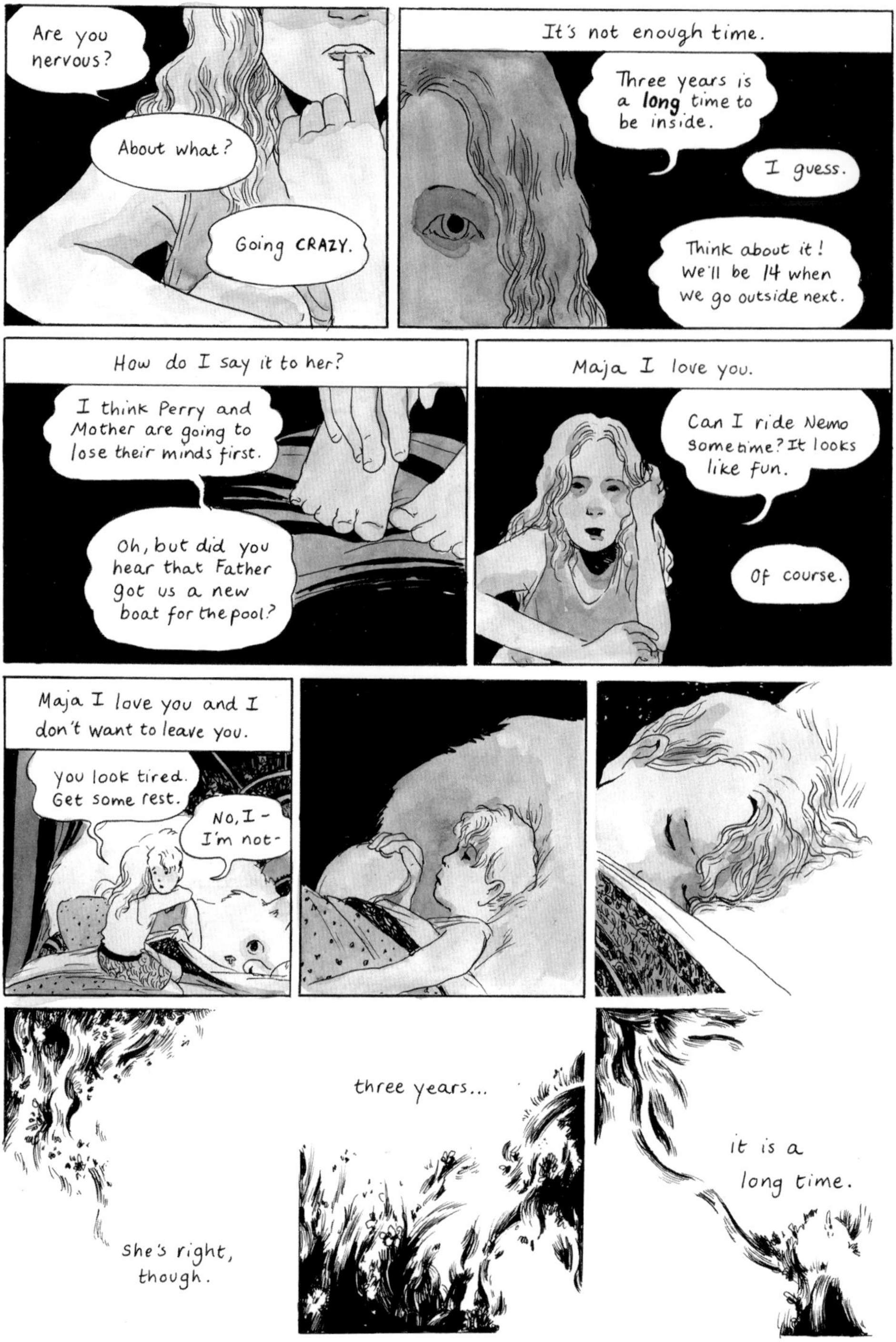

Are you nervous?
About what?
Going CRAZY.
It's not enough time.
Three years is a **long** time to be inside.
I guess.
Think about it! We'll be 14 when we go outside next.
How do I say it to her?
I think Perry and Mother are going to lose their minds first.
Oh, but did you hear that Father got us a new boat for the pool?
Maja I love you.
Can I ride Nemo sometime? It looks like fun.
Of course.
Maja I love you and I don't want to leave you.
you look tired. Get some rest.
No, I - I'm not-
she's right, though.
three years...
it is a long time.

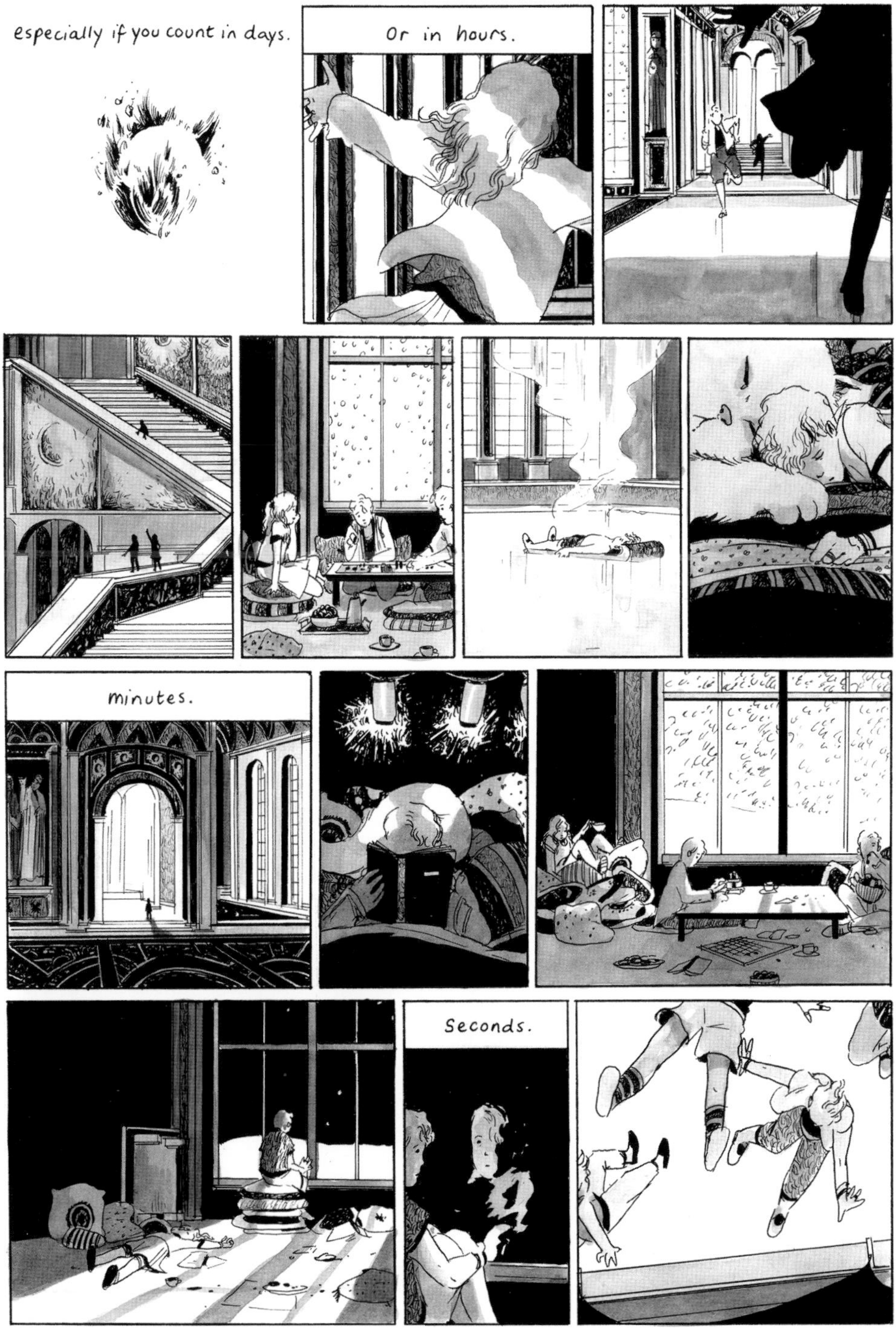
especially if you count in days.
Or in hours.
minutes.
Seconds.

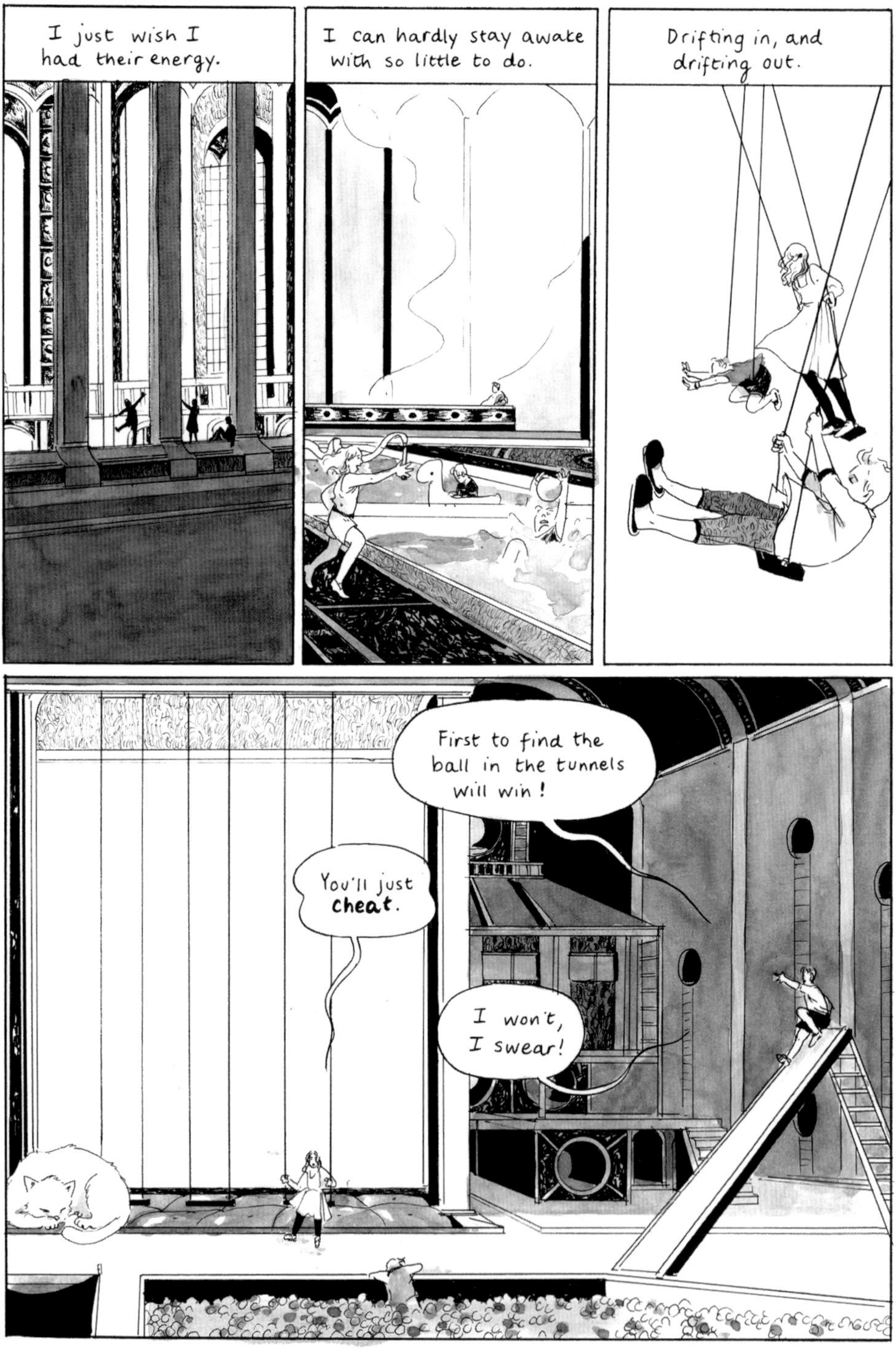
I just wish I had their energy.
I can hardly stay awake with so little to do.
Drifting in, and drifting out.
First to find the ball in the tunnels will win!
You'll just **cheat**.
I won't, I swear!

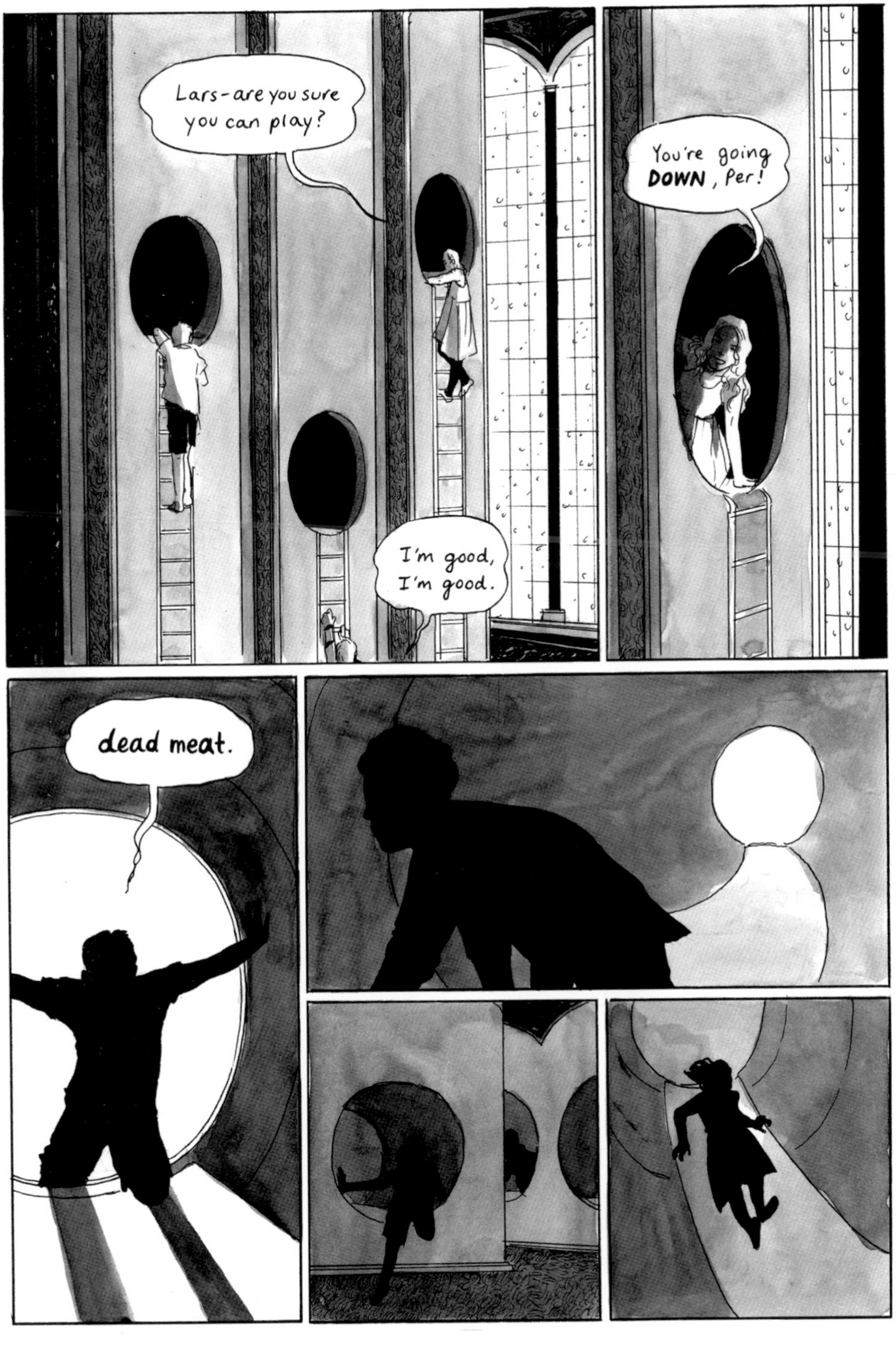
Lars-are you sure you can play?
I'm good, I'm good.
You're going DOWN, Per!
dead meat.

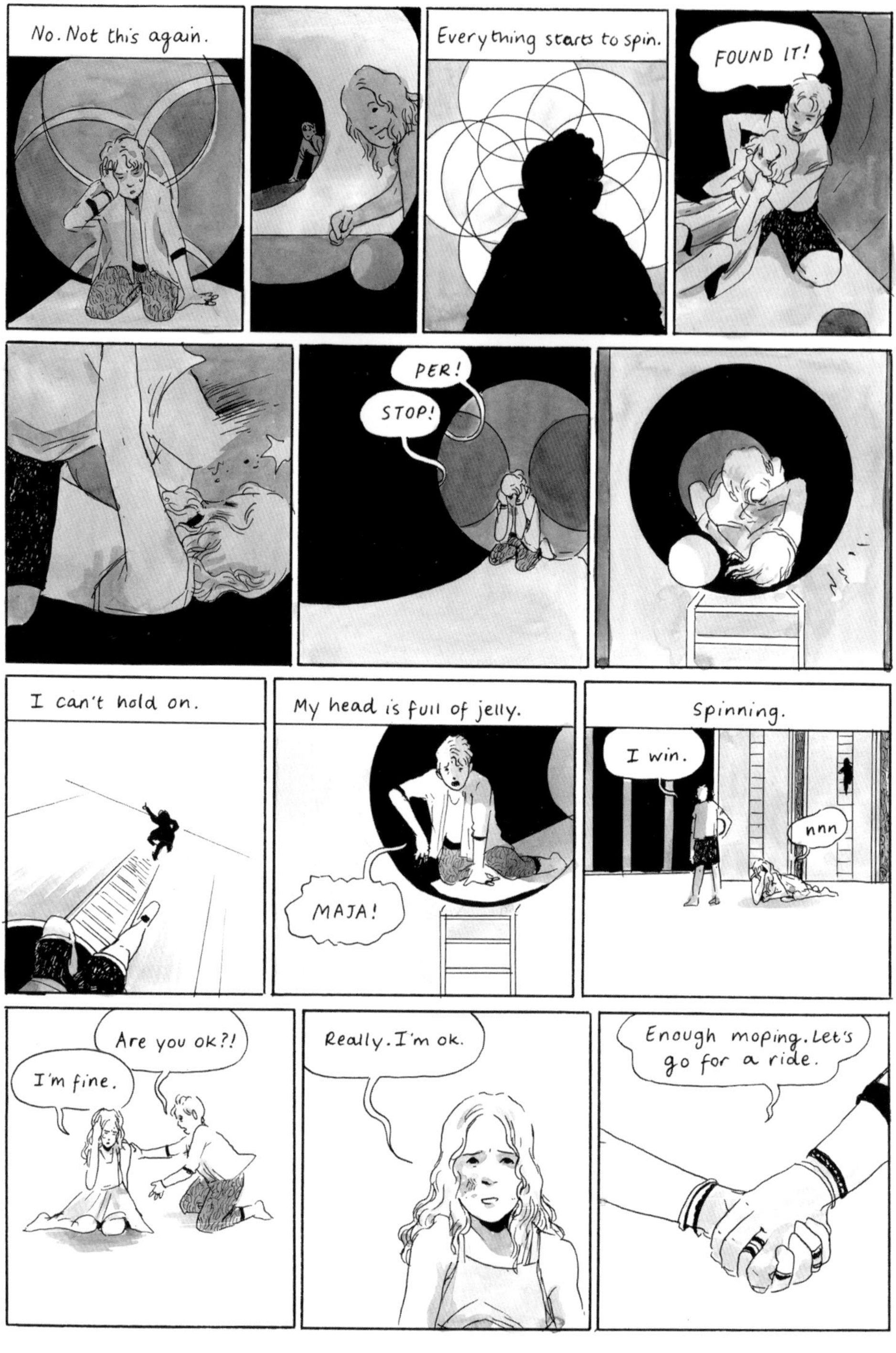
No. Not this again.
Everything starts to spin.
FOUND IT!
PER!
STOP!
I can't hold on.
My head is full of jelly.
MAJA!
Spinning.
I win.
nnn
Are you ok?!
I'm fine.
Really. I'm ok.
Enough moping. Let's go for a ride.

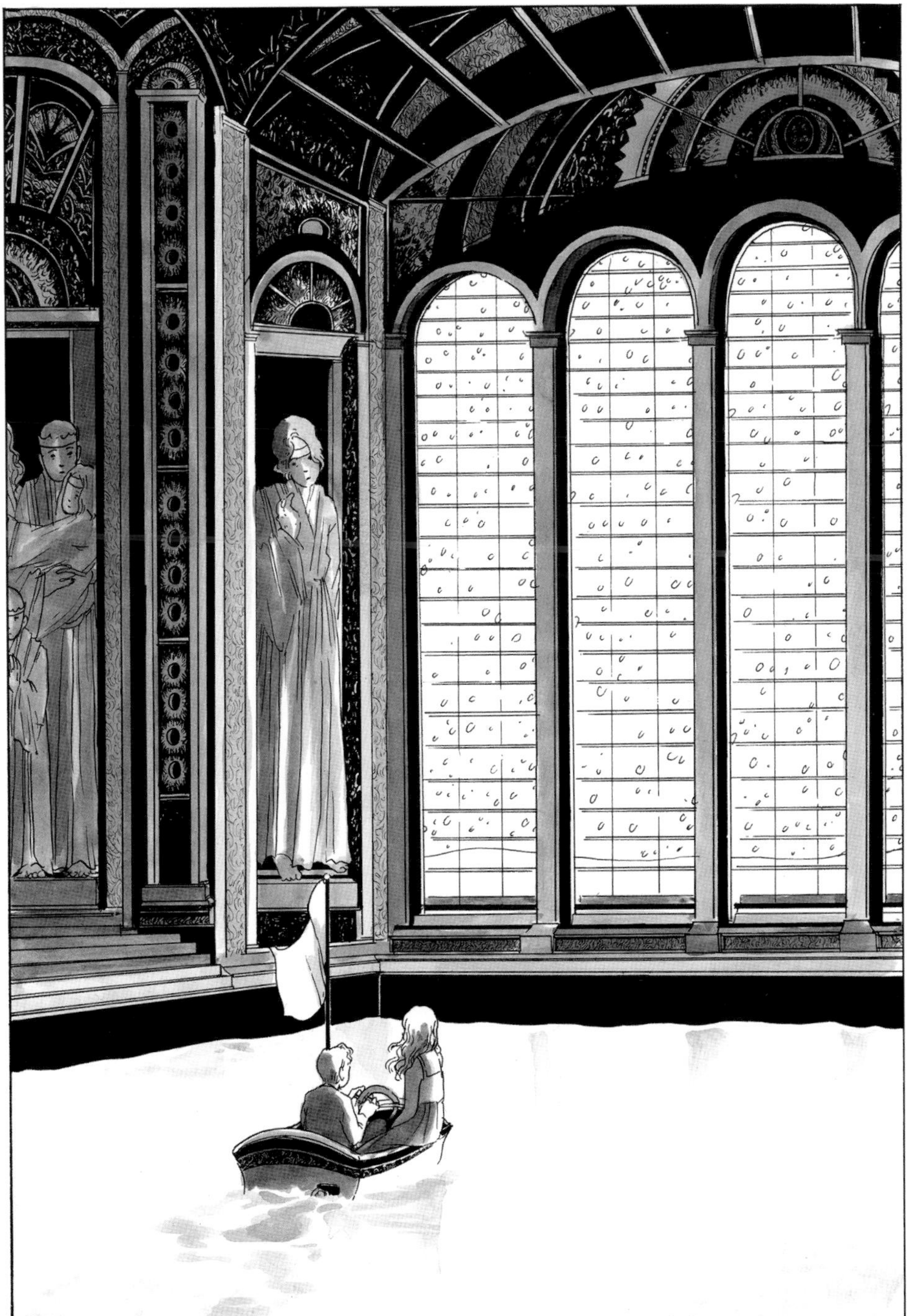

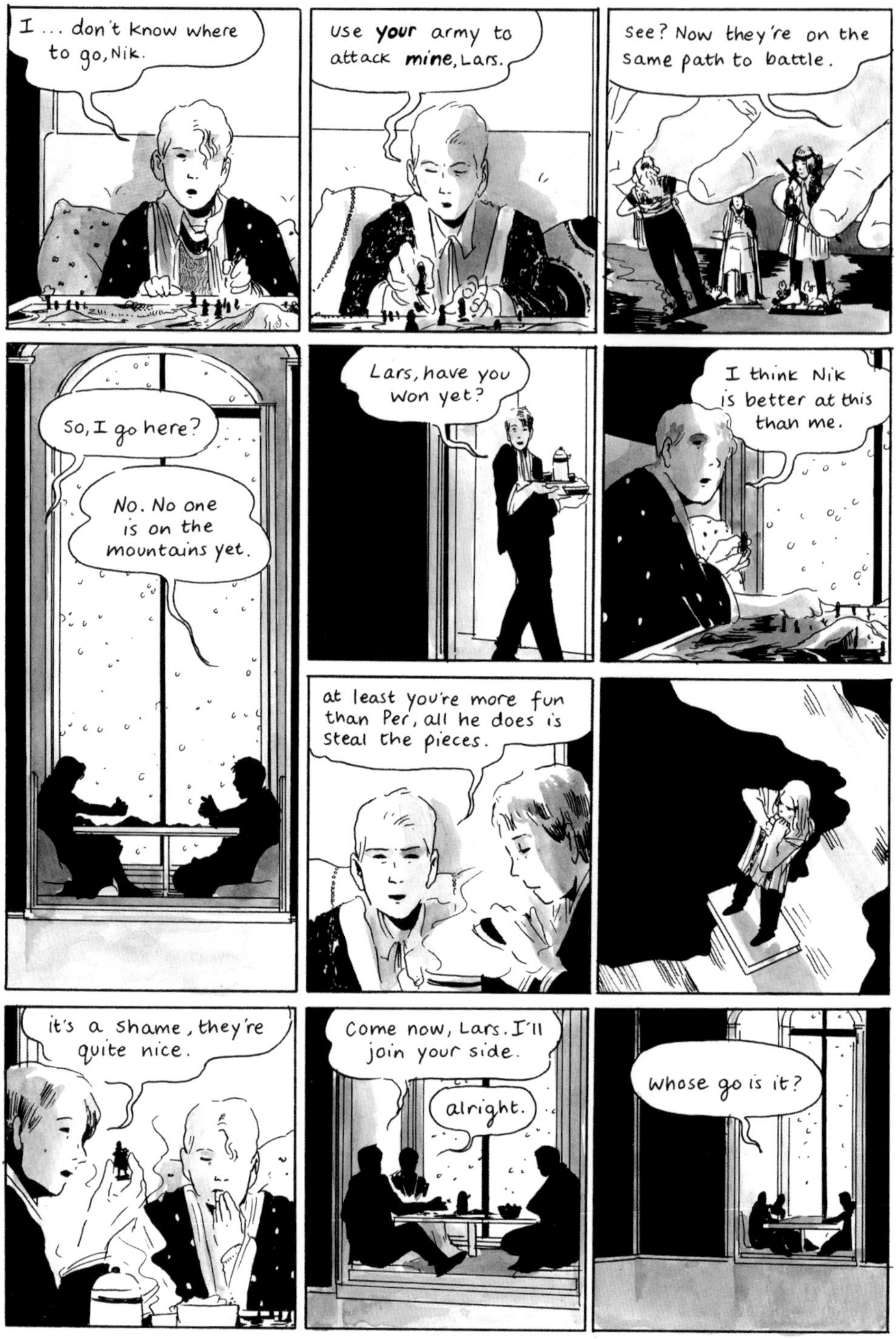
I ... don't know where to go, Nik.
Use **your** army to attack **mine**, Lars.
See? Now they're on the same path to battle.
So, I go here?
No. No one is on the mountains yet.
Lars, have you won yet?
I think Nik is better at this than me.
at least you're more fun than Per, all he does is steal the pieces.
it's a shame, they're quite nice.
Come now, Lars. I'll join your side.
alright.
Whose go is it?

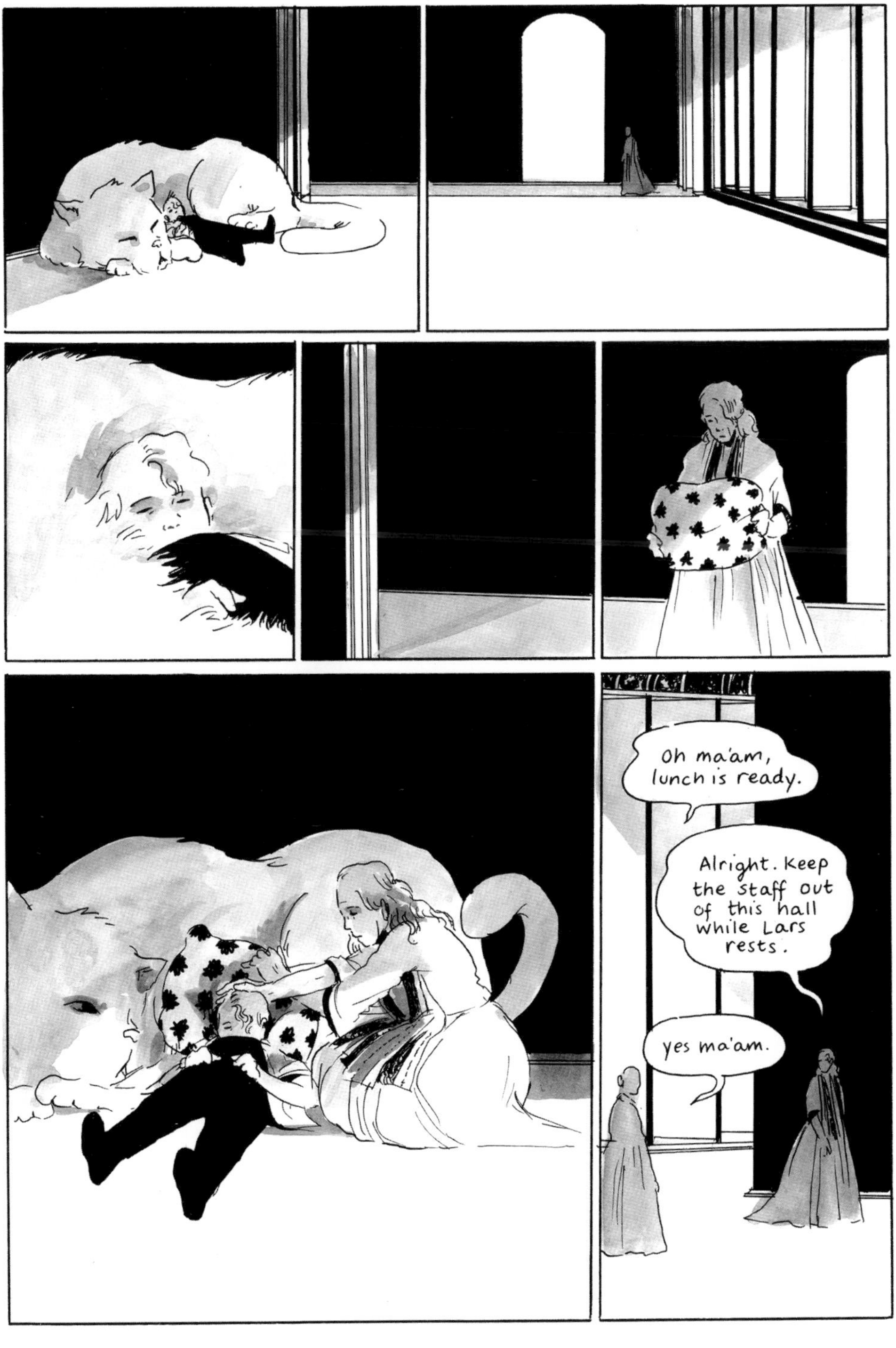
Oh ma'am, lunch is ready.
Alright. Keep the staff out of this hall while Lars rests.
yes ma'am.

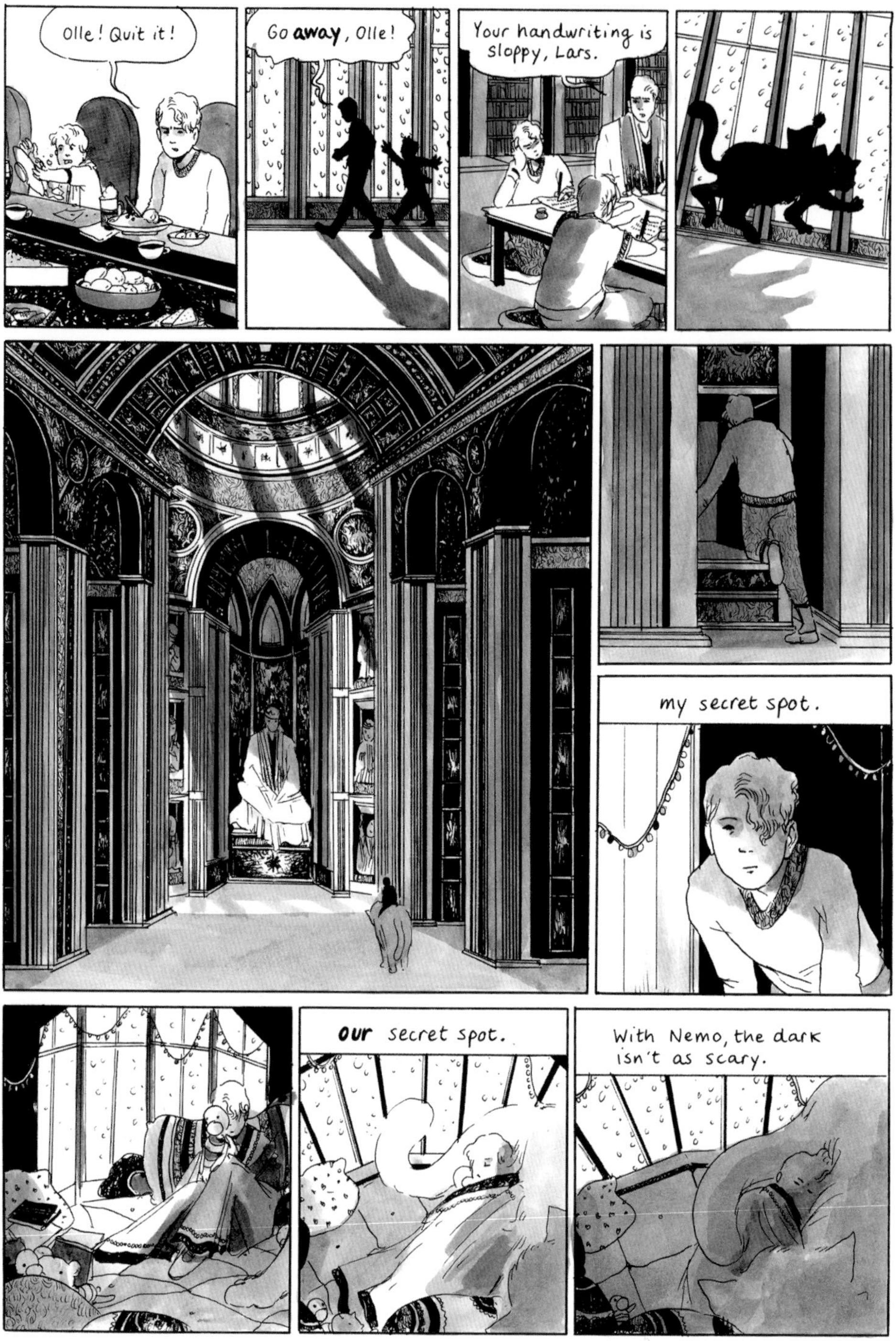
Olle! Quit it!
Go **away**, Olle!
Your handwriting is sloppy, Lars.
my secret spot.
our secret spot.
With Nemo, the dark isn't as scary.

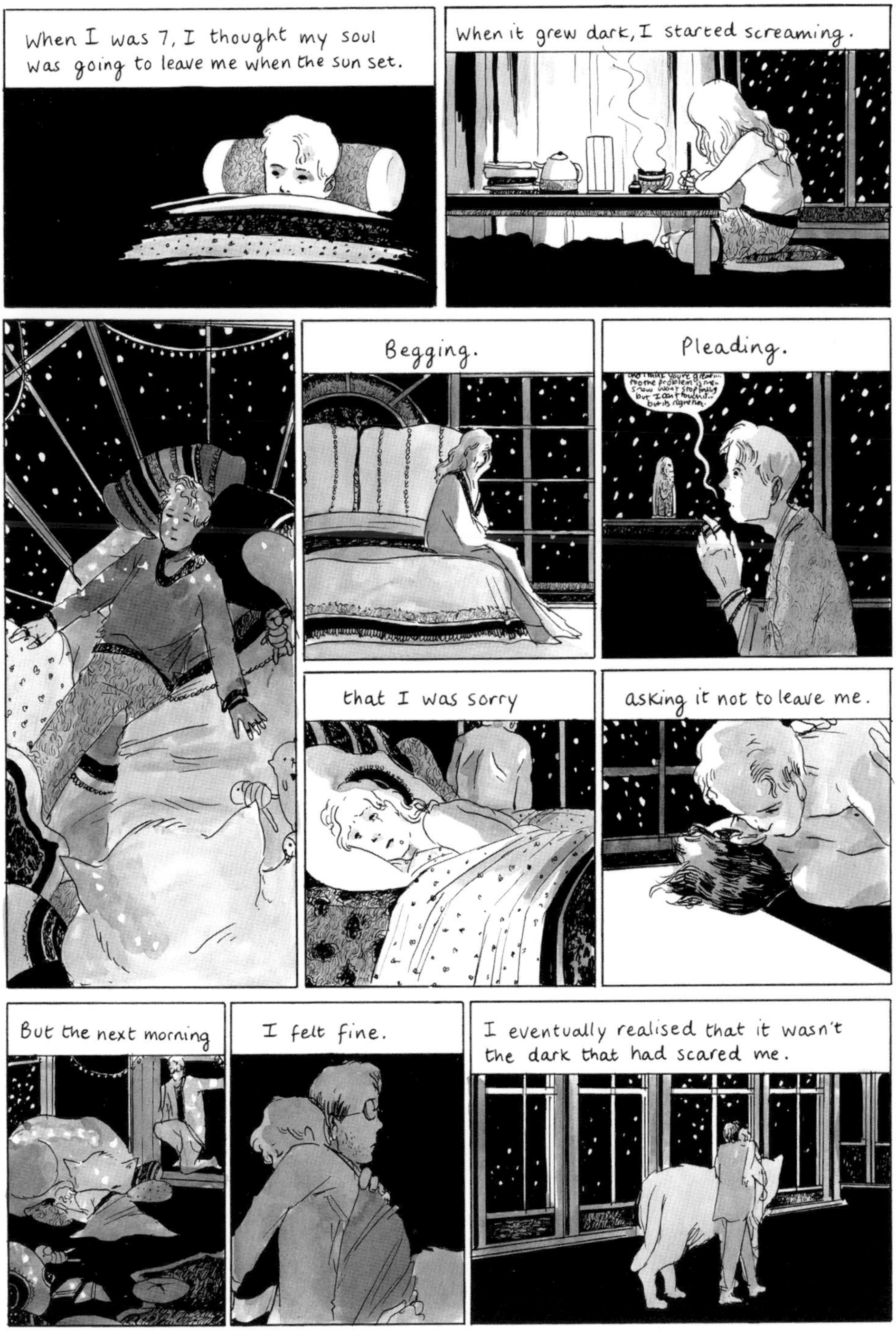
When I was 7, I thought my soul was going to leave me when the sun set.
When it grew dark, I started screaming.
Begging.
Pleading.
that I was sorry
asking it not to leave me.
But the next morning
I felt fine.
I eventually realised that it wasn't the dark that had scared me.

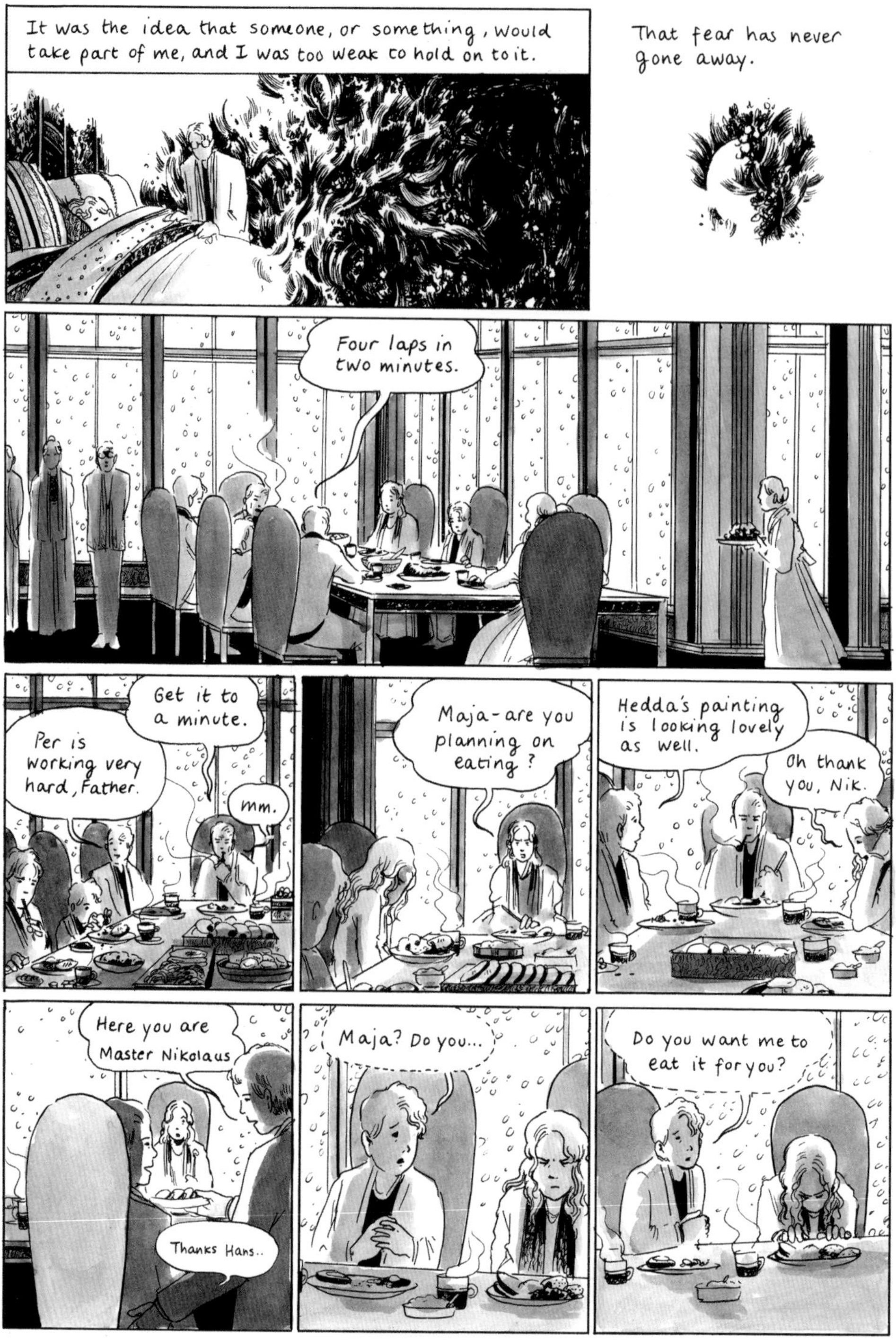

It was the idea that someone, or something, would take part of me, and I was too weak to hold on to it.
That fear has never gone away.
Four laps in two minutes.
Per is working very hard, Father.
Get it to a minute.
mm.
Maja- are you planning on eating ?
Hedda's painting is looking lovely as well.
Oh thank you, Nik.
Here you are Master Nikolaus
Thanks Hans..
Maja? Do you...
Do you want me to eat it for you?

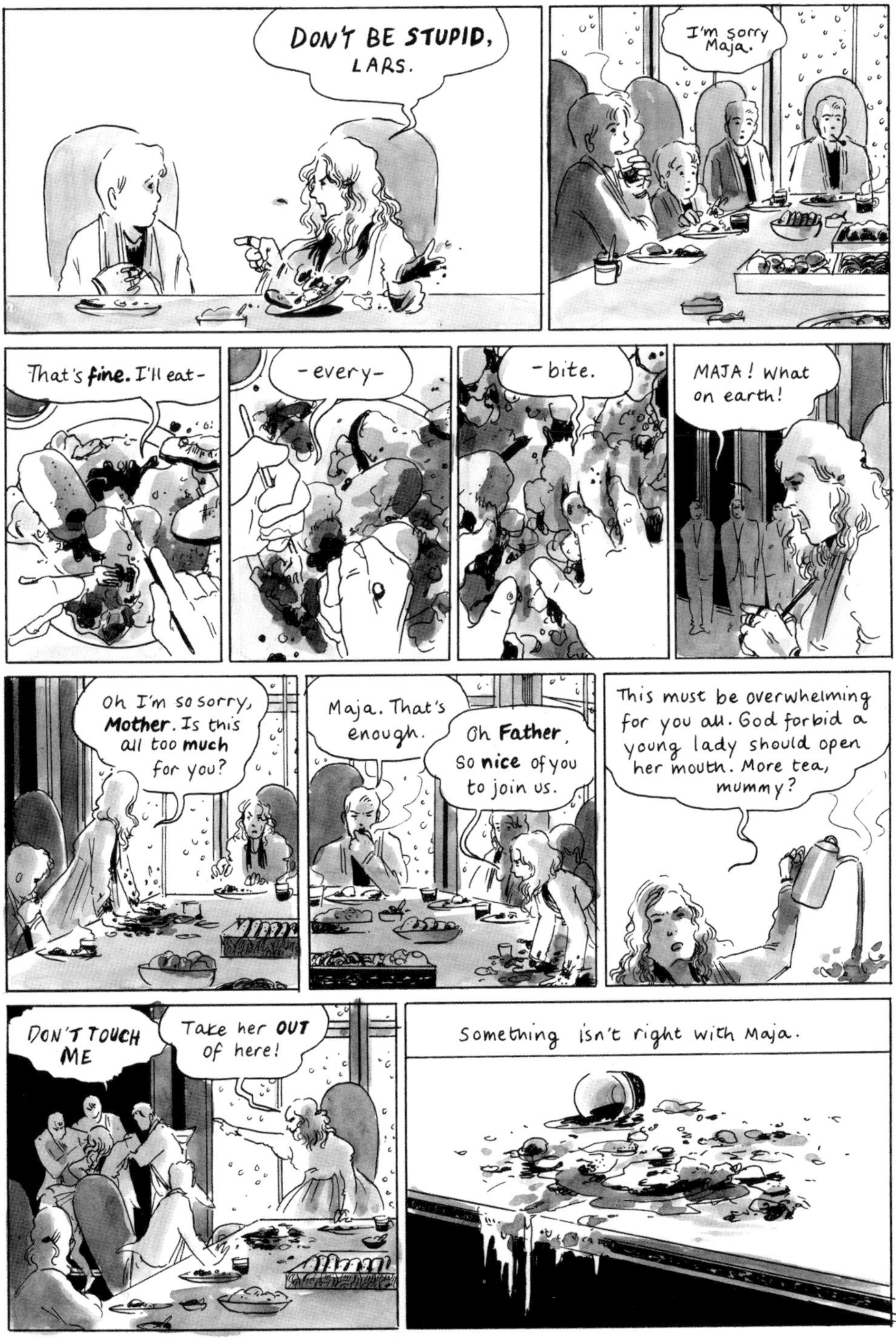
DON'T BE STUPID, LARS.
I'm sorry Maja.
That's fine. I'll eat-
-every-
-bite.
MAJA! What on earth!
Oh I'm so sorry, Mother. Is this all too much for you?
Maja. That's enough.
Oh Father, so nice of you to join us.
This must be overwhelming for you all. God forbid a young lady should open her mouth. More tea, mummy?
DON'T TOUCH ME
Take her OUT of here!
Something isn't right with Maja.

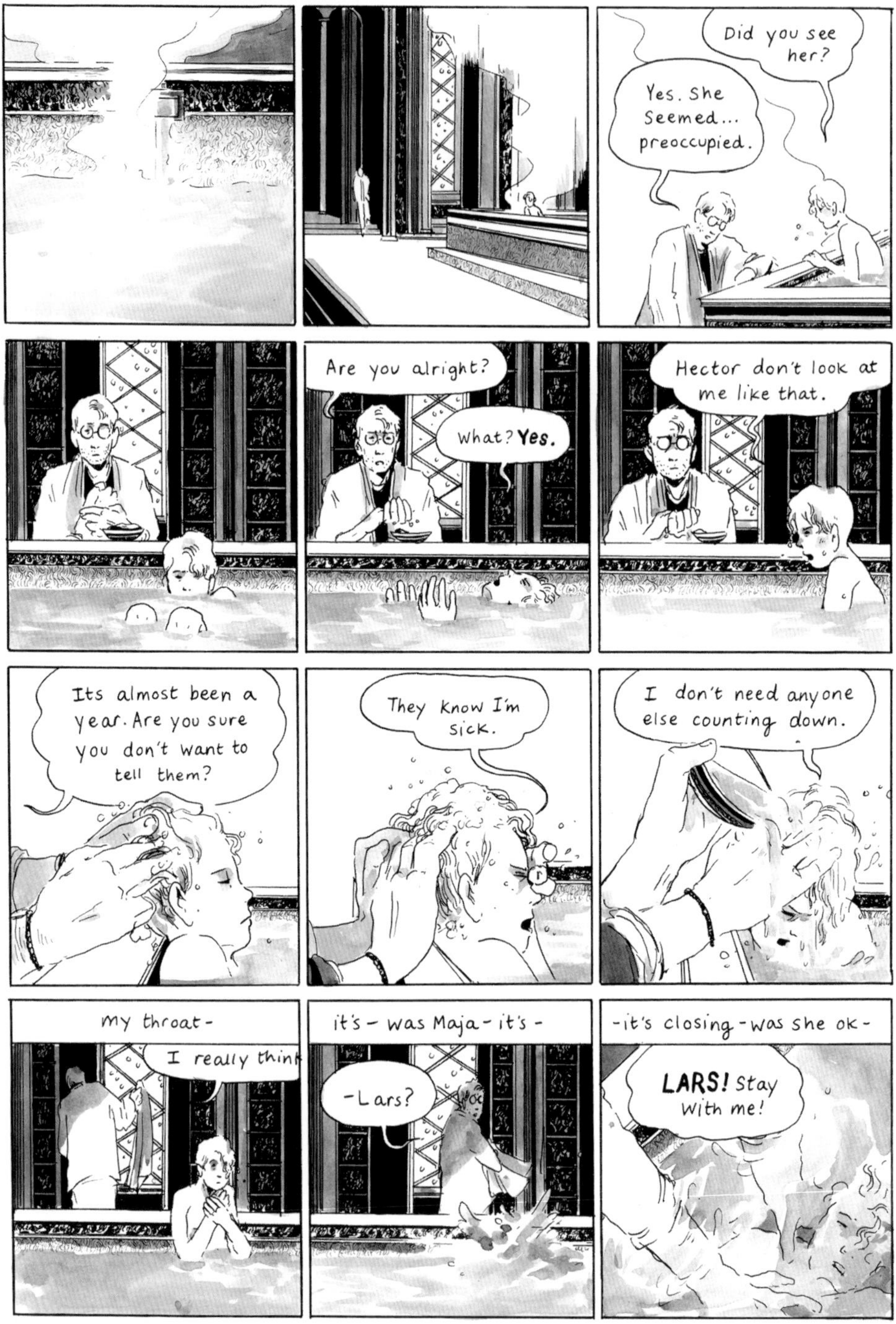
Did you see her?
Yes. She seemed... preoccupied.
Are you alright?
What? Yes.
Hector don't look at me like that.
Its almost been a year. Are you sure you don't want to tell them?
They know I'm sick.
I don't need anyone else counting down.
my throat-
I really think
it's - was Maja - it's -
-Lars?
-it's closing - was she ok-
LARS! Stay with me!

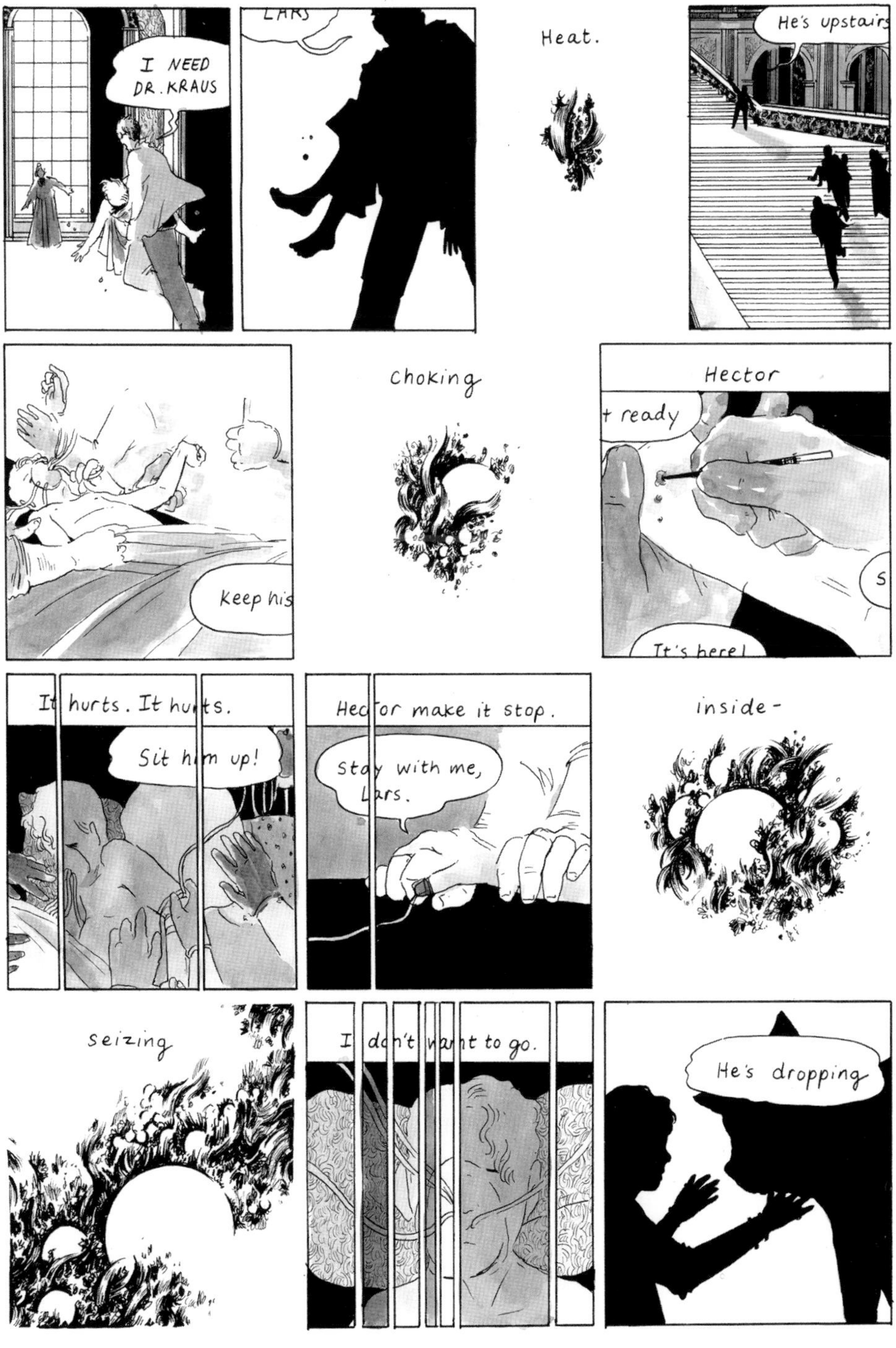
I NEED DR. KRAUS
LARS
Heat.
He's upstairs
Keep his
choking
Hector
t ready
S
It's here!
It hurts. It hurts.
Sit him up!
Hector make it stop.
Stay with me, Lars.
inside-
seizing
I don't want to go.
He's dropping

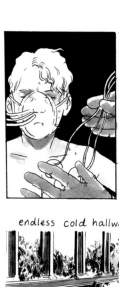

I'm riding Nemo   and I'm ok.

endless cold hallways  impossible windows   rooms that bellow

We don't know where we are

Hector?

and there is plenty of time.

20

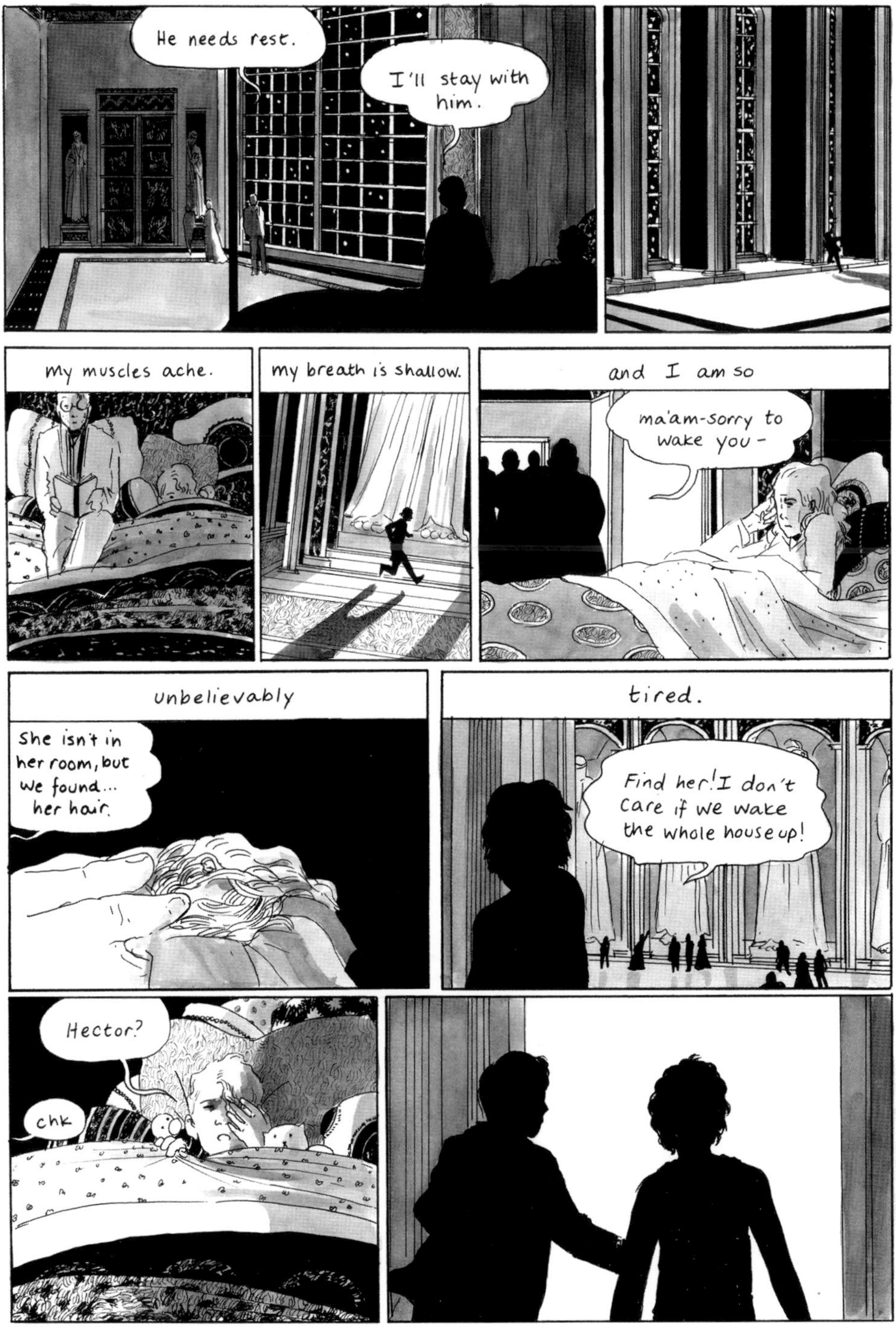

He needs rest.
I'll stay with him.
my muscles ache.
my breath is shallow.
and I am so
ma'am-sorry to wake you-
unbelievably
She isn't in her room, but we found... her hair.
tired.
Find her! I don't care if we wake the whole house up!
Hector?
chk

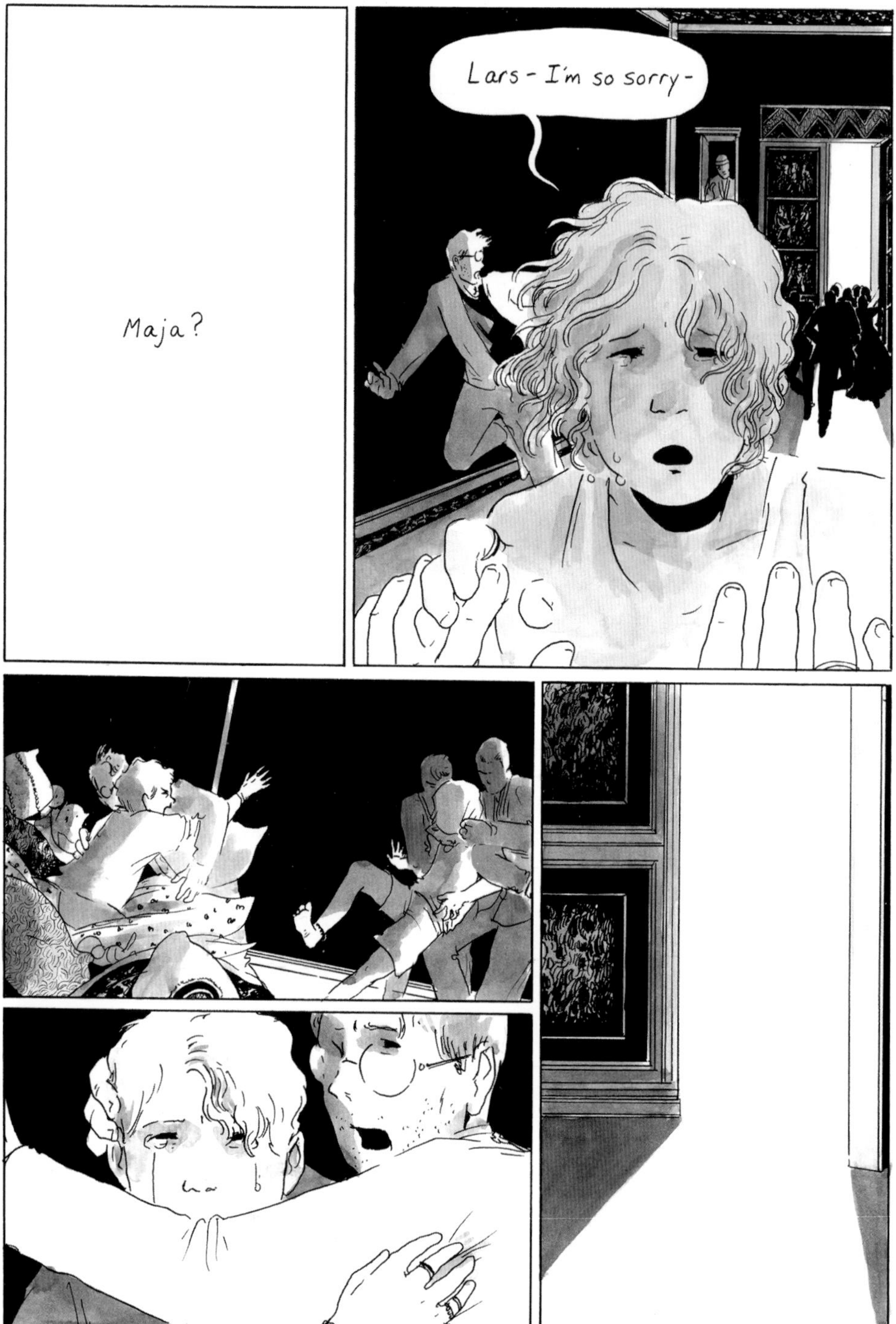
Maja?
Lars - I'm so sorry -

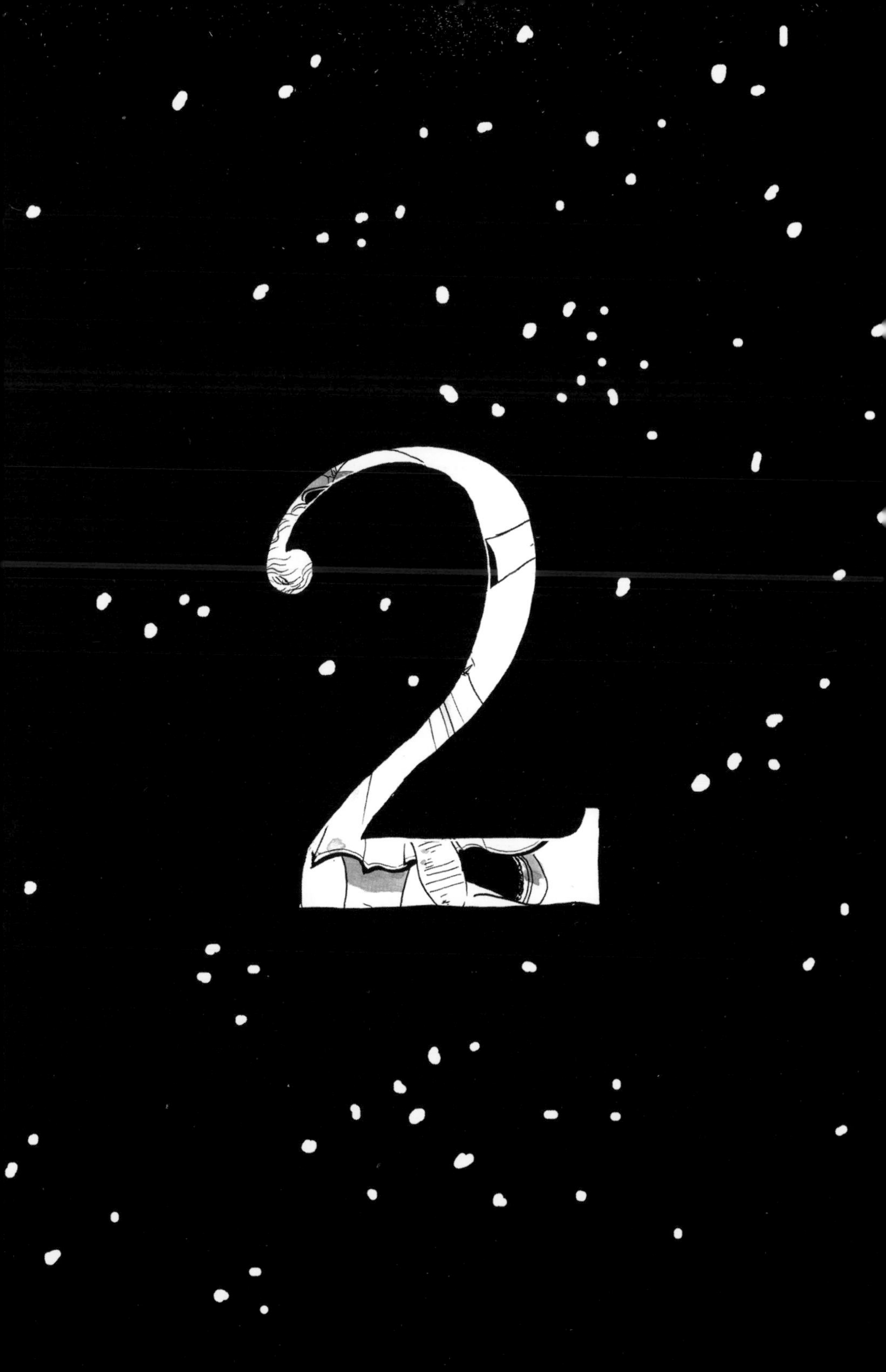
2

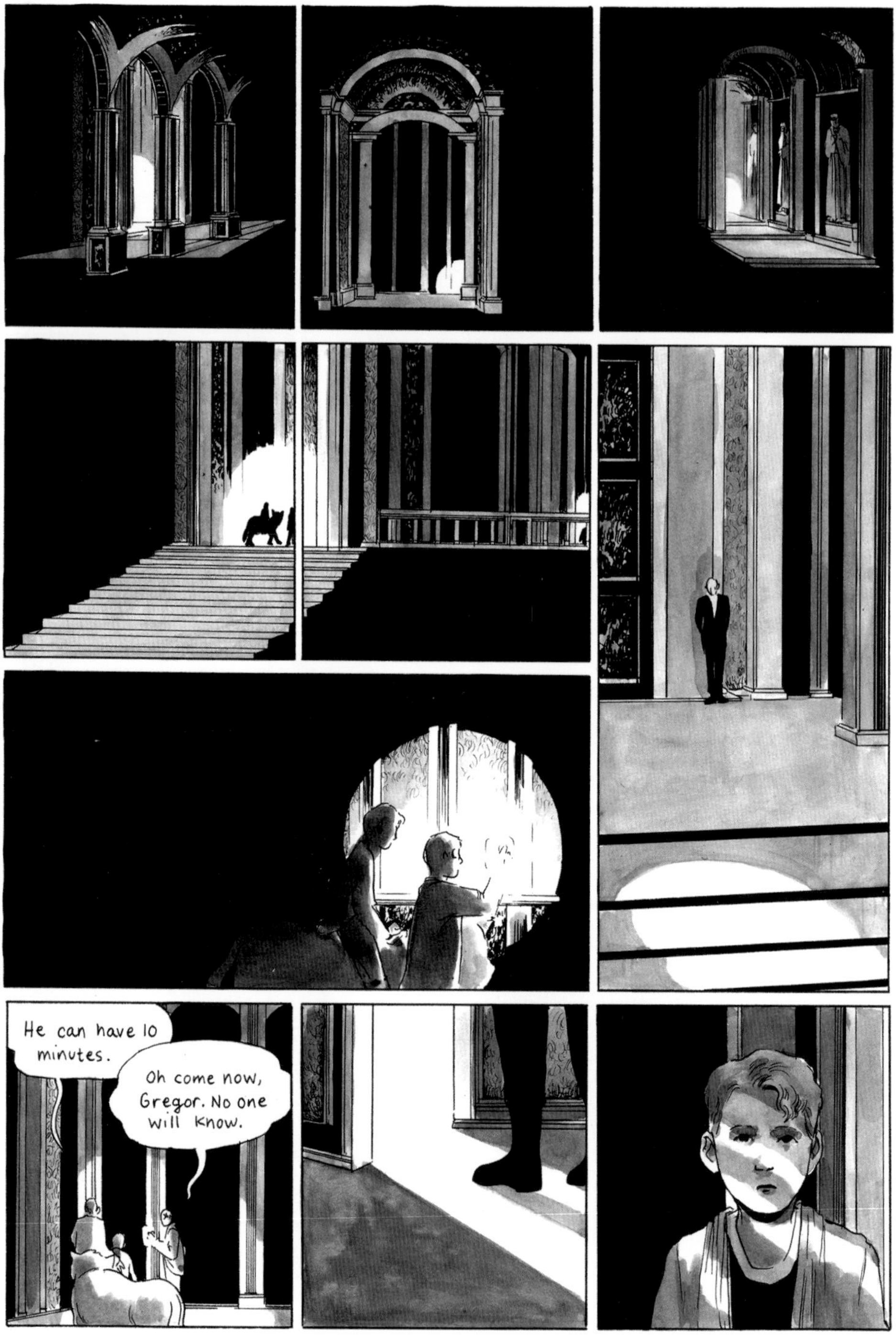
He can have 10 minutes.
Oh come now, Gregor. No one will know.

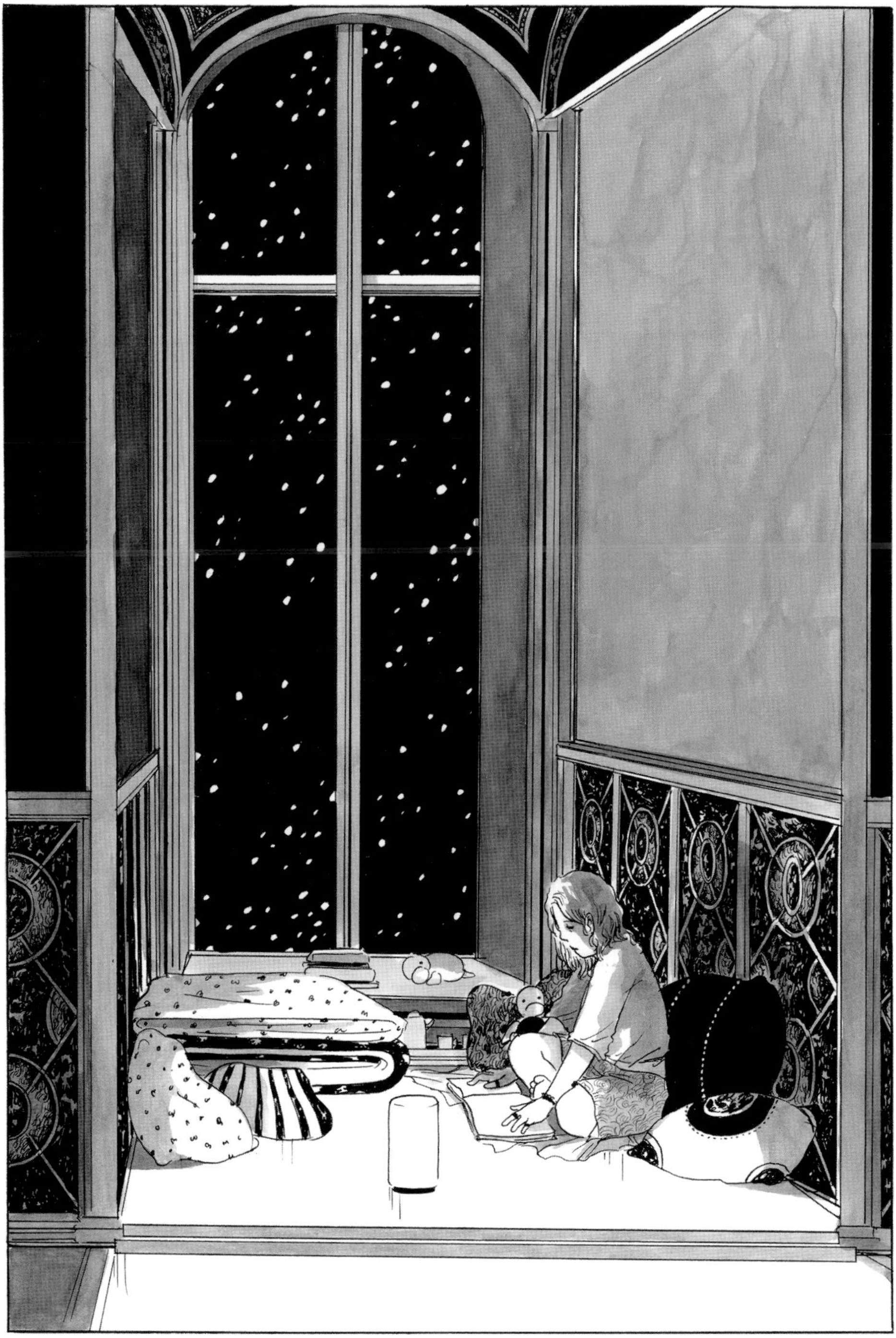

coffee?

sure.

You have to catch me up on everything. Gregor doesn't tell me squat.

everyone is fine.

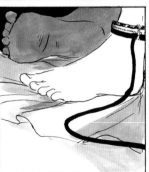

Oh come **on**, give me more than that.

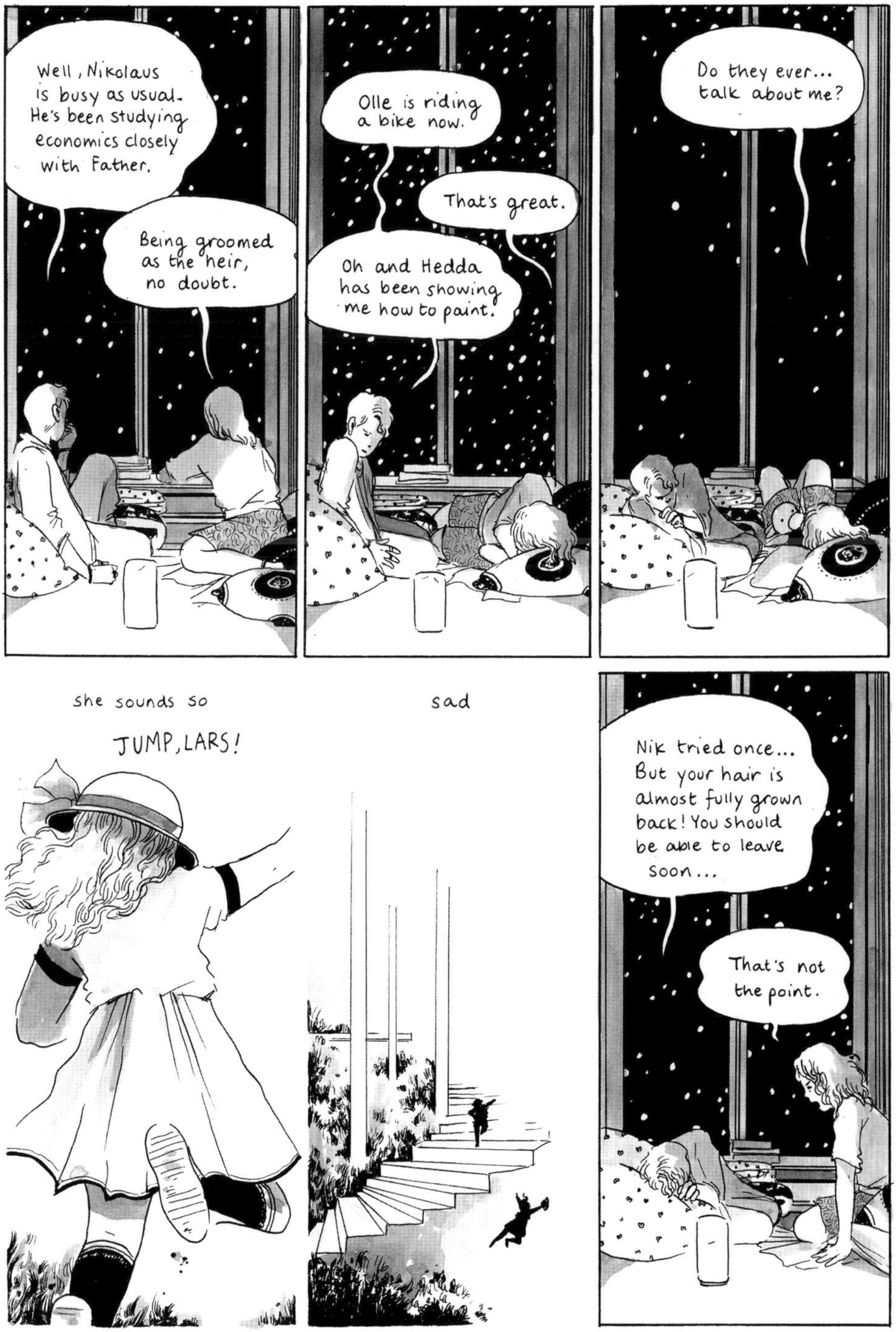
Well, Nikolaus is busy as usual. He's been studying economics closely with Father.
Being groomed as the heir, no doubt.
Olle is riding a bike now.
That's great.
Oh and Hedda has been showing me how to paint.
Do they ever... talk about me?
she sounds so
sad
JUMP, LARS!
Nik tried once... But your hair is almost fully grown back! You should be able to leave soon...
That's not the point.

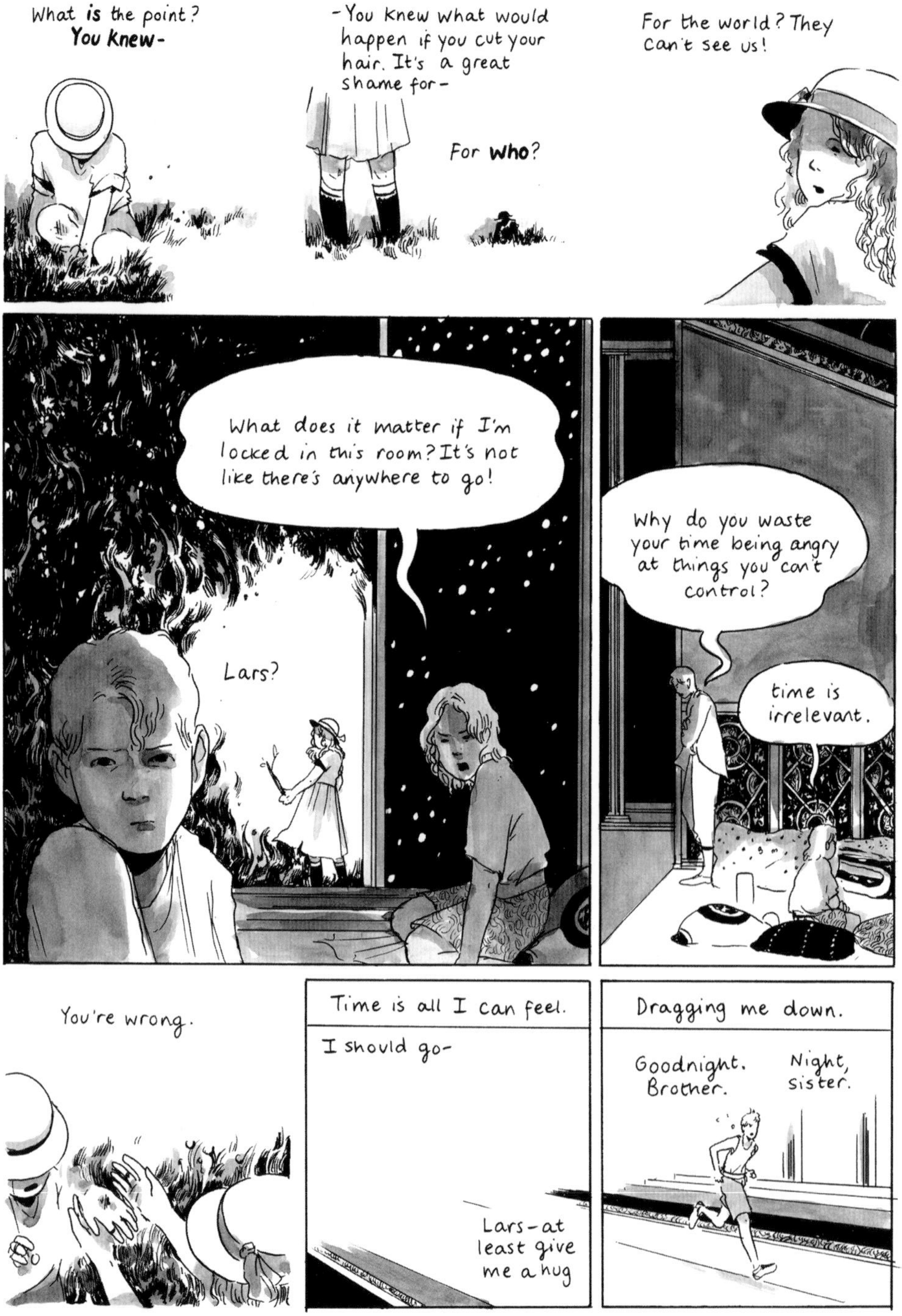
What is the point? You knew-
-You knew what would happen if you cut your hair. It's a great shame for-
For who?
For the world? They can't see us!
What does it matter if I'm locked in this room? It's not like there's anywhere to go!
Lars?
Why do you waste your time being angry at things you can't control?
time is irrelevant.
You're wrong.
Time is all I can feel.
I should go-
Lars-at least give me a hug
Dragging me down.
Goodnight. Brother.
Night, sister.

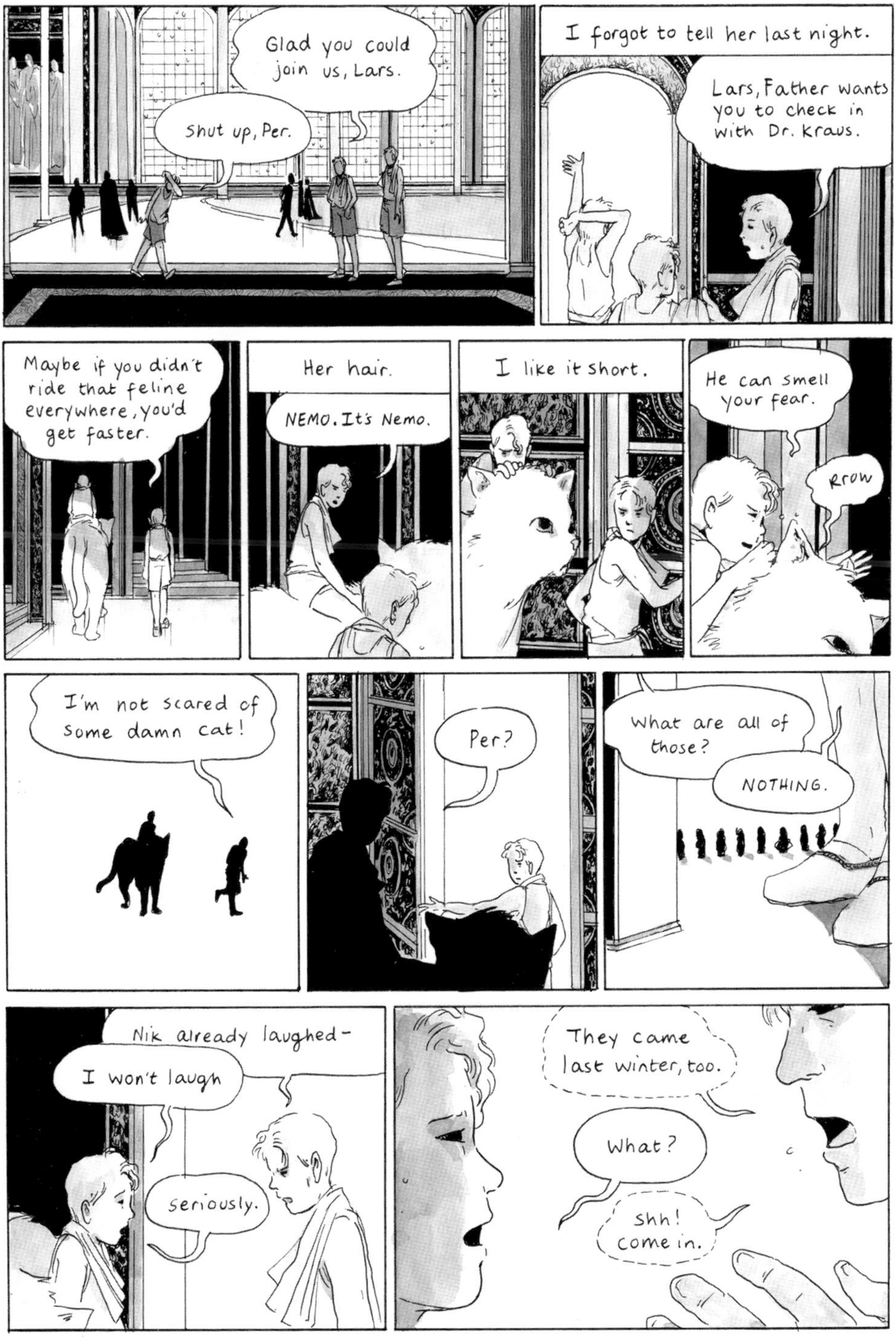
Glad you could join us, Lars.
Shut up, Per.
I forgot to tell her last night.
Lars, Father wants you to check in with Dr. Kraus.
Maybe if you didn't ride that feline everywhere, you'd get faster.
Her hair.
NEMO. It's Nemo.
I like it short.
He can smell your fear.
Rrow
I'm not scared of some damn cat!
Per?
What are all of those?
NOTHING.
Nik already laughed-
I won't laugh
seriously.
They came last winter, too.
What?
Shh! come in.

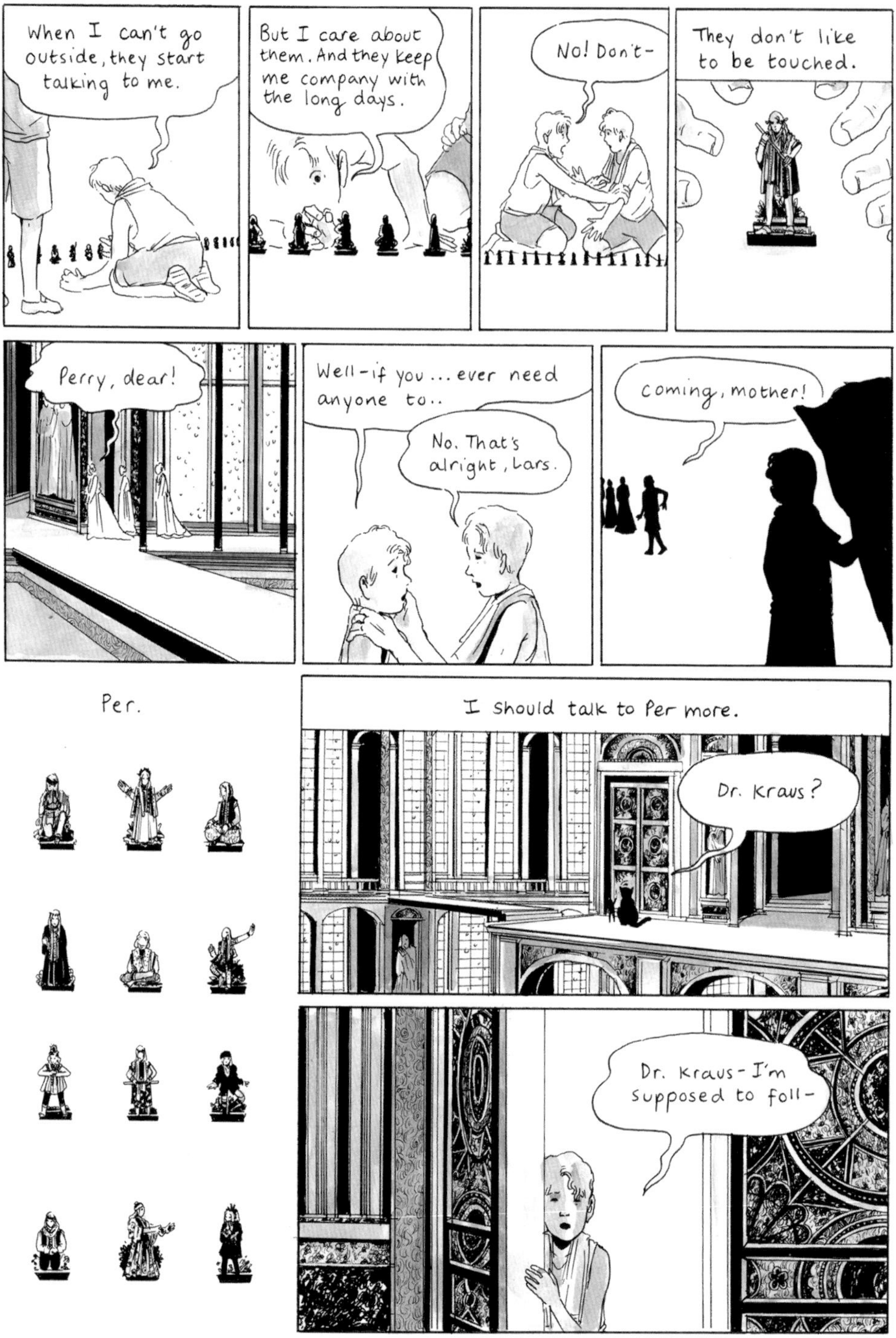

When I can't go outside, they start talking to me.
But I care about them. And they keep me company with the long days.
No! Don't-
They don't like to be touched.
Perry, dear!
Well-if you... ever need anyone to..
No. That's alright, Lars.
Coming, mother!
Per.
I should talk to Per more.
Dr. Kraus?
Dr. Kraus- I'm supposed to foll-

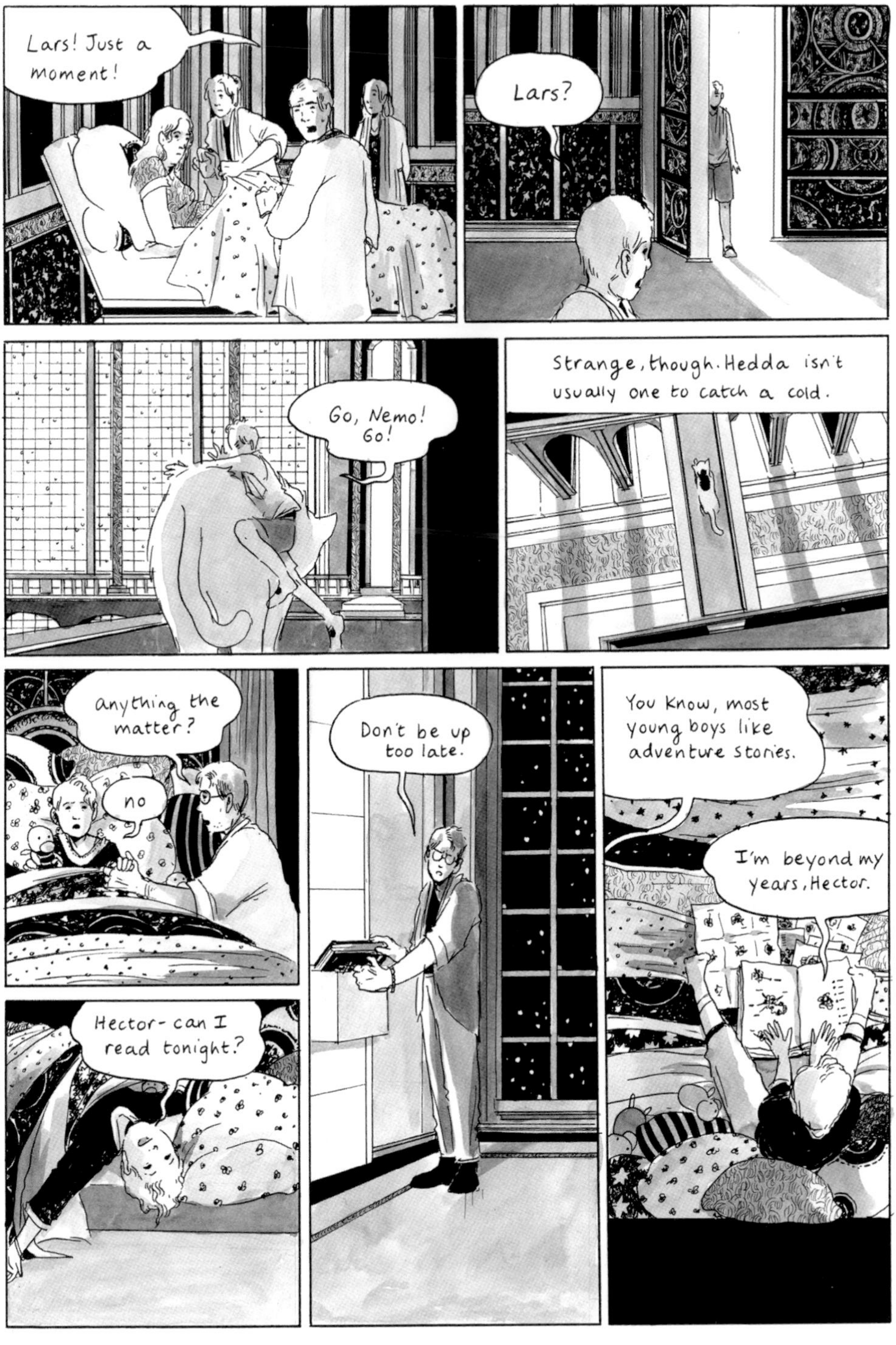

Lars! Just a moment!
Lars?
Go, Nemo! Go!
Strange, though. Hedda isn't usually one to catch a cold.
anything the matter?
no
Hector- can I read tonight?
Don't be up too late.
You know, most young boys like adventure stories.
I'm beyond my years, Hector.

I can't shut my brain off this time.

MAIN PUMP

Maja with short hair, tied to a wall.

FILTER UNIT

Pers' eyes on me. Gripping my shoulder.

FUEL INJECTOR HARNESS

Snow won't stop blowing and I'm getting thinner.

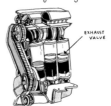

EXHAUST VALVE

After the last episode, I don't have the energy to think about it.

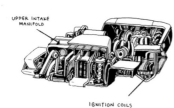

UPPER INTAKE MANIFOLD

IGNITION COILS

impending doom

I keep having these dreams that I'm in a war.

I fight valiantly.

When I get home, I go to a celebration. But I'm 30 minutes early.

No one comes and the food goes cold.

As I sit alone and eat, I suddenly remember the war isn't over yet.

An enemy shoots me, I don't fight back.

always the same.

night after night

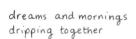

dreams and mornings dripping together

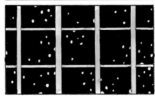

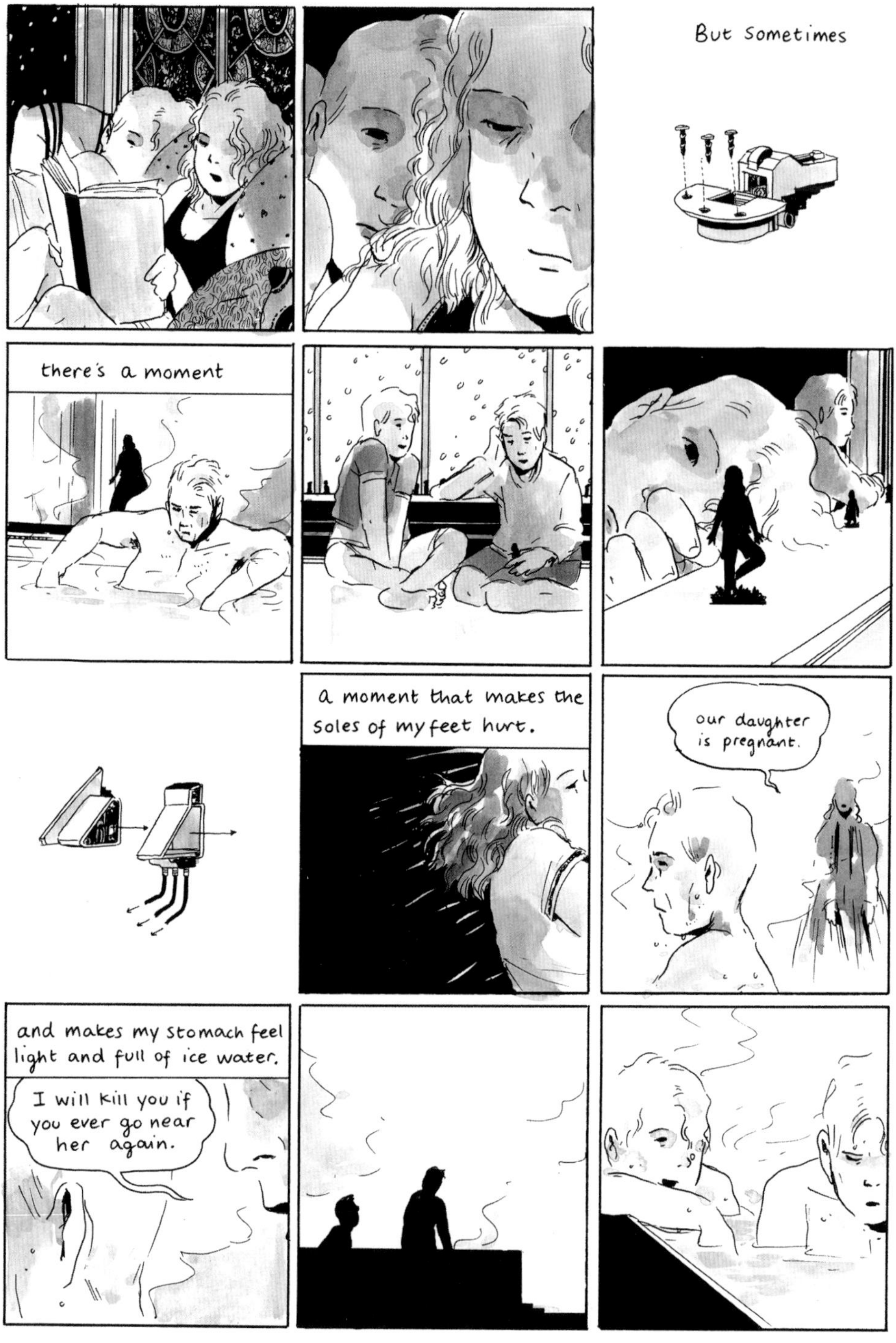
But Sometimes
there's a moment
a moment that makes the soles of my feet hurt.
our daughter is pregnant.
and makes my stomach feel light and full of ice water.
I will kill you if you ever go near her again.

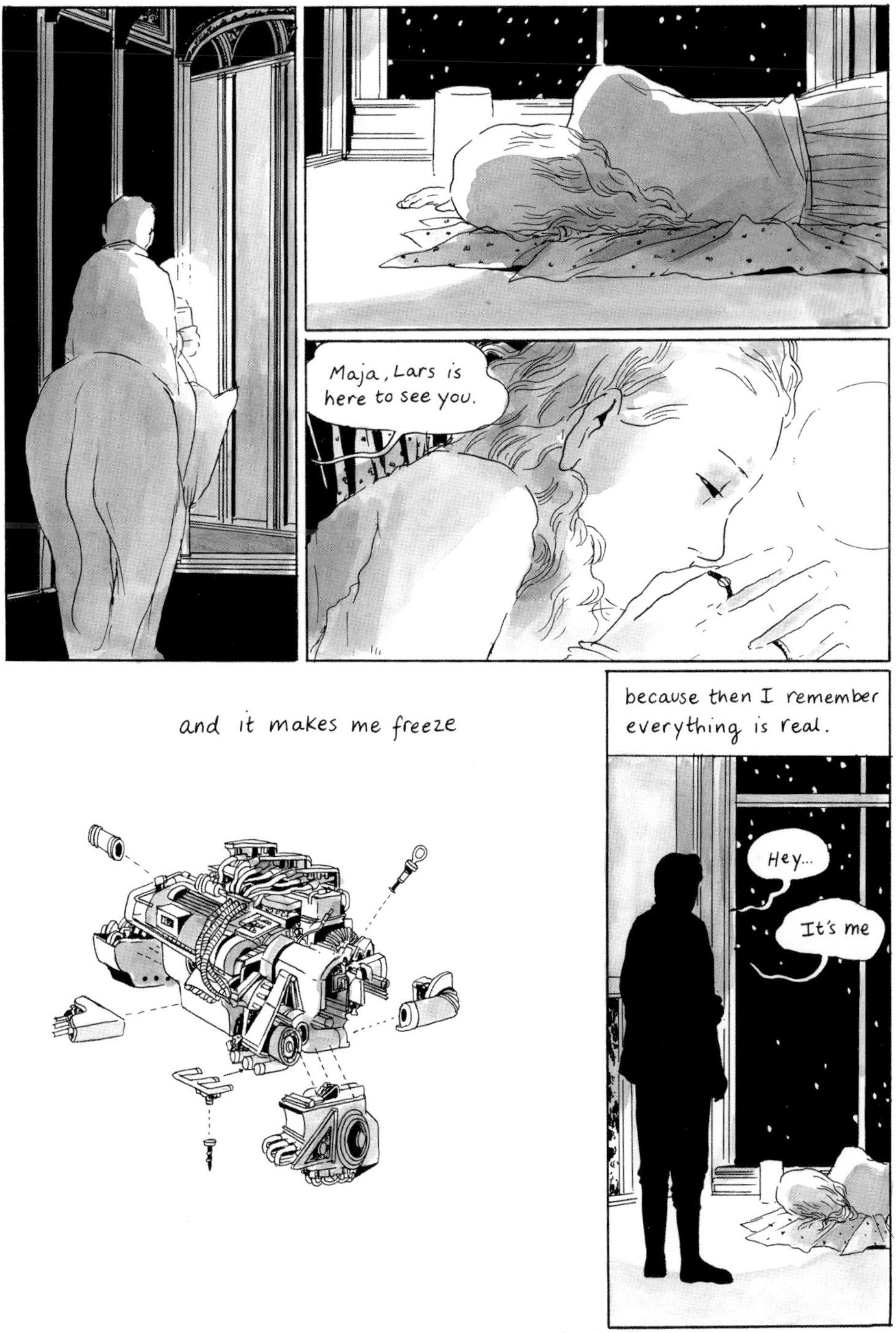

Maja, Lars is here to see you.
and it makes me freeze
because then I remember everything is real.
Hey...
It's me

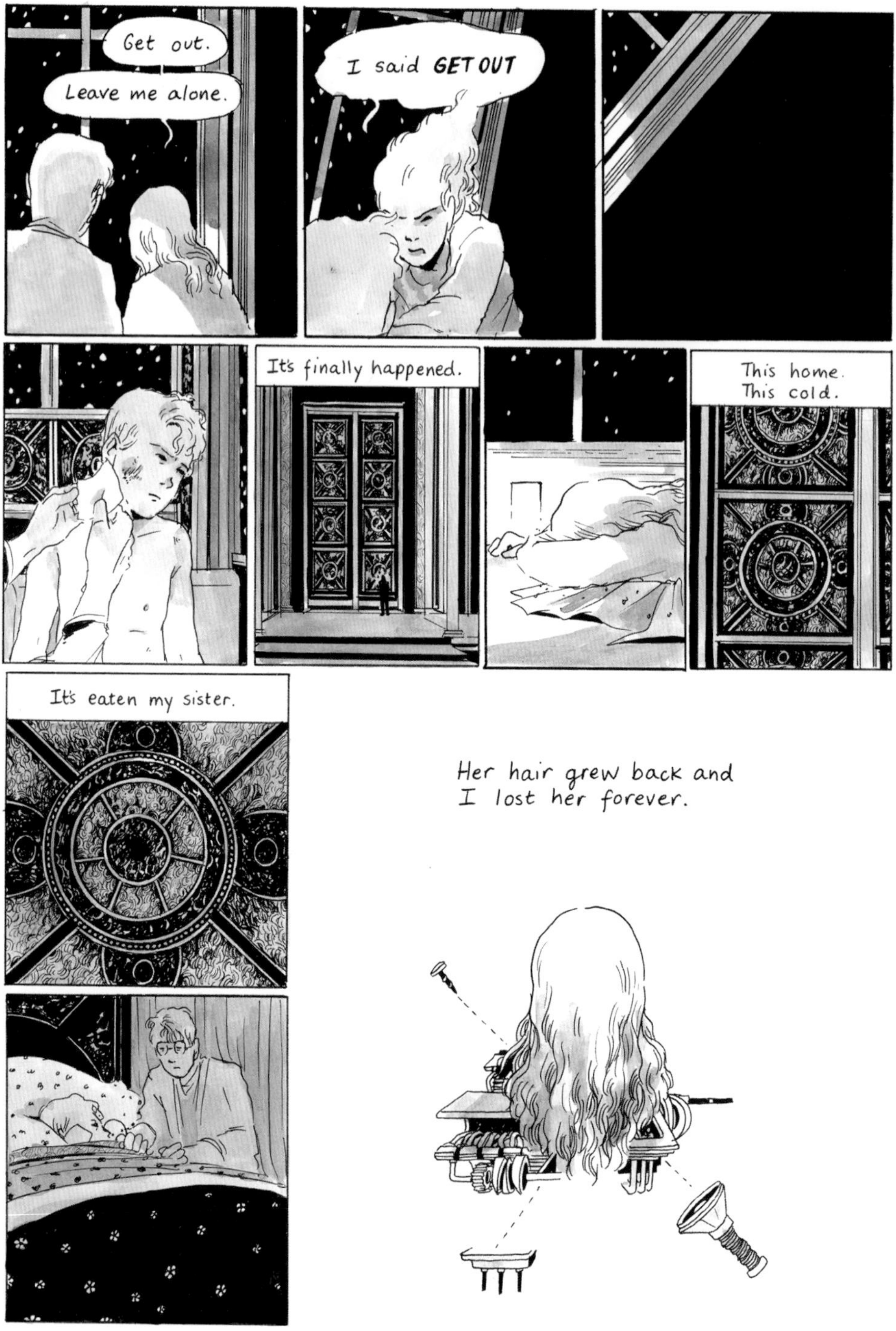
Get out.
Leave me alone.
I said GET OUT
It's finally happened.
This home.
This cold.
It's eaten my sister.
Her hair grew back and I lost her forever.

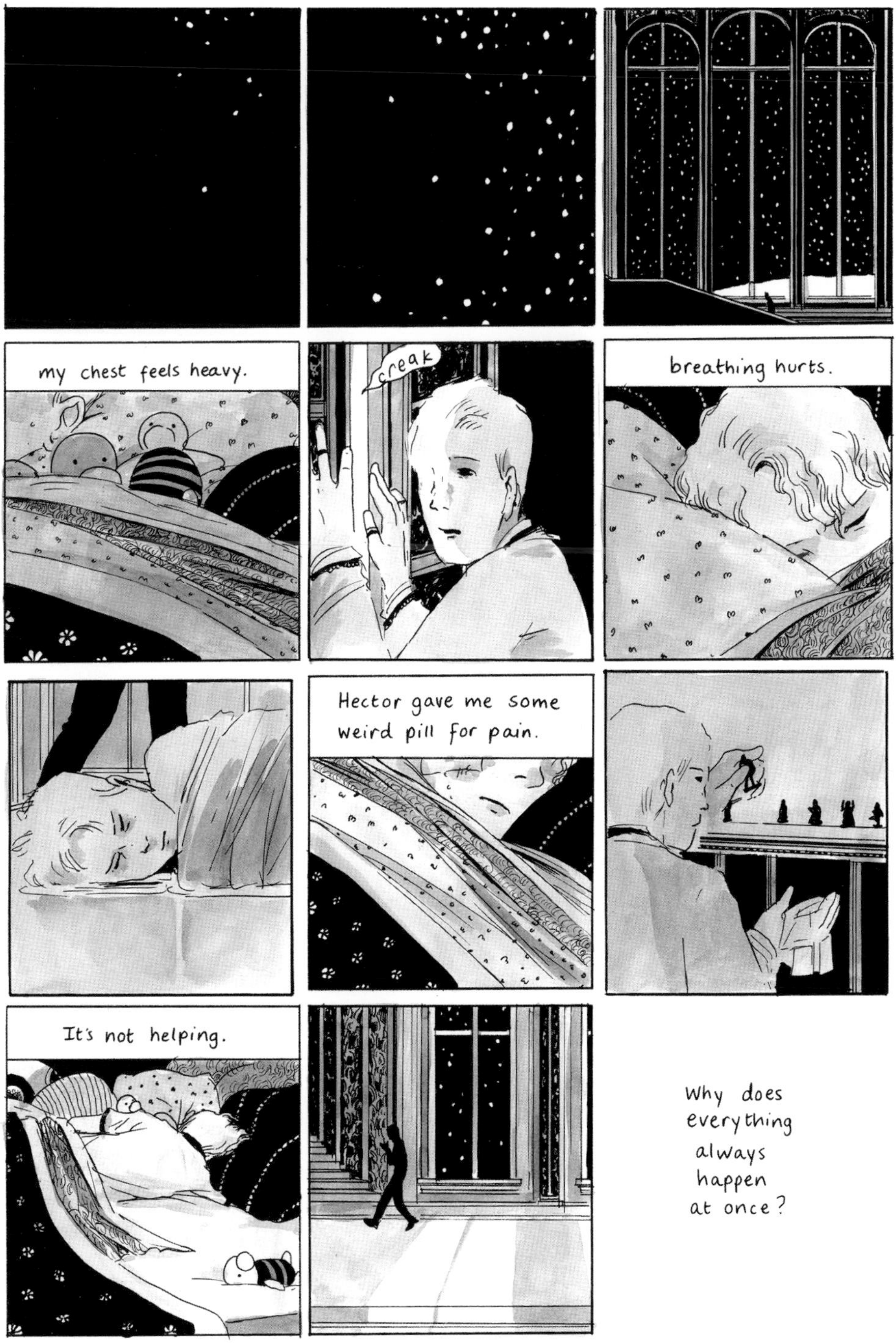
my chest feels heavy.
creak
breathing hurts.
Hector gave me some weird pill for pain.
It's not helping.
Why does everything always happen at once?

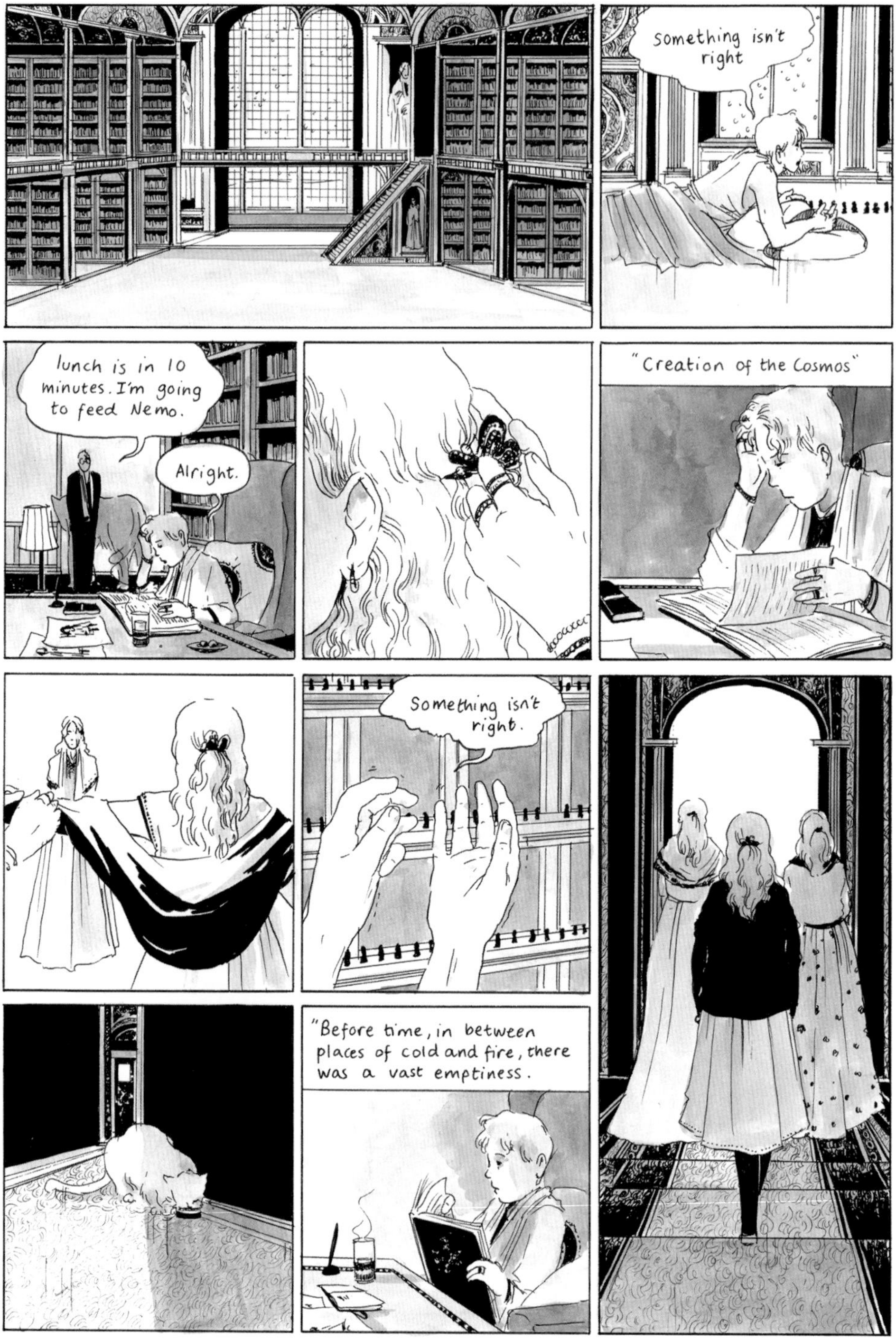
Something isn't right
lunch is in 10 minutes. I'm going to feed Nemo.
Alright.
"Creation of the Cosmos"
Something isn't right.
"Before time, in between places of cold and fire, there was a vast emptiness.

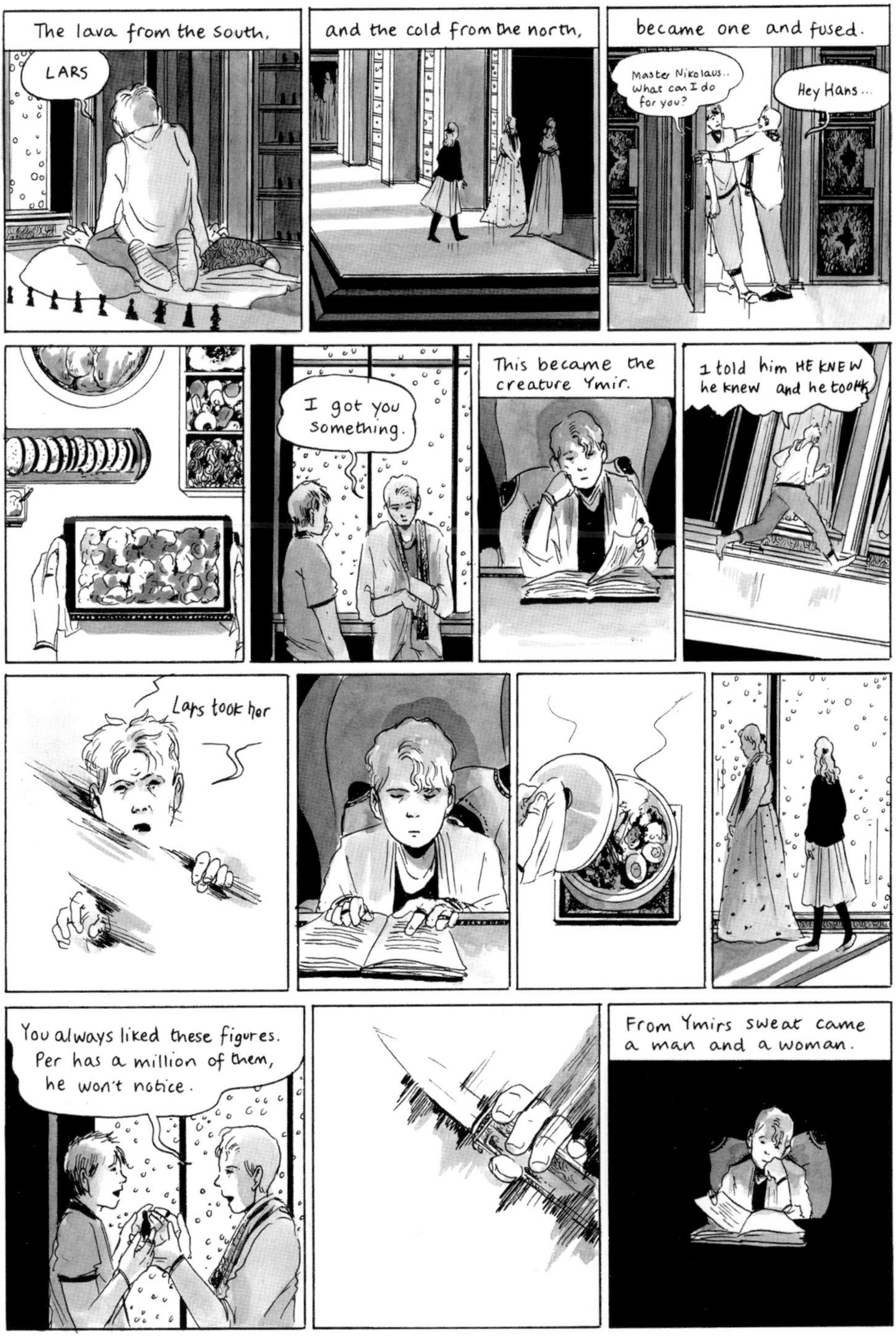
The lava from the south,
LARS
and the cold from the north,
became one and fused.
Master Nikolaus.. What can I do for you?
Hey Hans...
I got you something.
This became the creature Ymir.
I told him HE KNEW he knew and he took
Lars took her
You always liked these figures. Per has a million of them, he won't notice.
From Ymirs sweat came a man and a woman.

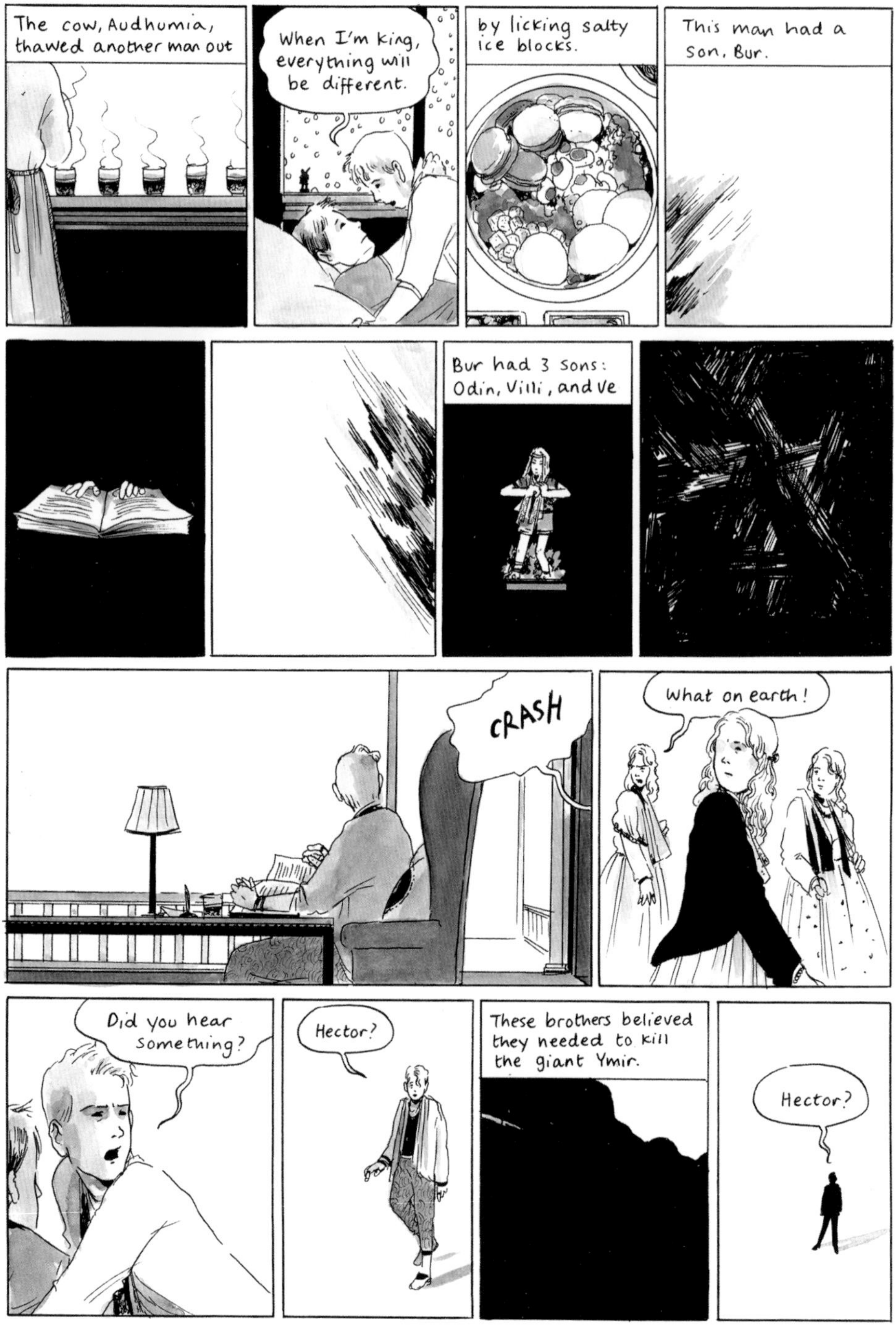
The cow, Audhumia, thawed another man out
When I'm king, everything will be different.
by licking salty ice blocks.
This man had a son, Bur.
Bur had 3 sons: Odin, Villi, and Ve
CRASH
What on earth!
Did you hear something?
Hector?
These brothers believed they needed to kill the giant Ymir.
Hector?

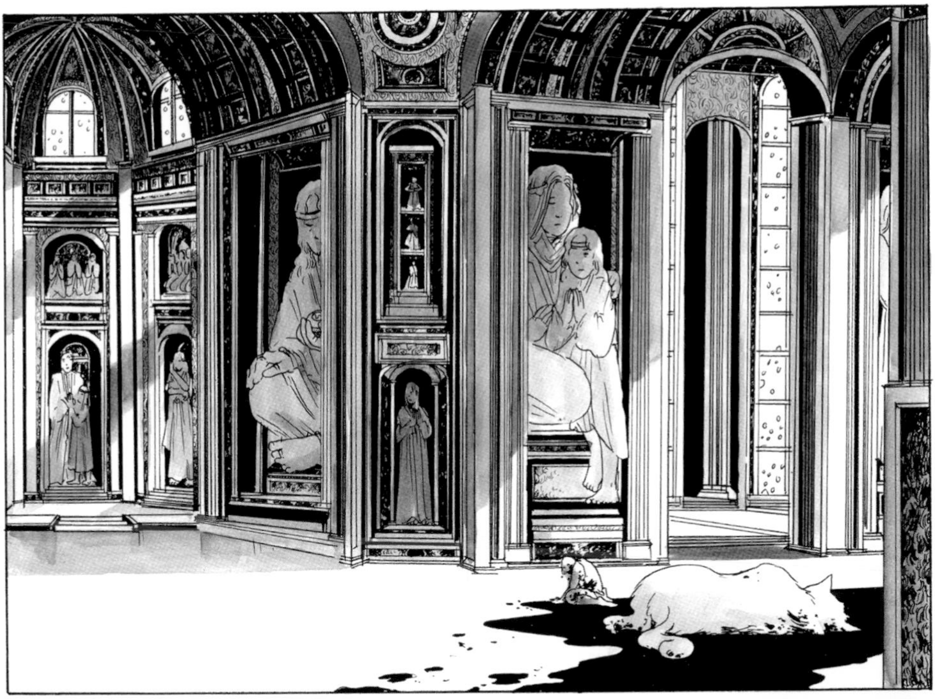

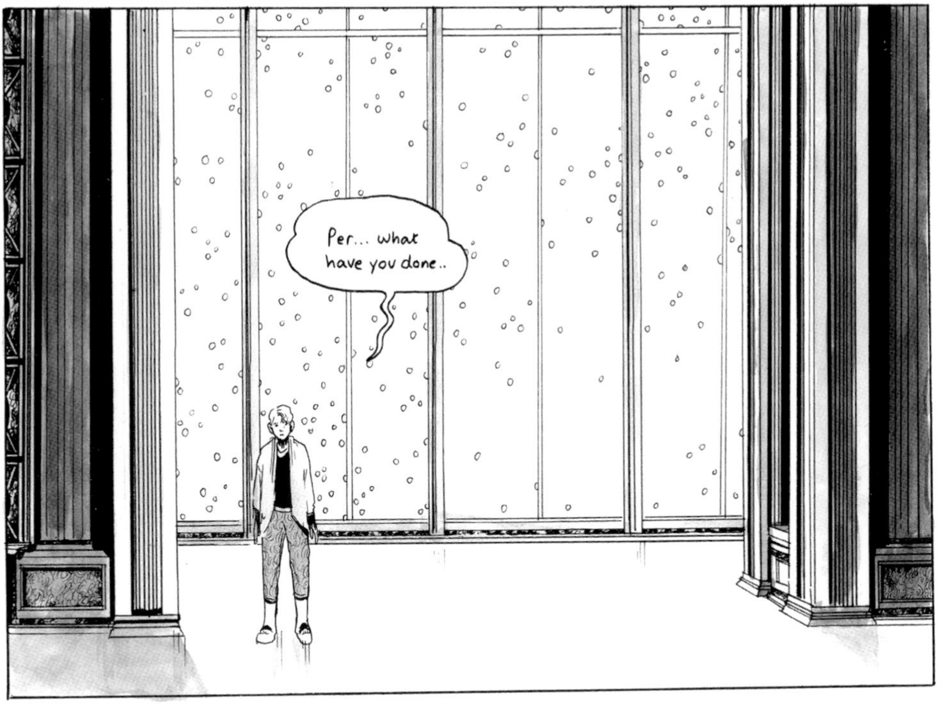
Per... what have you done..

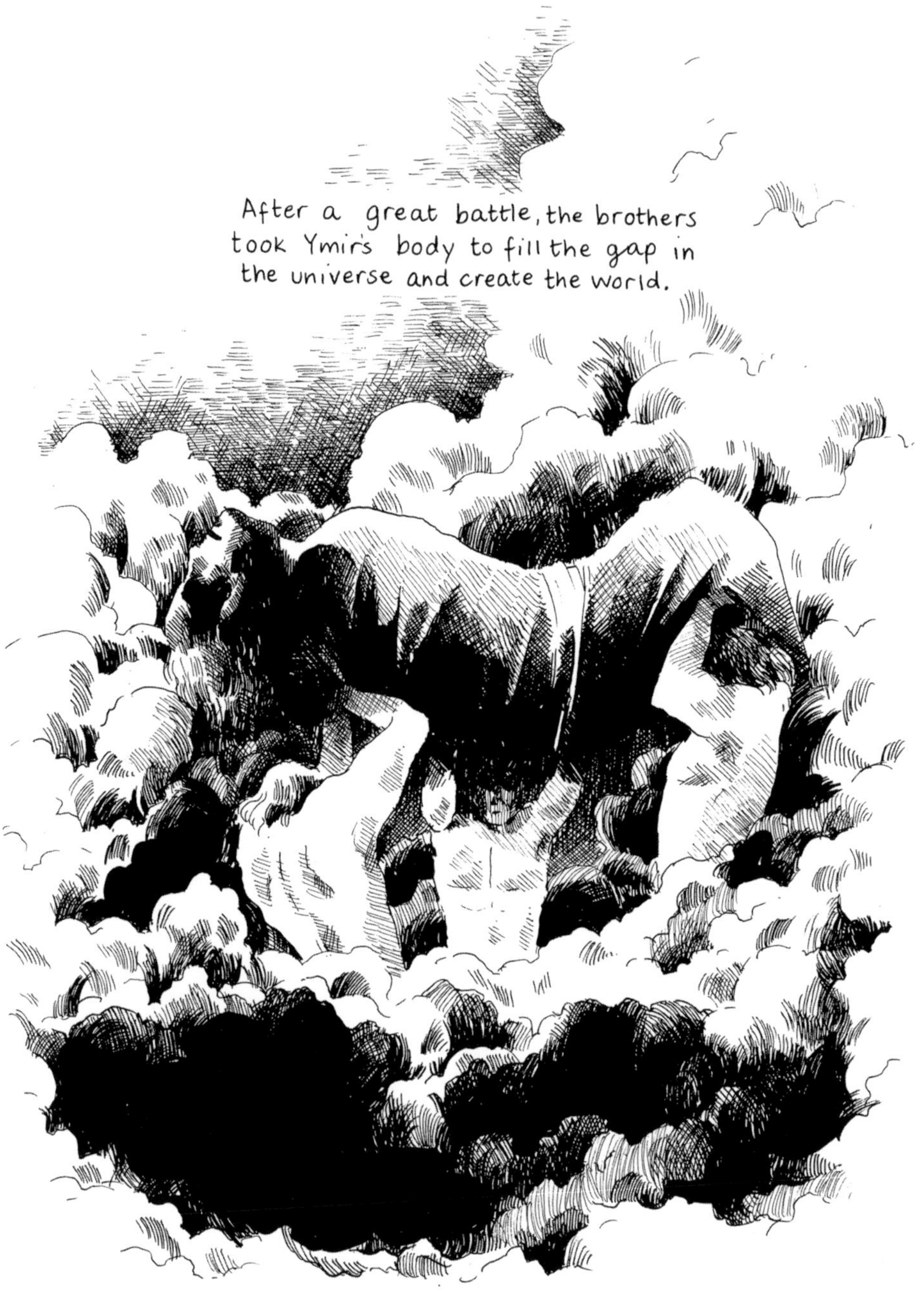
After a great battle, the brothers took Ymir's body to fill the gap in the universe and create the world.

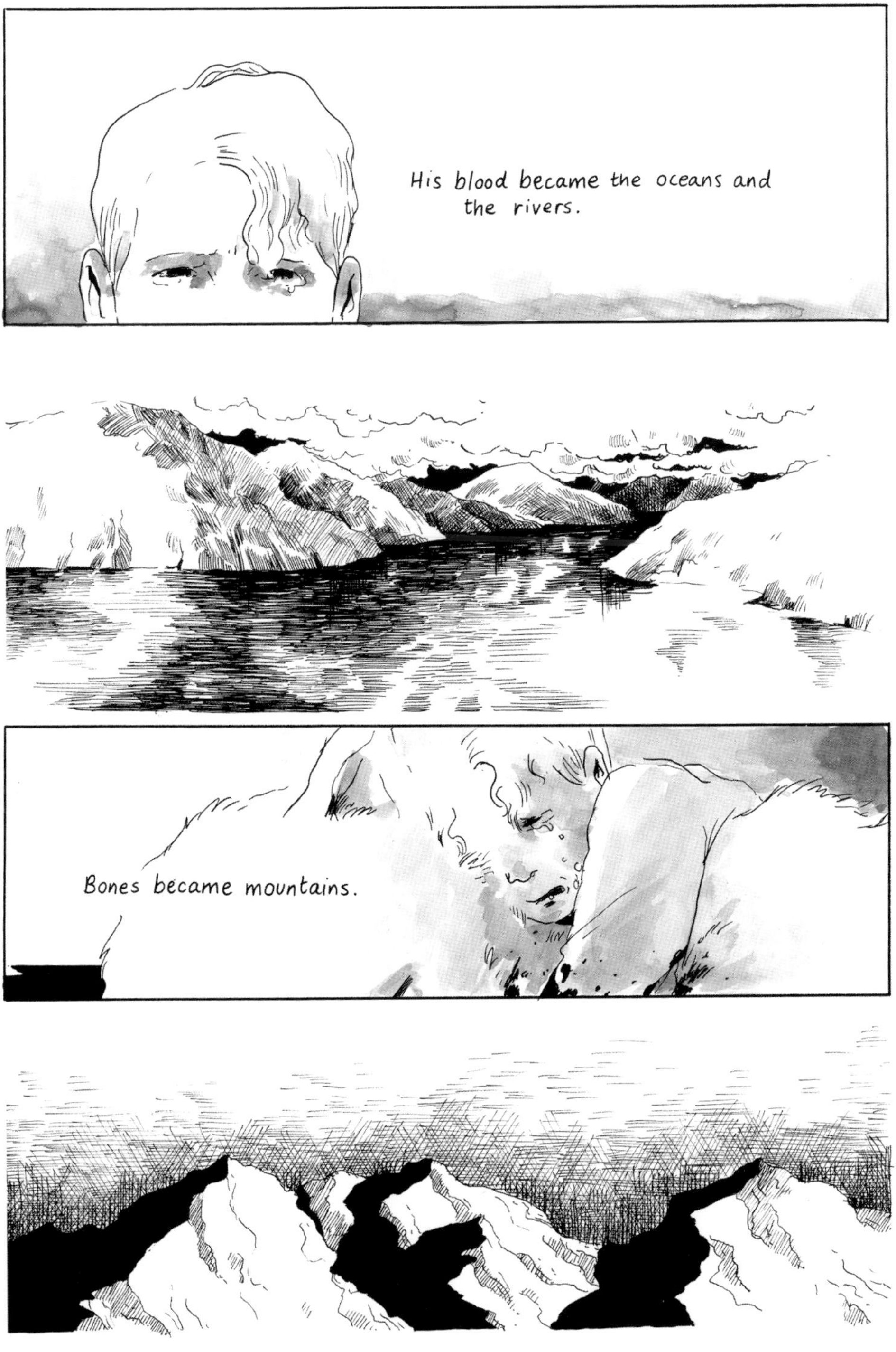
His blood became the oceans and the rivers.
Bones became mountains.

And flesh became the land.

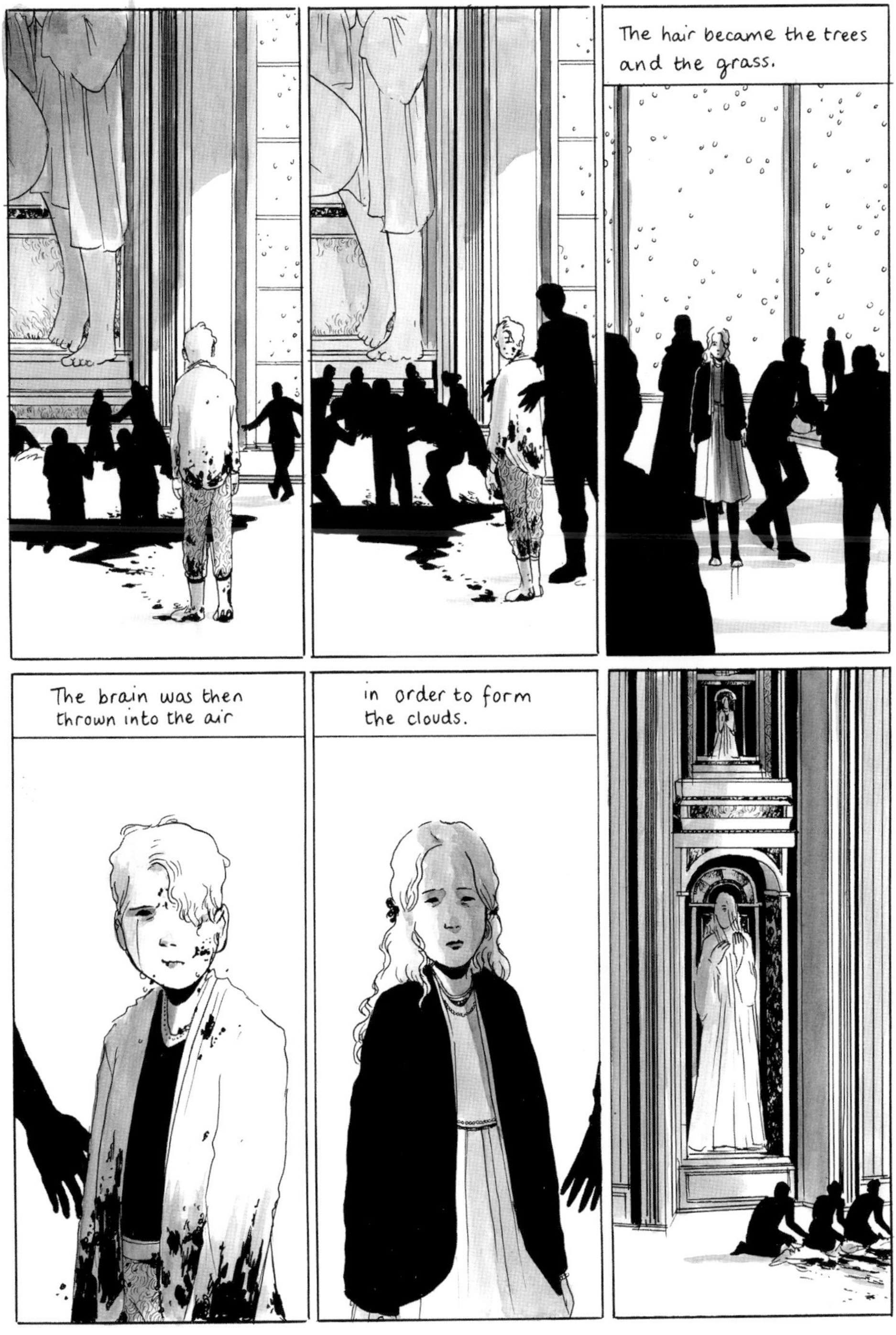
The hair became the trees and the grass.
The brain was then thrown into the air
in order to form the clouds.

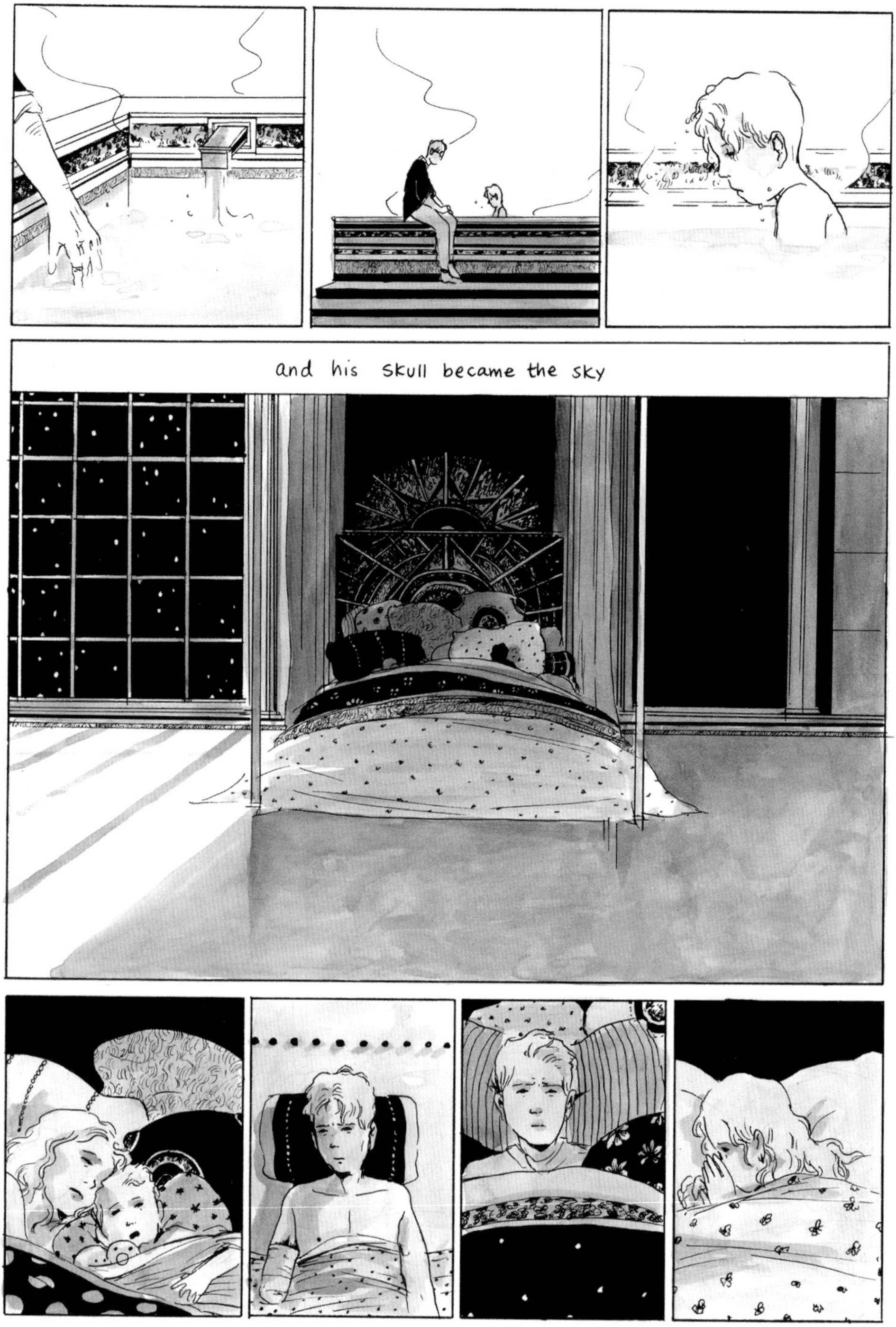
and his skull became the sky

When everything gets quiet, I can't understand that the world extends past me.

I can only see glimpses.

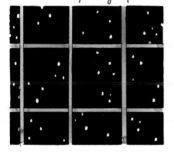

light

depth

chills

relief

color

The little Sounds he made when he was sleeping

reminding me that I am still alive.

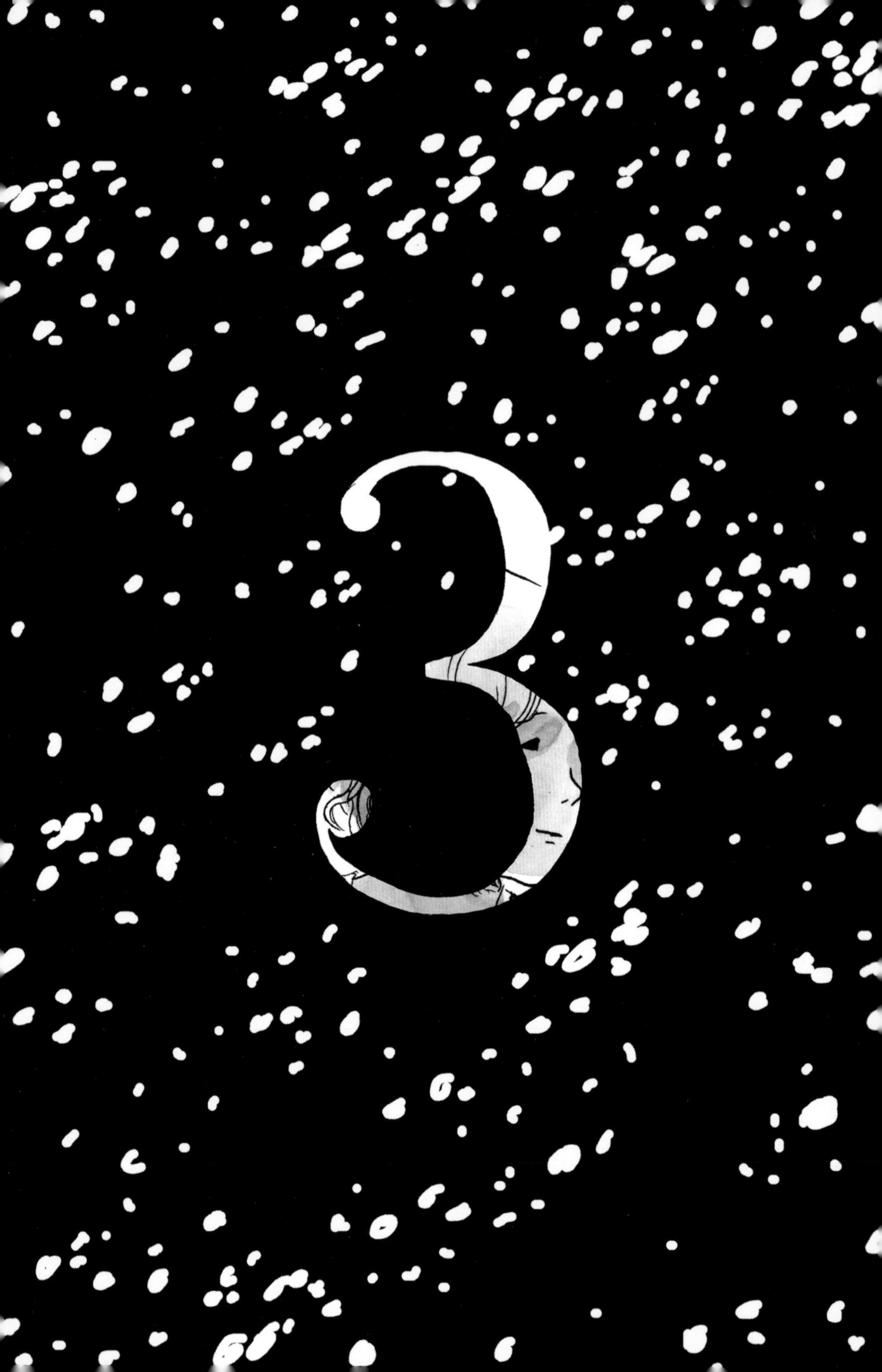
3

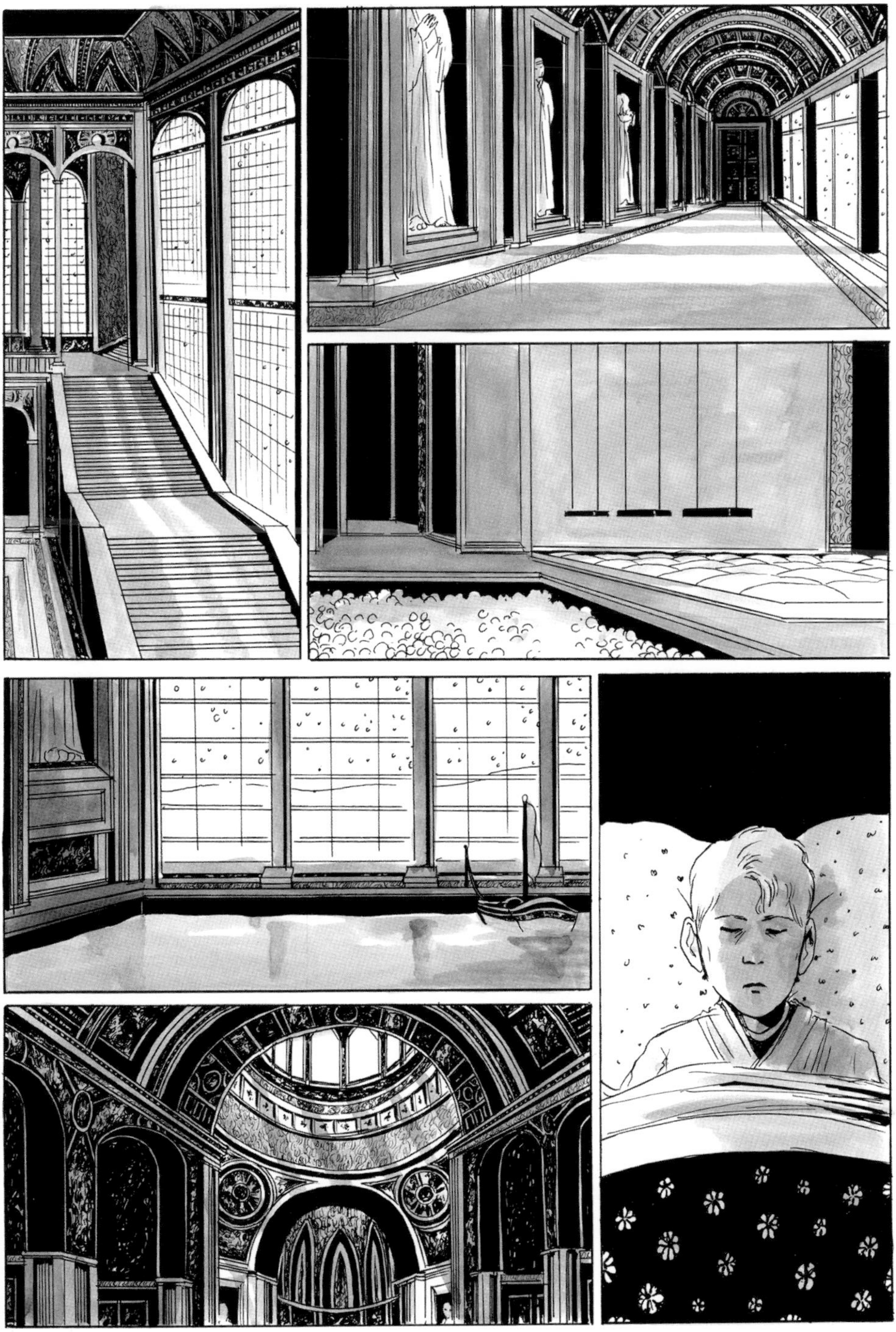

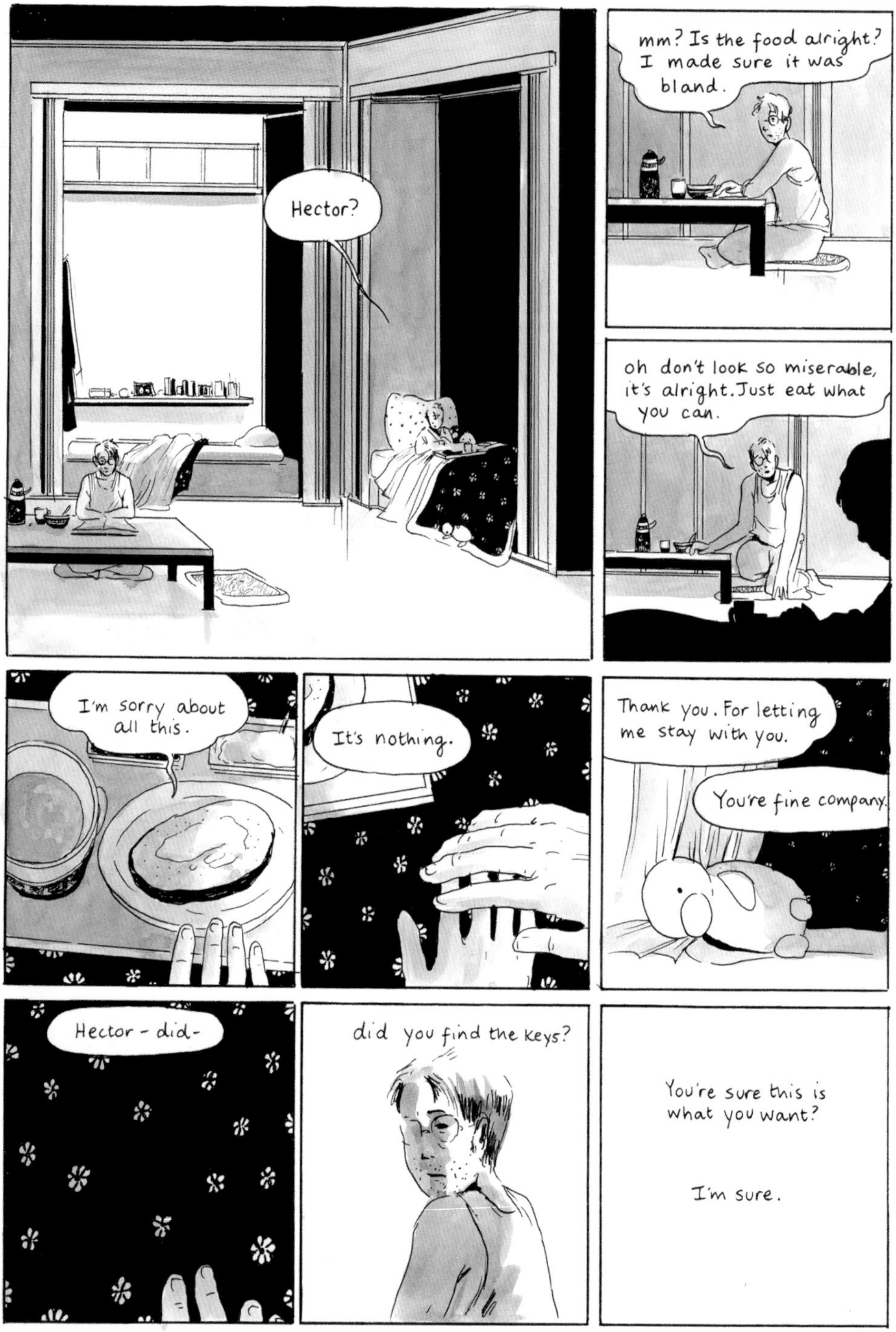
Hector?
mm? Is the food alright? I made sure it was bland.
oh don't look so miserable, it's alright. Just eat what you can.
I'm sorry about all this.
It's nothing.
Thank you. For letting me stay with you.
You're fine company.
Hector - did-
did you find the keys?
You're sure this is what you want?
I'm sure.

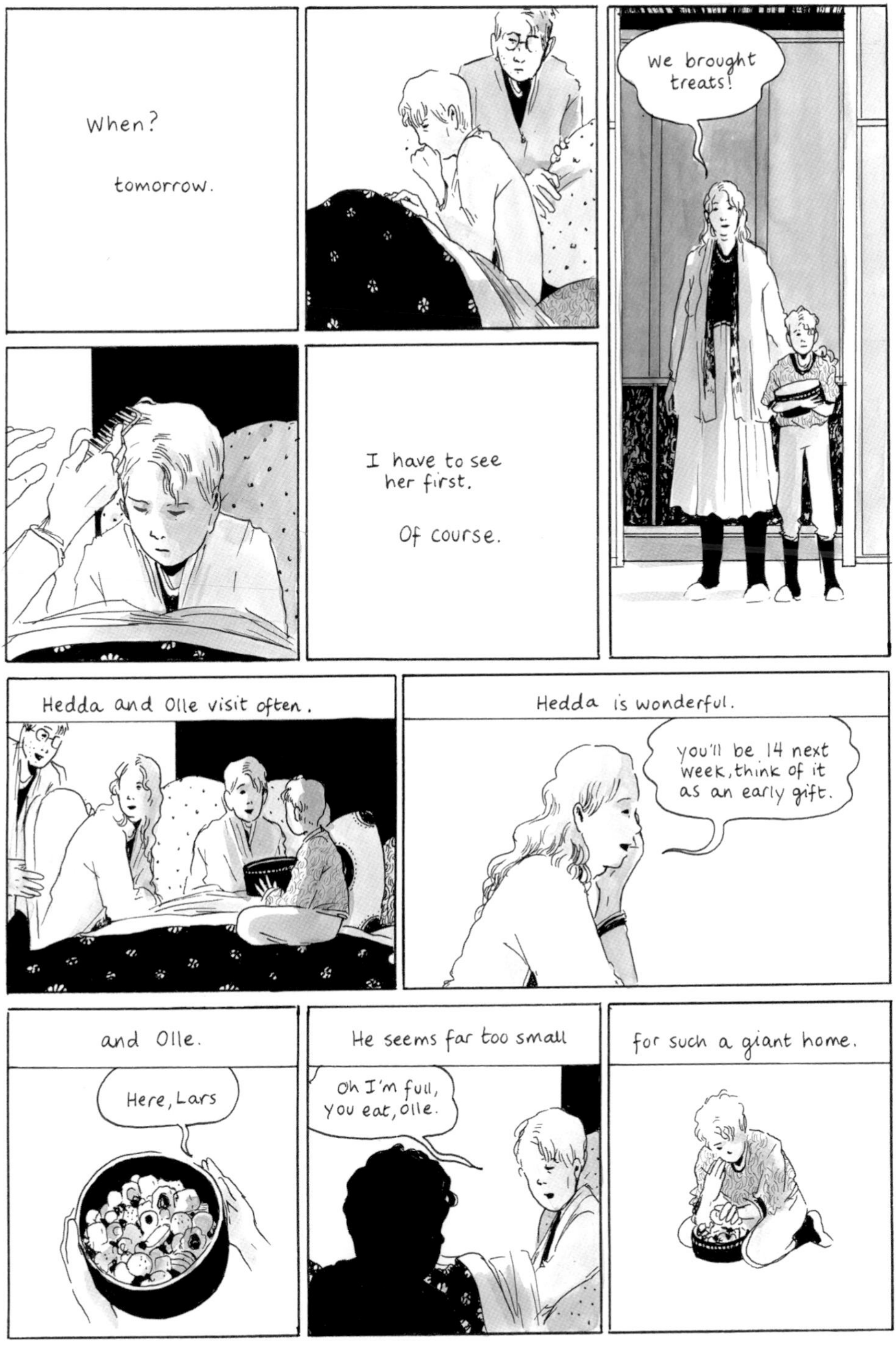
When?
tomorrow.
We brought treats!
I have to see her first.
Of course.
Hedda and Olle visit often.
Hedda is wonderful.
you'll be 14 next week, think of it as an early gift.
and Olle.
Here, Lars
He seems far too small
Oh I'm full, you eat, Olle.
for such a giant home.

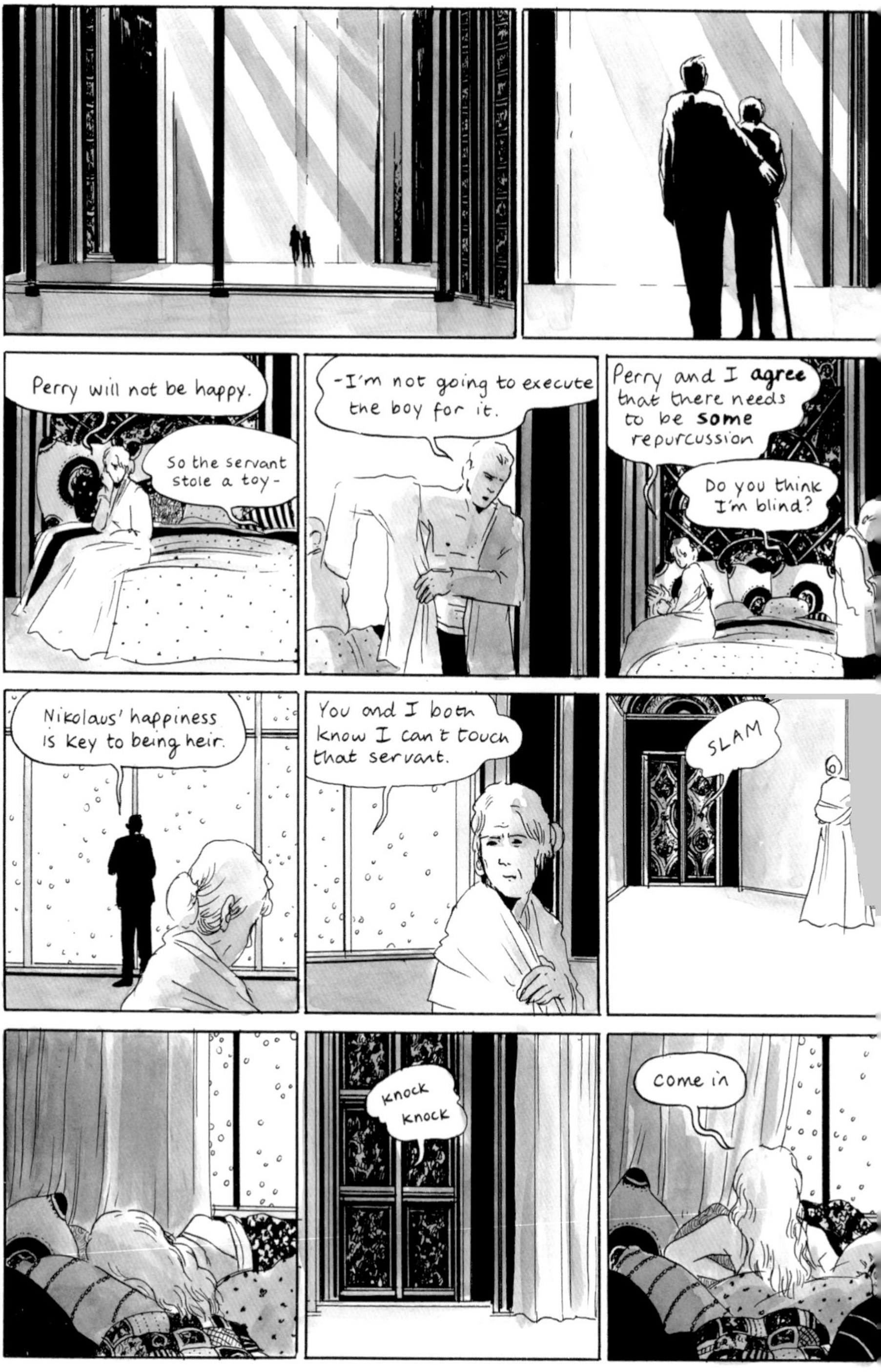
Perry will not be happy.
So the servant stole a toy-
-I'm not going to execute the boy for it.
Perry and I **agree** that there needs to be **some** repurcussion
Do you think I'm blind?
Nikolaus' happiness is key to being heir.
You and I both know I can't touch that servant.
SLAM
knock knock
Come in

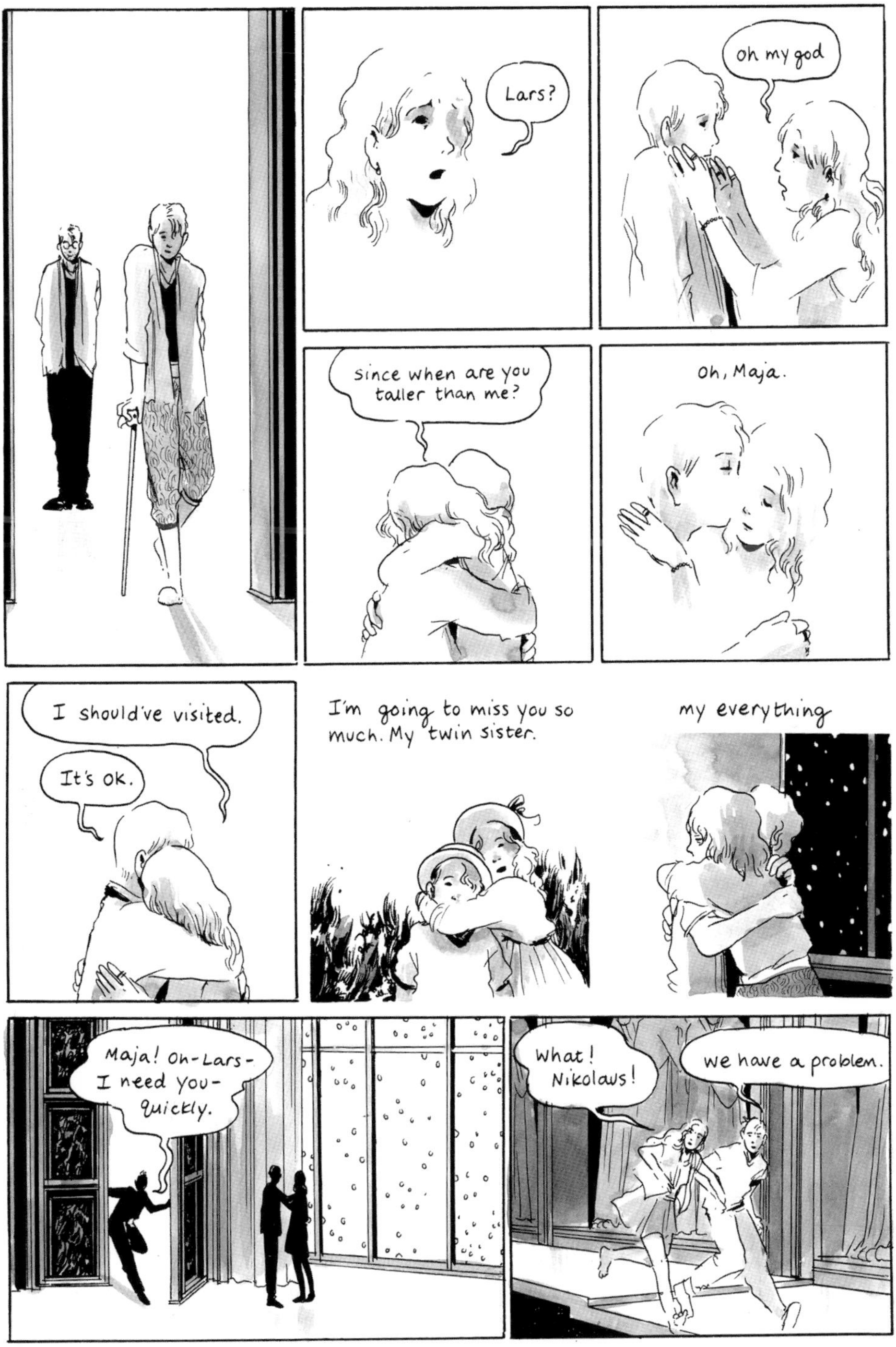
Lars?
oh my god
since when are you taller than me?
Oh, Maja.
I should've visited.
It's OK.
I'm going to miss you so much. My twin sister.
my everything
Maja! Oh-Lars- I need you- quickly.
What! Nikolaus!
we have a problem.

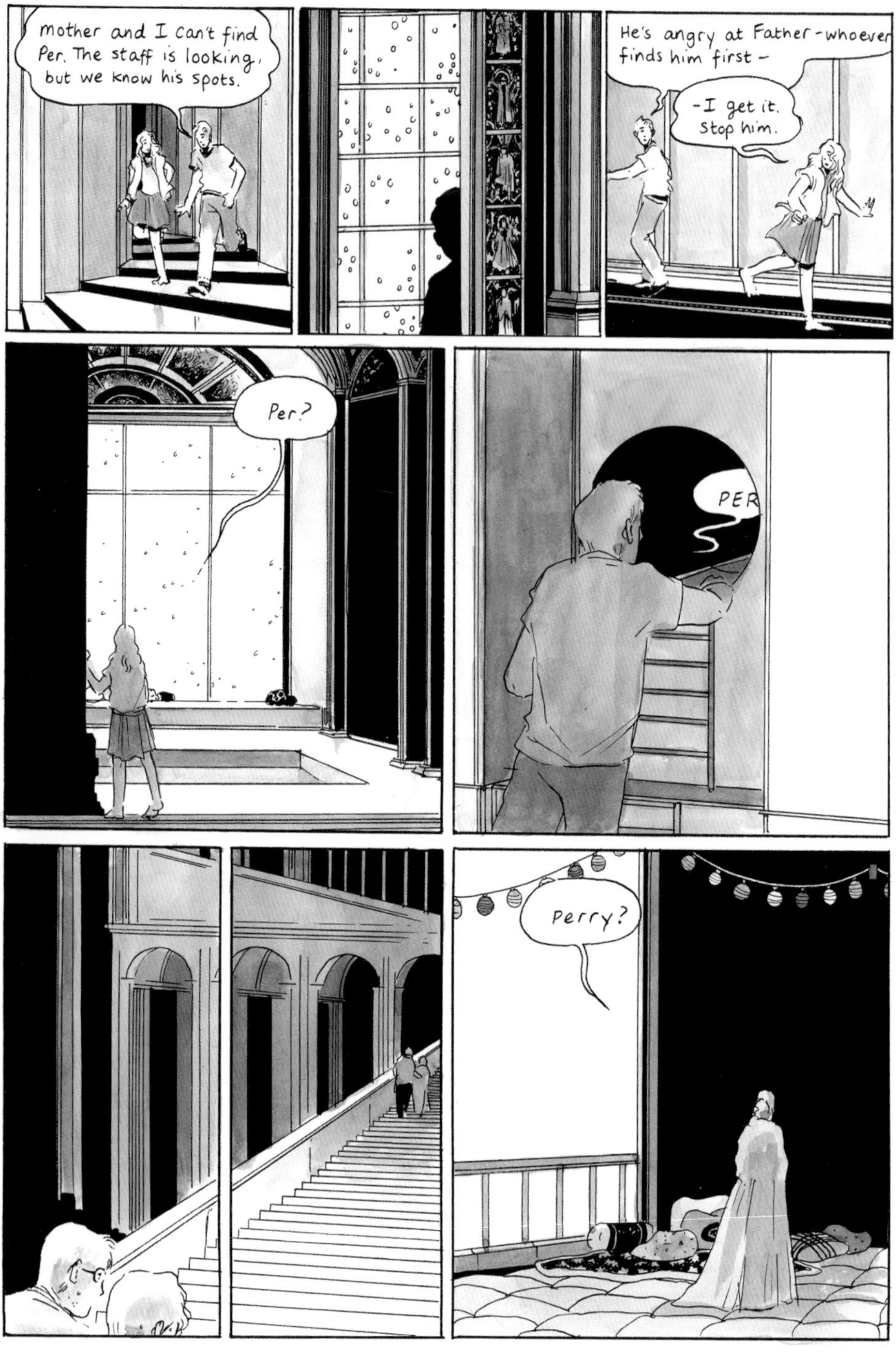
mother and I can't find Per. The staff is looking, but we know his spots.
He's angry at Father-whoever finds him first-
-I get it. Stop him.
Per?
PER
Perry?

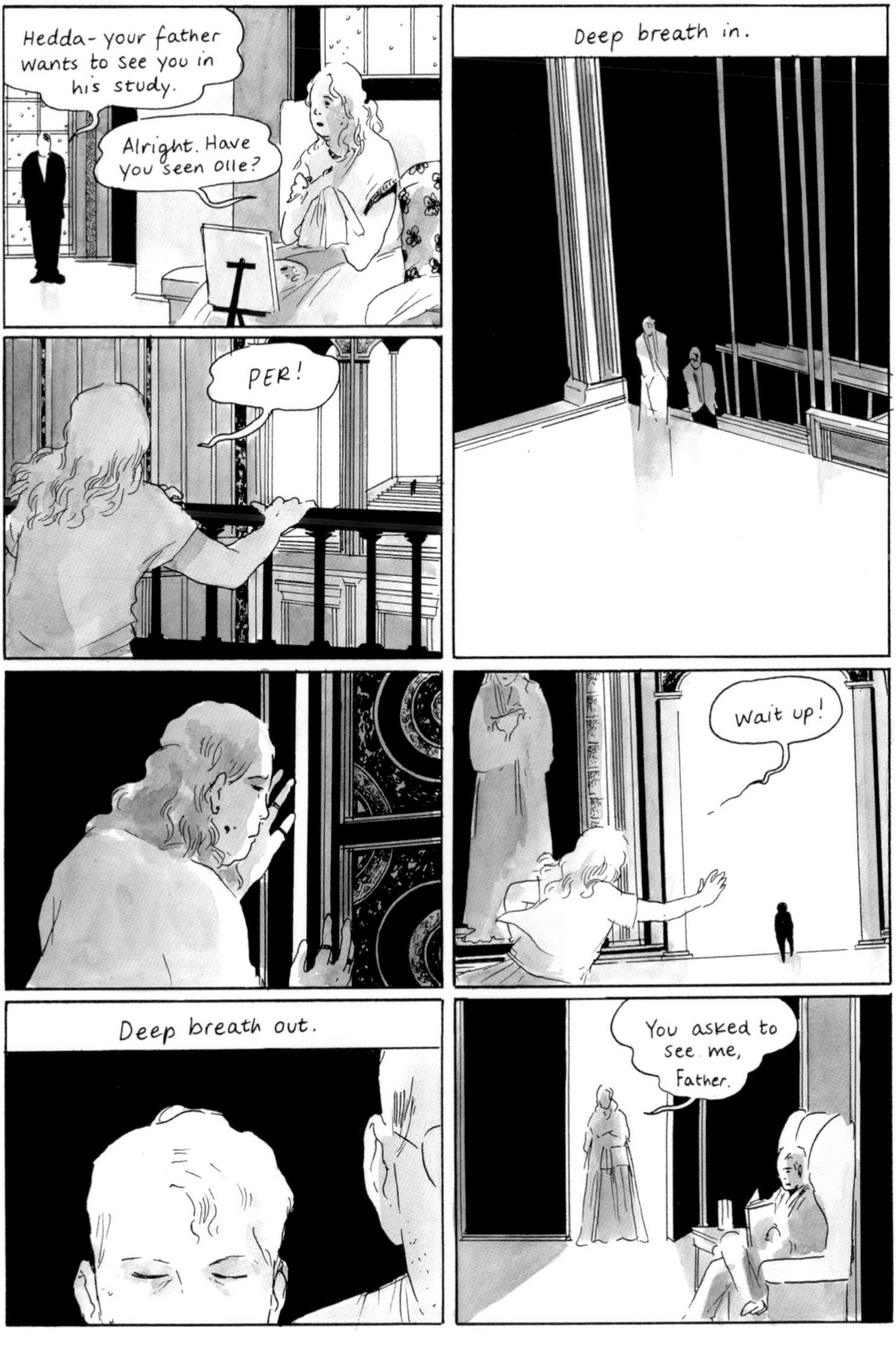
Hedda- your father wants to see you in his study.
Alright. Have you seen Olle?
Deep breath in.
PER!
Wait up!
Deep breath out.
You asked to see me, Father.

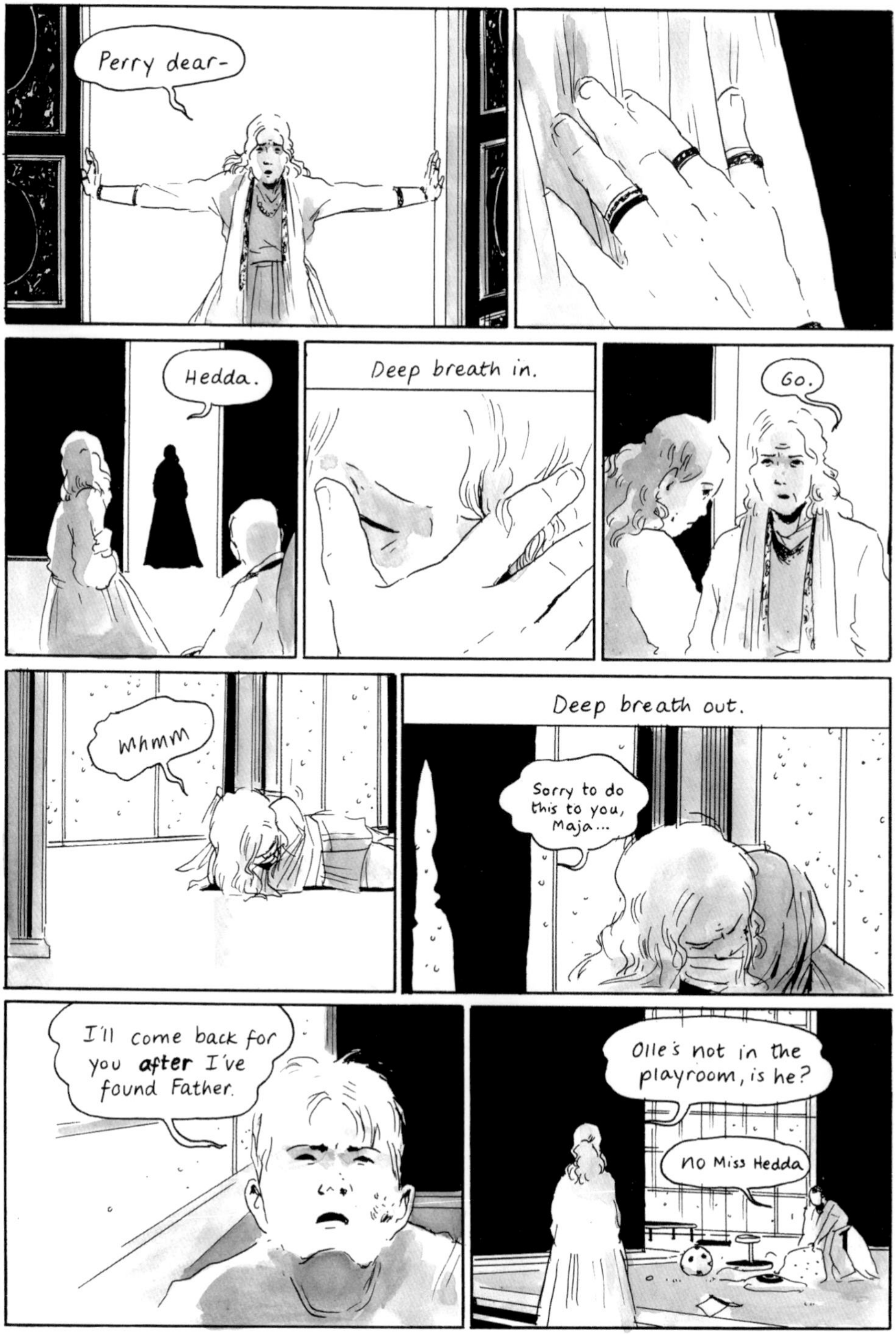
Perry dear-
Hedda.
Deep breath in.
Go.
Whmm
Deep breath out.
Sorry to do this to you, Maja...
I'll come back for you **after** I've found Father.
Olle's not in the playroom, is he?
No Miss Hedda

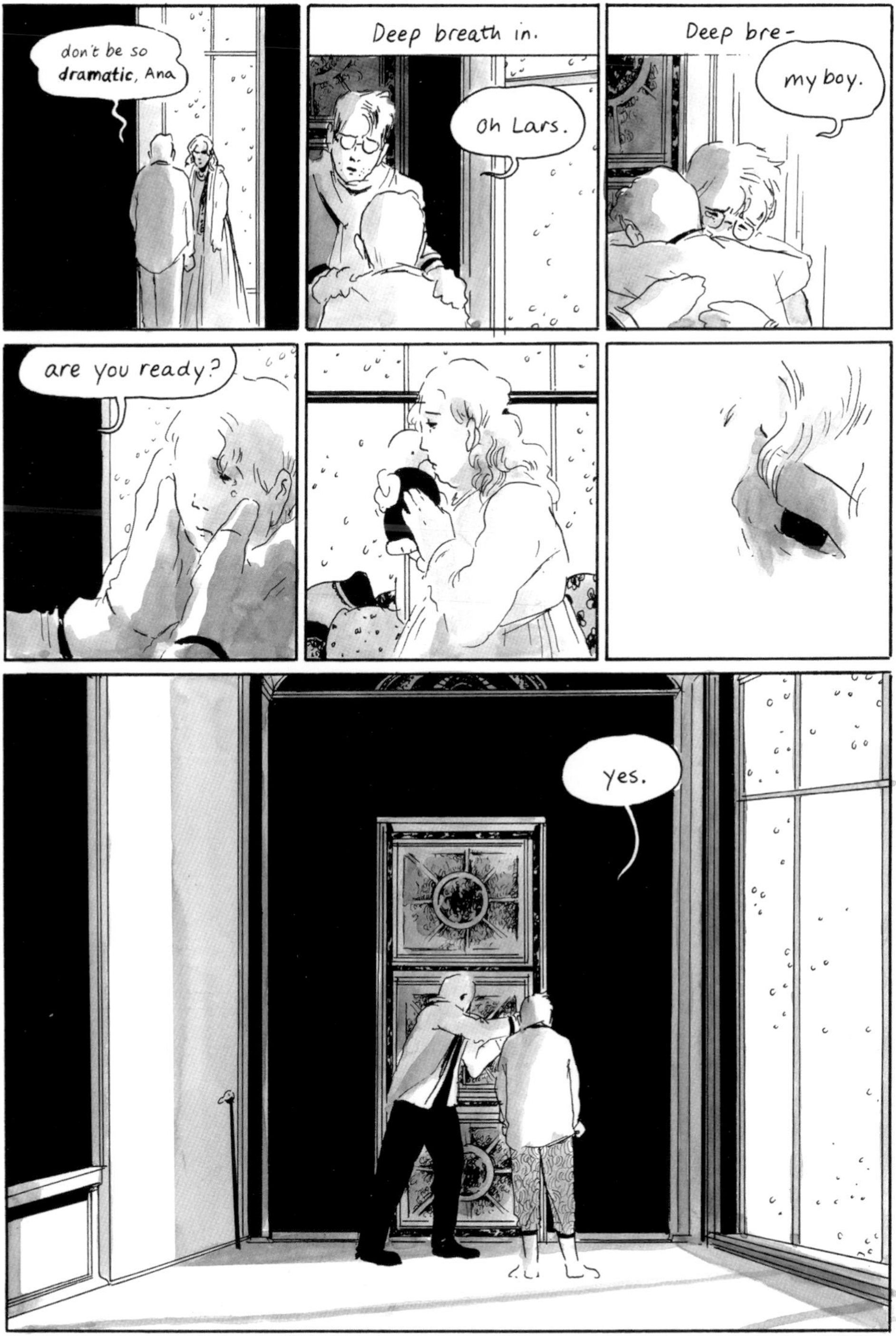

don't be so **dramatic**, Ana
Deep breath in.
Oh Lars.
Deep bre-
my boy.
are you ready?
yes.

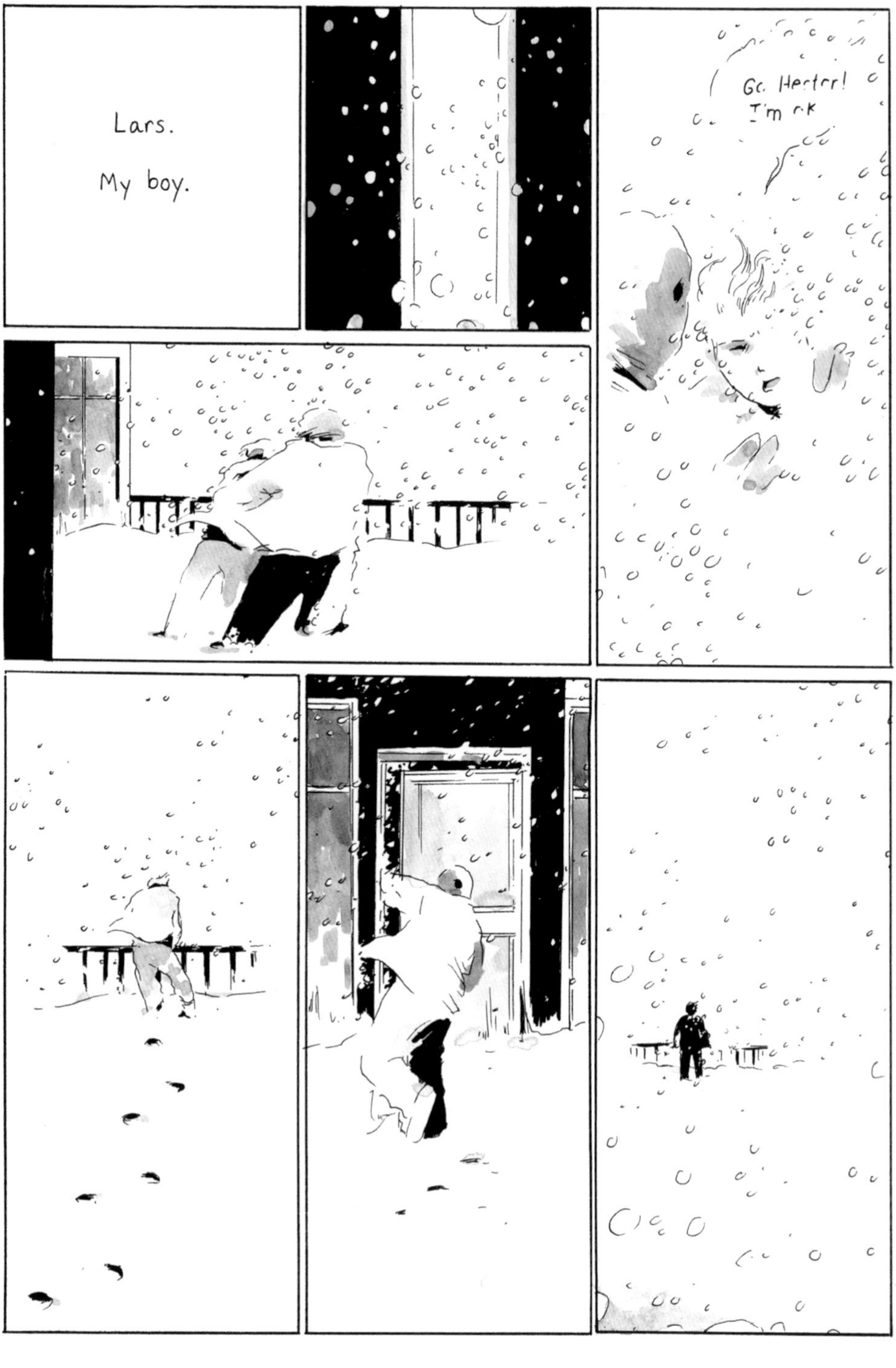
Lars.
My boy.

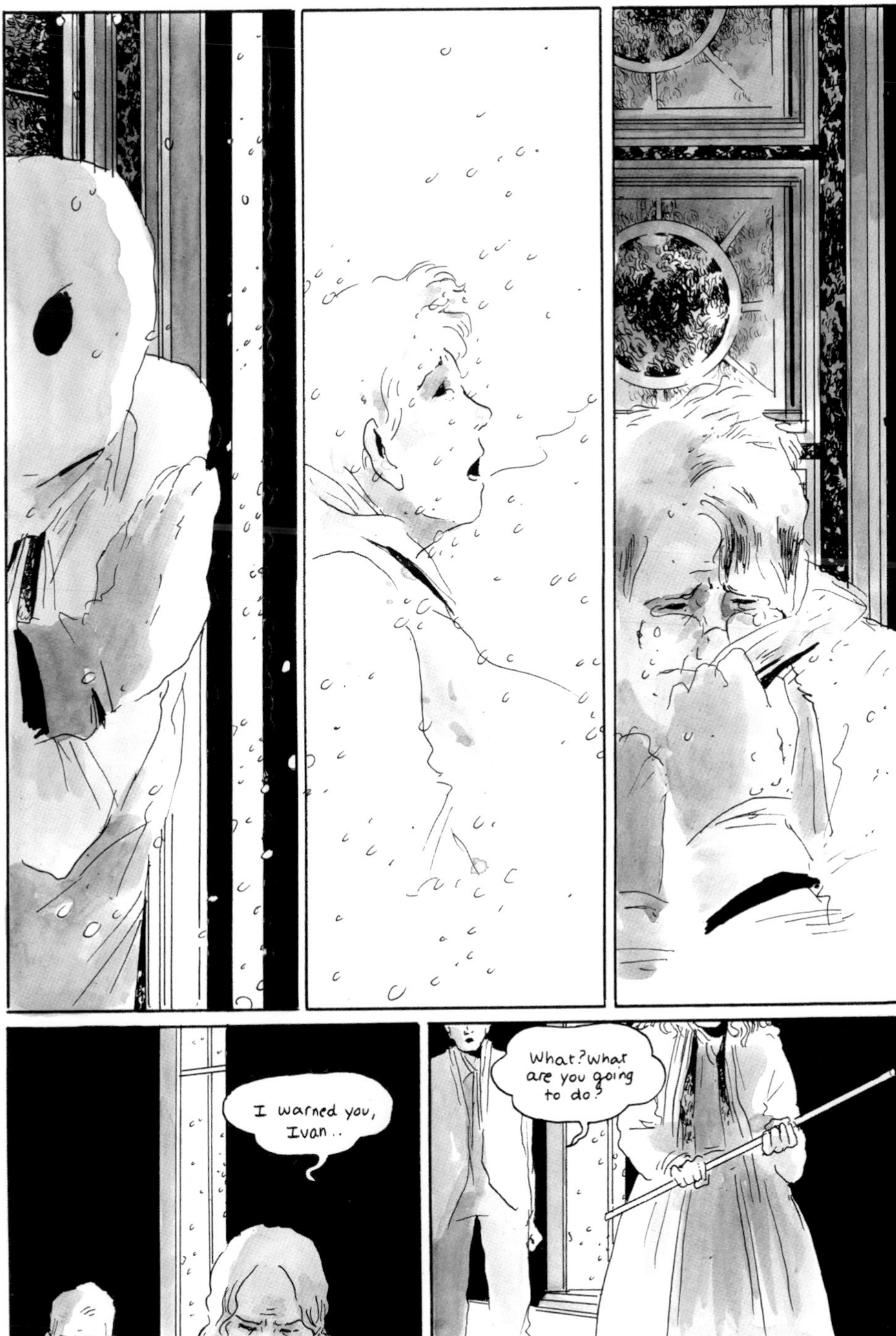
I warned you, Ivan..
What? what are you going to do?

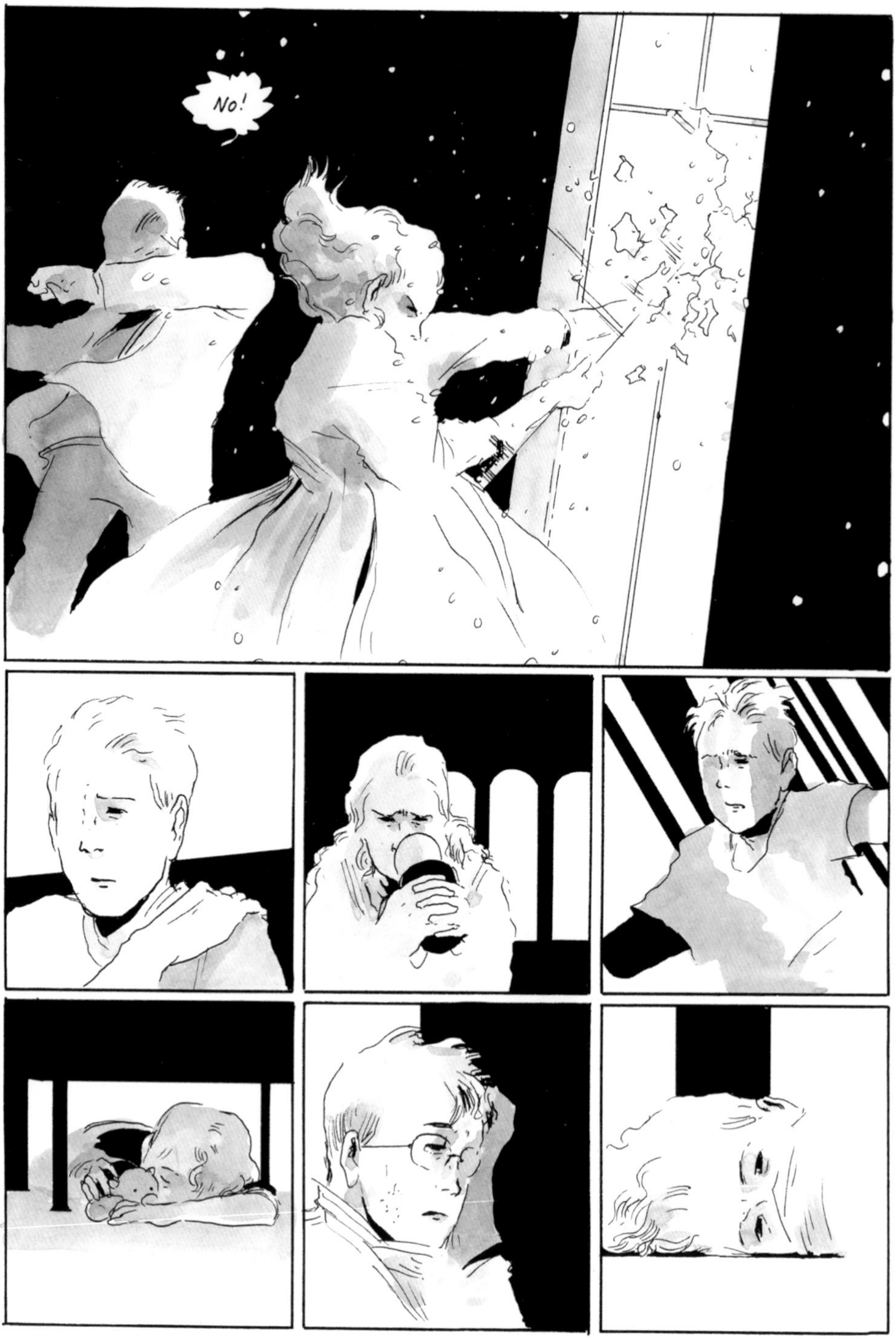
No!

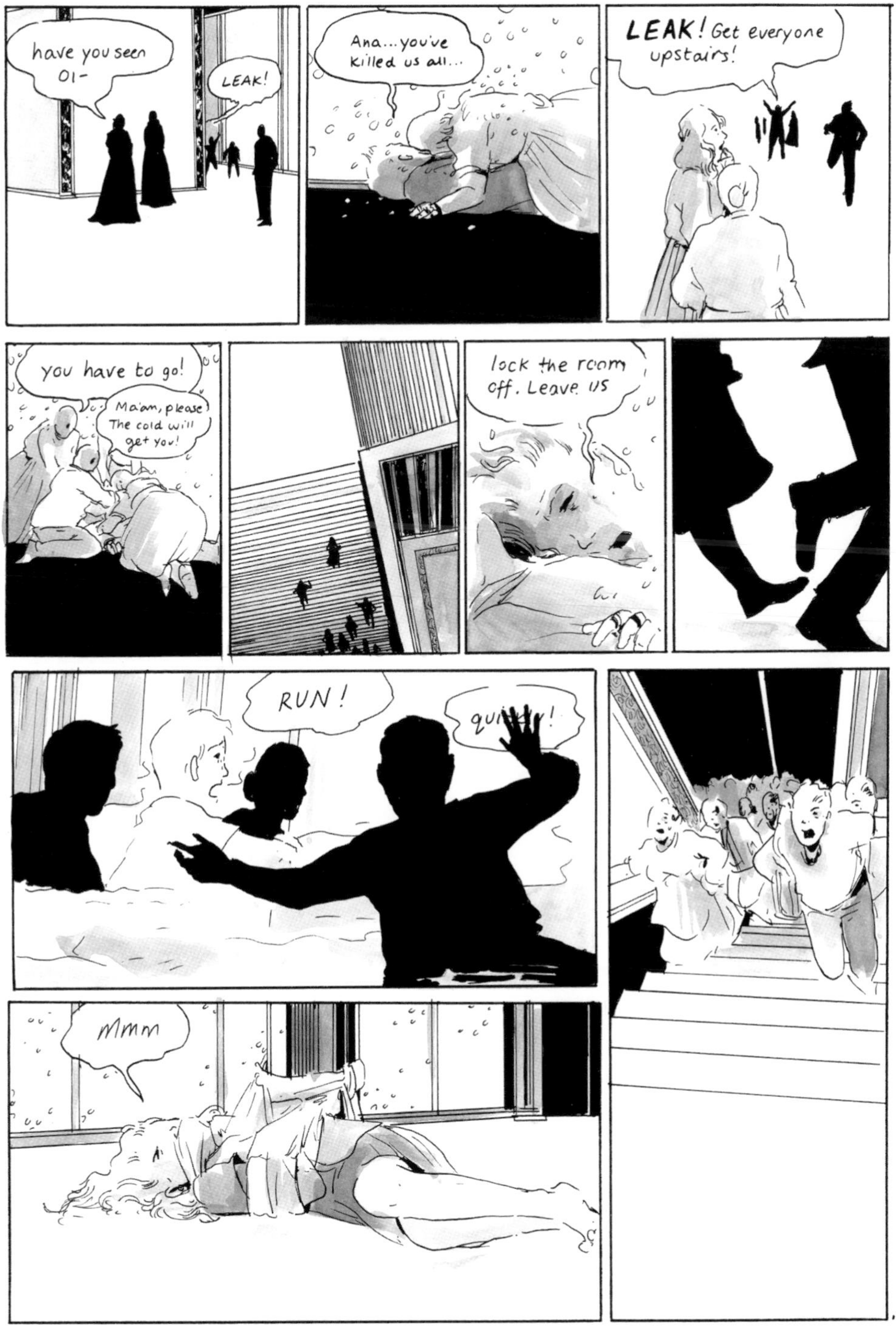
have you seen Ol-
LEAK!
Ana... you've killed us all...
LEAK! Get everyone upstairs!
you have to go!
Ma'am, please! The cold will get you!
lock the room off. Leave us
RUN!
qui y!
Mmm

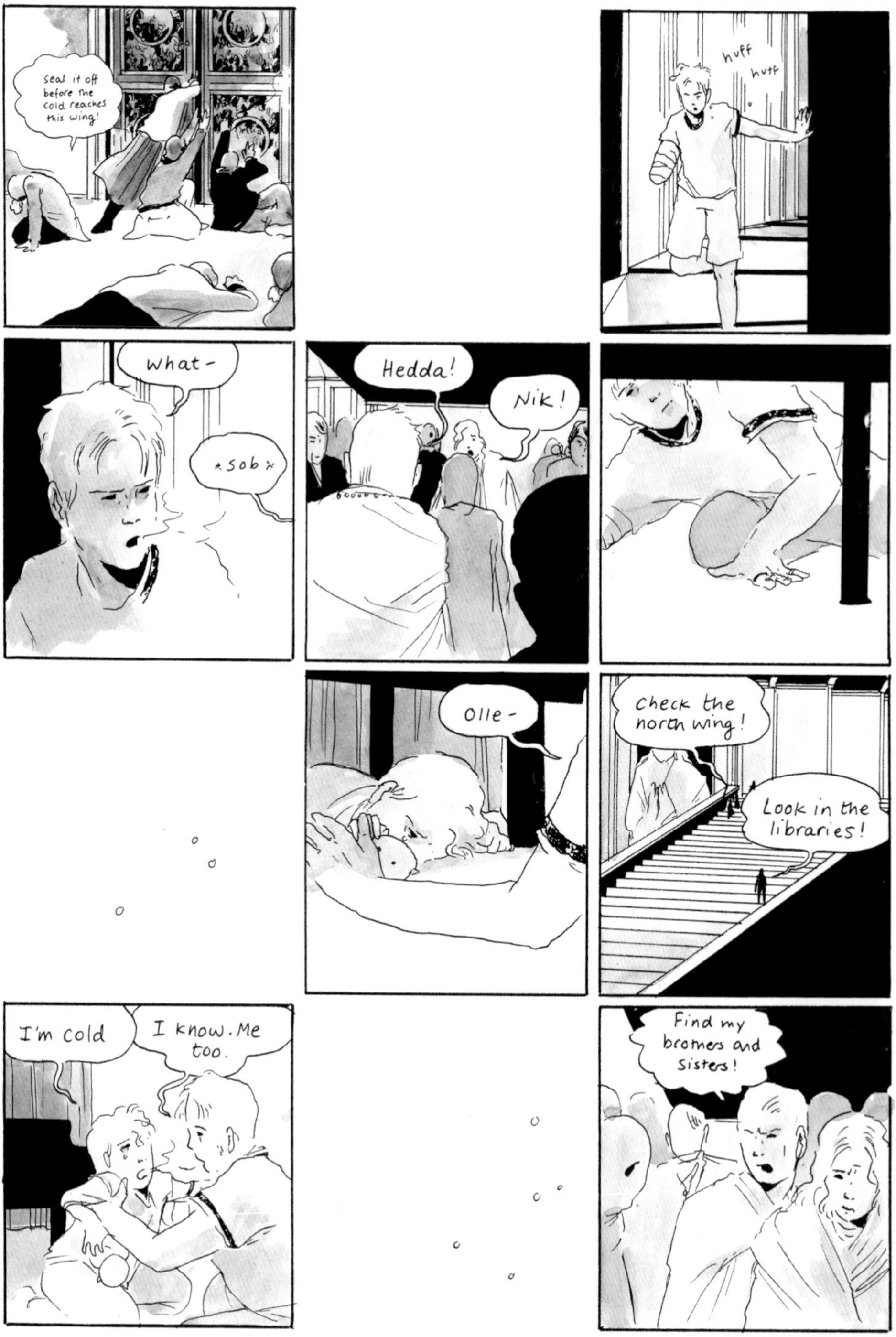
Seal it off before the cold reaches this wing!
huff
huff
What-
sob
Hedda!
Nik!
Olle-
Check the north wing!
Look in the libraries!
I'm cold
I know. Me too.
Find my brothers and sisters!

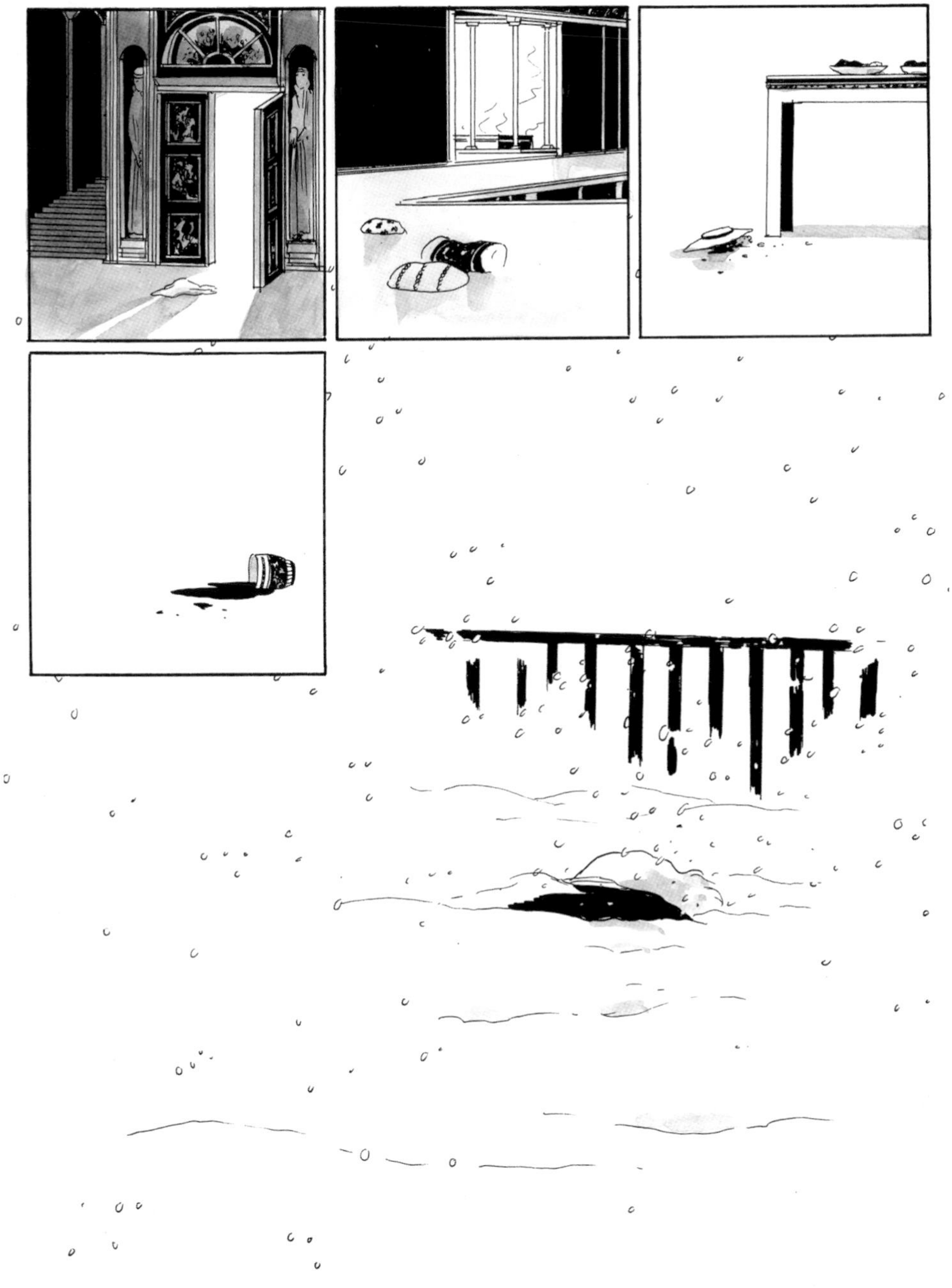

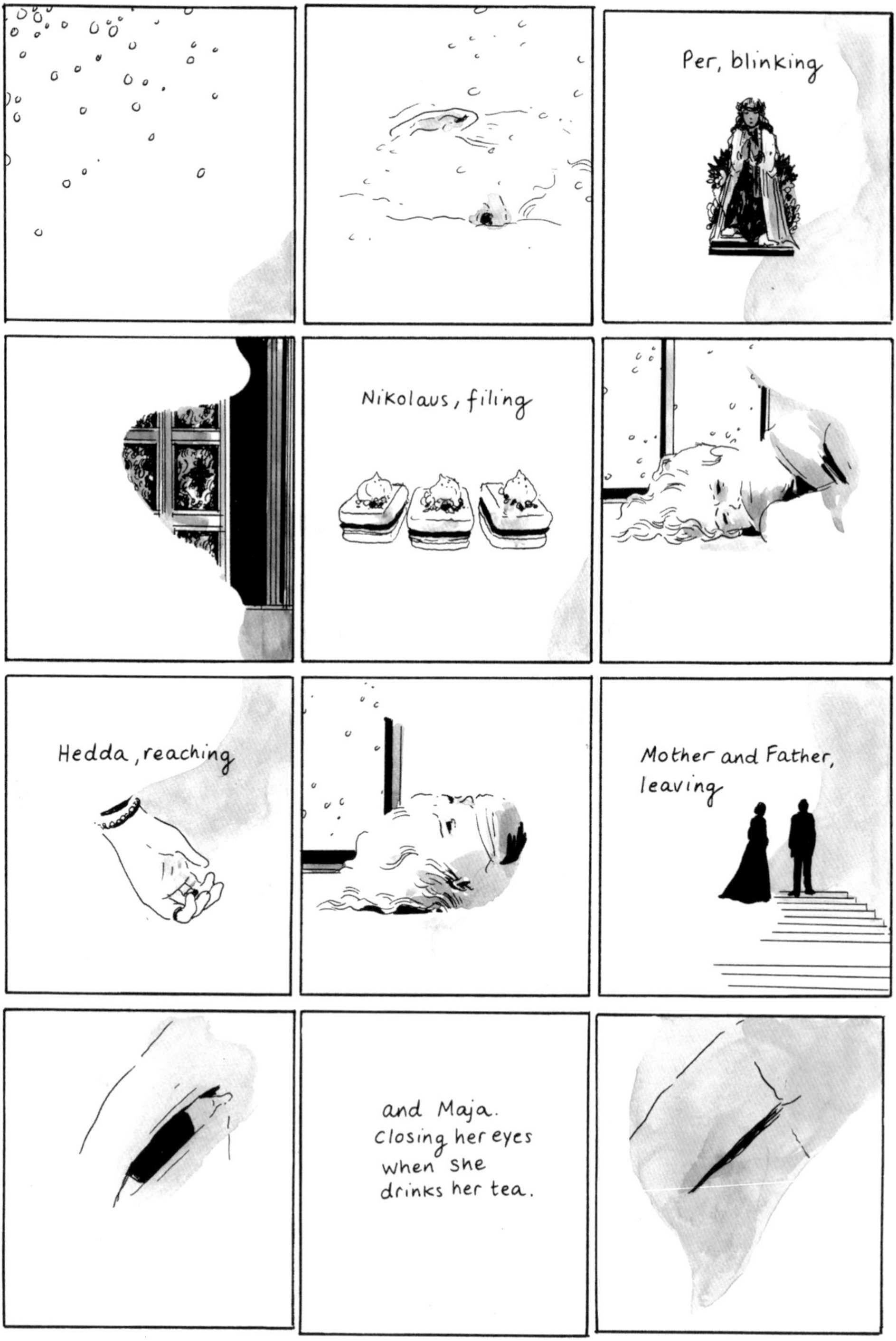

Per, blinking
Nikolaus, filing
Hedda, reaching
Mother and Father, leaving
and Maja.
Closing her eyes when she drinks her tea.

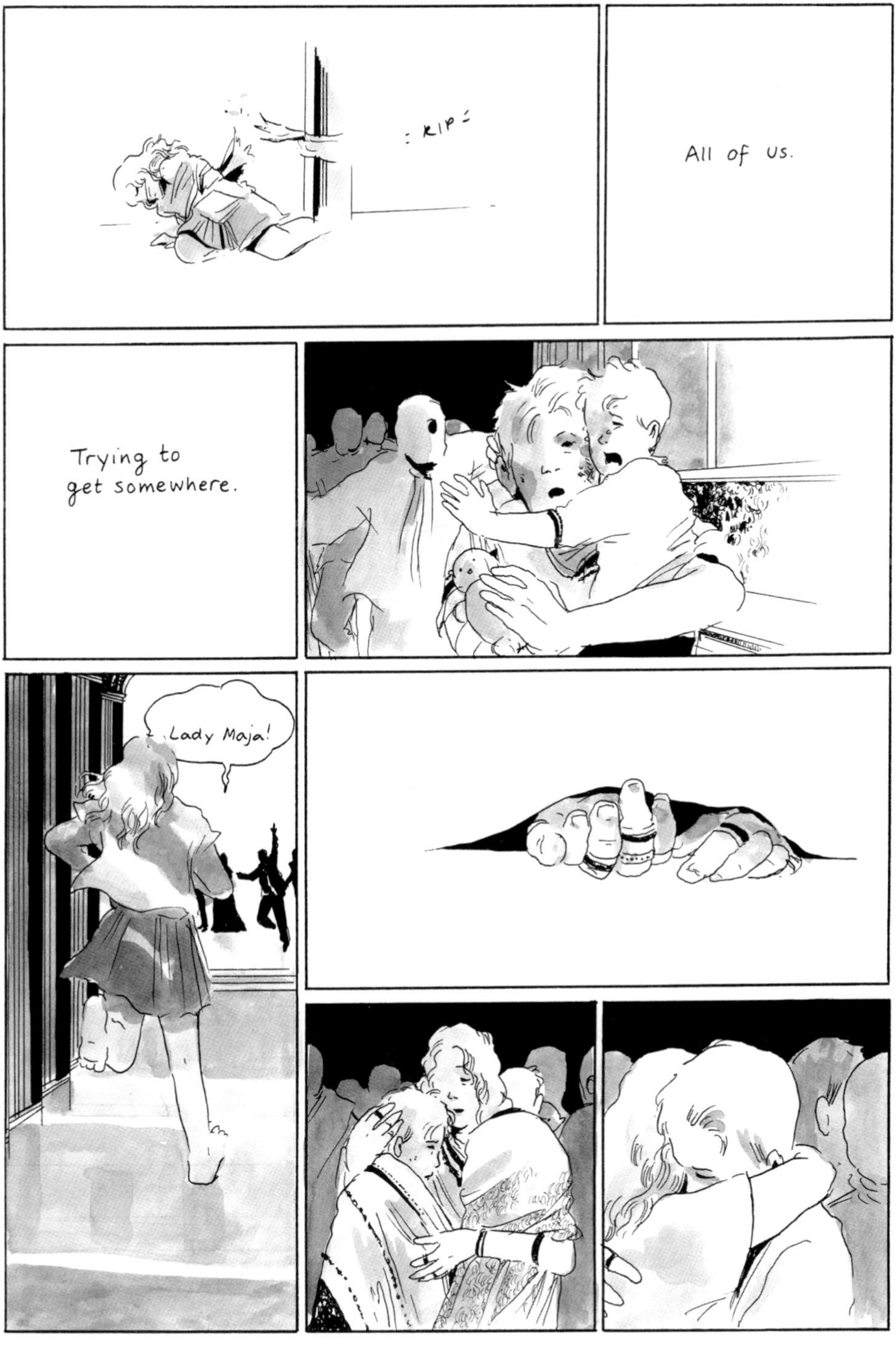
RIP
All of us.
Trying to get somewhere.
Lady Maja!

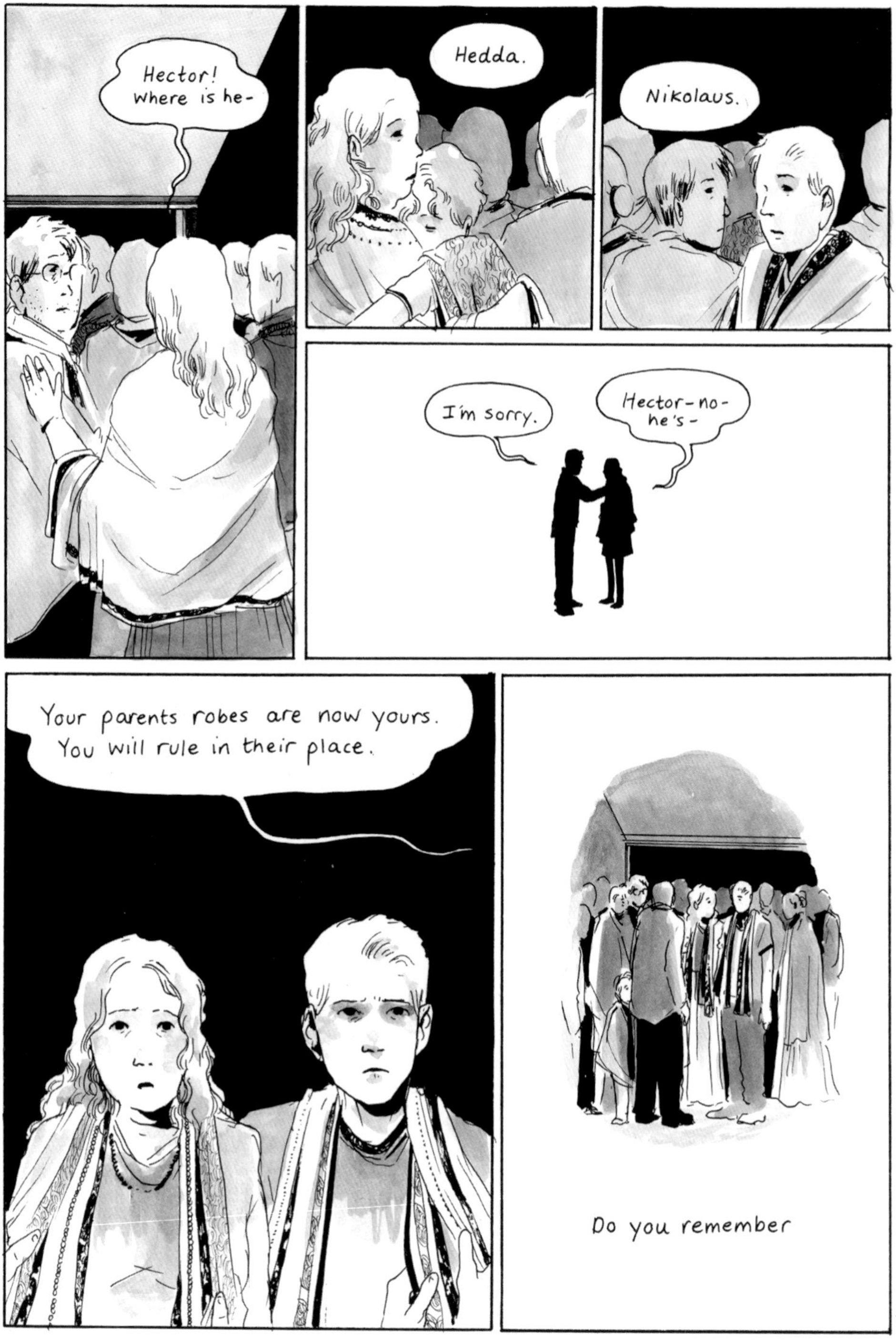
Hector! where is he-
Hedda.
Nikolaus.
I'm sorry.
Hector-no-he's-
Your parents robes are now yours. You will rule in their place.
Do you remember

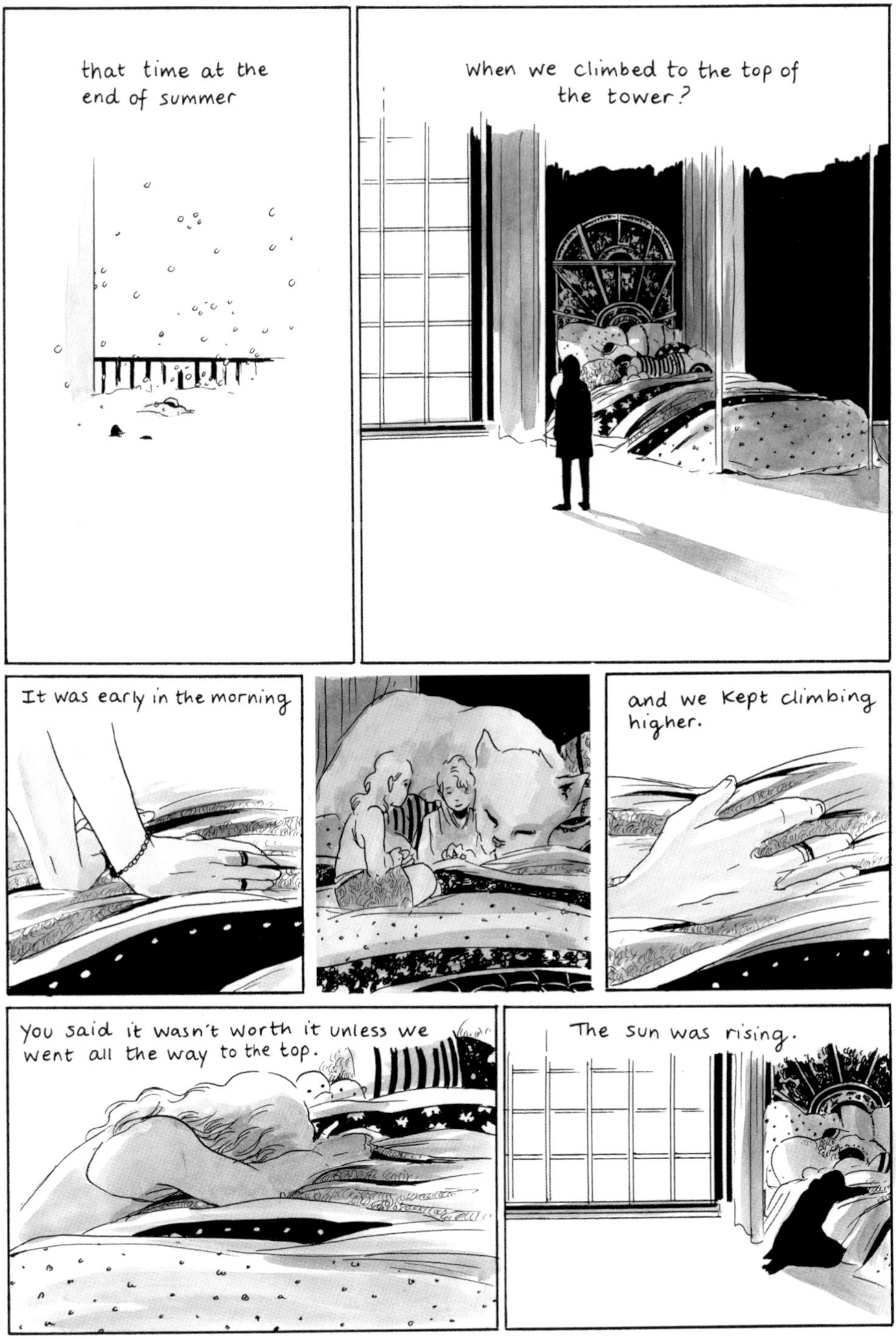
that time at the end of summer
when we climbed to the top of the tower?
It was early in the morning
and we kept climbing higher.
You said it wasn't worth it unless we went all the way to the top.
The sun was rising.

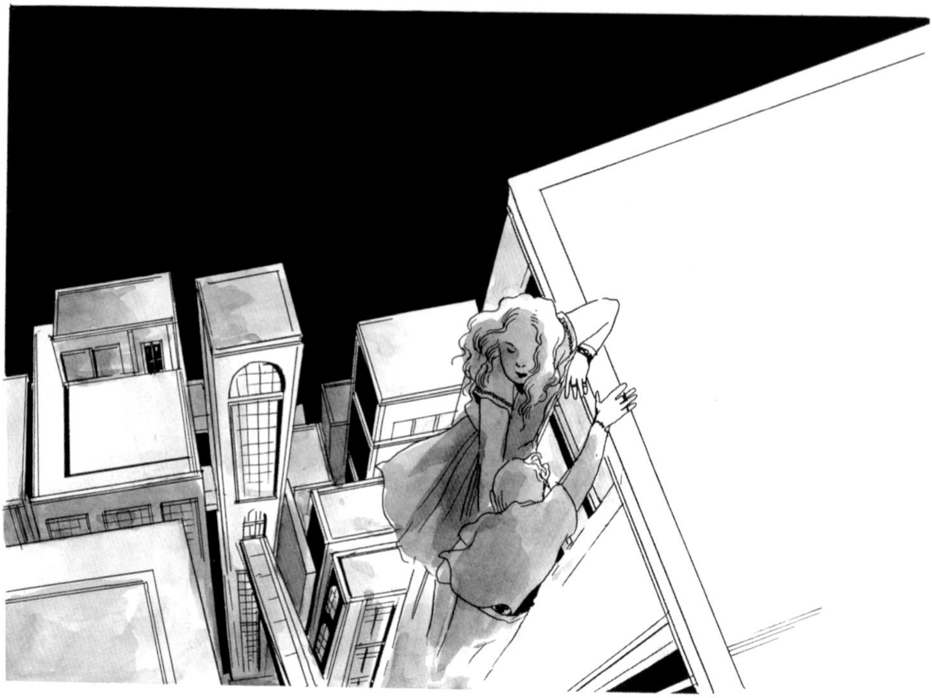
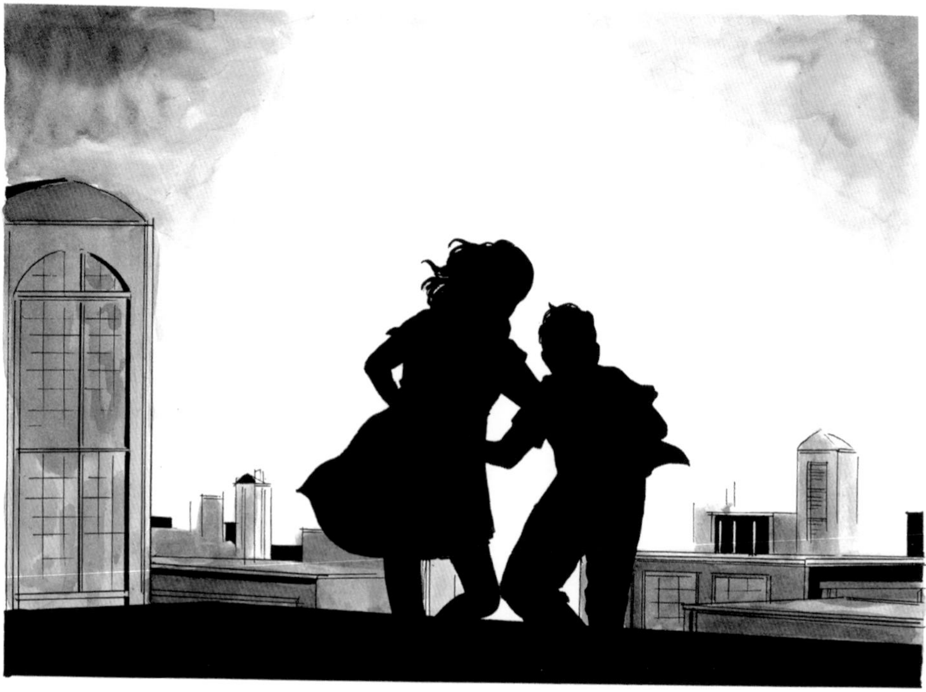

Your hands were sweaty when you told me this was why you were alive.

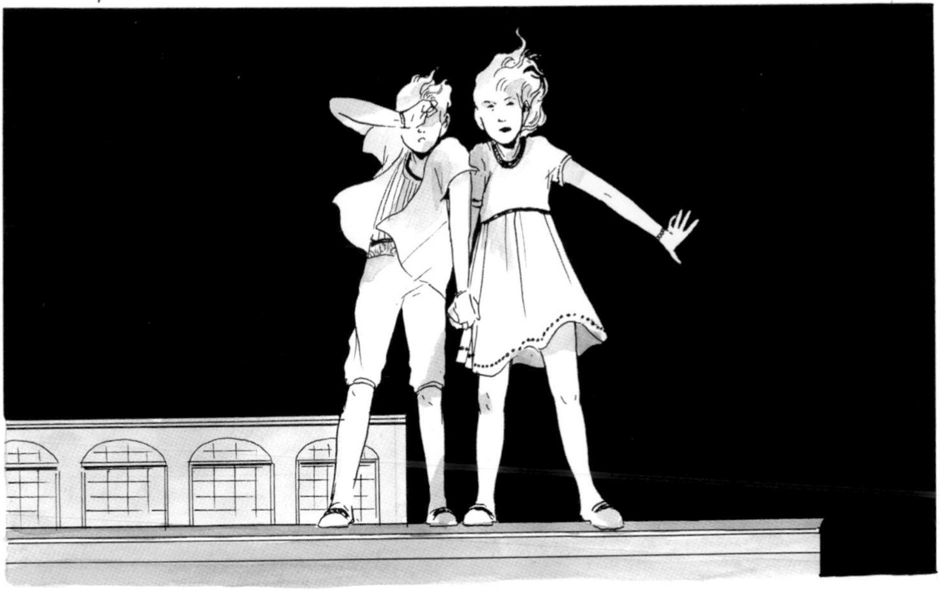

We tried to stand as close to the edge as we could. But a gust of wind hit us and we weren't ready for it.

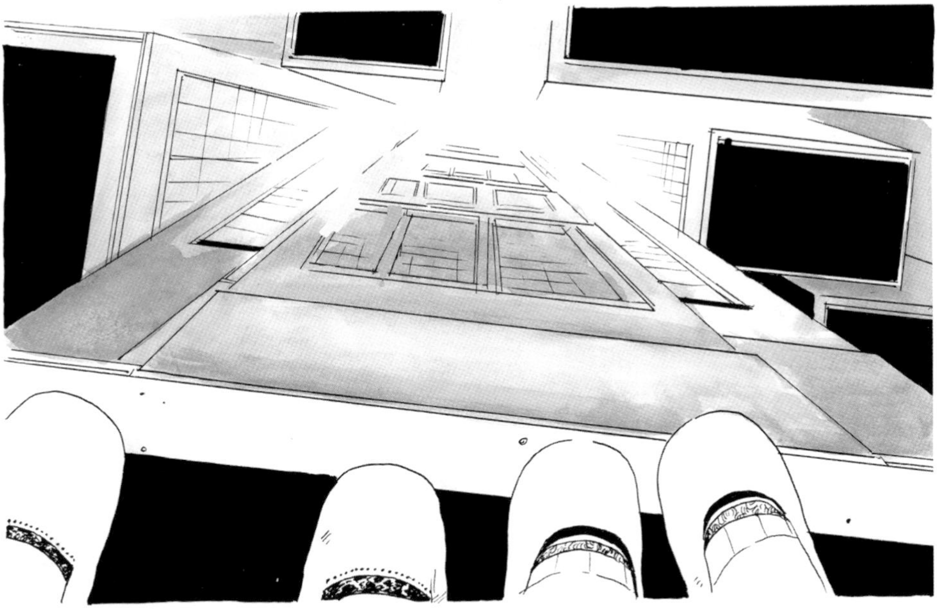

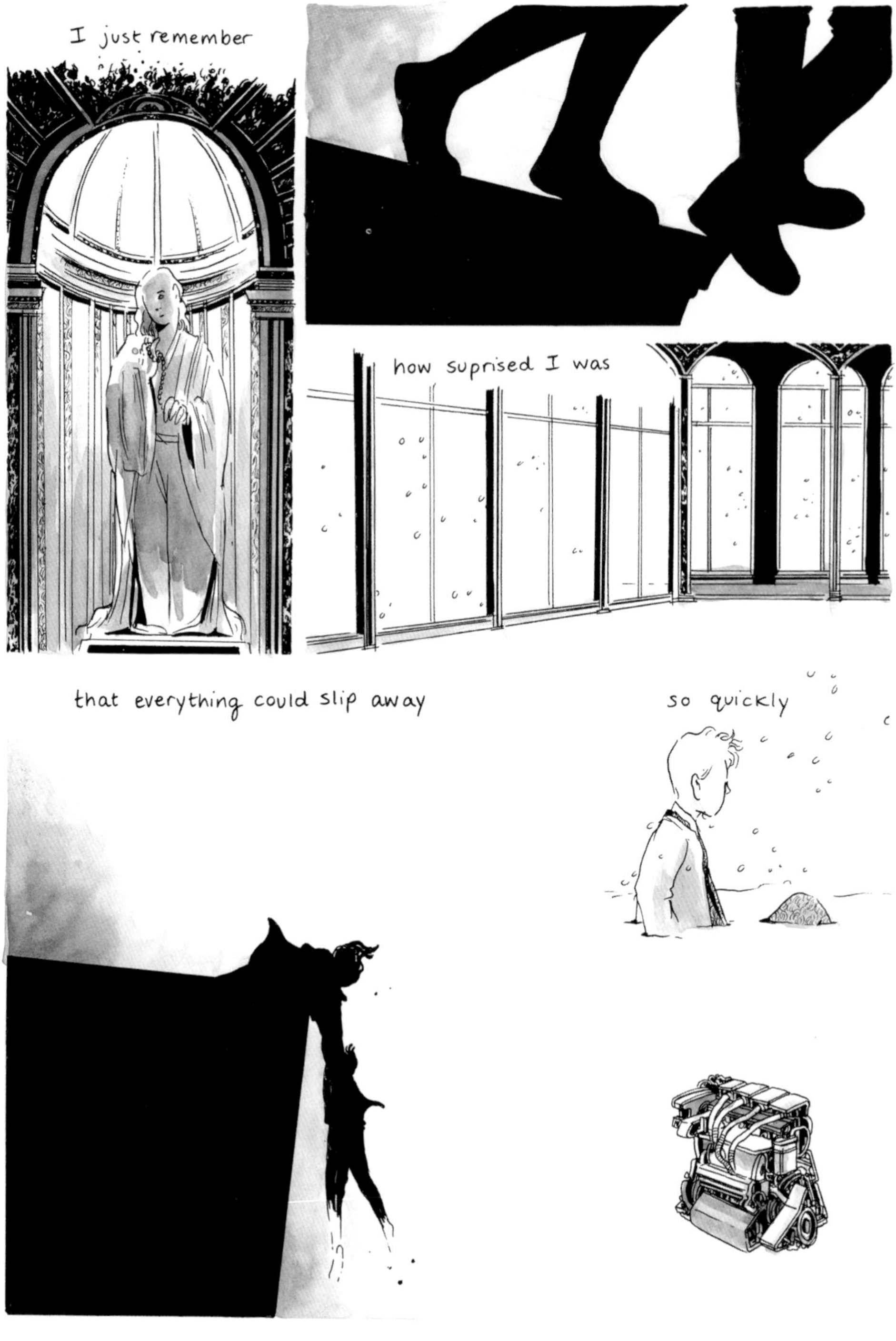
I just remember
how suprised I was
that everything could slip away
so quickly

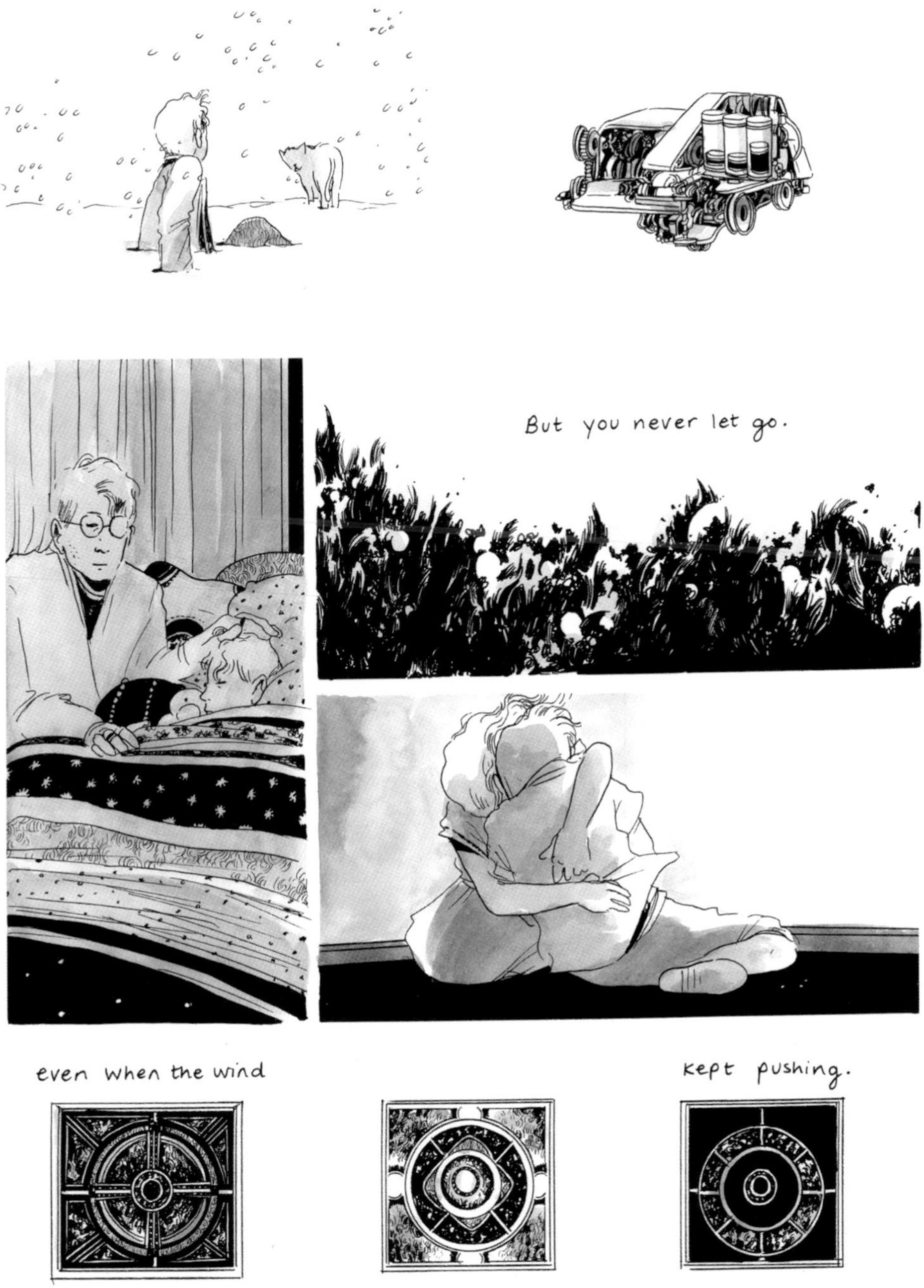
But you never let go.
even when the wind
kept pushing.

Tirelessly.

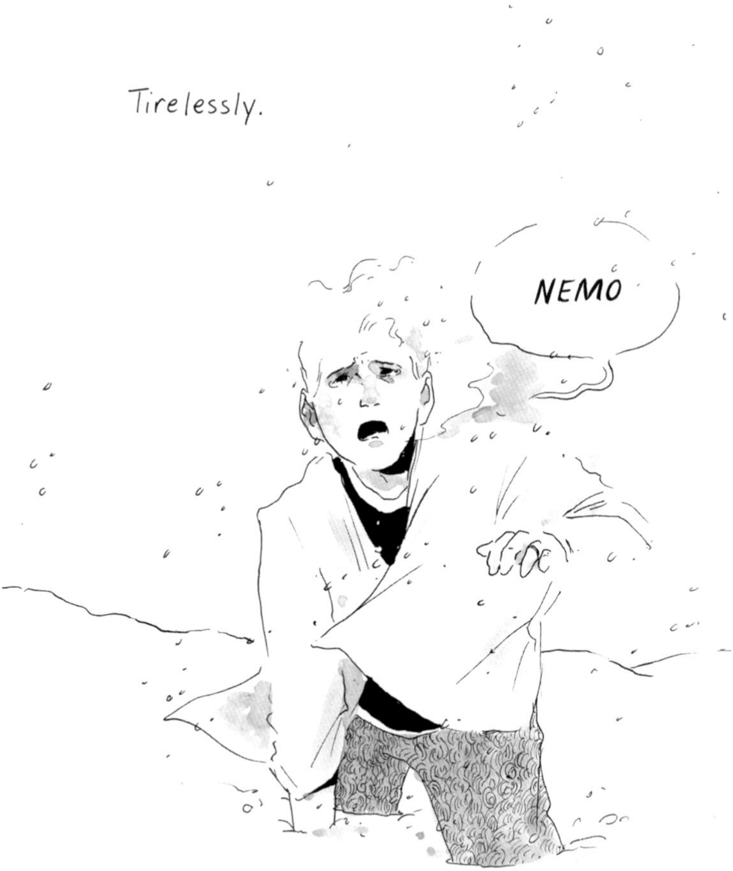
NEMO

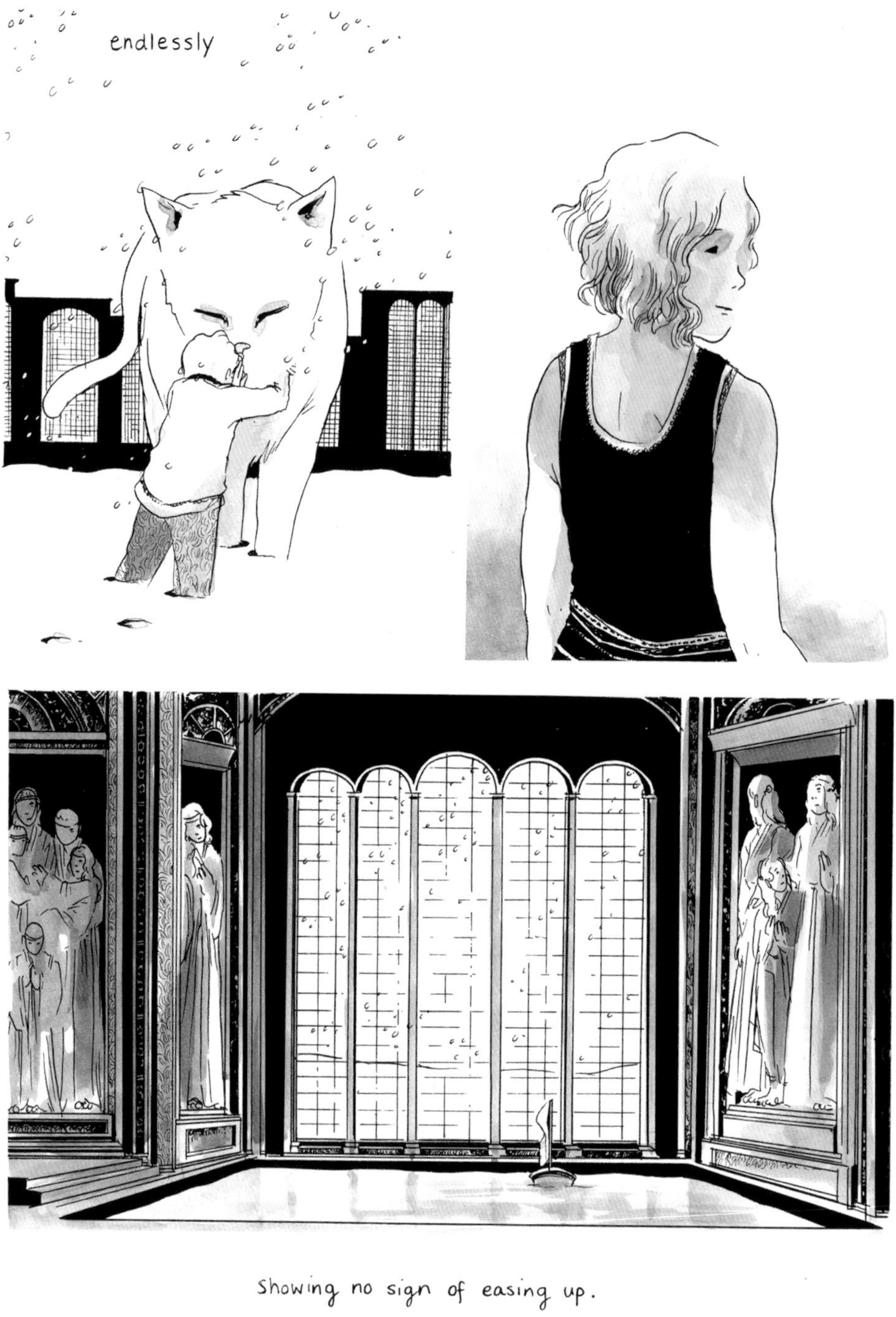
endlessly
Showing no sign of easing up.

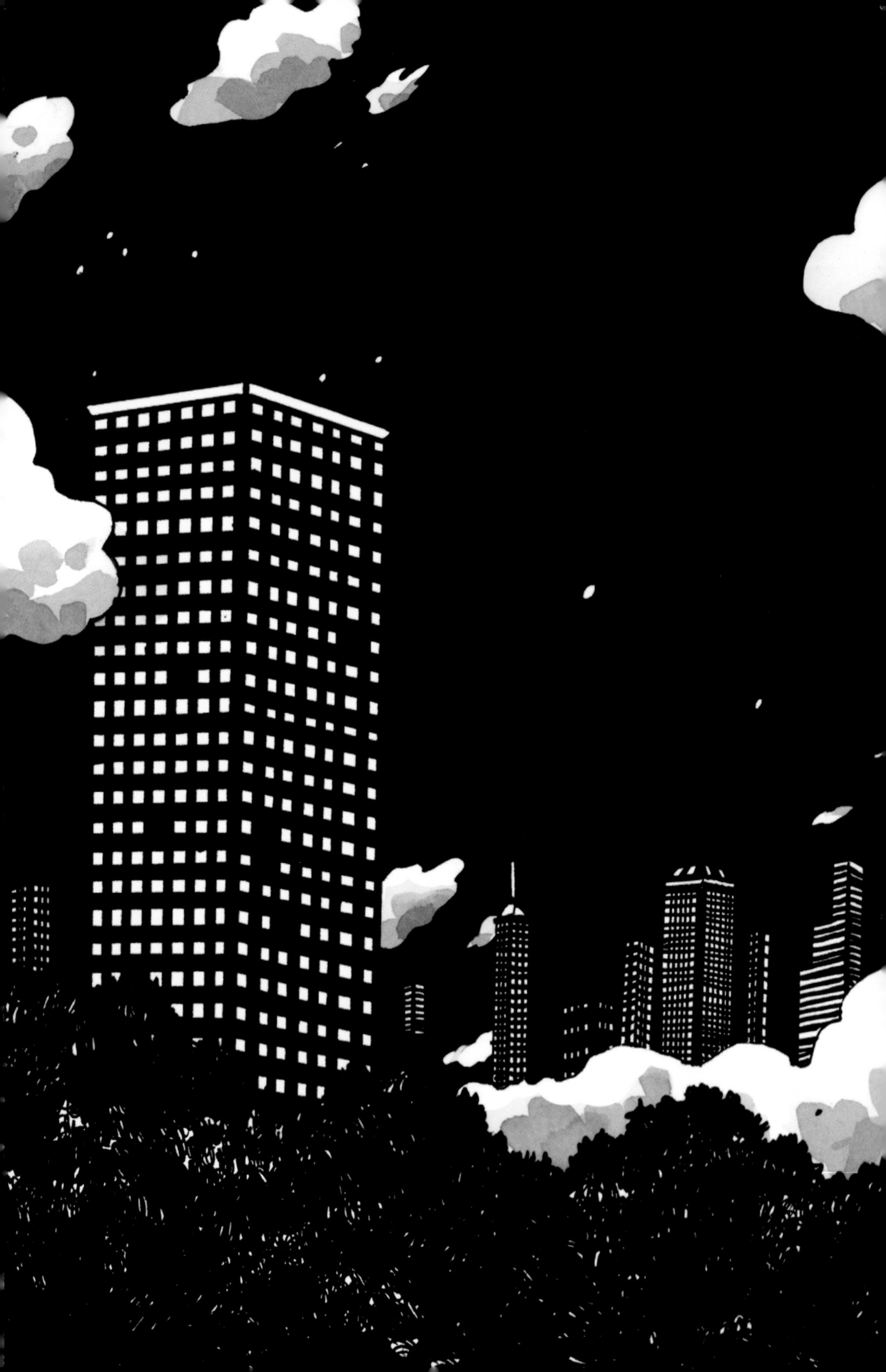

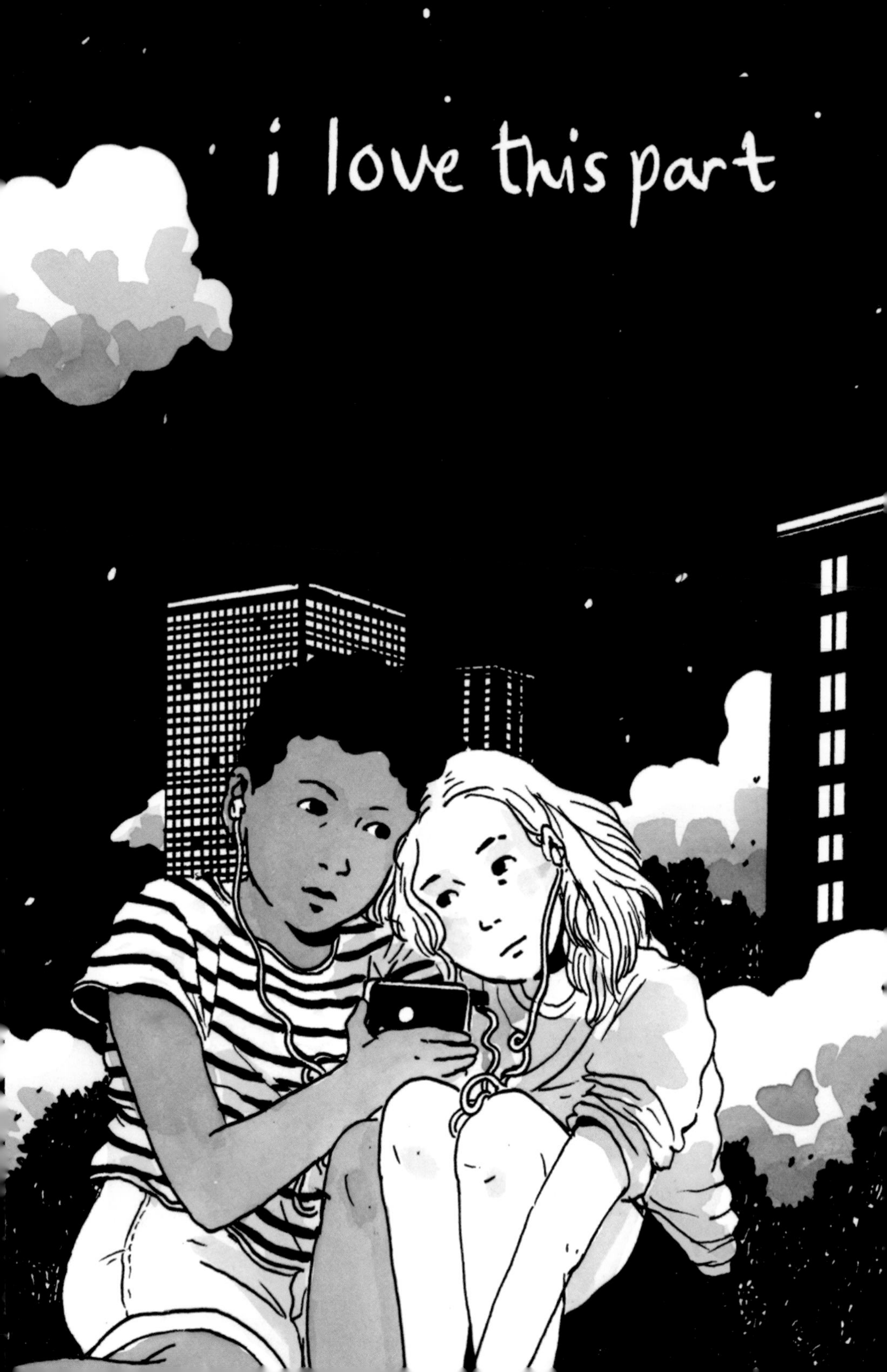
i love this part

i love
this part

tillie walden

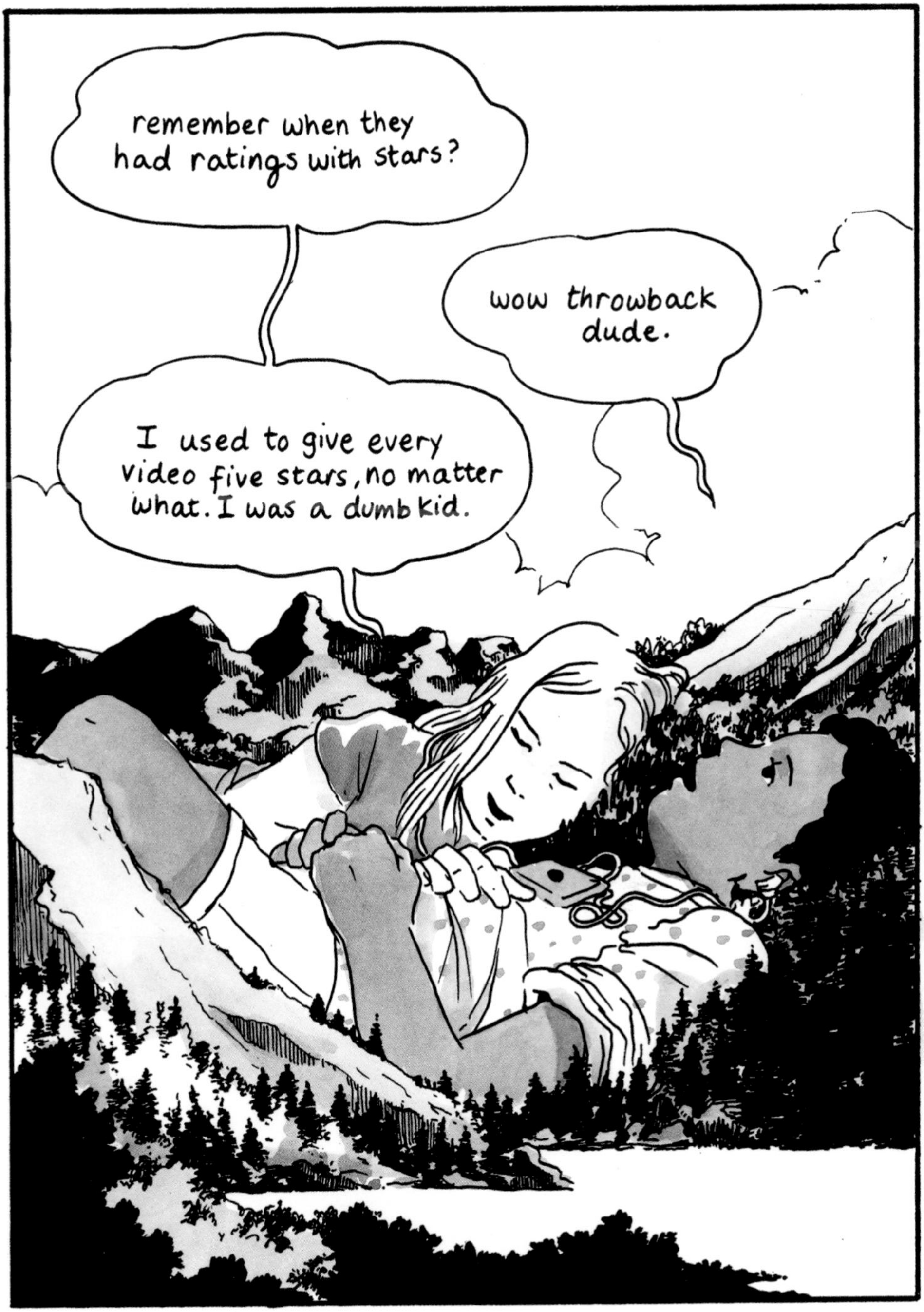
remember when they had ratings with stars?
I used to give every video five stars, no matter what. I was a dumb kid.
wow throwback dude.

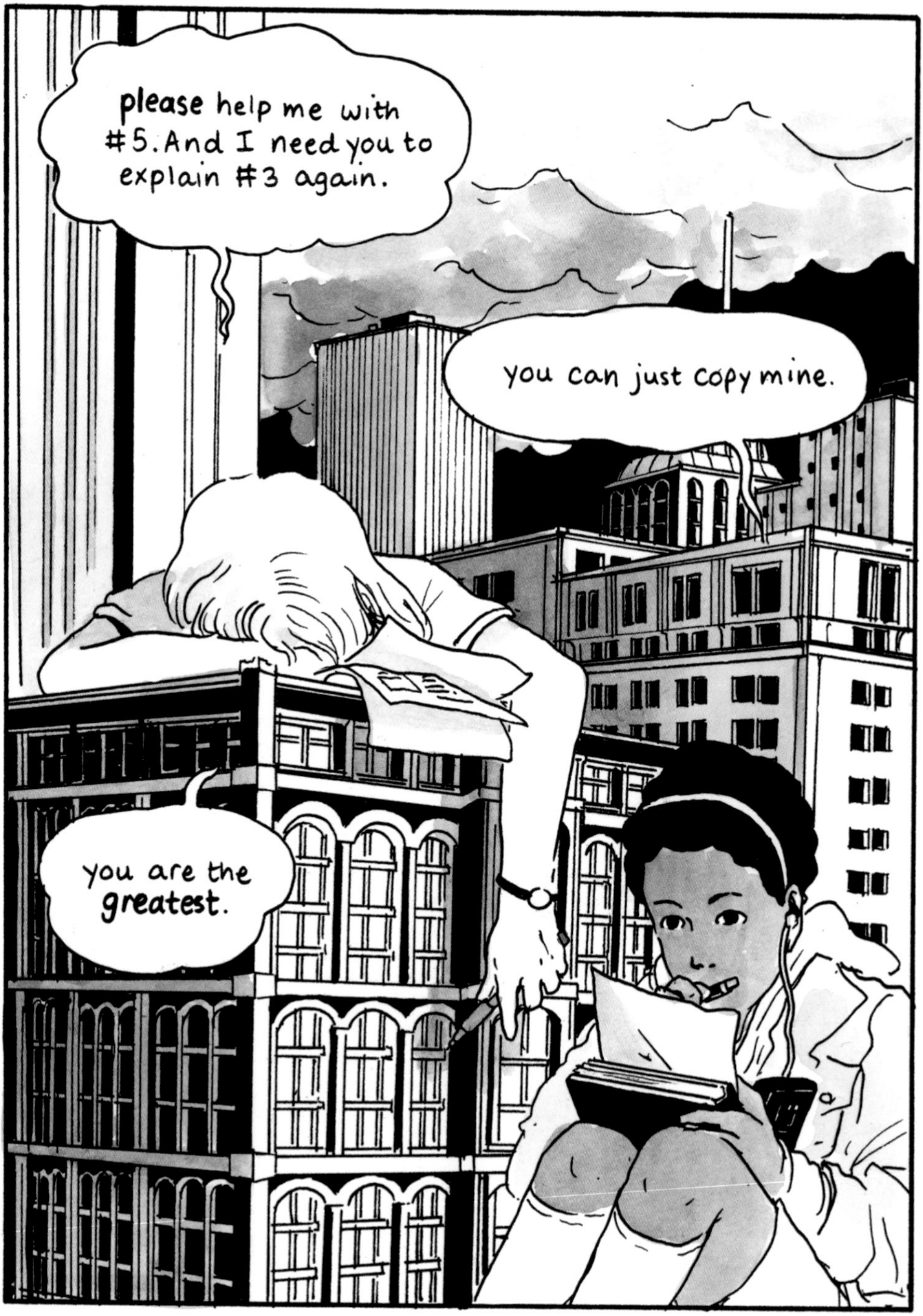
please help me with #5. And I need you to explain #3 again.
you can just copy mine.
you are the greatest.

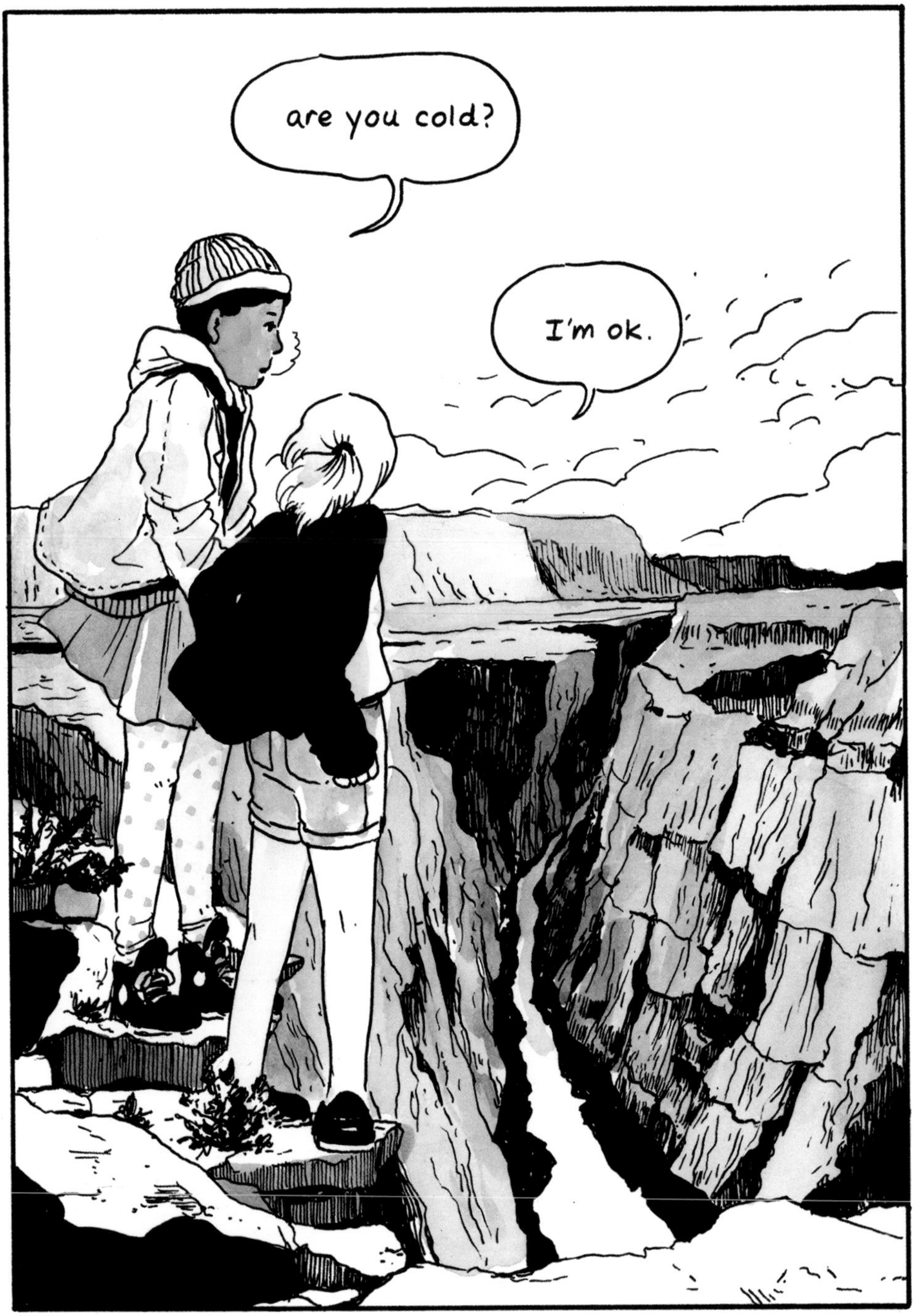
are you cold?
I'm ok.

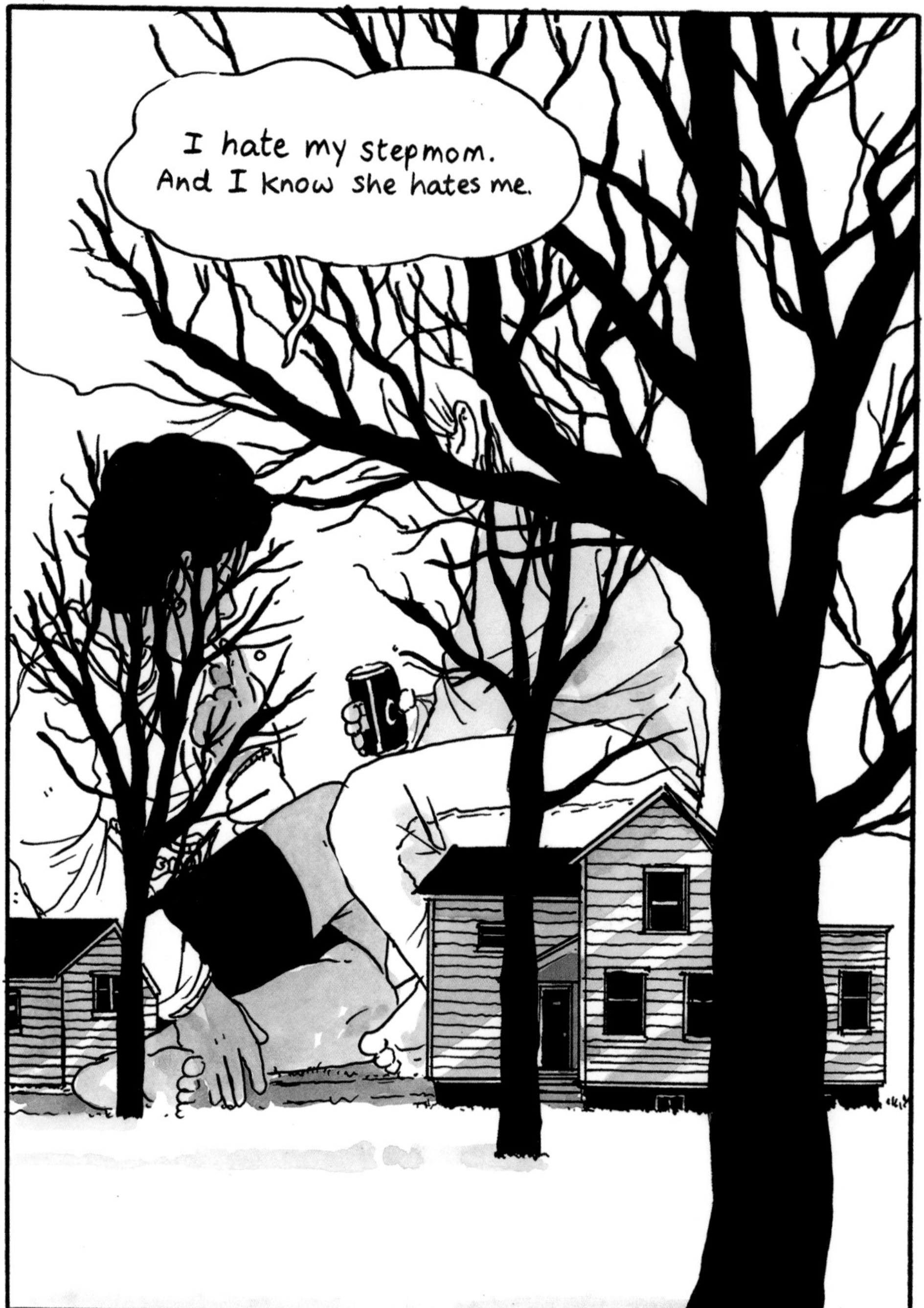
I hate my stepmom.
And I know she hates me.

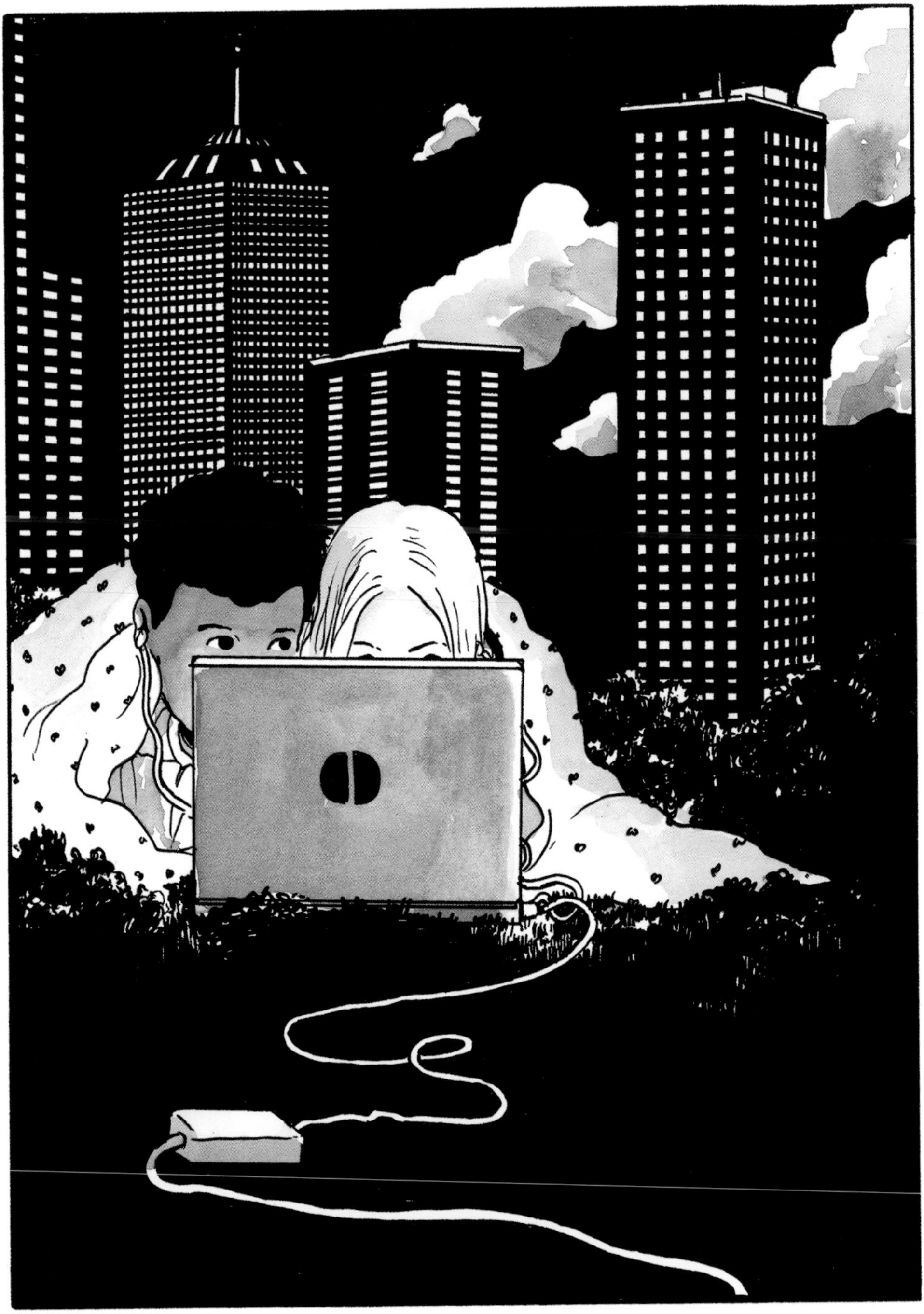

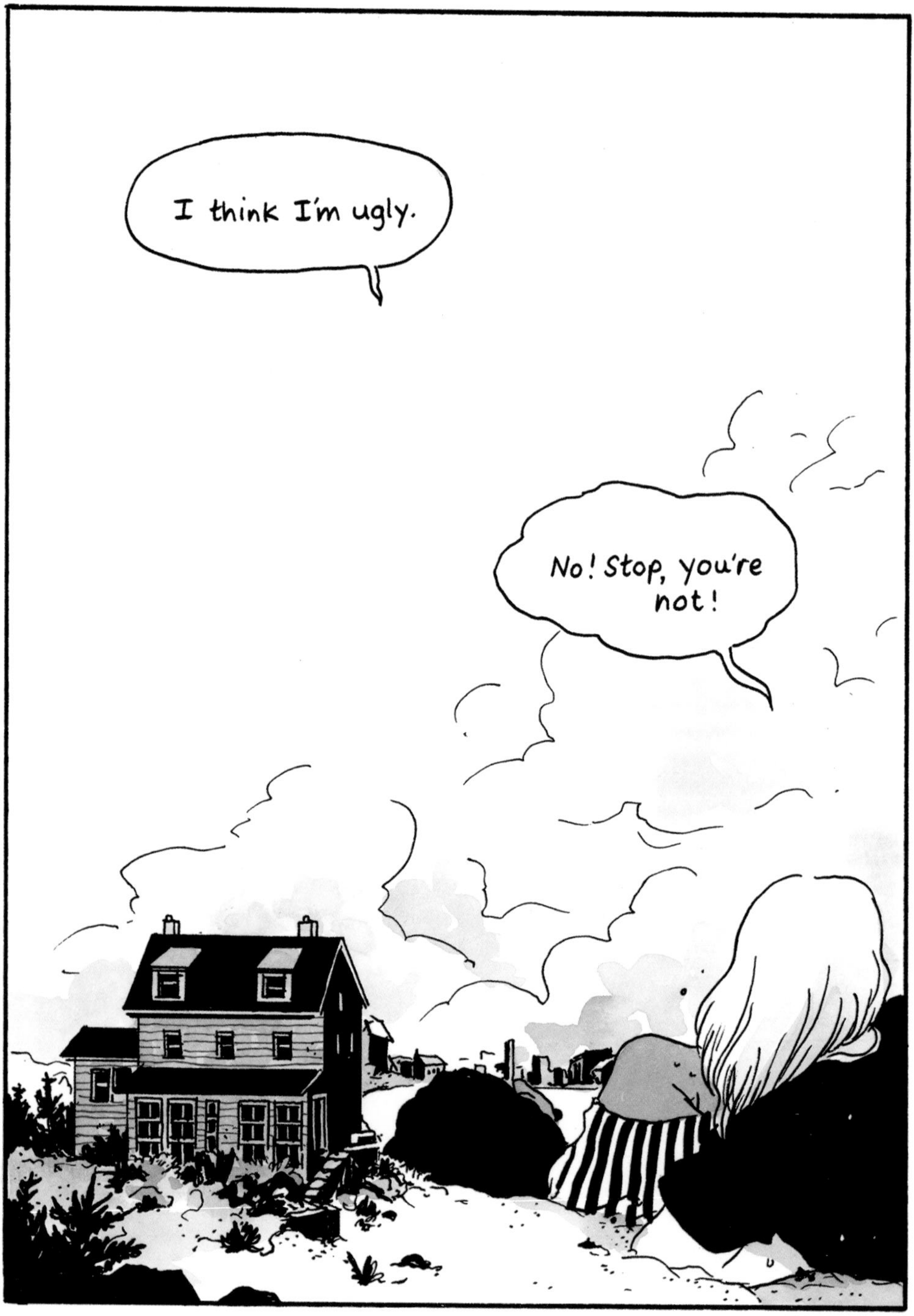
I think I'm ugly.
No! Stop, you're not!

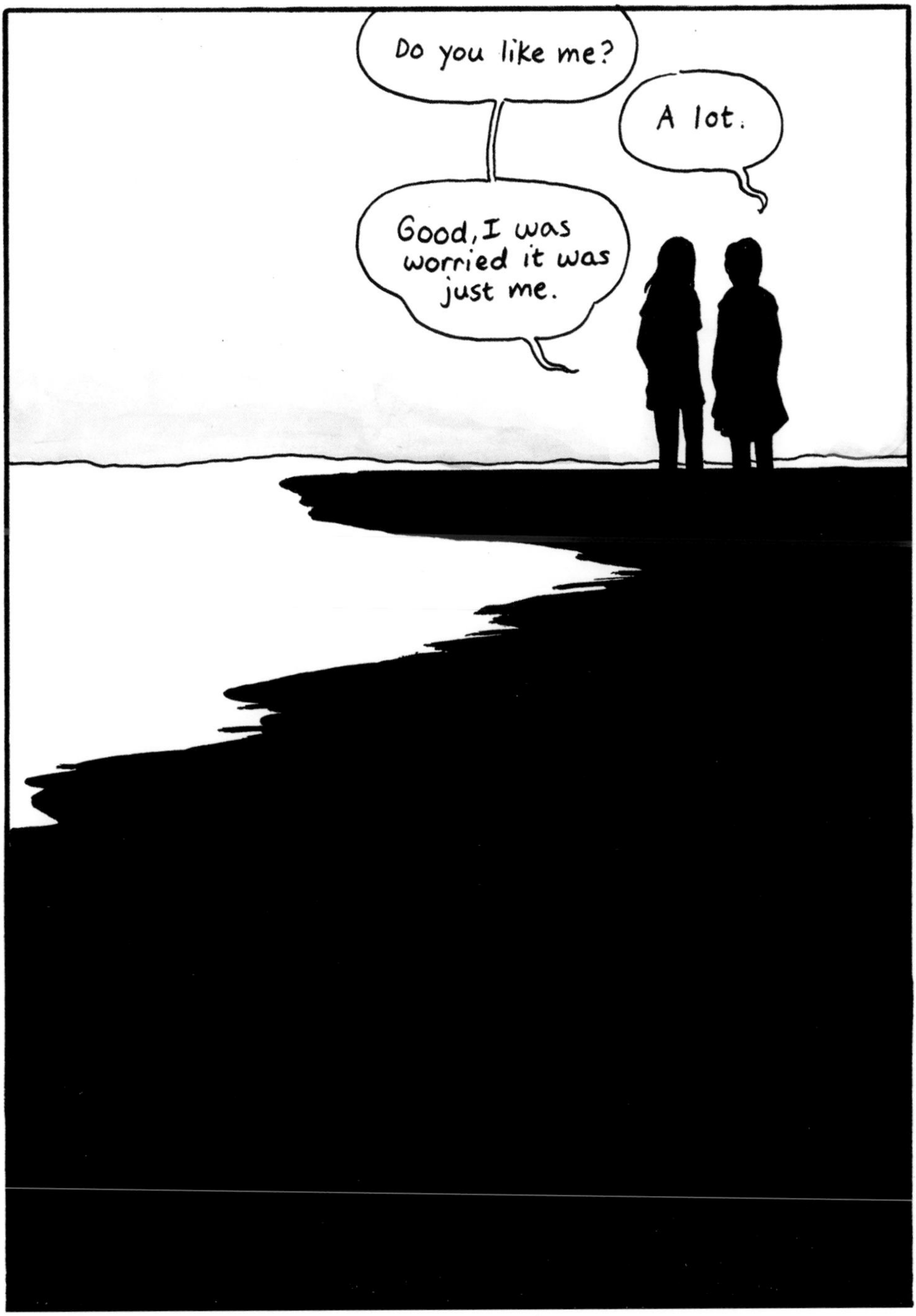
Do you like me?
A lot.
Good, I was worried it was just me.

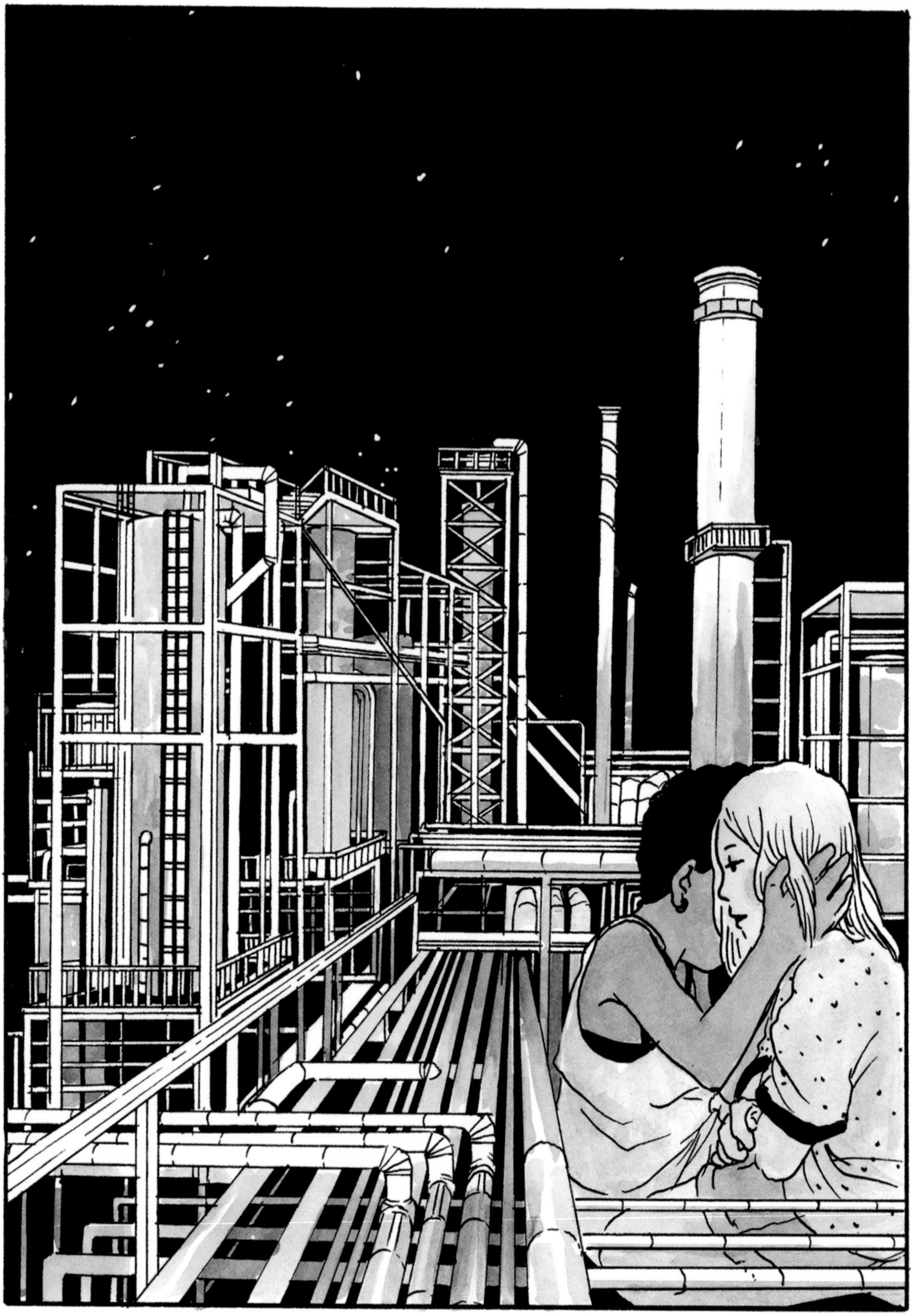

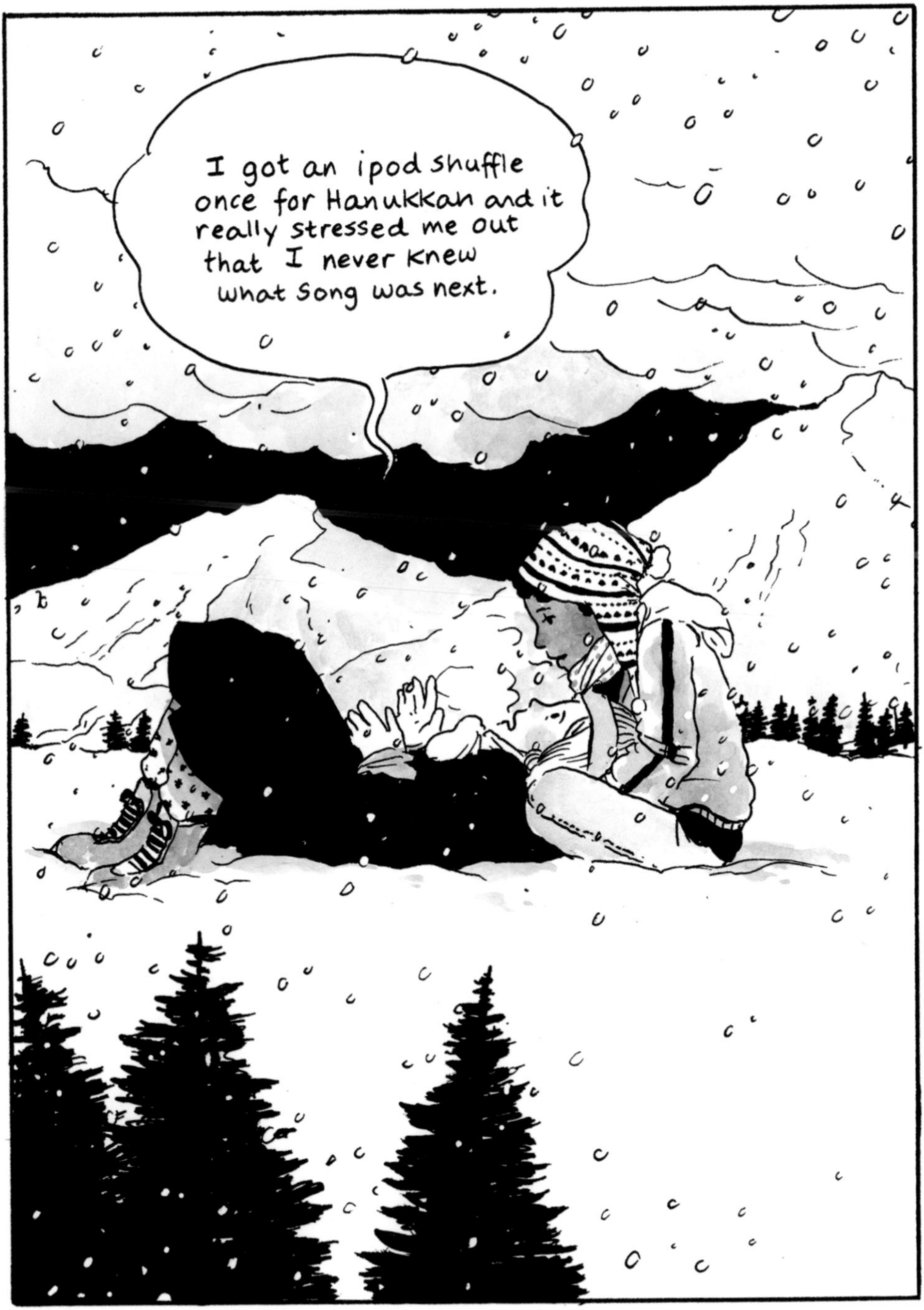
I got an ipod shuffle once for Hanukkah and it really stressed me out that I never knew what Song was next.

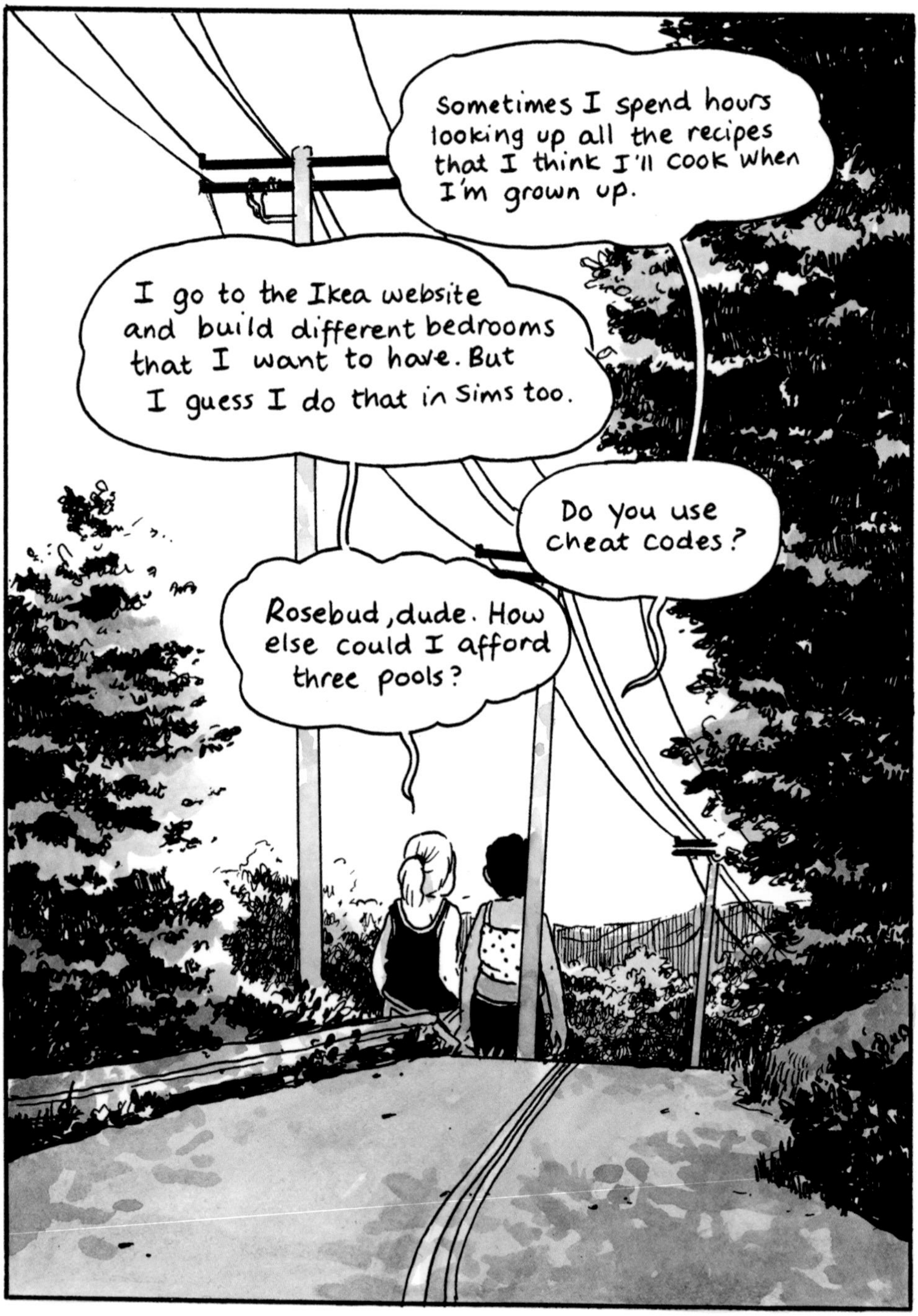
Sometimes I spend hours looking up all the recipes that I think I'll cook when I'm grown up.
I go to the Ikea website and build different bedrooms that I want to have. But I guess I do that in Sims too.
Do you use cheat codes?
Rosebud, dude. How else could I afford three pools?

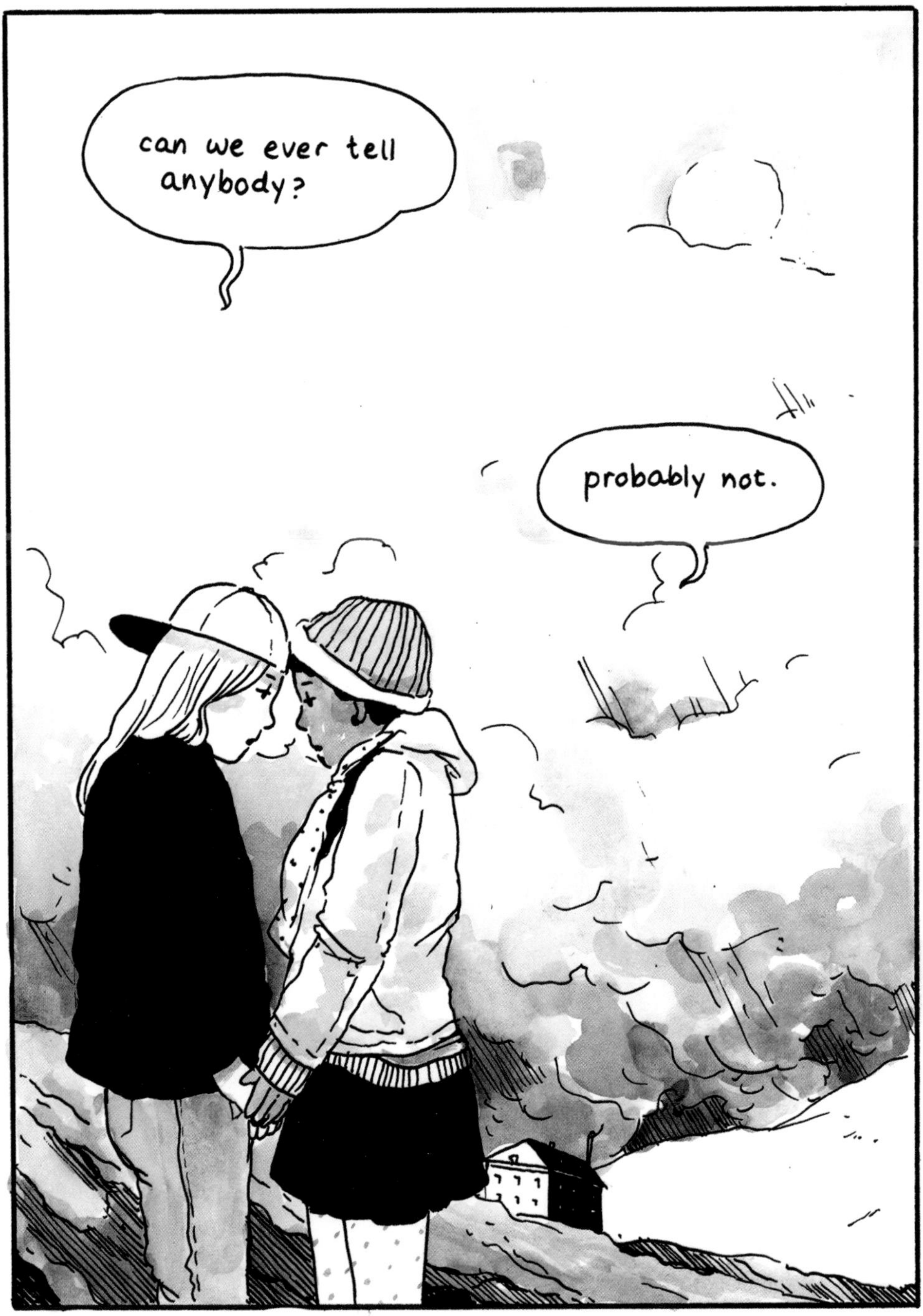
can we ever tell anybody?
probably not.

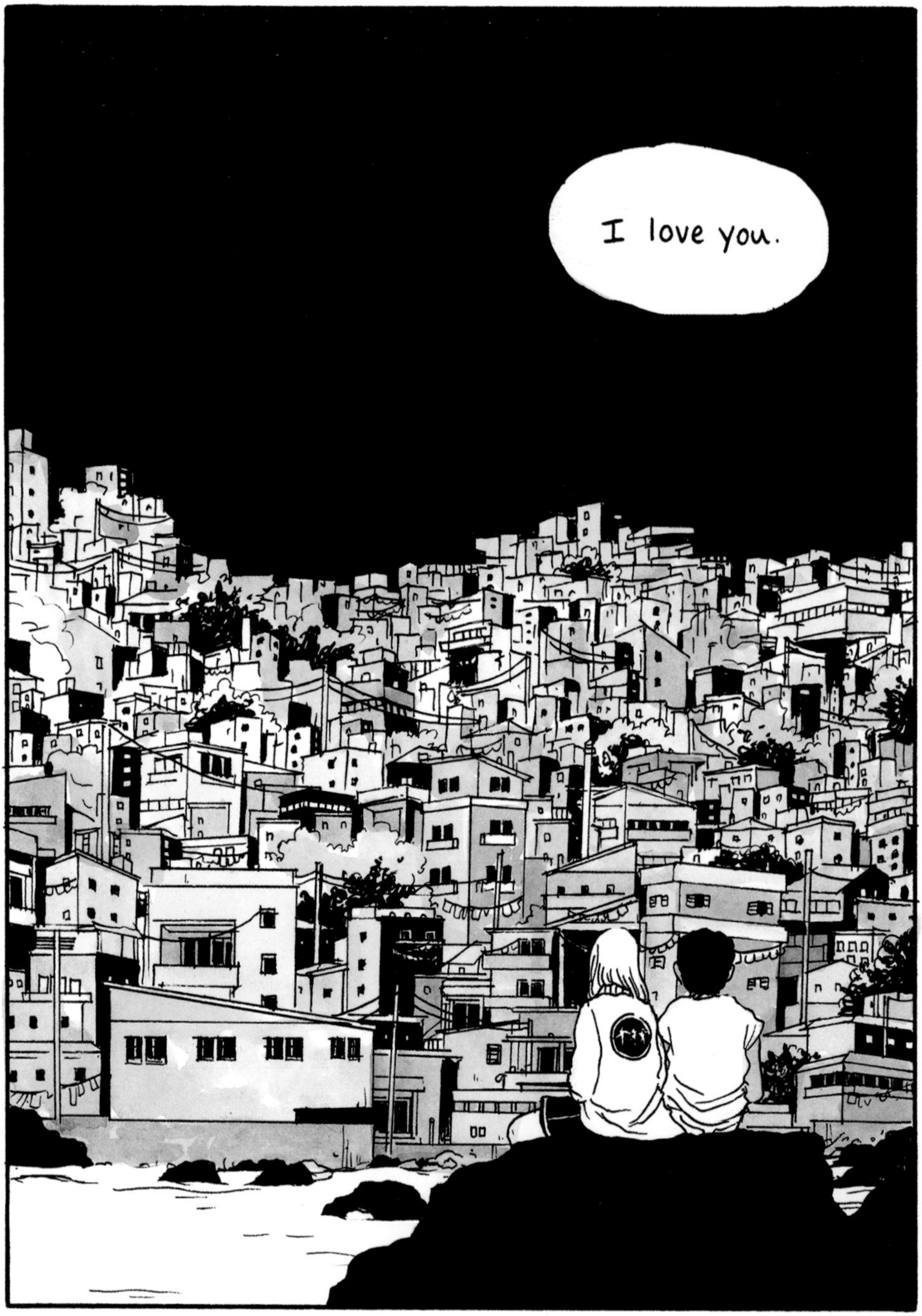
I love you.

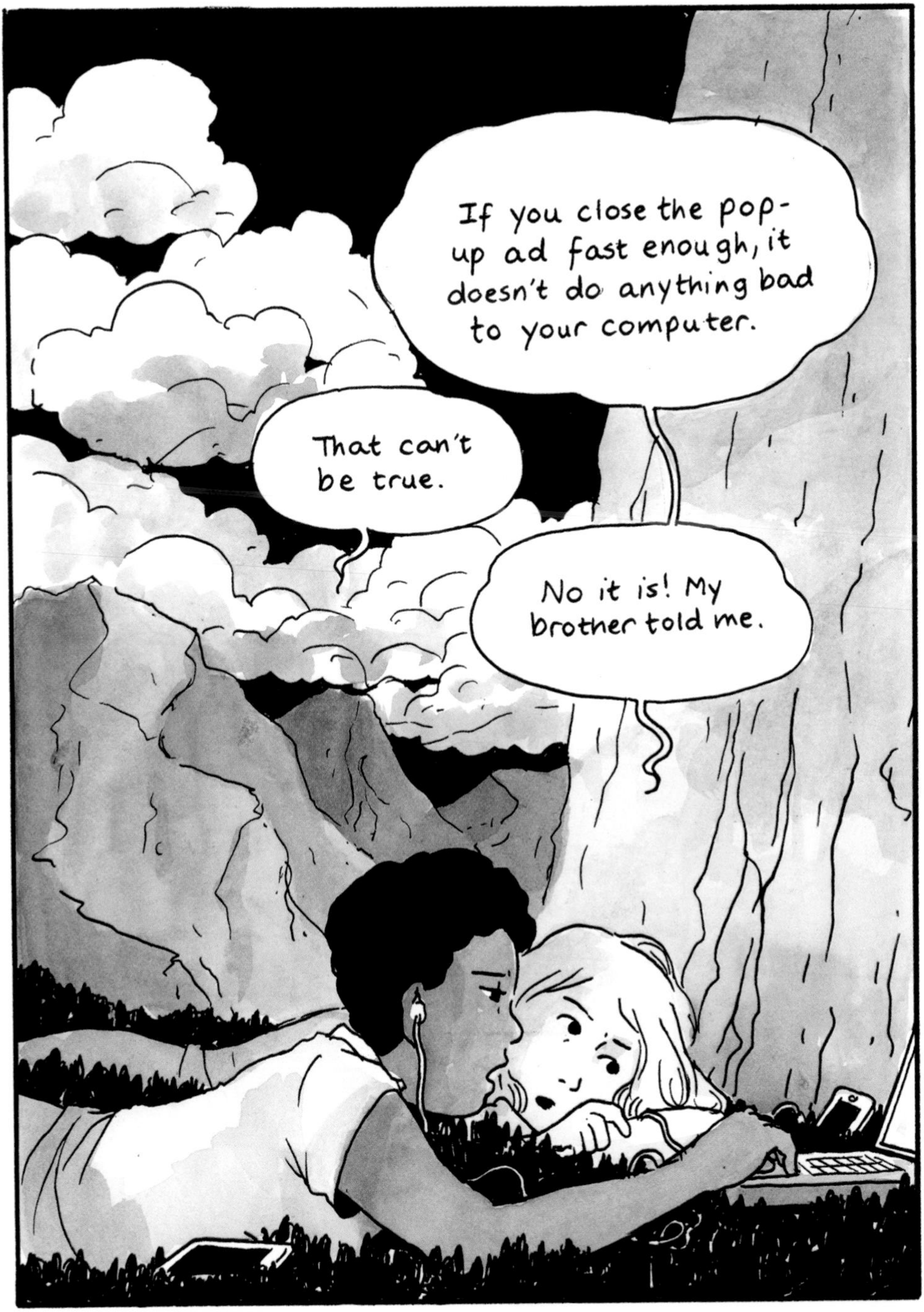
If you close the pop-up ad fast enough, it doesn't do anything bad to your computer.
That can't be true.
No it is! My brother told me.

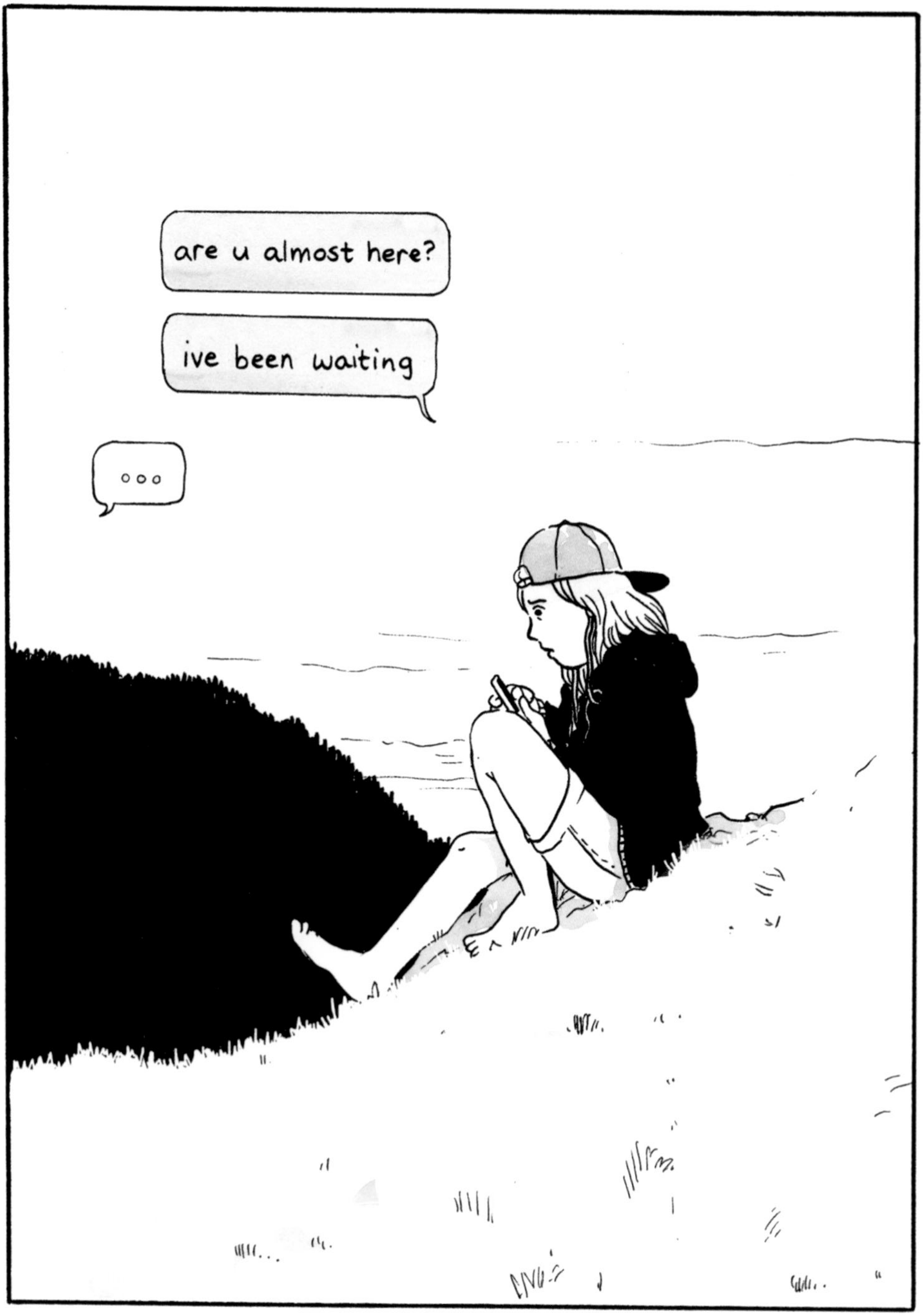
are u almost here?
ive been waiting
...

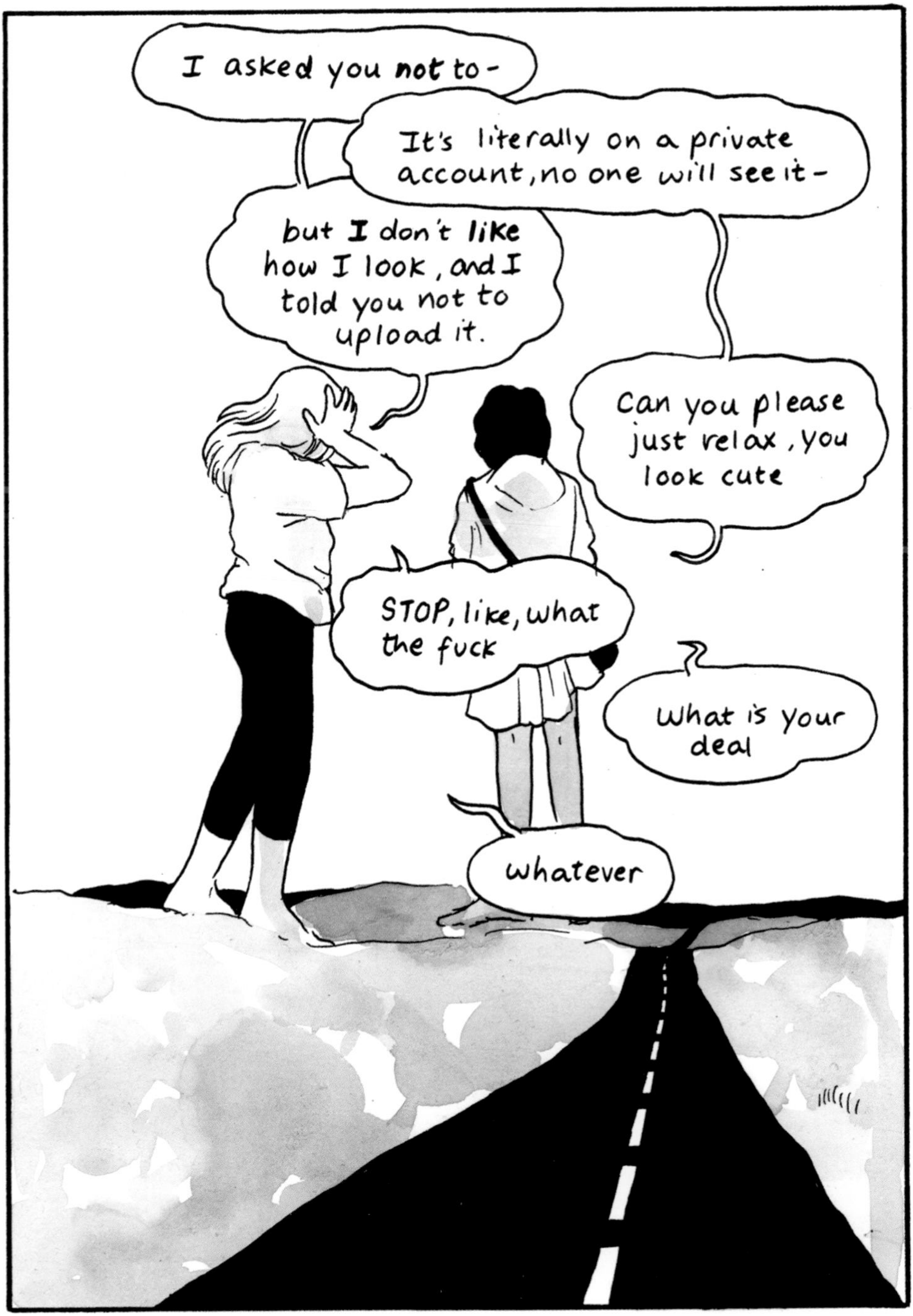
I asked you not to-
It's literally on a private account, no one will see it-
but I don't like how I look, and I told you not to upload it.
Can you please just relax, you look cute
STOP, like, what the fuck
What is your deal
whatever

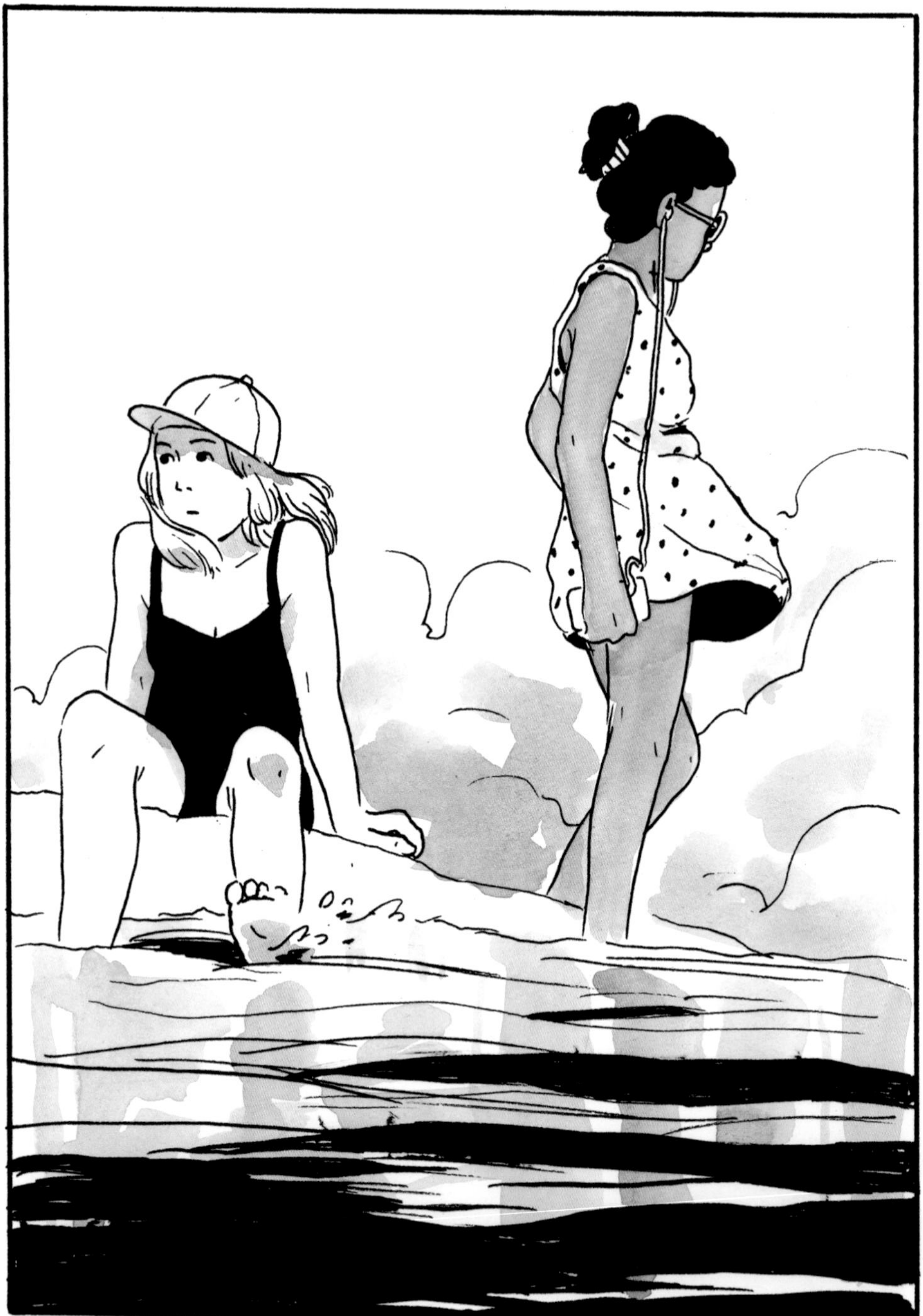

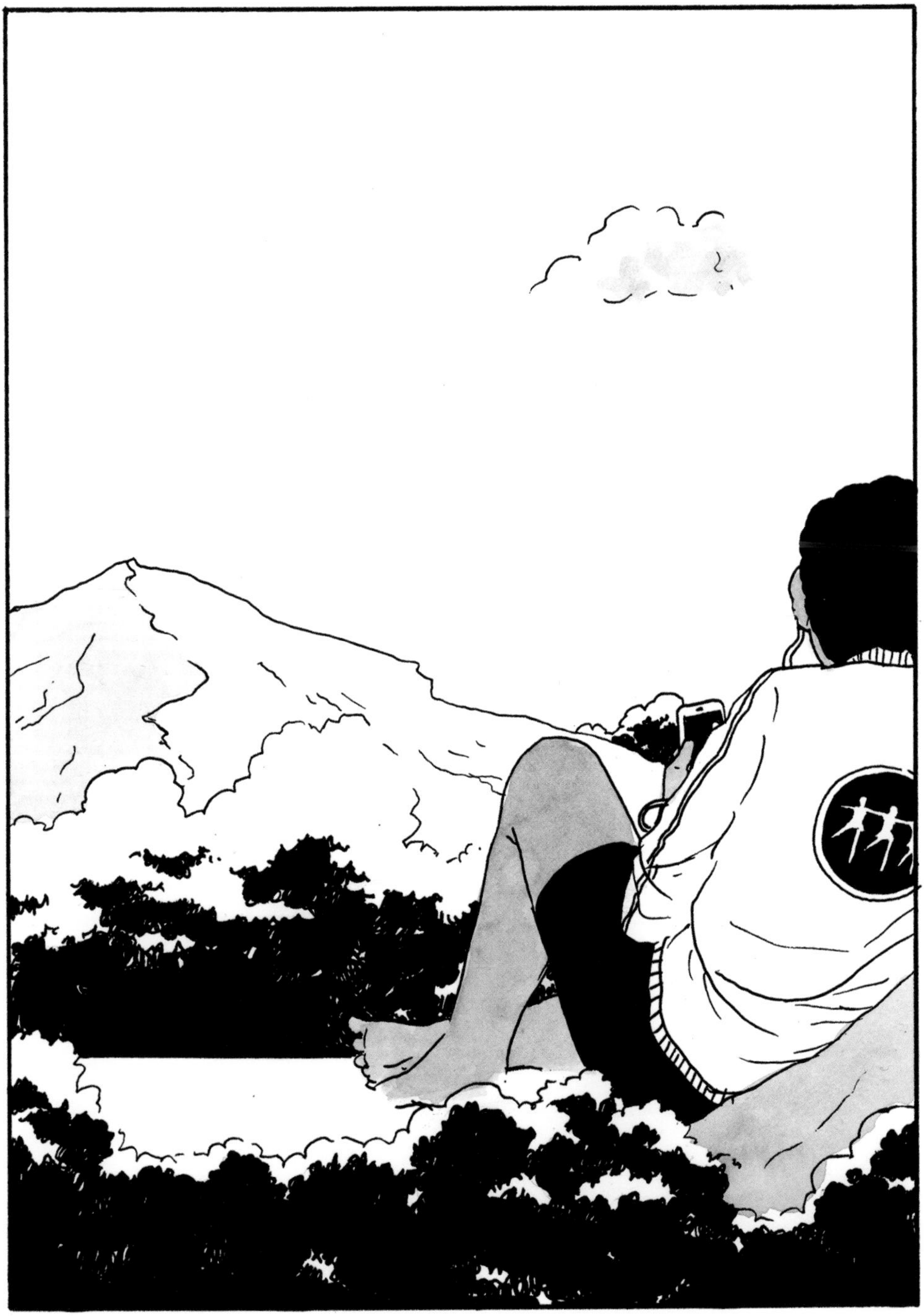

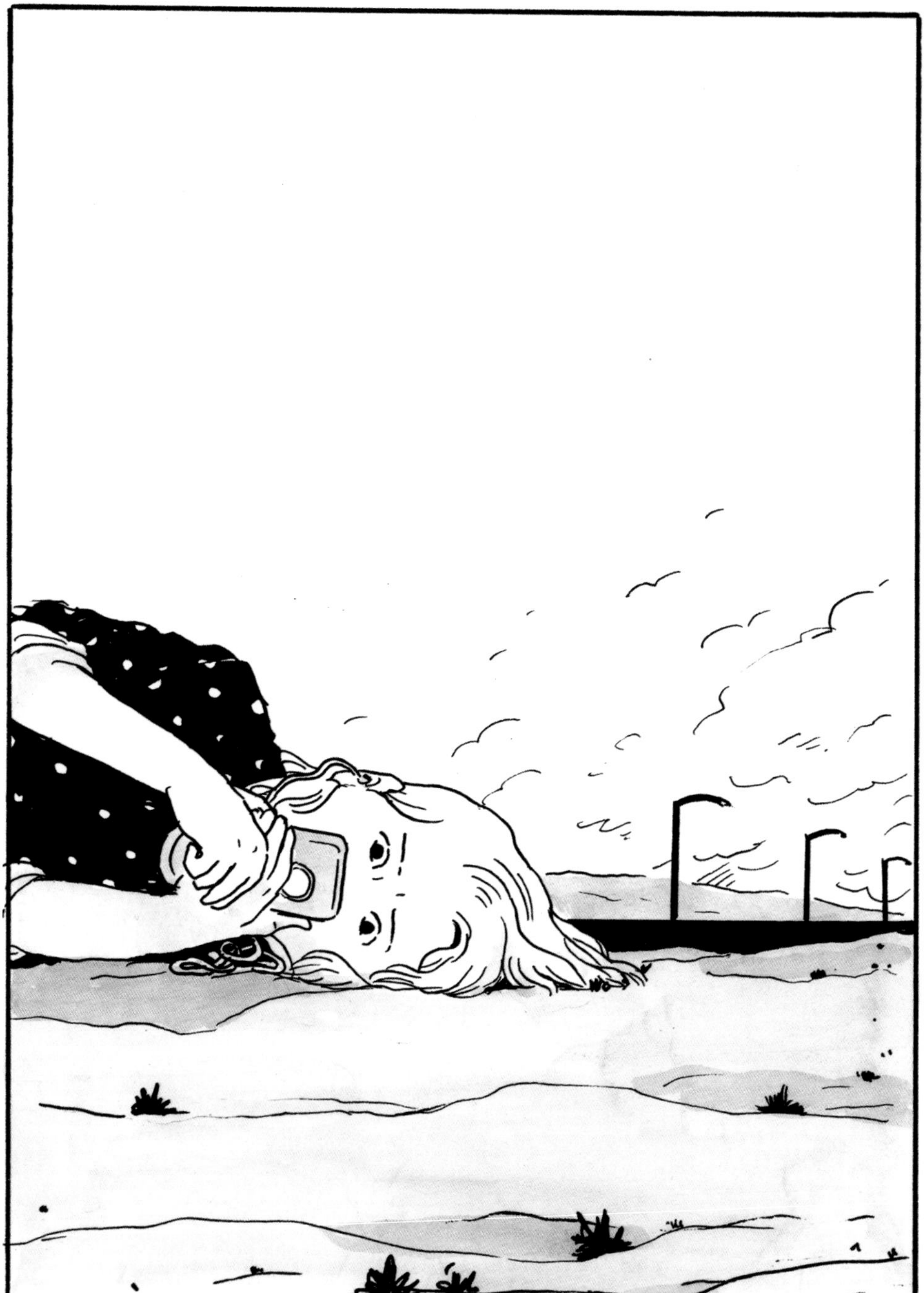

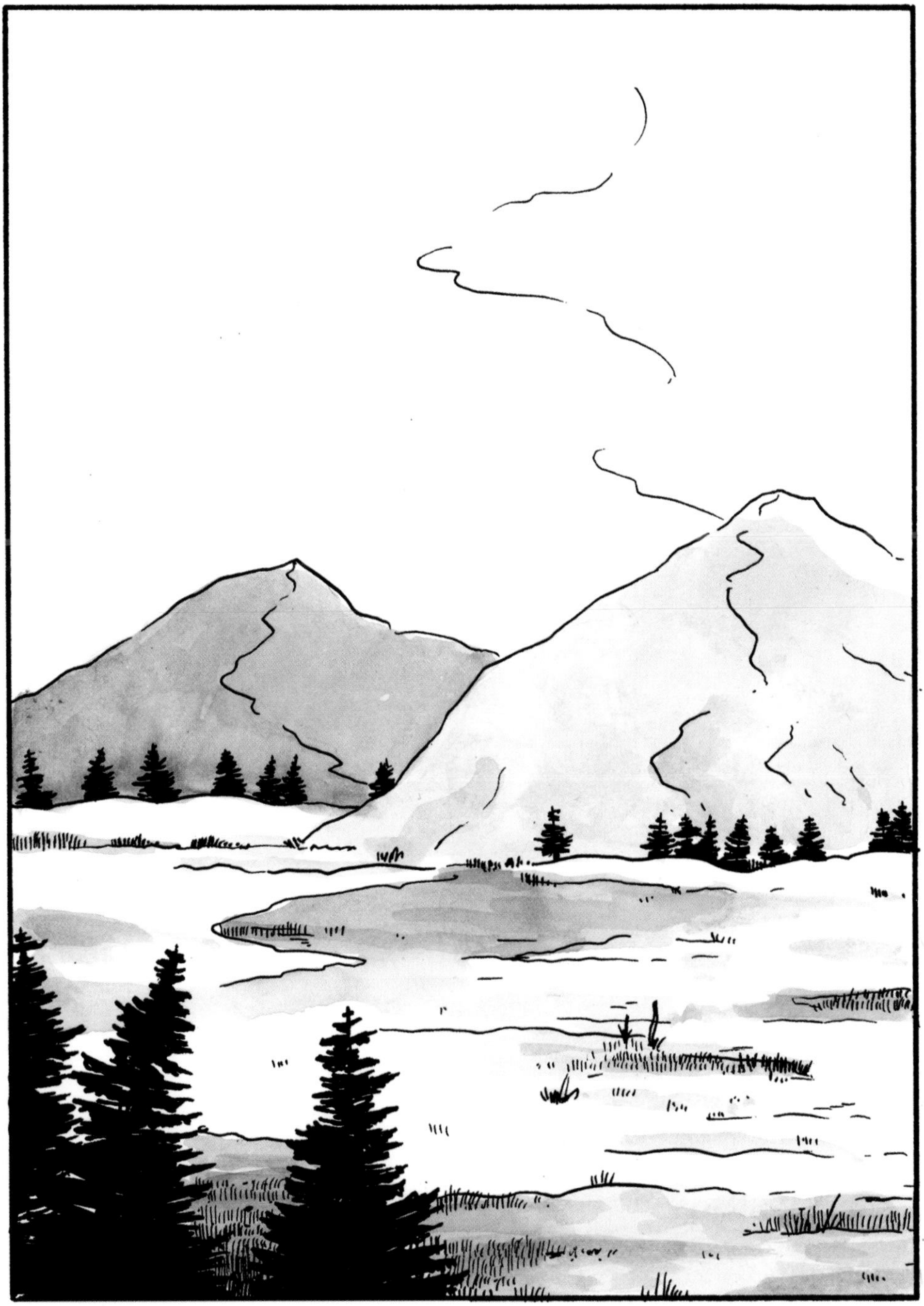

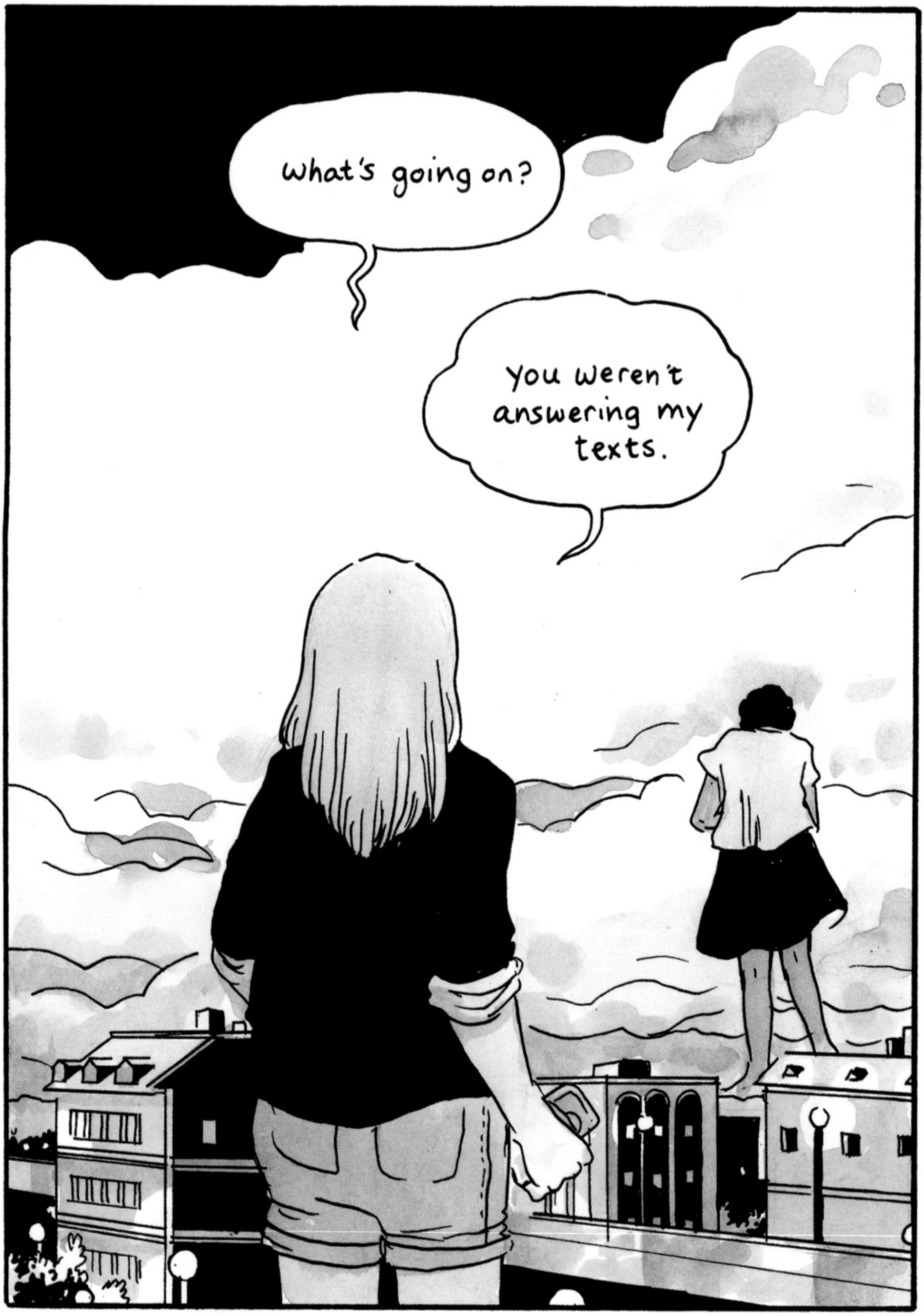
what's going on?
you weren't answering my texts.

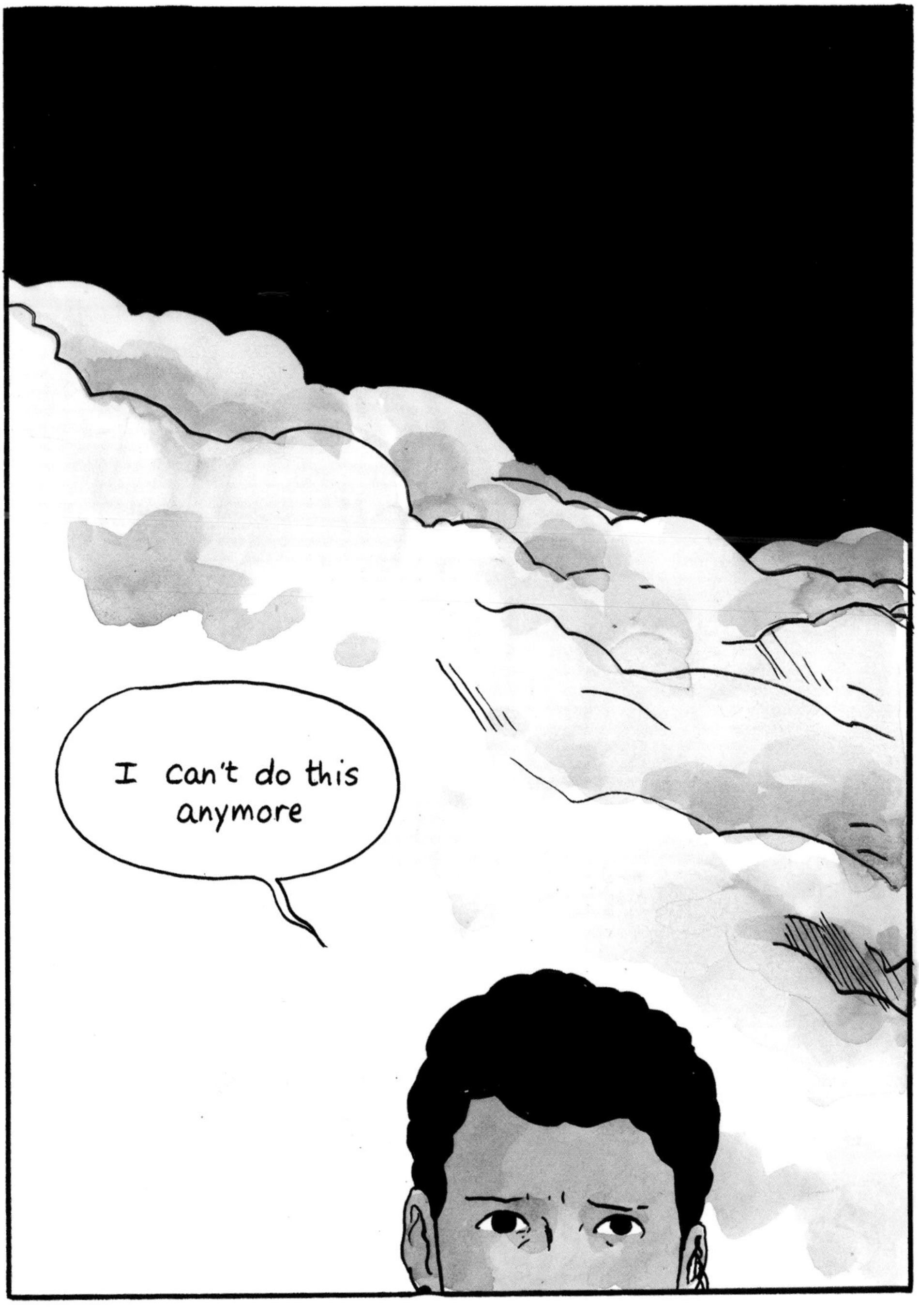
I can't do this anymore

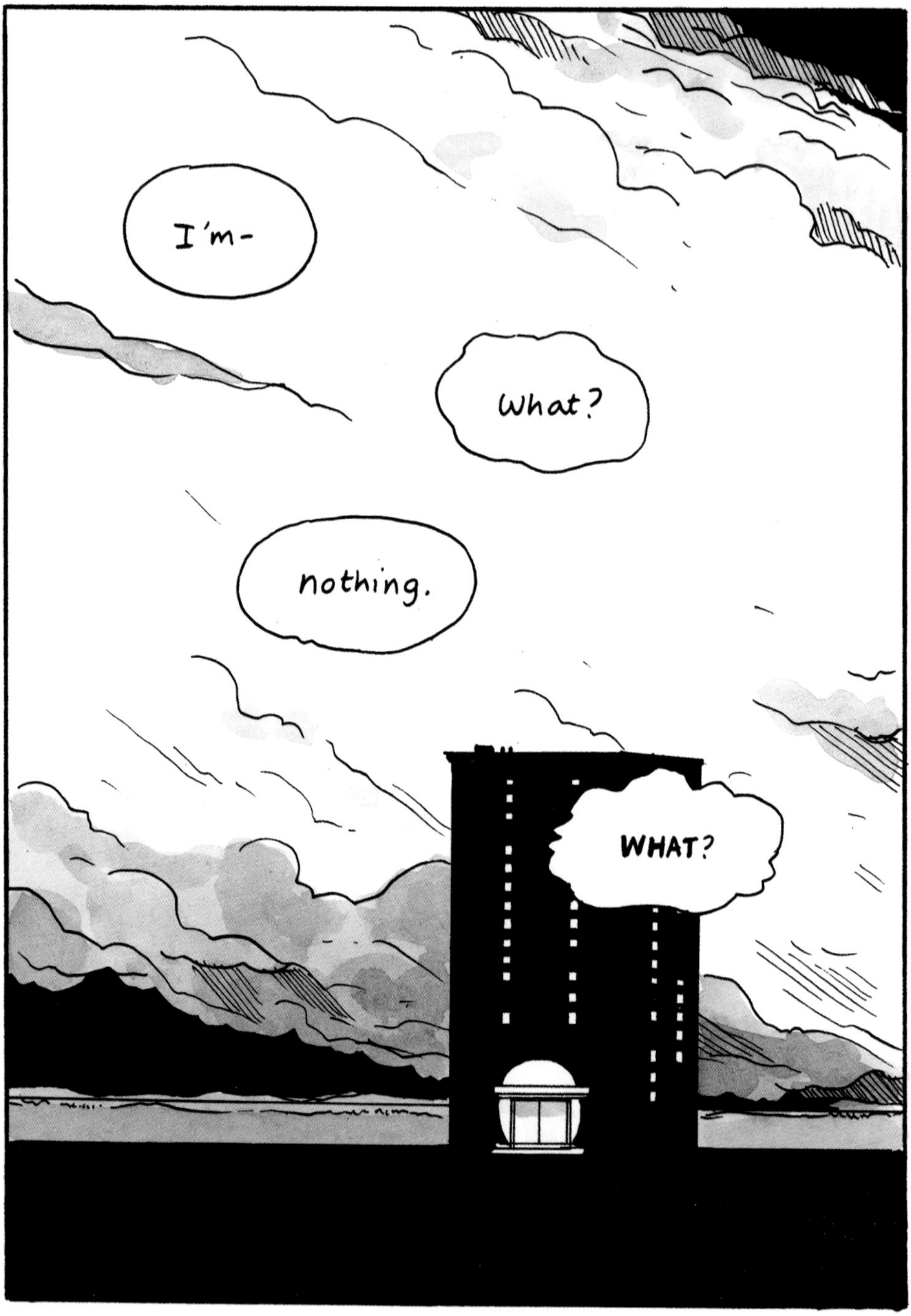
I'm-
What?
nothing.
WHAT?

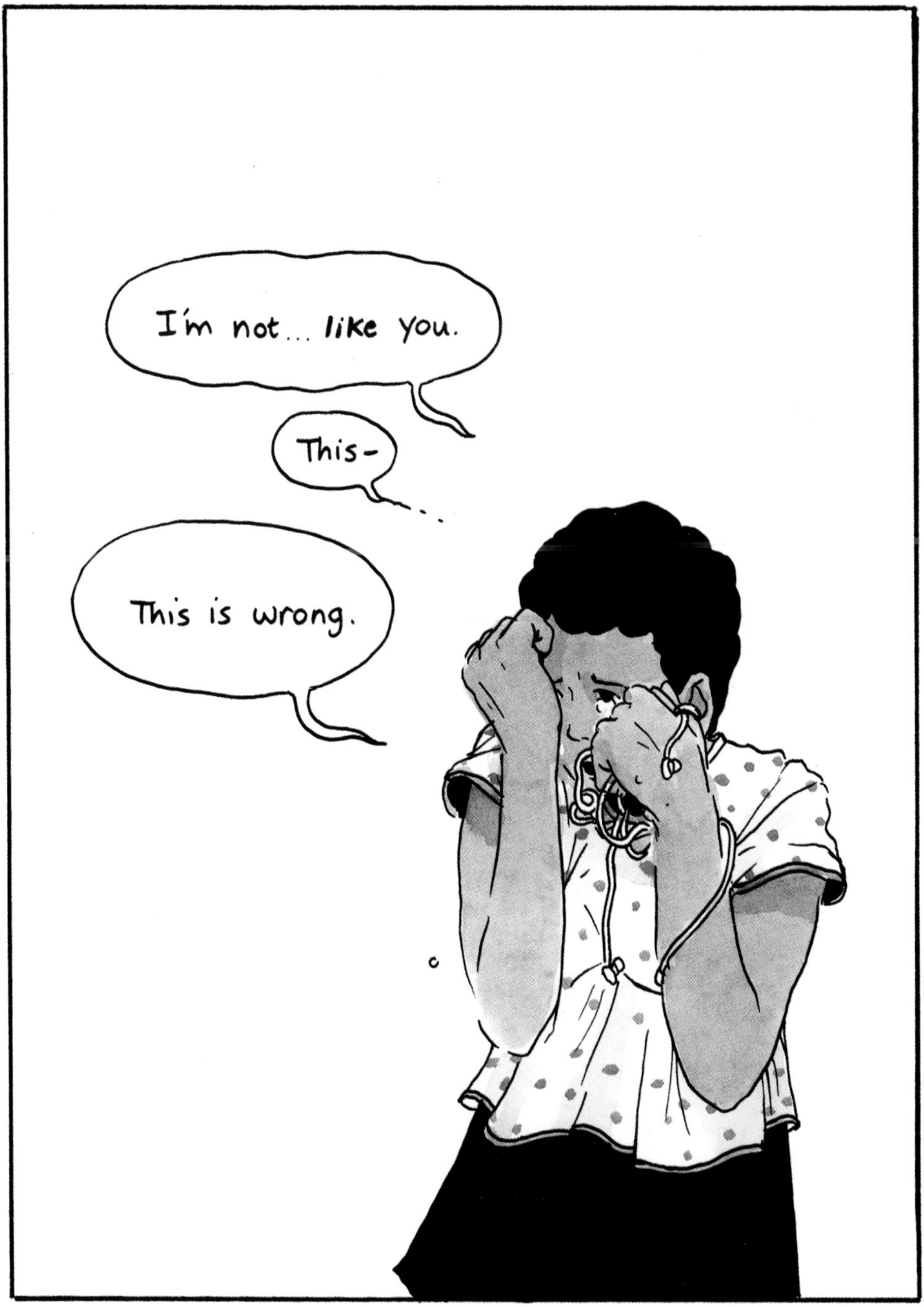
I'm not... like you.
This-
This is wrong.

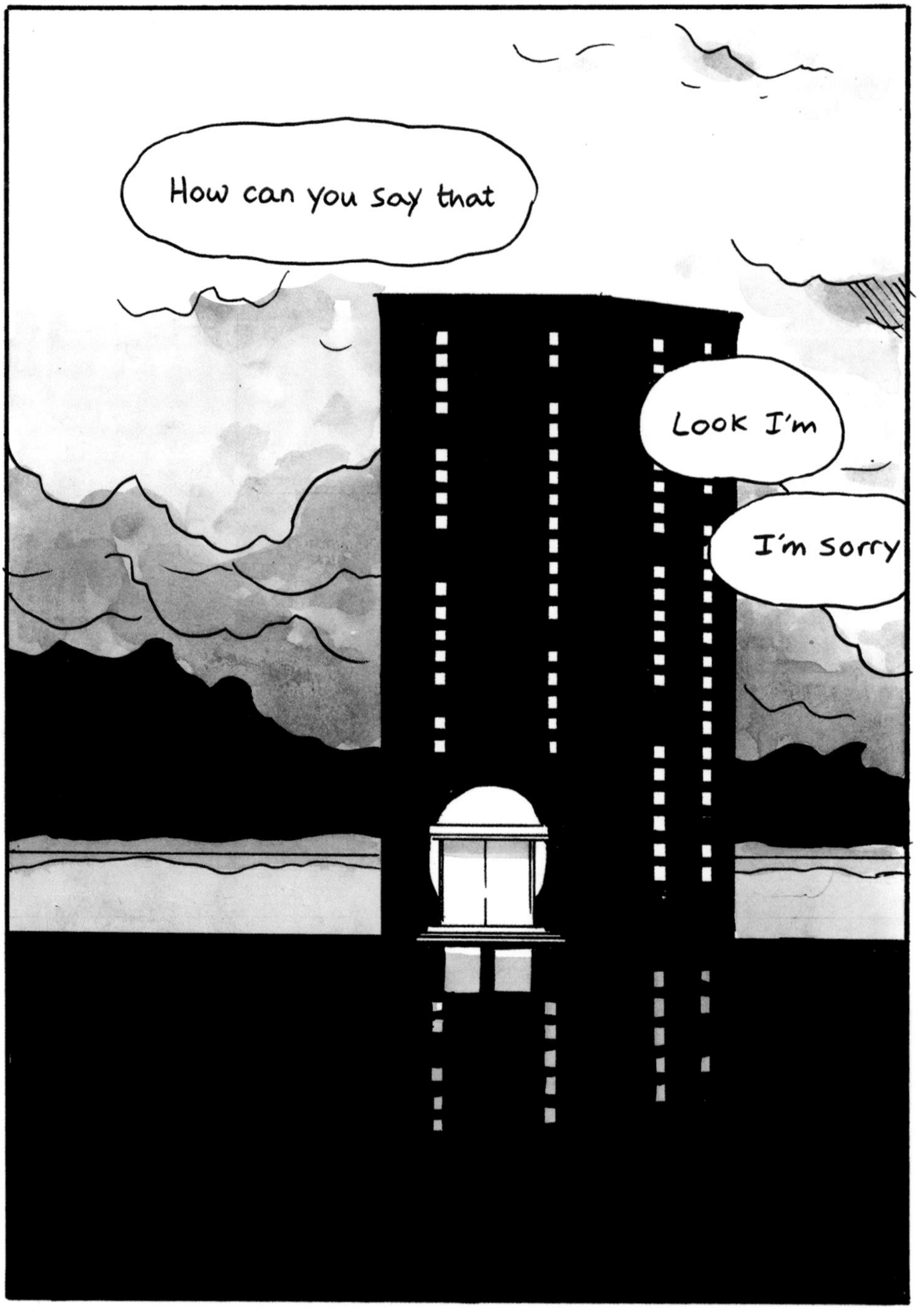
How can you say that
Look I'm
I'm sorry

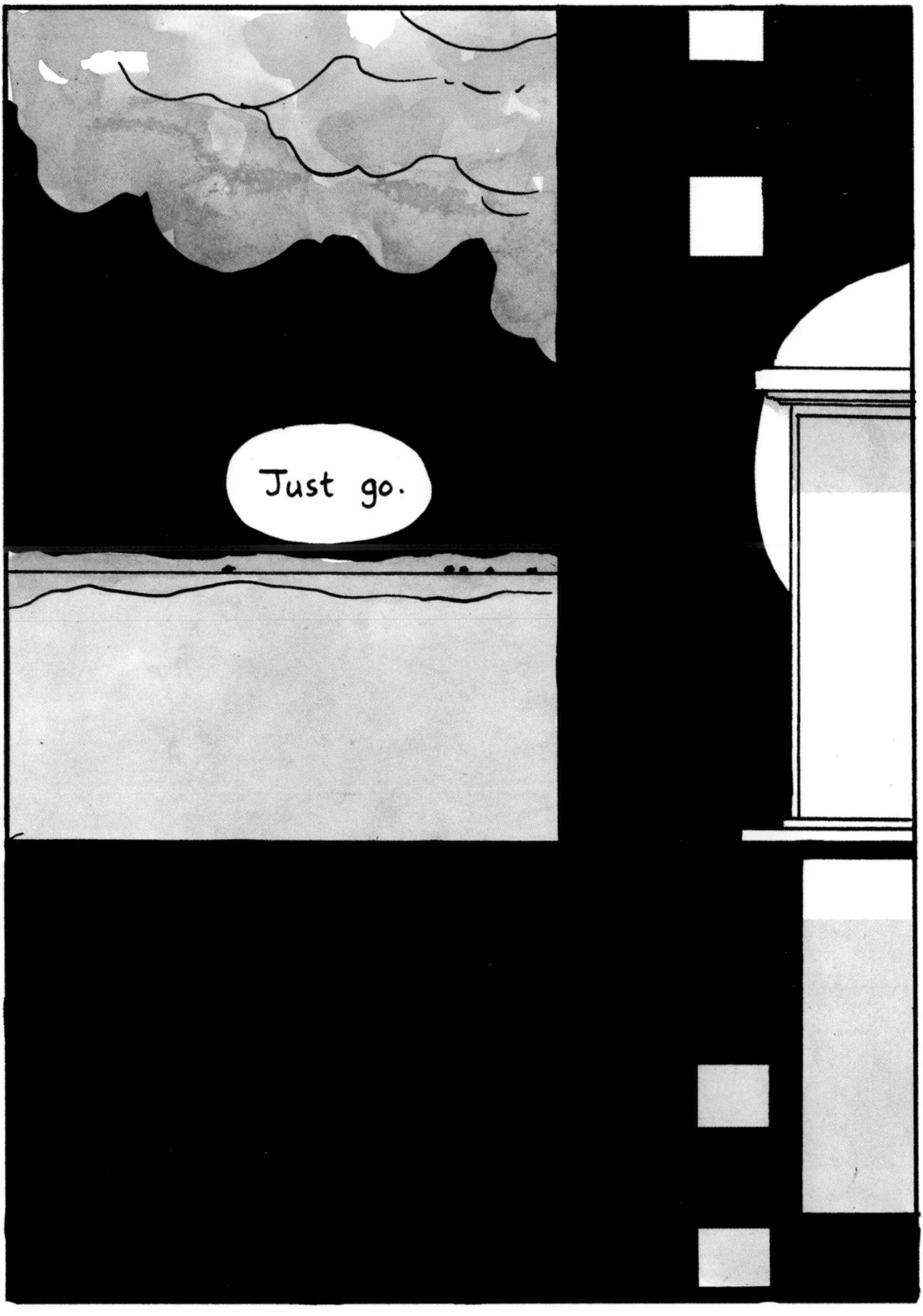
Just go.

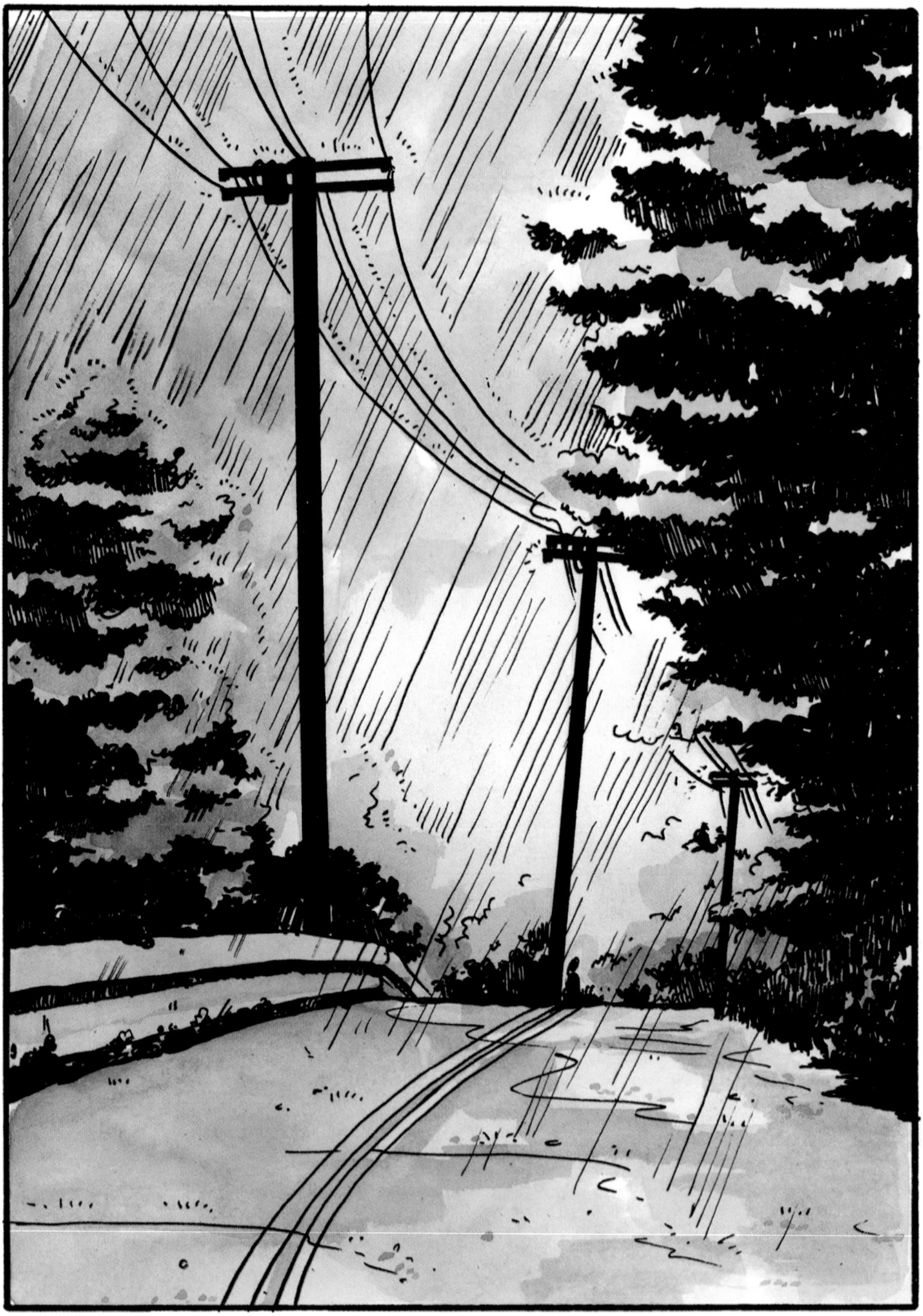

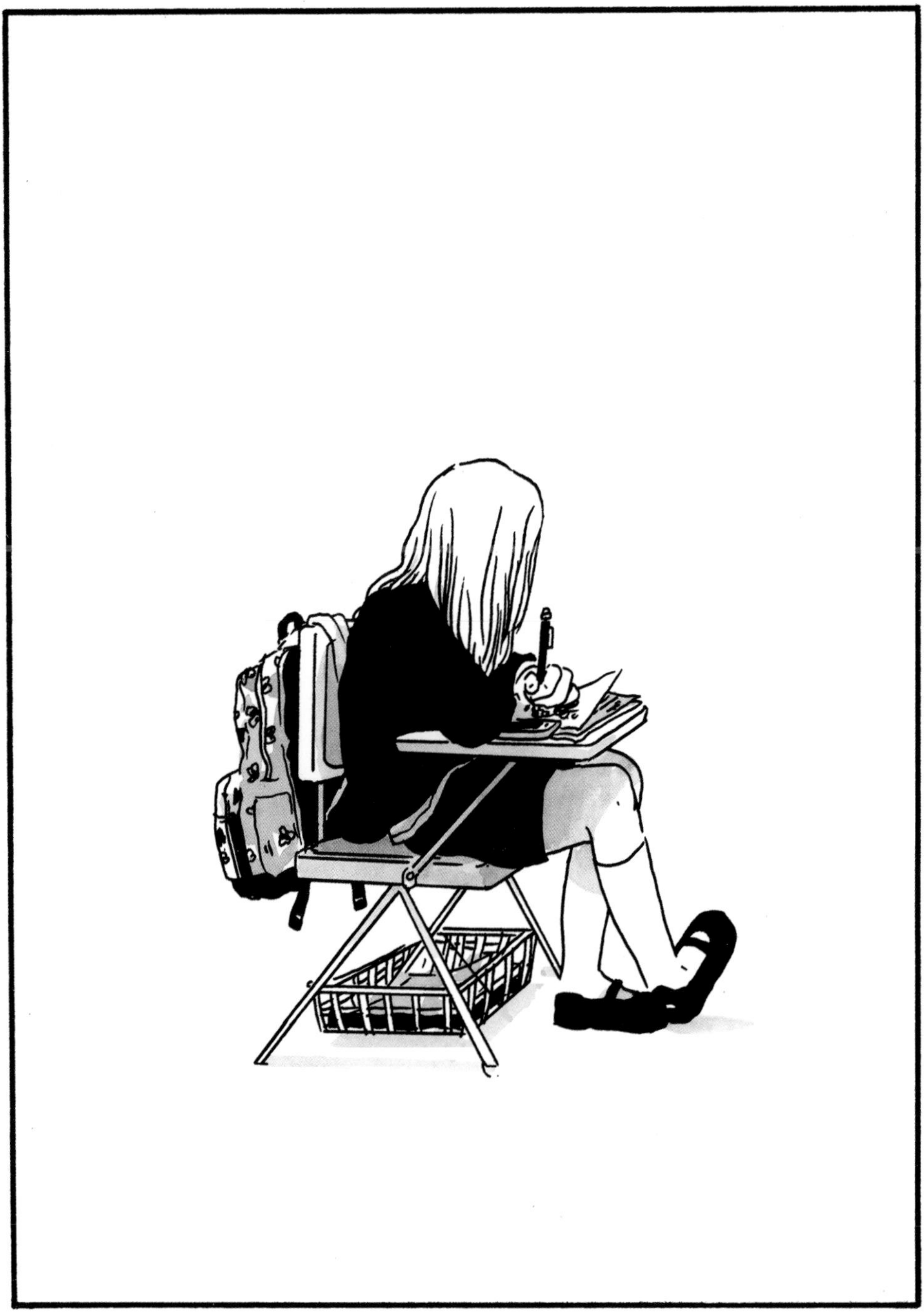

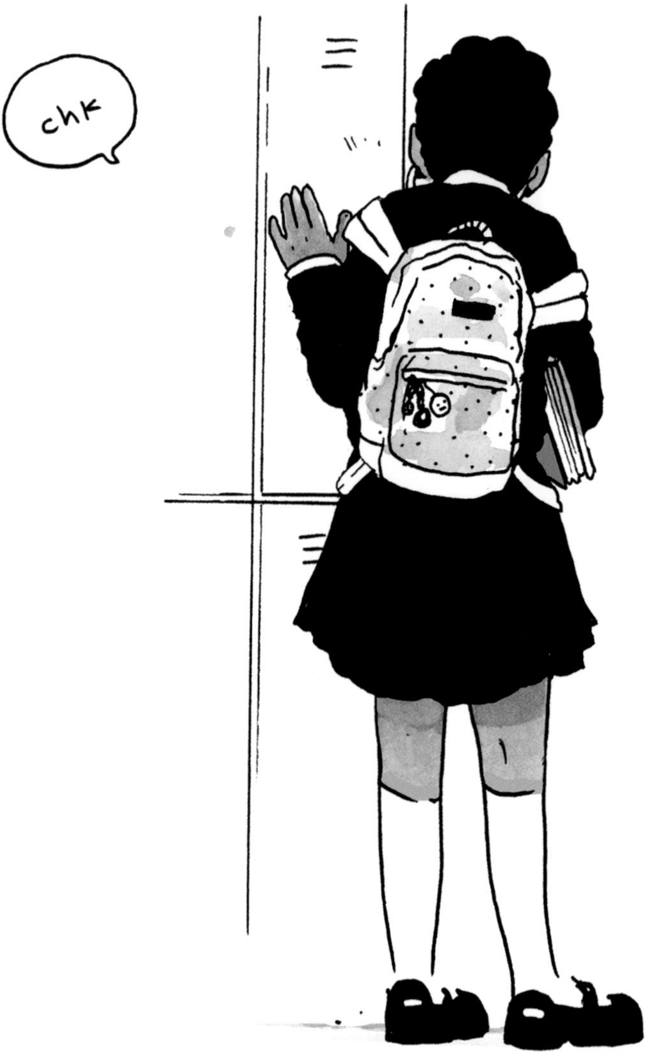
chk

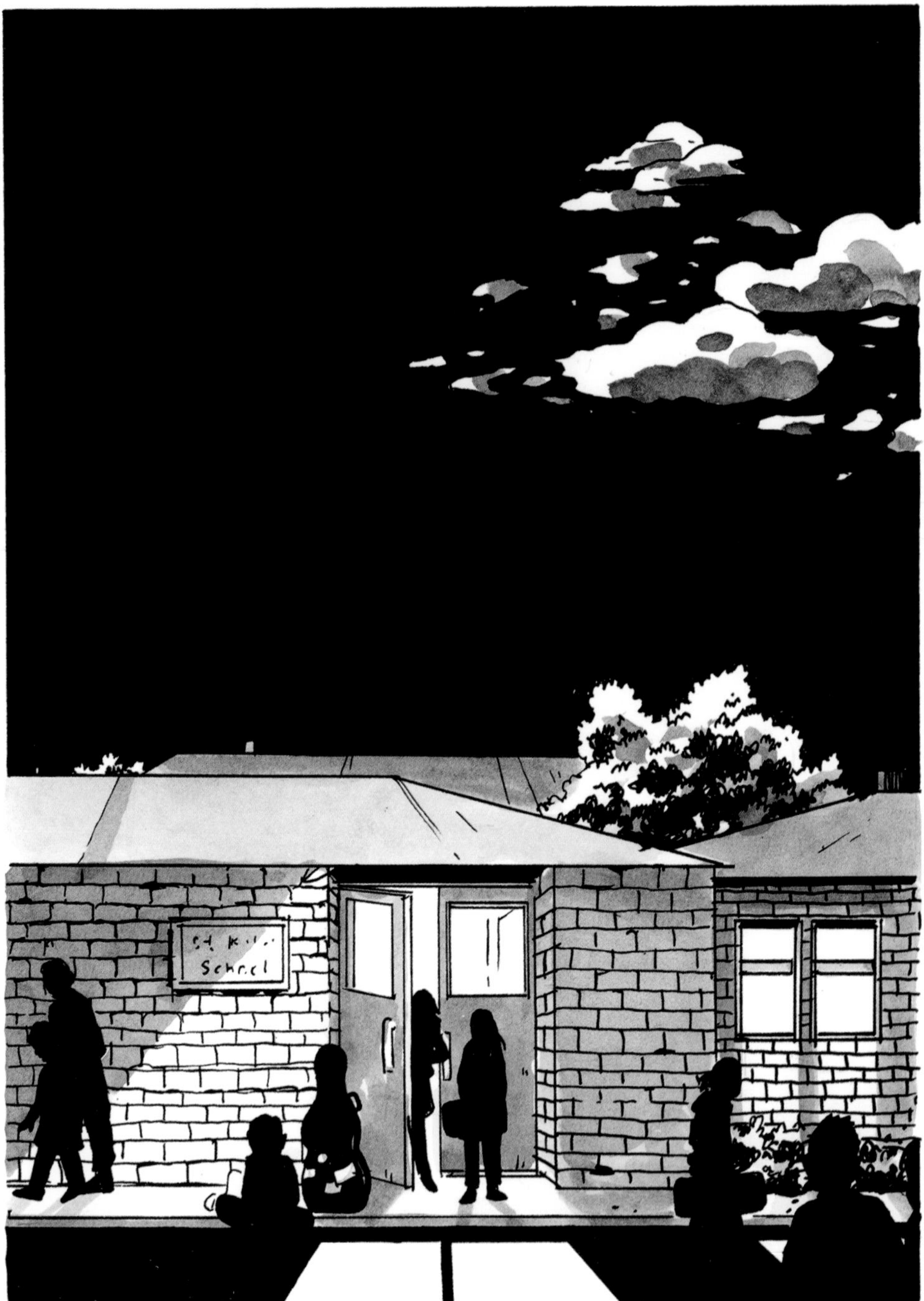

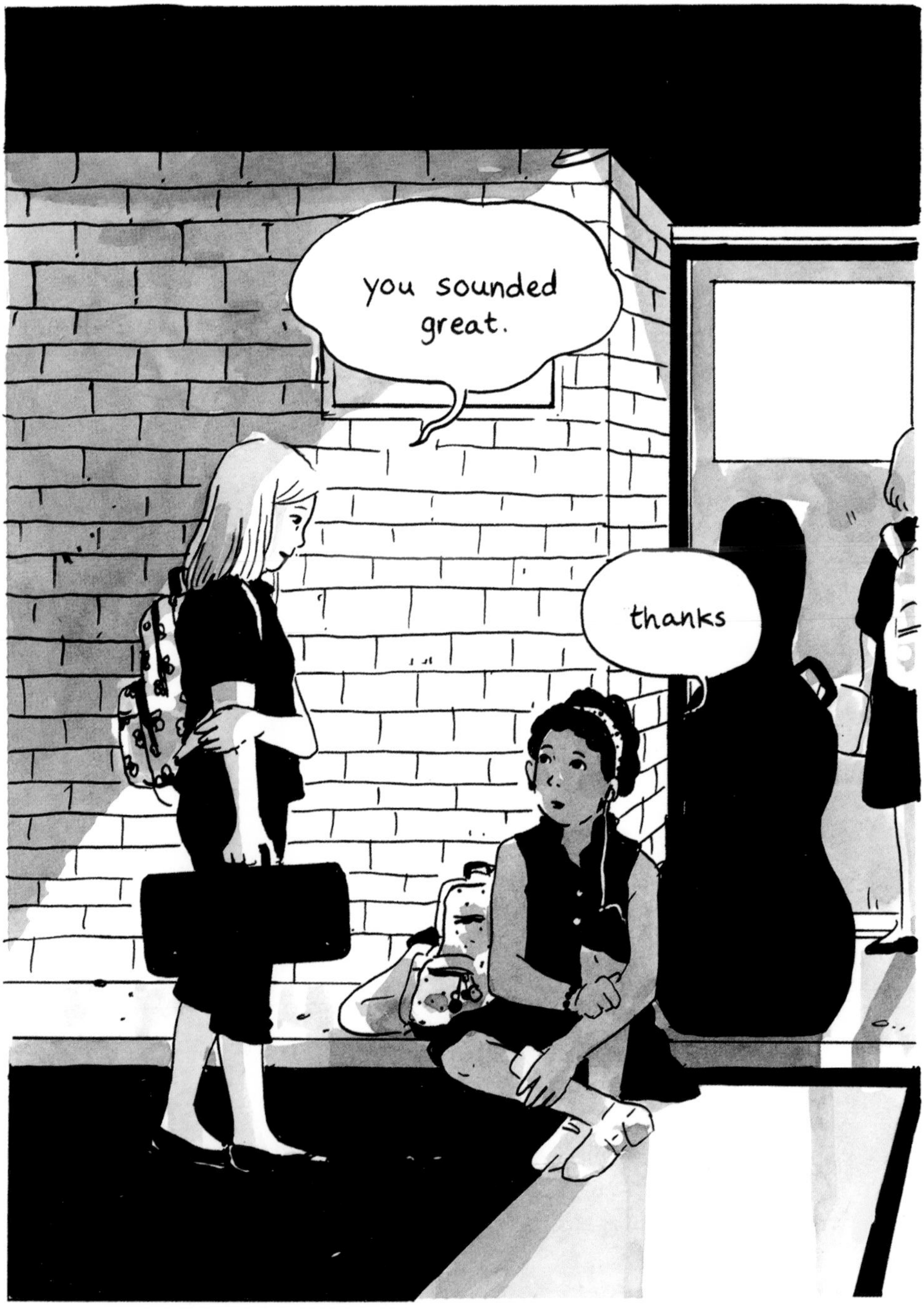
you sounded great.
thanks

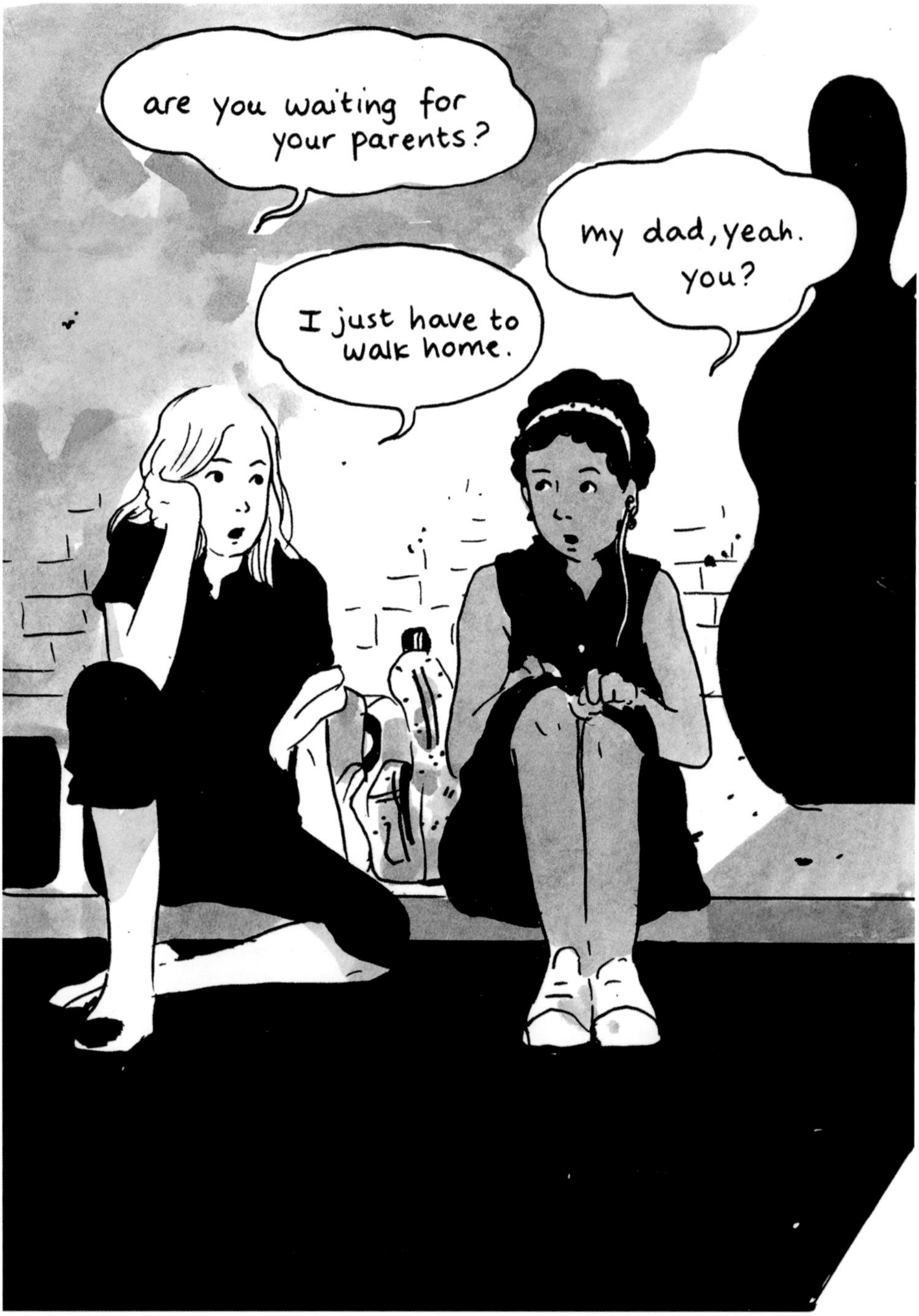
are you waiting for your parents?
my dad, yeah. you?
I just have to walk home.

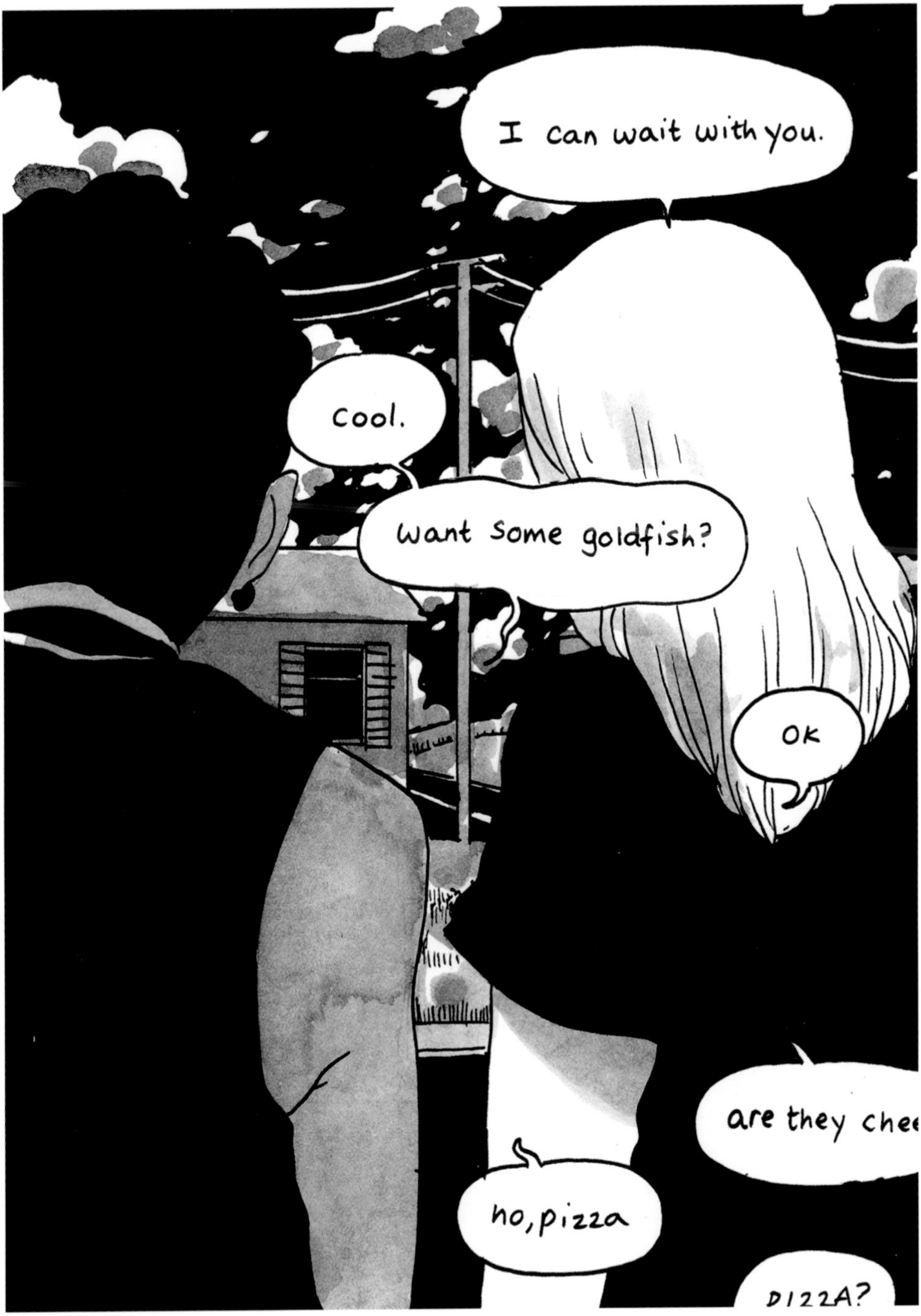
I can wait with you.
Cool.
Want some goldfish?
Ok
are they chee
no, pizza
PIZZA?

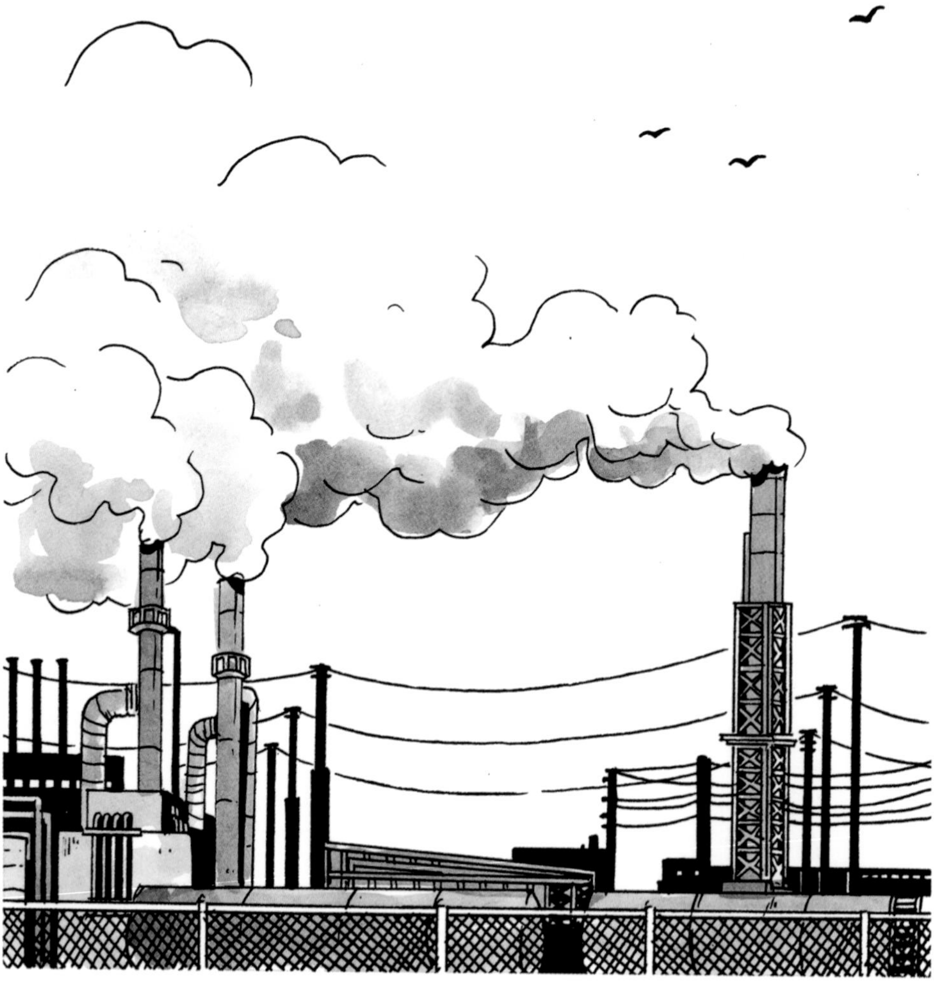

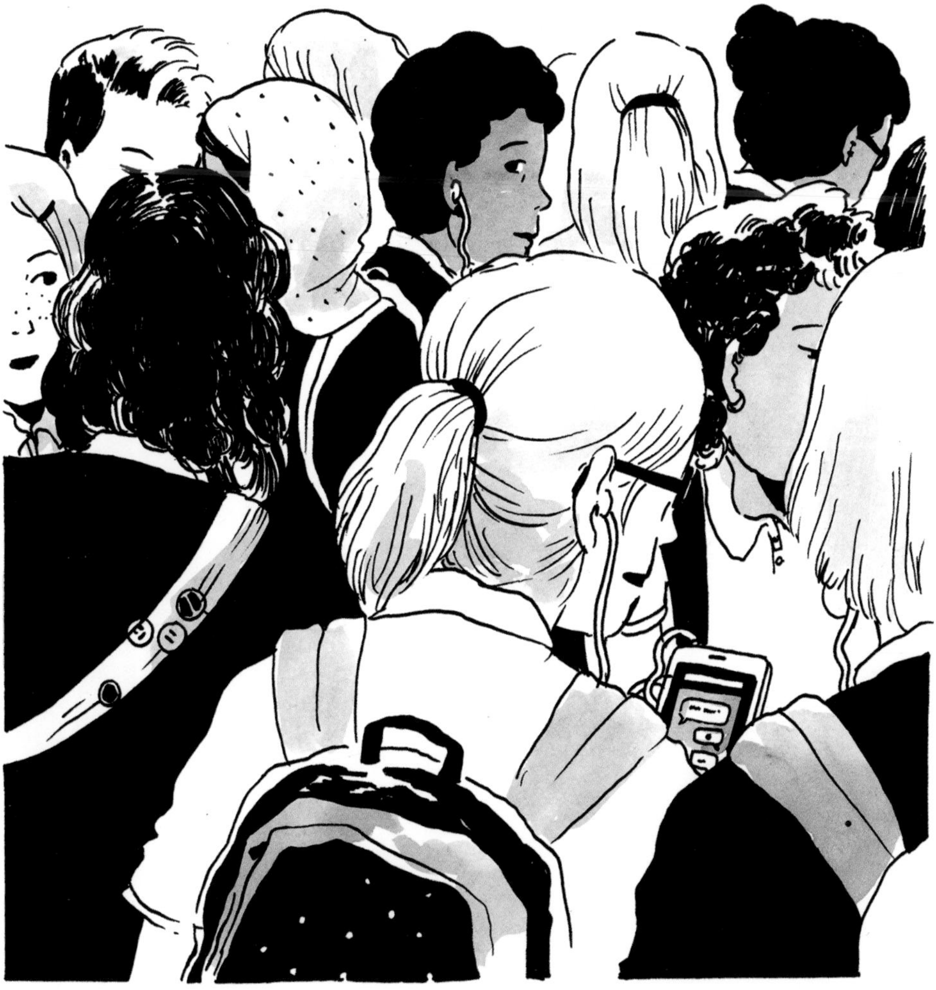

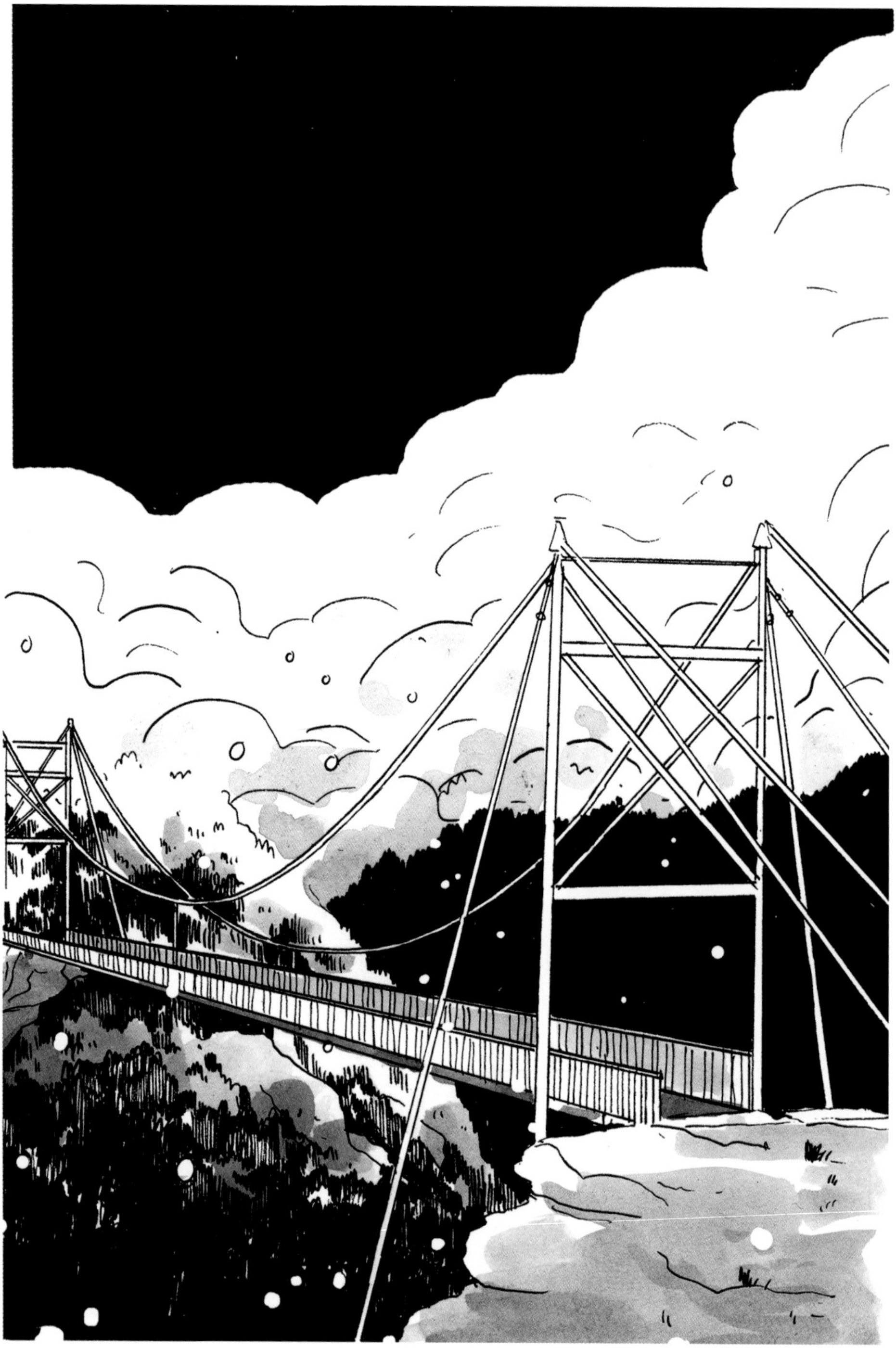

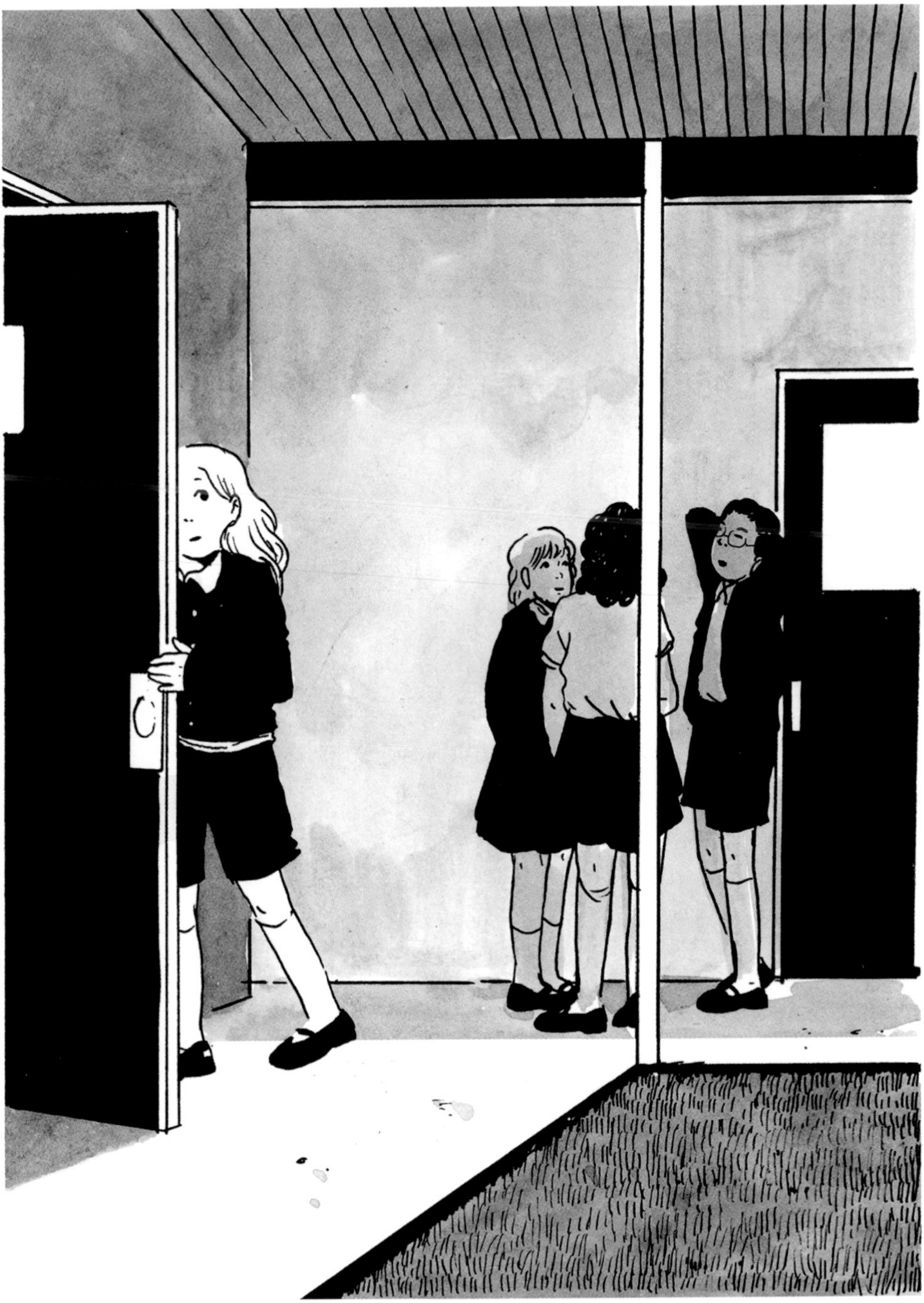

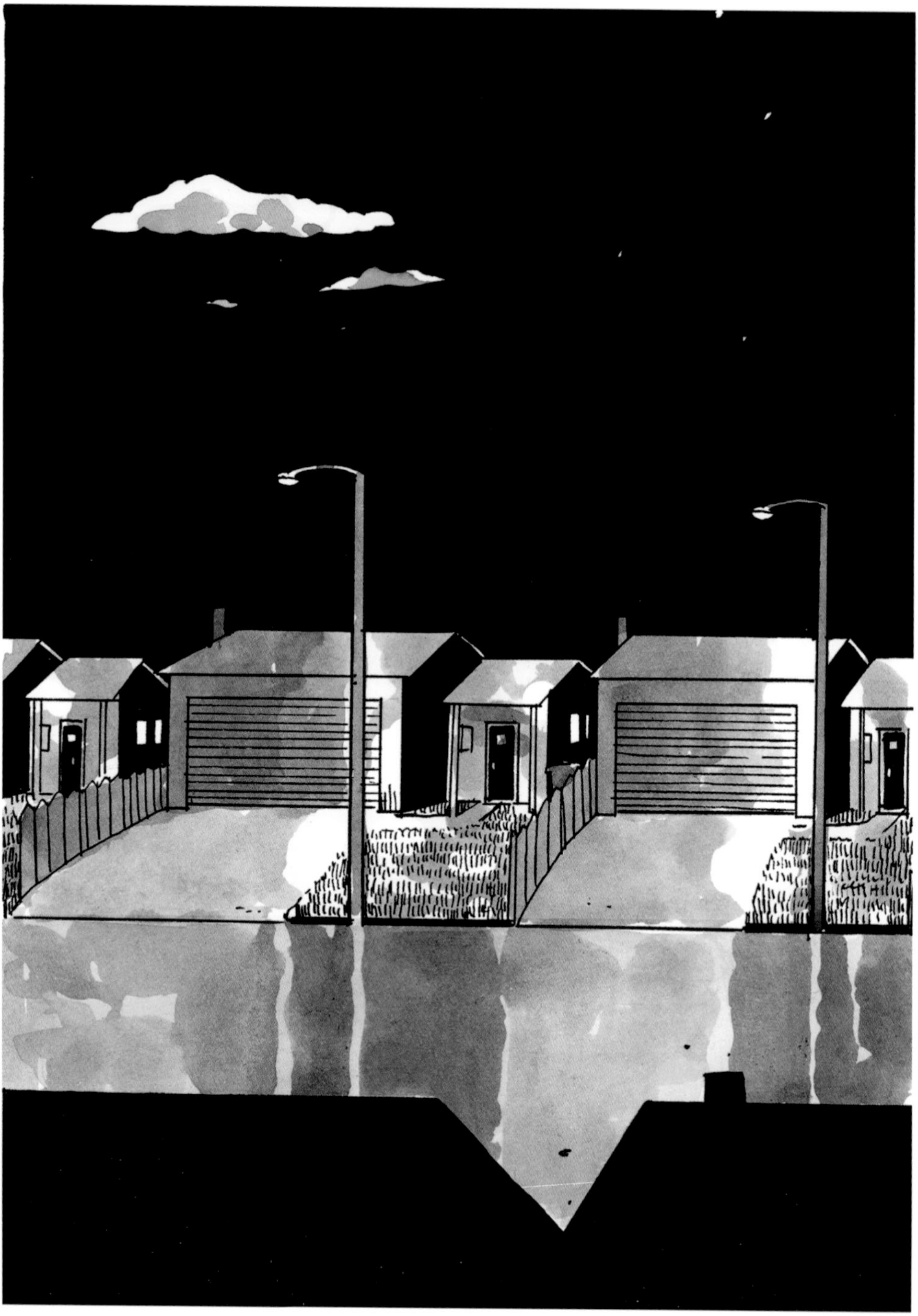

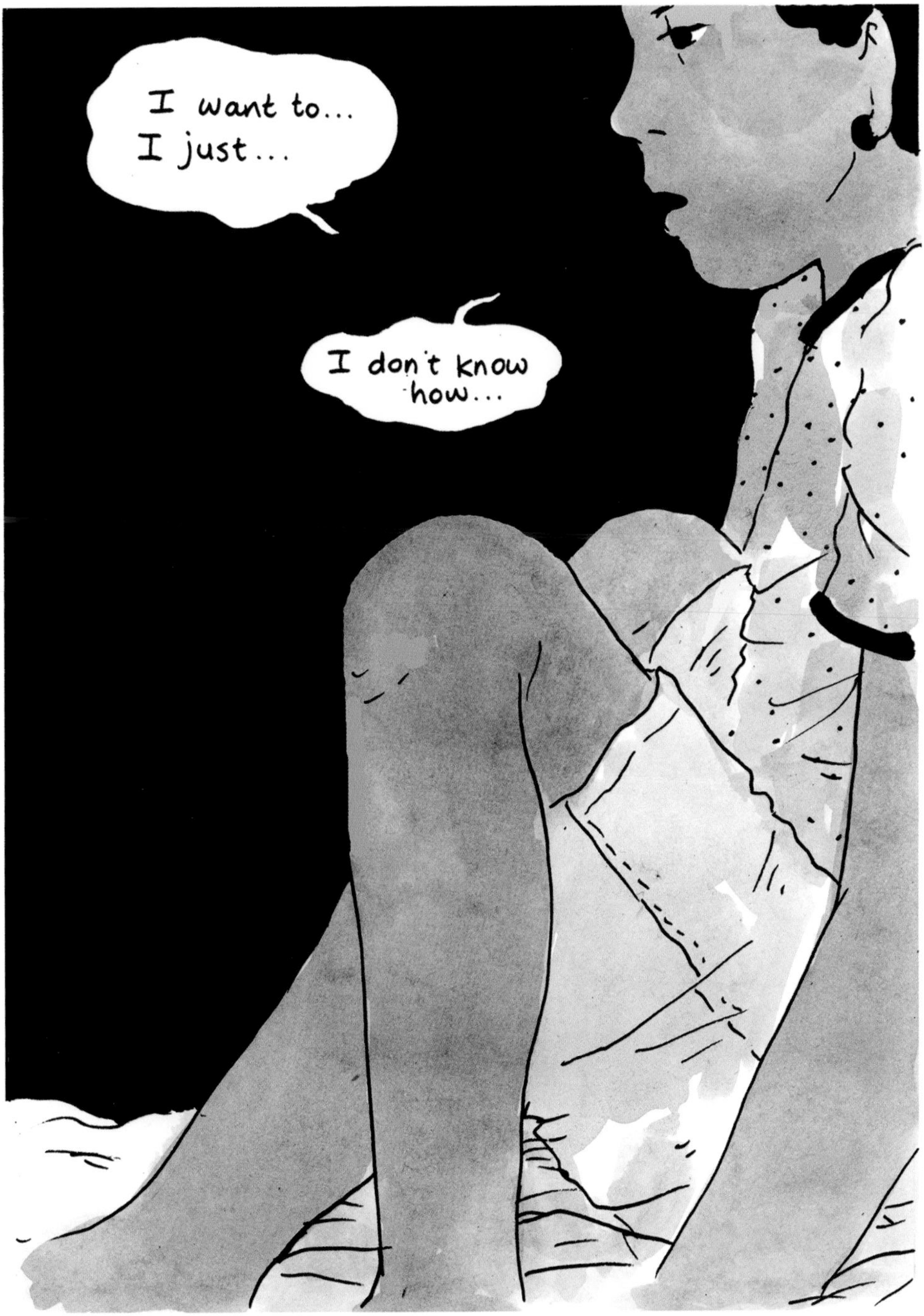
I want to... I just...
I don't know how...

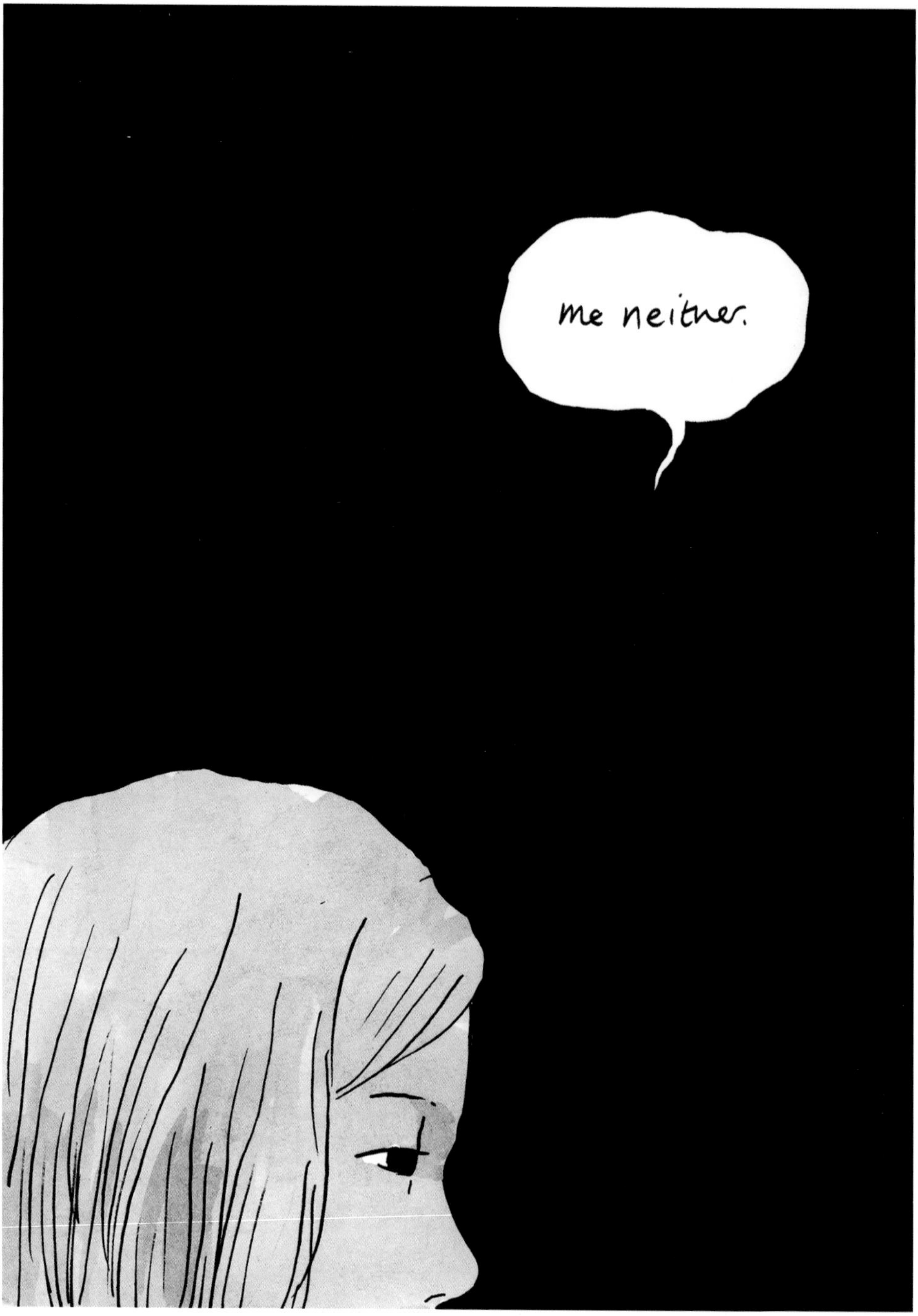
me neither.

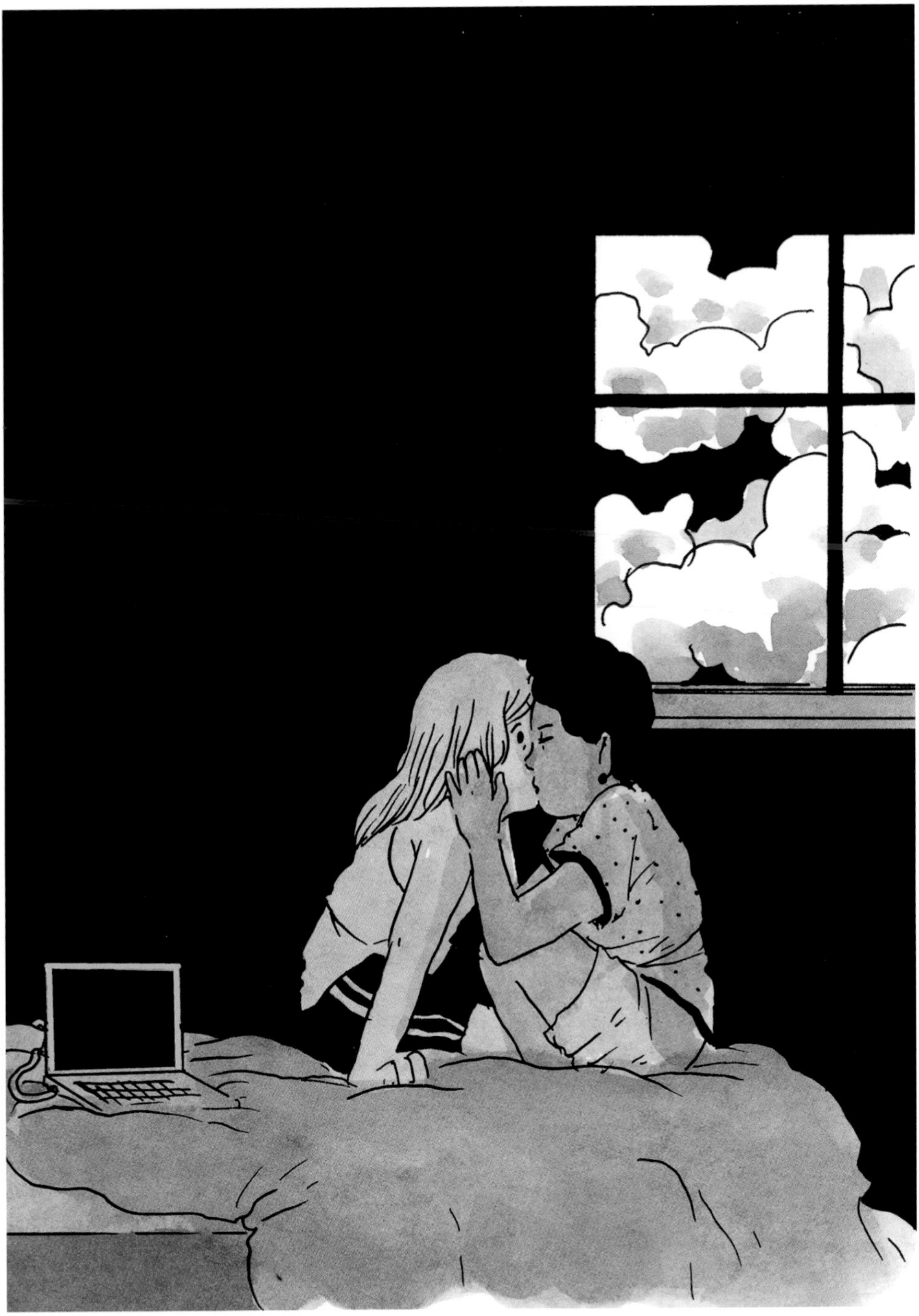

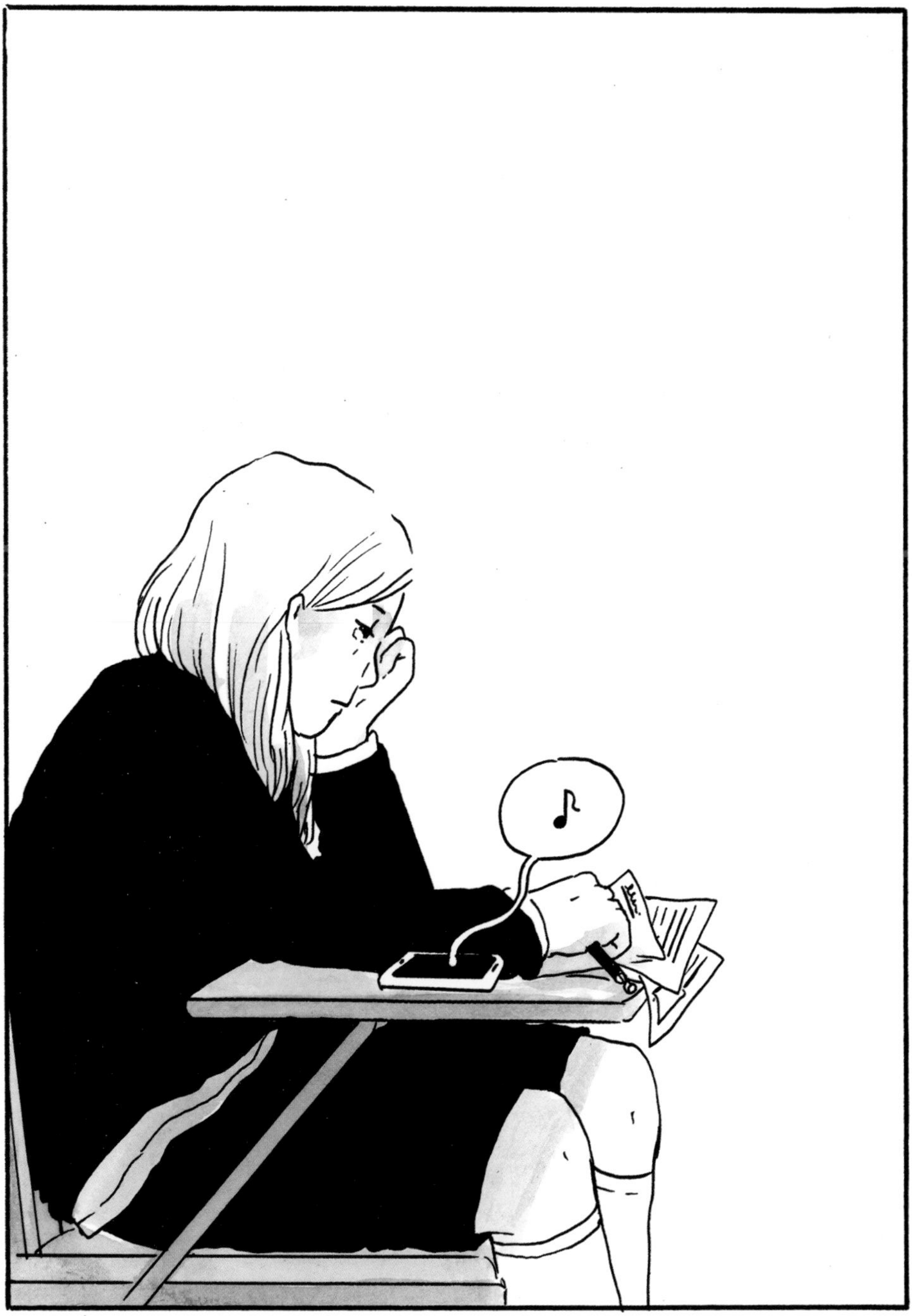

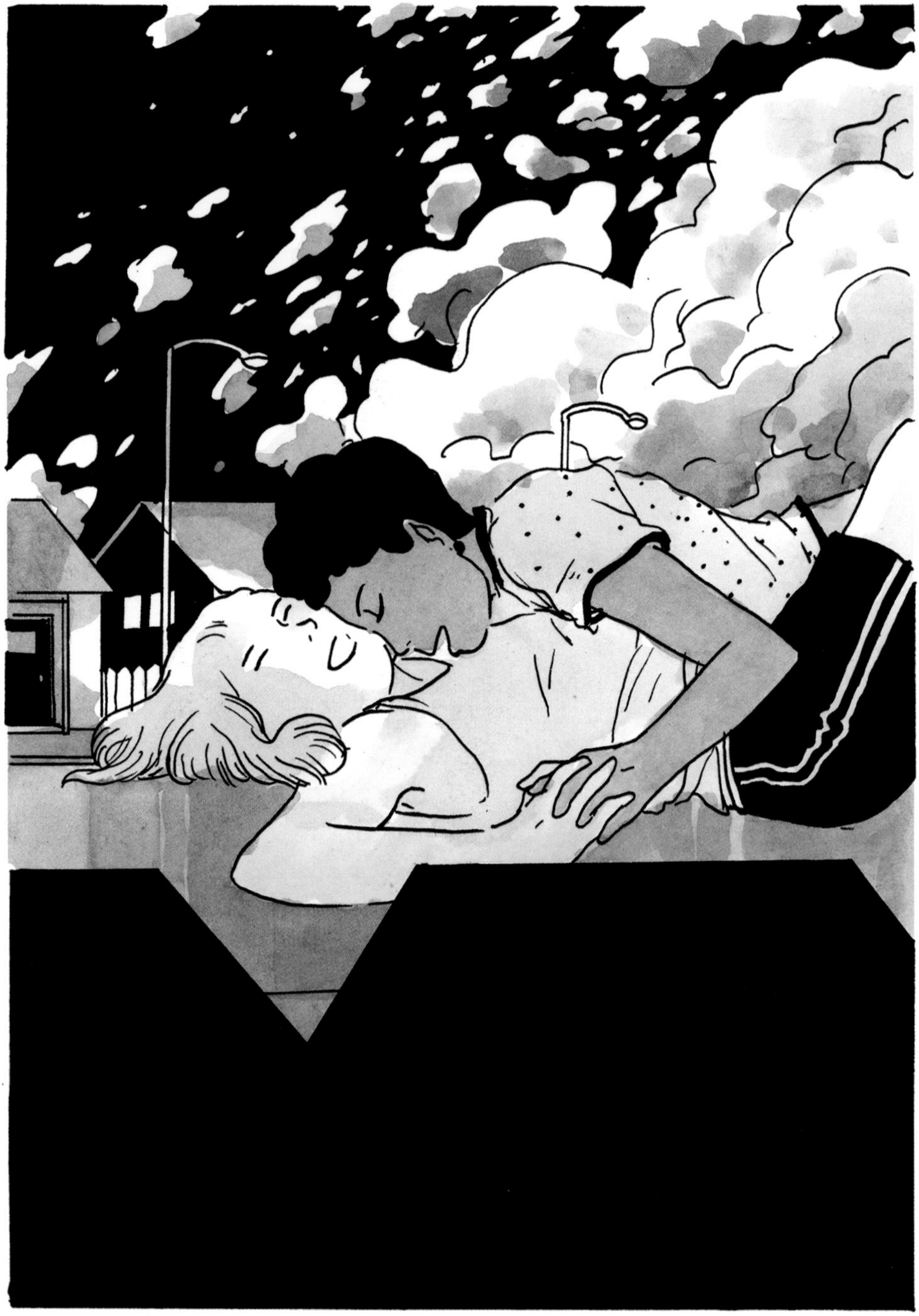

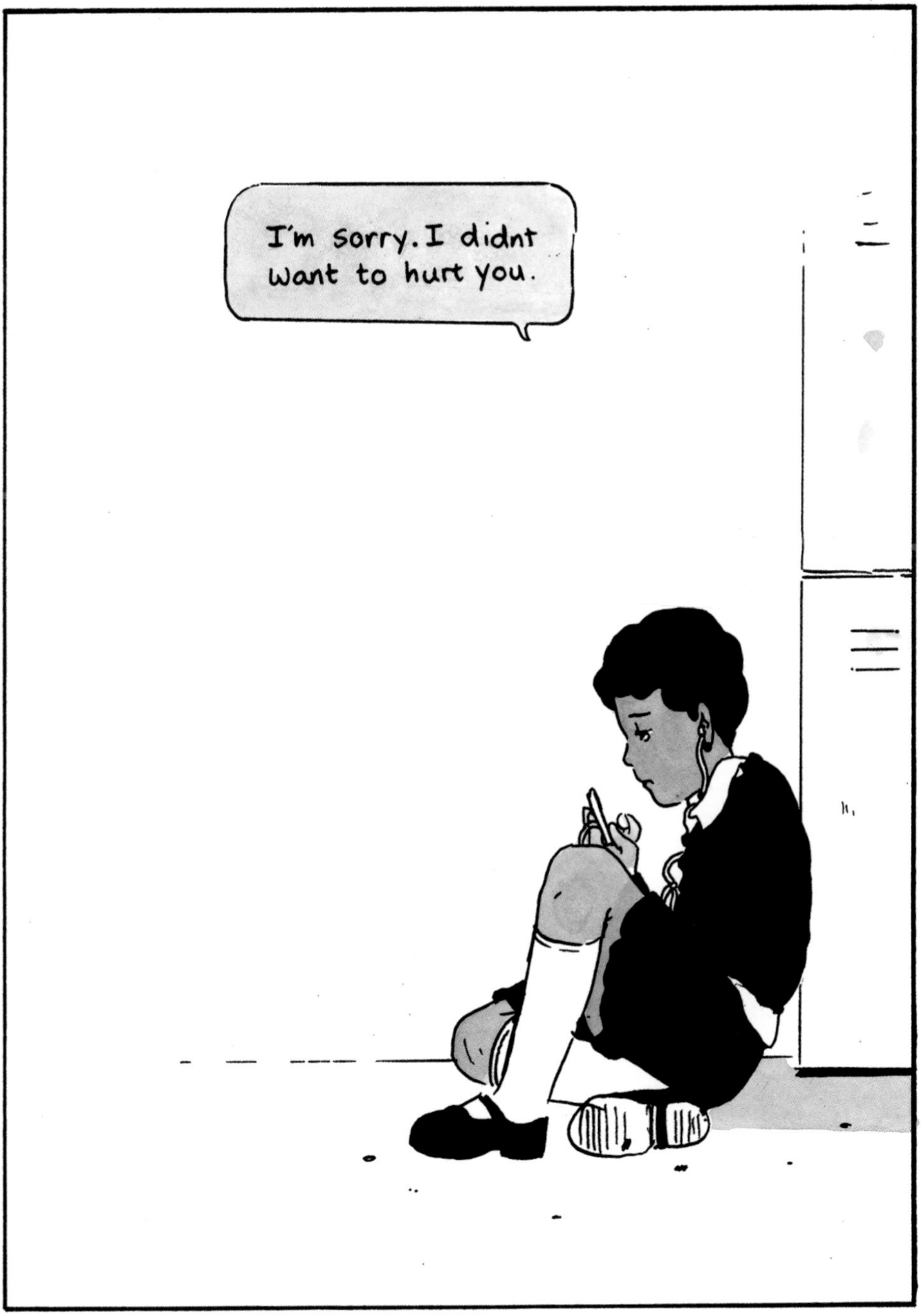
I'm sorry. I didnt want to hurt you.

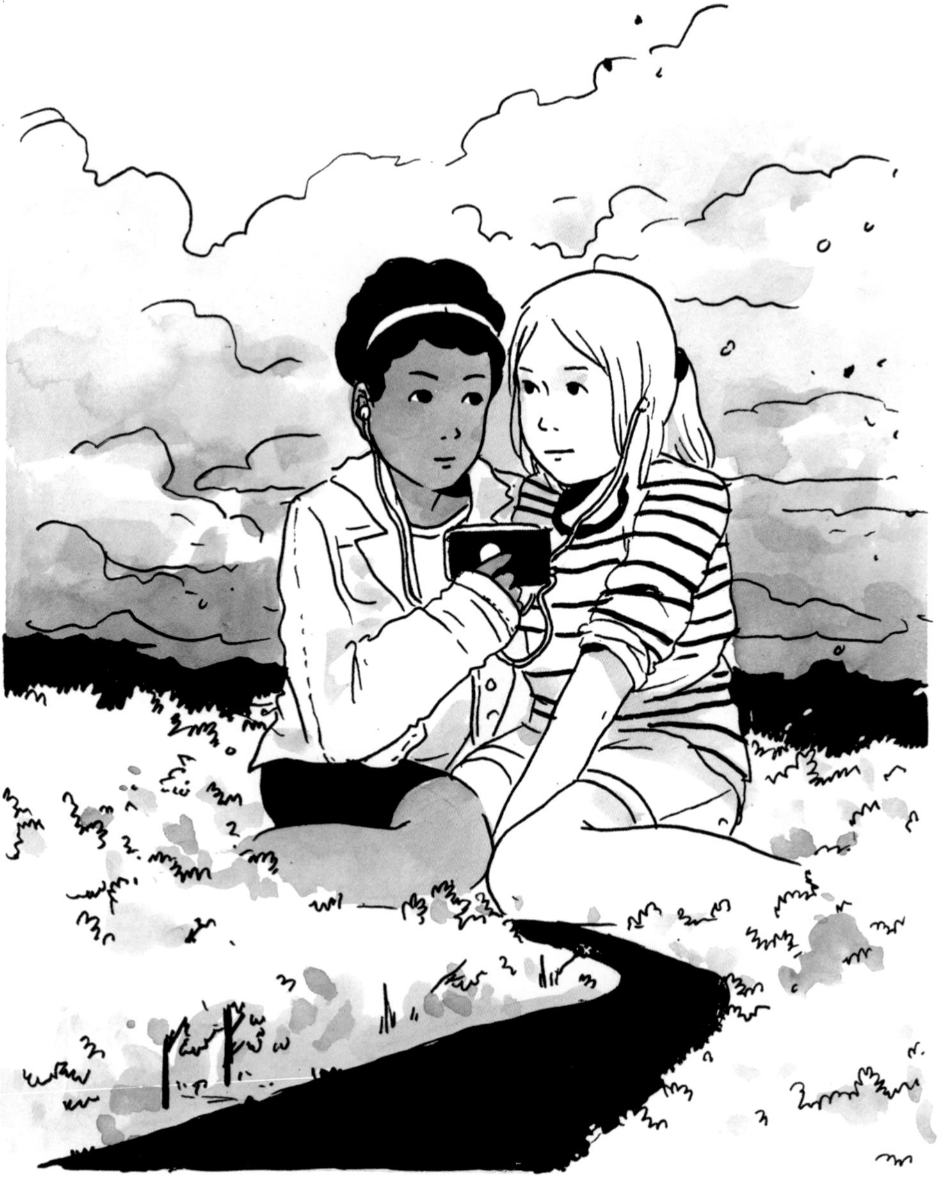

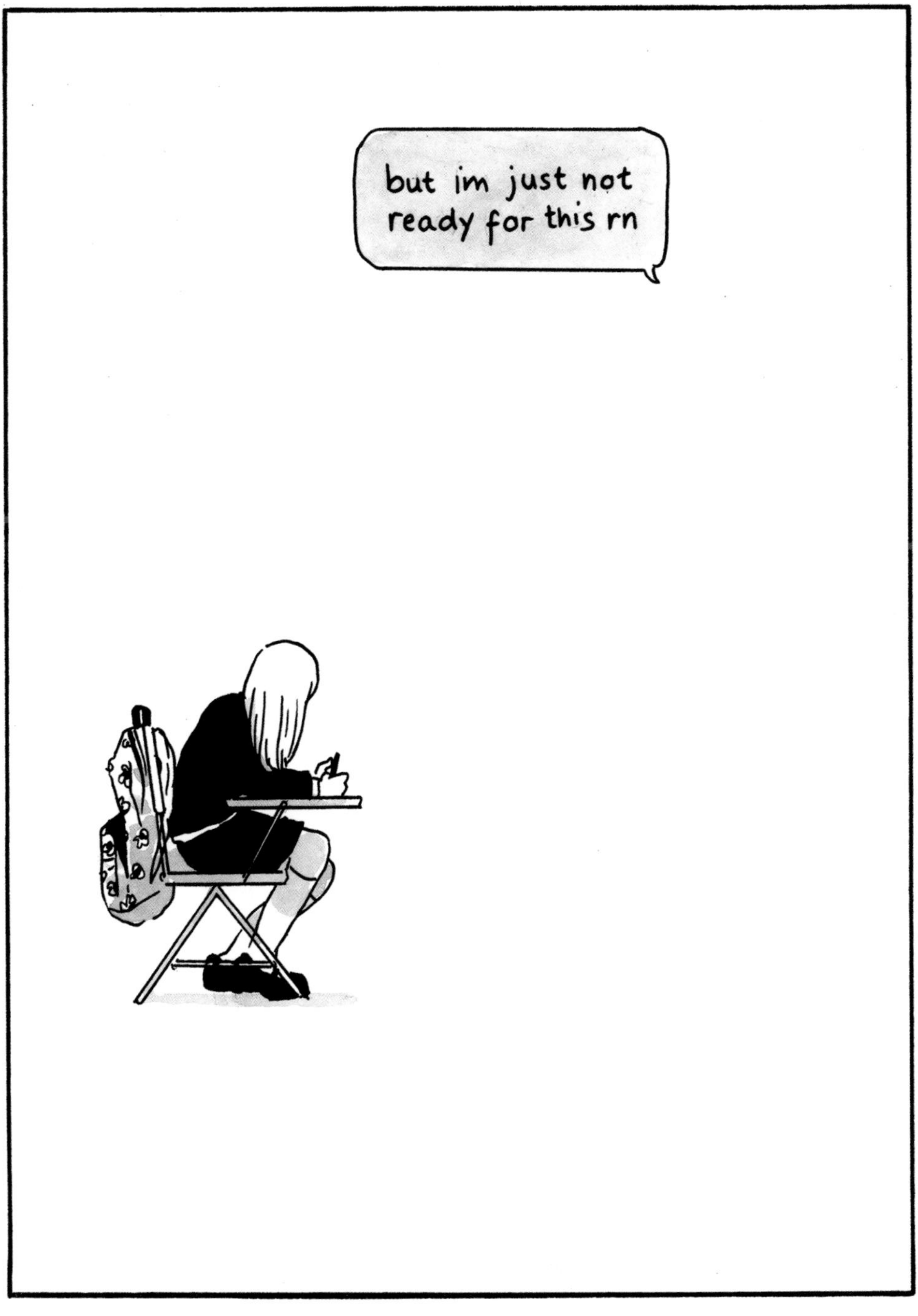
but im just not ready for this rn

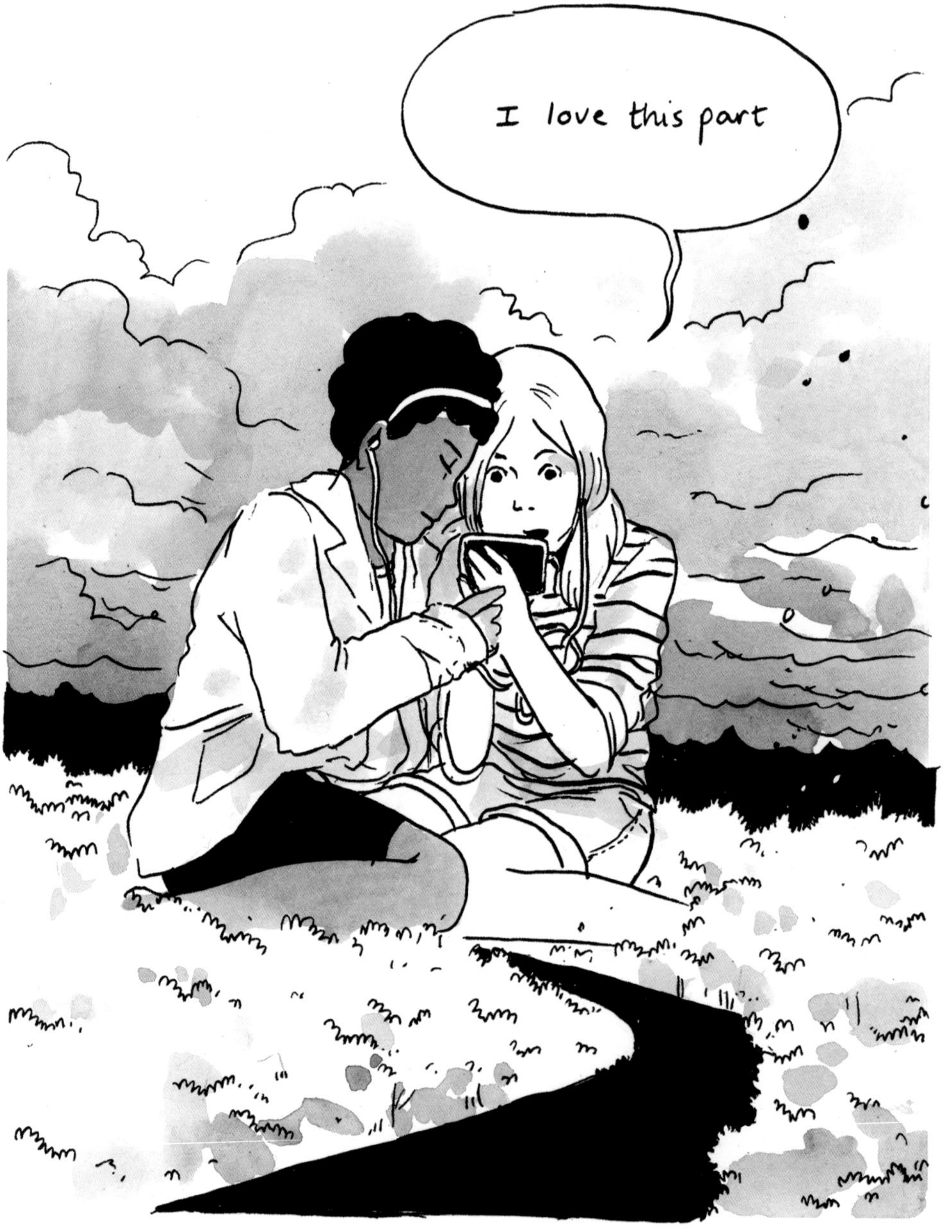
I love this part

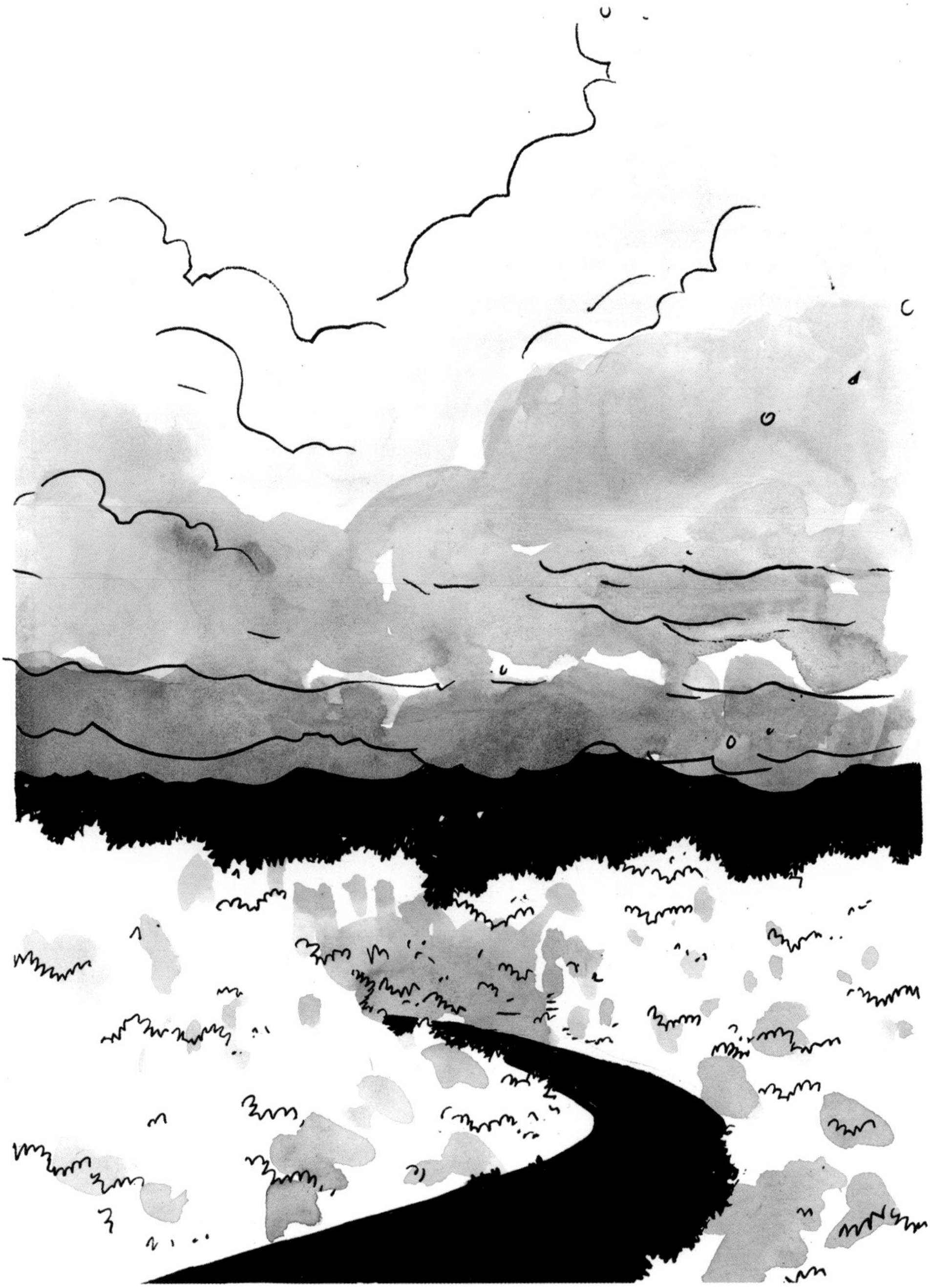

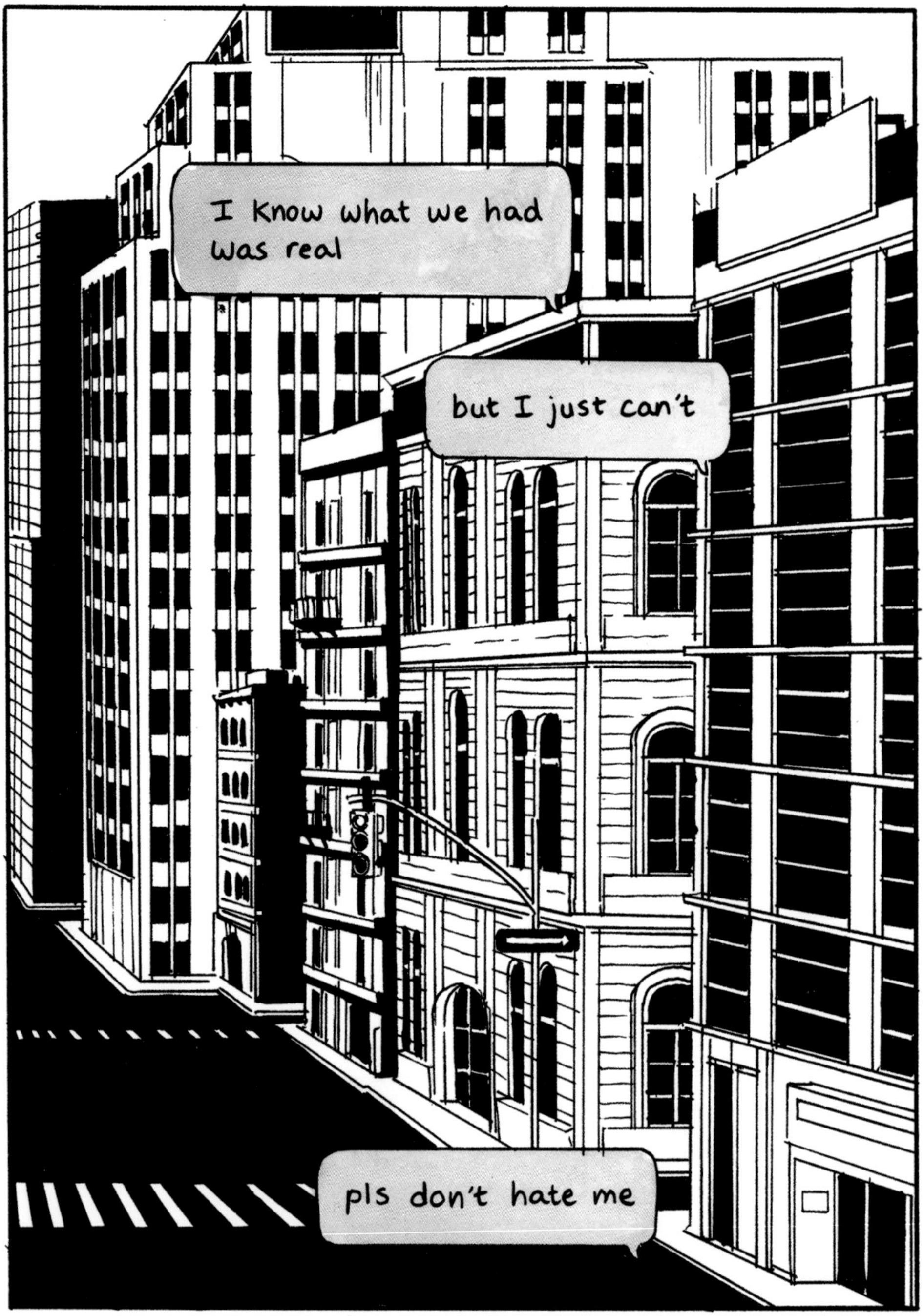
I know what we had was real
but I just can't
pls don't hate me

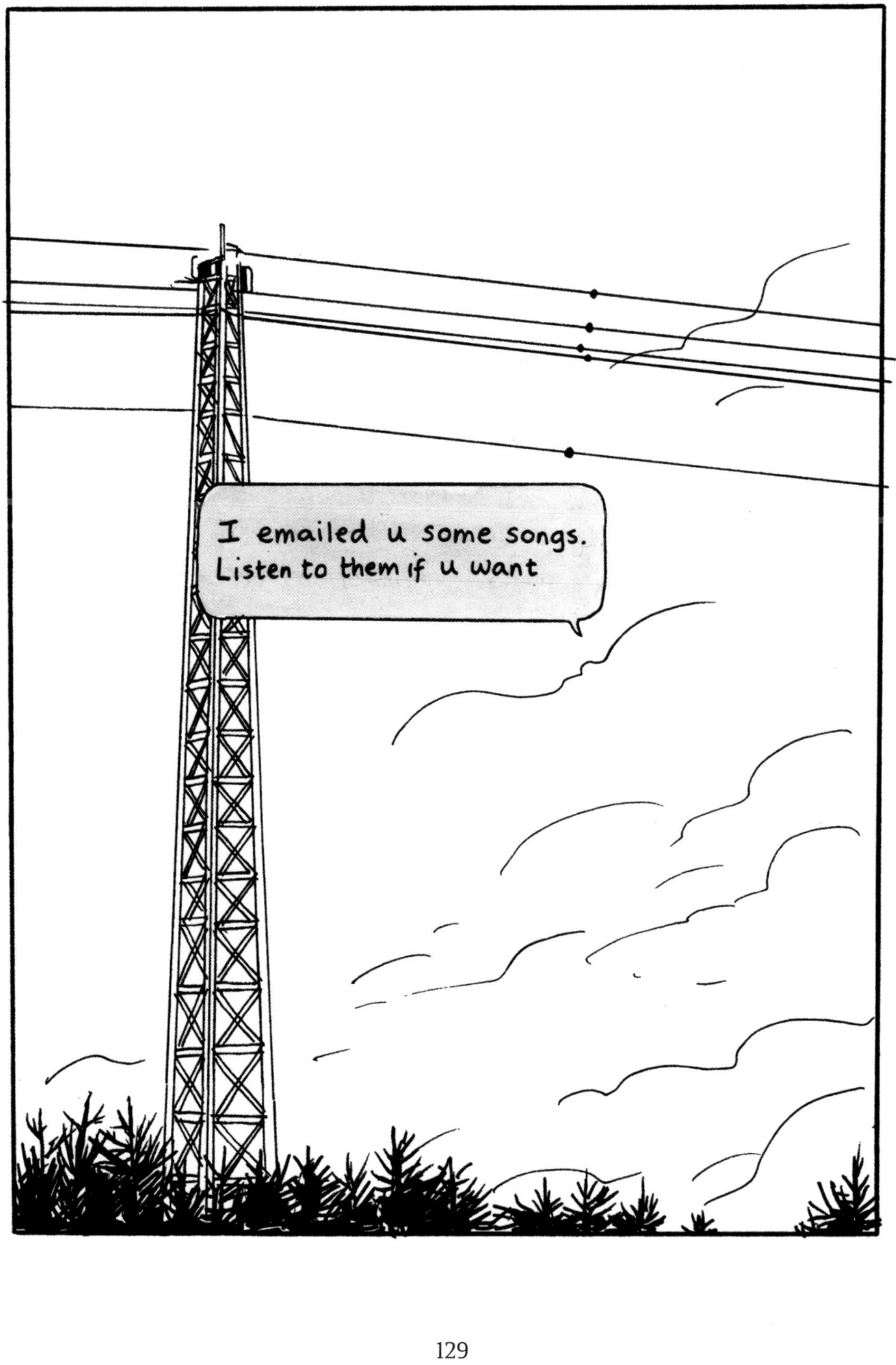
I emailed u some songs. Listen to them if u want

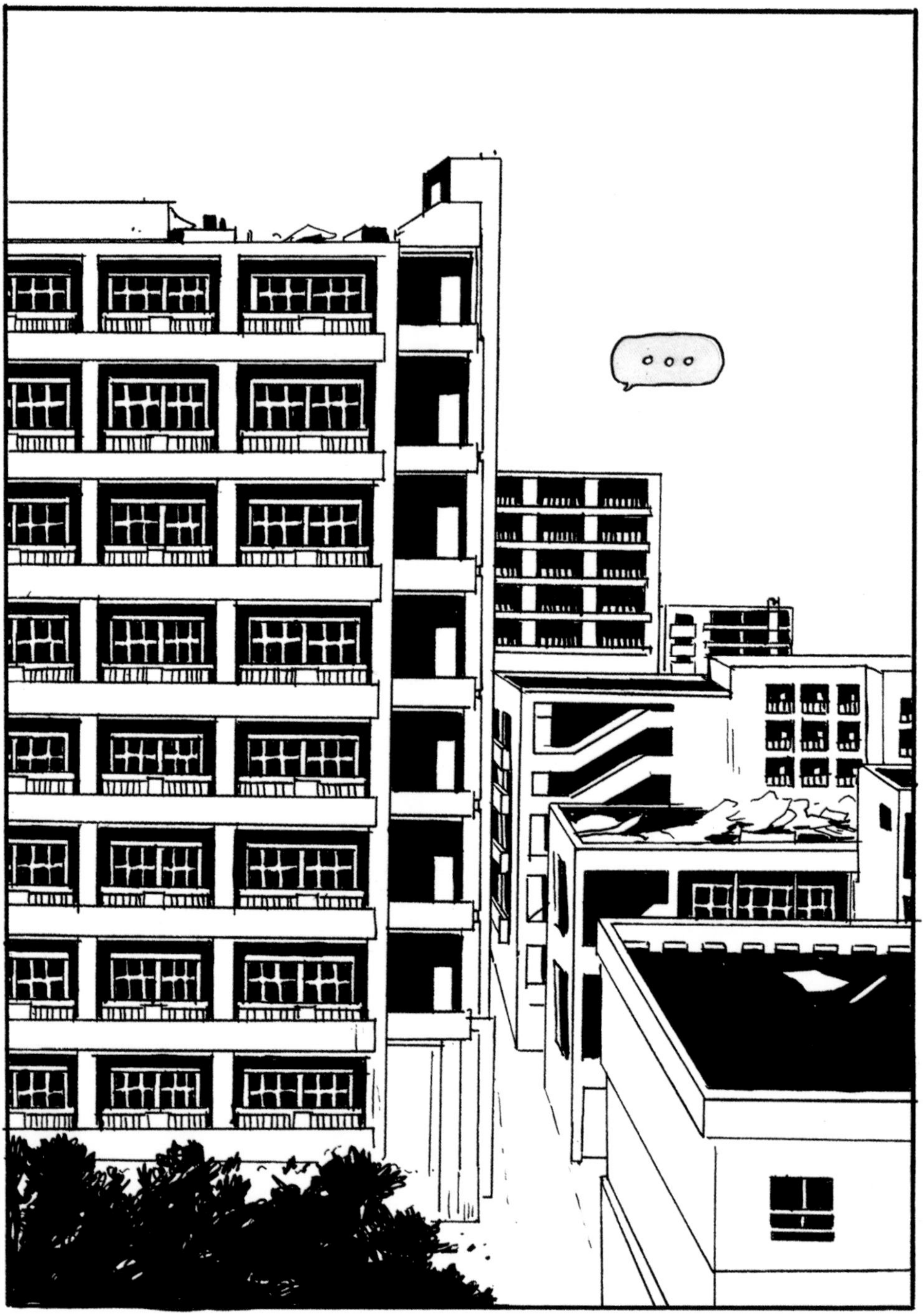
...

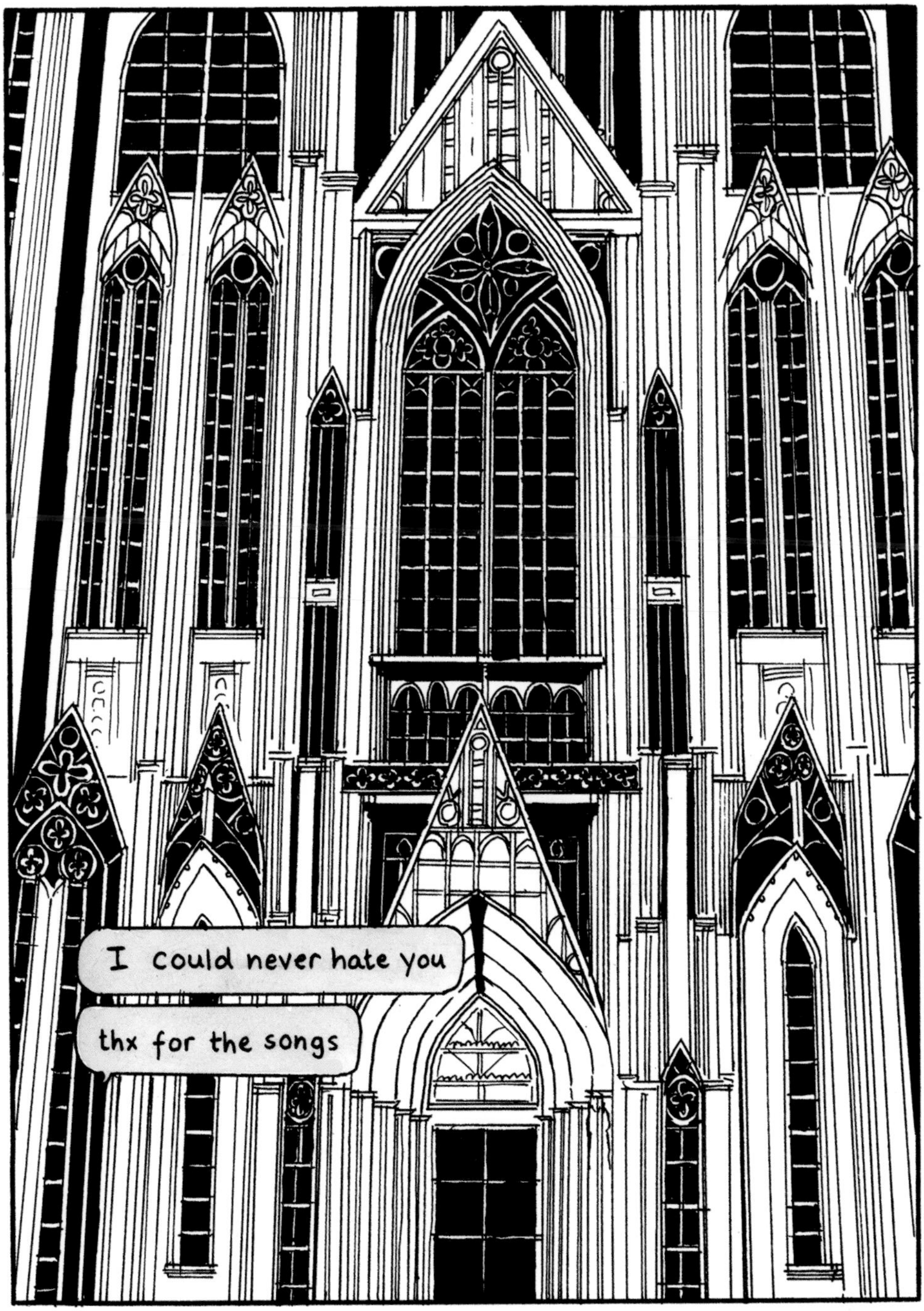
I could never hate you
thx for the songs

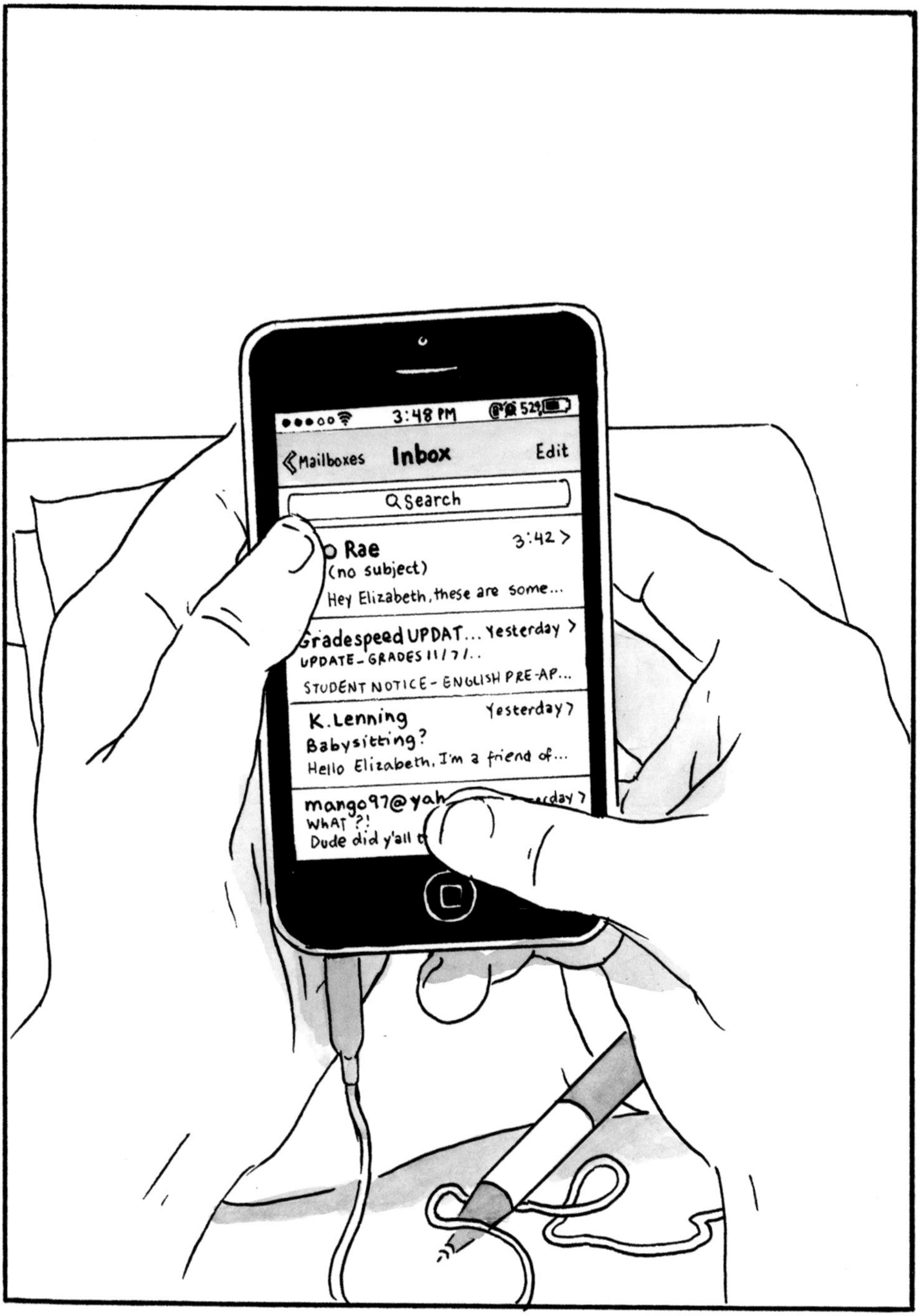
3:48 PM
Mailboxes
Inbox
Edit
Search
Rae
3:42
(no subject)
Hey Elizabeth, these are some...
Gradespeed UPDAT... Yesterday
UPDATE_GRADES 11/7/..
STUDENT NOTICE - ENGLISH PRE-AP...
K. Lenning
Yesterday
Babysitting?
Hello Elizabeth, I'm a friend of...
mango97@yah
WHAT?!
Dude did y'all t

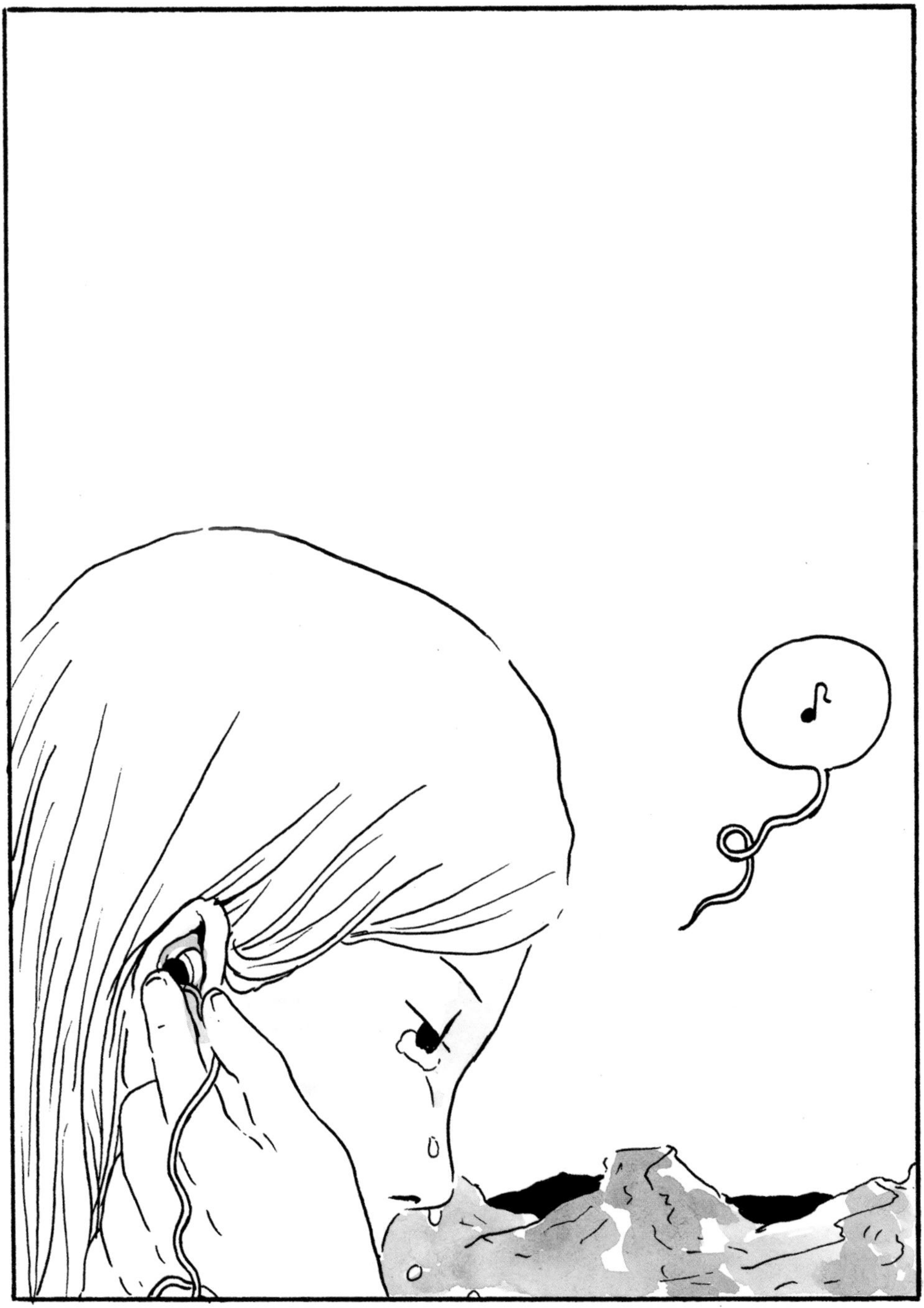

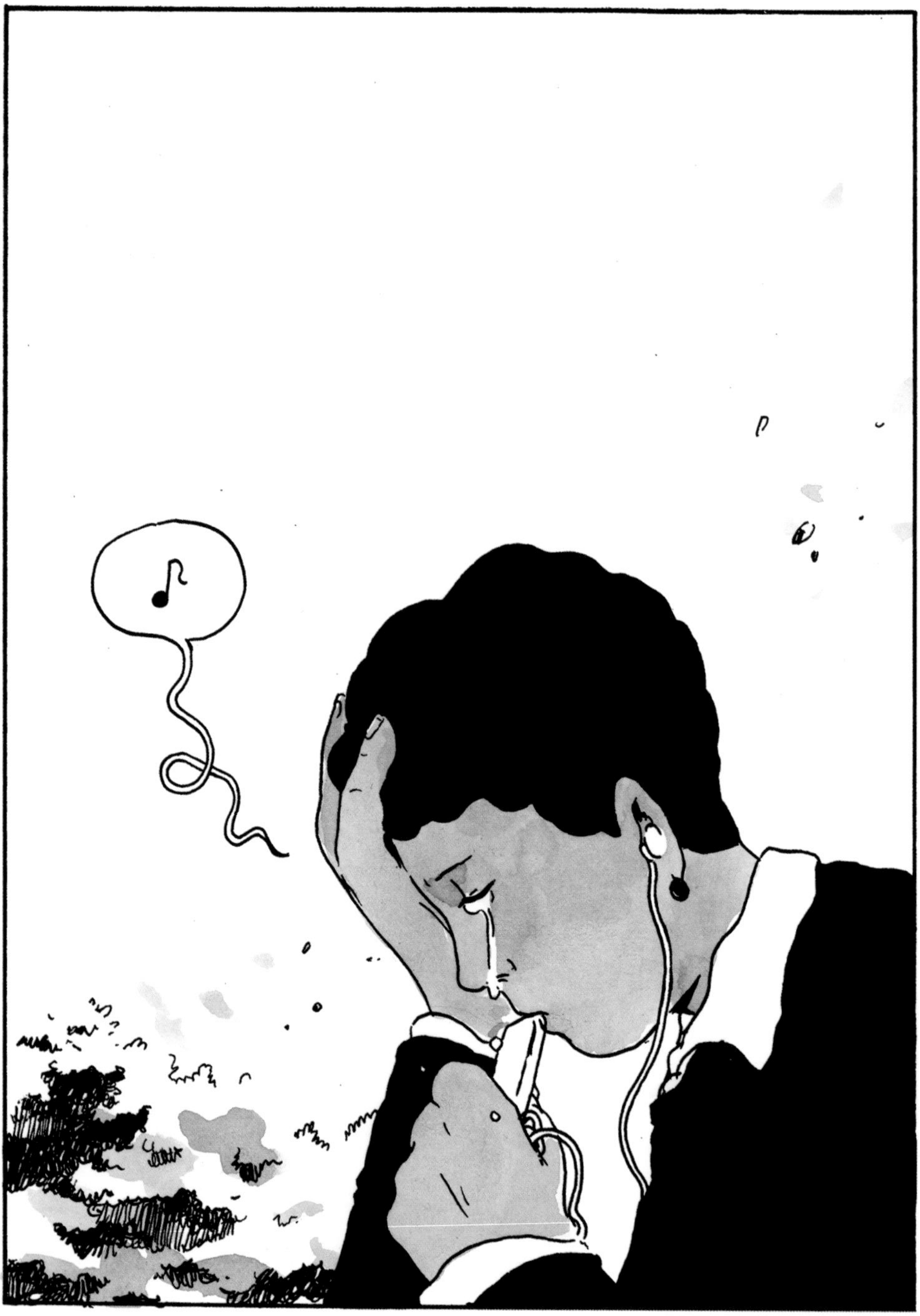

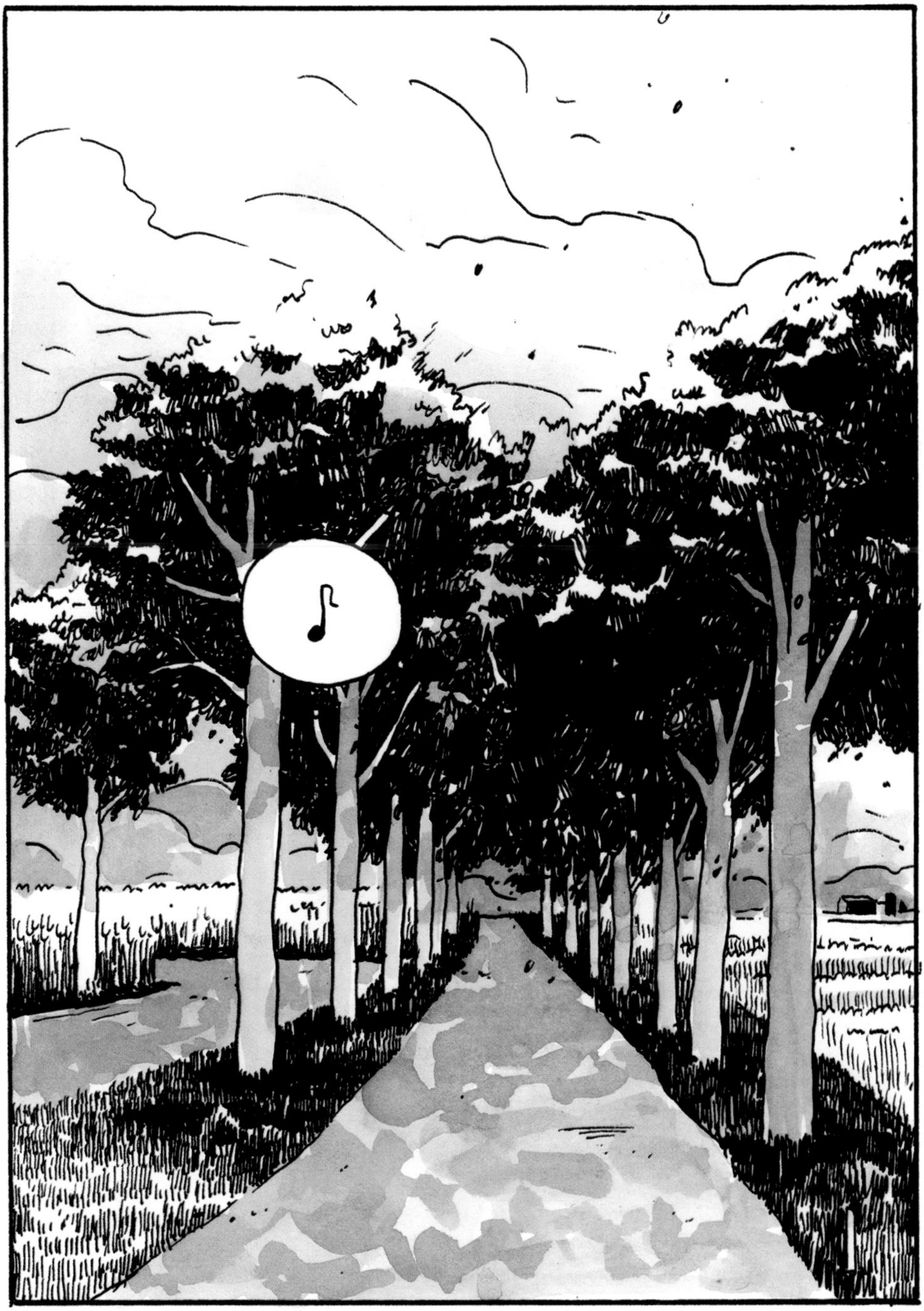

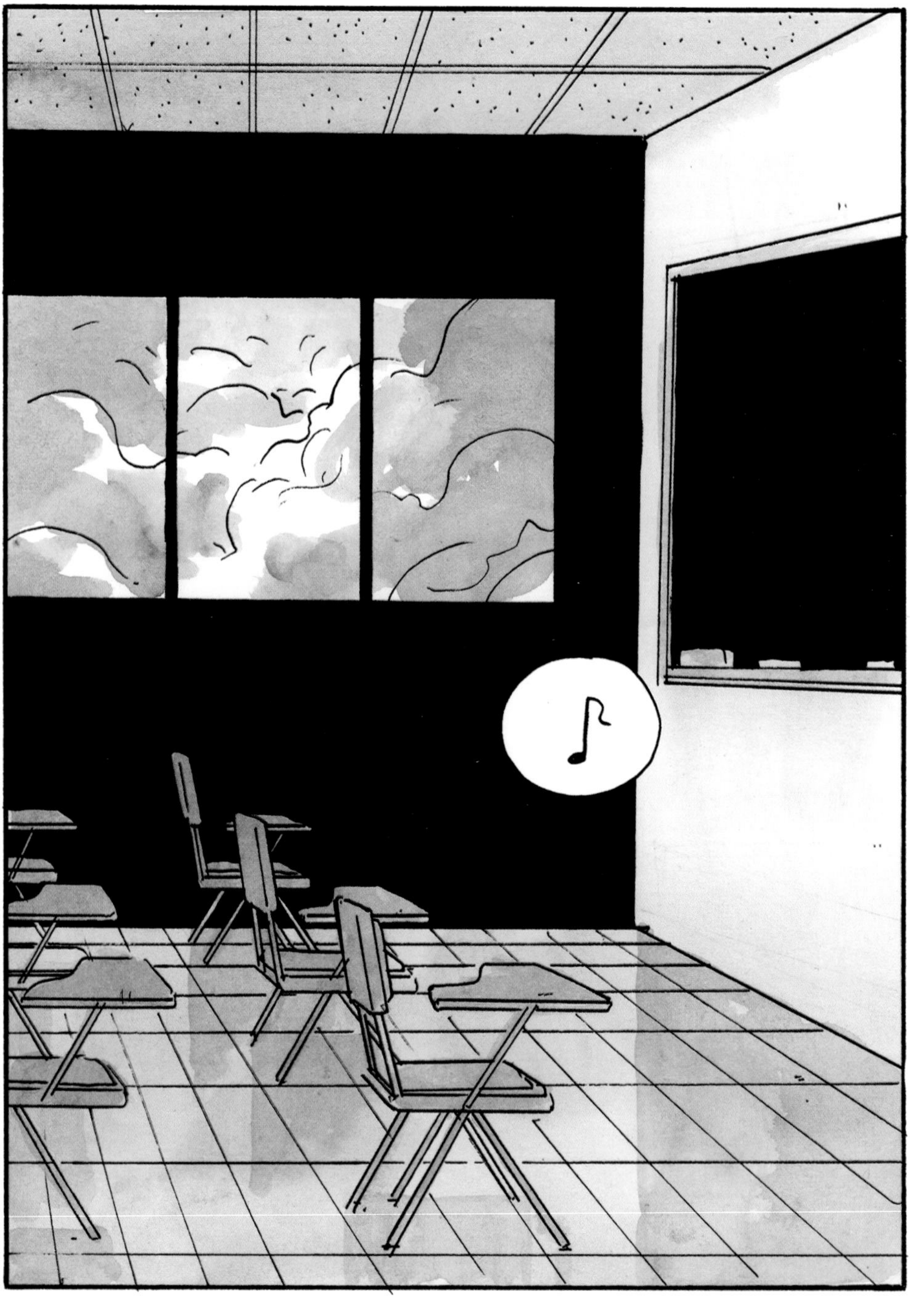

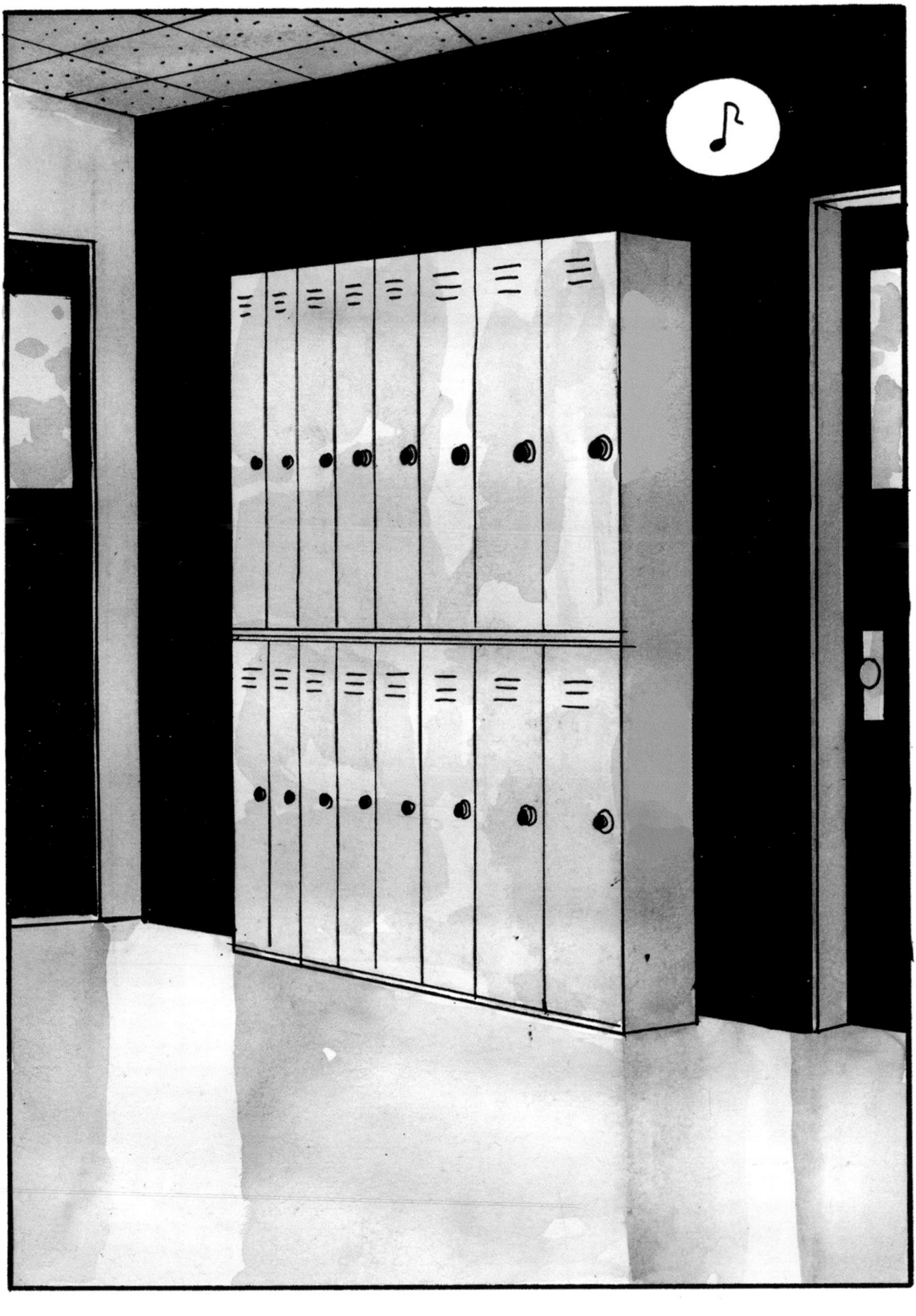

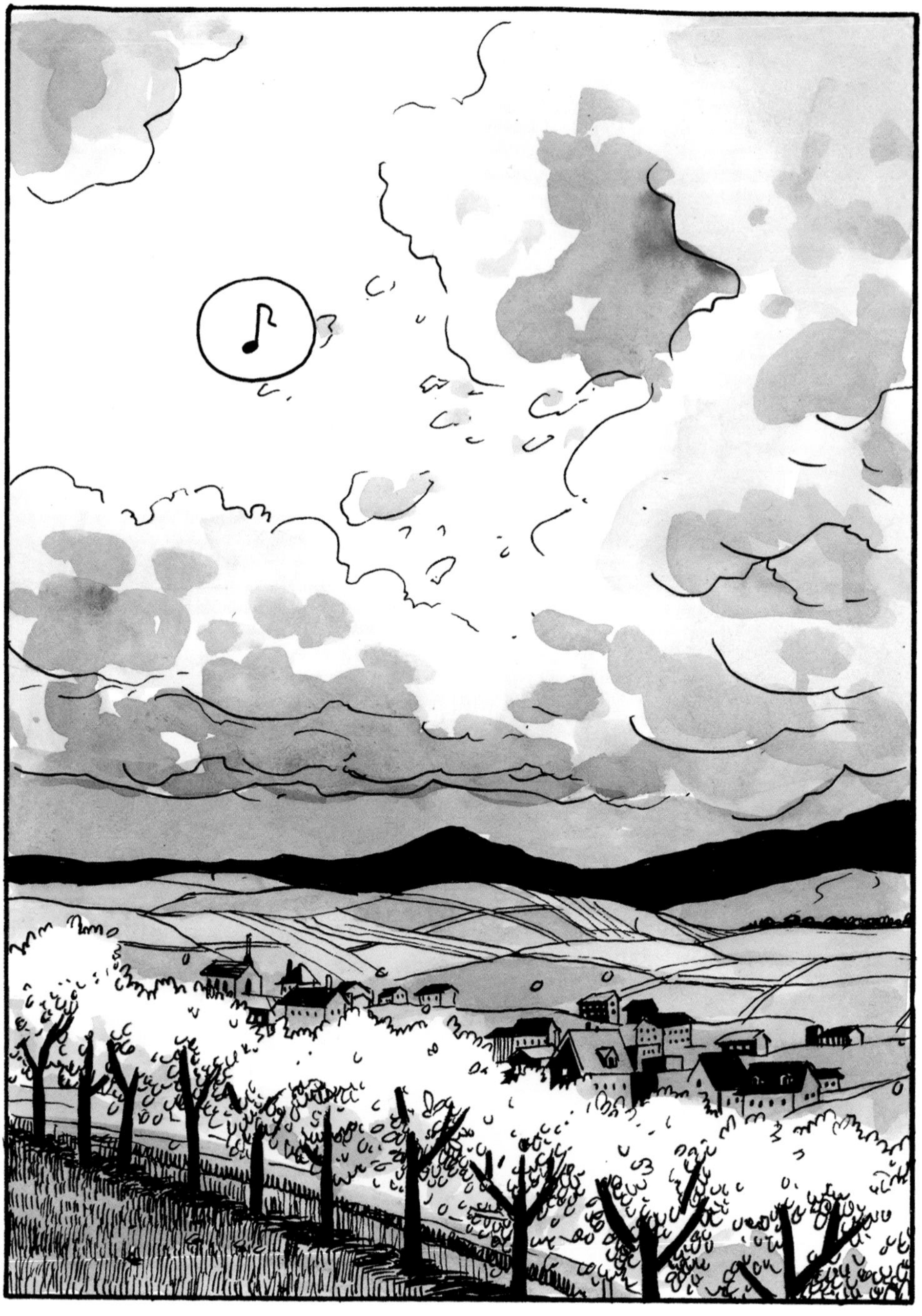

end

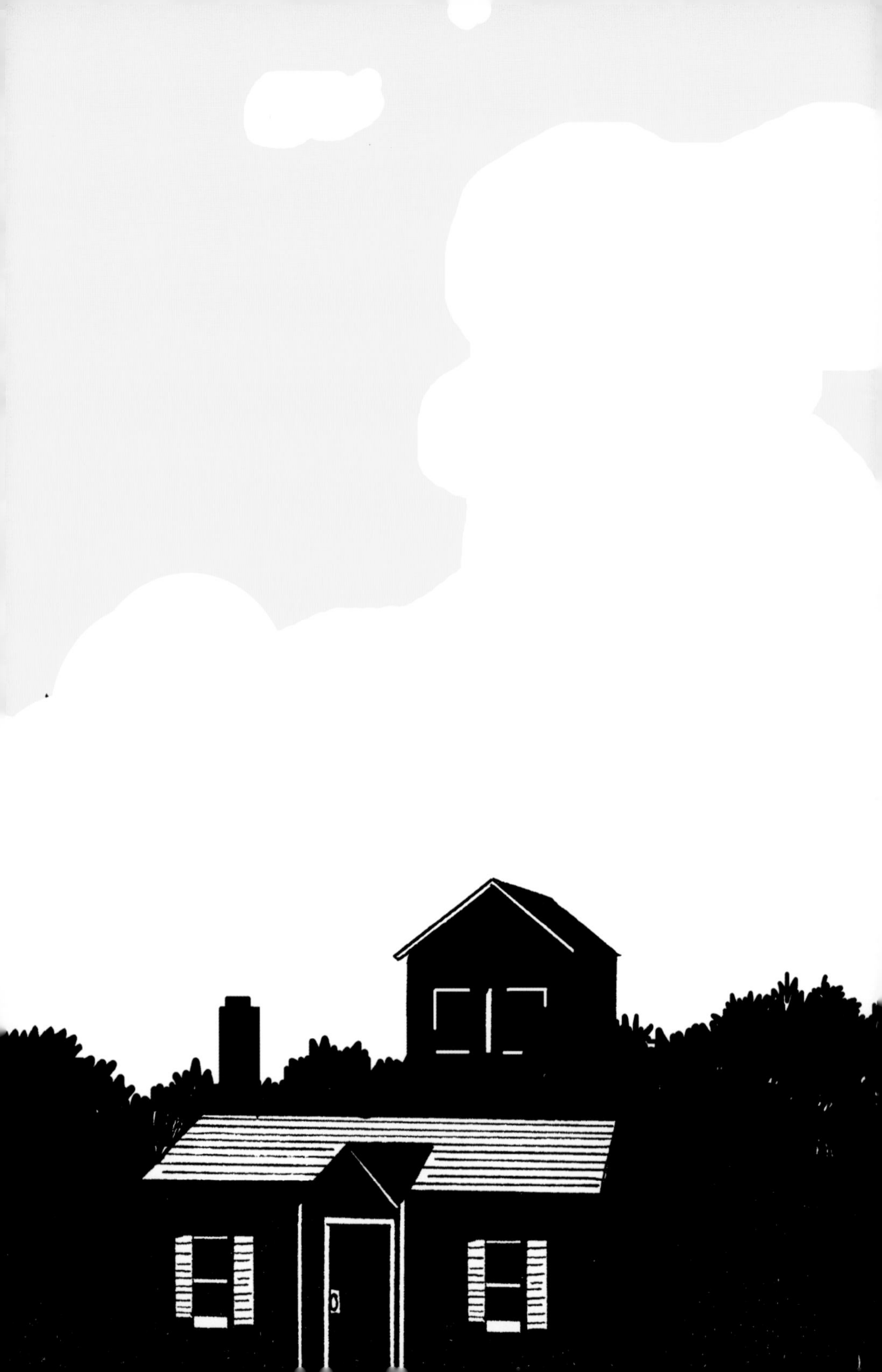

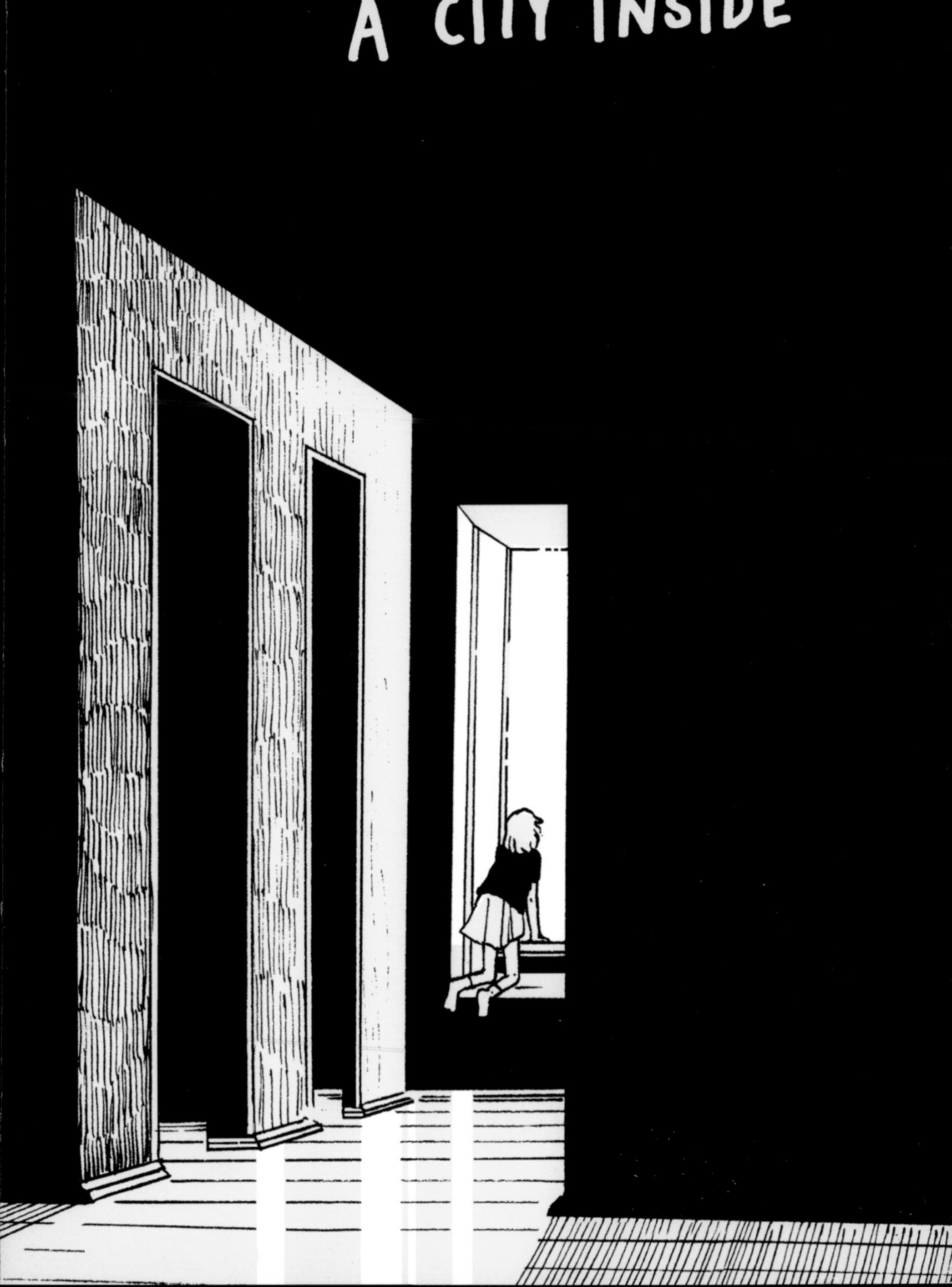
A CITY INSIDE

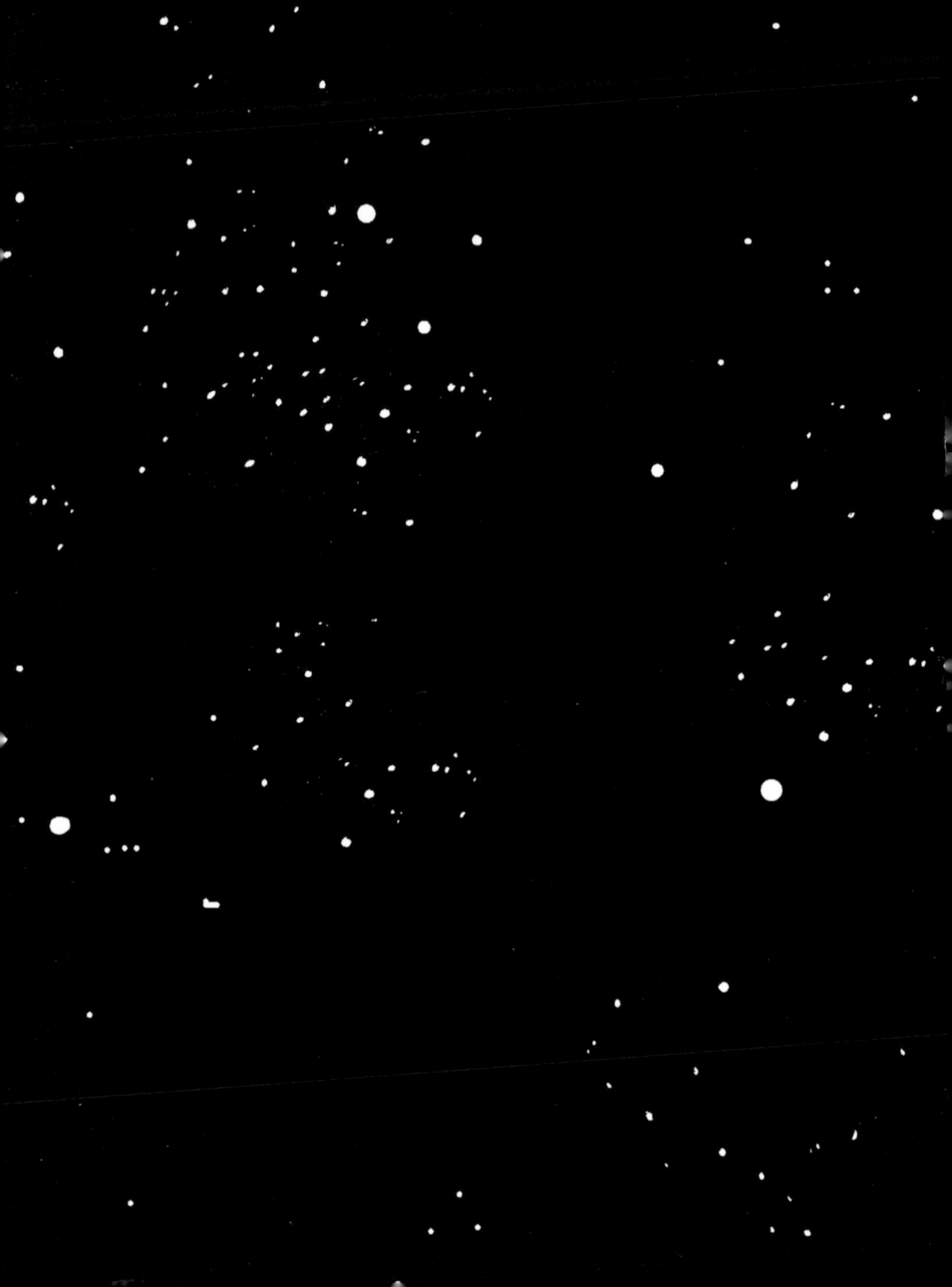

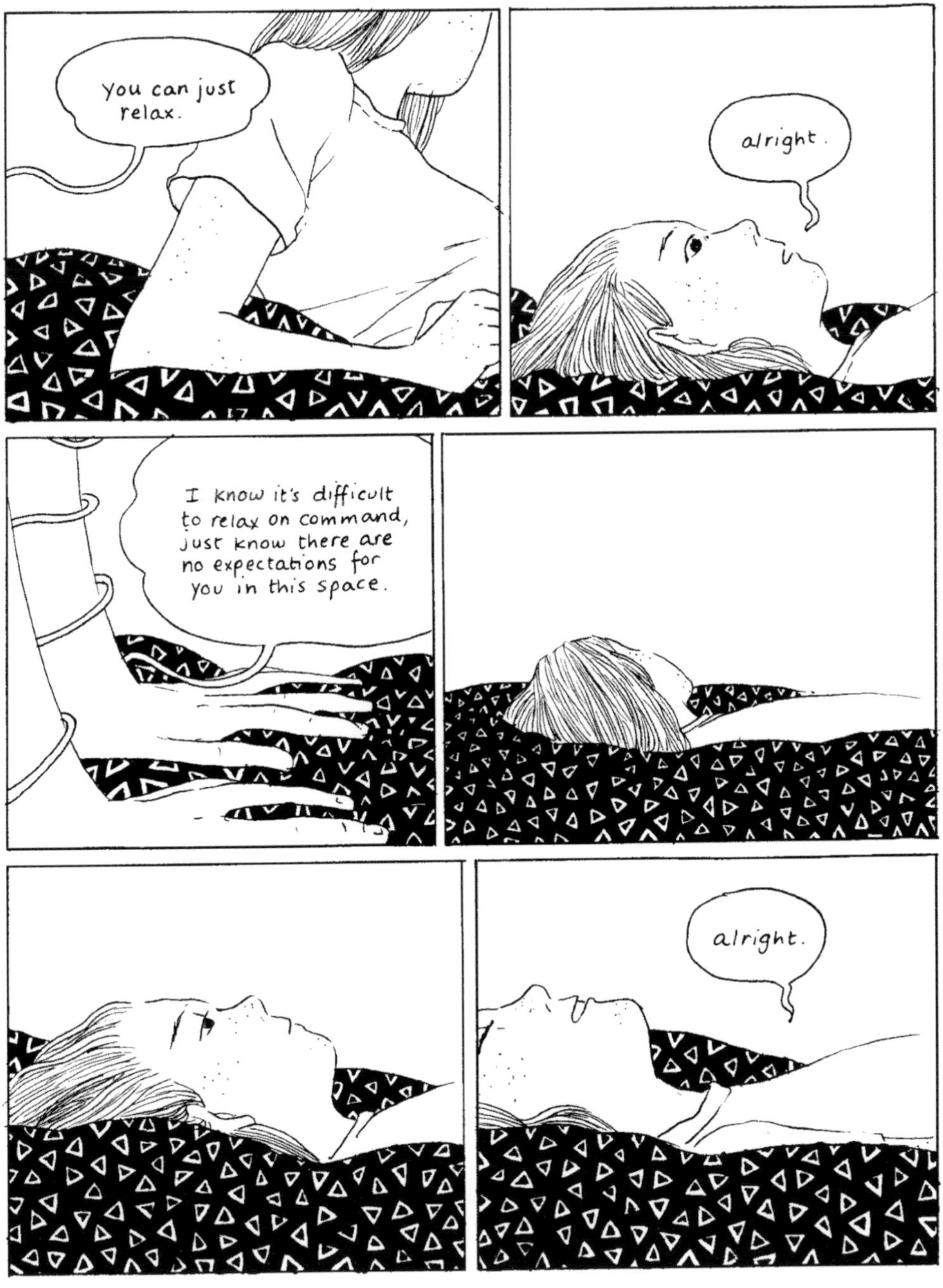
you can just relax.
alright.
I know it's difficult to relax on command, just know there are no expectations for you in this space.
alright.

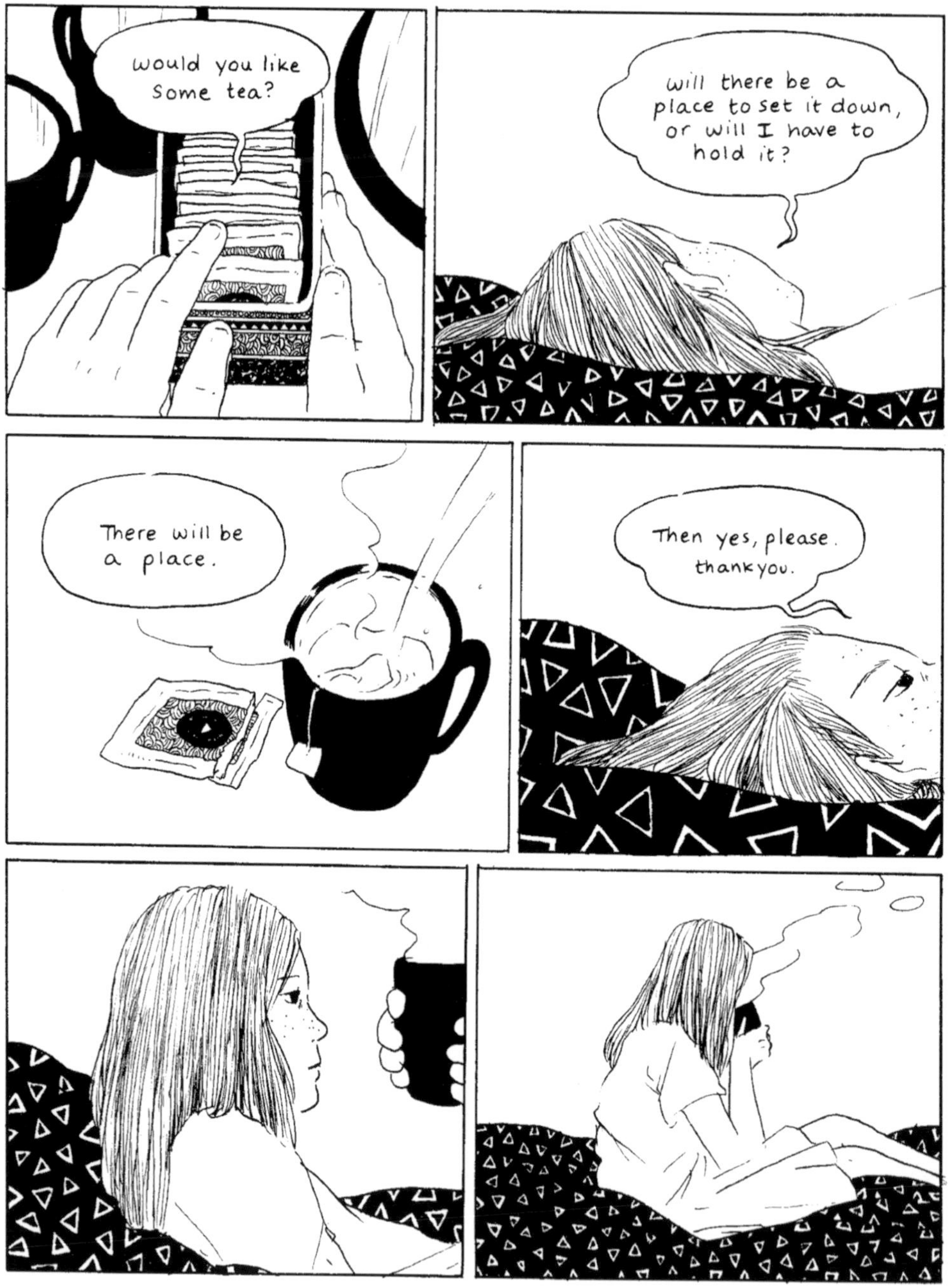
would you like some tea?
will there be a place to set it down, or will I have to hold it?
There will be a place.
Then yes, please. thankyou.

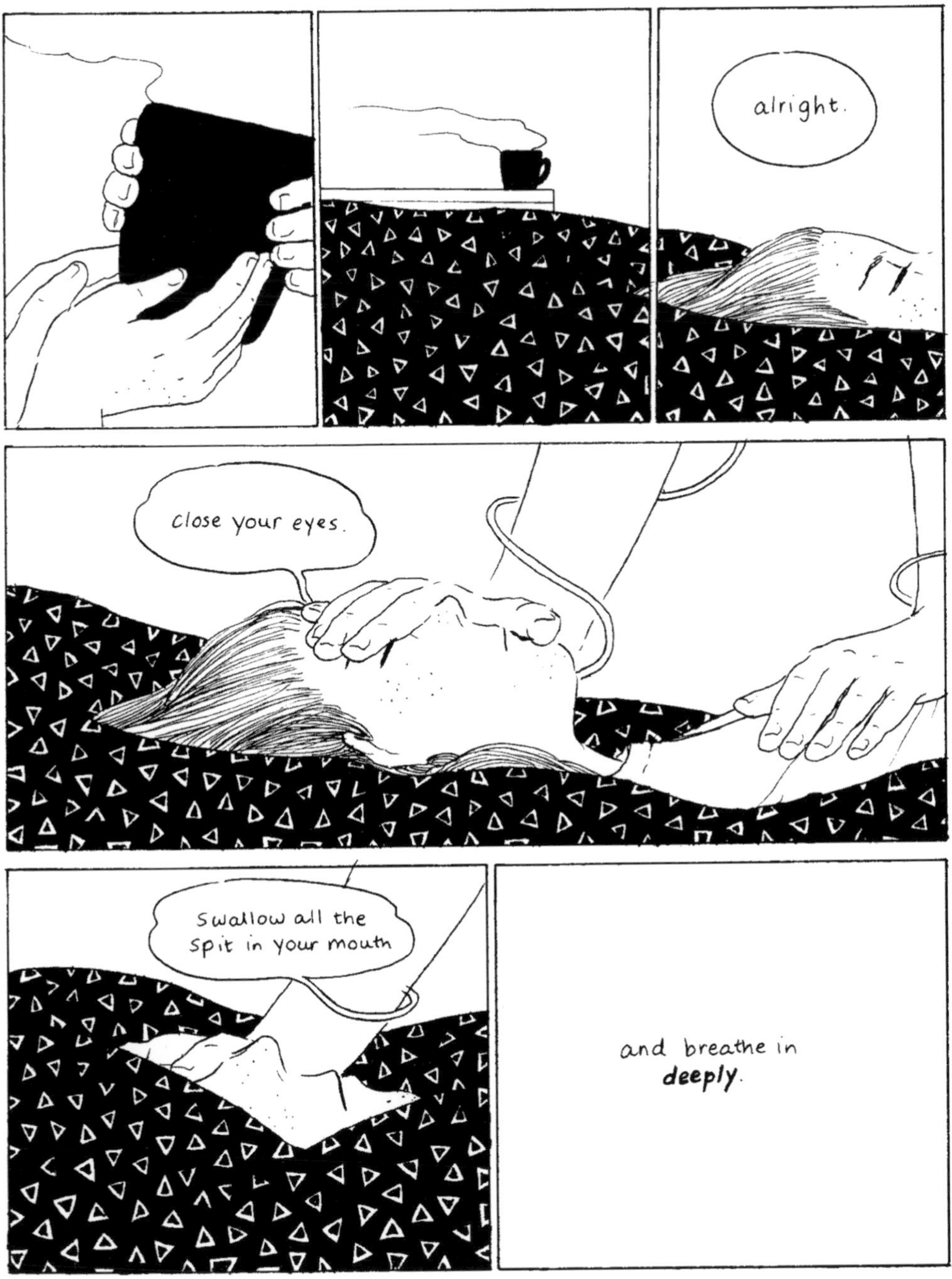
alright.
close your eyes.
swallow all the spit in your mouth
and breathe in deeply.

A CITY

INSIDE

you grew up in the south

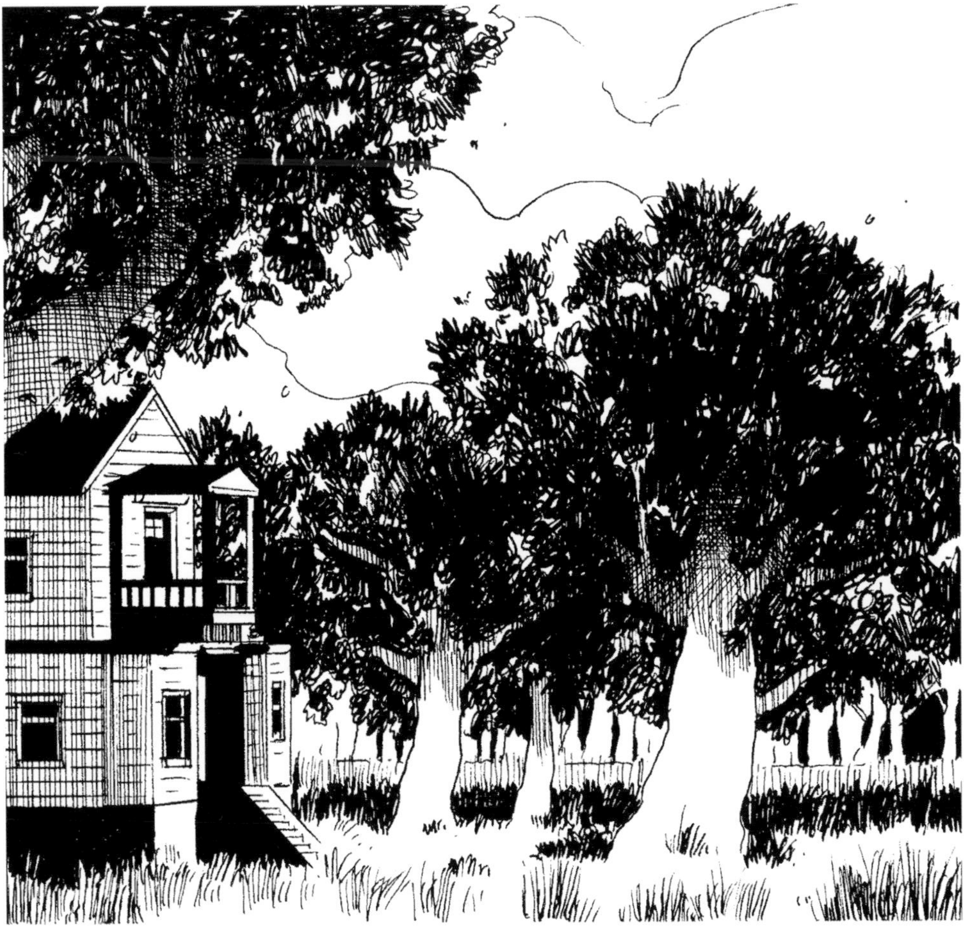

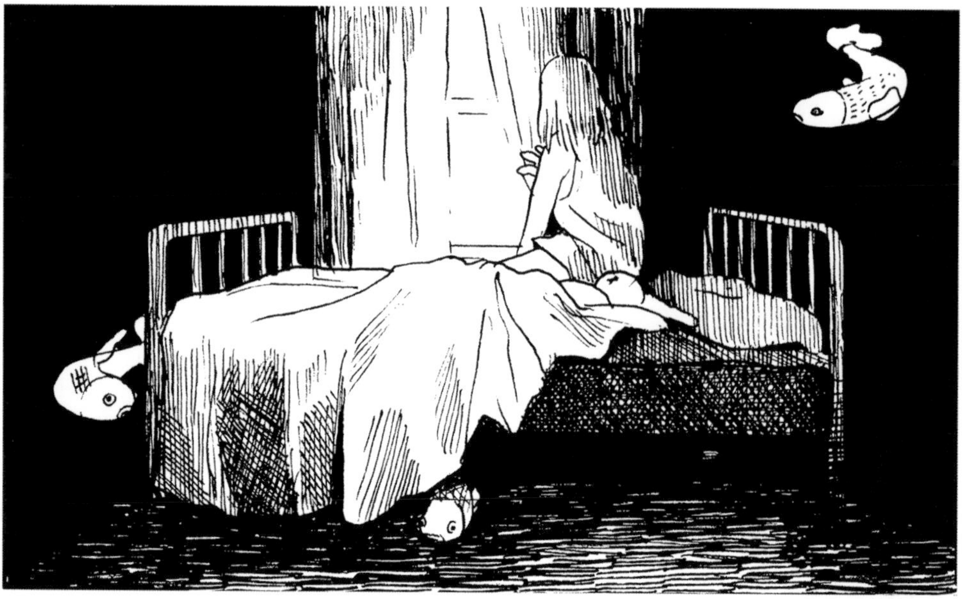

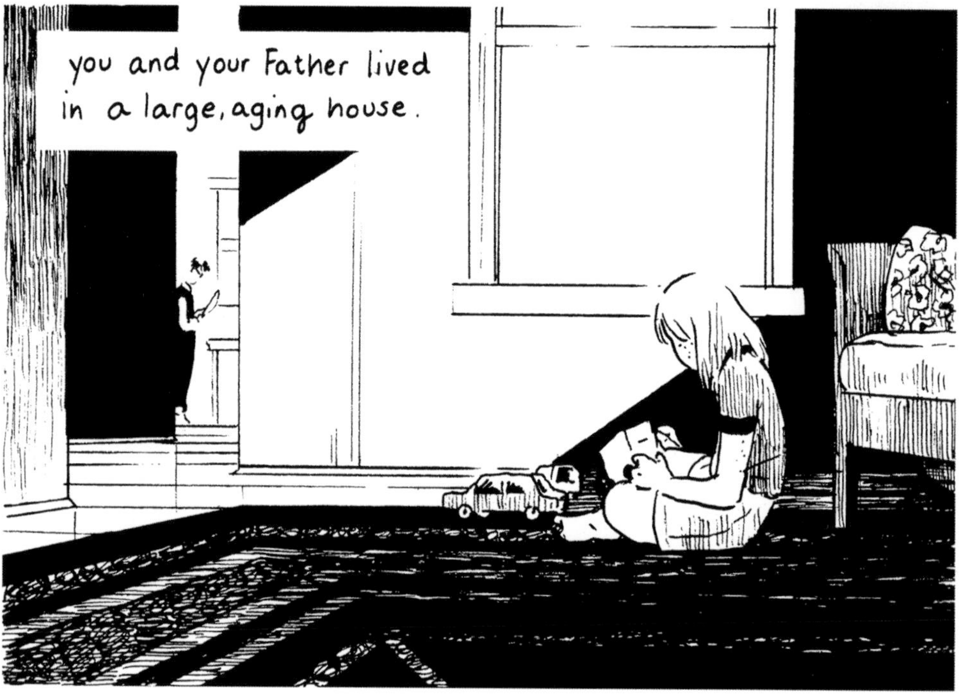
you and your Father lived in a large, aging house.

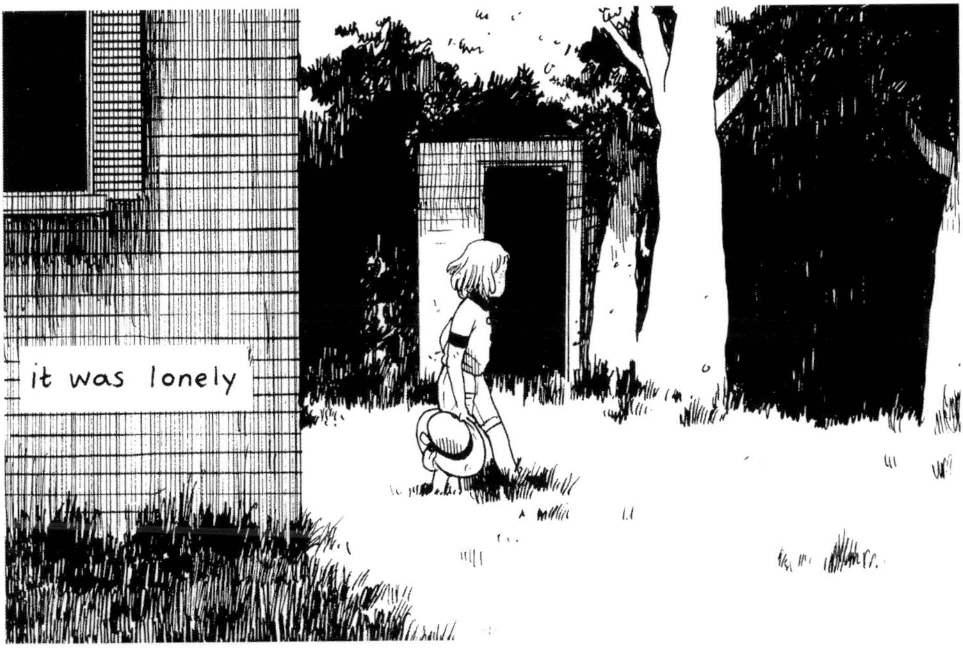
it was lonely

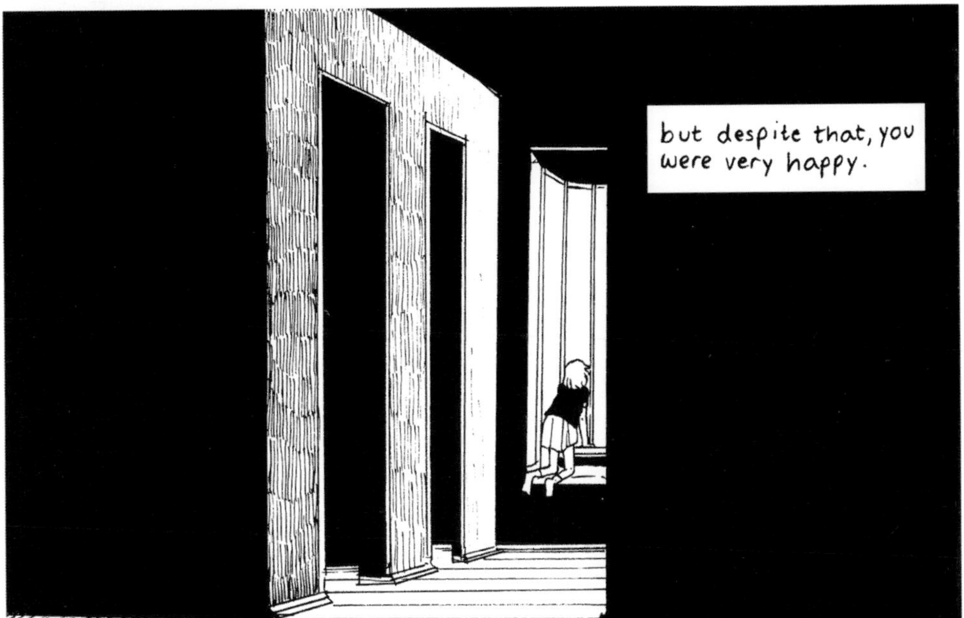
but despite that, you were very happy.

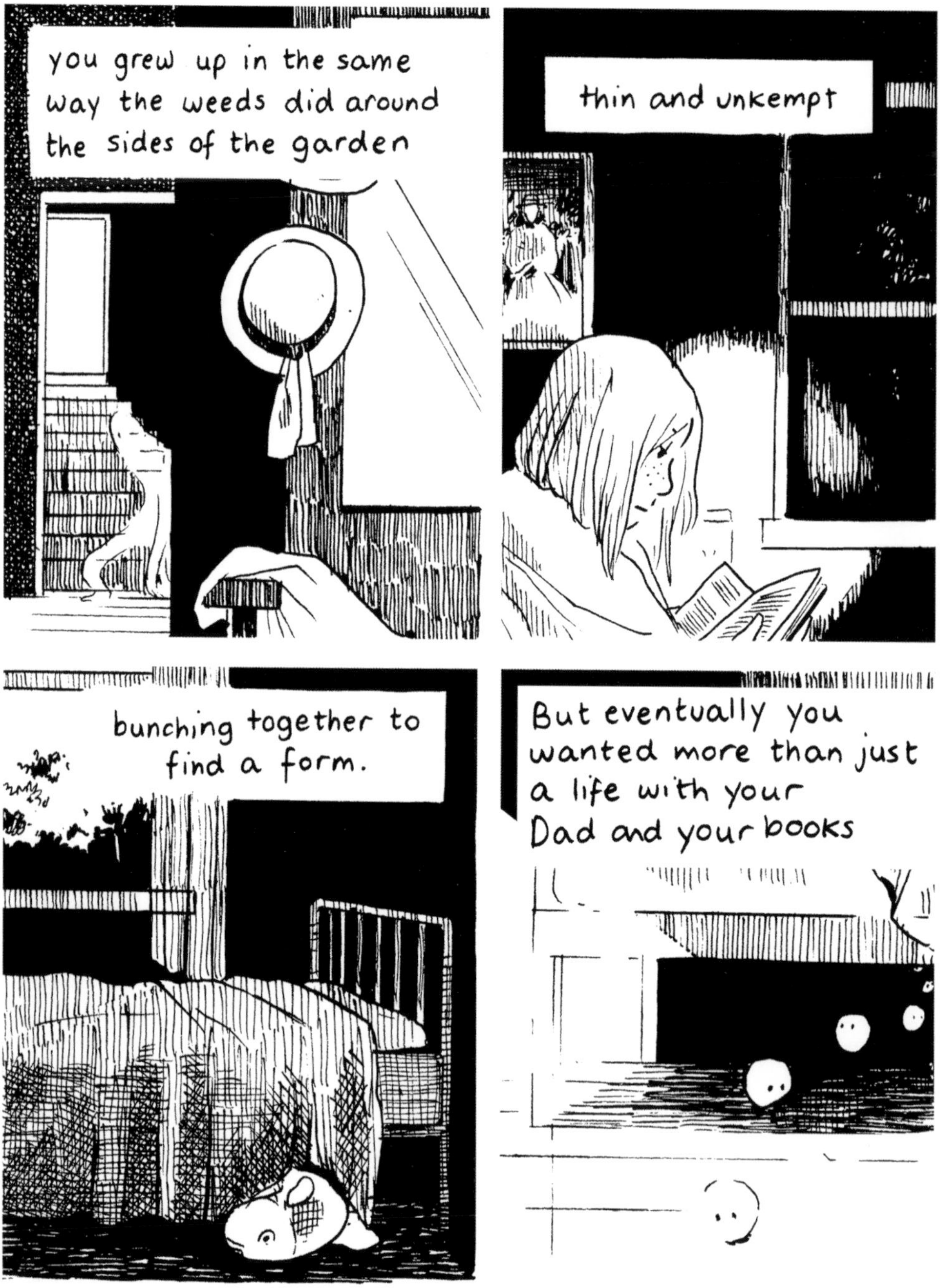
you grew up in the same way the weeds did around the sides of the garden
thin and unkempt
bunching together to find a form.
But eventually you wanted more than just a life with your Dad and your books

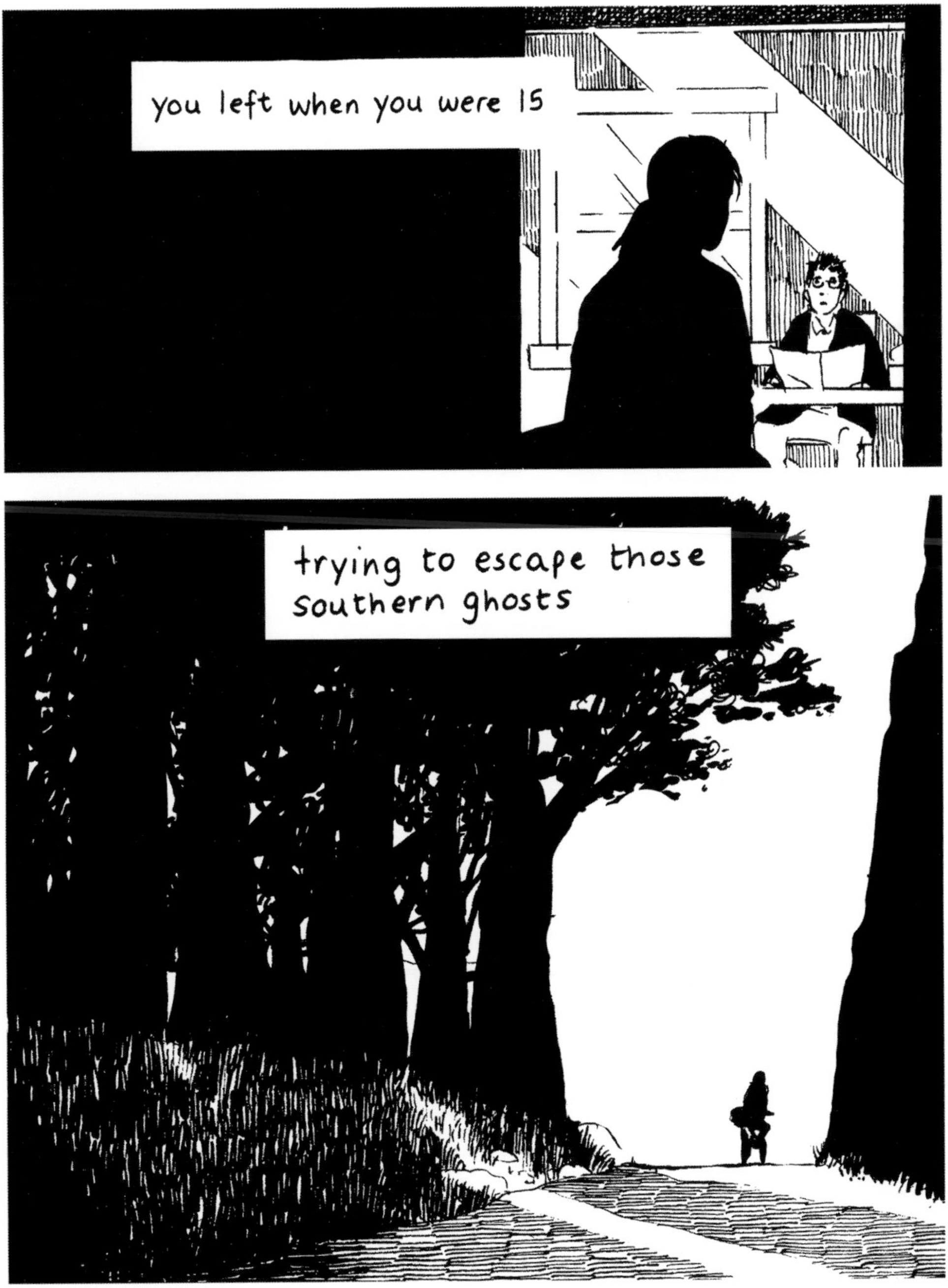
you left when you were 15
trying to escape those southern ghosts

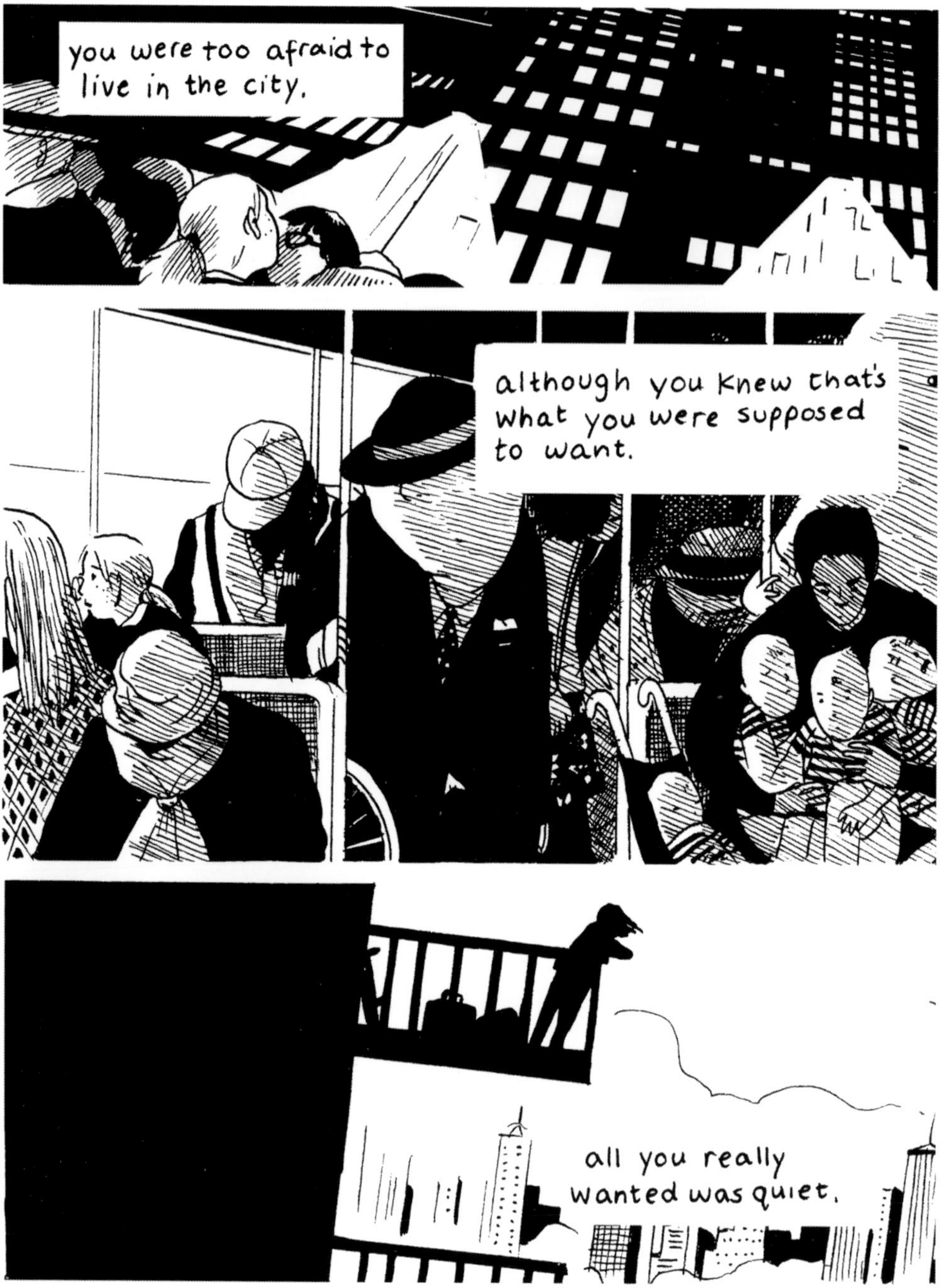
you were too afraid to live in the city.
although you knew that's what you were supposed to want.
all you really wanted was quiet.

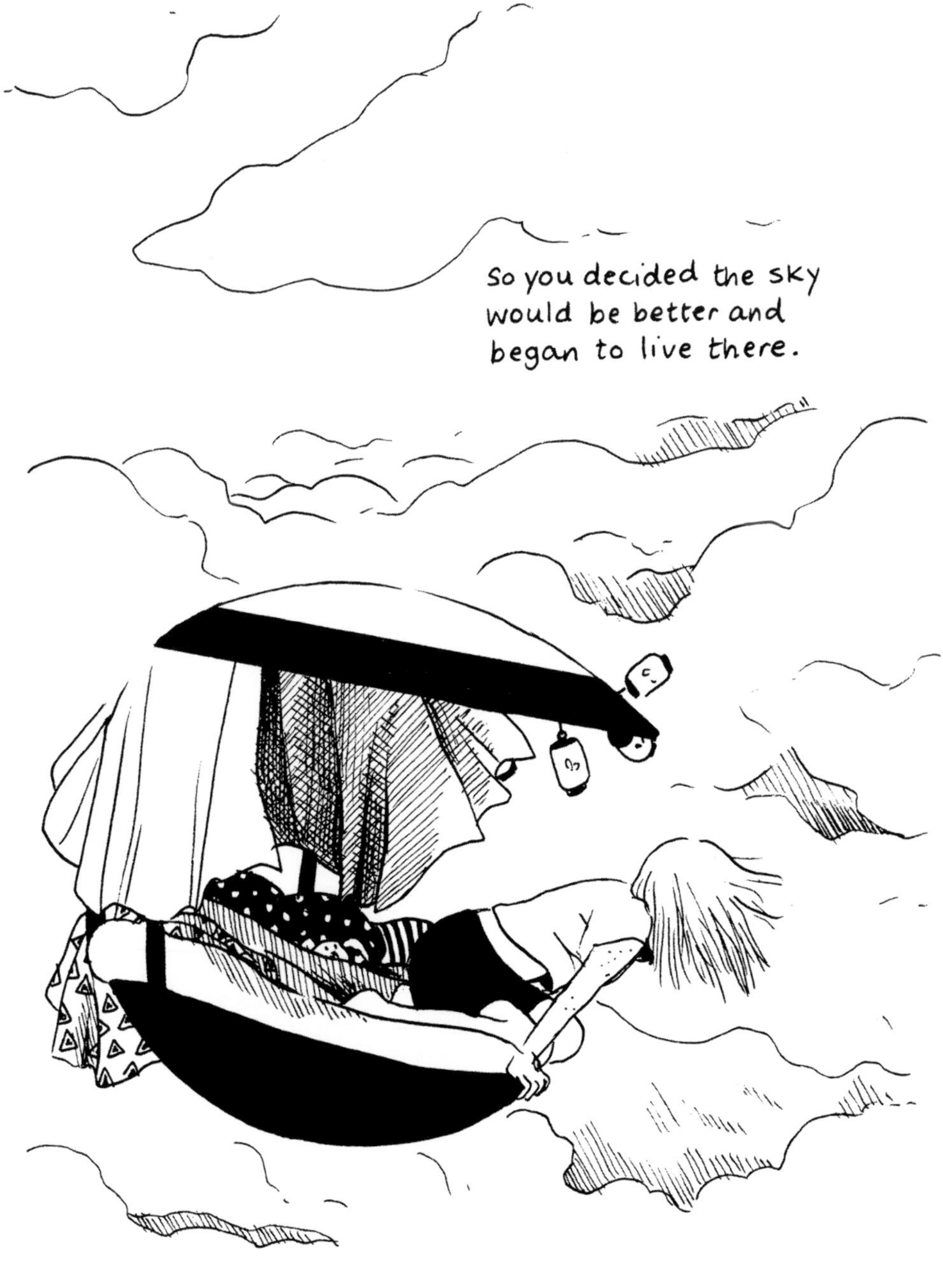
So you decided the sky would be better and began to live there.

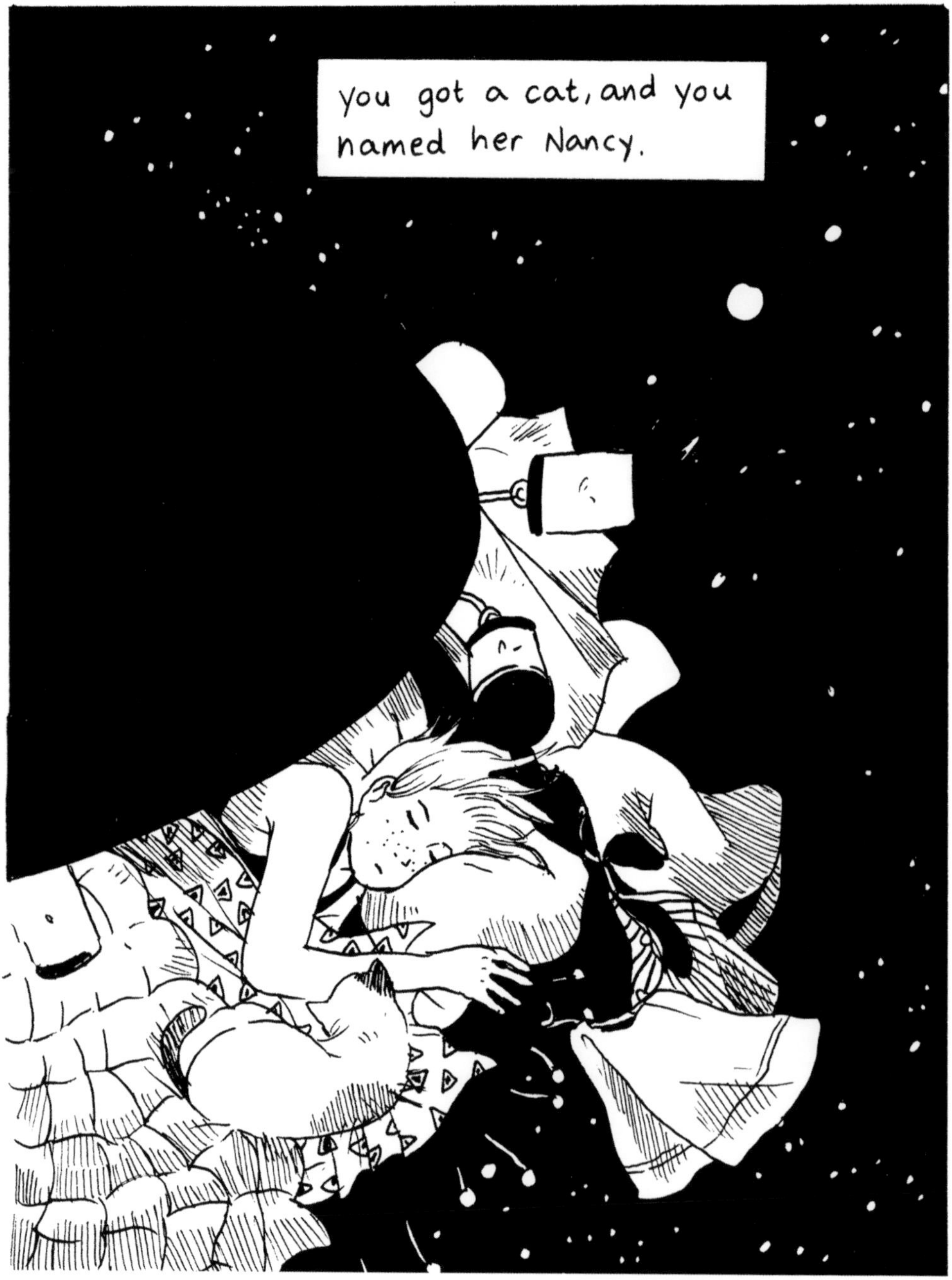
you got a cat, and you named her Nancy.

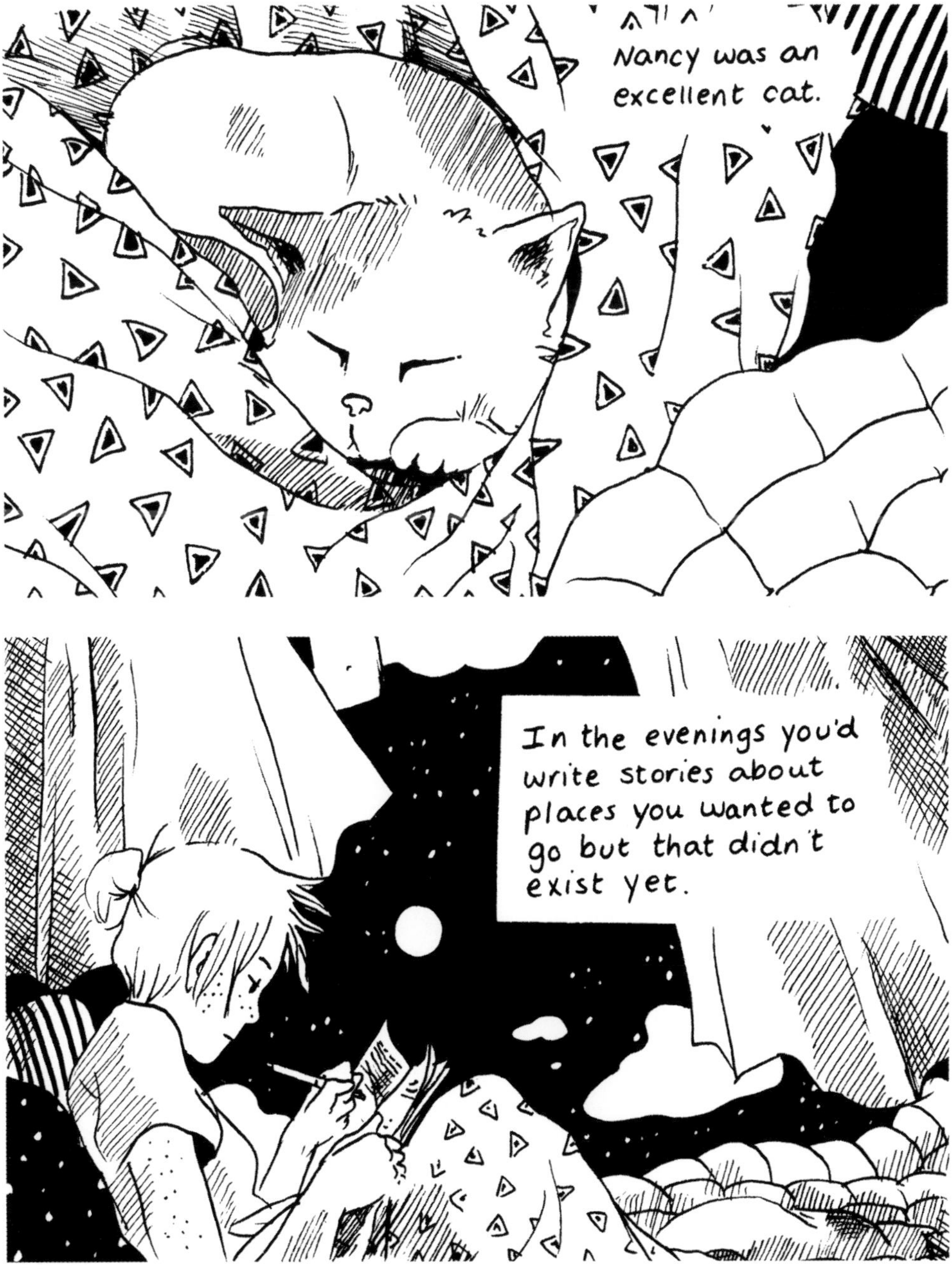
Nancy was an excellent cat.
In the evenings you'd write stories about places you wanted to go but that didn't exist yet.

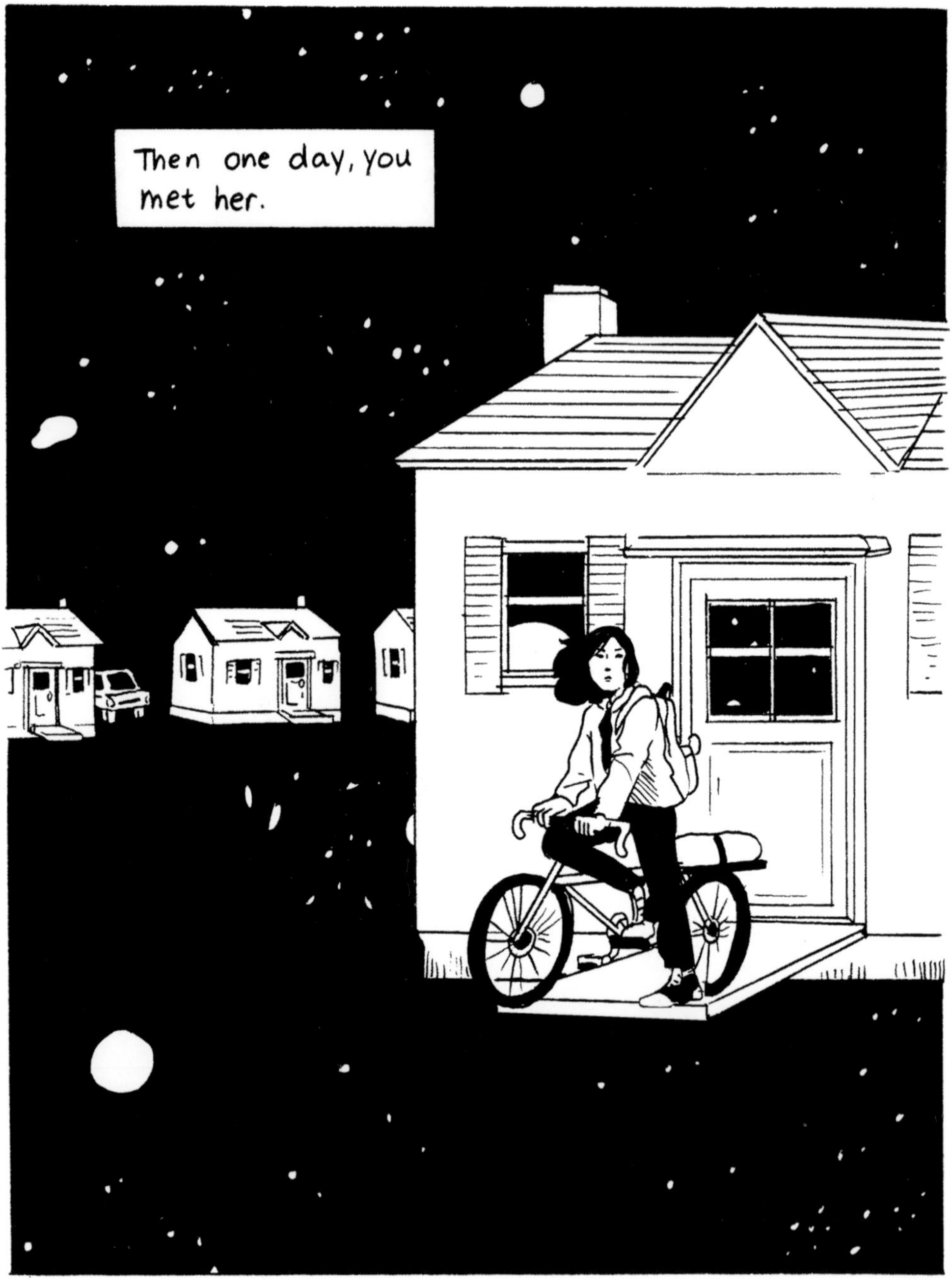
Then one day, you met her.

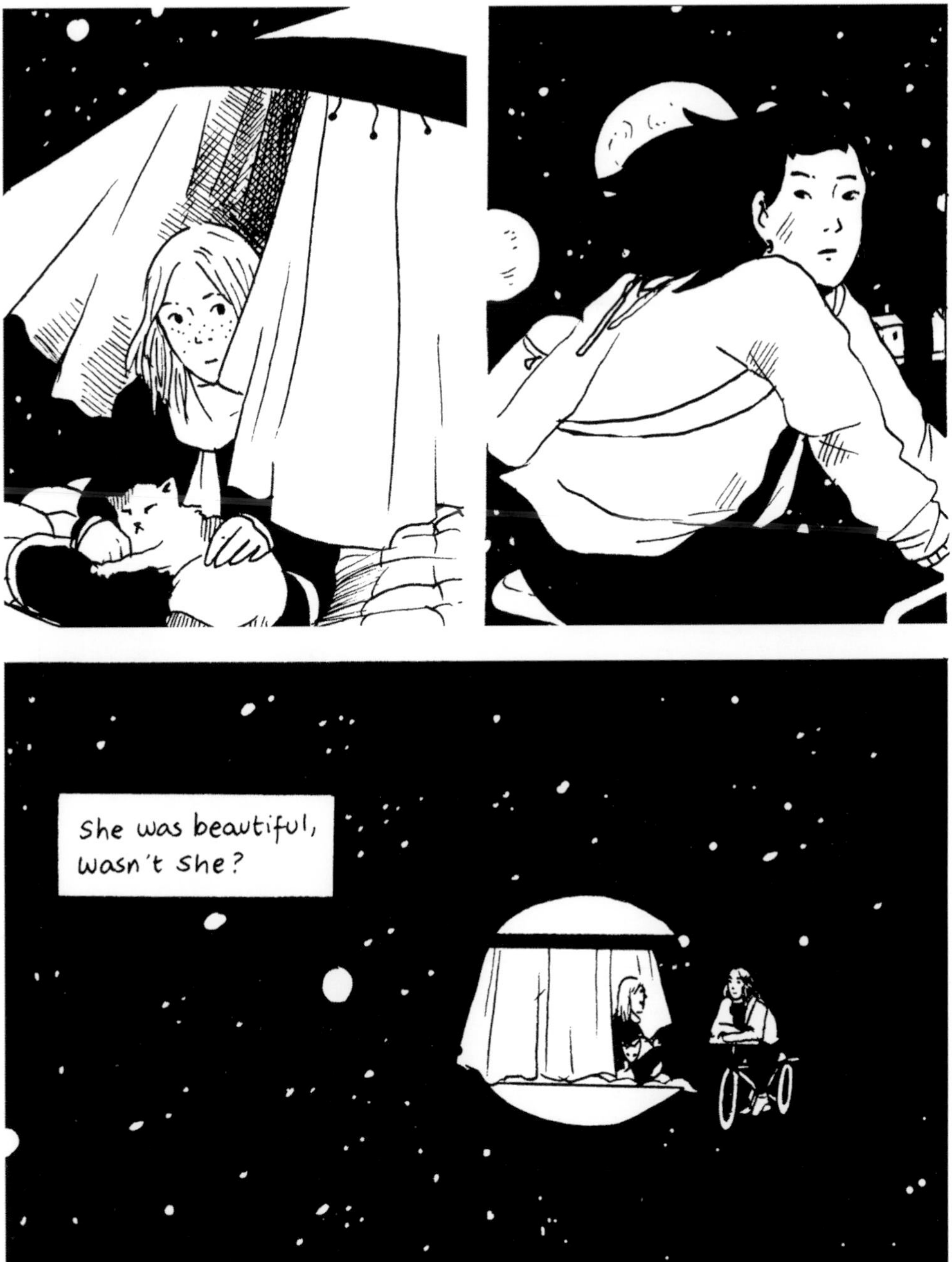
She was beautiful,
wasn't she?

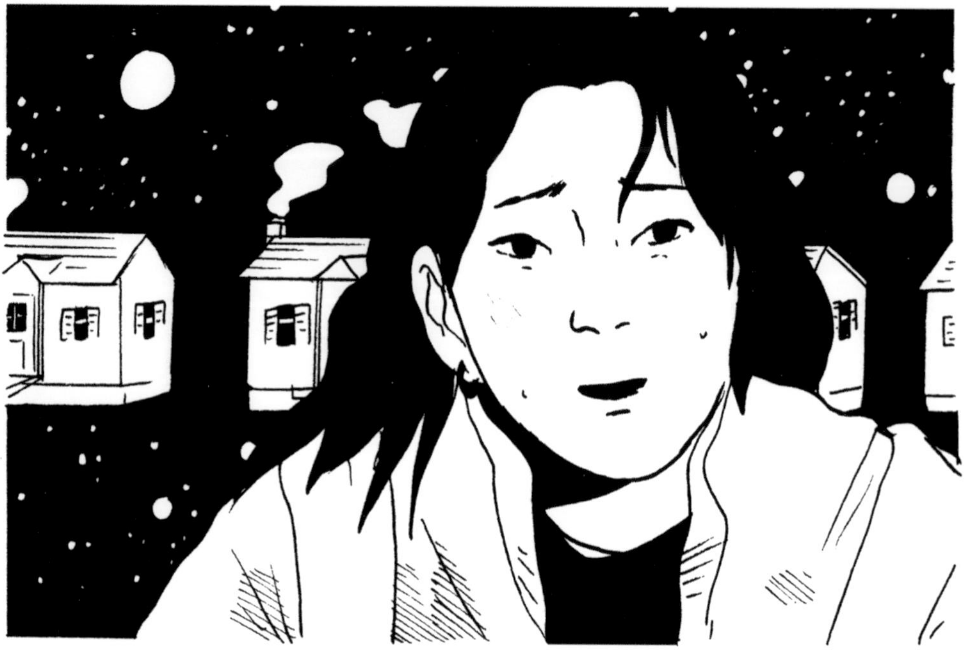

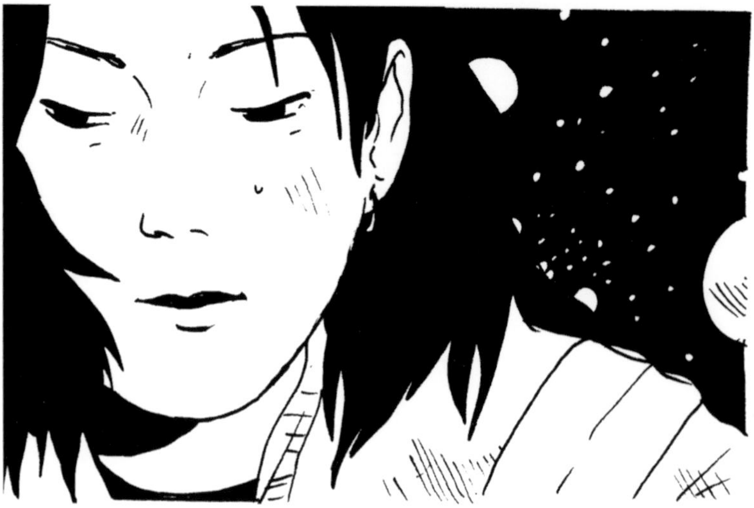

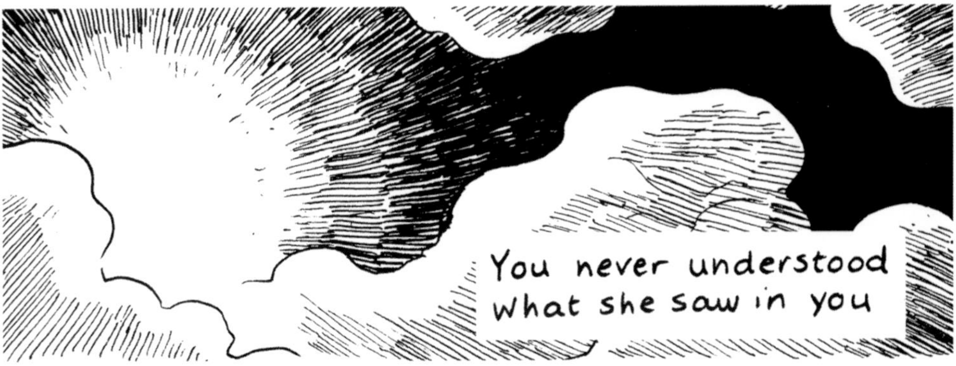
You never understood
what she saw in you

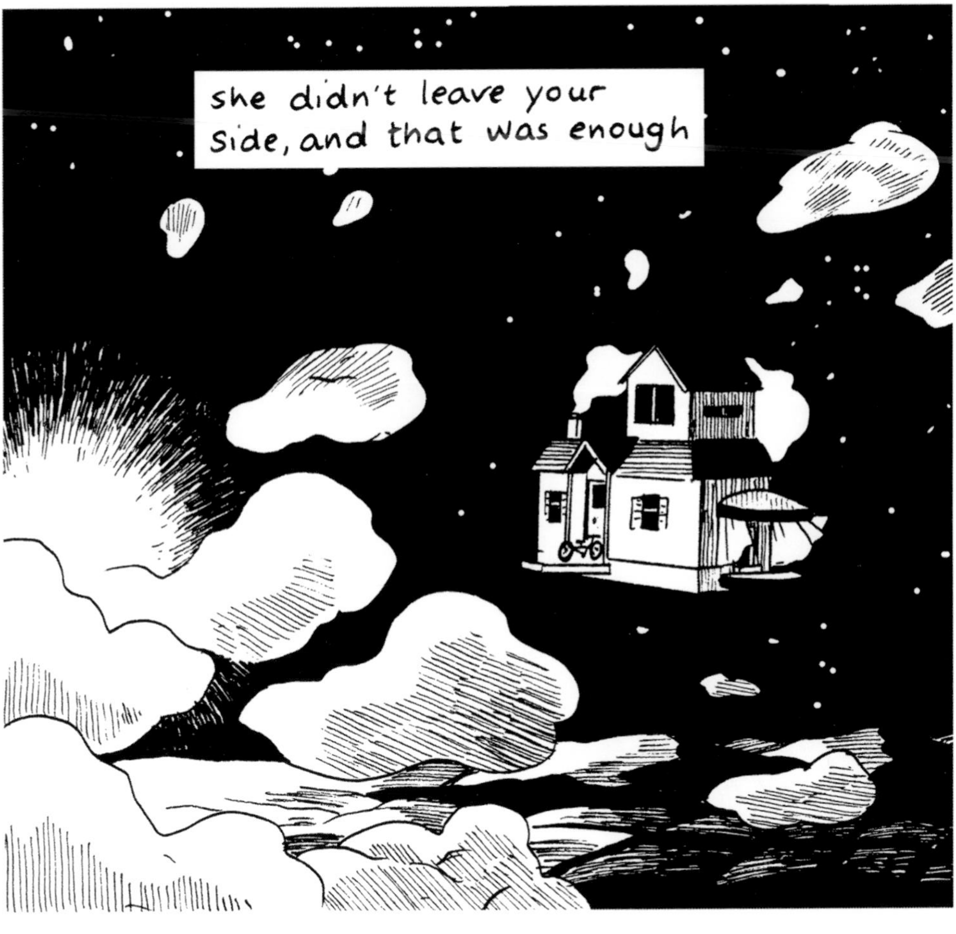
she didn't leave your
side, and that was enough

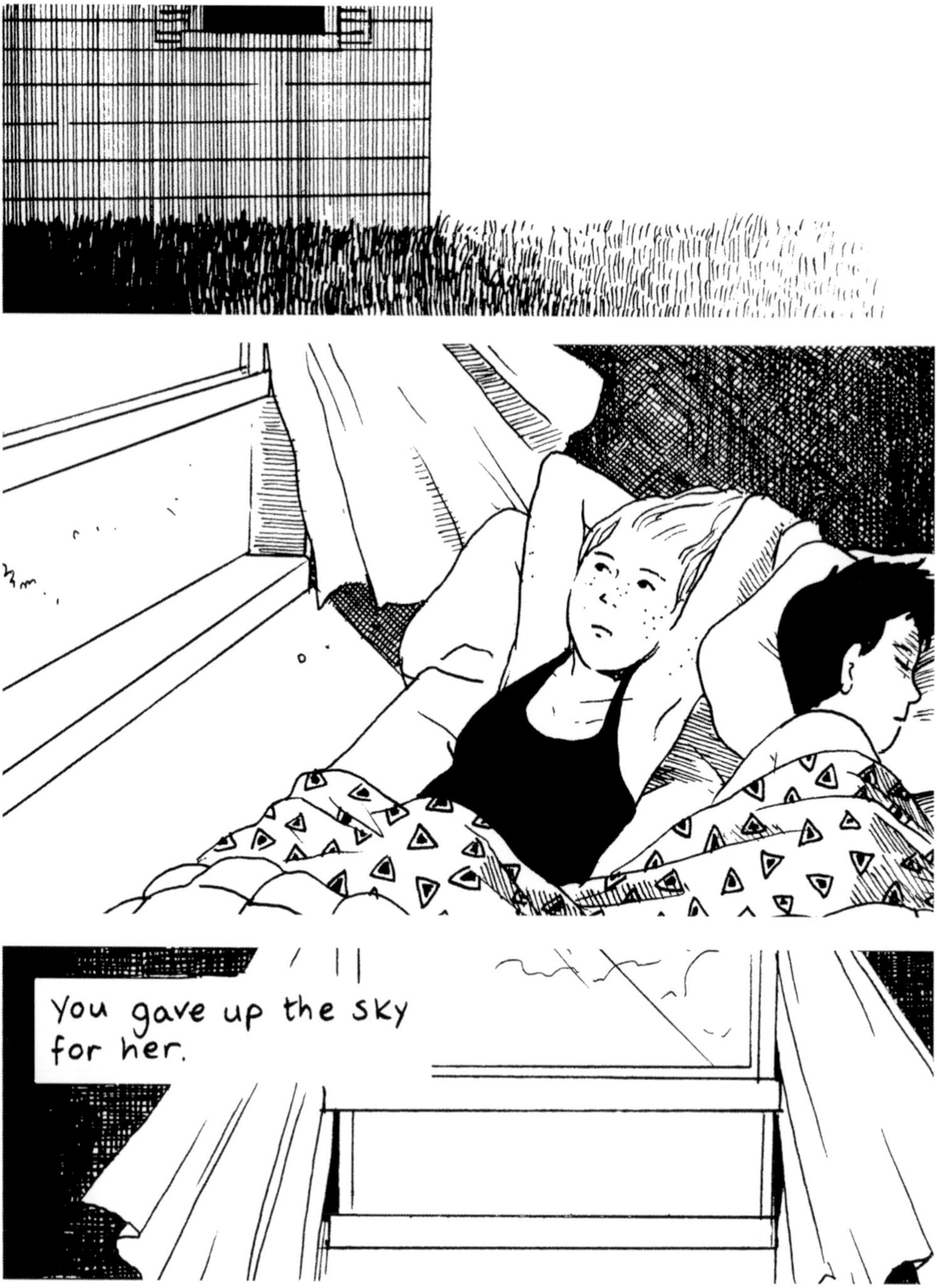
You gave up the sky for her.

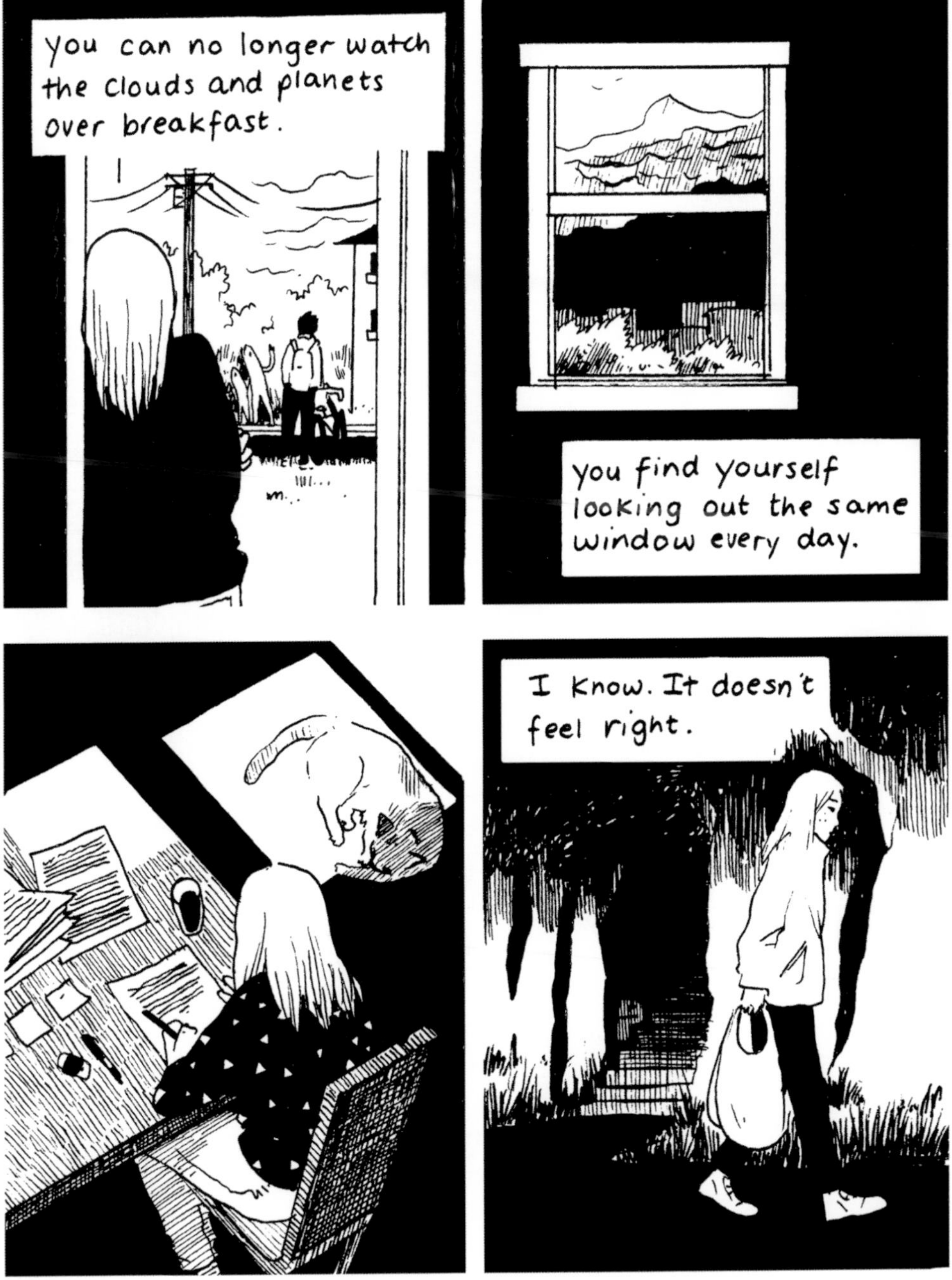
you can no longer watch the clouds and planets over breakfast.
you find yourself looking out the same window every day.
I know. It doesn't feel right.

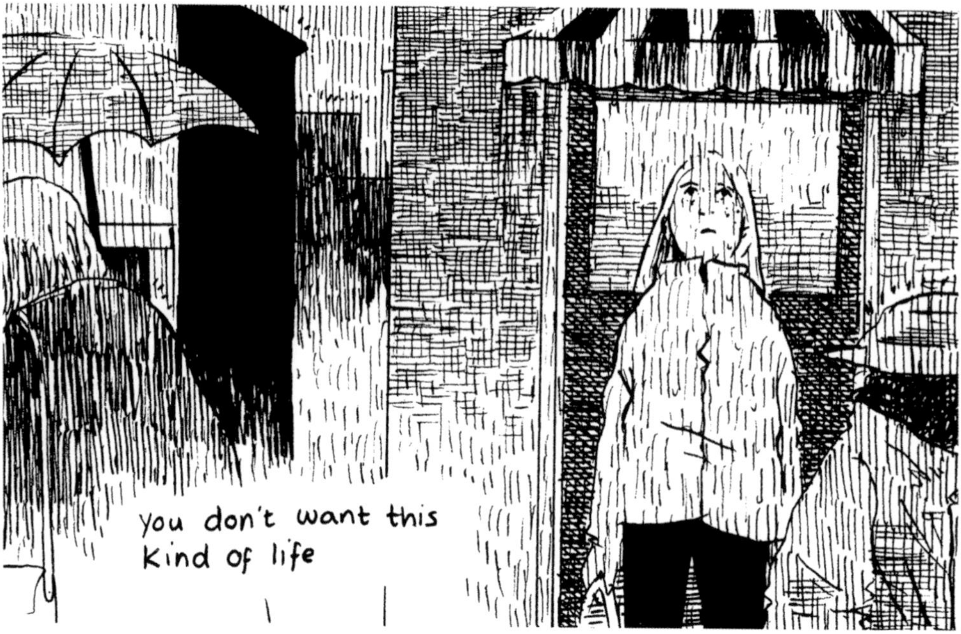
you don't want this
kind of life

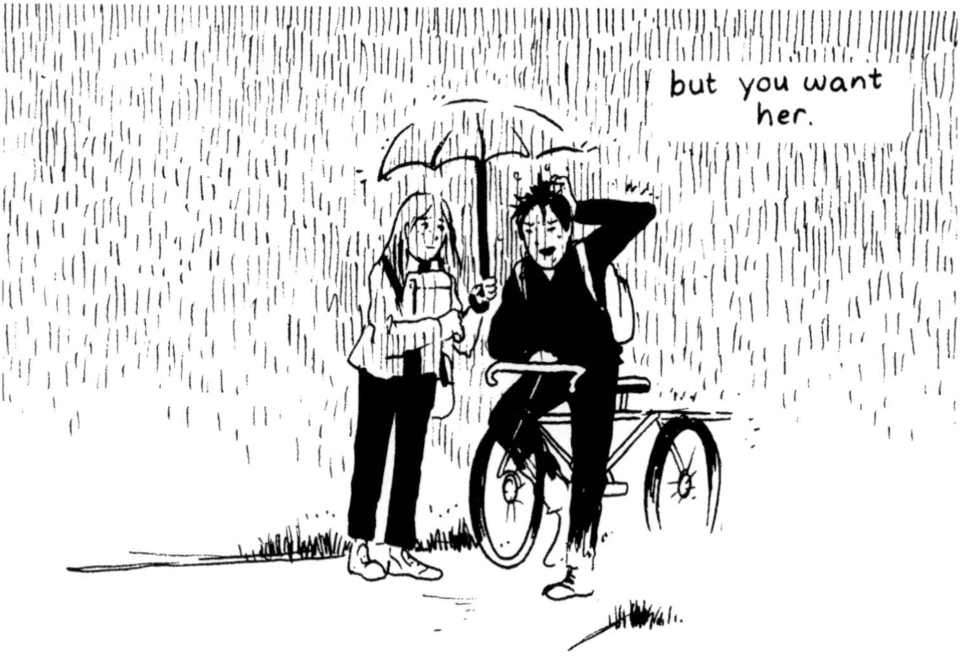
but you want
her.

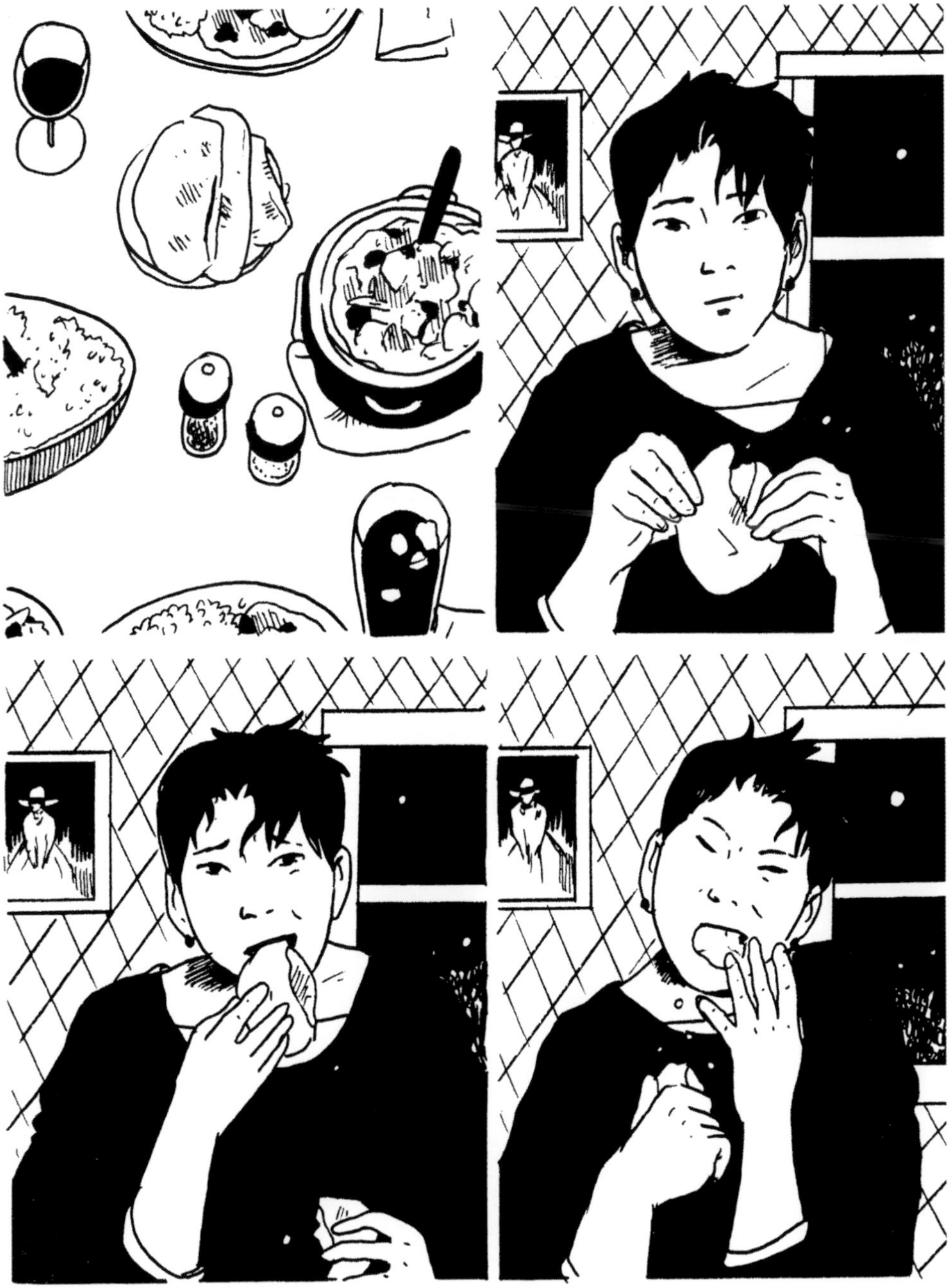

But in time, you'll leave.

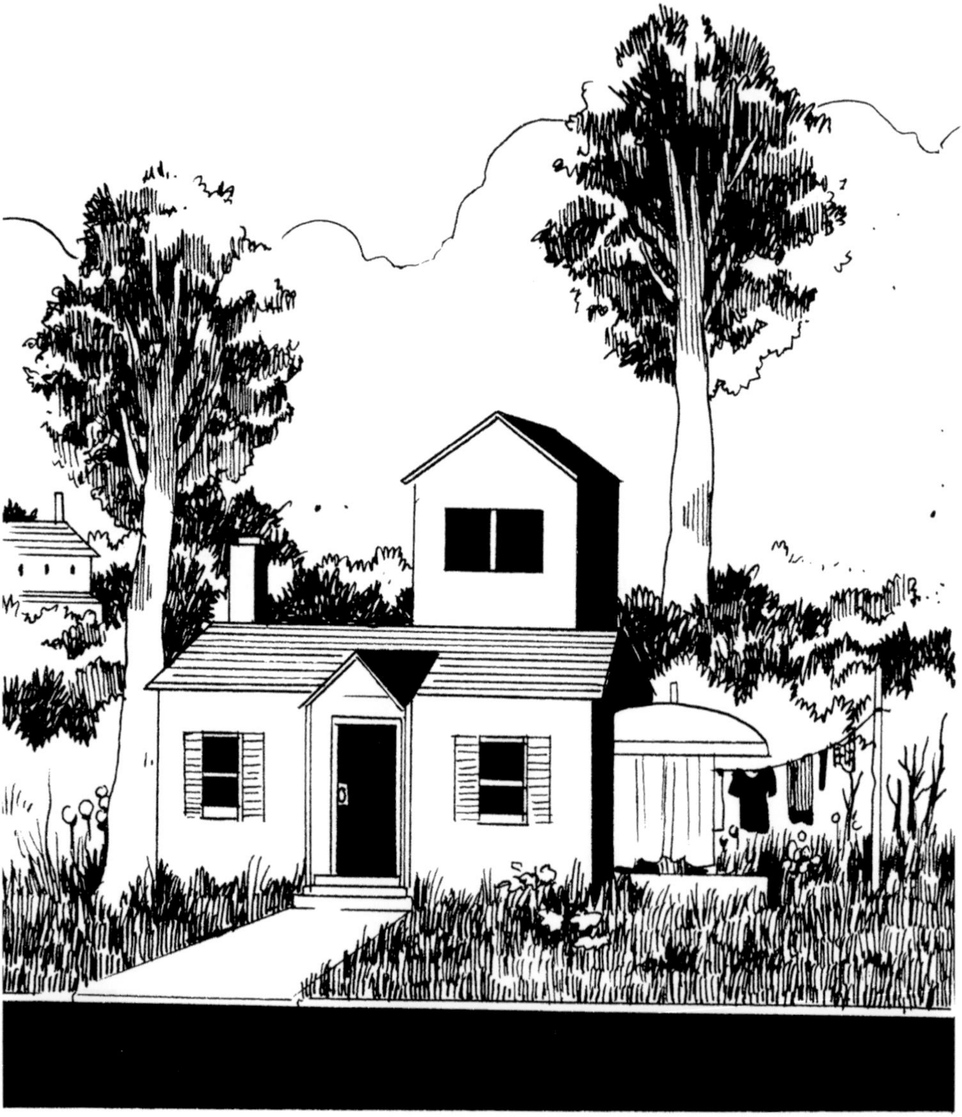

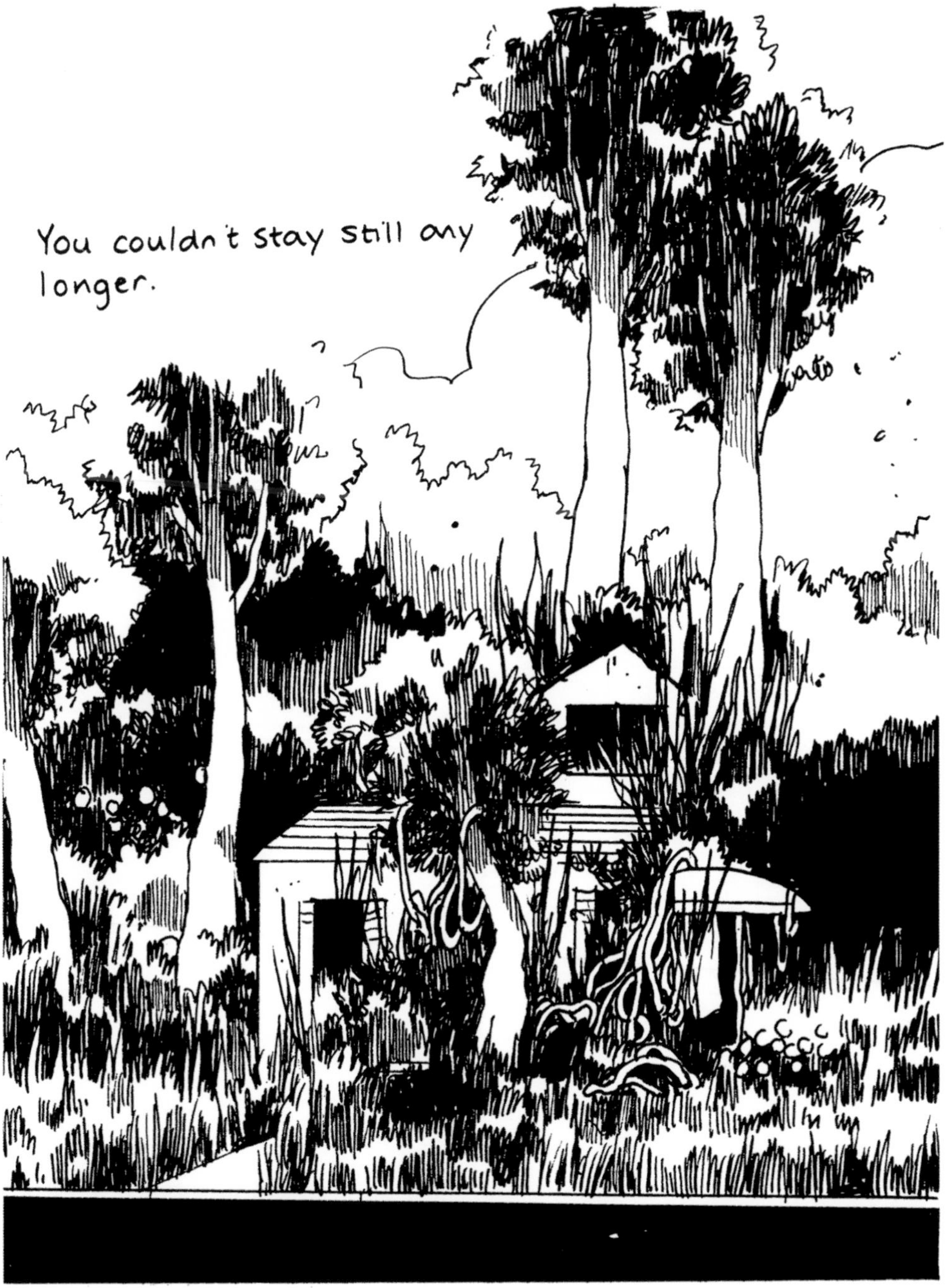
You couldn't stay still any longer.

you'll leave Nancy
with her, feeling like
you don't deserve
such a fine-spirited
cat.

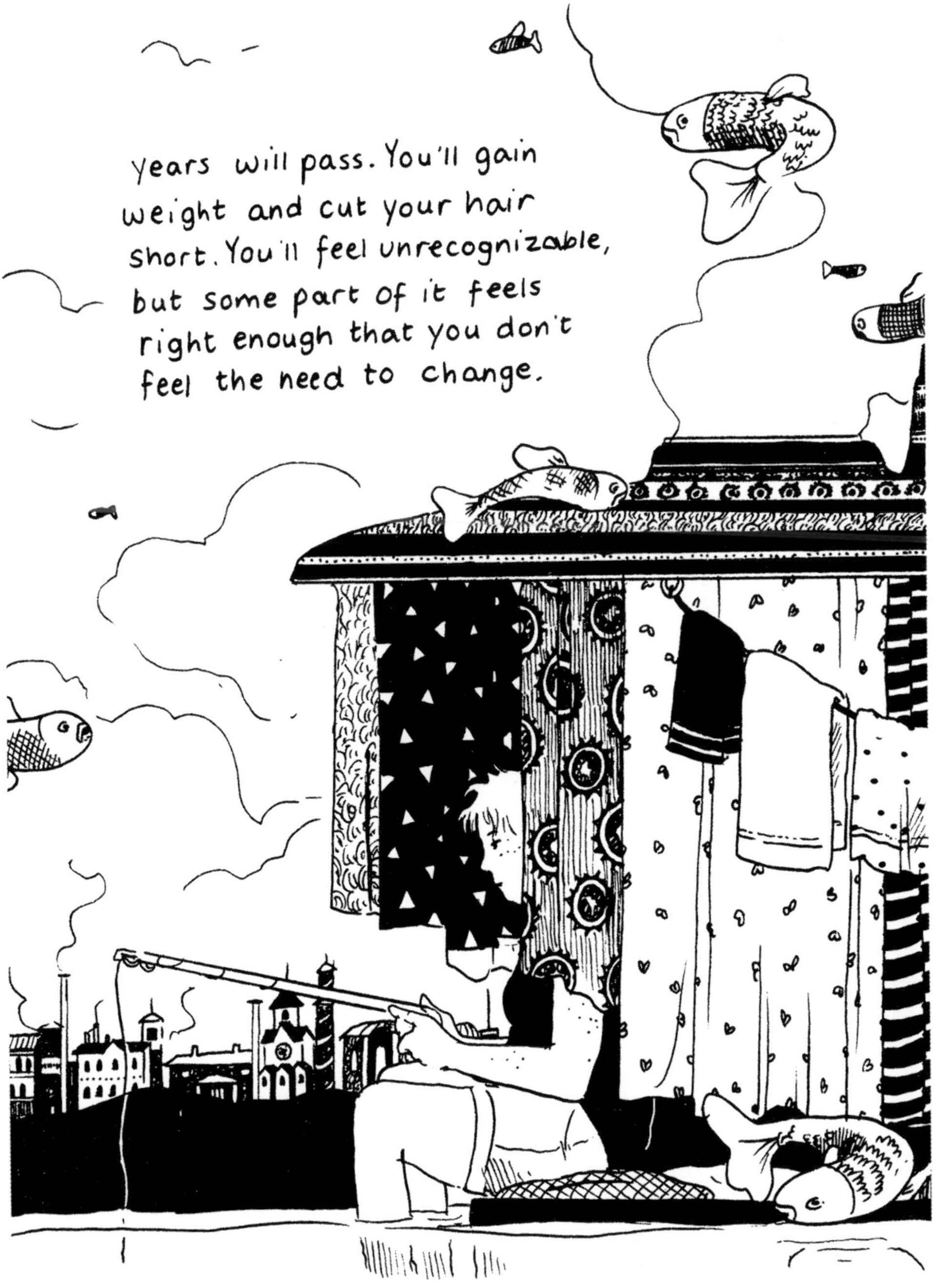
years will pass. You'll gain weight and cut your hair short. You'll feel unrecognizable, but some part of it feels right enough that you don't feel the need to change.

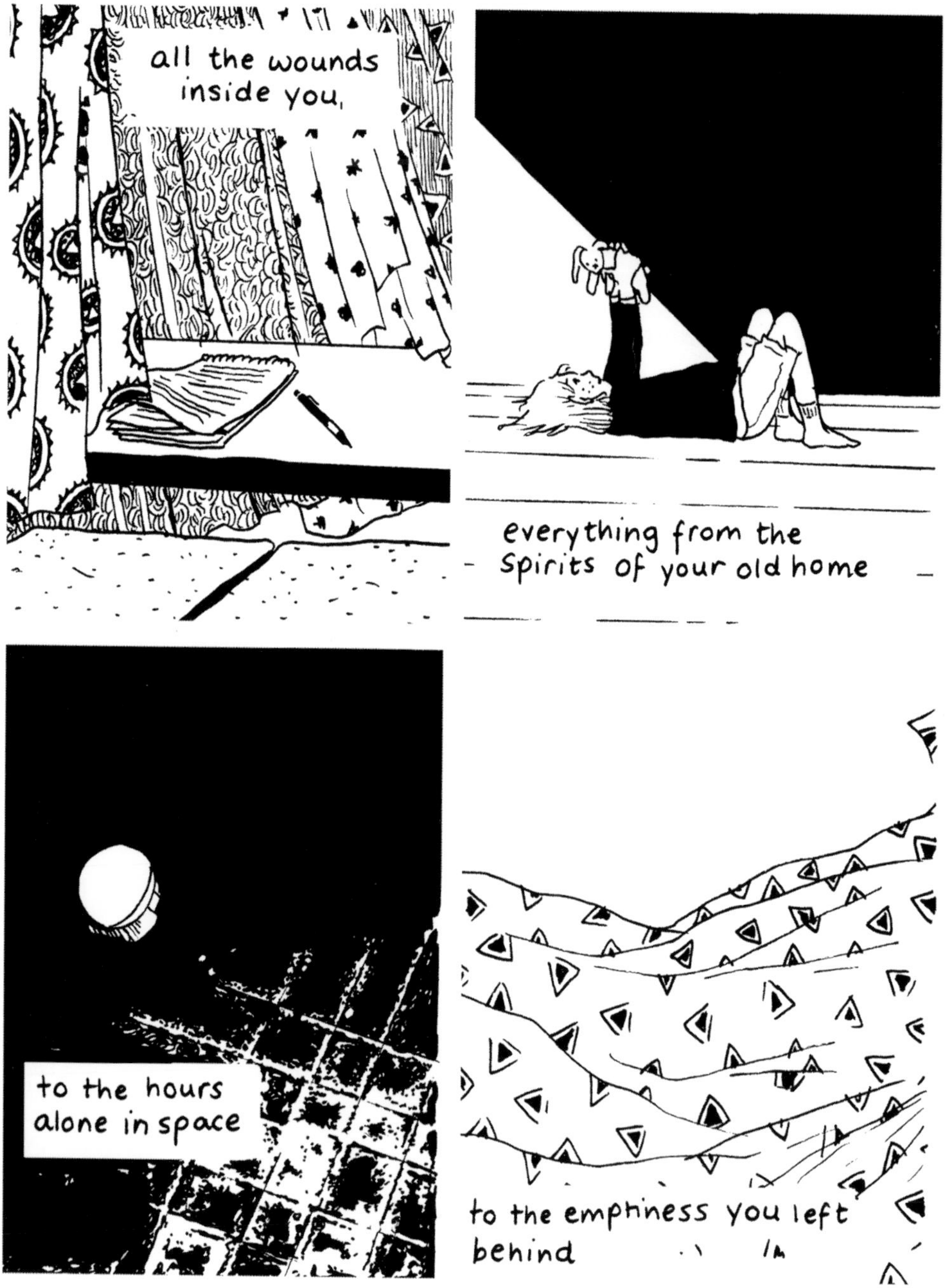
all the wounds inside you,
everything from the spirits of your old home
to the hours alone in space
to the emptiness you left behind

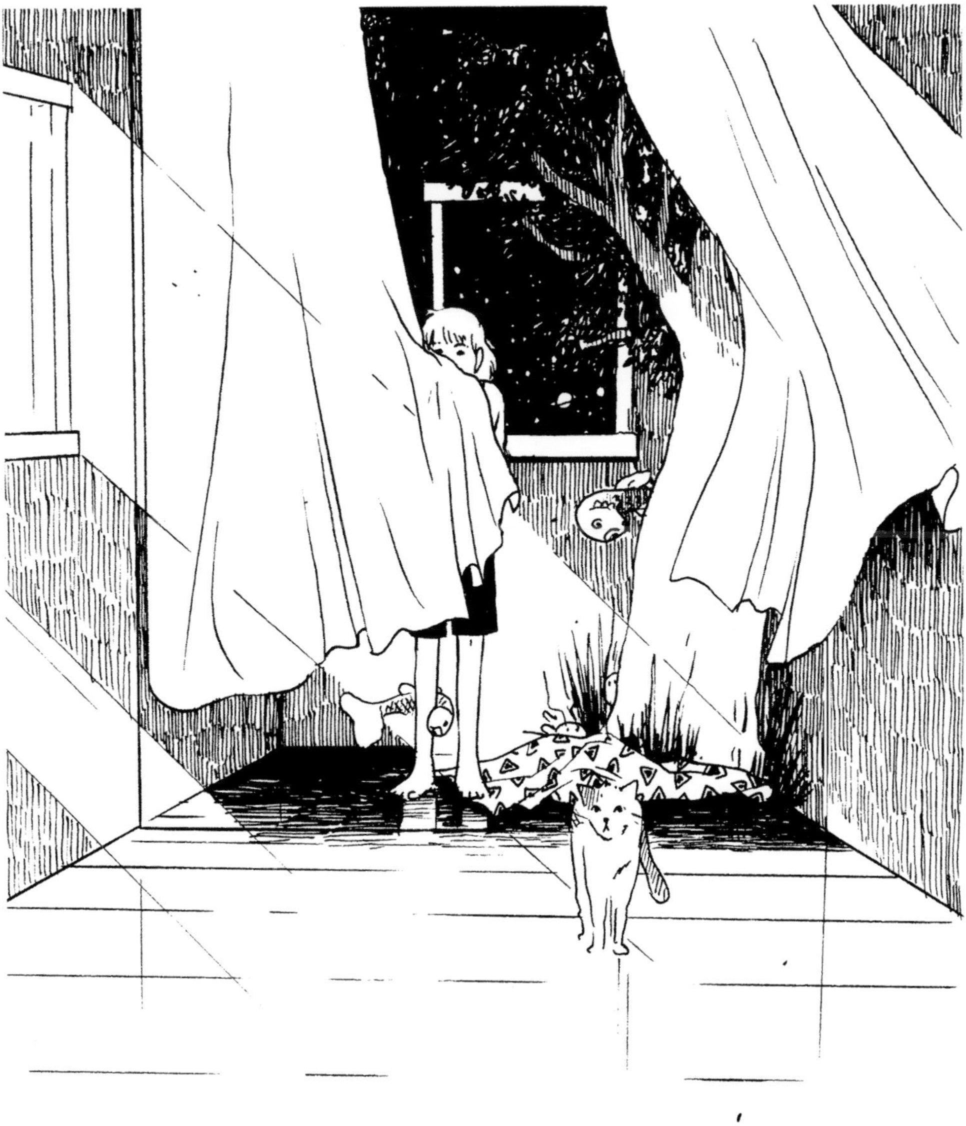

start to fill every room
you're in

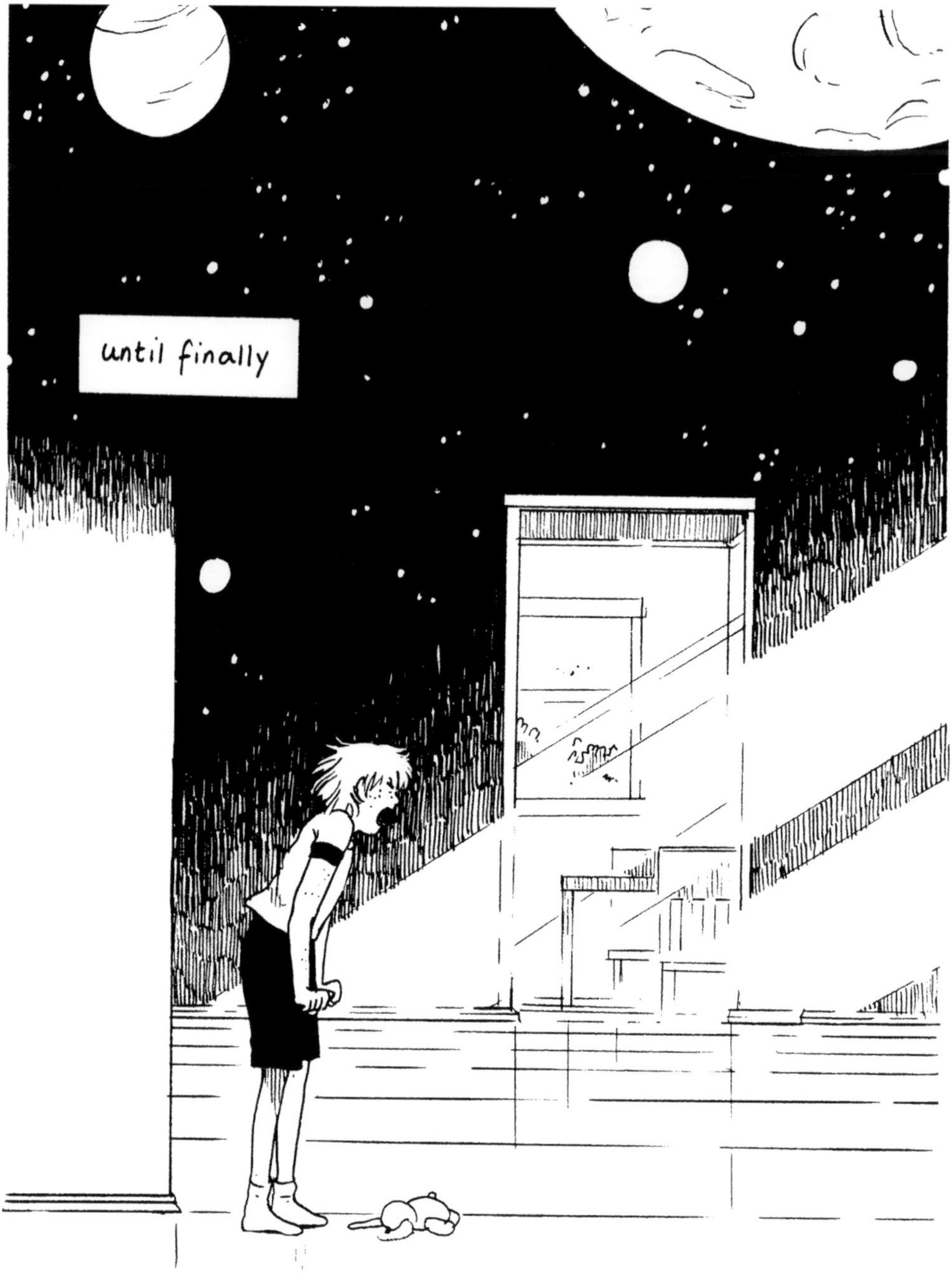
until finally

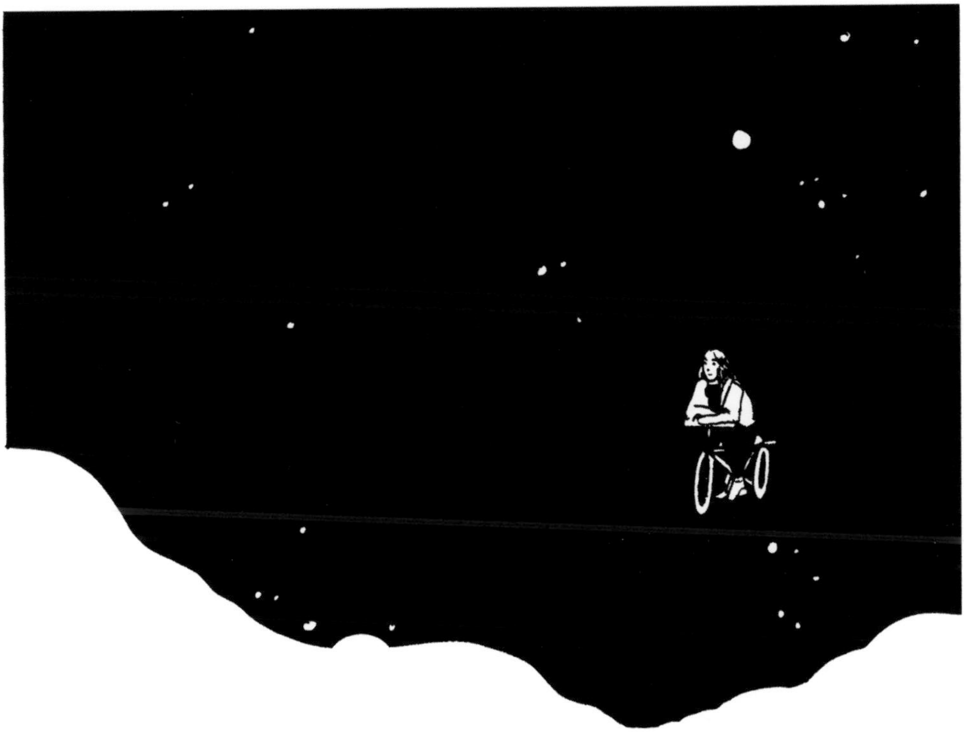

they crack open,
like a chunk of ice

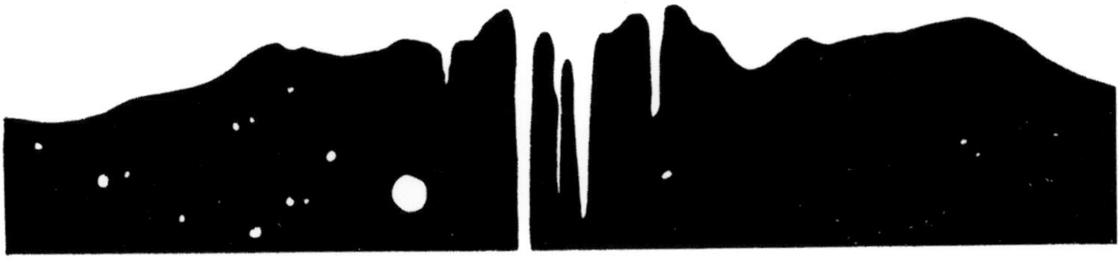

a massive space will form

a new city will be built

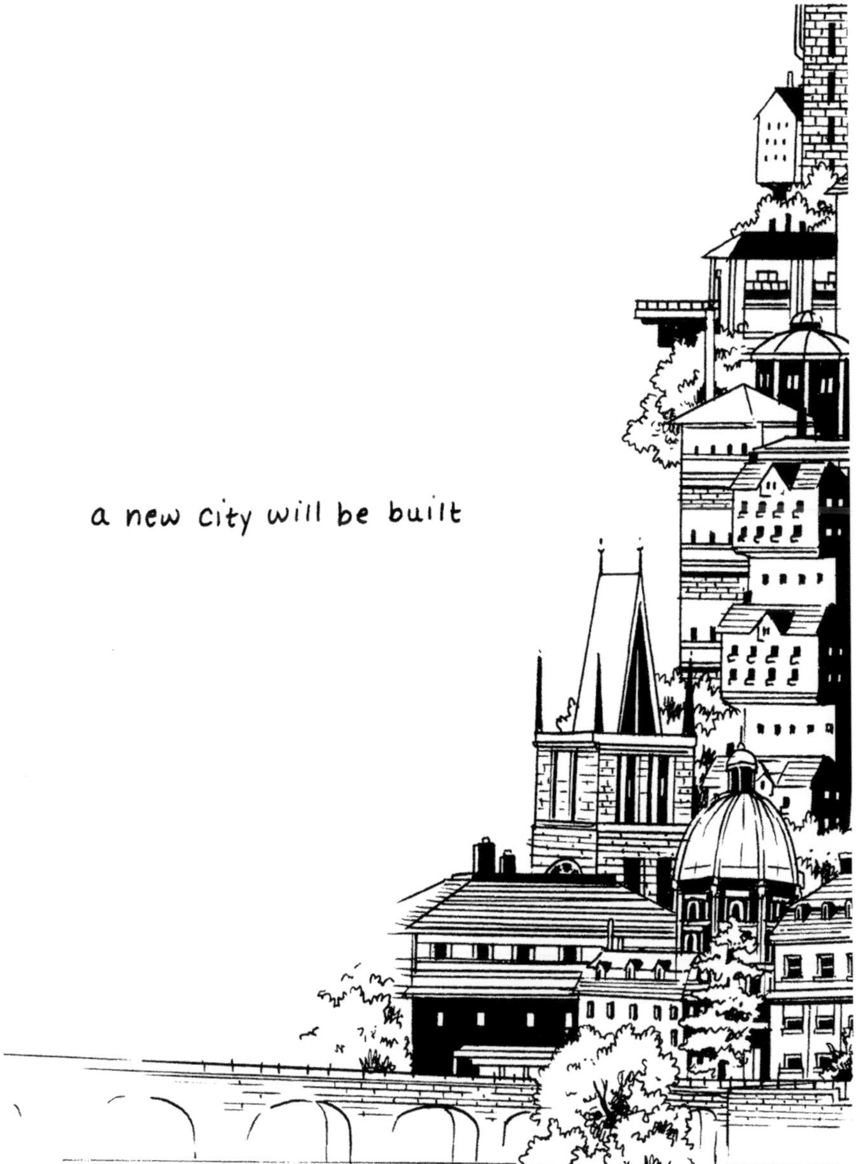

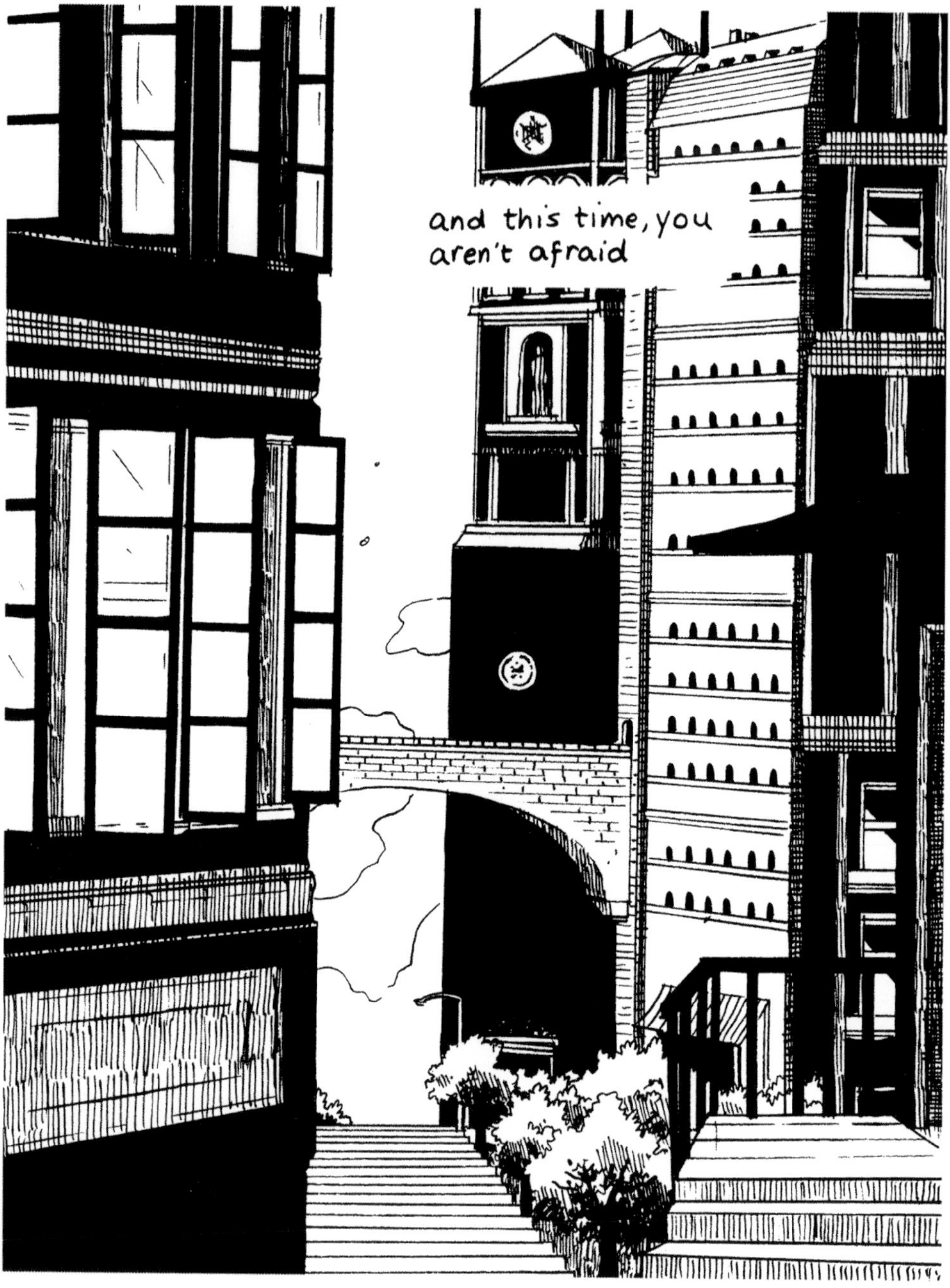
and this time, you aren't afraid

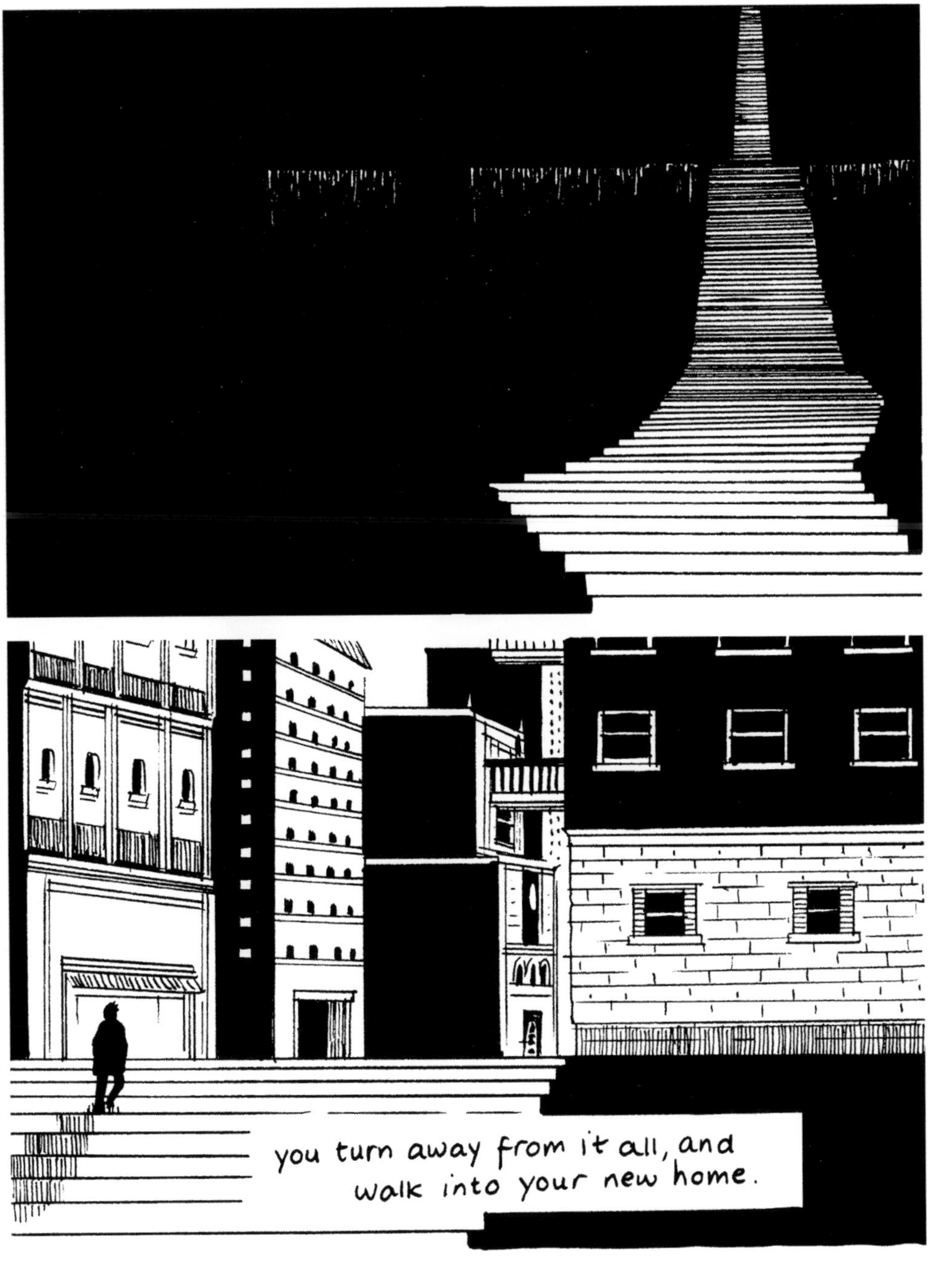
you turn away from it all, and
walk into your new home.

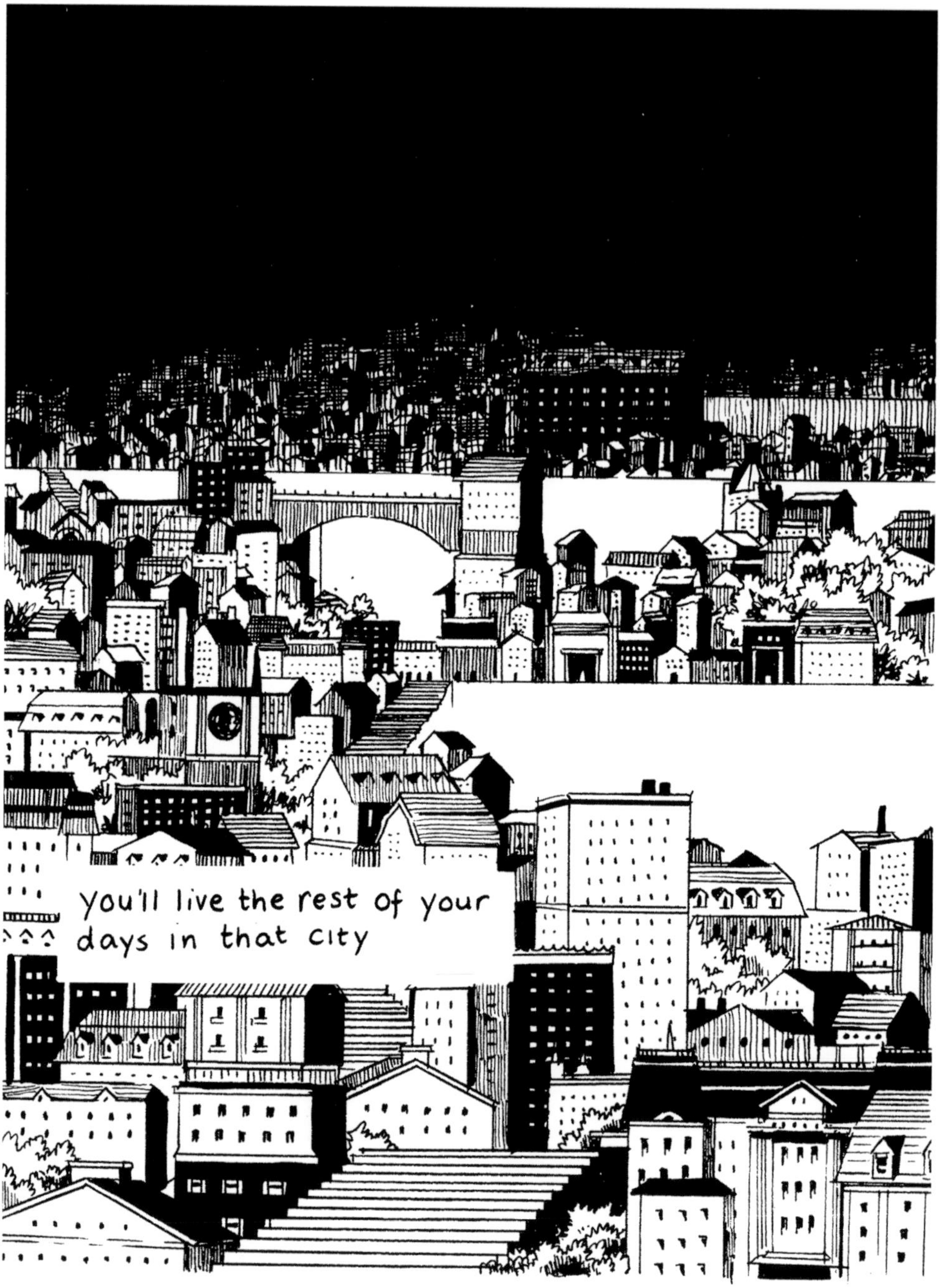
you'll live the rest of your days in that city

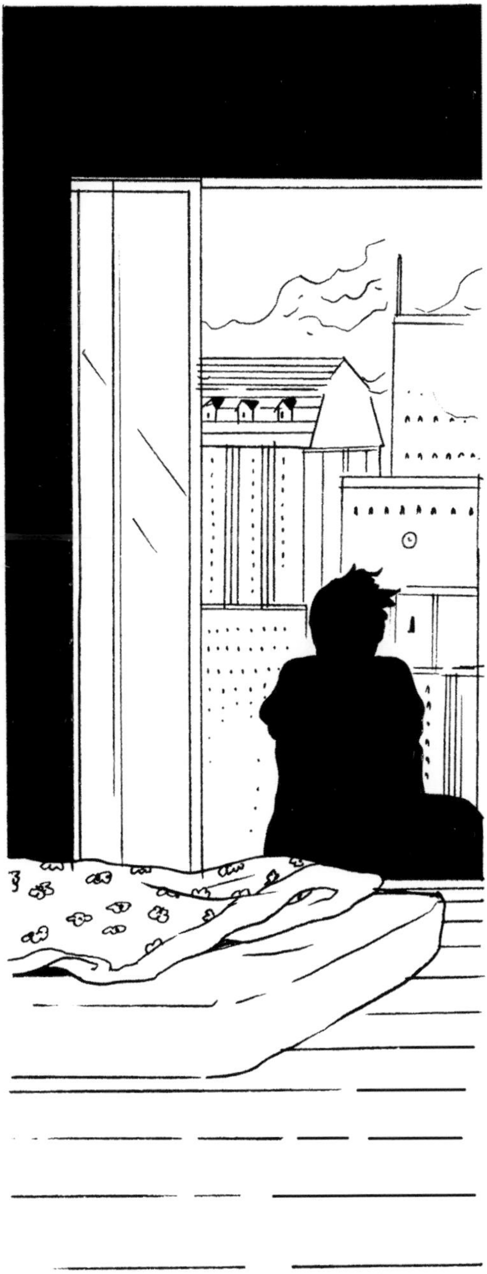

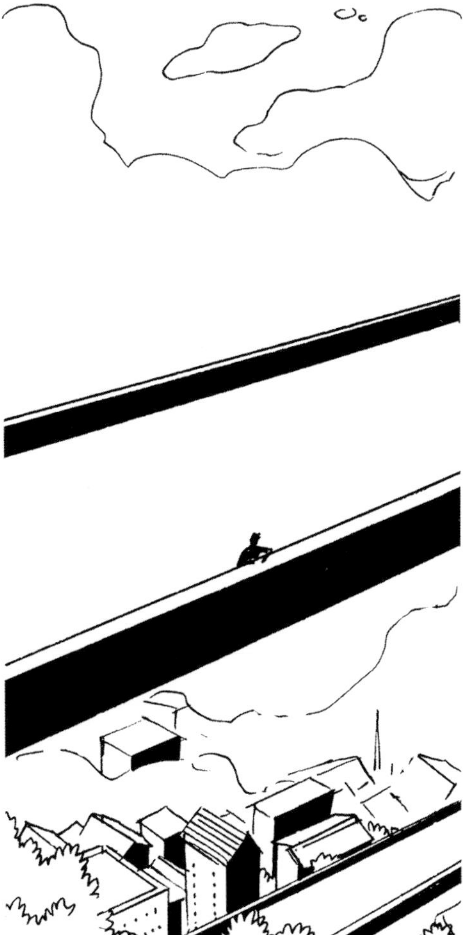

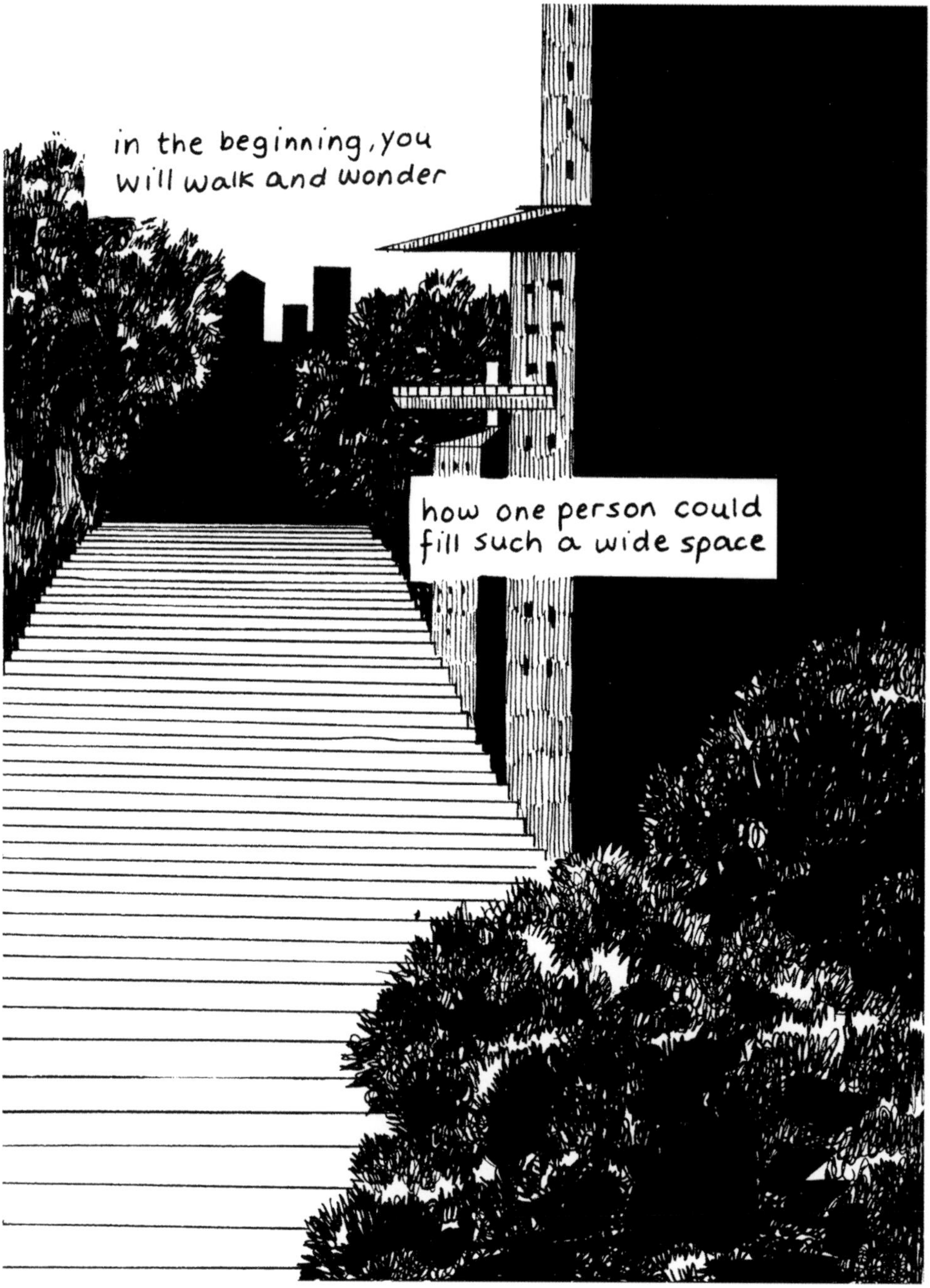
in the beginning, you will walk and wonder
how one person could fill such a wide space

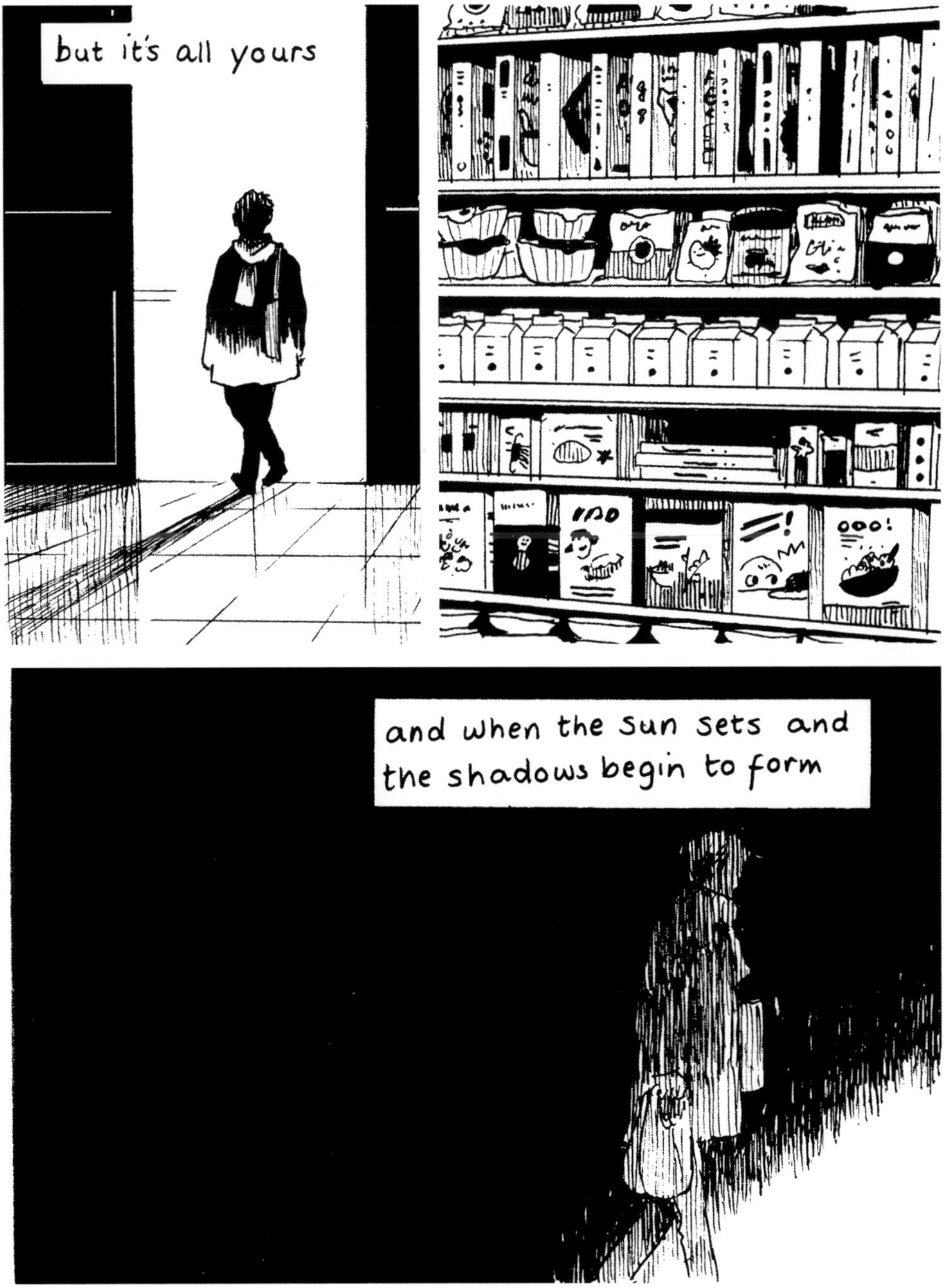
but it's all yours
and when the sun sets and the shadows begin to form

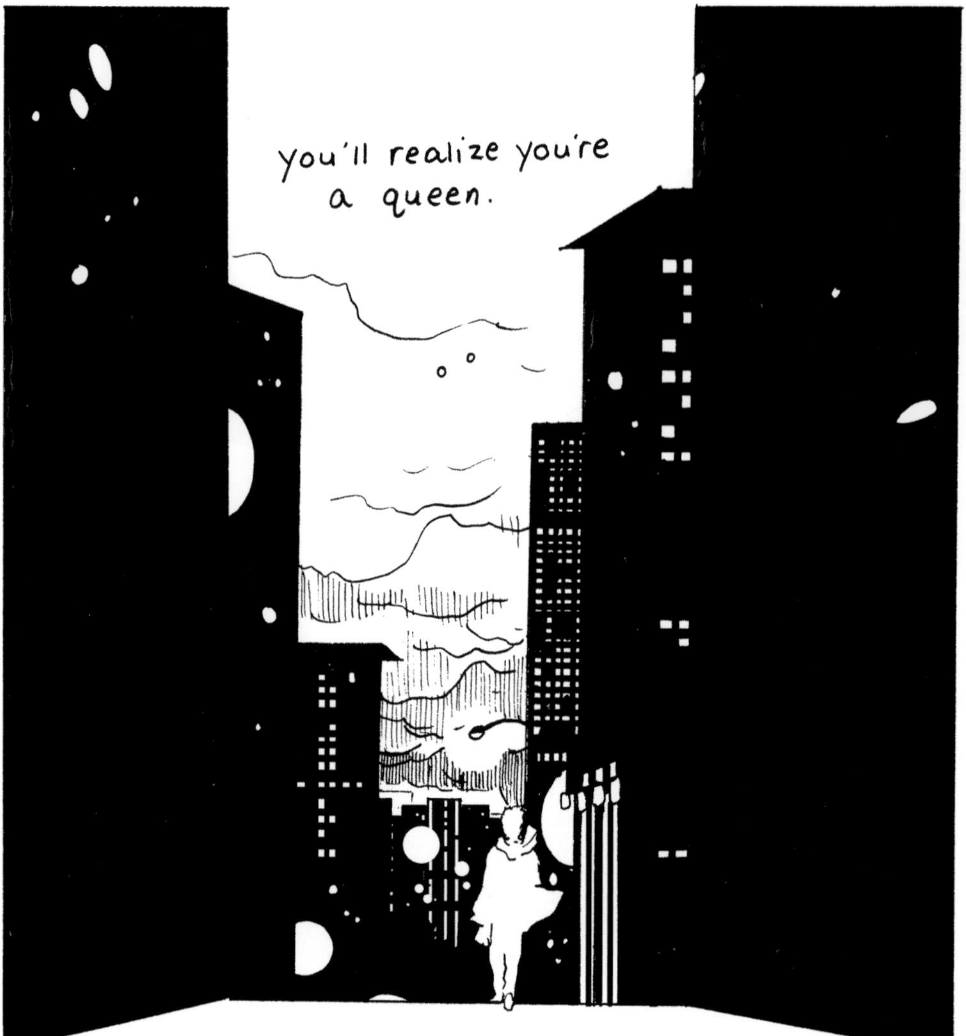
you'll realize you're
a queen.

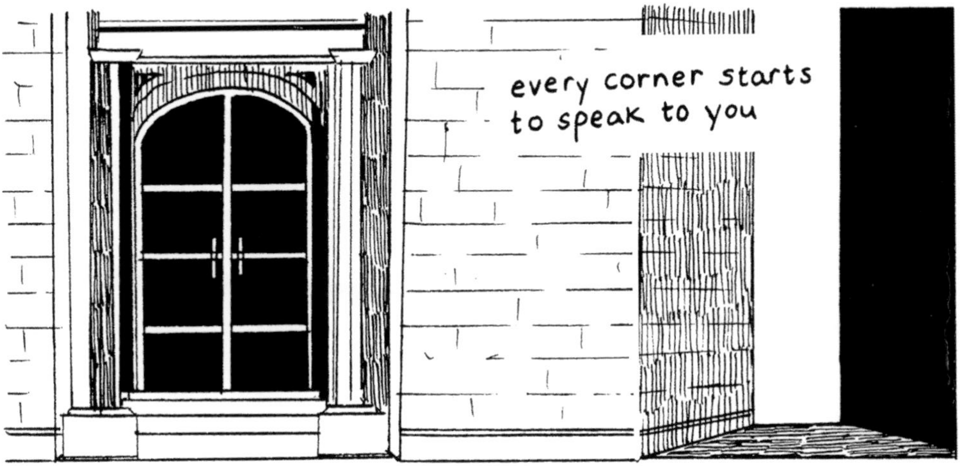
every corner starts to speak to you

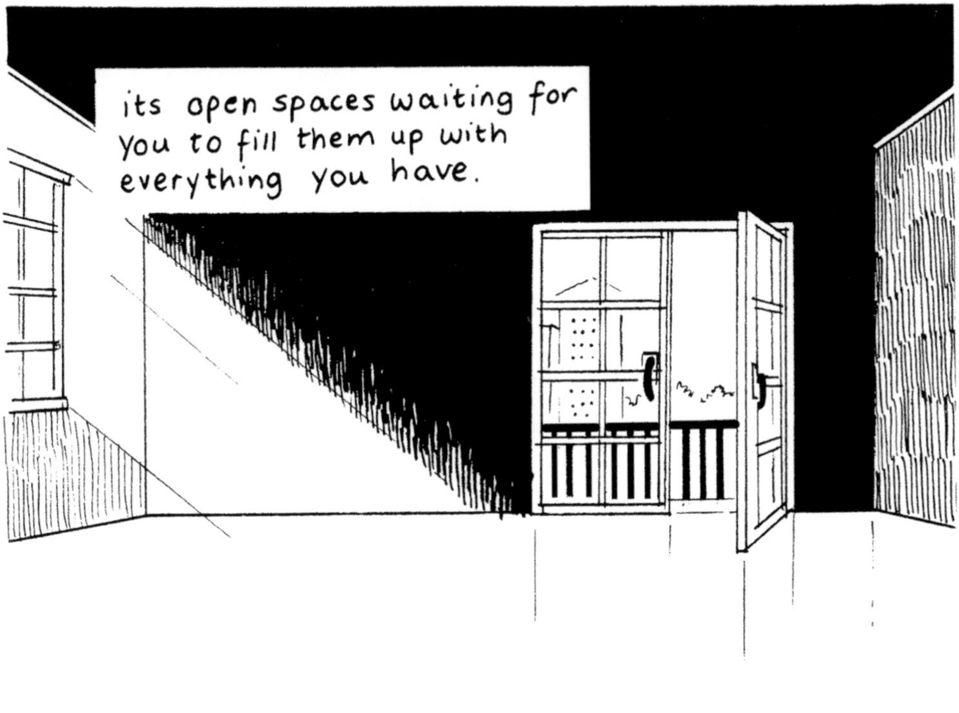
its open spaces waiting for you to fill them up with everything you have.

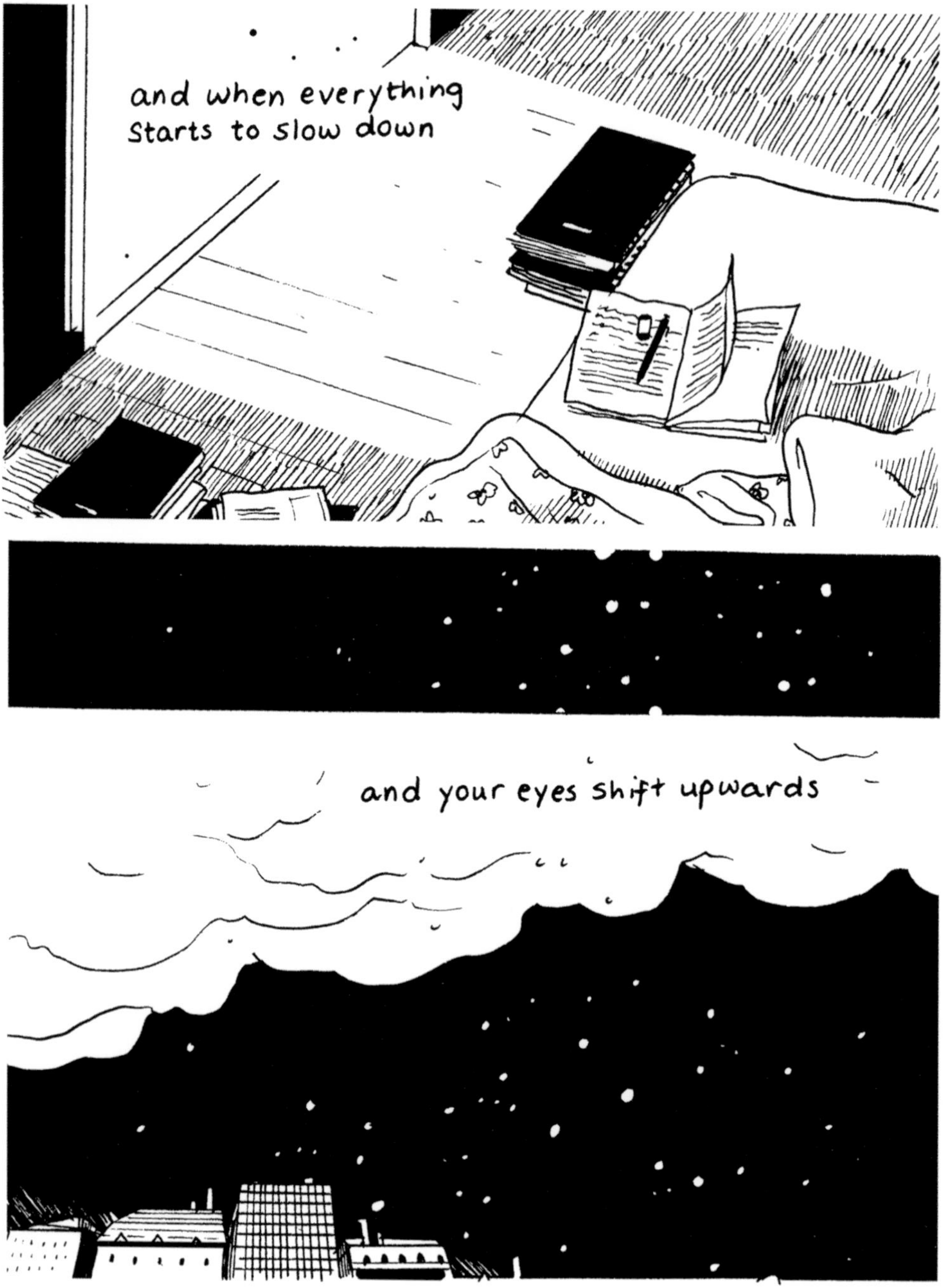
and when everything
starts to slow down
and your eyes shift upwards

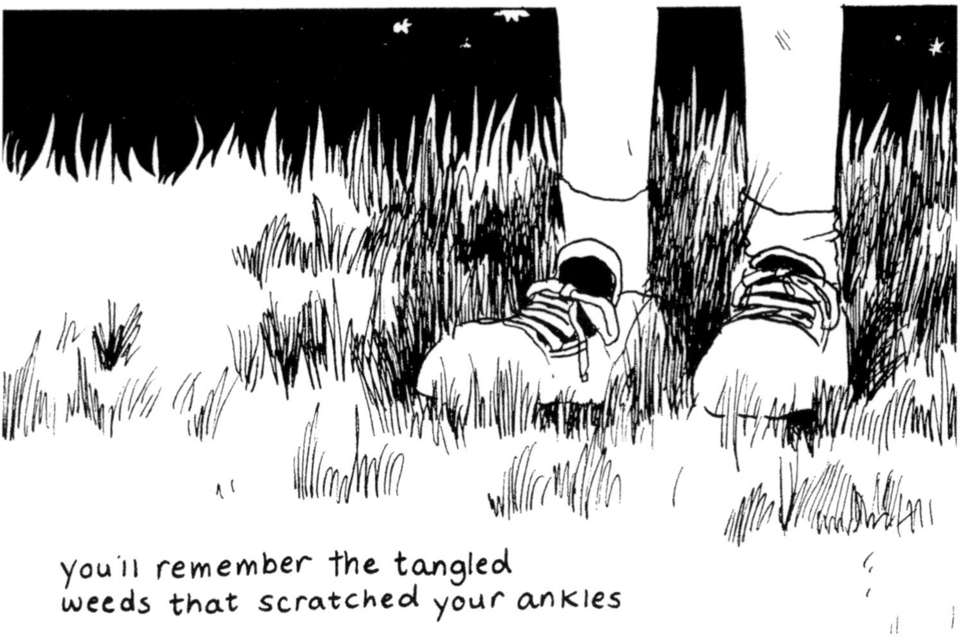
you'll remember the tangled
weeds that scratched your ankles

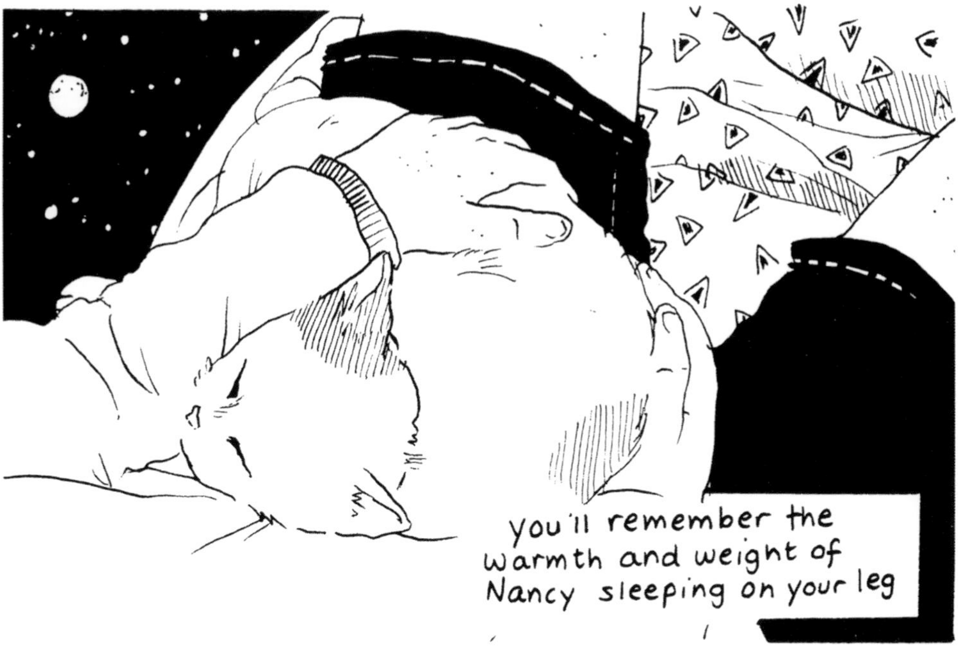
you'll remember the
warmth and weight of
Nancy sleeping on your leg

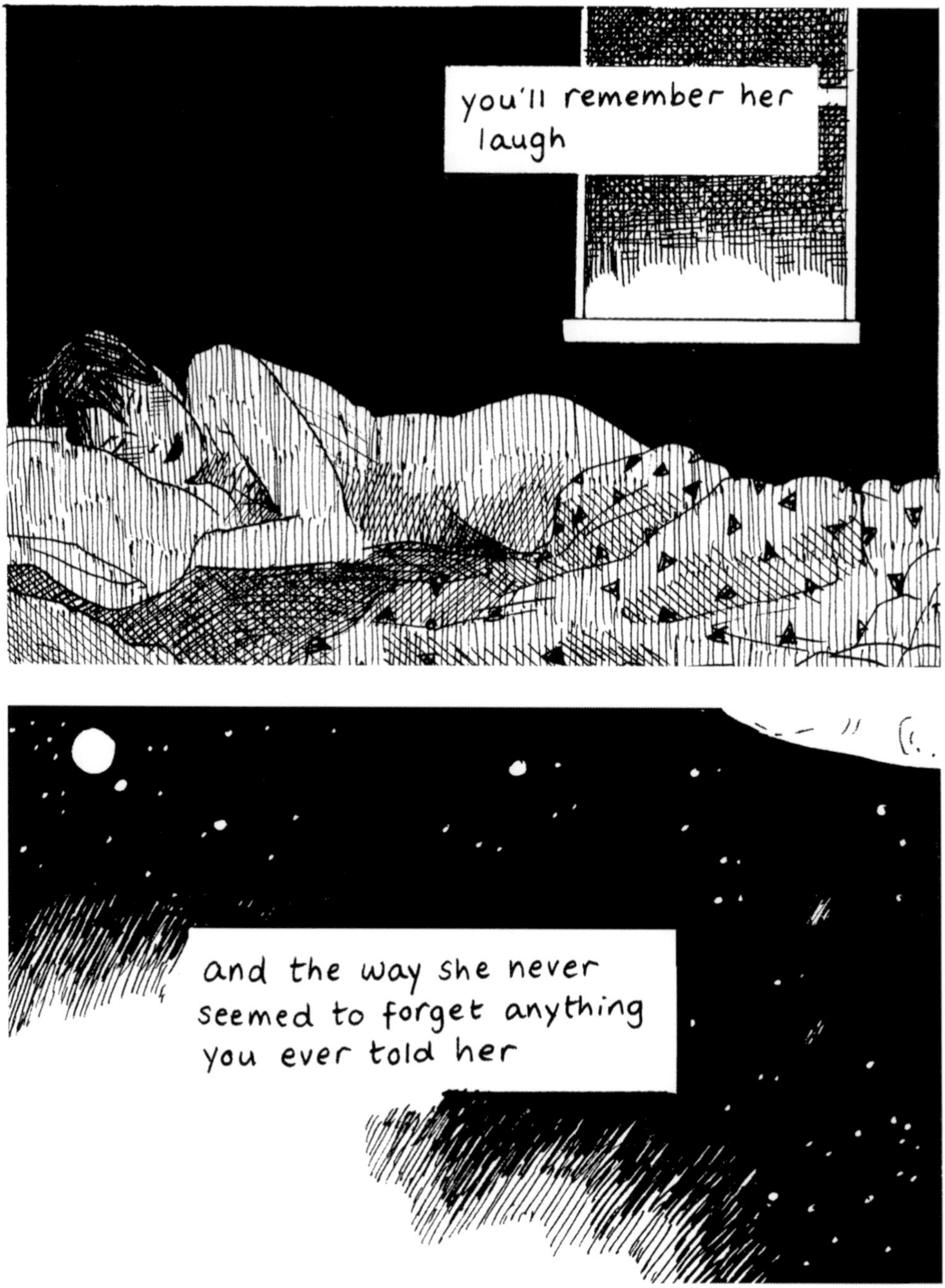
you'll remember her laugh
and the way she never seemed to forget anything you ever told her

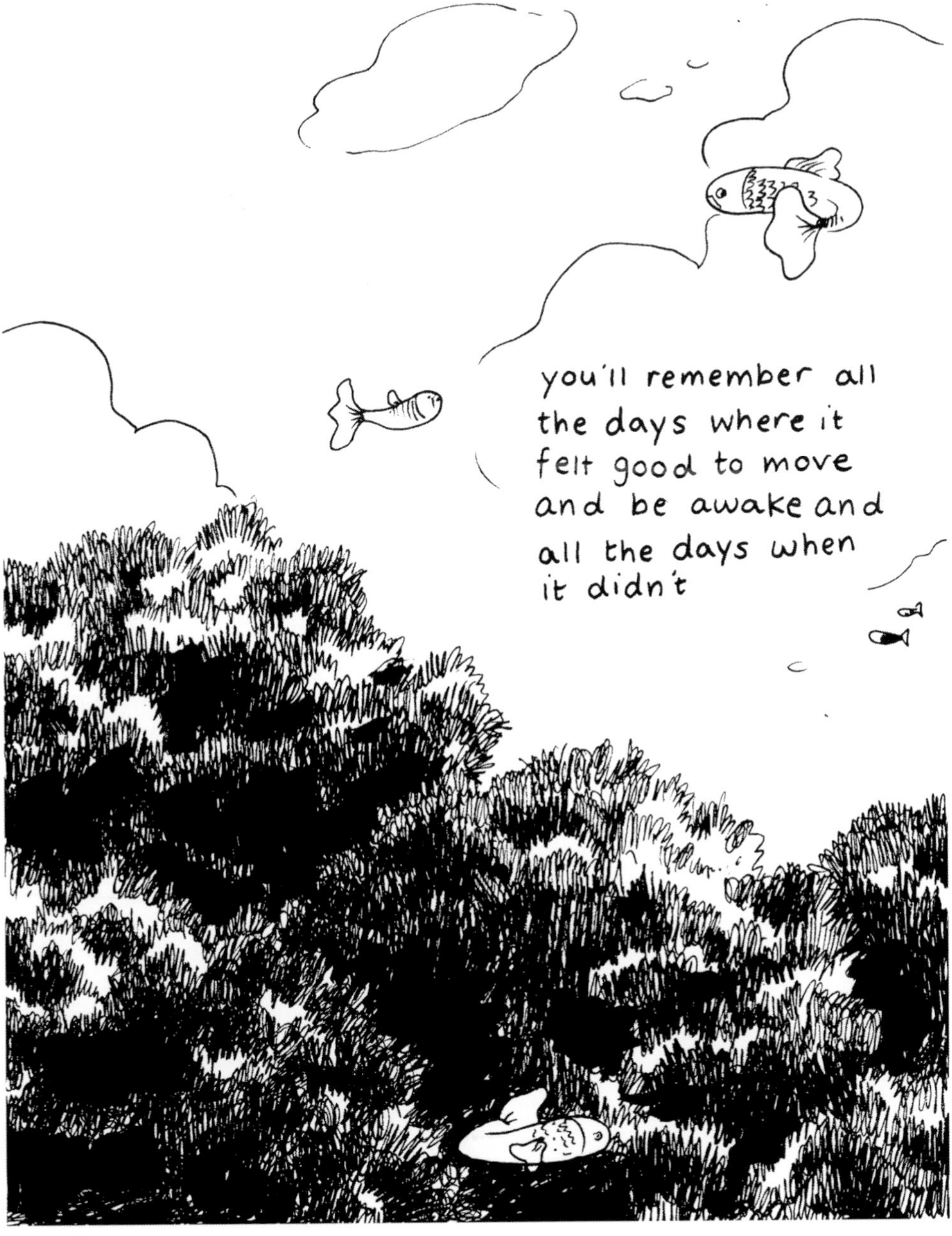
you'll remember all the days where it felt good to move and be awake and all the days when it didn't

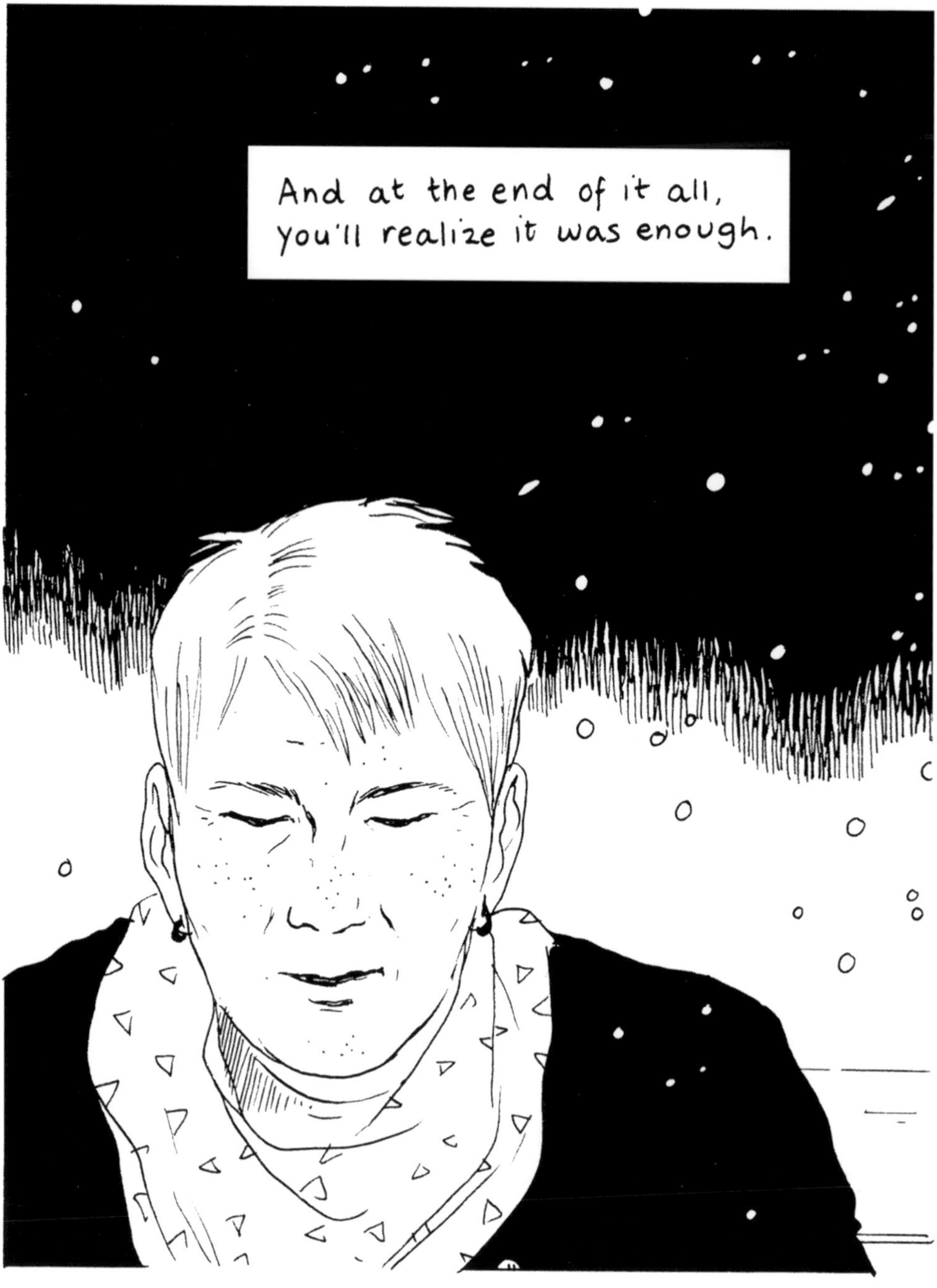
And at the end of it all, you'll realize it was enough.

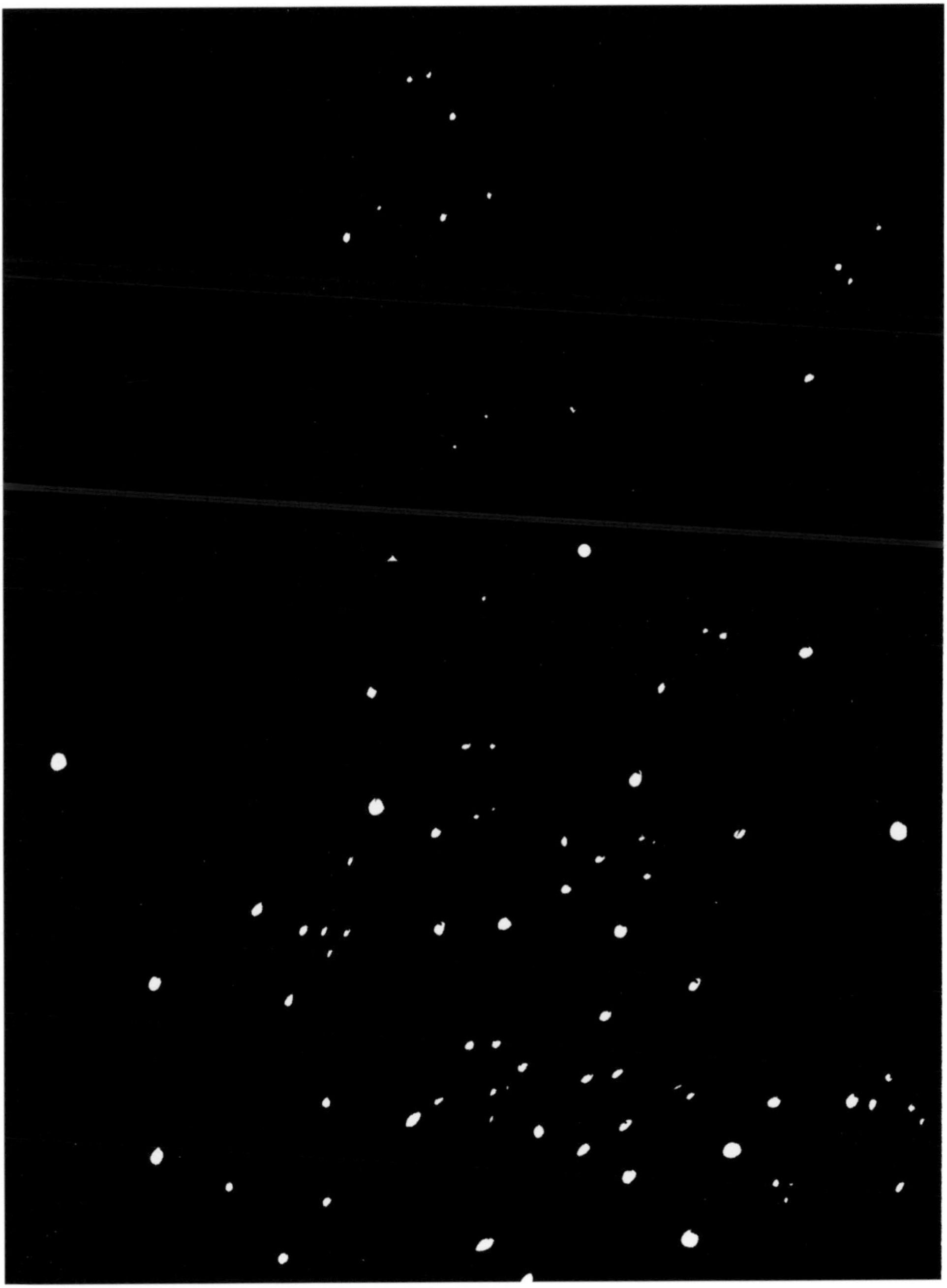

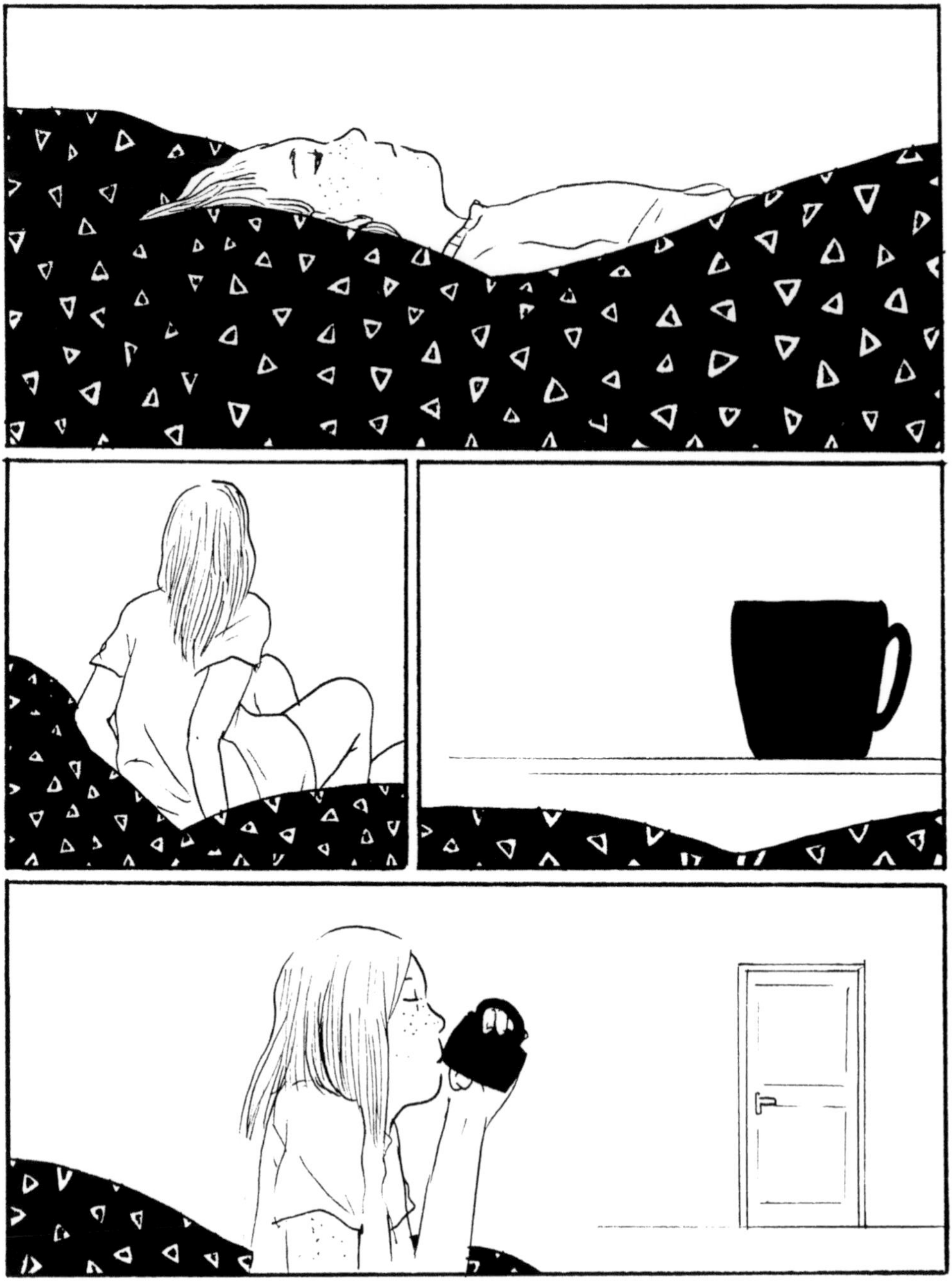

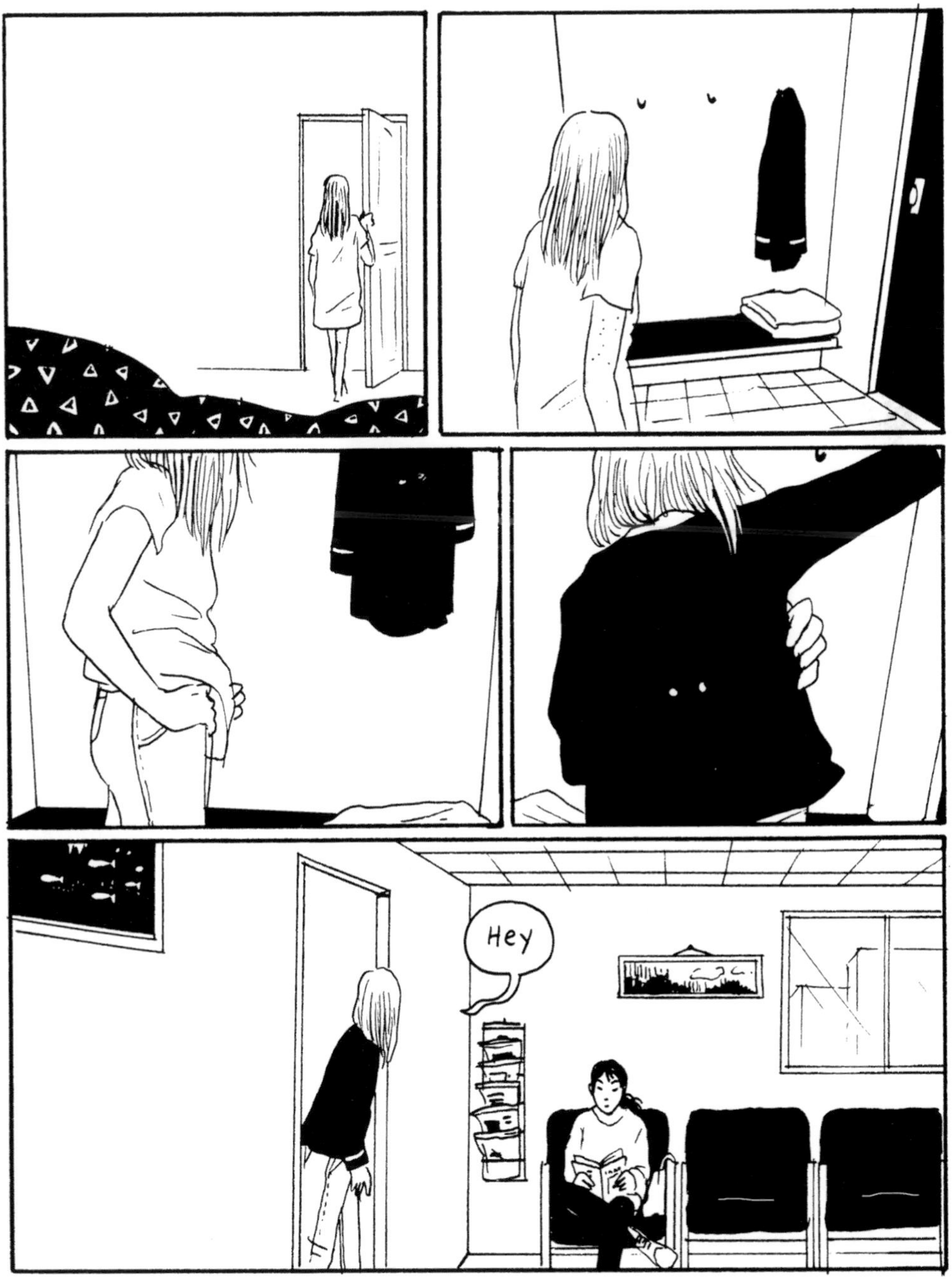
Hey

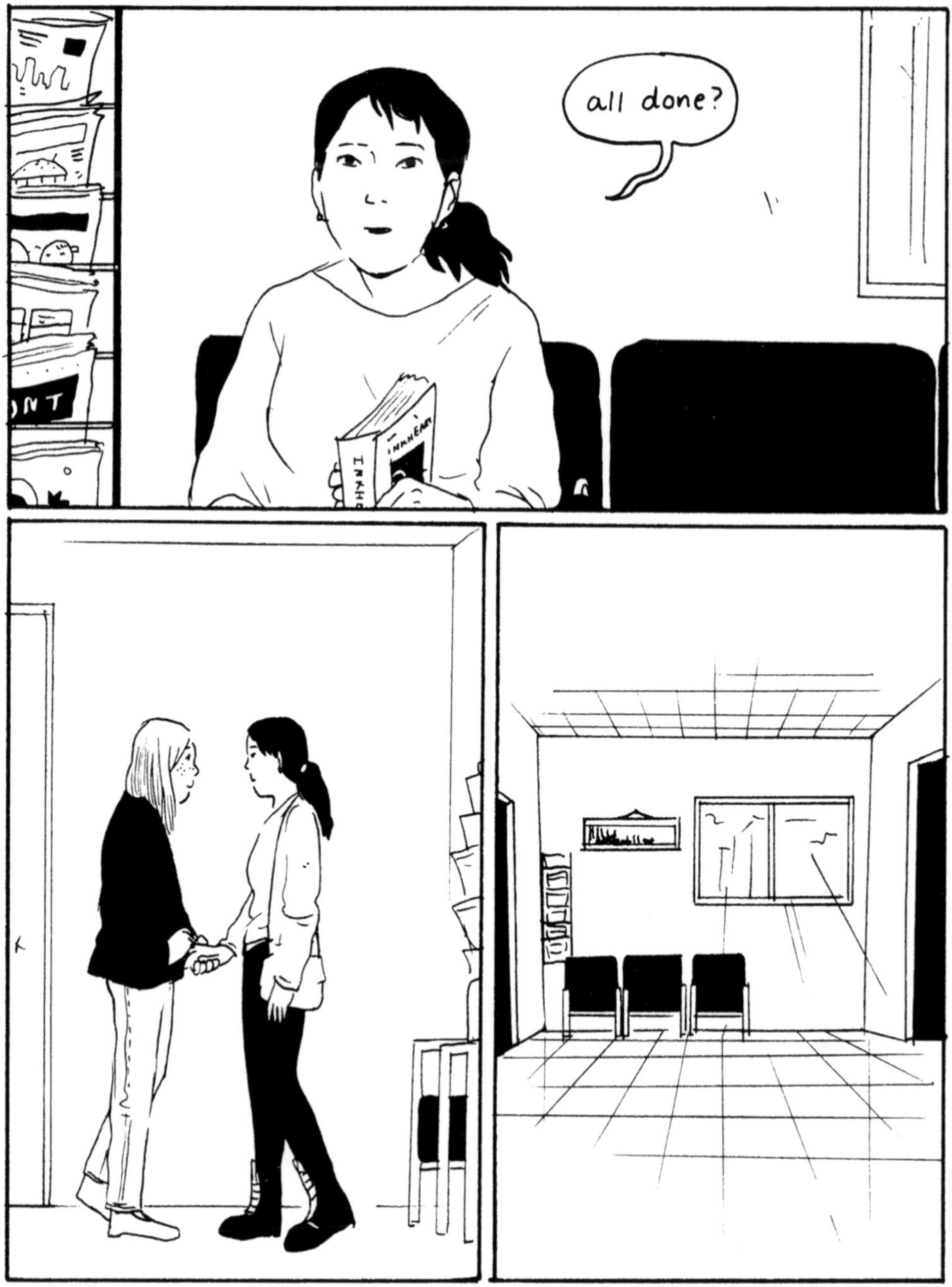
all done?

COMICS BY TILLIE WALDEN
AGED 16-20
YEARS OLD

Glare (2013)

The work of a moody, unhappy teen.
(Though drawing made me happy.) This
comic is so bleak, but it is how I felt
at the time. Growing up is vicious.

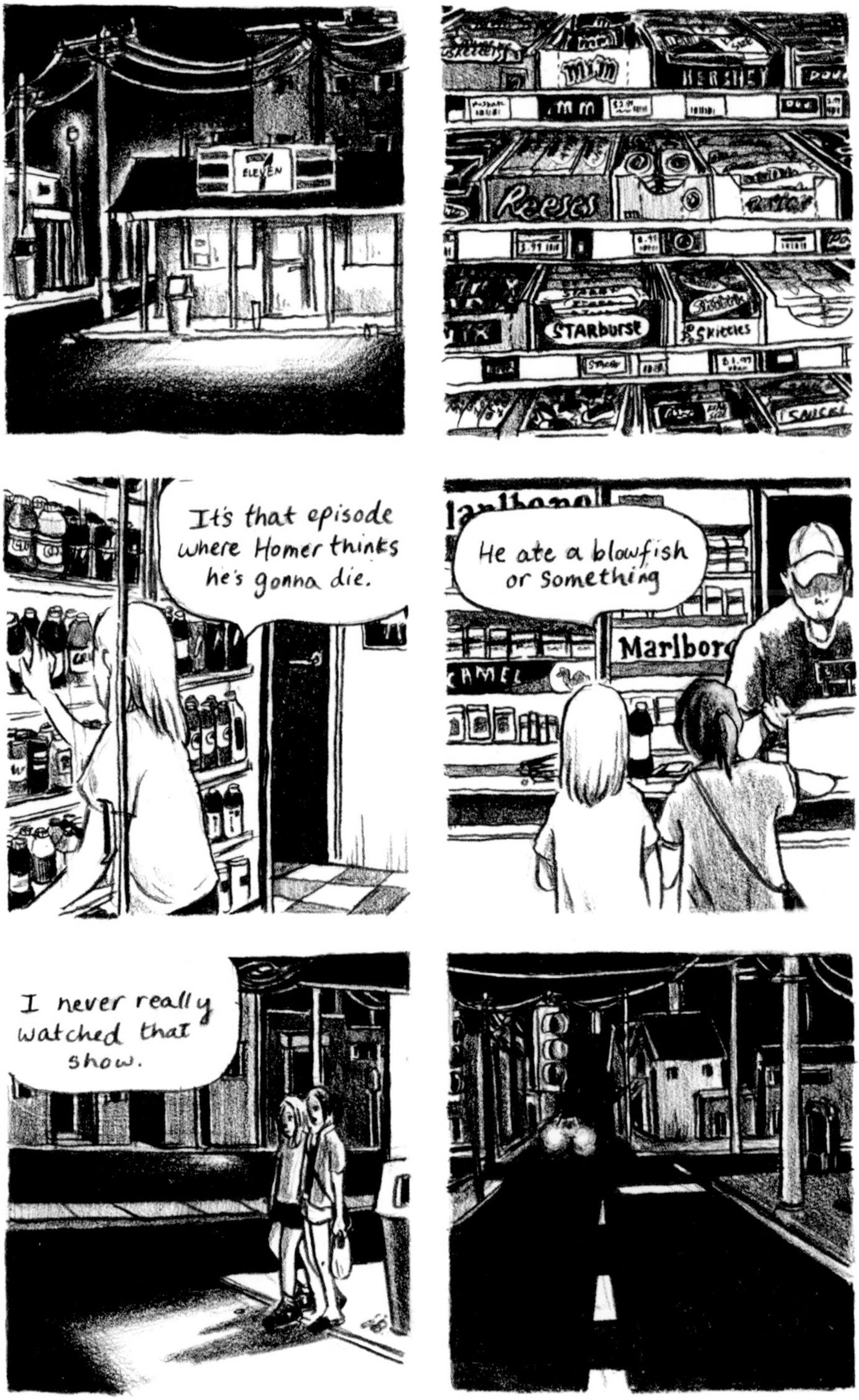
ELEVEN
HERSHEY
Reeses
It's that episode where Homer thinks he's gonna die.
He ate a blowfish or something
Marlboro
CAMEL
I never really watched that show.

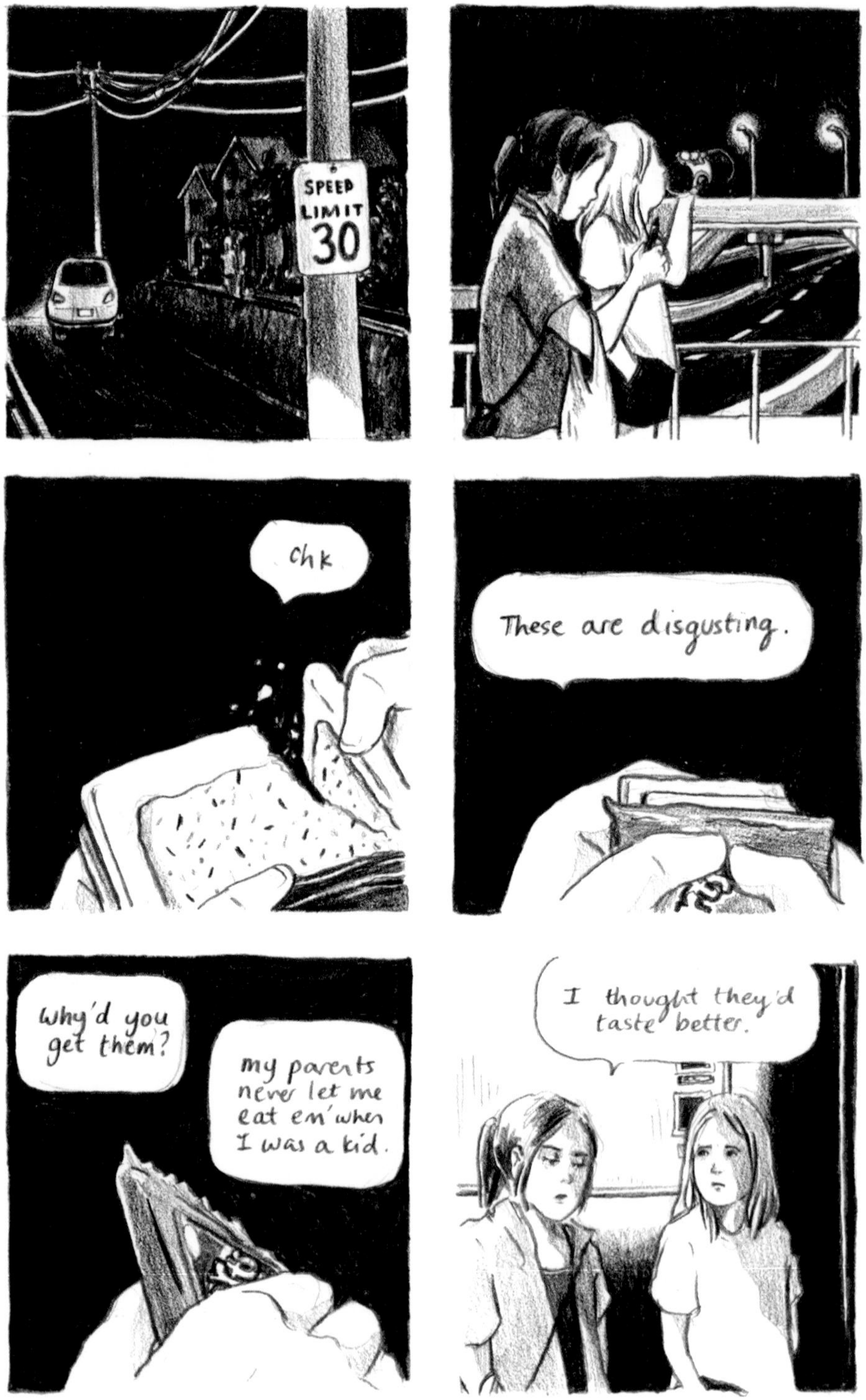
SPEED LIMIT 30
chk
These are disgusting.
why'd you get them?
my parents never let me eat em' when I was a kid.
I thought they'd taste better.

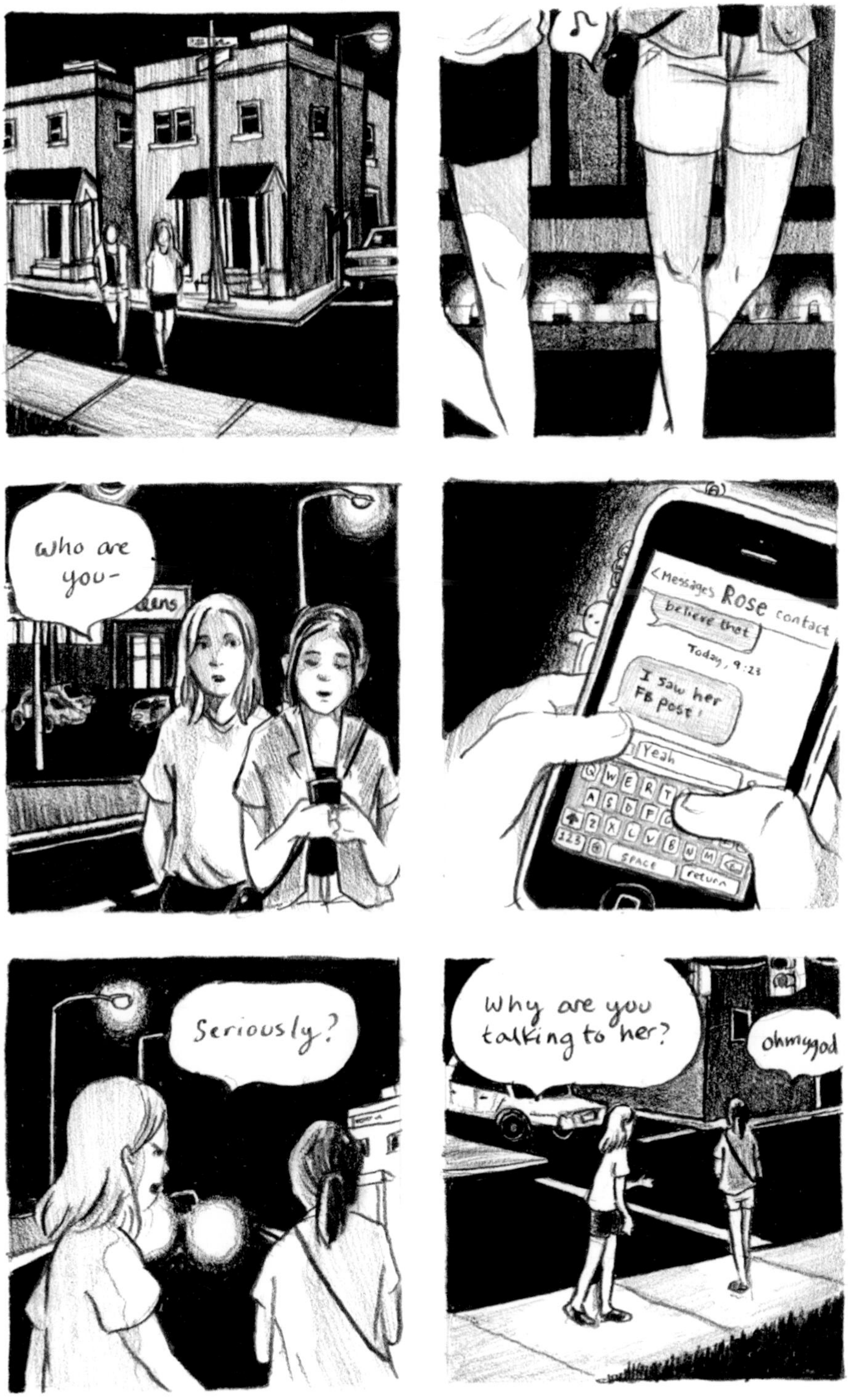
who are you-
<Messages Rose contact
believe that
Today, 9:23
I saw her FB post!
Yeah
Seriously?
Why are you talking to her?
ohmygod

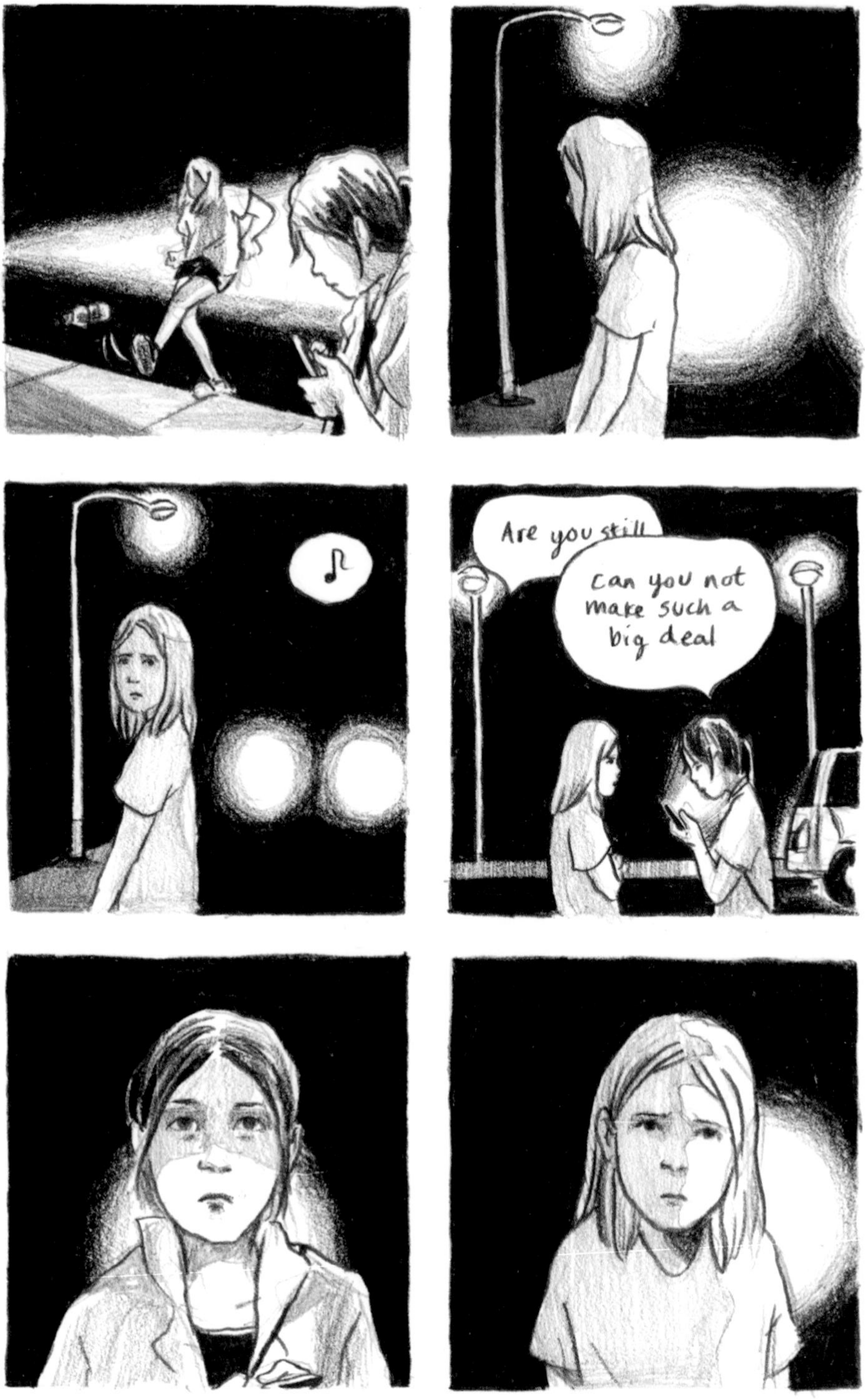
♪
Are you still
Can you not make such a big deal

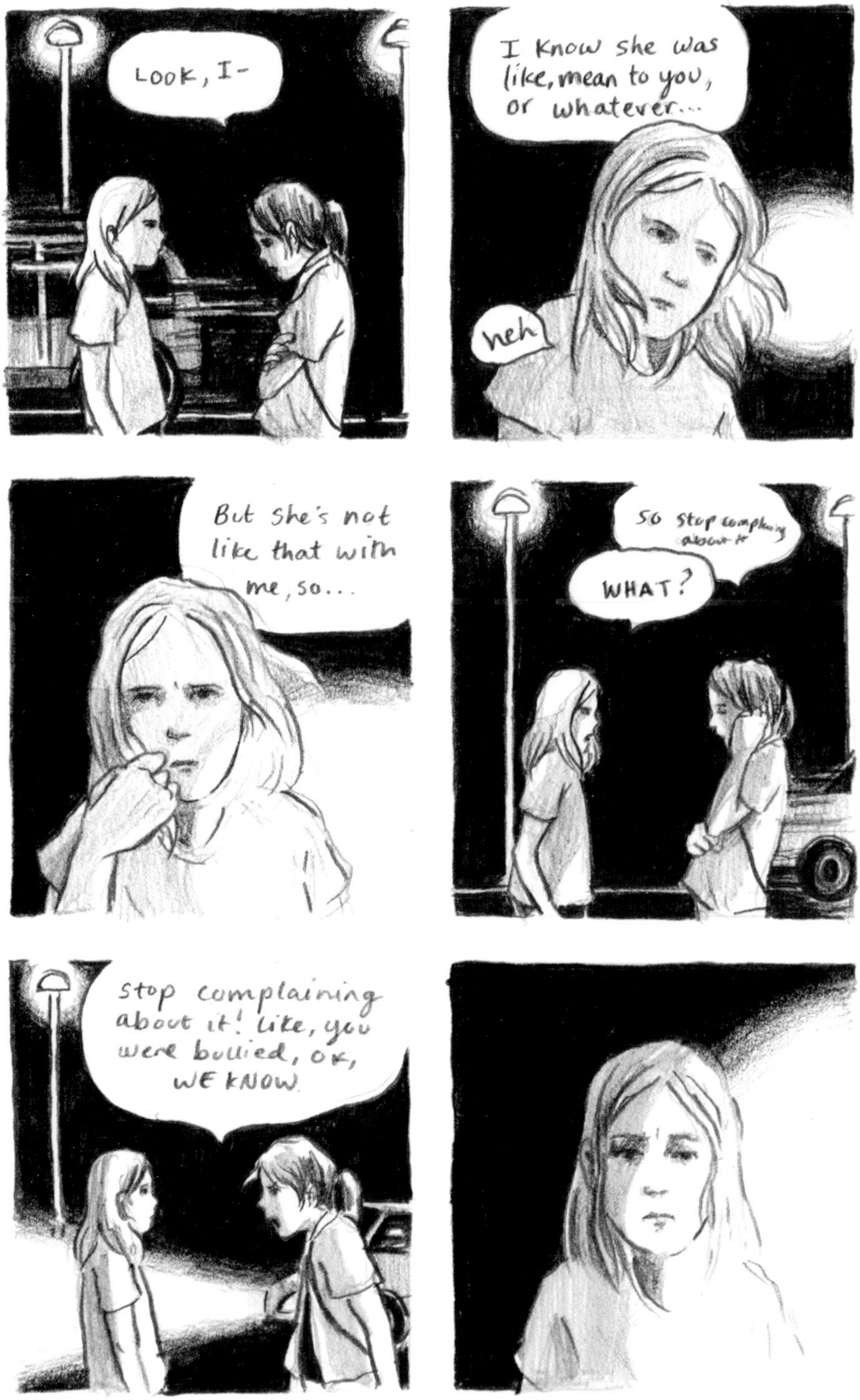

LOOK, I-
I know she was like, mean to you, or whatever...
heh
But she's not like that with me, so...
So stop
WHAT?
stop complaining about it! Like, you were bullied, OK, WE KNOW.

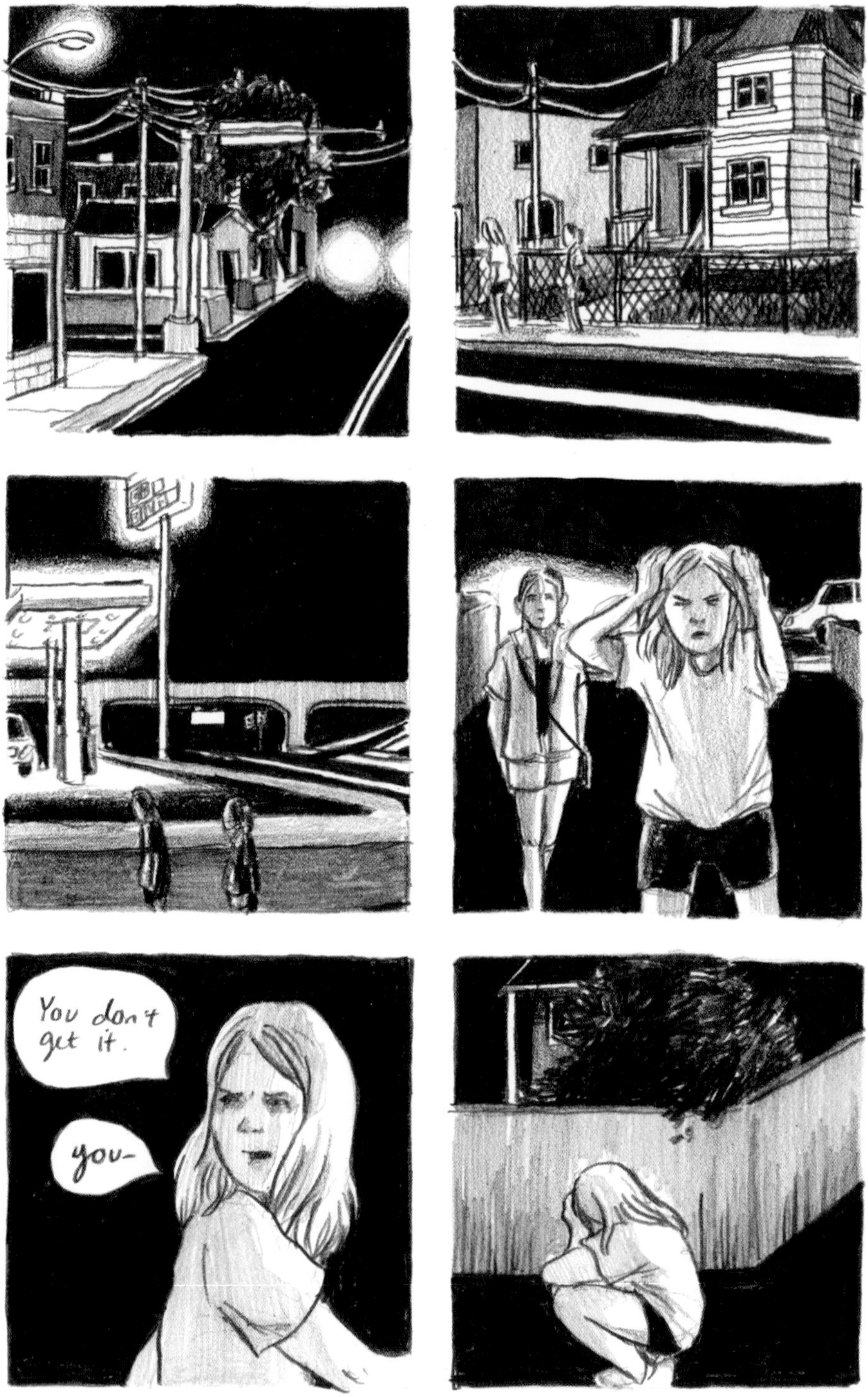
You don't get it.
you-

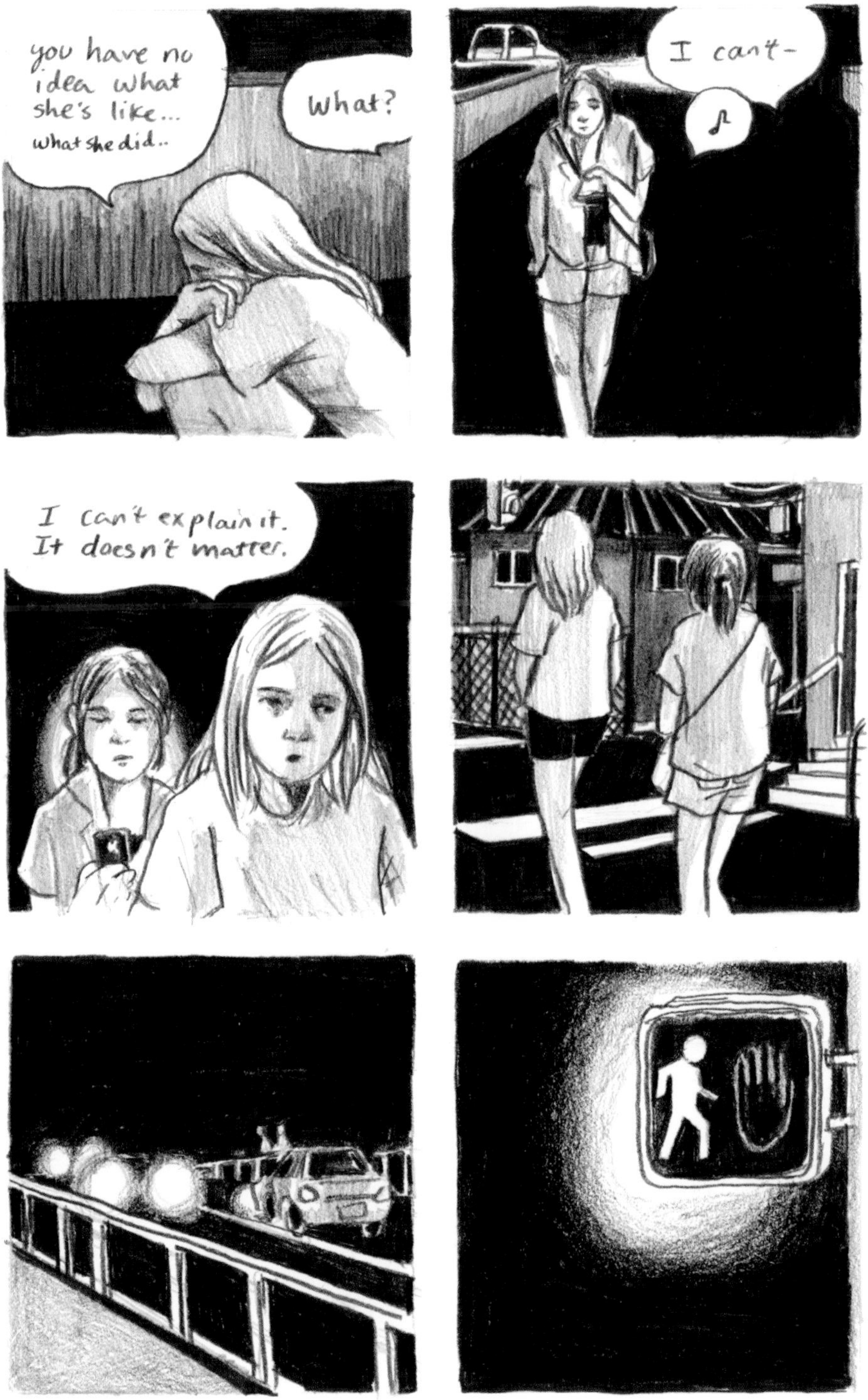
you have no idea what she's like... what she did..
What?
I can't-
♪
I can't explain it. It doesn't matter.

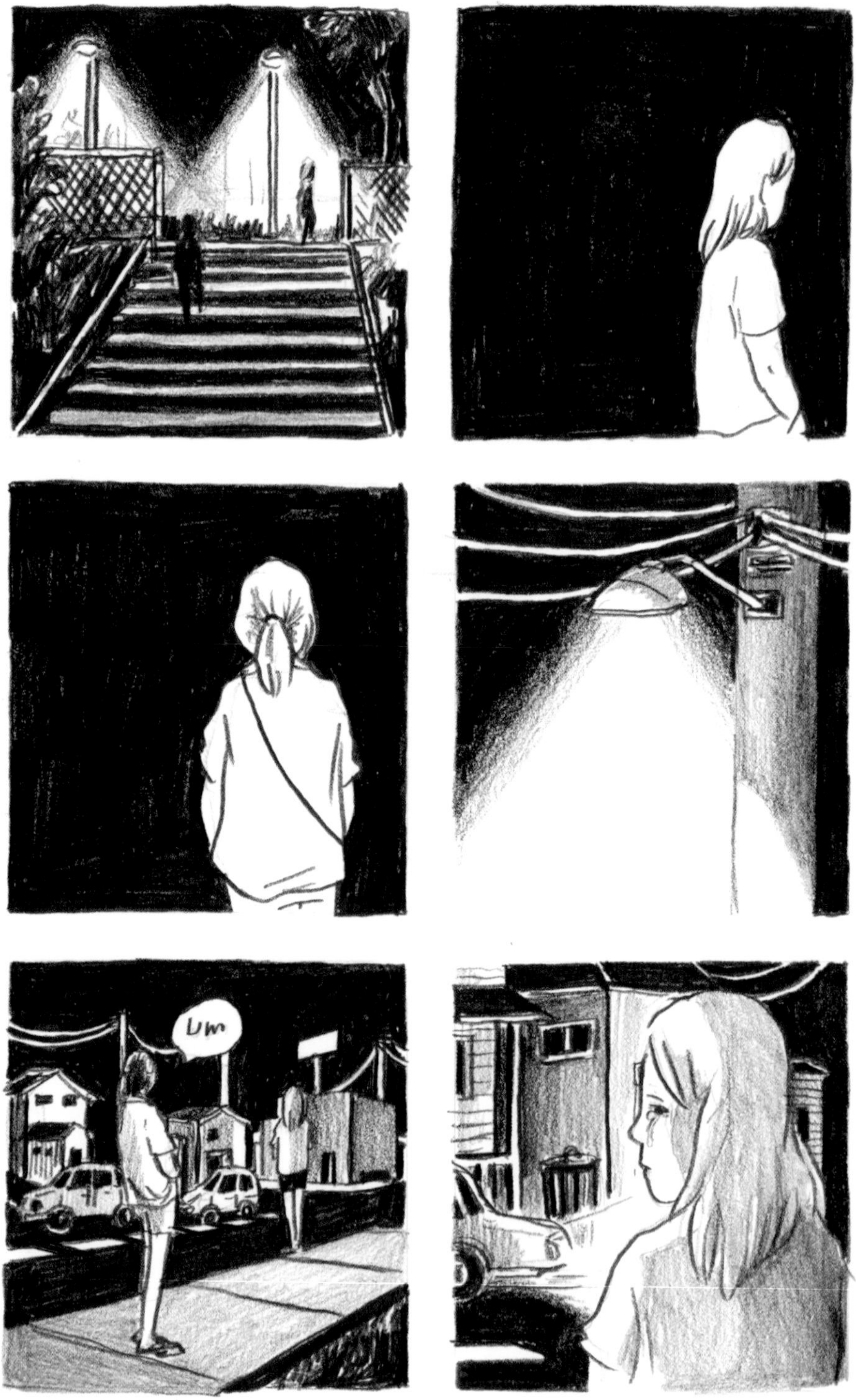
Um

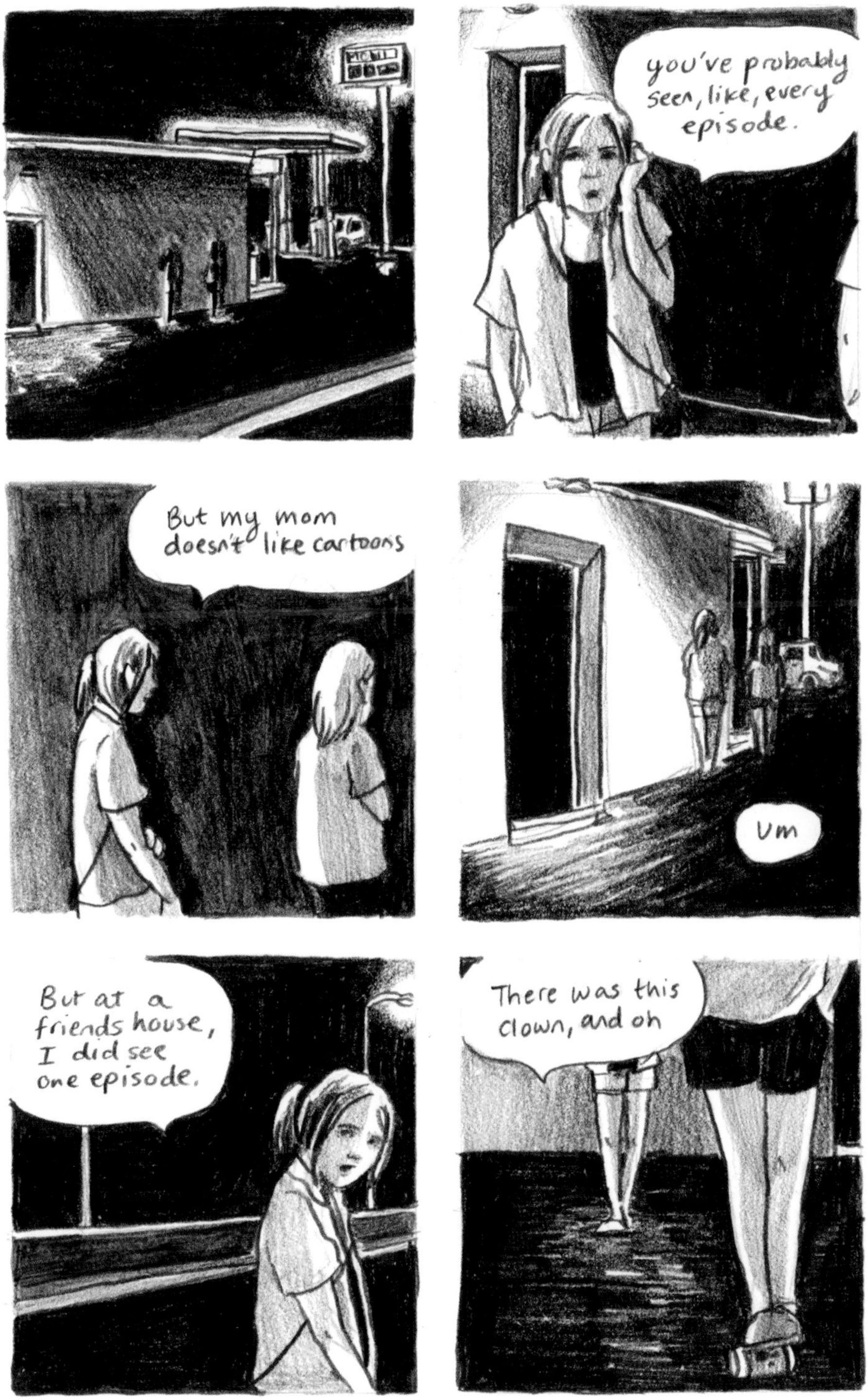
you've probably seen, like, every episode.
But my mom doesn't like cartoons
Um
But at a friends house, I did see one episode.
There was this clown, and oh

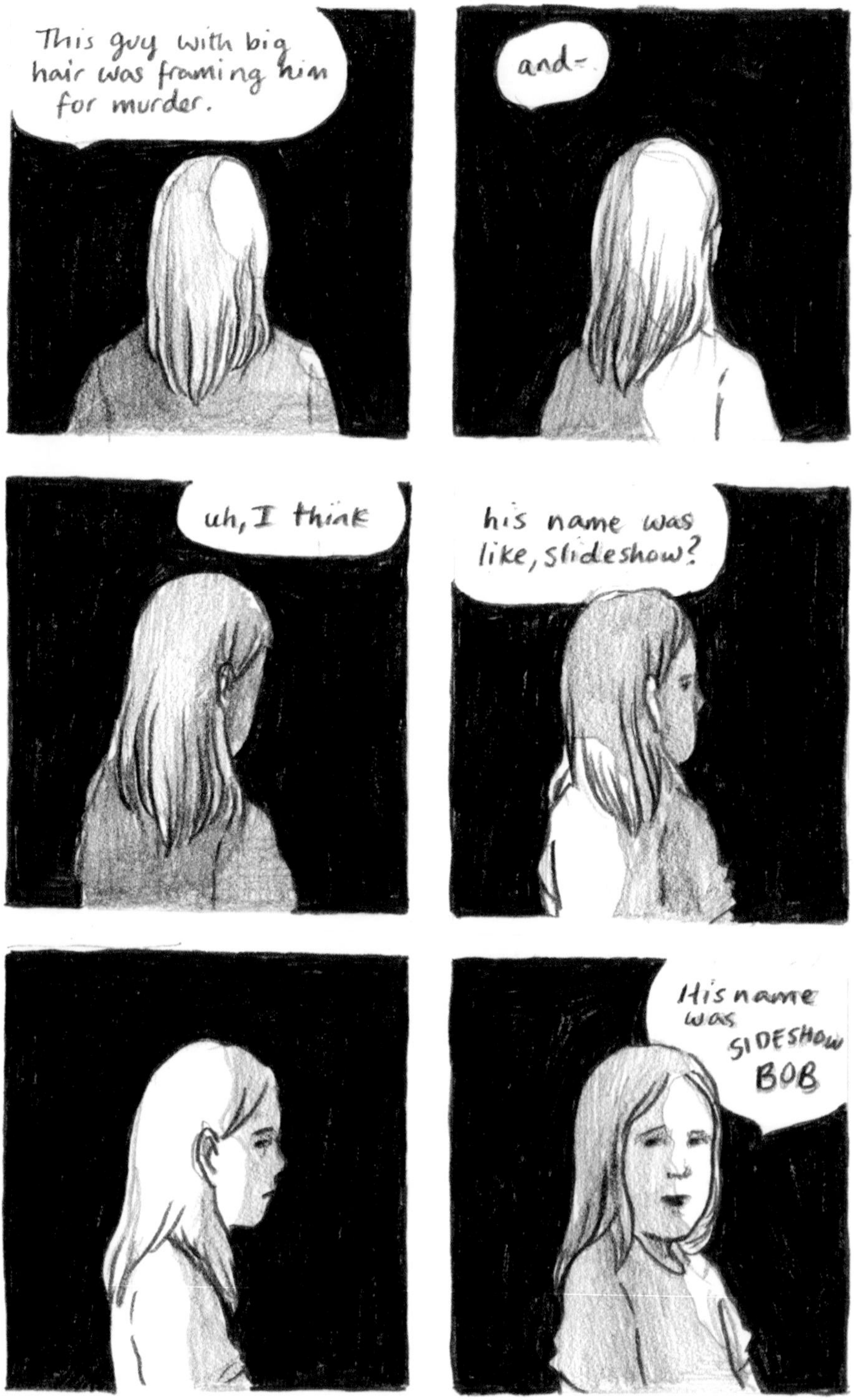
This guy with big hair was framing him for murder.
and-
uh, I think
his name was like, slideshow?
His name was SIDESHOW BOB

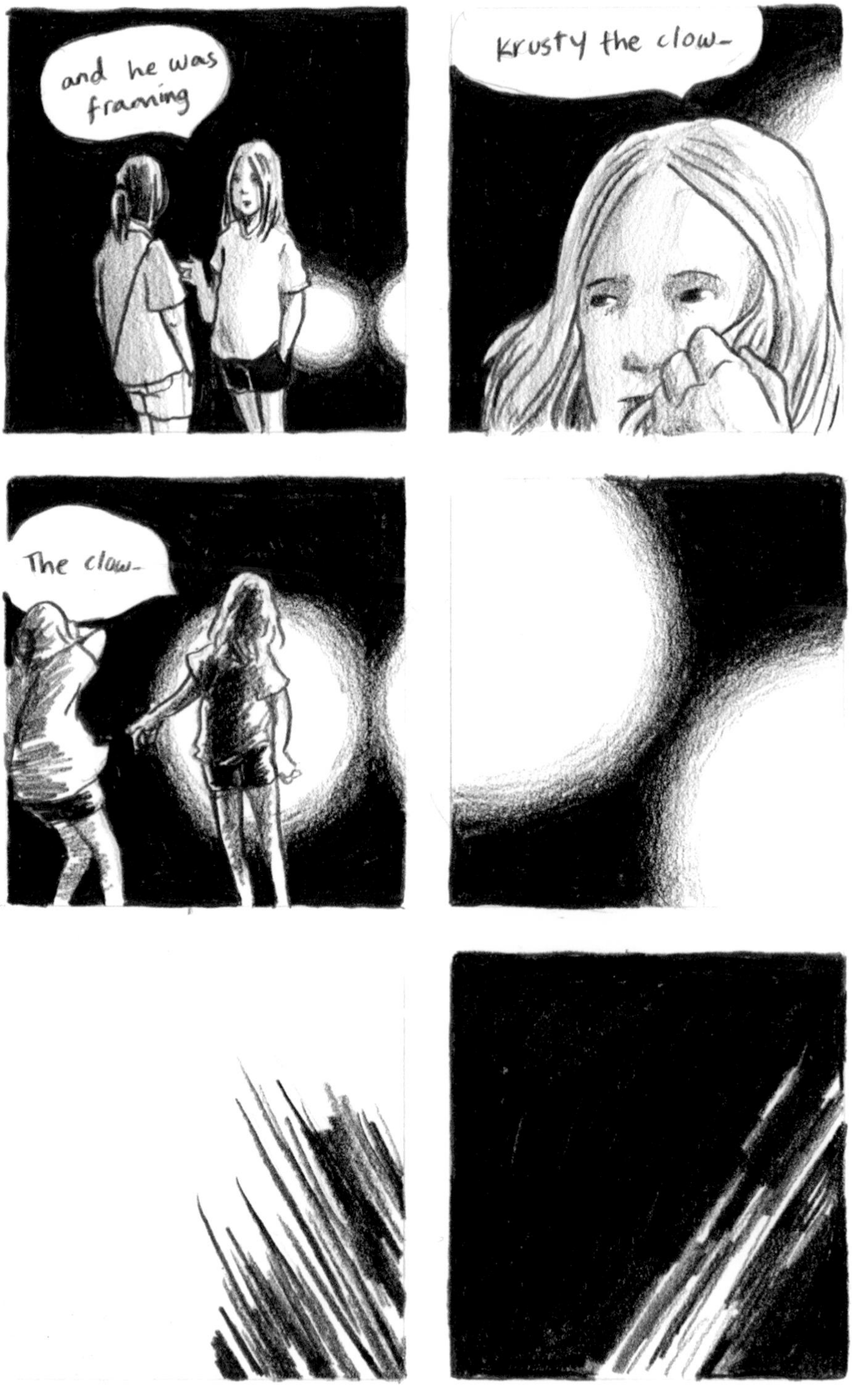
and he was framing
Krusty the clow-
The clow-

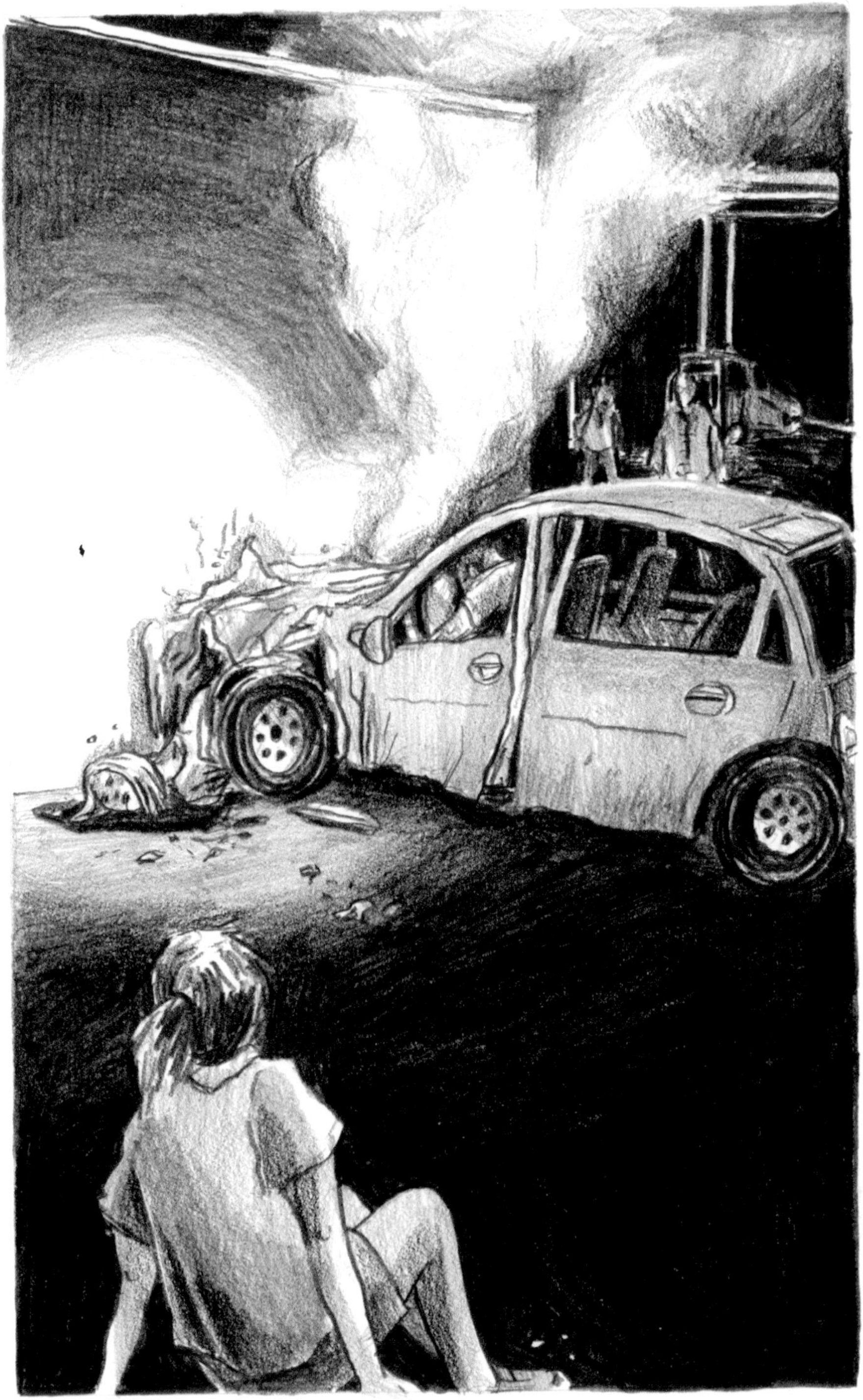

My Name Is... (2014)

This was my first assignment at CCS.
We had to make a page introducing ourselves.

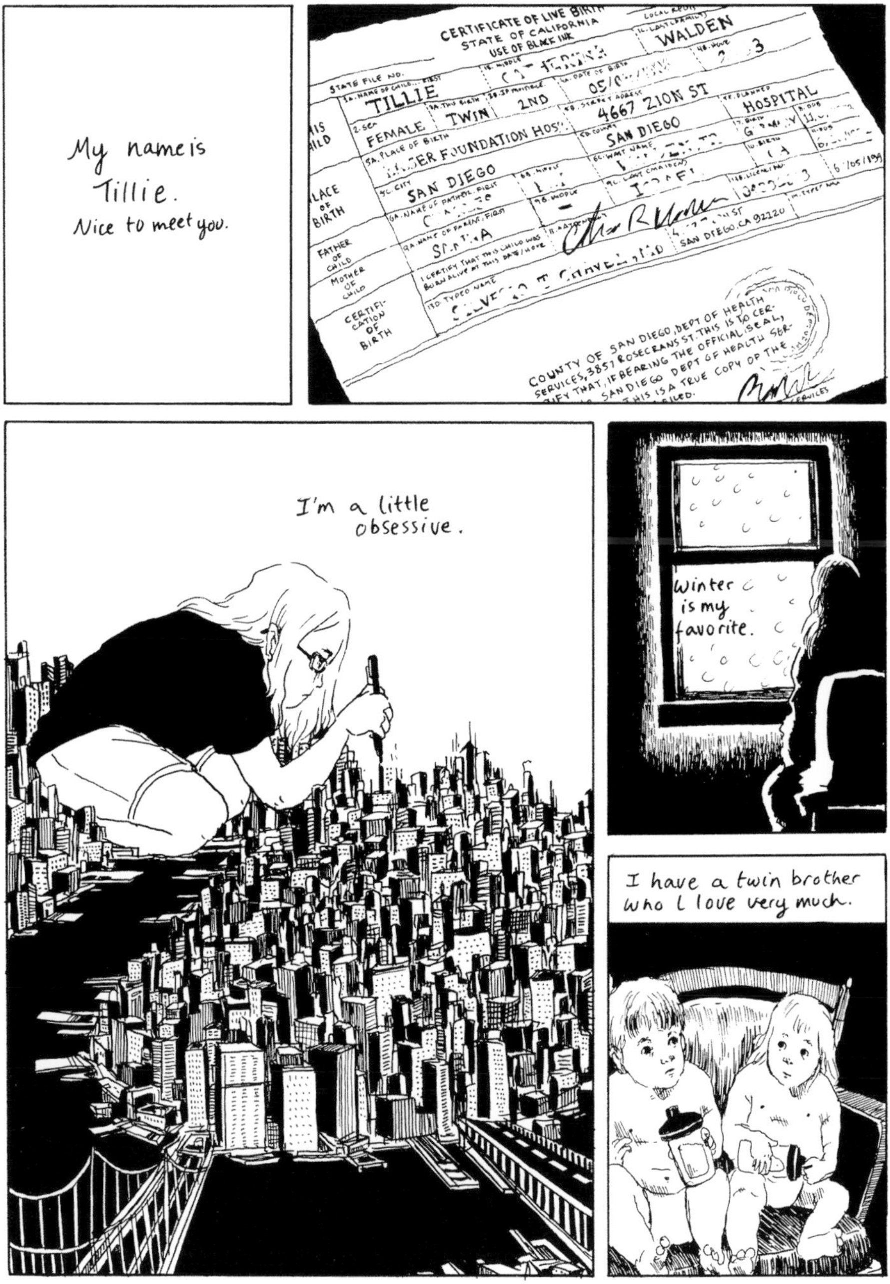
My name is Tillie.
Nice to meet you.
CERTIFICATE OF LIVE BIRTH
STATE OF CALIFORNIA
USE OF BLACK INK
WALDEN
TILLIE
TWIN
2ND
4667 ZION ST
HOSPITAL
FEMALE
SAN DIEGO
SAN DIEGO
STATE FILE NO.
PLACE OF BIRTH
FATHER OF CHILD
MOTHER OF CHILD
CERTIFICATION OF BIRTH
SAN DIEGO, CA 92220
I'm a little obsessive.
Winter is my favorite.
I have a twin brother who I love very much.

Slumberland (2014)

Another CCS assignment, given to me by
Jason Lutes. He asked me to tell an autobio
story in the style of Winsor McCay.

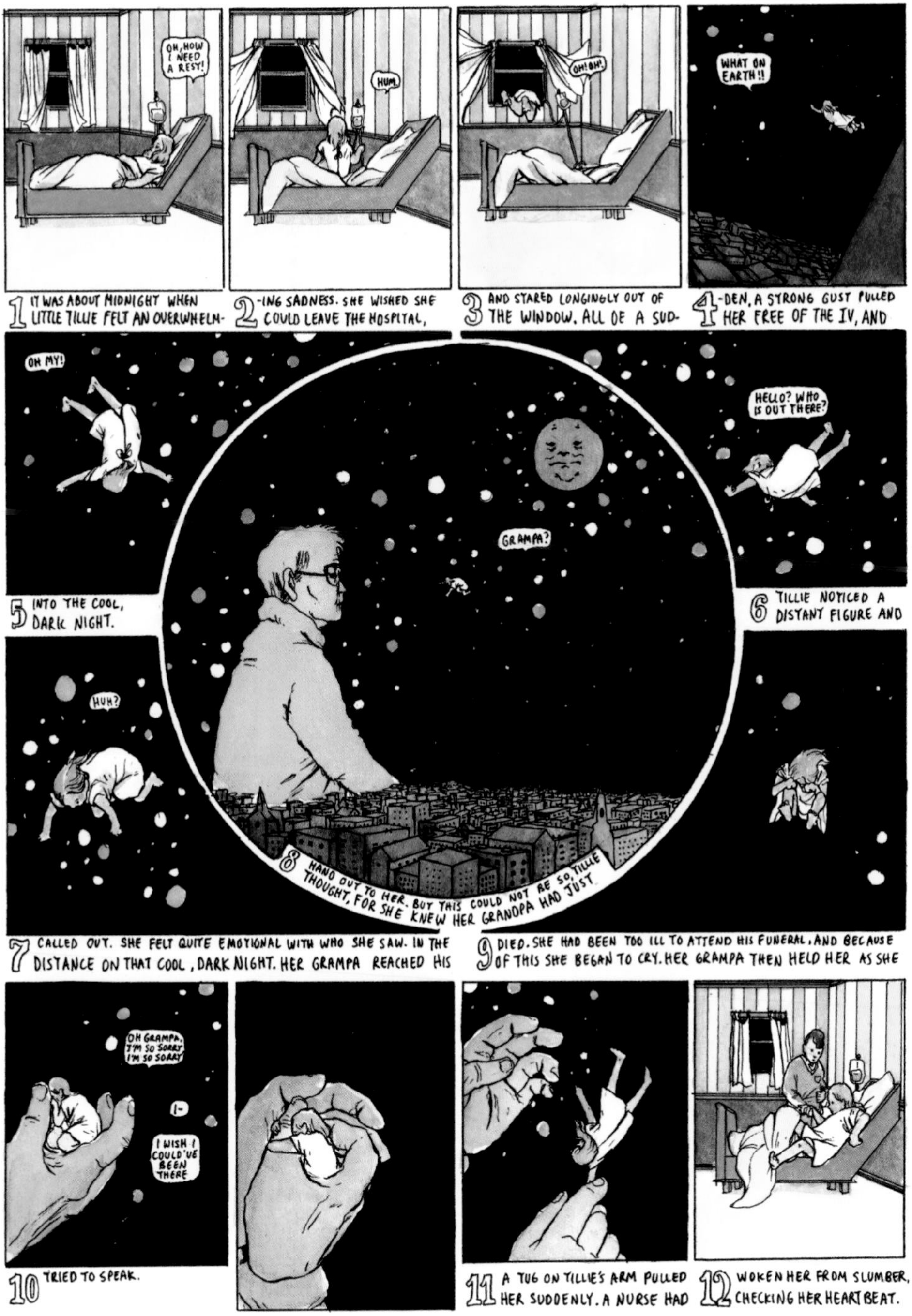
OH, HOW I NEED A REST!
1 IT WAS ABOUT MIDNIGHT WHEN LITTLE TILLIE FELT AN OVERWHELM-
HUM.
2 -ING SADNESS. SHE WISHED SHE COULD LEAVE THE HOSPITAL,
OH! OH!
3 AND STARED LONGINGLY OUT OF THE WINDOW. ALL OF A SUD-
WHAT ON EARTH!!
4 -DEN, A STRONG GUST PULLED HER FREE OF THE IV, AND
OH MY!
5 INTO THE COOL, DARK NIGHT.
HELLO? WHO IS OUT THERE?
6 TILLIE NOTICED A DISTANT FIGURE AND
HUH?
7 CALLED OUT. SHE FELT QUITE EMOTIONAL WITH WHO SHE SAW. IN THE DISTANCE ON THAT COOL, DARK NIGHT. HER GRAMPA REACHED HIS
GRAMPA?
8 HAND OUT TO HER. BUT THIS COULD NOT BE SO, TILLIE THOUGHT, FOR SHE KNEW HER GRANDPA HAD JUST
9 DIED. SHE HAD BEEN TOO ILL TO ATTEND HIS FUNERAL. AND BECAUSE OF THIS SHE BEGAN TO CRY. HER GRAMPA THEN HELD HER AS SHE
OH GRAMPA, I'M SO SORRY I'M SO SORRY
I-
I WISH I COULD'VE BEEN THERE
10 TRIED TO SPEAK.
11 A TUG ON TILLIE'S ARM PULLED HER SUDDENLY. A NURSE HAD
12 WOKEN HER FROM SLUMBER, CHECKING HER HEARTBEAT.

Cramped (2014)

I had just moved to Vermont. I was using the grid a lot and spot color, which would show up in I Love This Part. This was one of my first times drawing big people and tiny buildings.

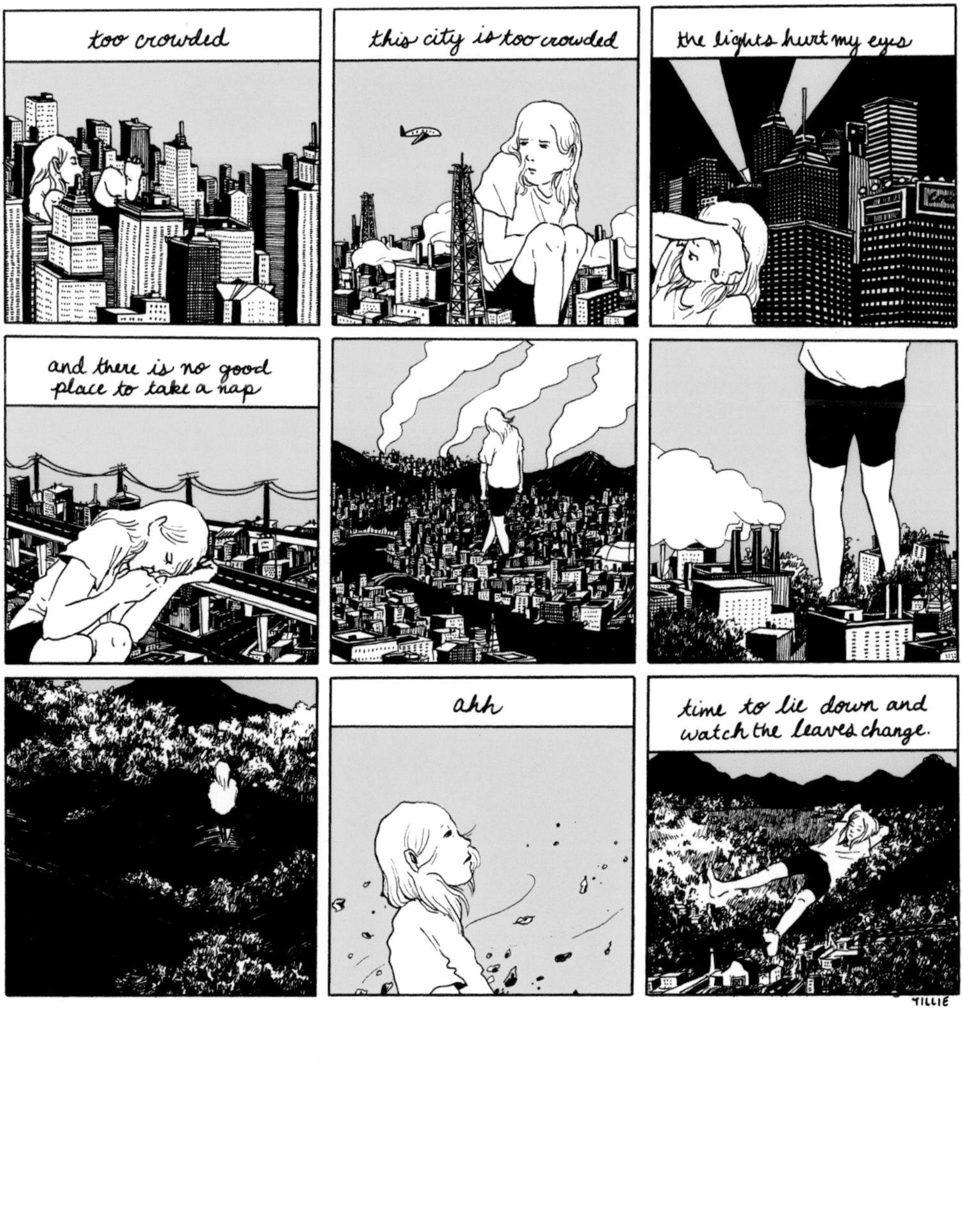
too crowded
this city is too crowded
the lights hurt my eyes
and there is no good place to take a nap
ahh
time to lie down and watch the leaves change.
TILLIE

Journal Entry (2014)
I had just started keeping a sketchbook.
I was trying to make faster and looser comics.

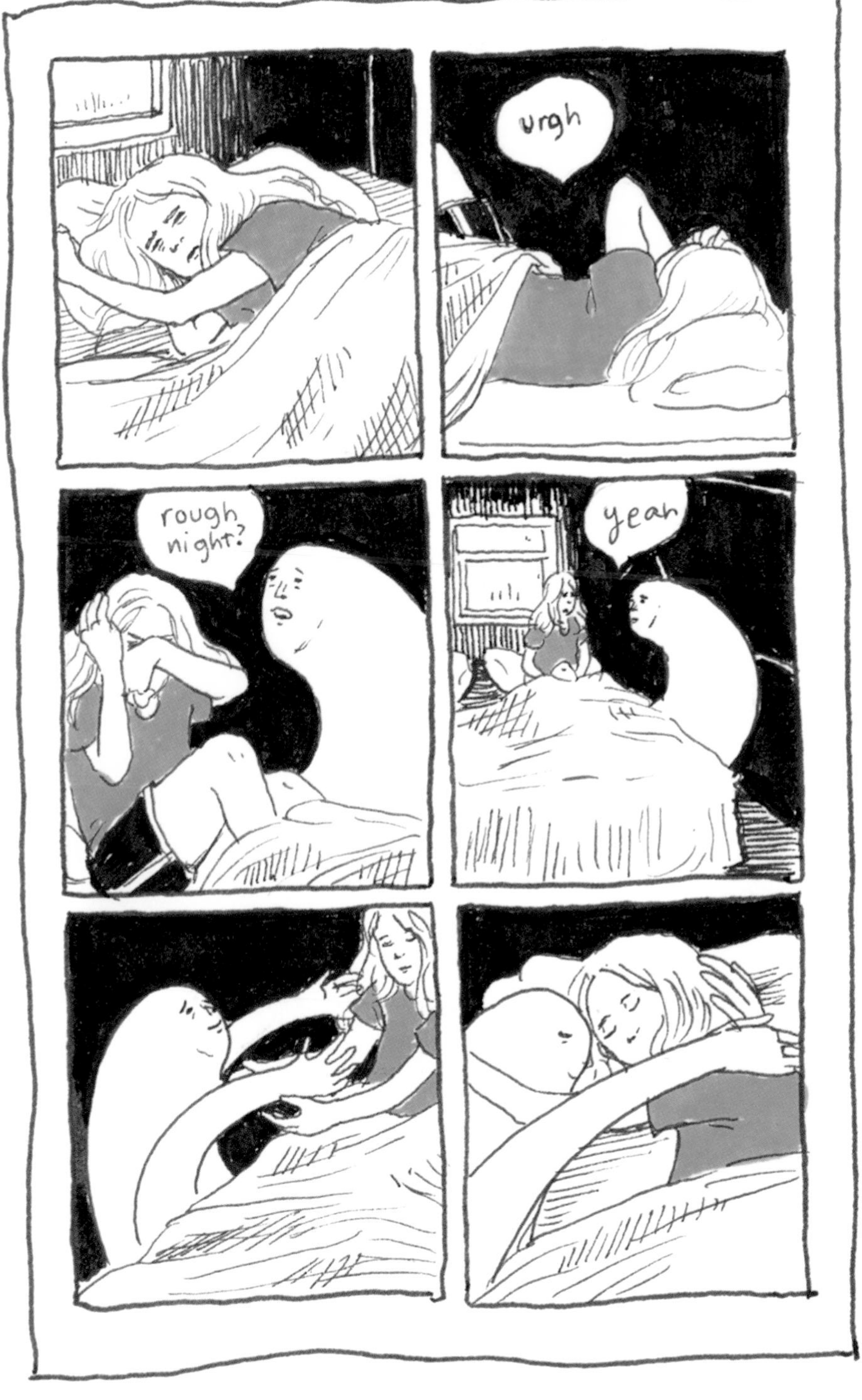
urgh
rough night?
yeah

The Graduate (2014)

I was 18, a little distraught about being on my own. Comics helped.

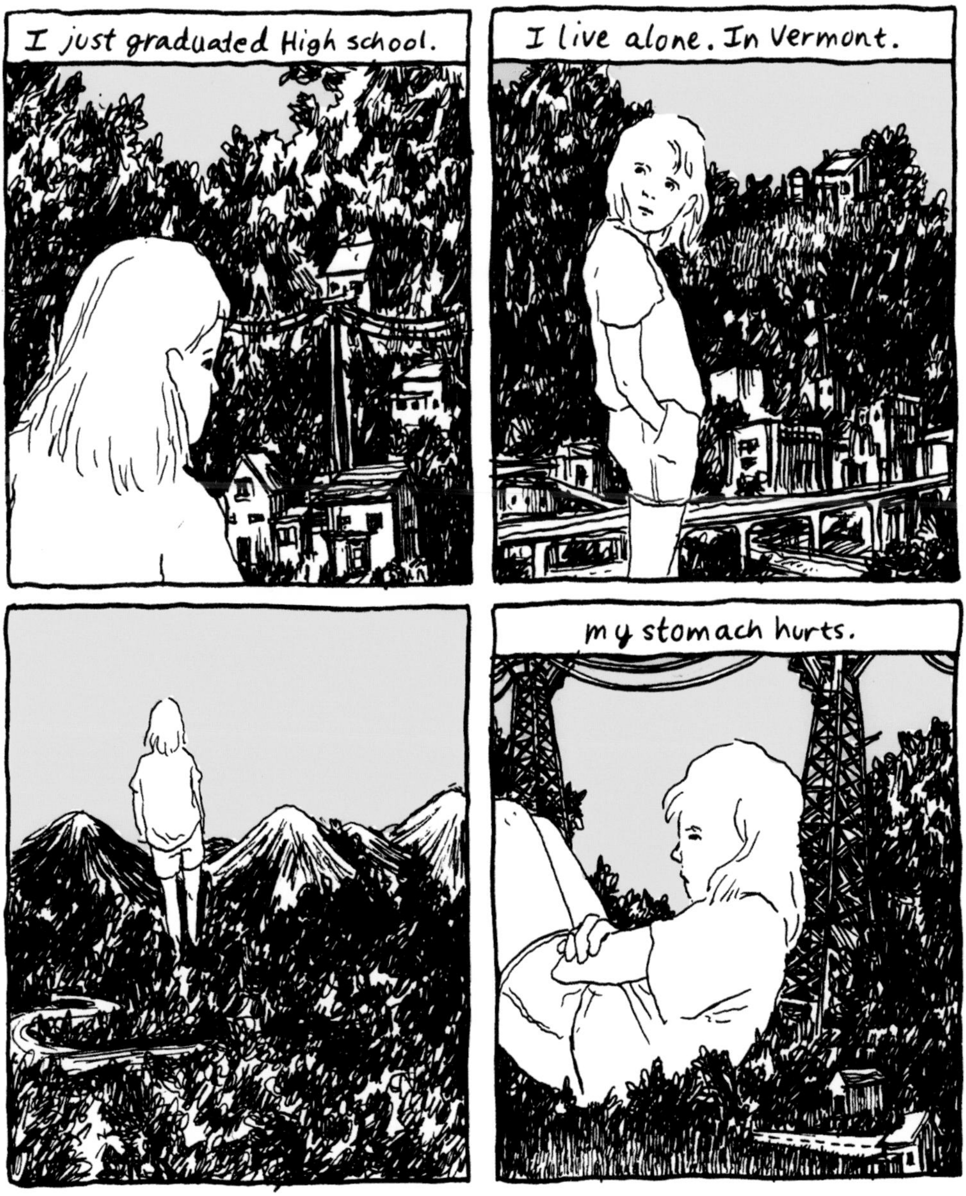
I just graduated High school.
I live alone. In Vermont.
my stomach hurts.

Ghibli (2015)

This was commissioned for an exhibition at Orbital Comics. All my work is deeply influenced by Studio Ghibli movies.

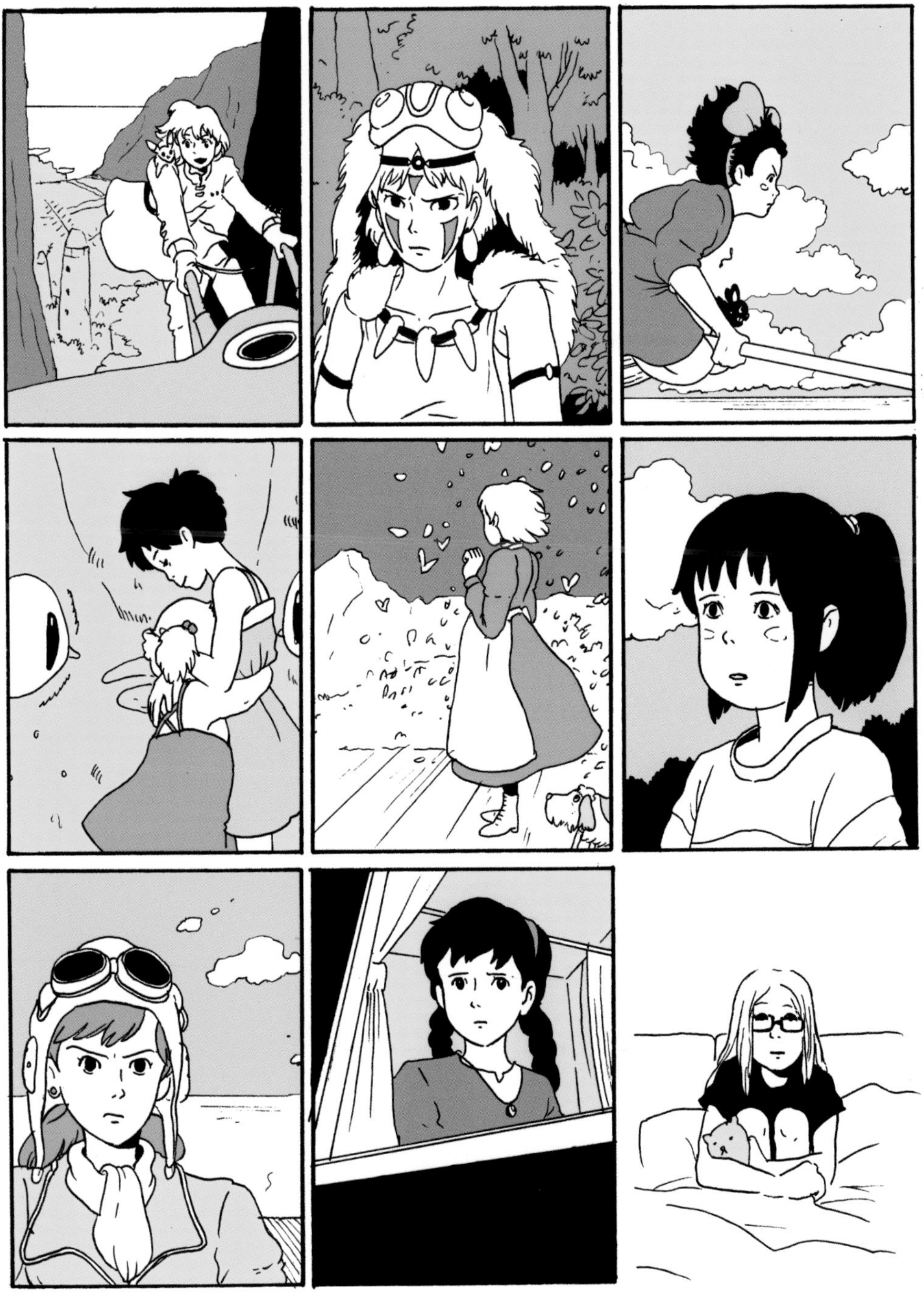

Lost Trees (2015)

I made this for a comics competition on tumblr, but in the end I didn't submit it. I like this comic!

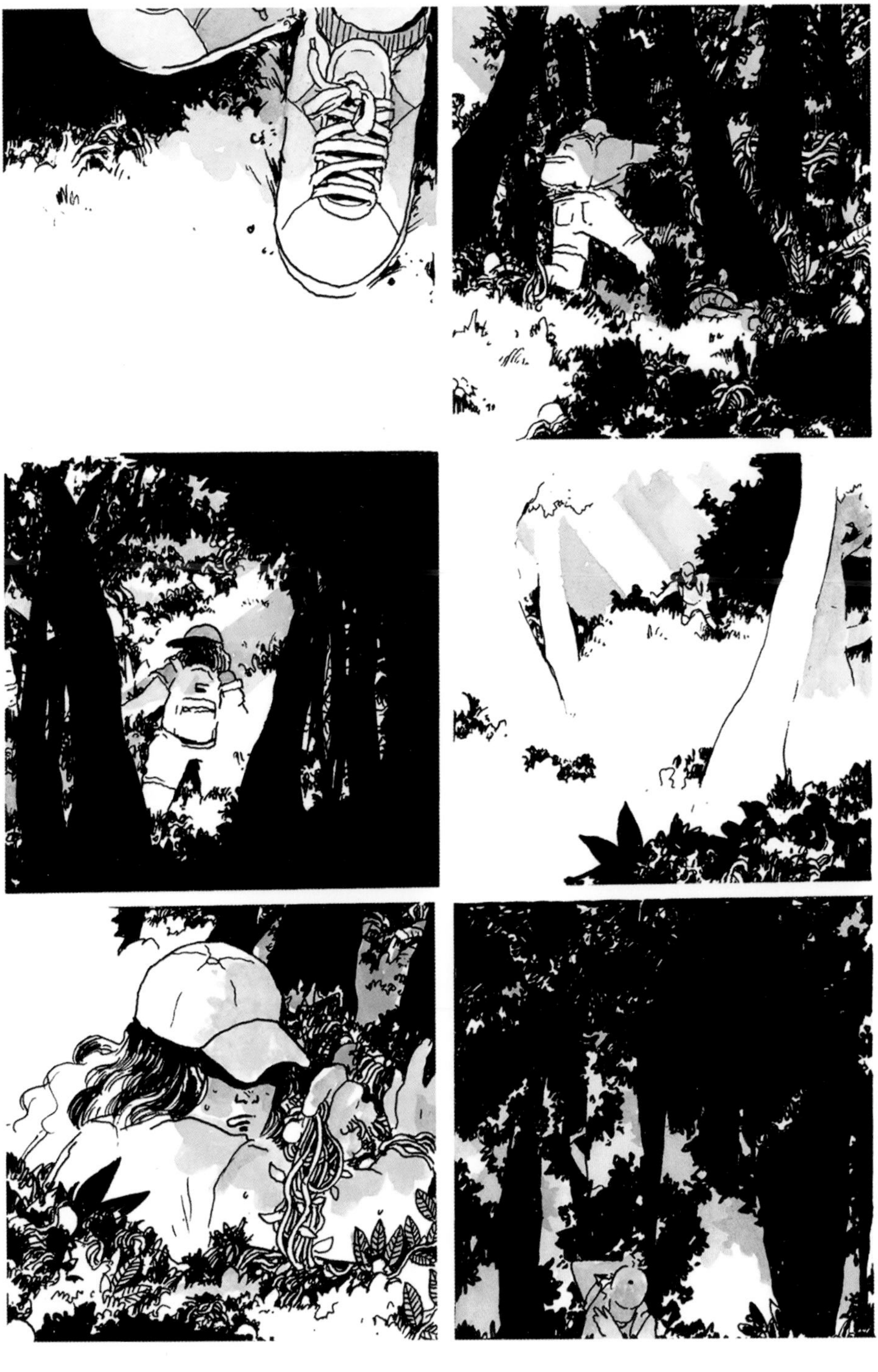

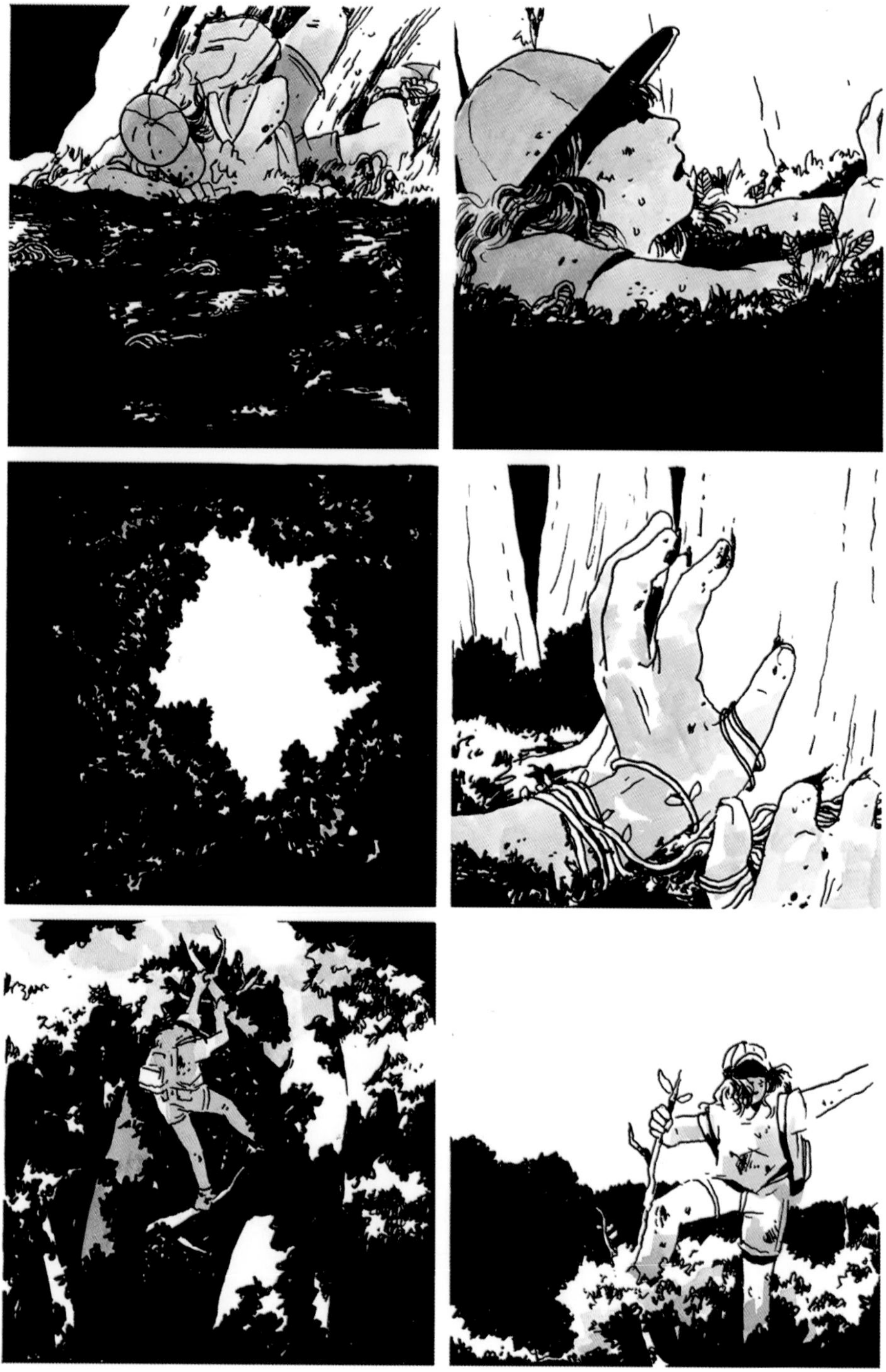

Dreaming (2015)

Drew this for an assignment in my
2nd year at CCS. It was based on a real
dream I had at the time. I'm still
really proud of it, apart from those chairs...

dreaming

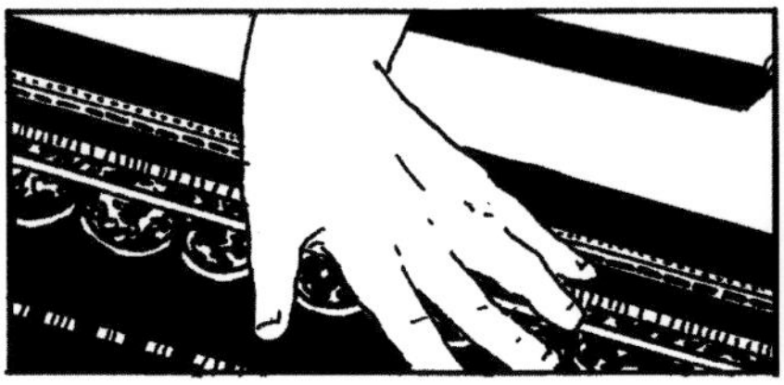

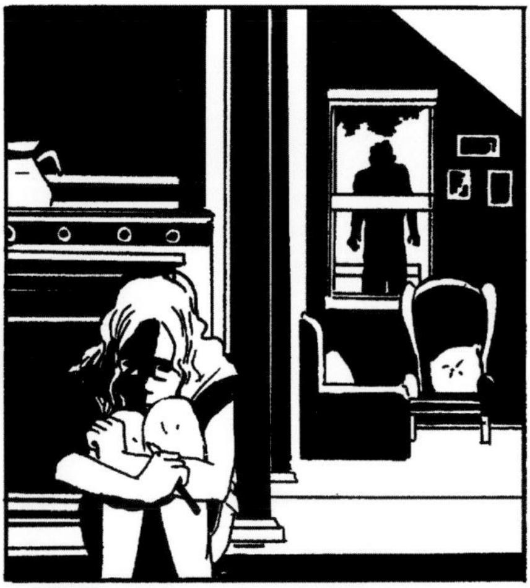

TILLIE WALDEN

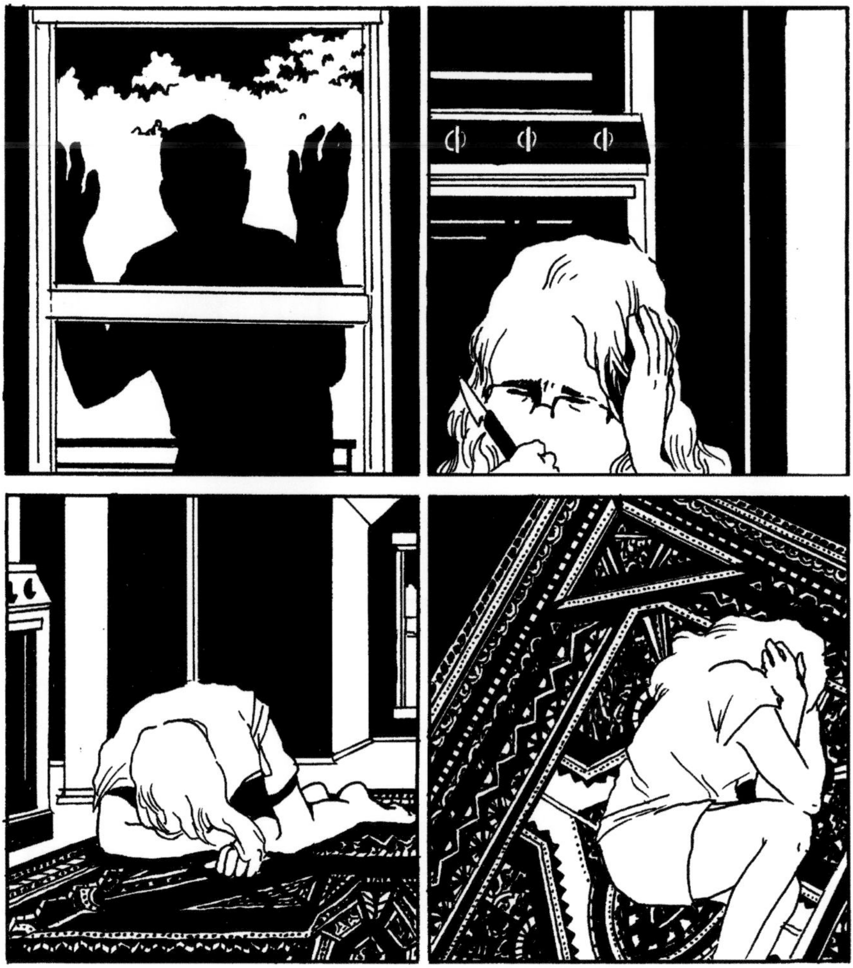

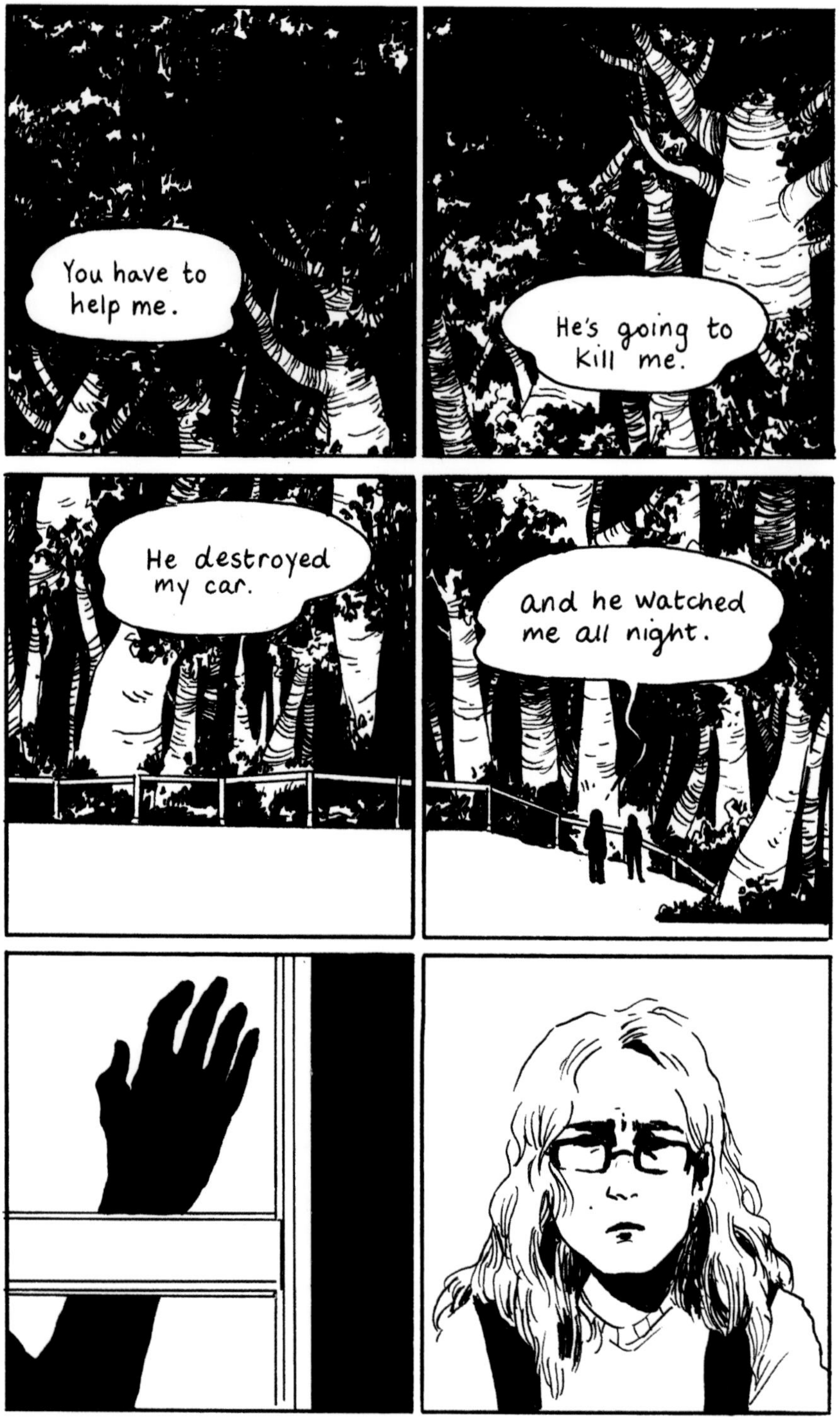
You have to help me.
He's going to kill me.
He destroyed my car.
and he watched me all night.

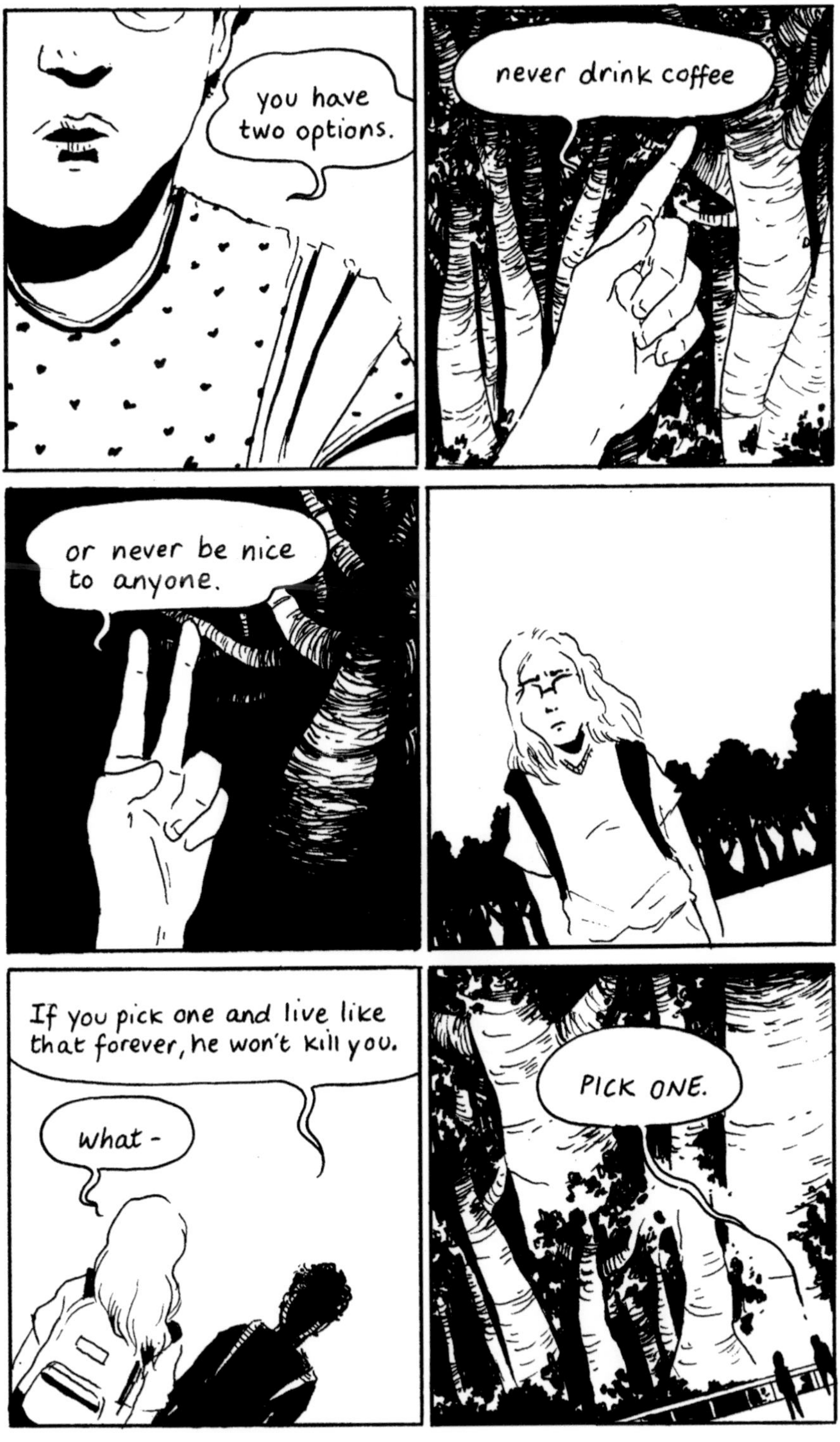
you have two options.
never drink coffee
or never be nice to anyone.
If you pick one and live like that forever, he won't kill you.
what -
PICK ONE.

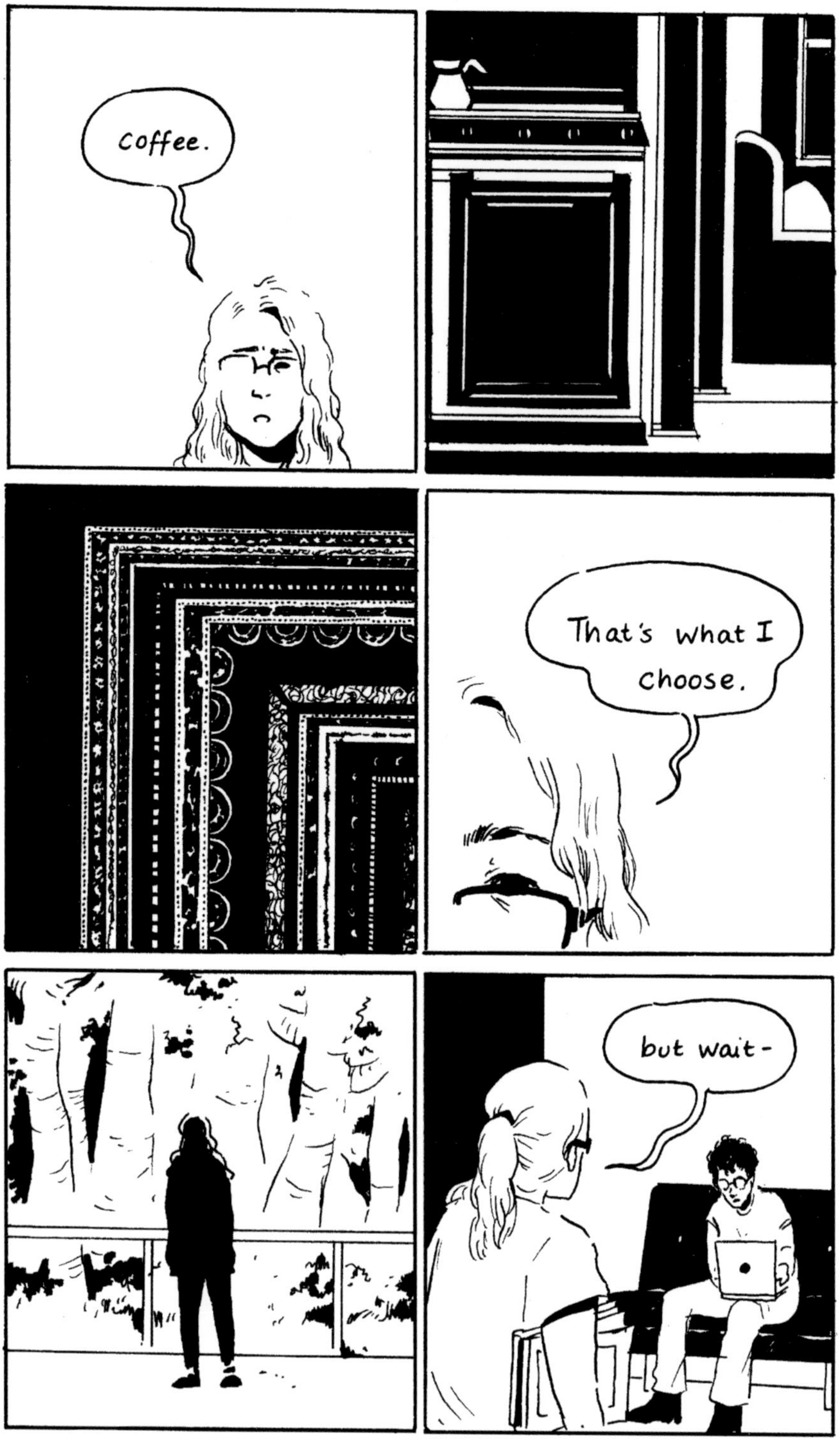
Coffee.
That's what I choose.
but wait-

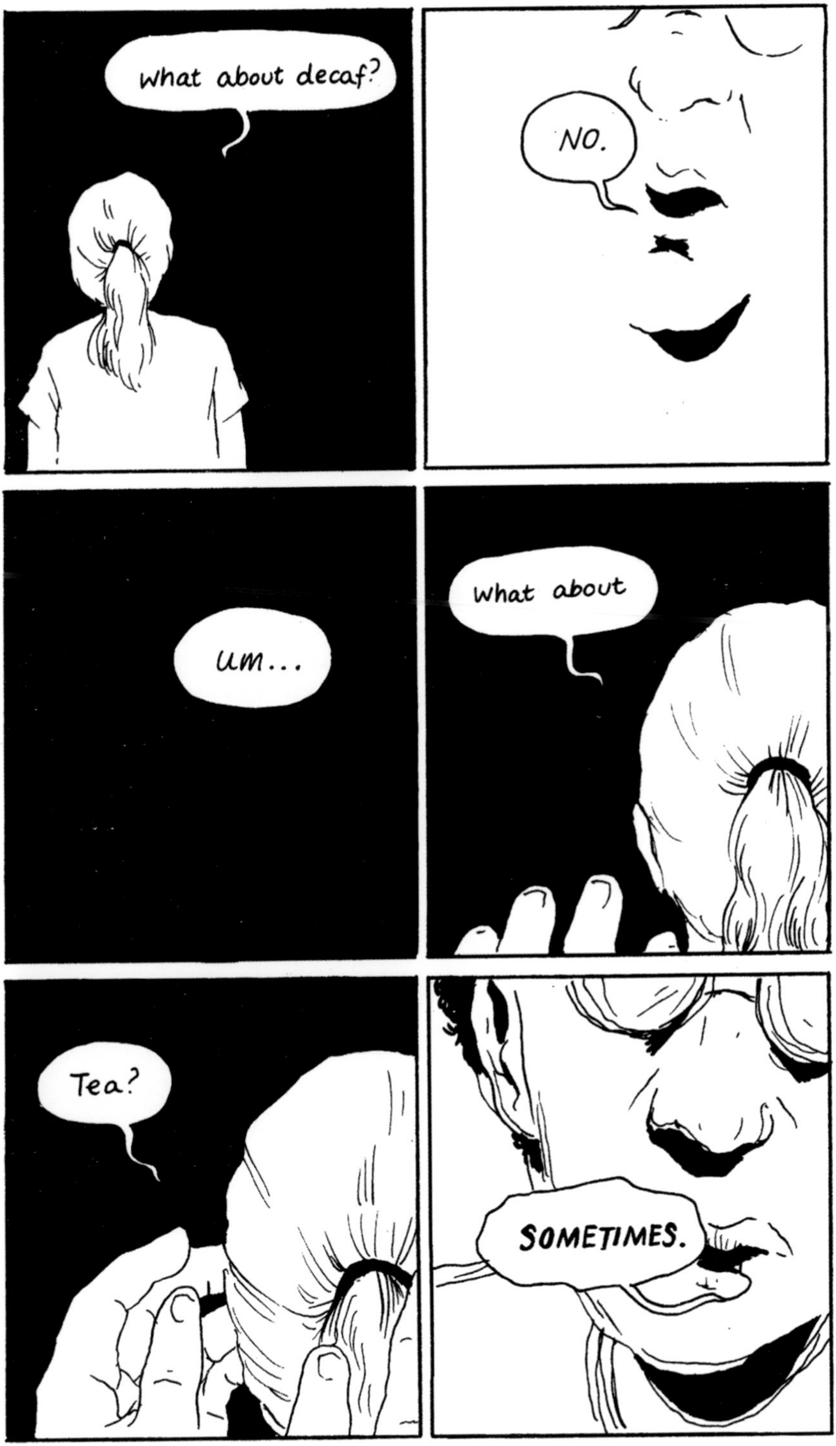
What about decaf?
NO.
um...
What about
Tea?
SOMETIMES.

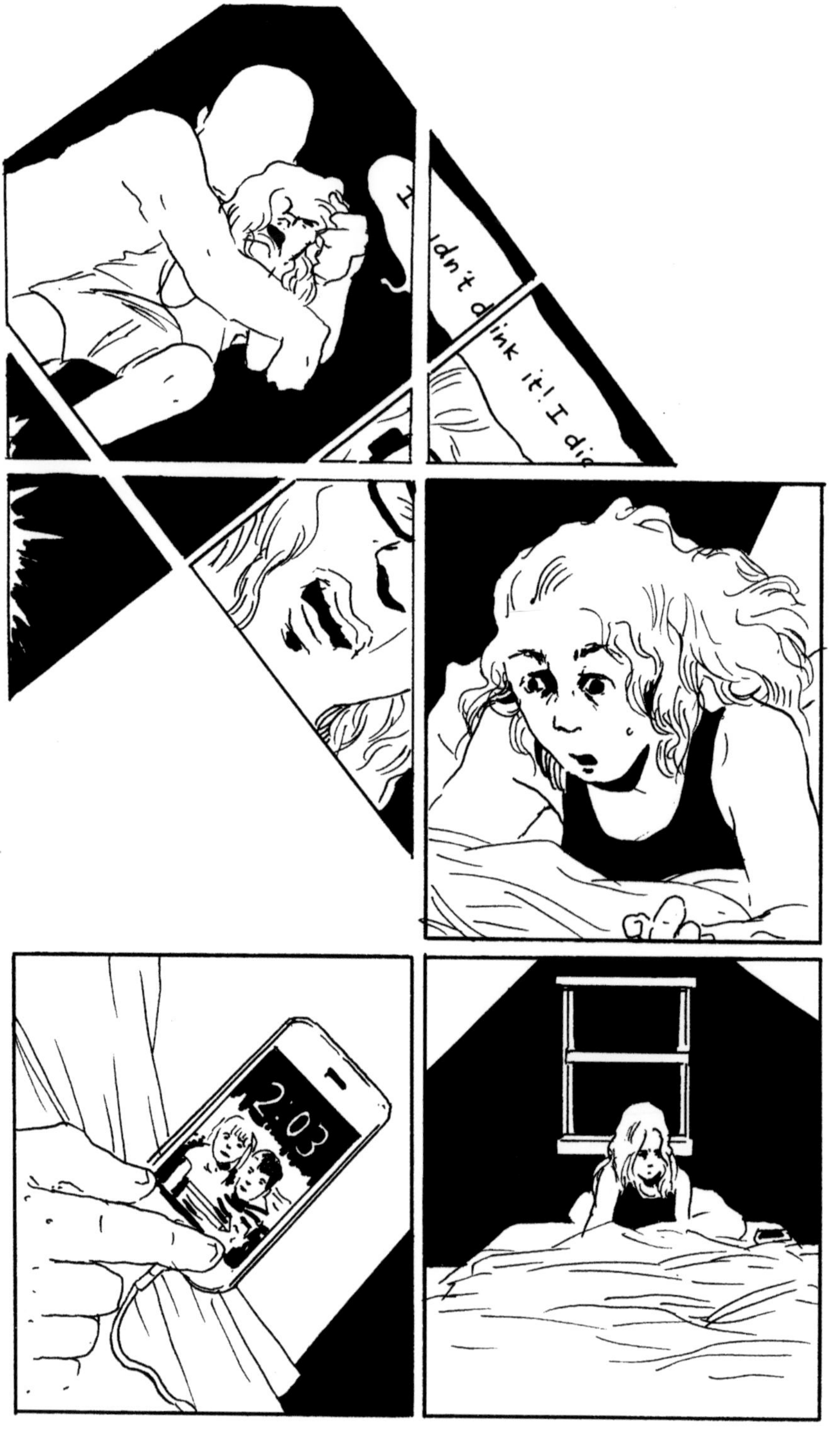
I dn't d ink it! I di
2:03

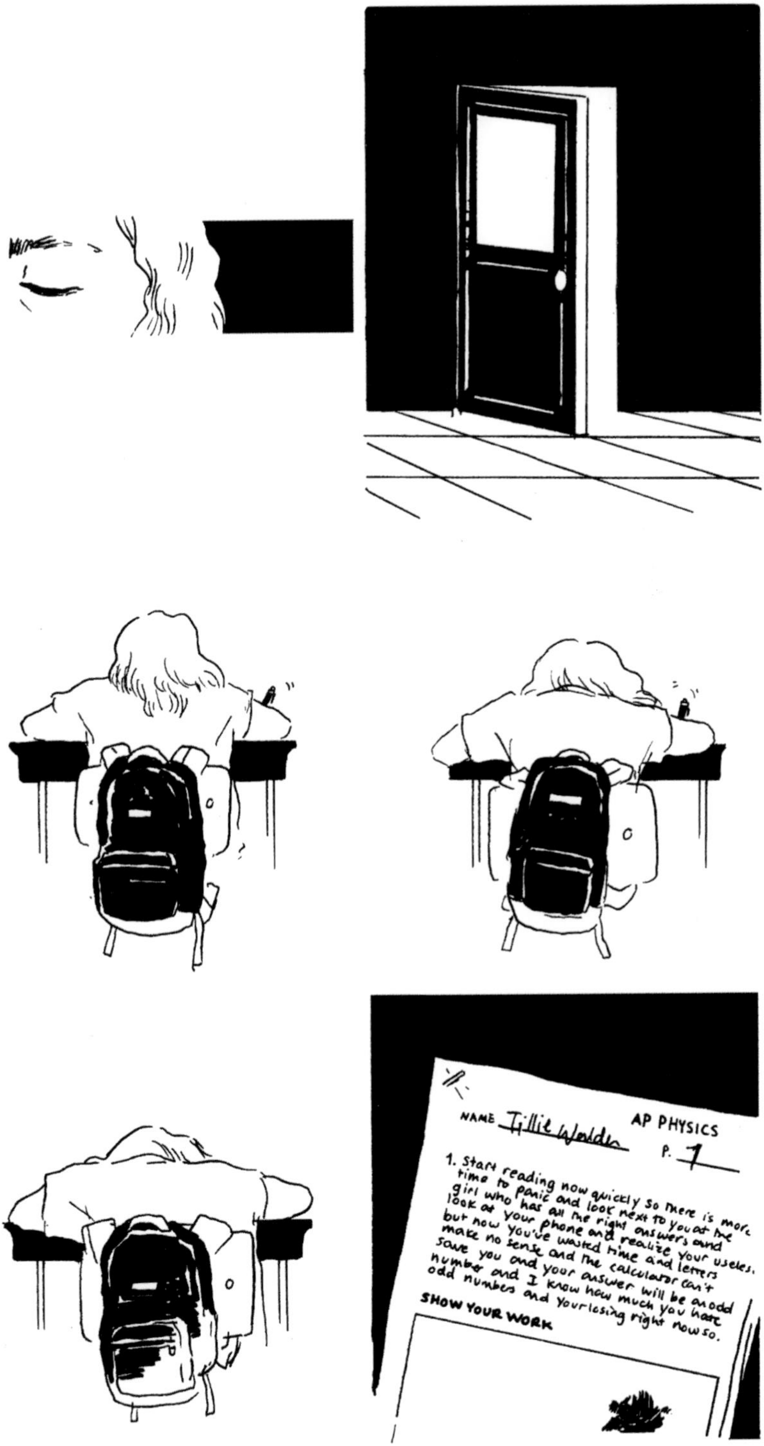
NAME Tillie Walden
AP PHYSICS
P. 7
1. Start reading now quickly so there is more time to panic and look next to you at the girl who has all the right answers and look at your phone and realize your useles. but now you've wasted time and letters make no sense and the calculator can't save you and your answer will be an odd number and I know how much you hate odd numbers and your losing right now so.
SHOW YOUR WORK

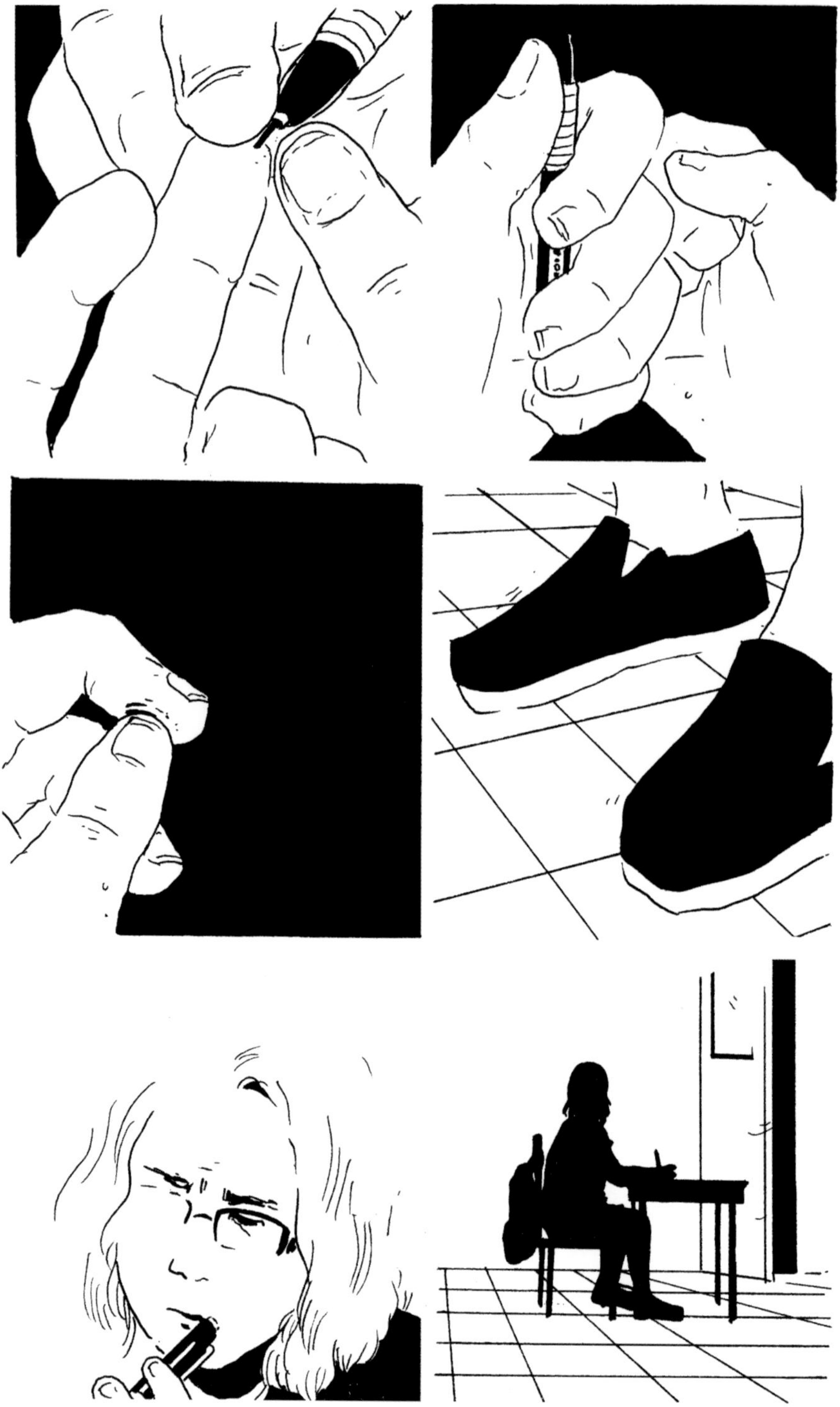

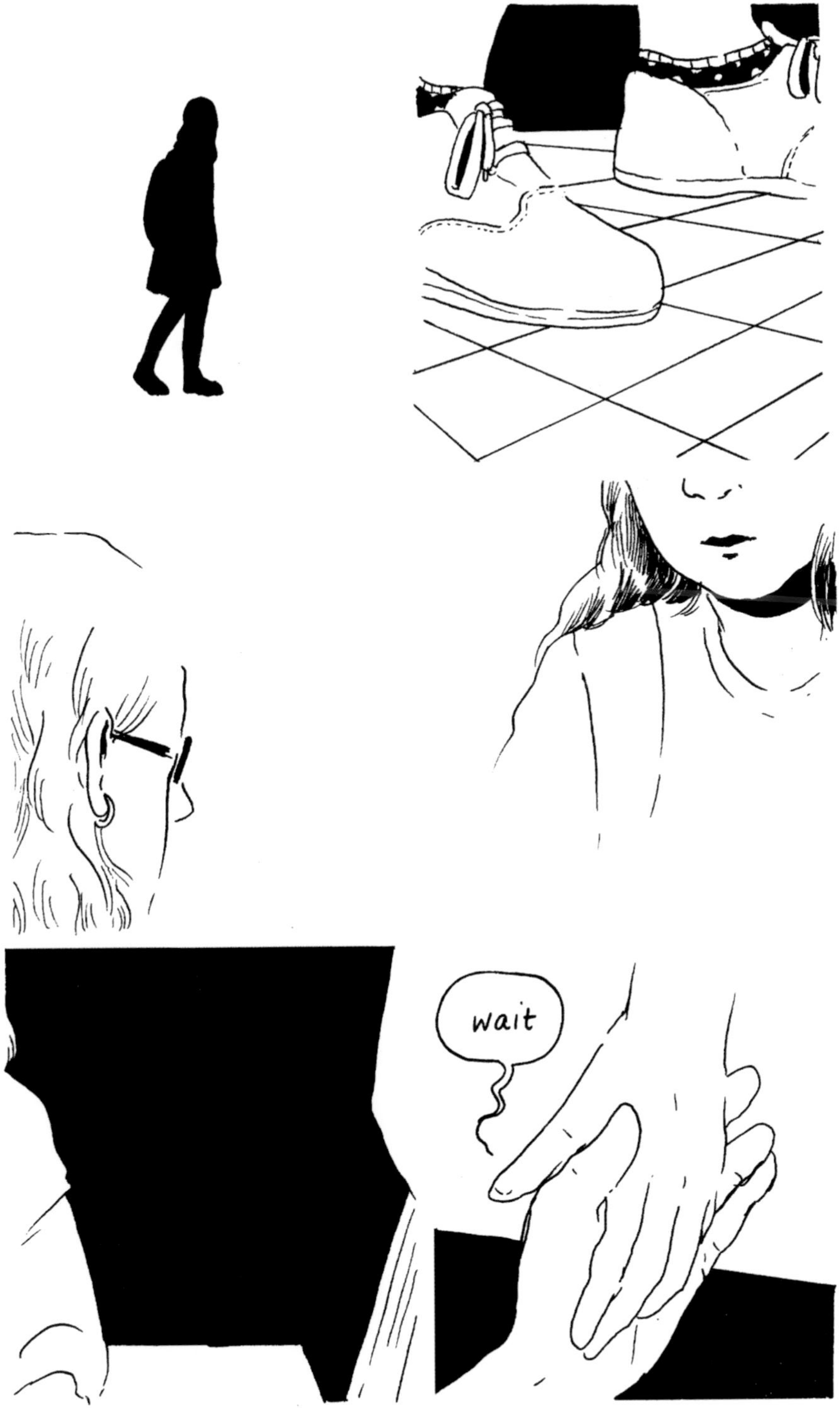
wait

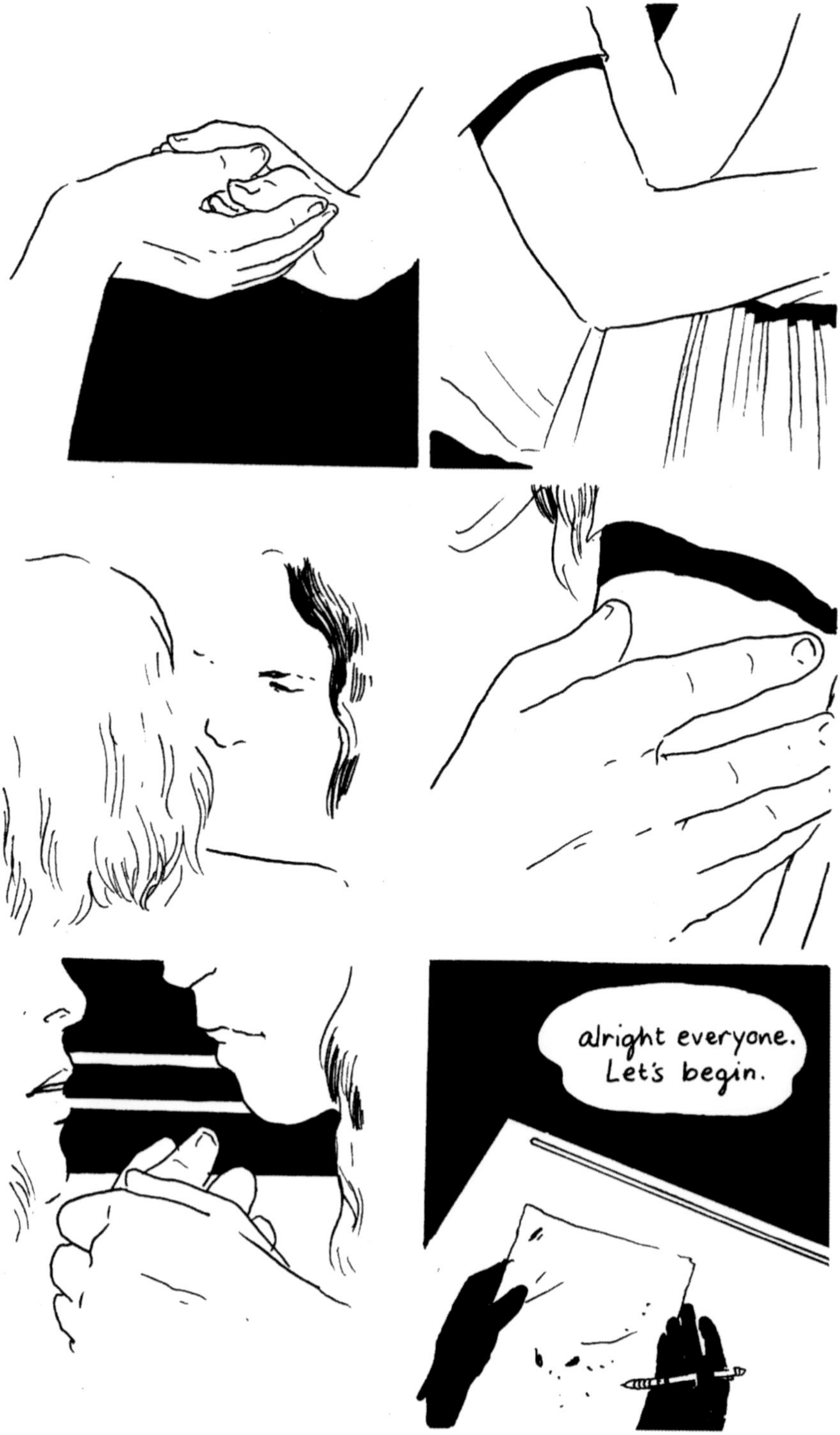
alright everyone. Let's begin.

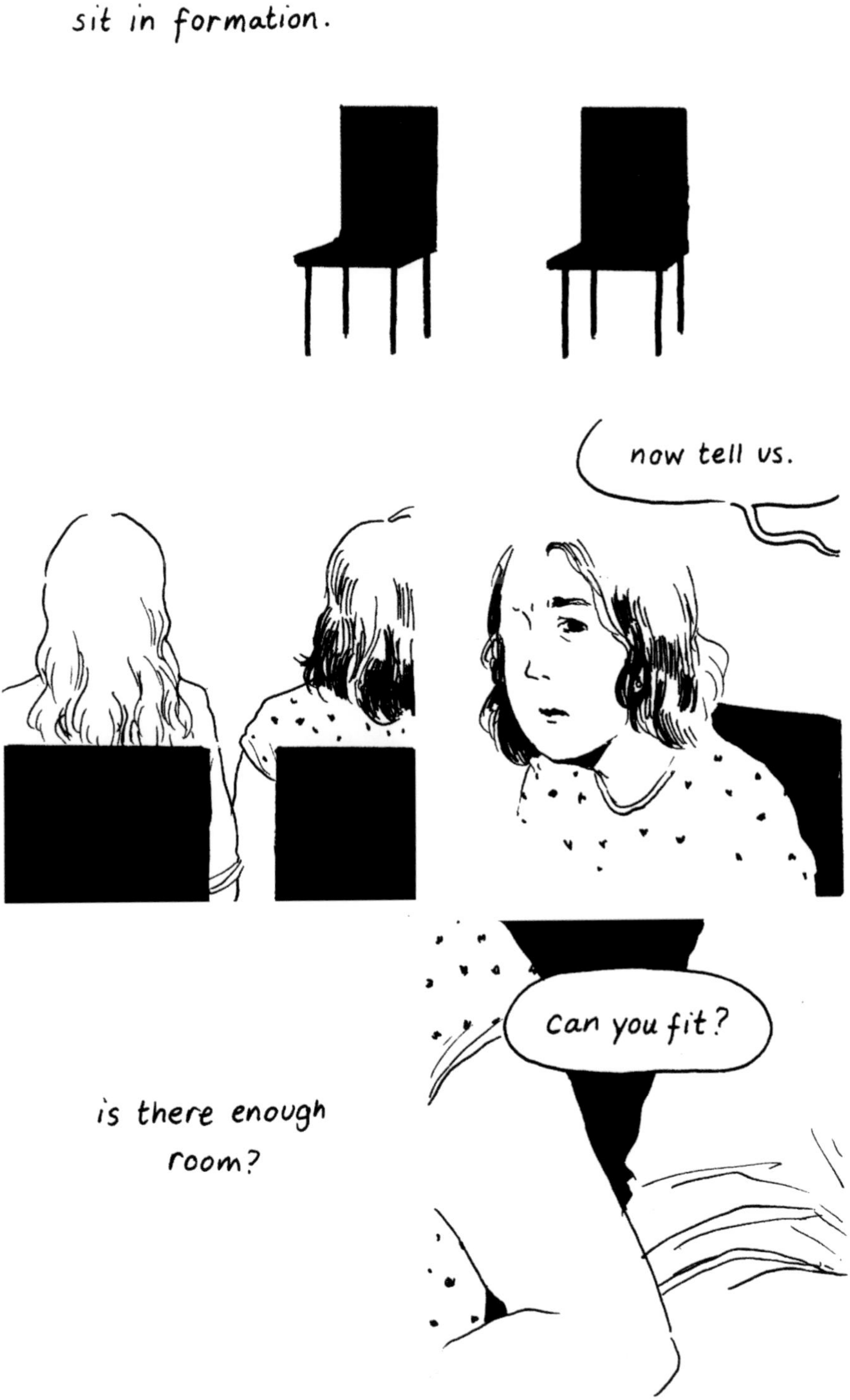
sit in formation.
now tell us.
is there enough room?
can you fit?

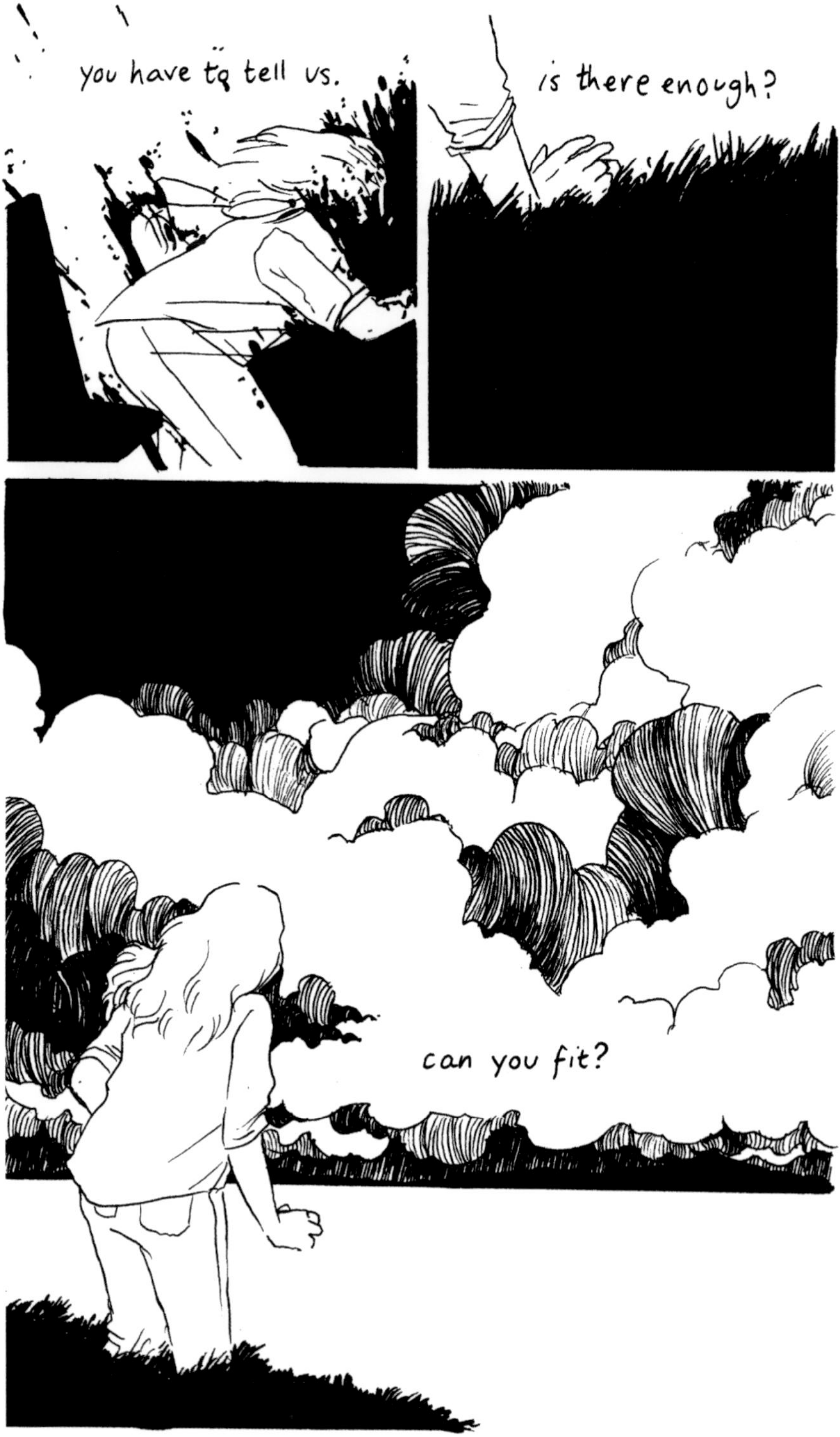
you have to tell us.
is there enough?
can you fit?

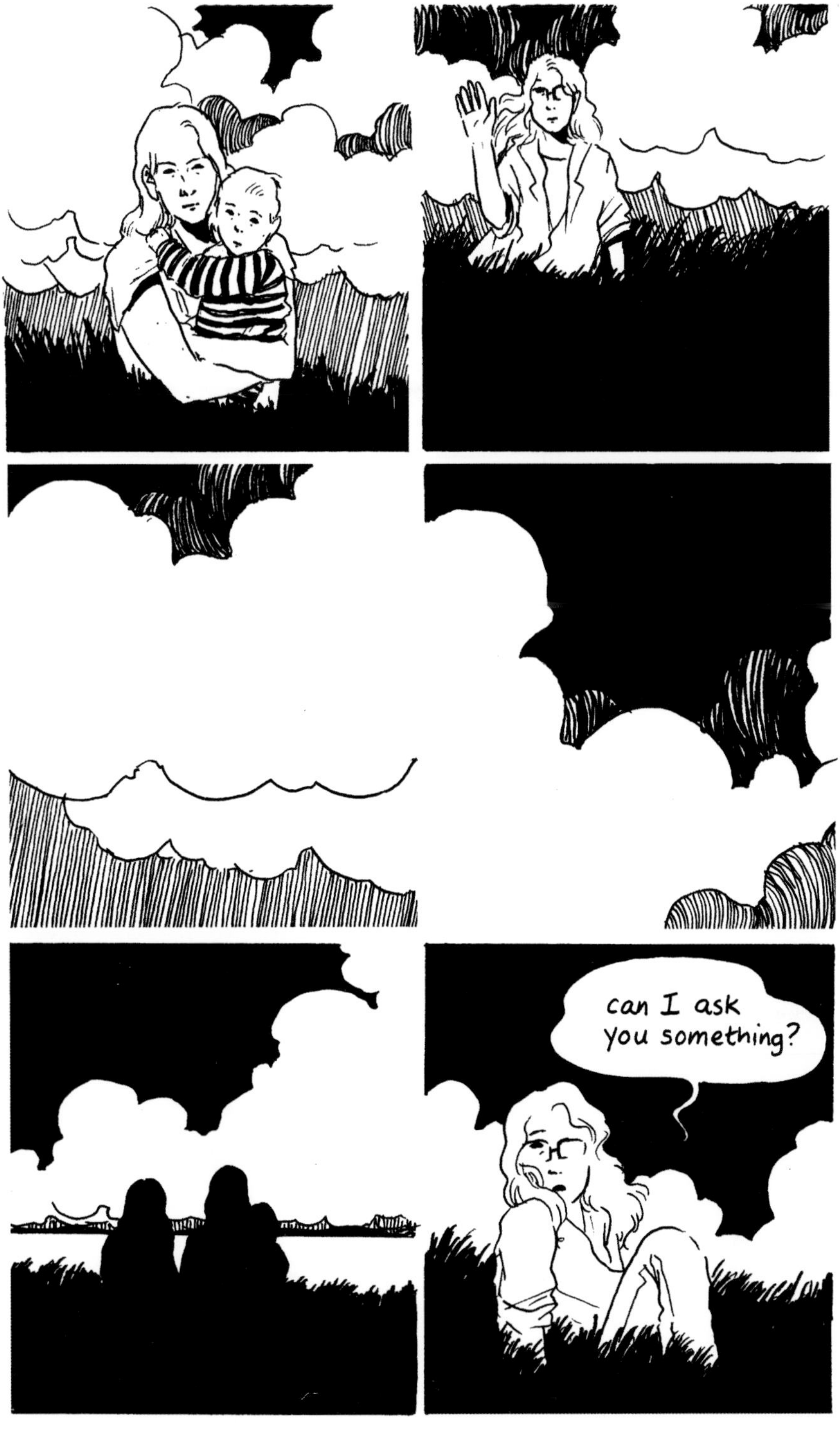
can I ask
you something?

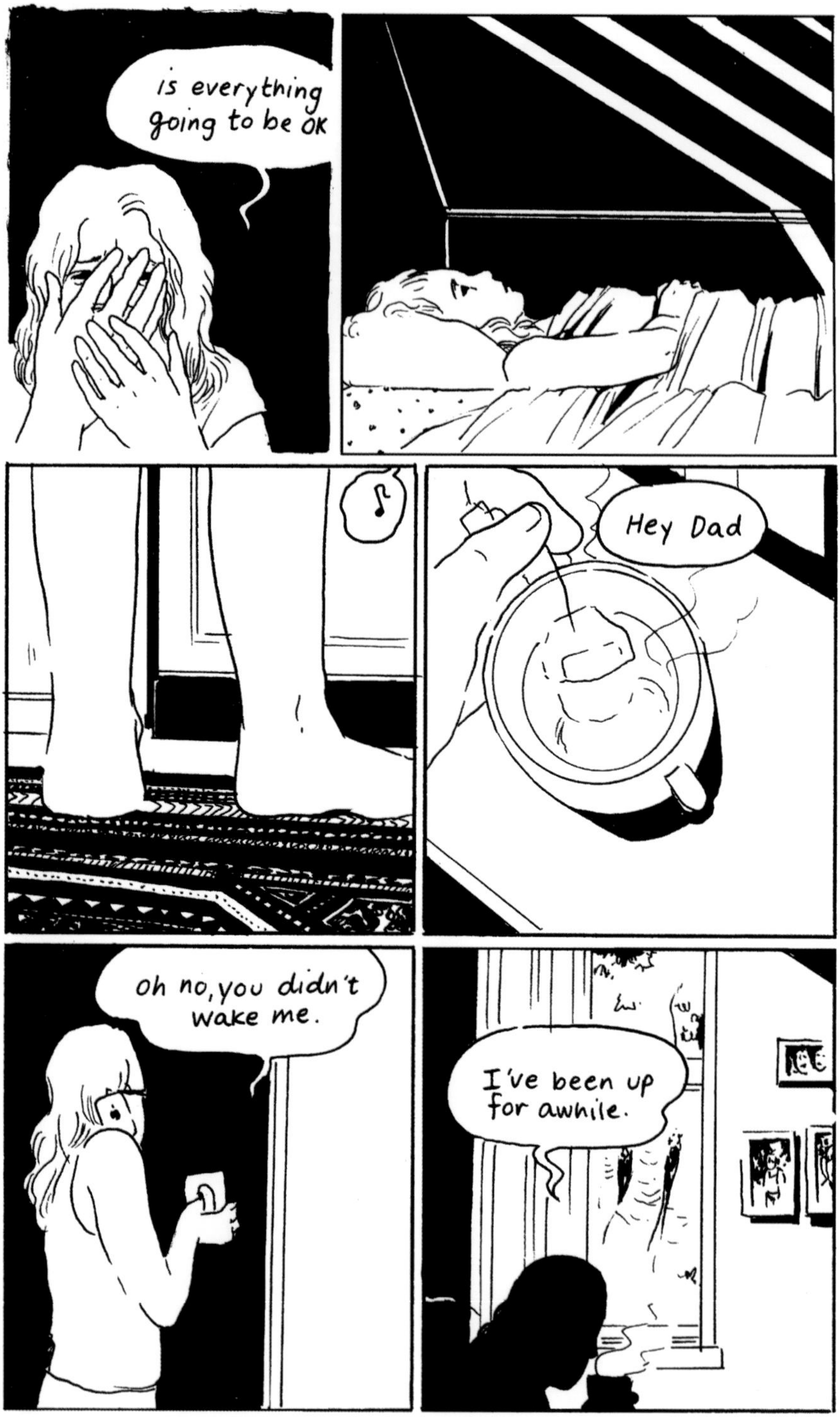
is everything going to be OK
♪
Hey Dad
oh no, you didn't wake me.
I've been up for awhile.

Sun In My Eyes (2015)

Made for Issue 12 of Off Life. I've always hated heat. Living in Texas was sweaty business.

I haven't been getting enough sleep lately.

The heat crawls all over me, keeping my eyes open.

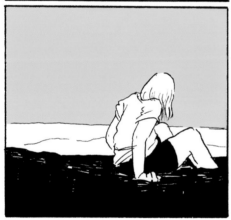

Summer makes me feel lost.

Buildings look too sharp in the sun and every plant is bursting with repulsive energy.

Everything hot

undefined

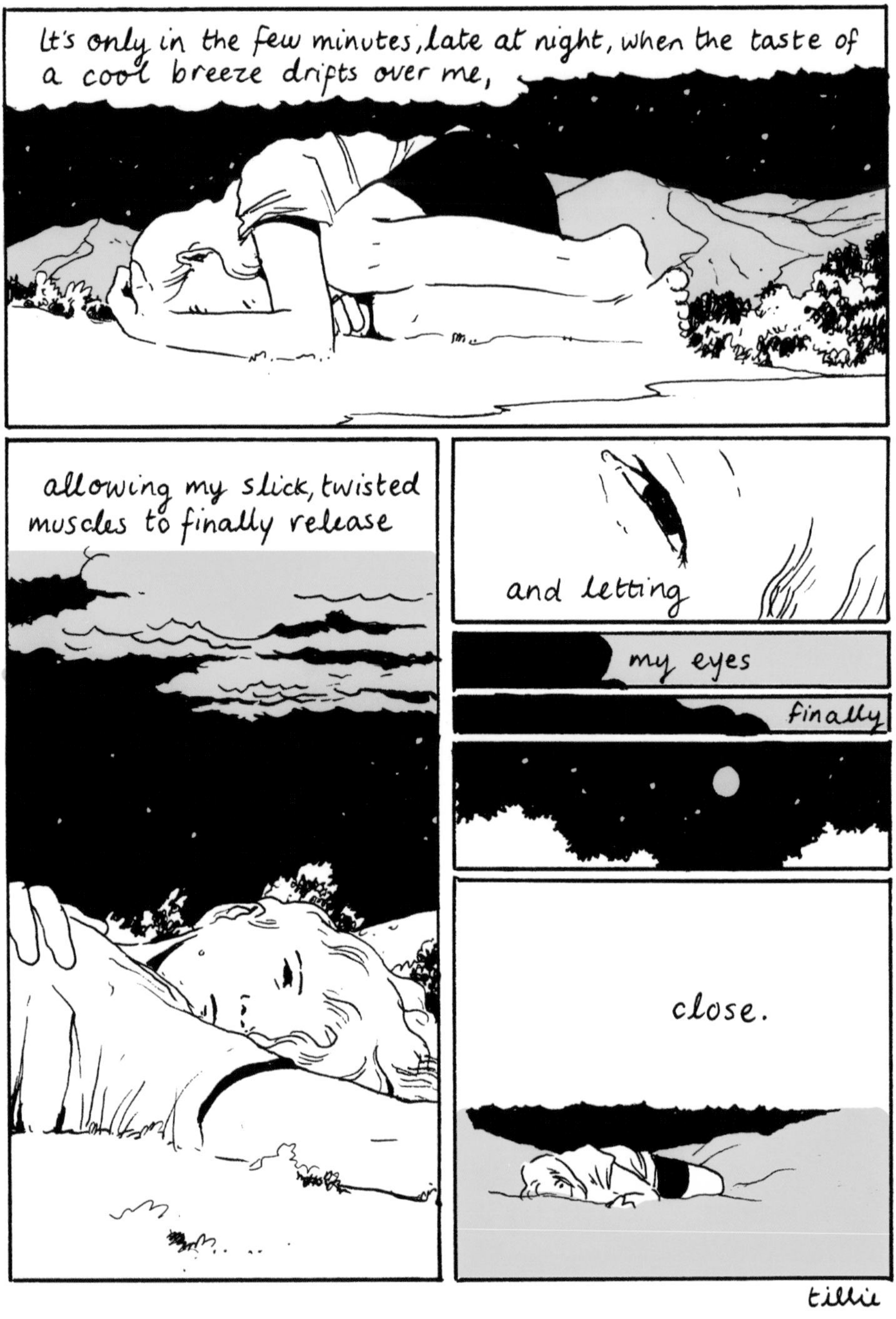
It's only in the few minutes, late at night, when the taste of a cool breeze drifts over me,
allowing my slick, twisted muscles to finally release
and letting
my eyes
finally
close.
tillie

In the Palm of Your Hand (2015)

This was my final project for my 1st year at CCS. At first I tried to make a comic about ice skating but I got super overwhelmed, and I ran out of time. At the last minute I made this, and used elements I was comfortable with (girls, purple.) I remember being especially happy with how I drew city lights.

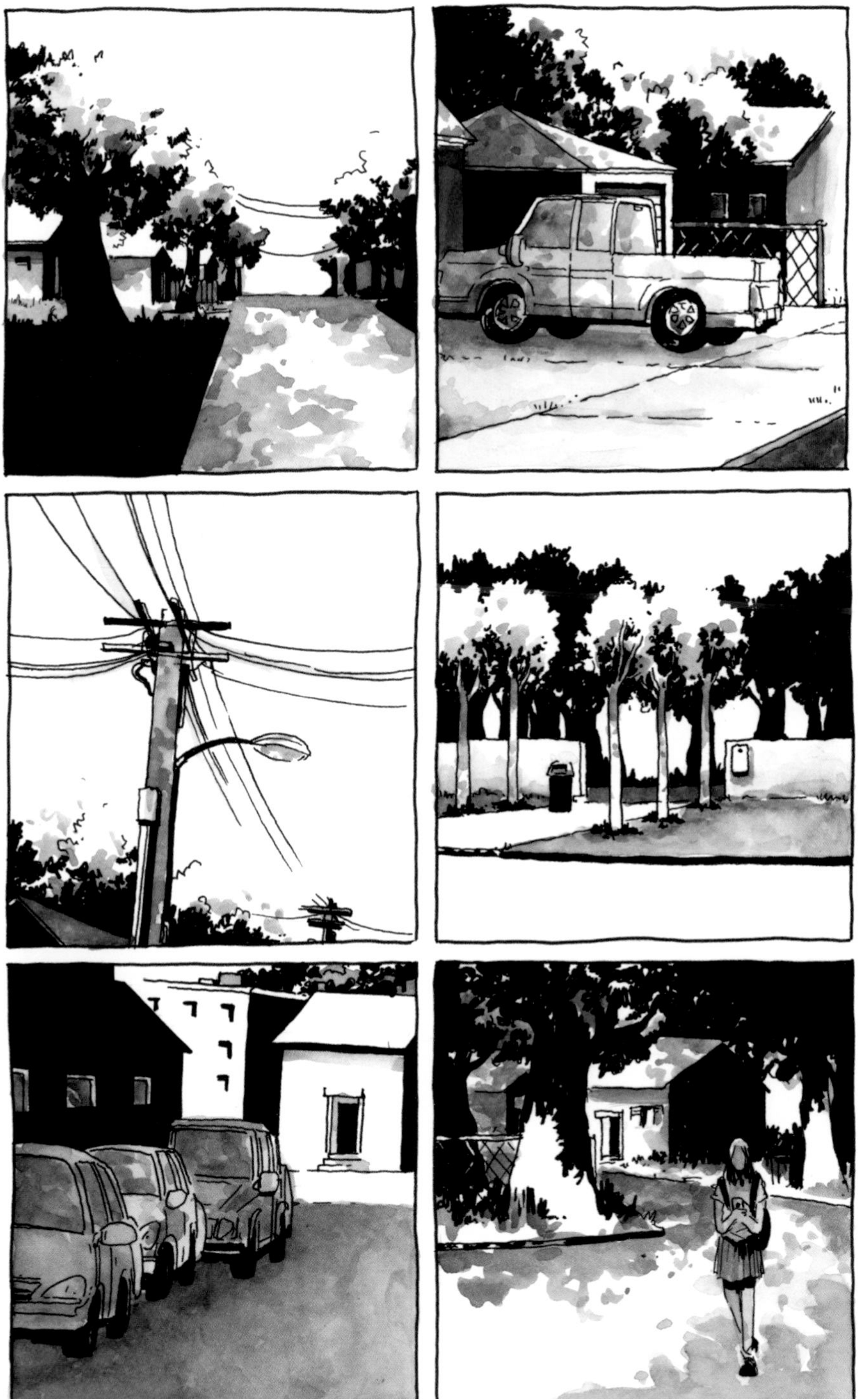

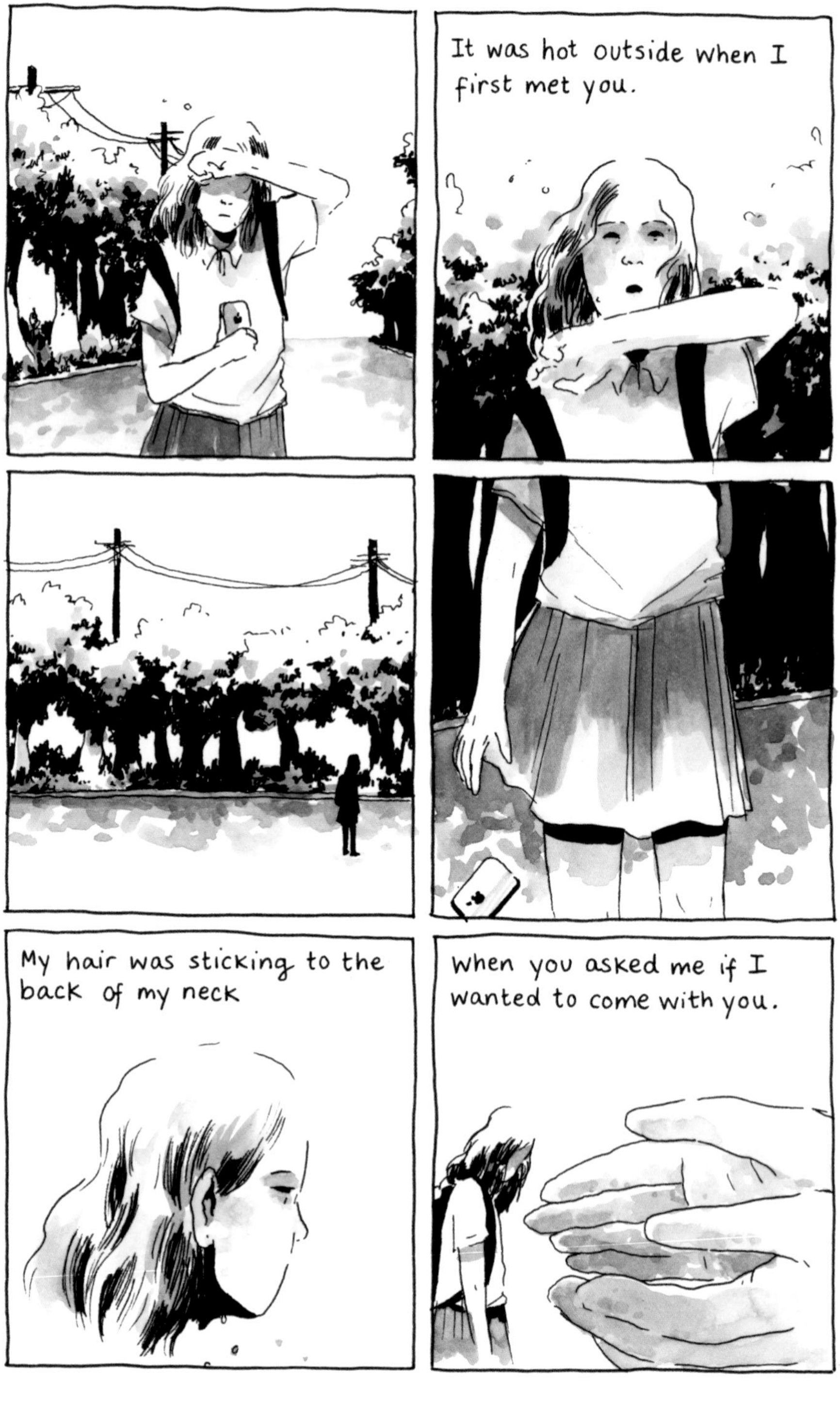
It was hot outside when I first met you.
My hair was sticking to the back of my neck
when you asked me if I wanted to come with you.

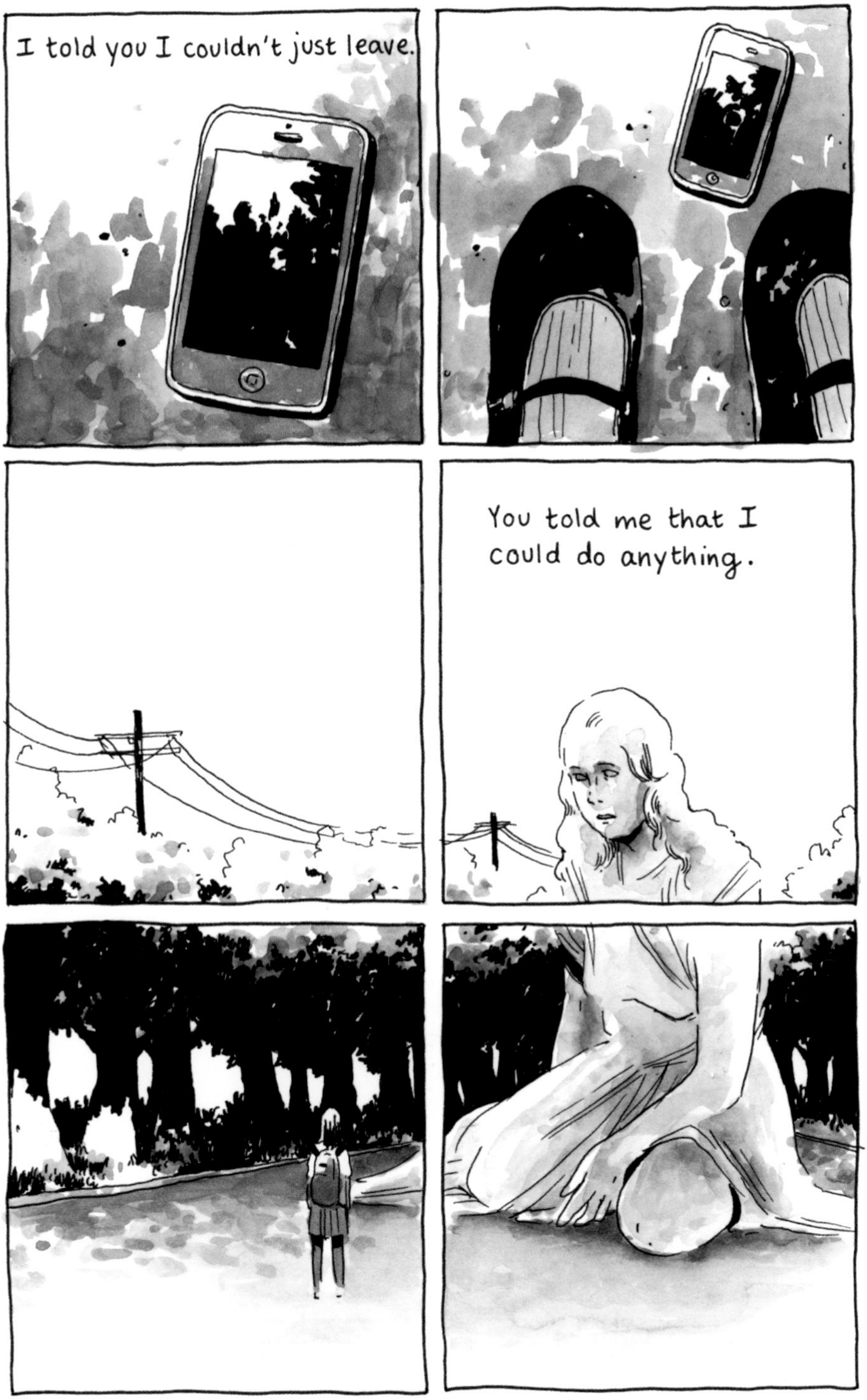
I told you I couldn't just leave.
You told me that I could do anything.

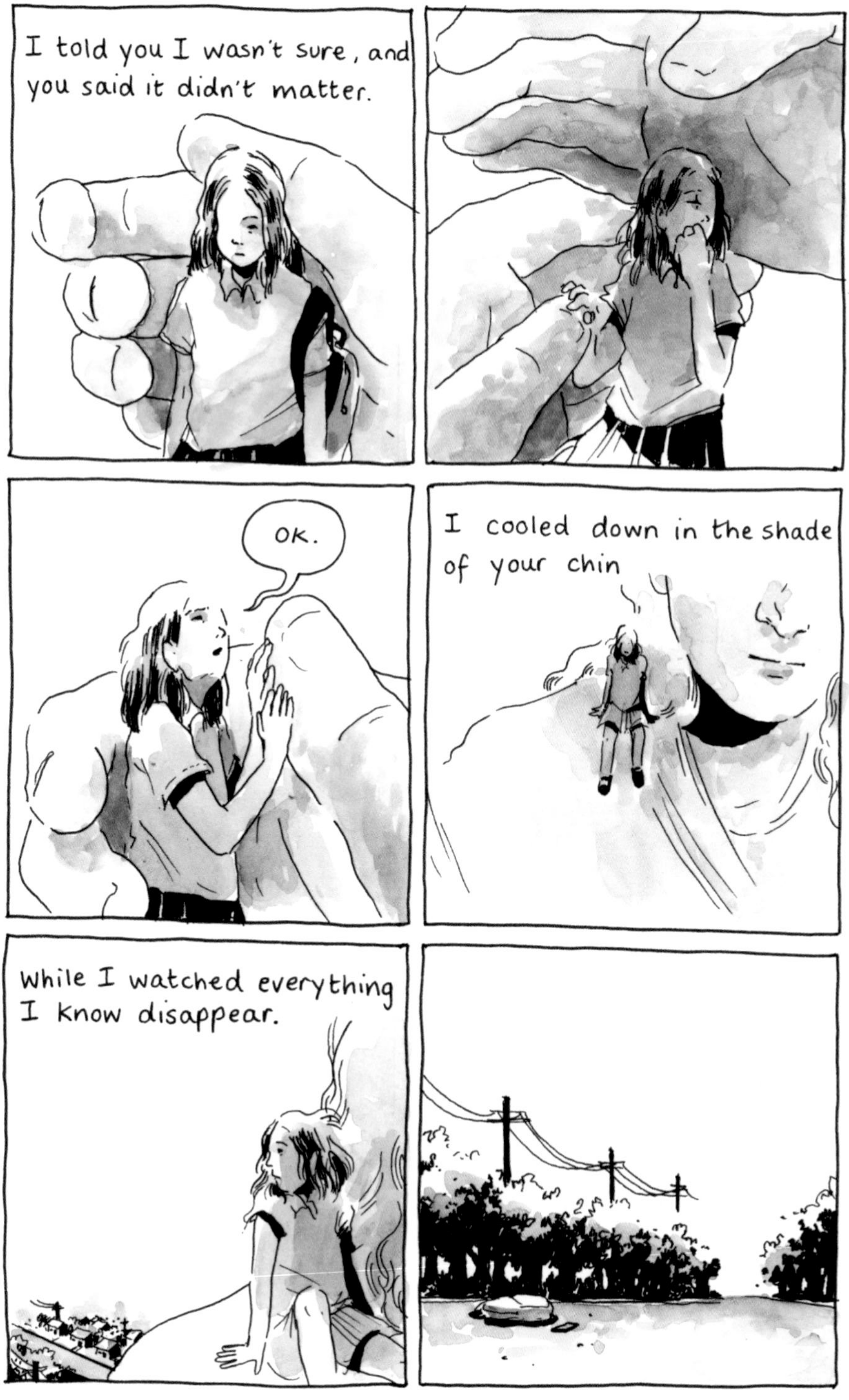
I told you I wasn't sure, and you said it didn't matter.
OK.
I cooled down in the shade of your chin
While I watched everything I know disappear.

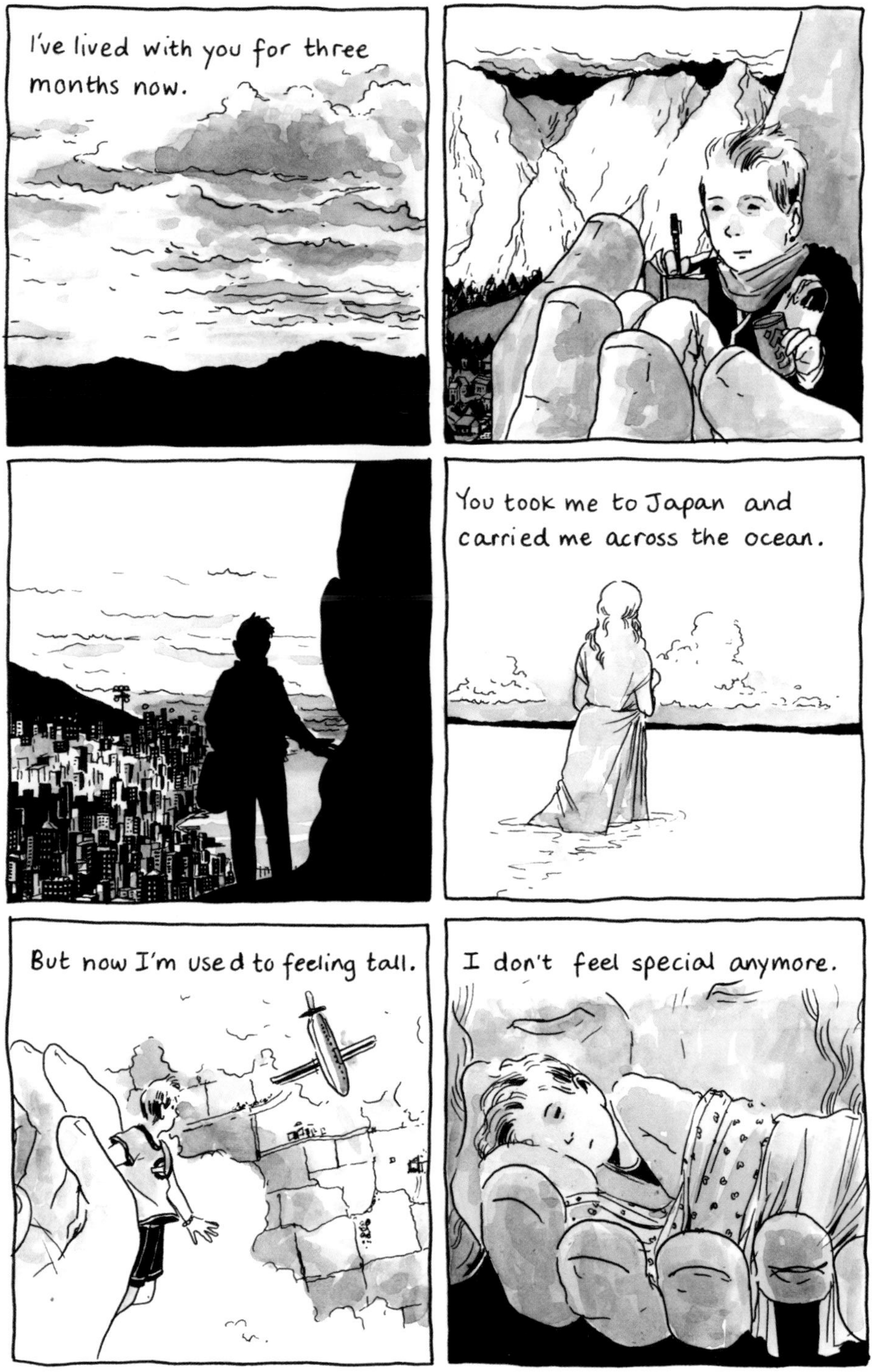
I've lived with you for three months now.
You took me to Japan and carried me across the ocean.
But now I'm used to feeling tall.
I don't feel special anymore.

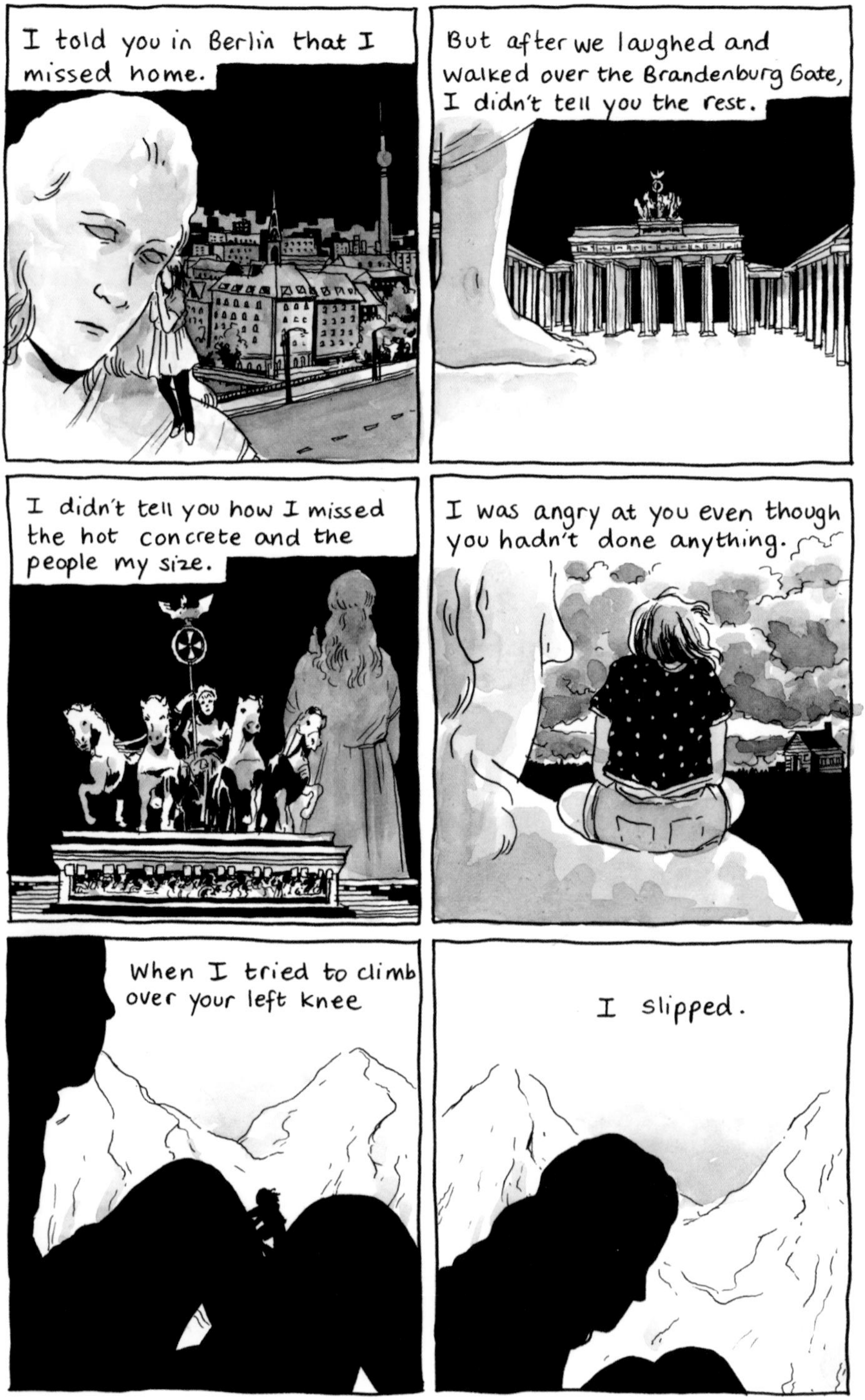
I told you in Berlin that I missed home.
But after we laughed and walked over the Brandenburg Gate, I didn't tell you the rest.
I didn't tell you how I missed the hot concrete and the people my size.
I was angry at you even though you hadn't done anything.
When I tried to climb over your left knee
I slipped.

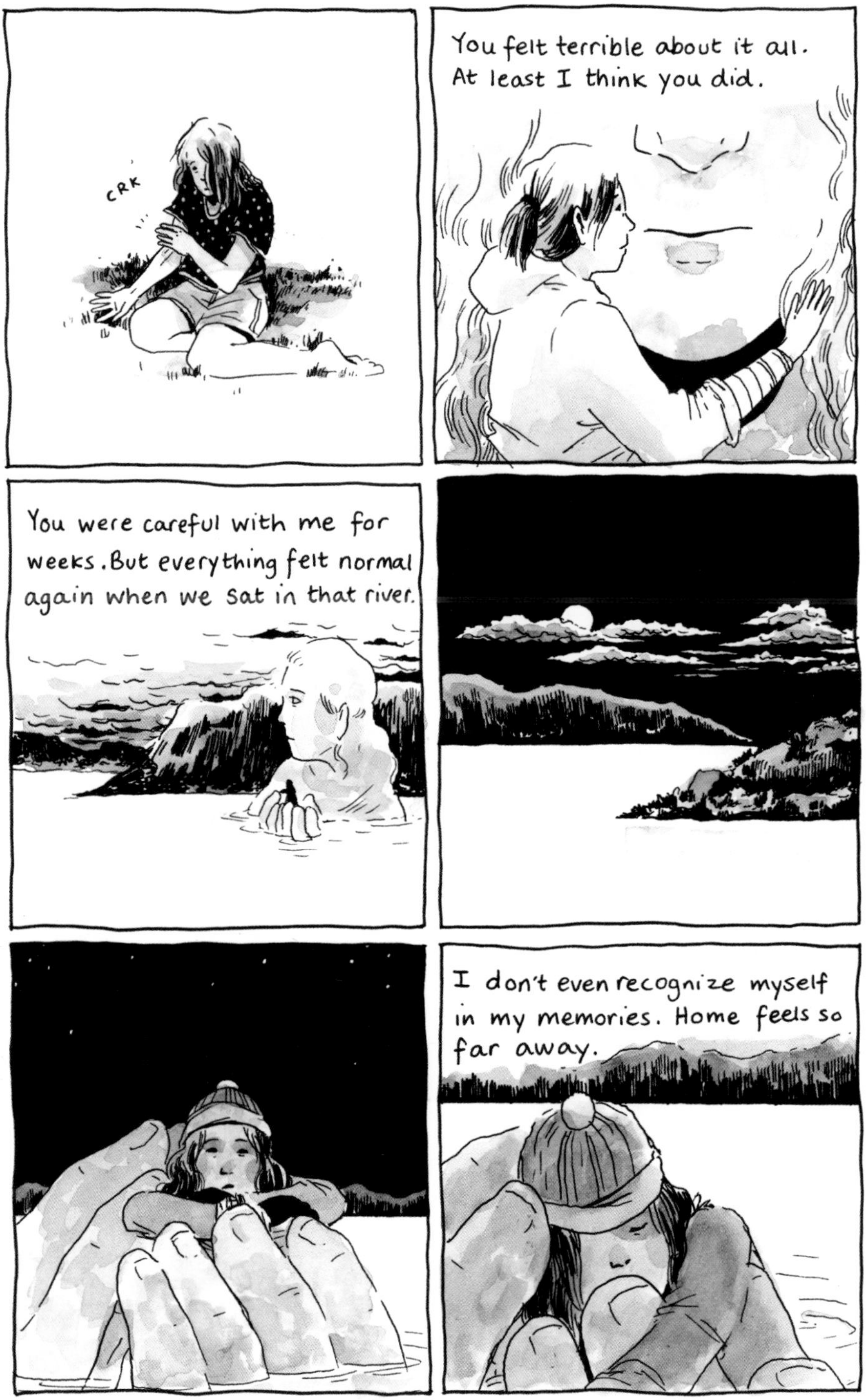
CRK
You felt terrible about it all. At least I think you did.
You were careful with me for weeks. But everything felt normal again when we sat in that river.
I don't even recognize myself in my memories. Home feels so far away.

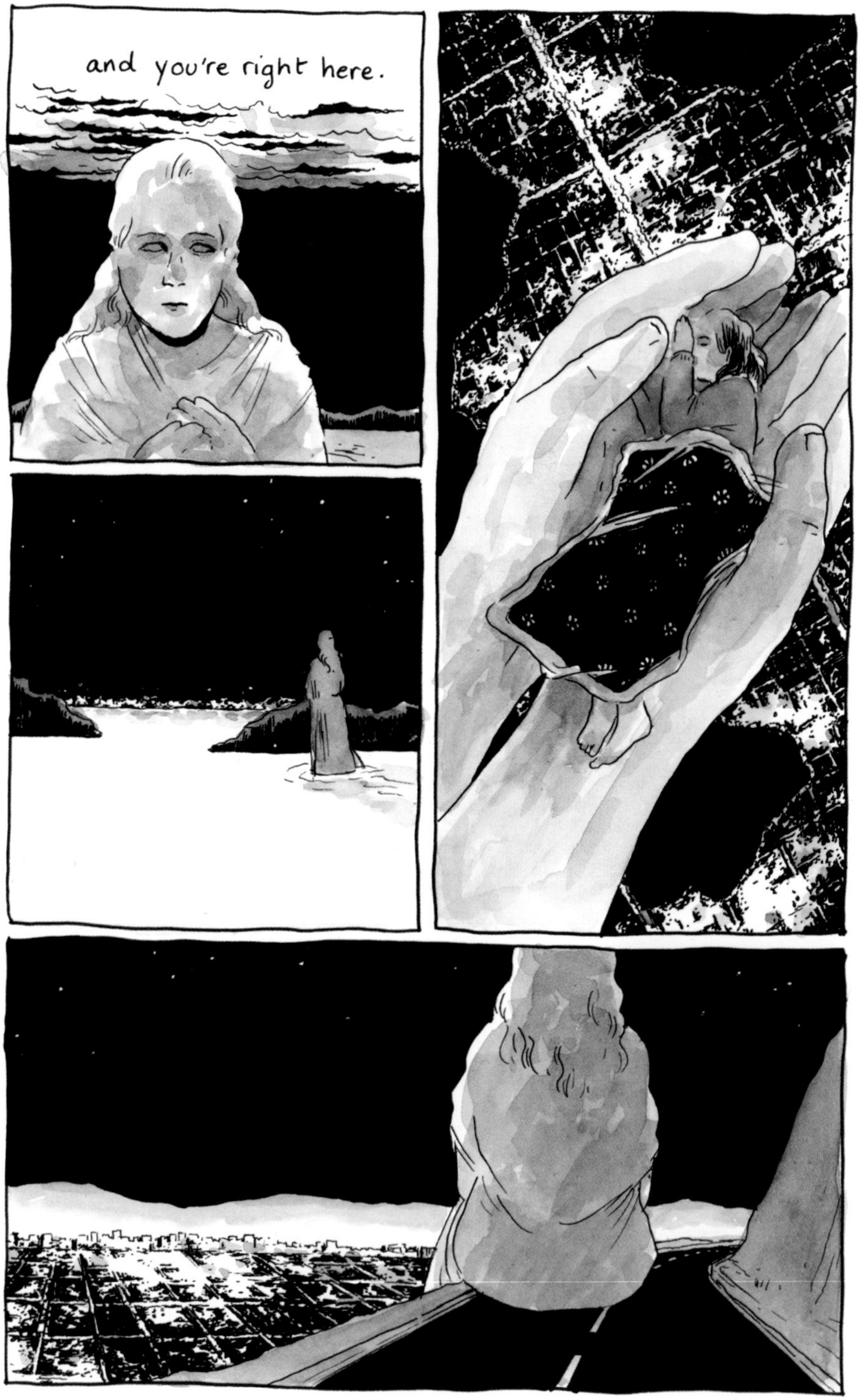
and you're right here.

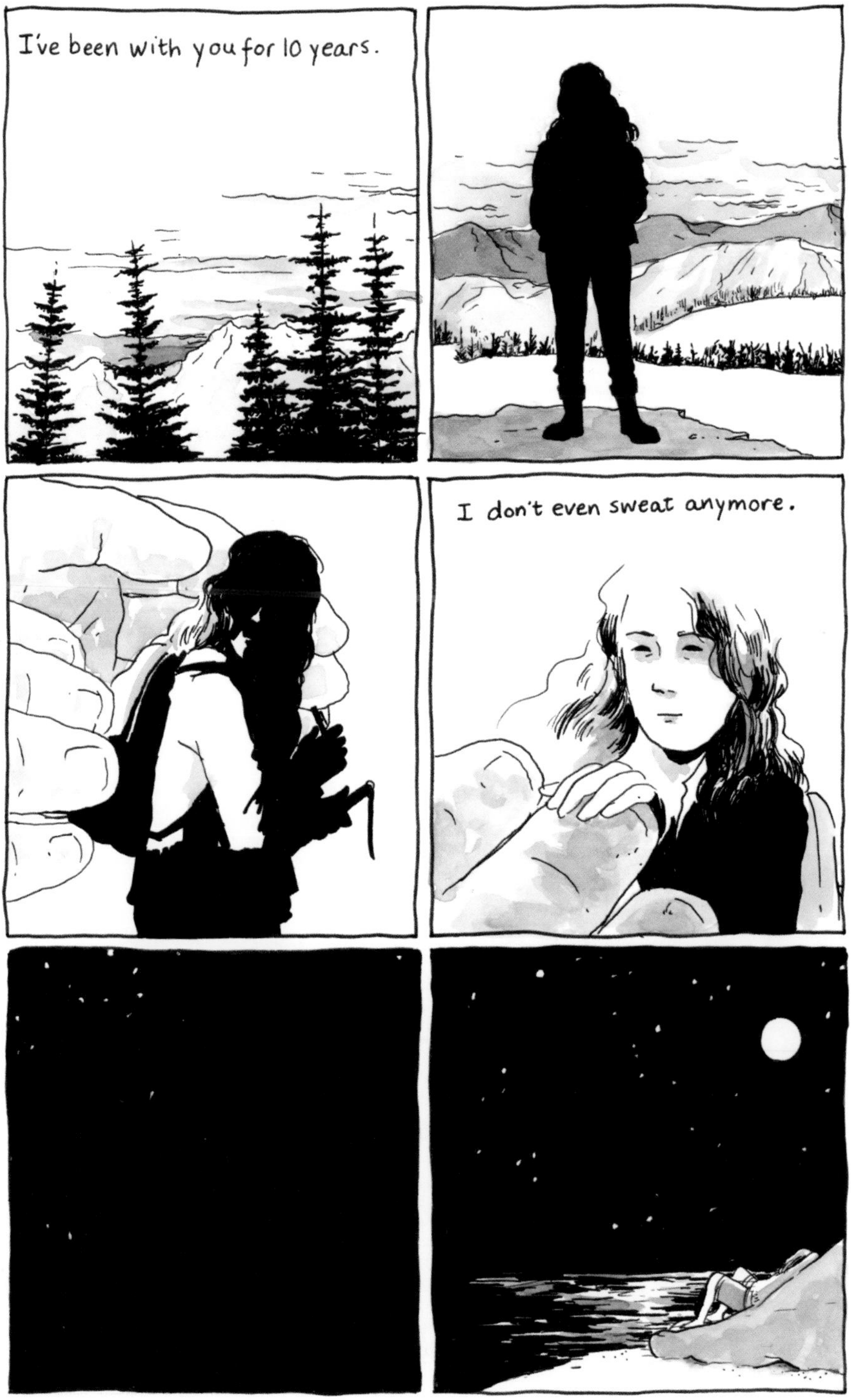
I've been with you for 10 years.
I don't even sweat anymore.

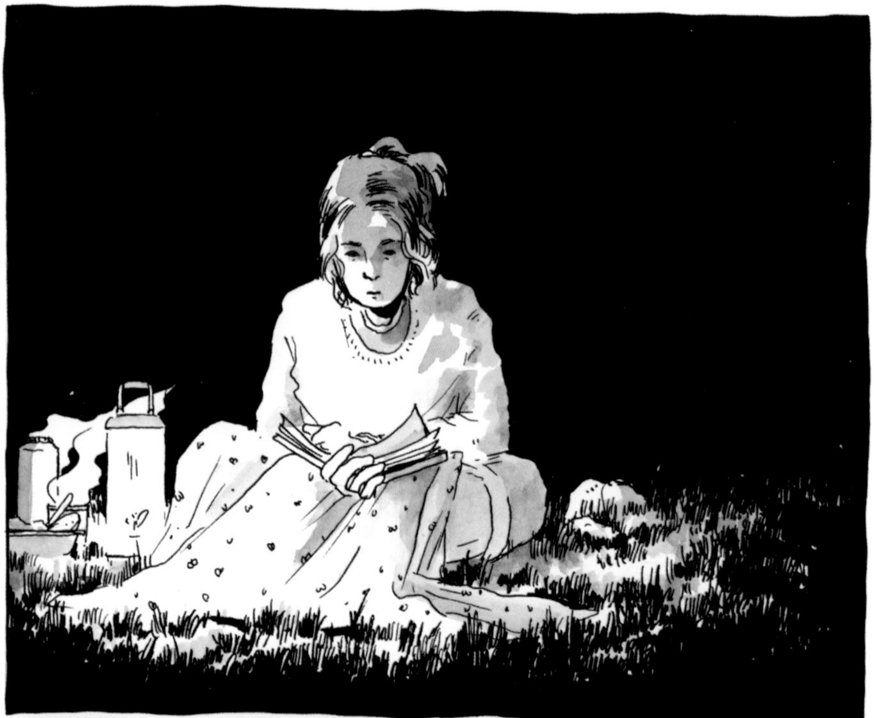

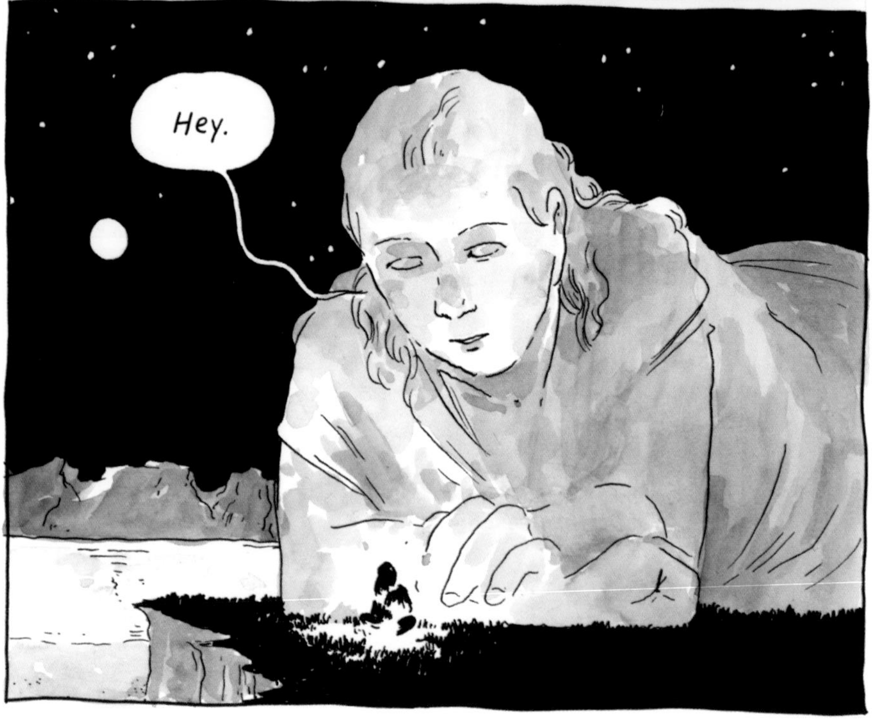
Hey.

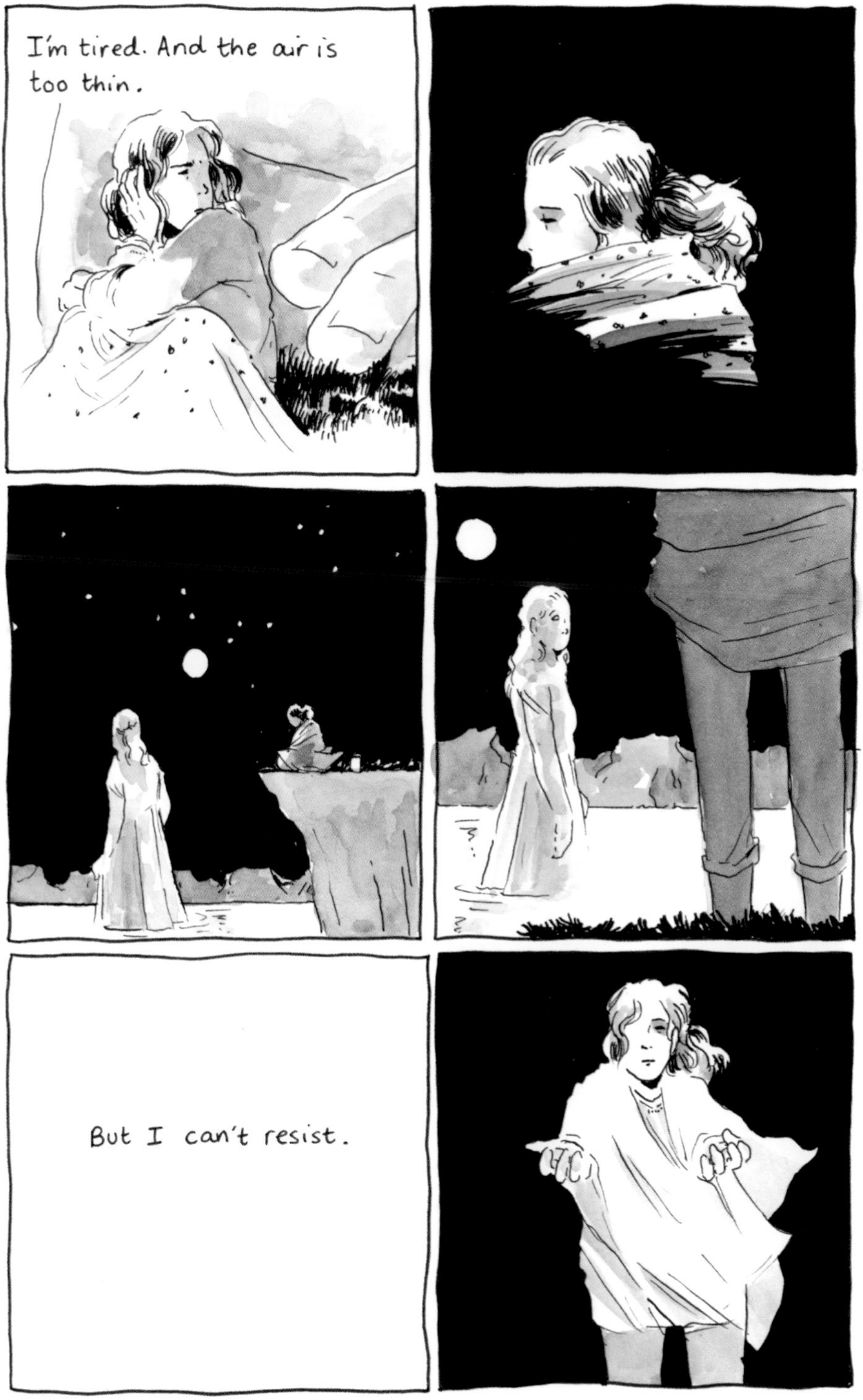
I'm tired. And the air is too thin.
But I can't resist.

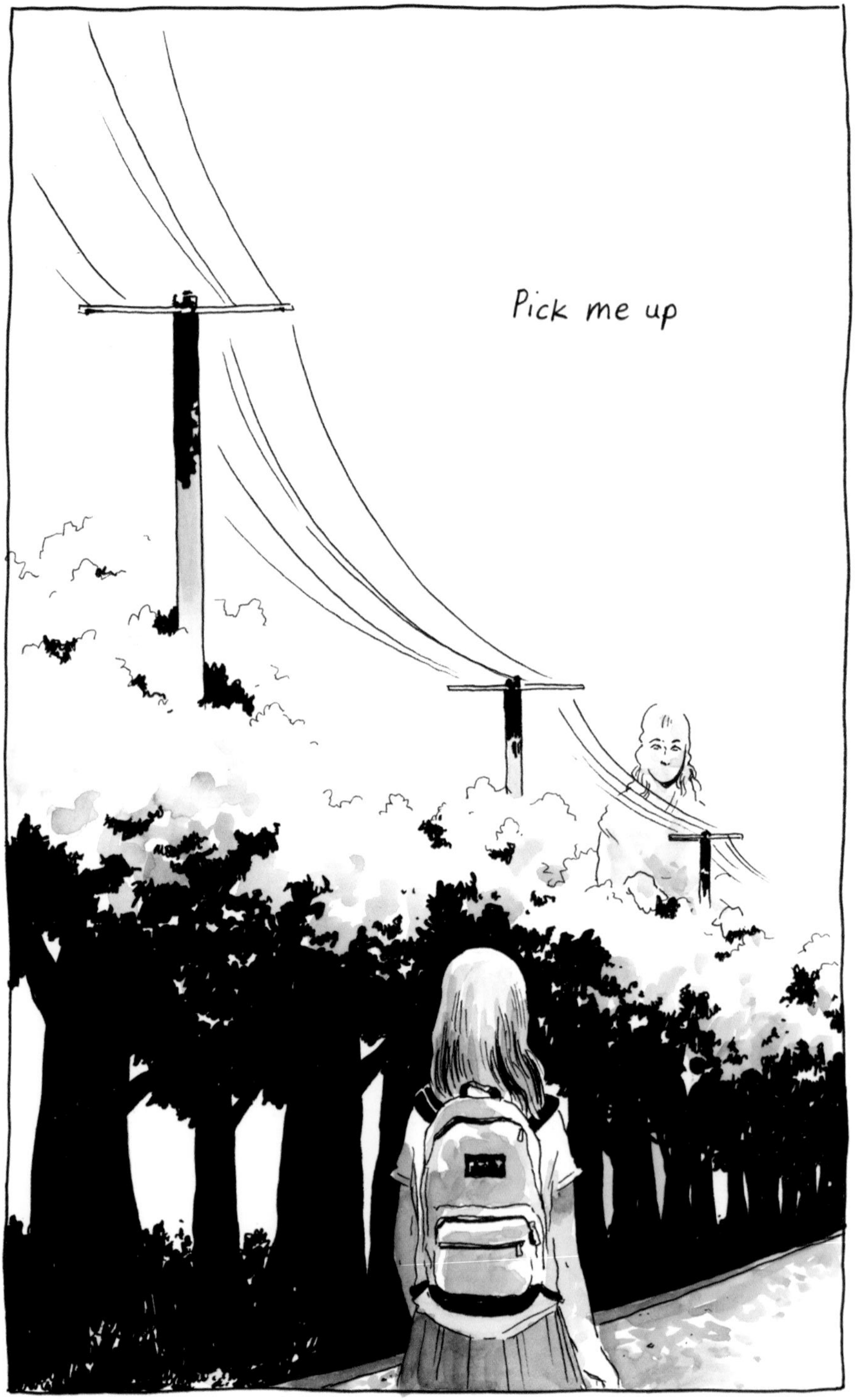
Pick me up

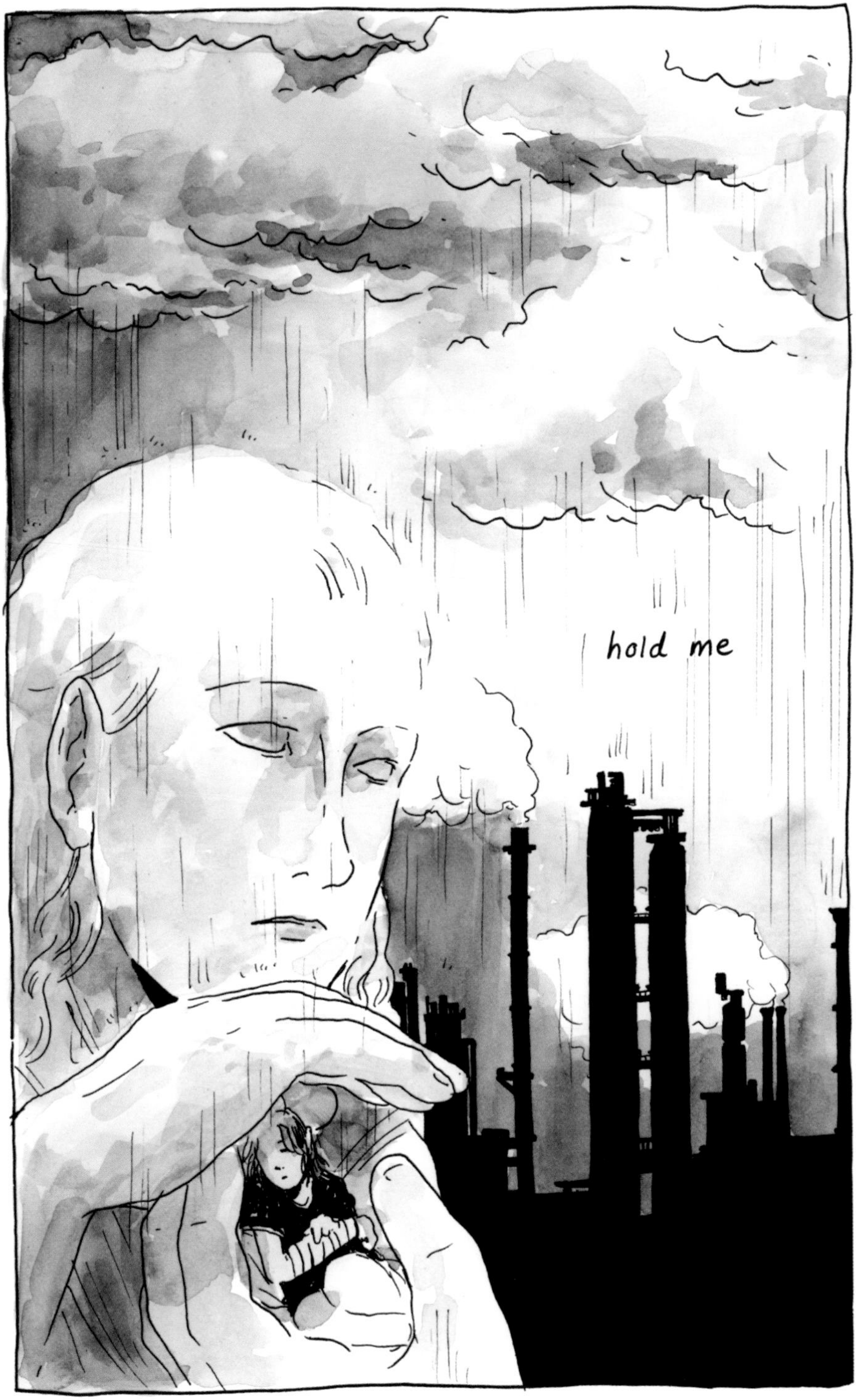
hold me

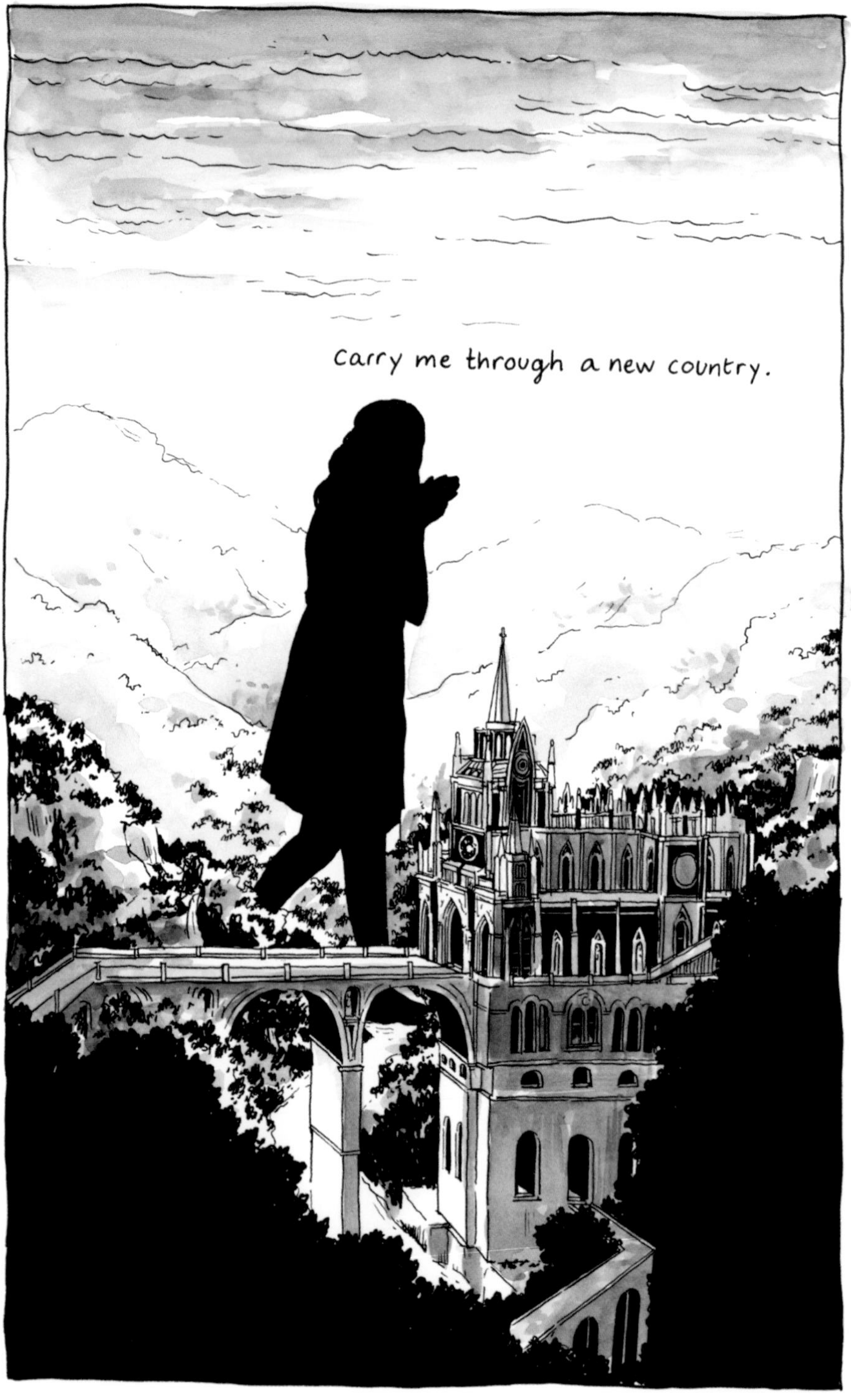
carry me through a new country.

The Weather Woman (2016)

Made this comic SUPER fast. It was good
practice for coloring digitally.

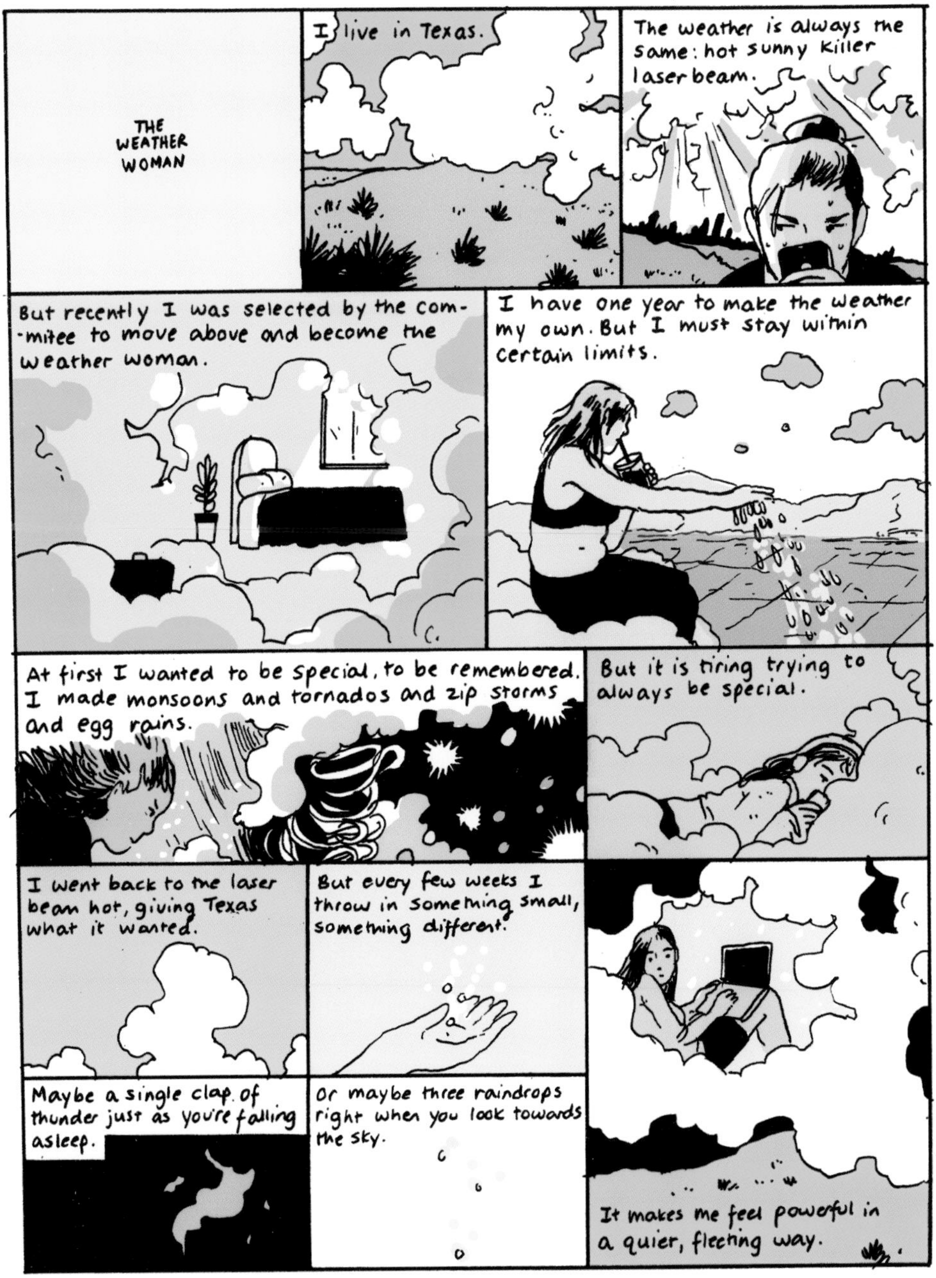
THE WEATHER WOMAN
I live in Texas.
The weather is always the same: hot sunny killer laserbeam.
But recently I was selected by the com-mitee to move above and become the weather woman.
I have one year to make the weather my own. But I must stay within certain limits.
At first I wanted to be special, to be remembered. I made monsoons and tornados and zip storms and egg rains.
But it is tiring trying to always be special.
I went back to the laser beam hot, giving Texas what it wanted.
But every few weeks I throw in something small, something different.
Maybe a single clap of thunder just as you're falling asleep.
Or maybe three raindrops right when you look towards the sky.
It makes me feel powerful in a quiet, fleeting way.

Lars + Nemo (2016)

Ricky made me do this. It was for a new edition of The End of Summer, a year or so after the original came out. I was right in the midst of a stylistic change- kind of in between the more detailed/realistic style of TEOS and the looser/more cartoony drawing I would find in On a Sunbeam.

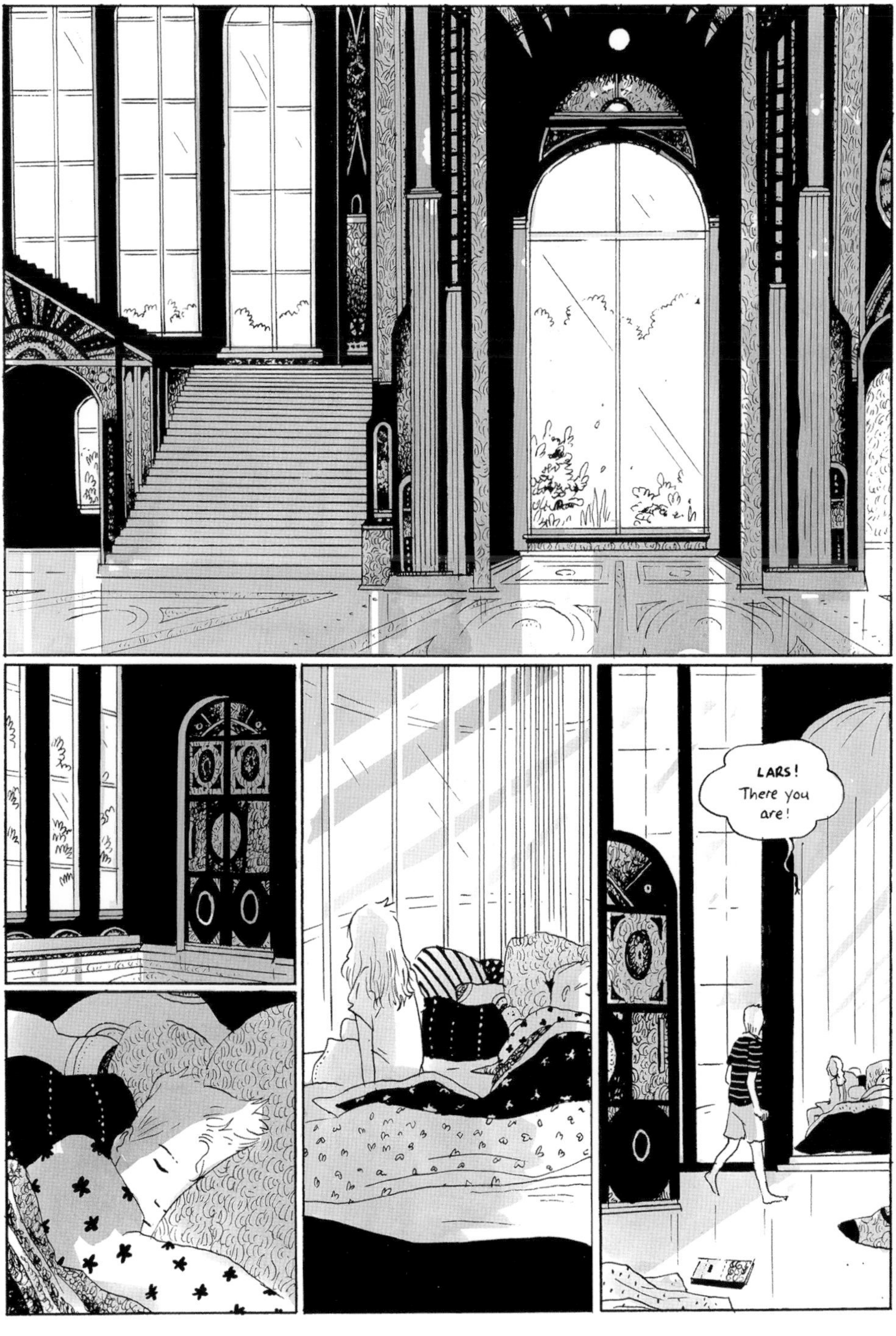
LARS!
There you are!

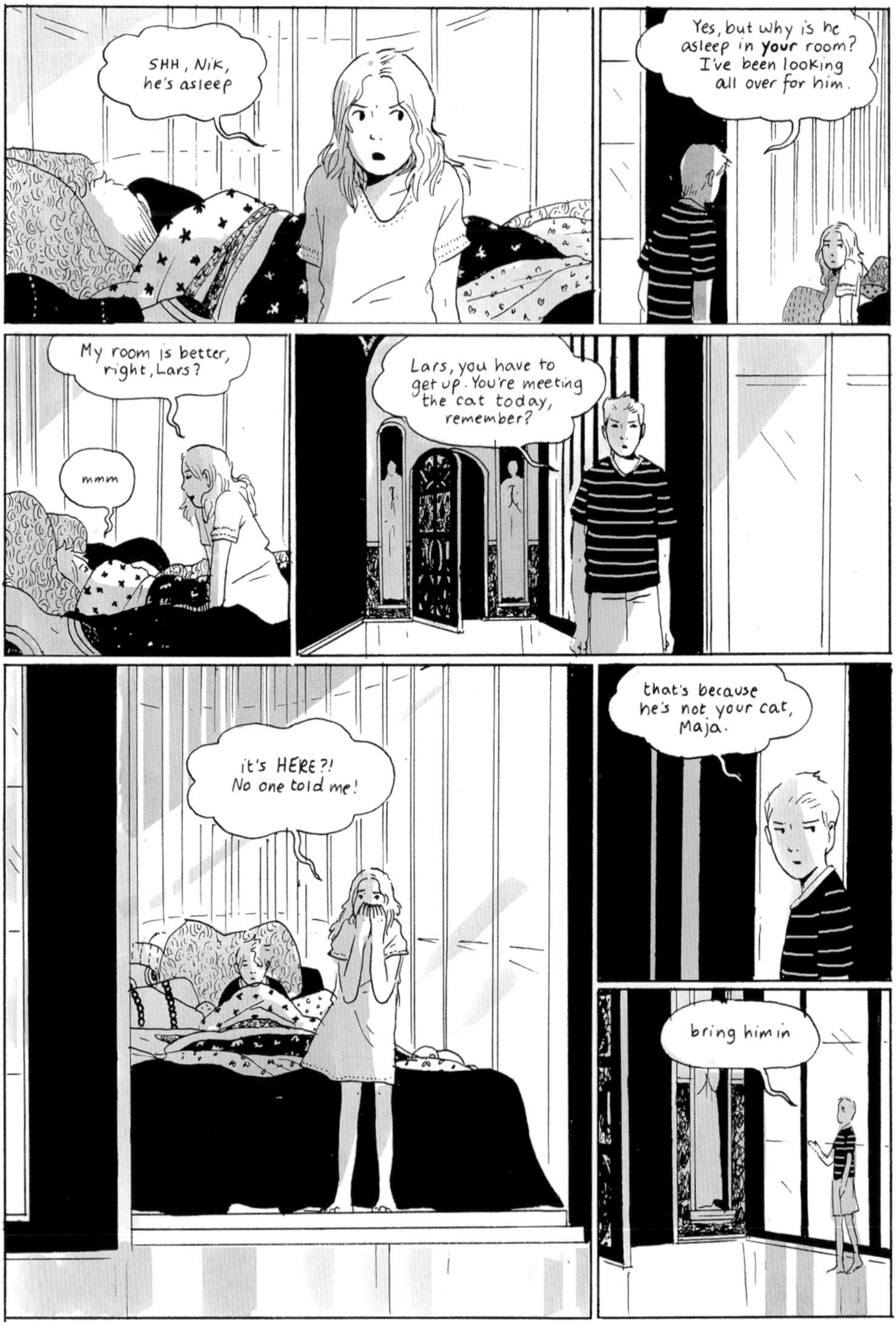
SHH, Nik, he's asleep
Yes, but why is he asleep in your room? I've been looking all over for him.
My room is better, right, Lars?
mmm
Lars, you have to get up. You're meeting the cat today, remember?
it's HERE?! No one told me!
that's because he's not your cat, Maja.
bring him in

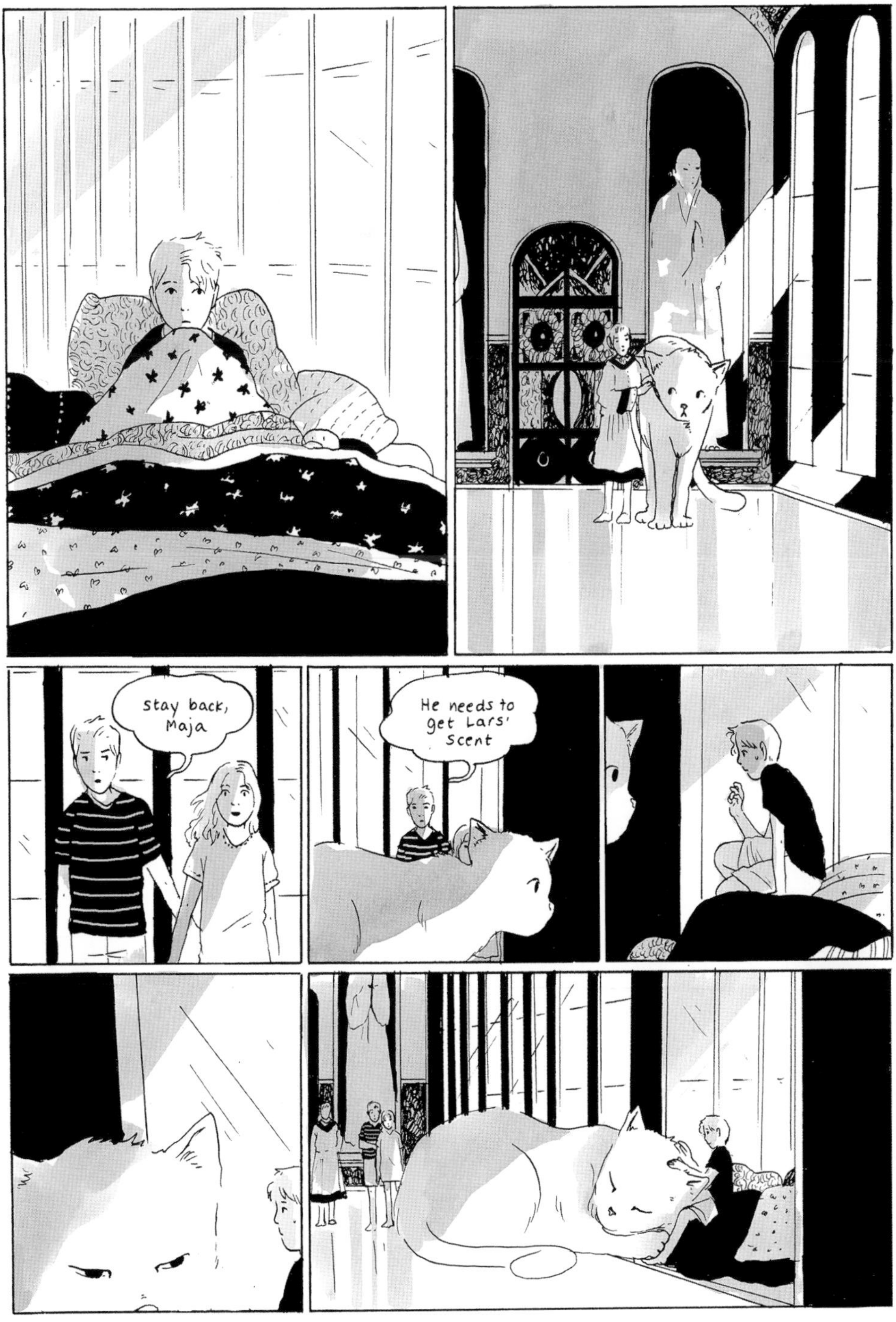
stay back, Maja
He needs to get Lars' scent

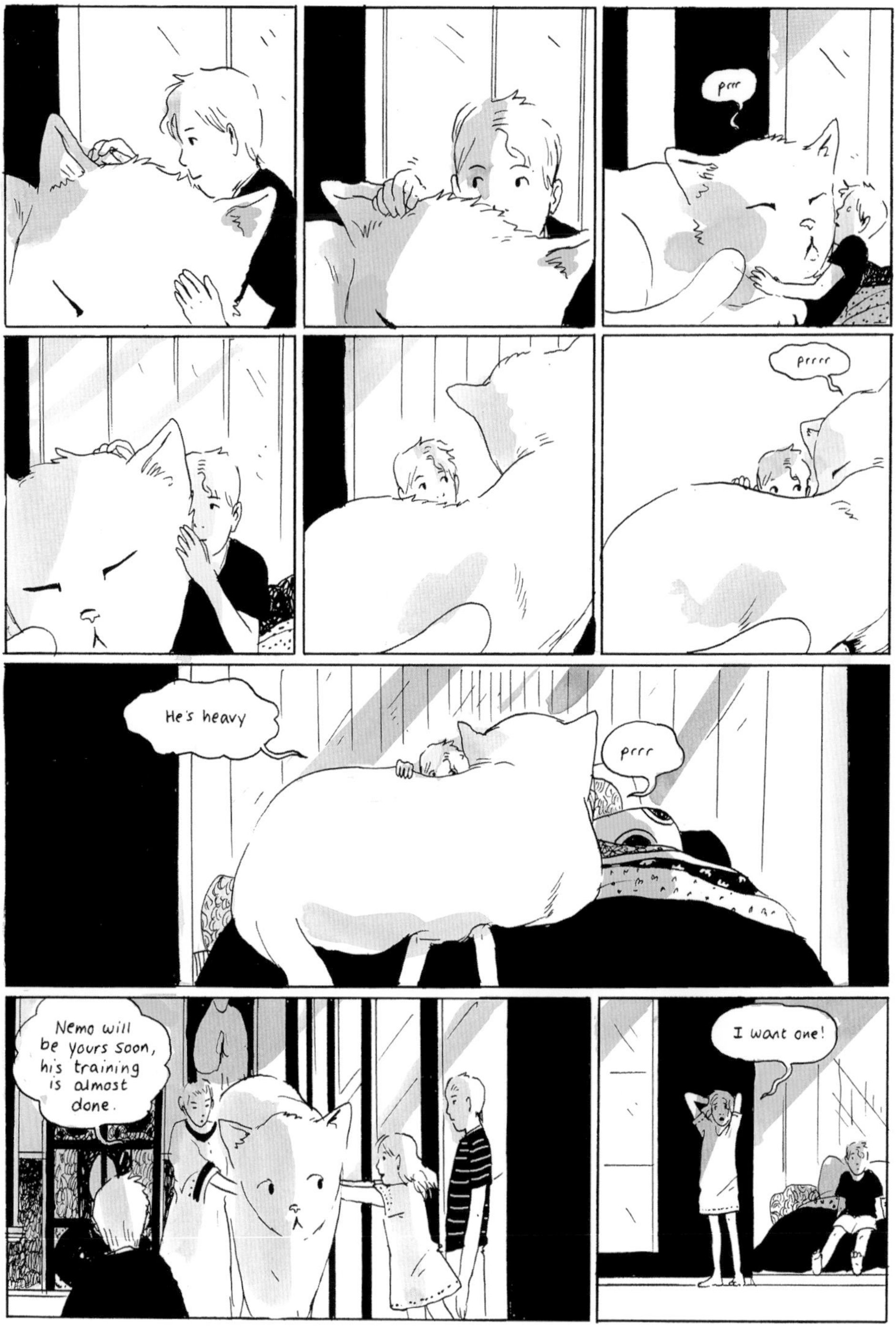
prrr
prrrr
He's heavy
prrr
Nemo will be yours soon, his training is almost done.
I want one!

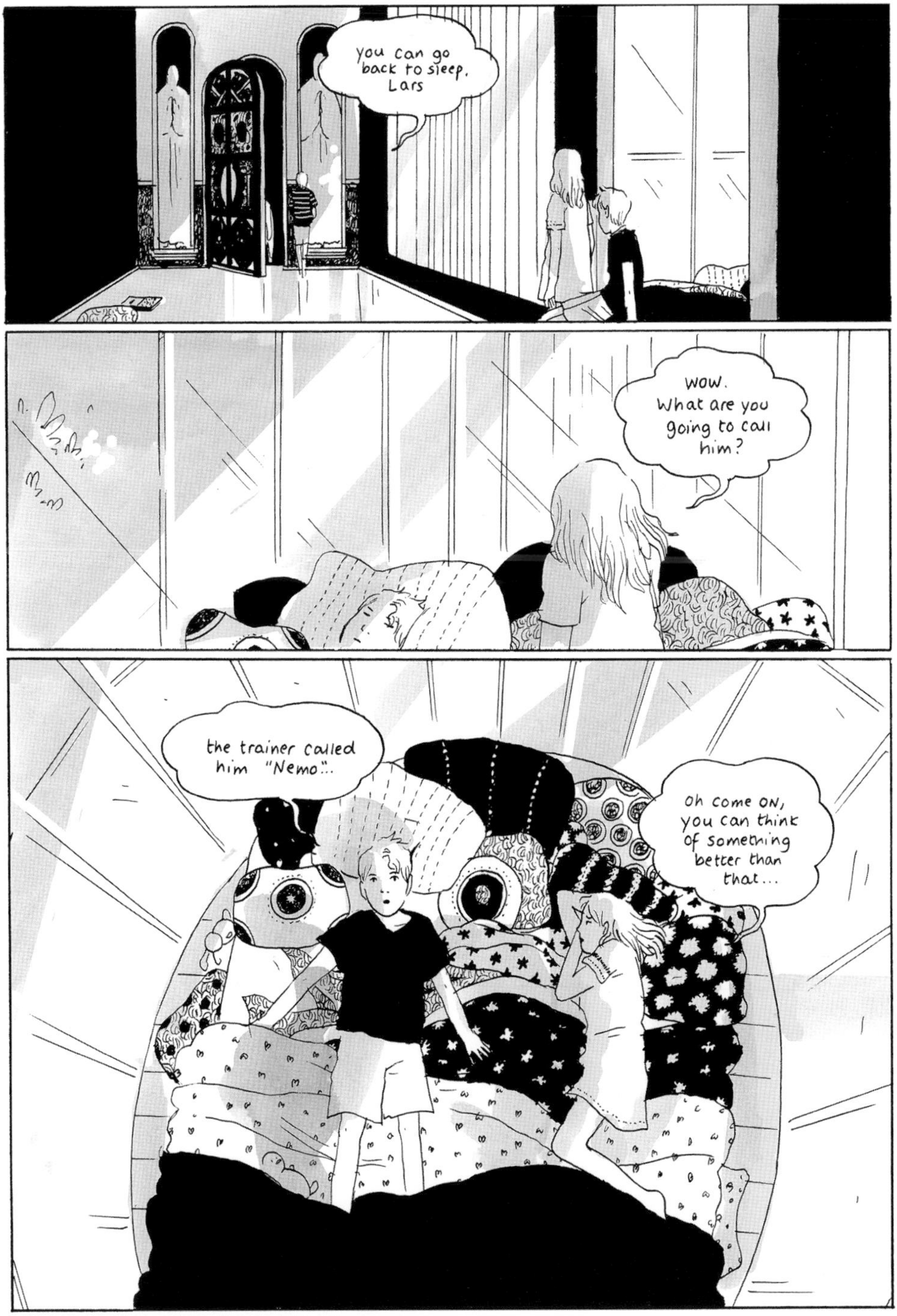
you can go back to sleep, Lars
wow. What are you going to call him?
the trainer called him "Nemo"..
Oh come ON, you can think of something better than that...

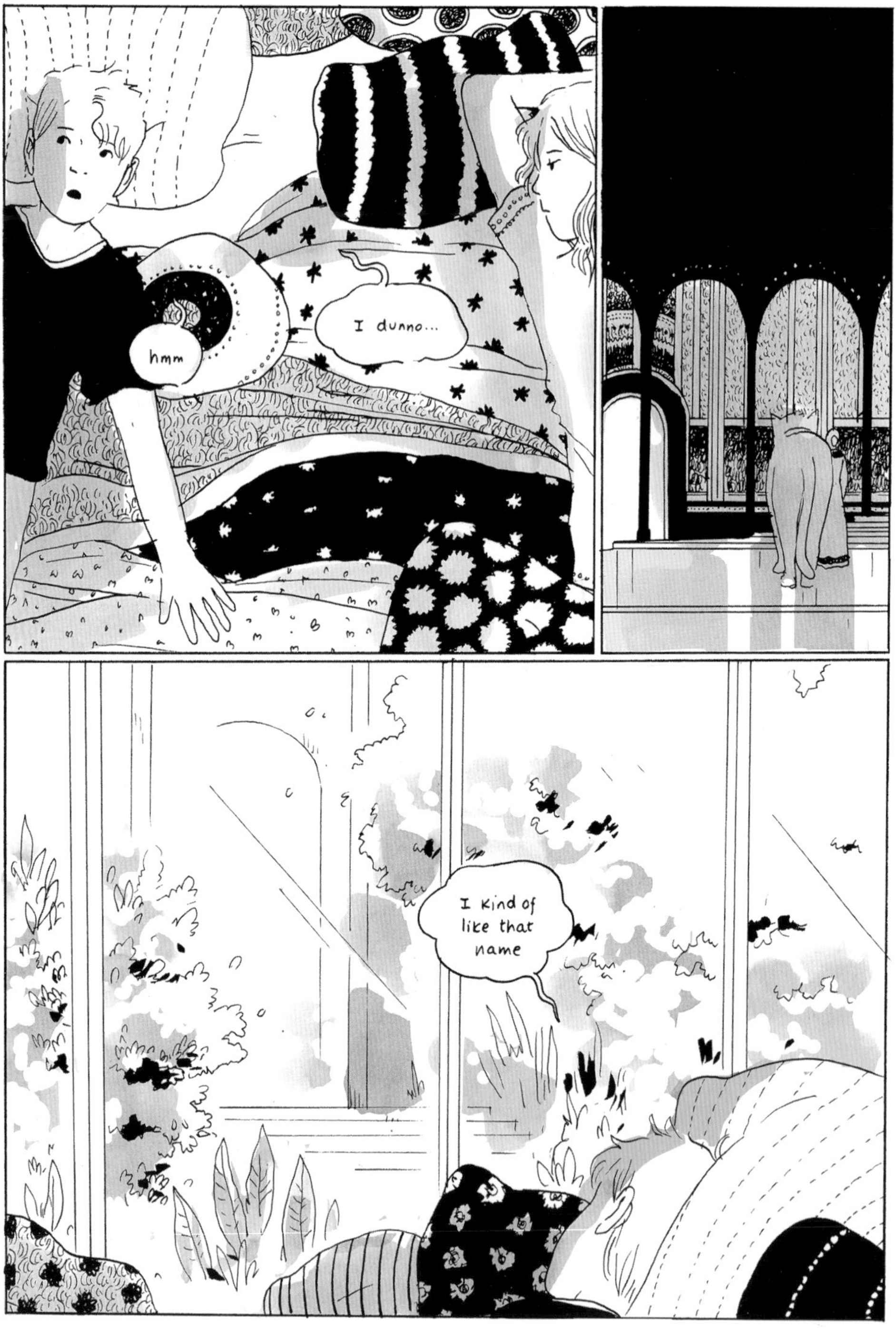
hmm
I dunno...
I kind of like that name

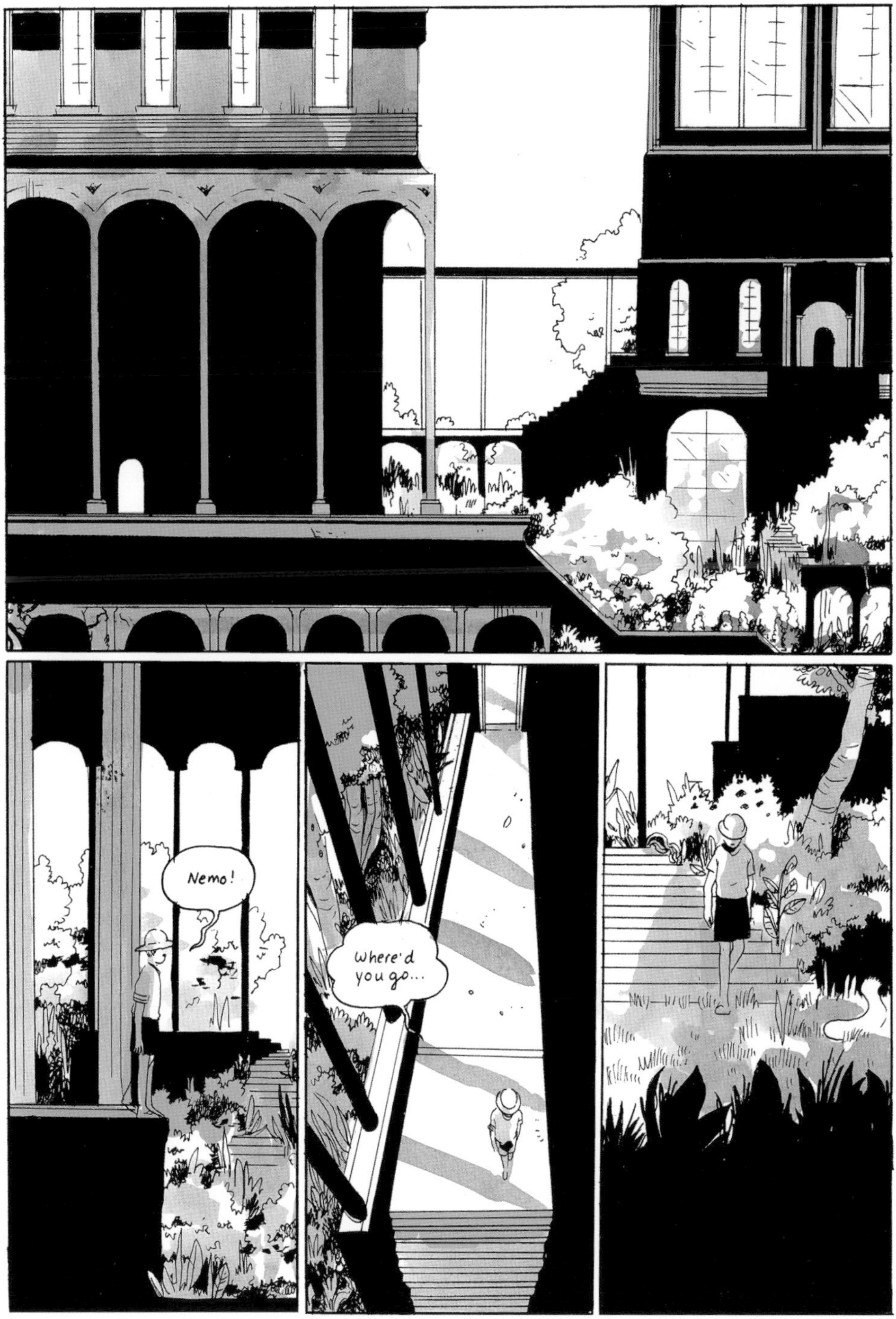
Nemo!
Where'd you go...

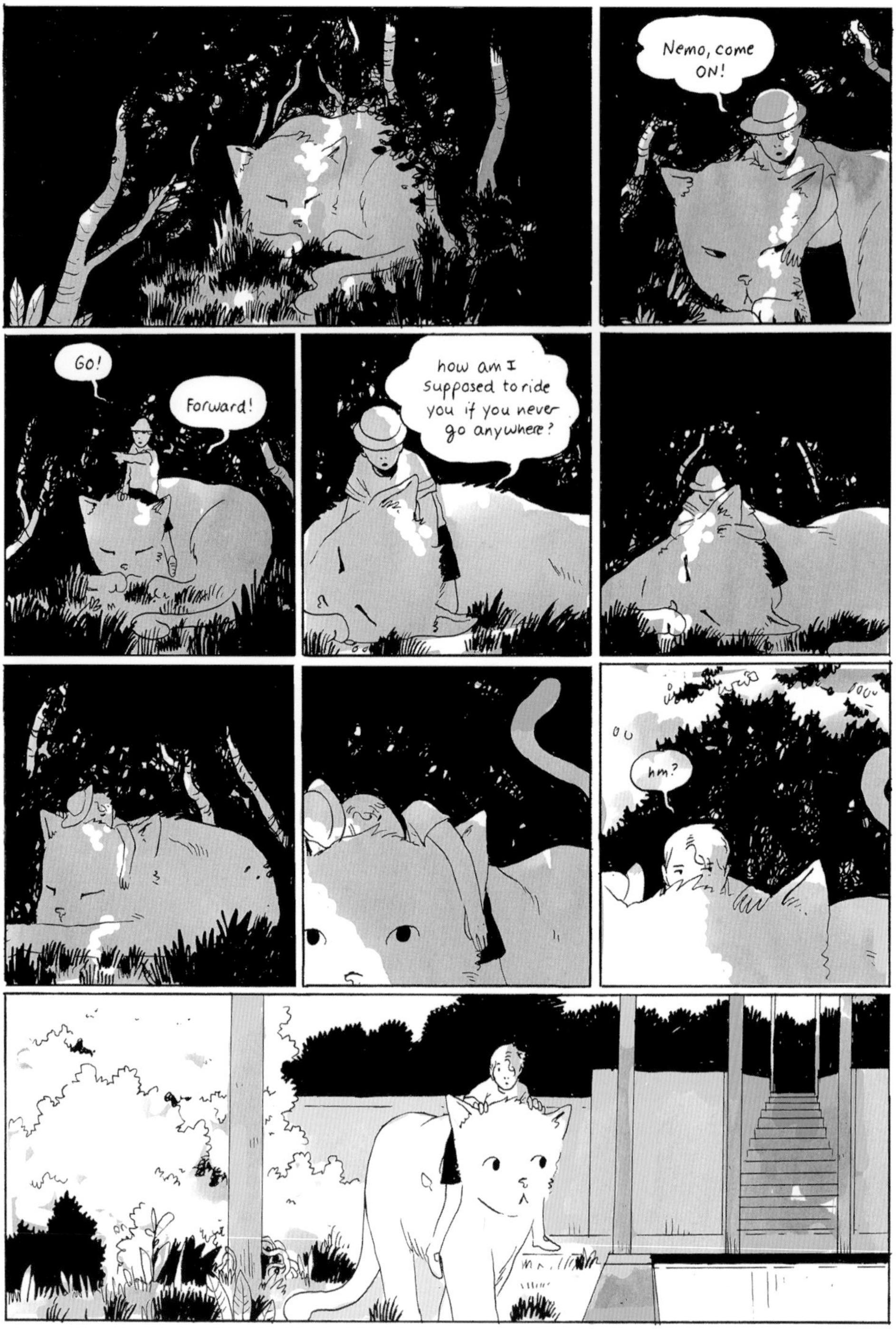
Nemo, come ON!
Go!
Forward!
how am I supposed to ride you if you never go anywhere?
hm?

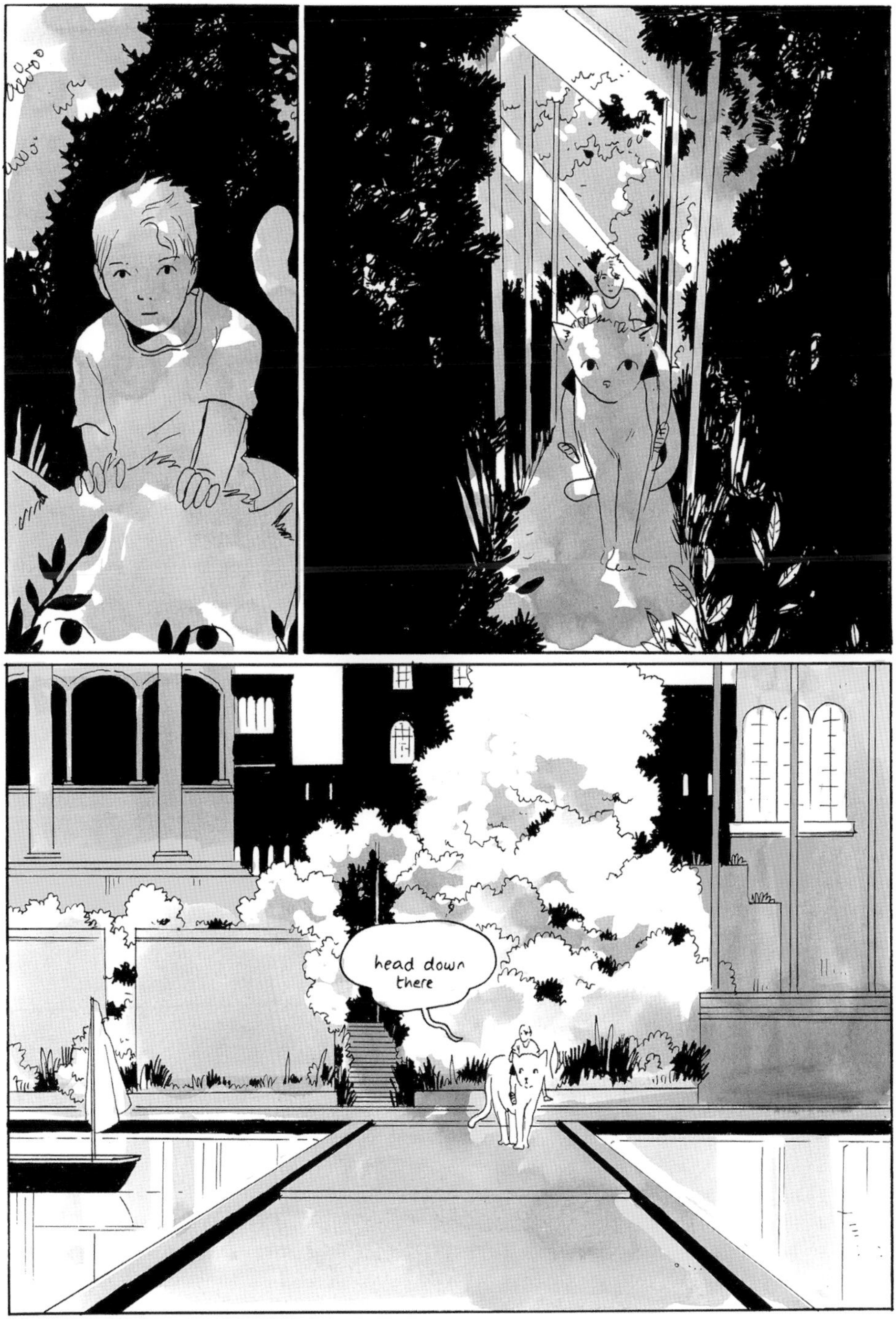
head down there

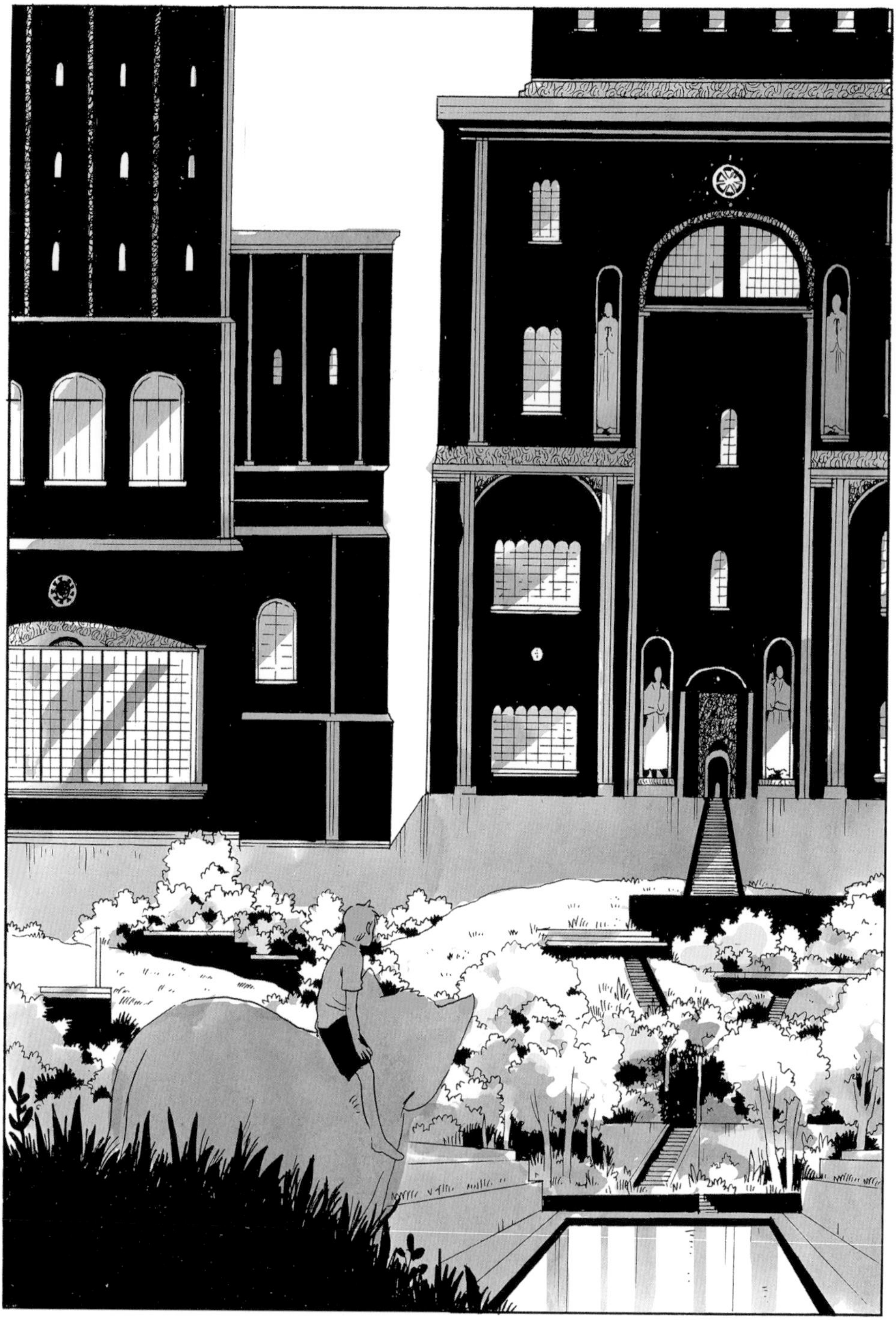

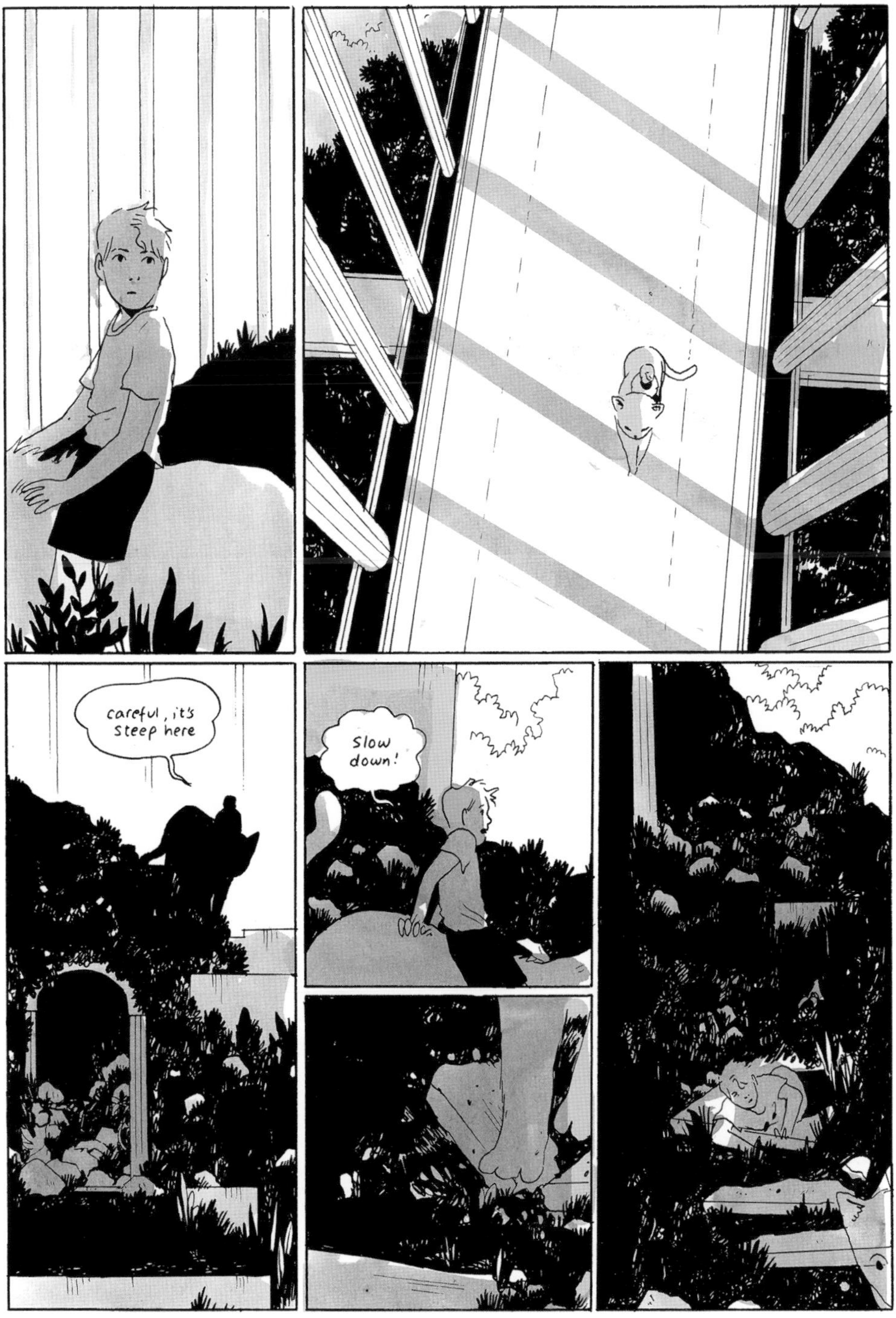
careful, it's steep here
slow down!

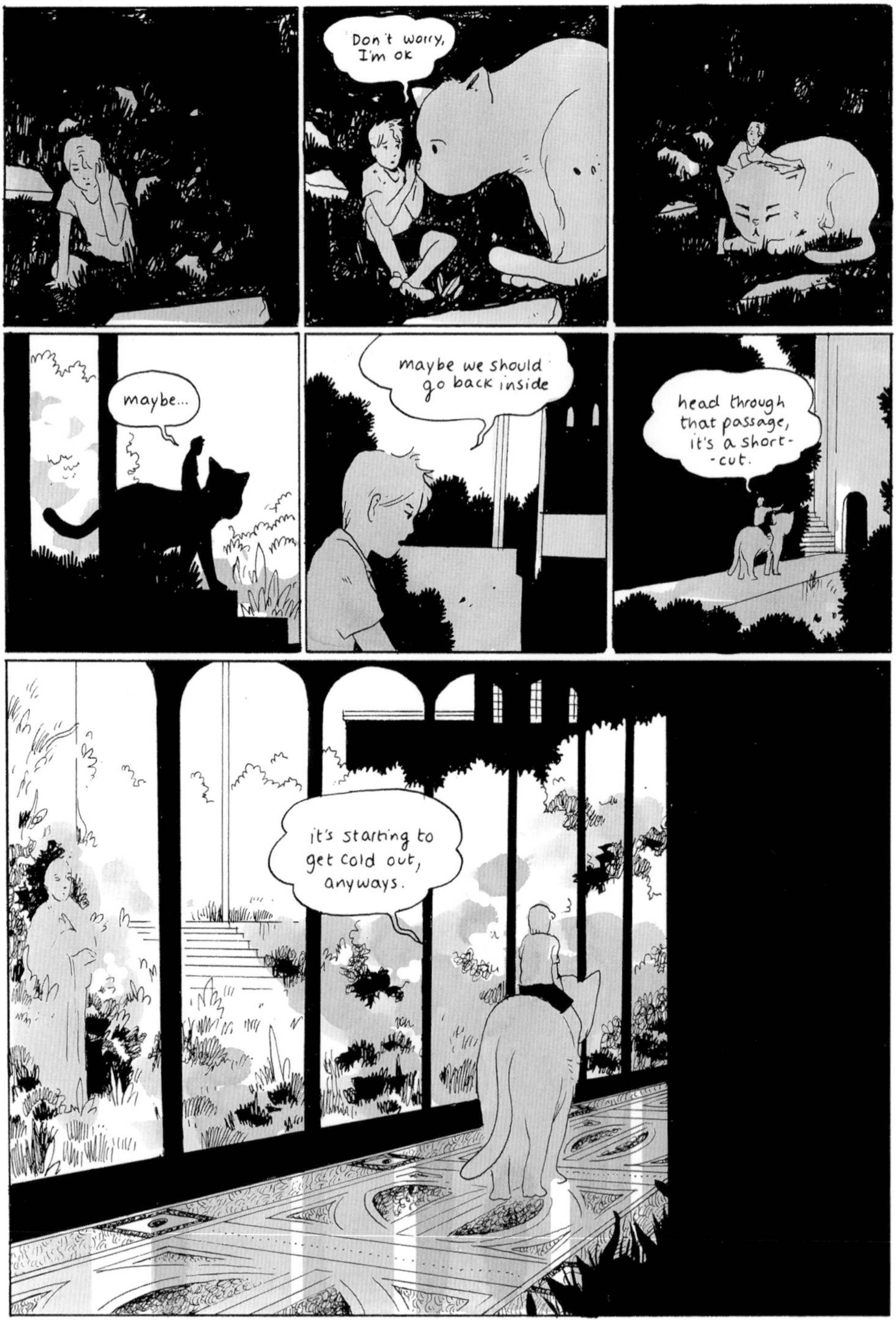
Don't worry, I'm ok
maybe...
maybe we should go back inside
head through that passage, it's a short-cut.
it's starting to get cold out, anyways.

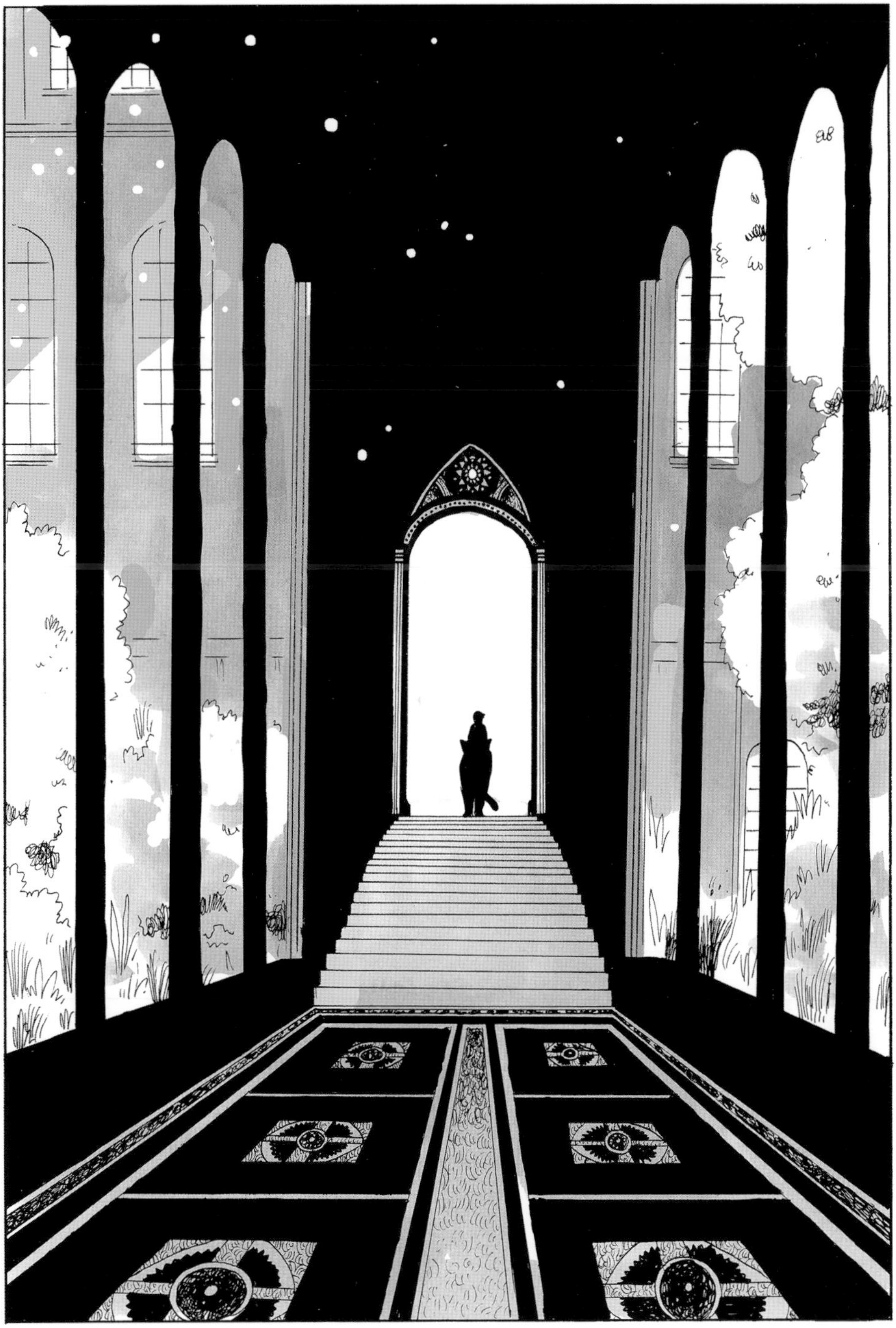

Alive (2016)

Made for Art Review Magazine. This is the first time I drew outer space! (I had just watched 2001: A Space Odyssey) The message of the comic doesn't really feel right anymore (I need people) but I appreciate the positivity. Also it shows my continued interest in drawing machinery.

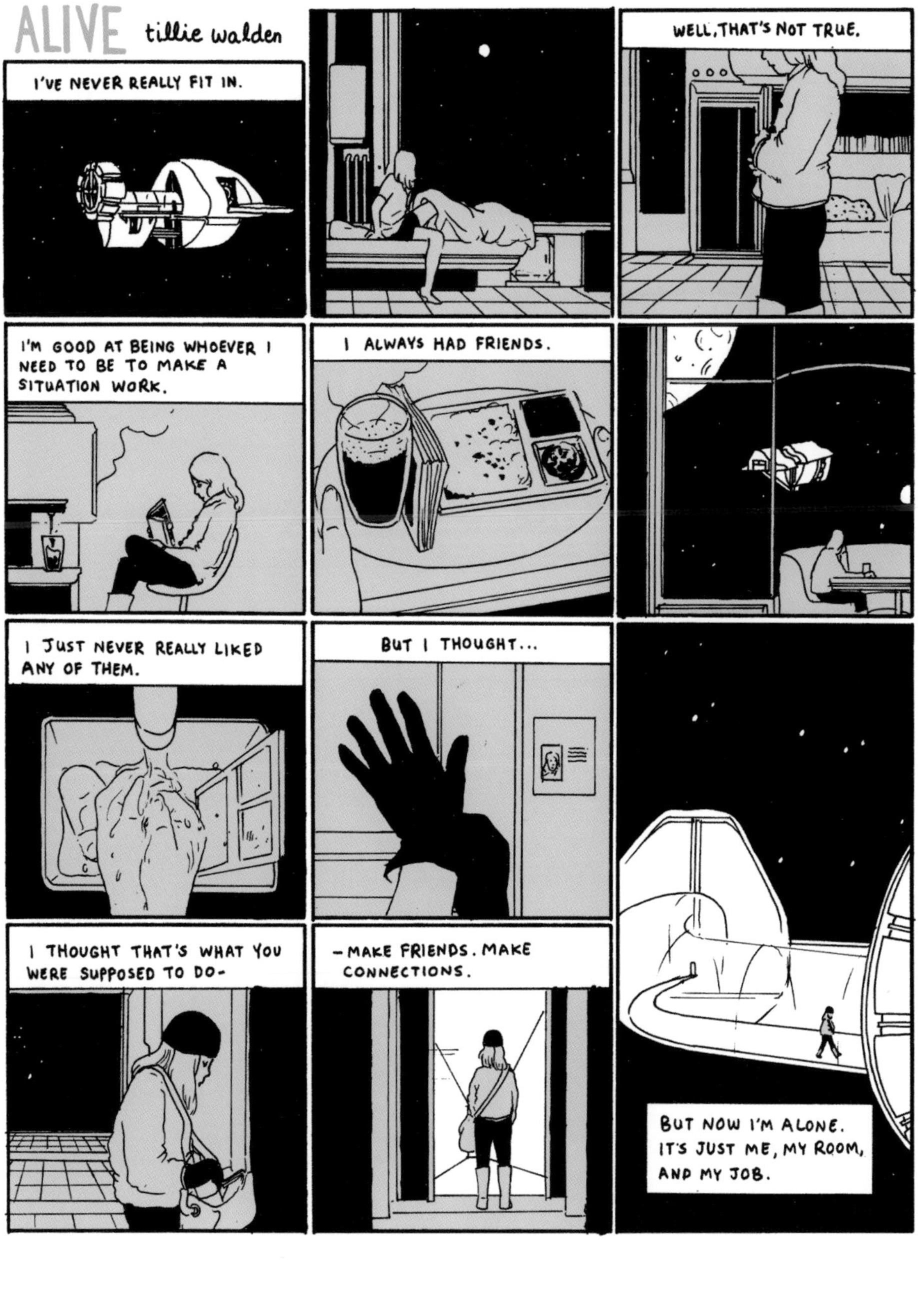
ALIVE
tillie walden
I'VE NEVER REALLY FIT IN.
WELL, THAT'S NOT TRUE.
I'M GOOD AT BEING WHOEVER I NEED TO BE TO MAKE A SITUATION WORK.
I ALWAYS HAD FRIENDS.
I JUST NEVER REALLY LIKED ANY OF THEM.
BUT I THOUGHT...
I THOUGHT THAT'S WHAT YOU WERE SUPPOSED TO DO-
-MAKE FRIENDS. MAKE CONNECTIONS.
BUT NOW I'M ALONE. IT'S JUST ME, MY ROOM, AND MY JOB.

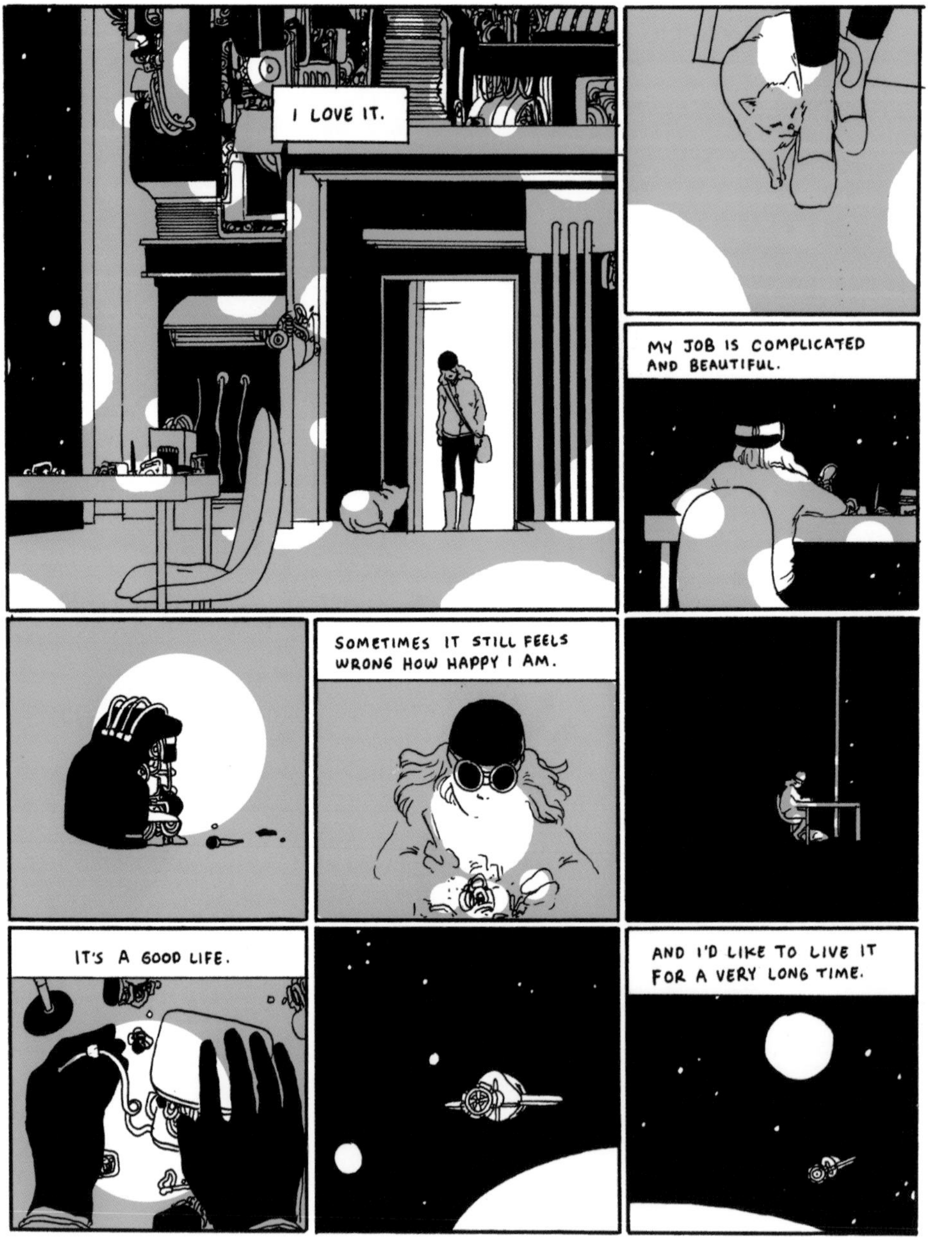
I LOVE IT.
MY JOB IS COMPLICATED AND BEAUTIFUL.
SOMETIMES IT STILL FEELS WRONG HOW HAPPY I AM.
IT'S A GOOD LIFE.
AND I'D LIKE TO LIVE IT FOR A VERY LONG TIME.

What It's Like to be Gay in an
All Girls Middle School (2016)

This was made for Vox.com and helped
my internet popularity grow. Ricky, my editor
on all these books, likes this one a lot. I really
like the pacing.

What it's like to be gay in an all-girls middle school
tillie walden

I always knew middle school was an unwinnable situation. I was too young to be myself and not yet old enough to be okay with standing out.

I knew I was gay the whole time. There was never any question in my mind about that. What I didn't know was how to be gay, or if it was even allowed.

Edward or Jacob?

I like Alice

but.. Edward or Jacob?

To make matters more confusing, I was at an all-girls school where experimentation was the norm.

I dare u 2 kiss for 10 seconds

3... 4... 5...

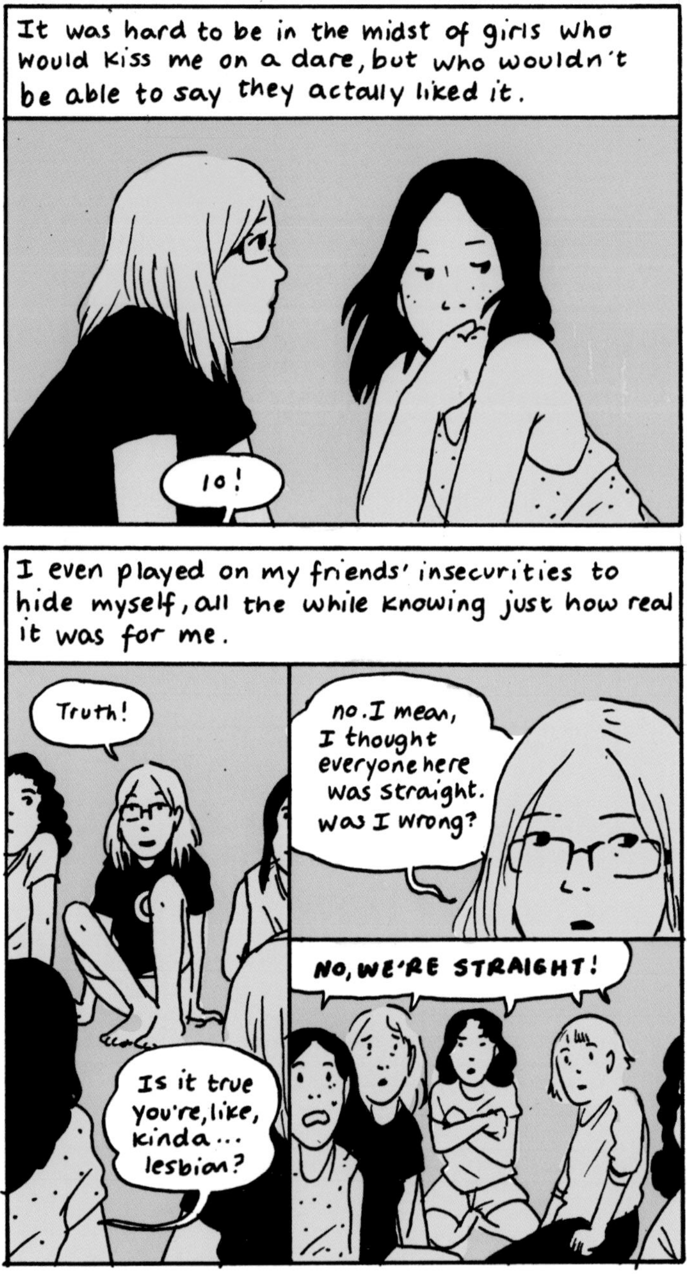
It was hard to be in the midst of girls who would kiss me on a dare, but who wouldn't be able to say they actally liked it.
10!
I even played on my friends' insecurities to hide myself, all the while knowing just how real it was for me.
Truth!
Is it true you're, like, kinda... lesbian?
no. I mean, I thought everyone here was straight. Was I wrong?
NO, WE'RE STRAIGHT!

The question I wanted an answer to was... was it real for anyone else?

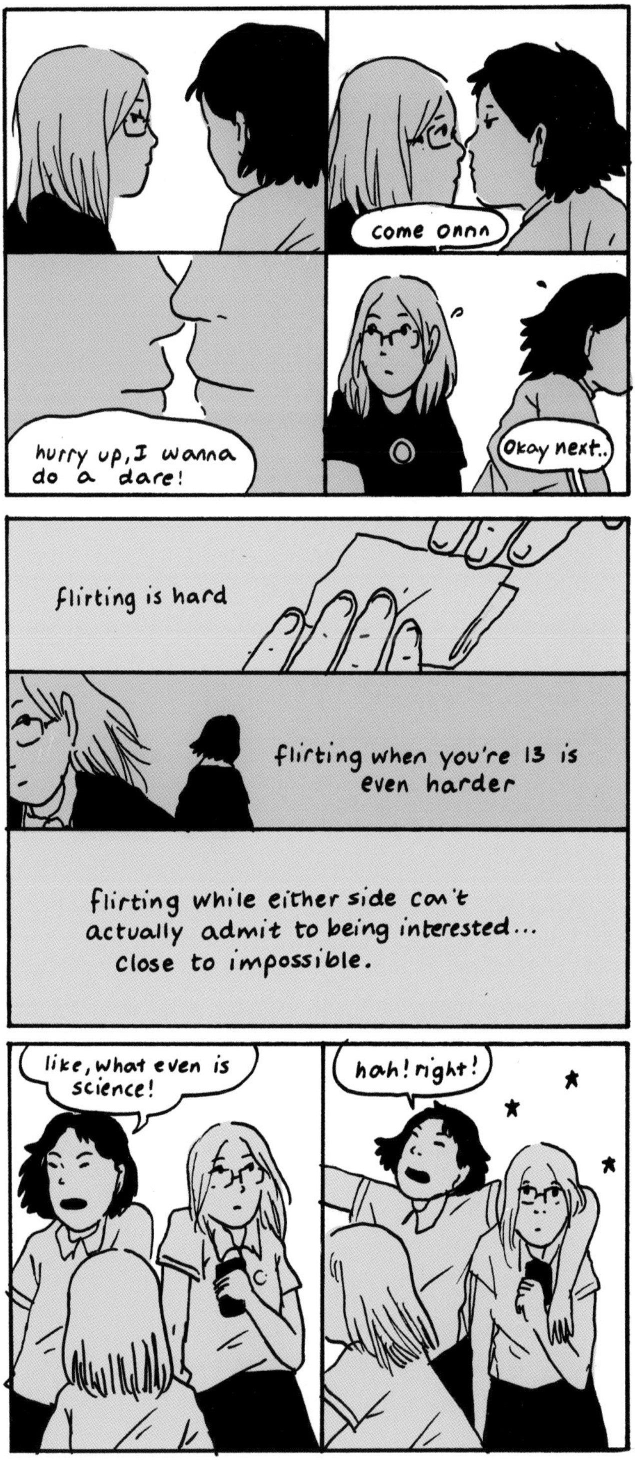
come Onnn
hurry up, I wanna do a dare!
Okay next..
flirting is hard
flirting when you're 13 is even harder
flirting while either side can't actually admit to being interested... close to impossible.
like, what even is science!
hah! right!

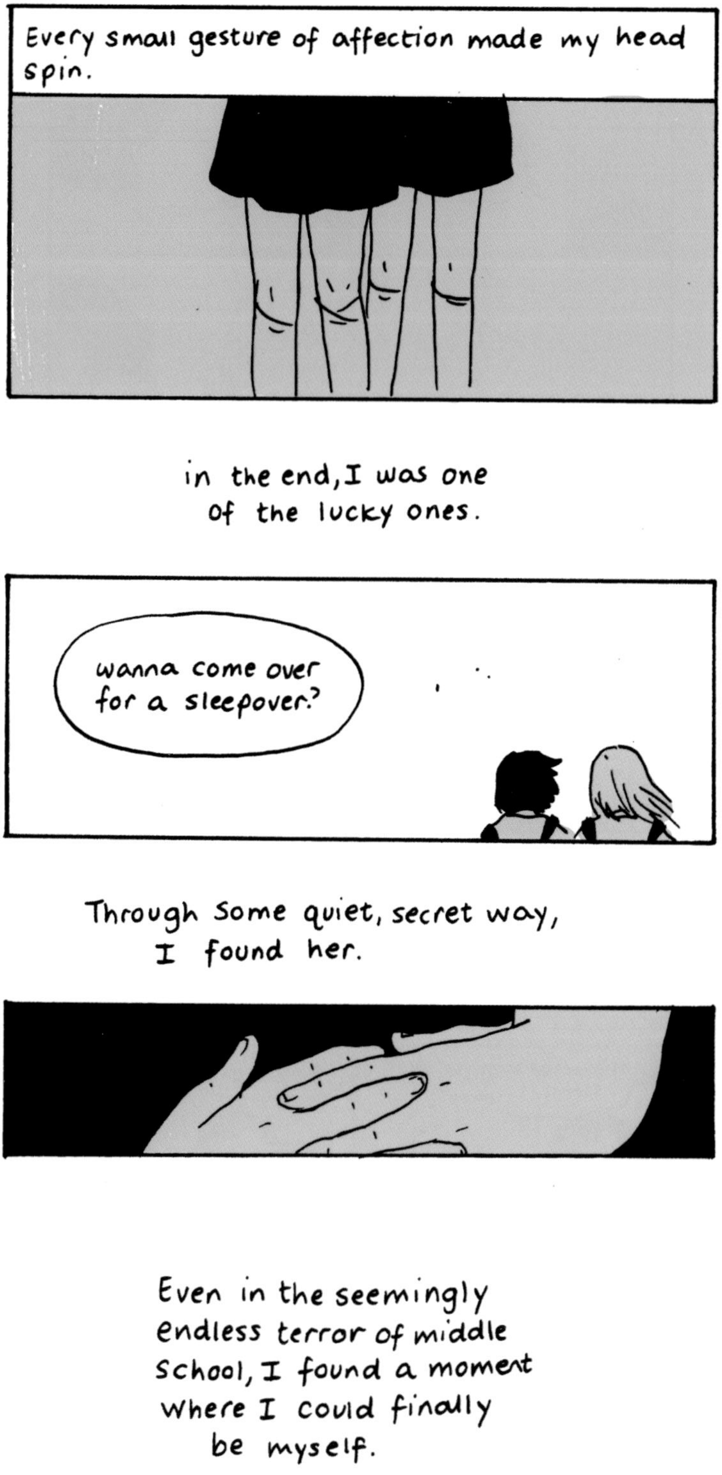
Every small gesture of affection made my head spin.
in the end, I was one of the lucky ones.
wanna come over for a sleepover?
. . .
Through some quiet, secret way, I found her.
Even in the seemingly endless terror of middle school, I found a moment where I could finally be myself.

Q&A (2017)

First time doing colored line art. James Sturm came up with the concept. A lot of CCS grads do pamphlets like these!

the Center for Cartoon Studies
PRESENTS

Q&A

WITH *tillie walden*

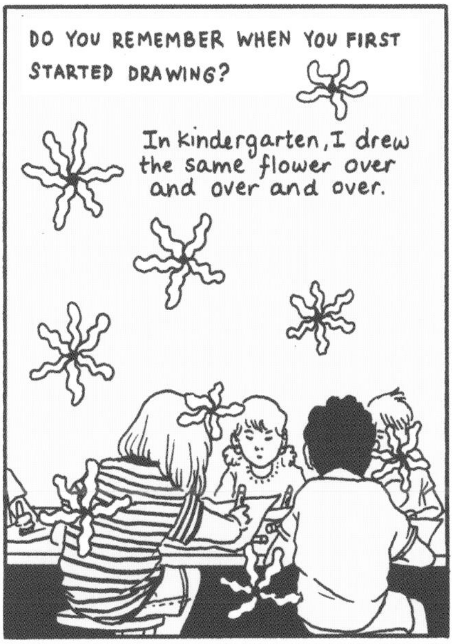
DO YOU REMEMBER WHEN YOU FIRST STARTED DRAWING?
In kindergarten, I drew the same flower over and over and over.

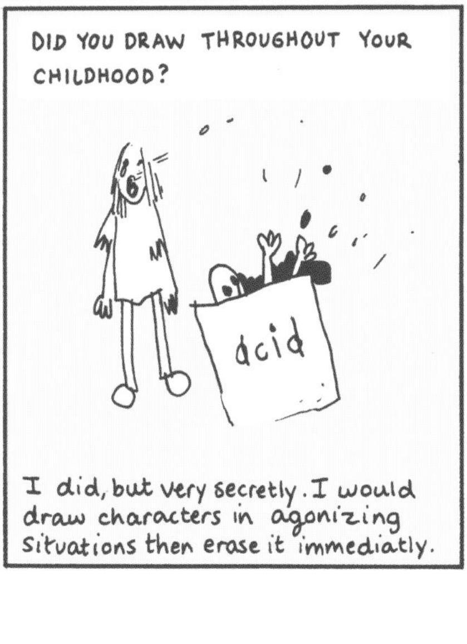
DID YOU DRAW THROUGHOUT YOUR CHILDHOOD?
acid
I did, but very secretly. I would draw characters in agonizing situations then erase it immediatly.

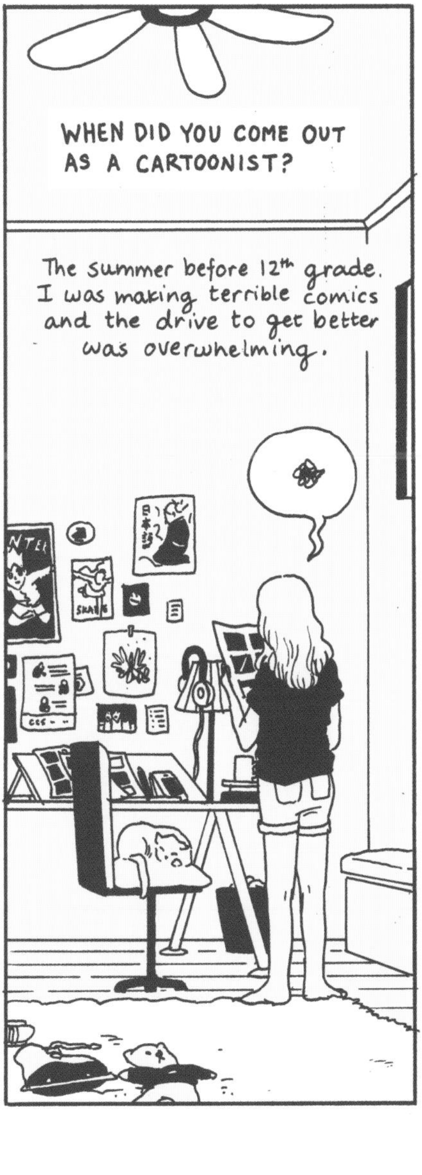
WHEN DID YOU COME OUT AS A CARTOONIST?
The summer before 12th grade. I was making terrible comics and the drive to get better was overwhelming.

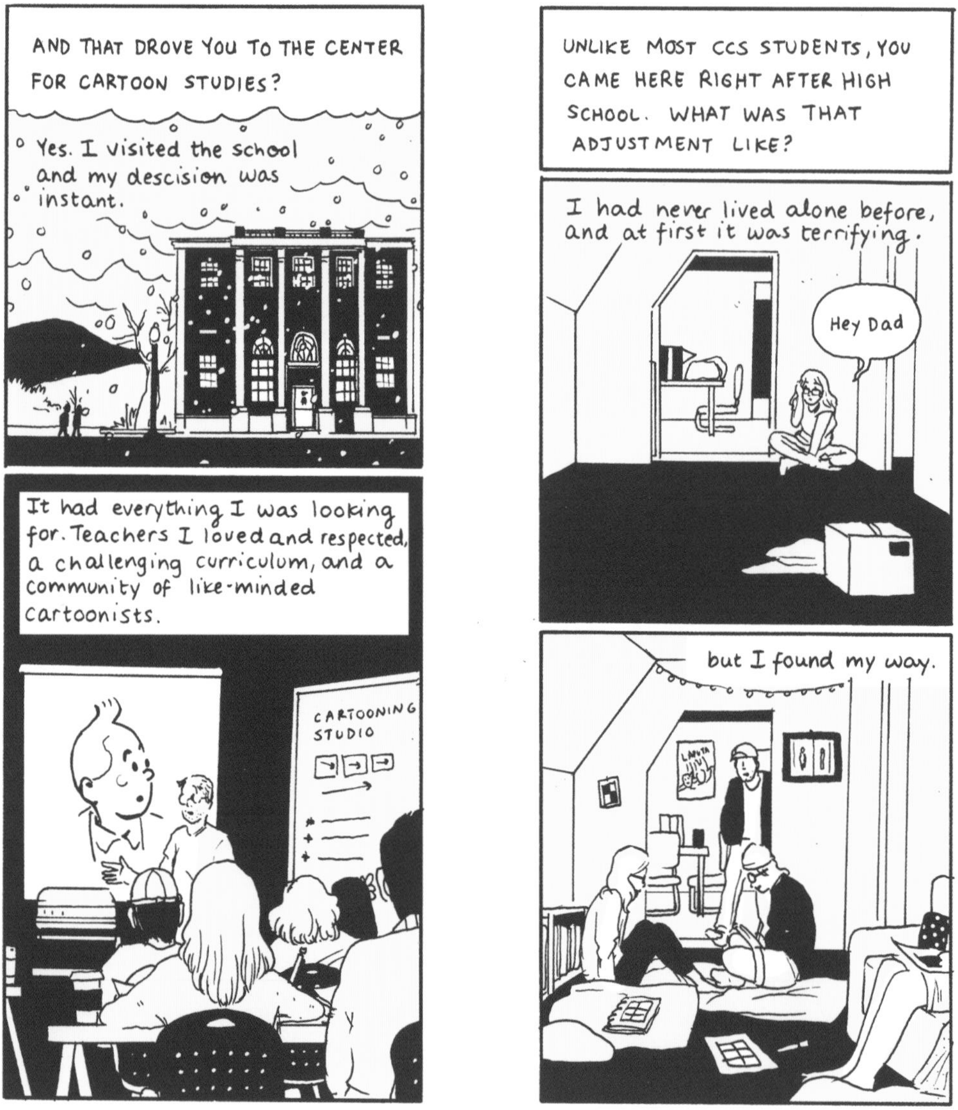
AND THAT DROVE YOU TO THE CENTER FOR CARTOON STUDIES?
Yes. I visited the school and my descision was instant.
It had everything I was looking for. Teachers I loved and respected, a challenging curriculum, and a community of like-minded cartoonists.
CARTOONING STUDIO
UNLIKE MOST CCS STUDENTS, YOU CAME HERE RIGHT AFTER HIGH SCHOOL. WHAT WAS THAT ADJUSTMENT LIKE?
I had never lived alone before, and at first it was terrifying.
Hey Dad
but I found my way.

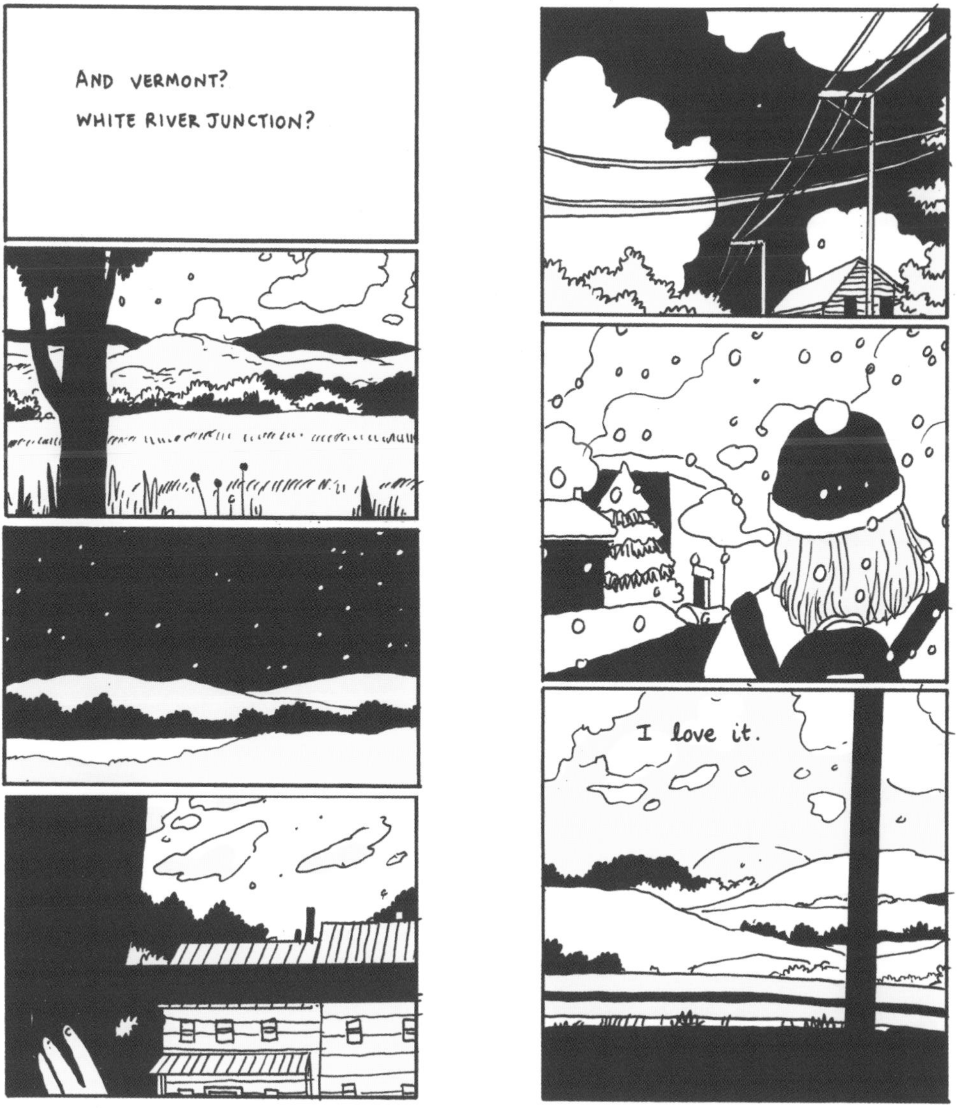
AND VERMONT?
WHITE RIVER JUNCTION?
I love it.

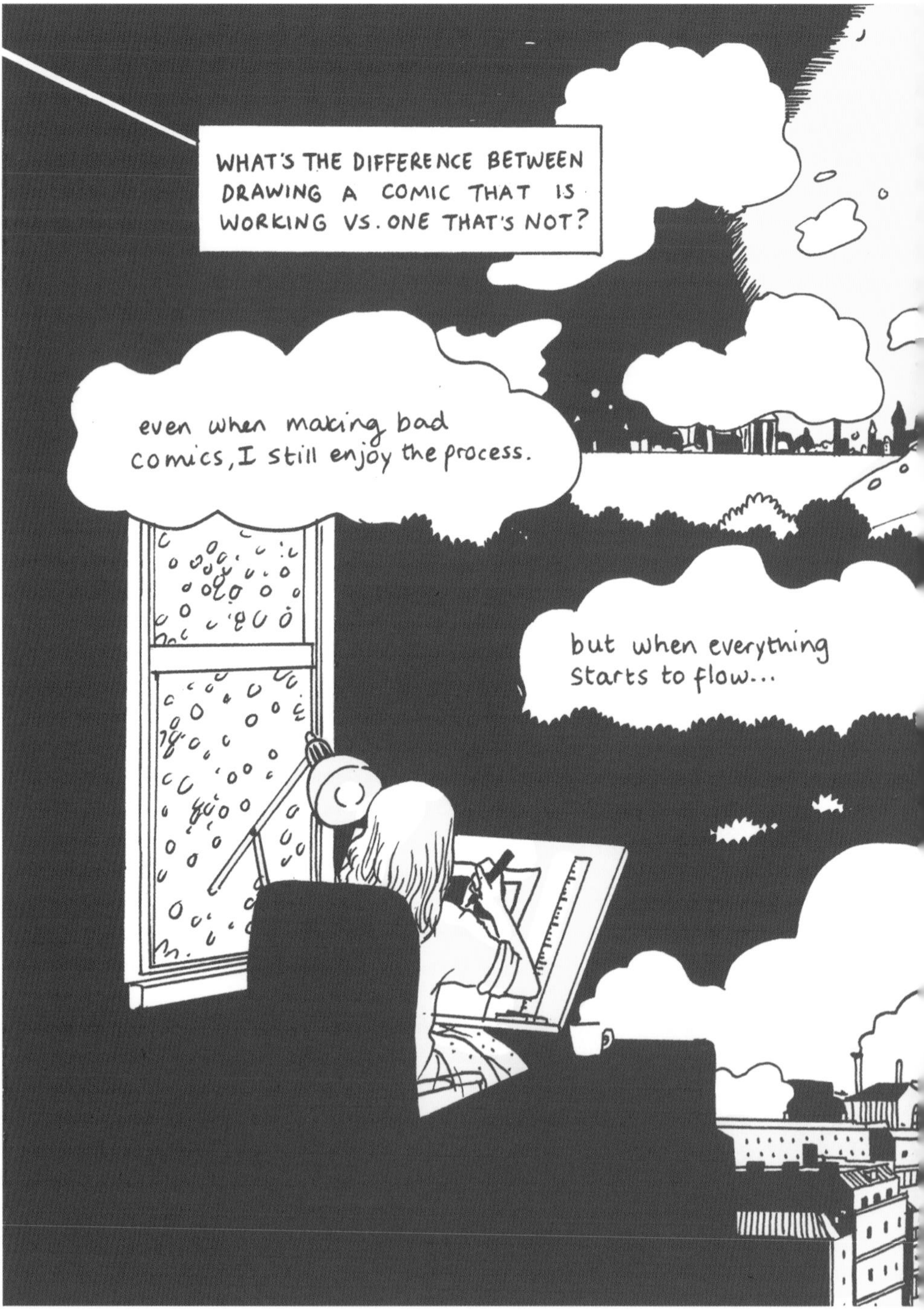
WHAT'S THE DIFFERENCE BETWEEN DRAWING A COMIC THAT IS WORKING VS. ONE THAT'S NOT?
even when making bad comics, I still enjoy the process.
but when everything starts to flow...

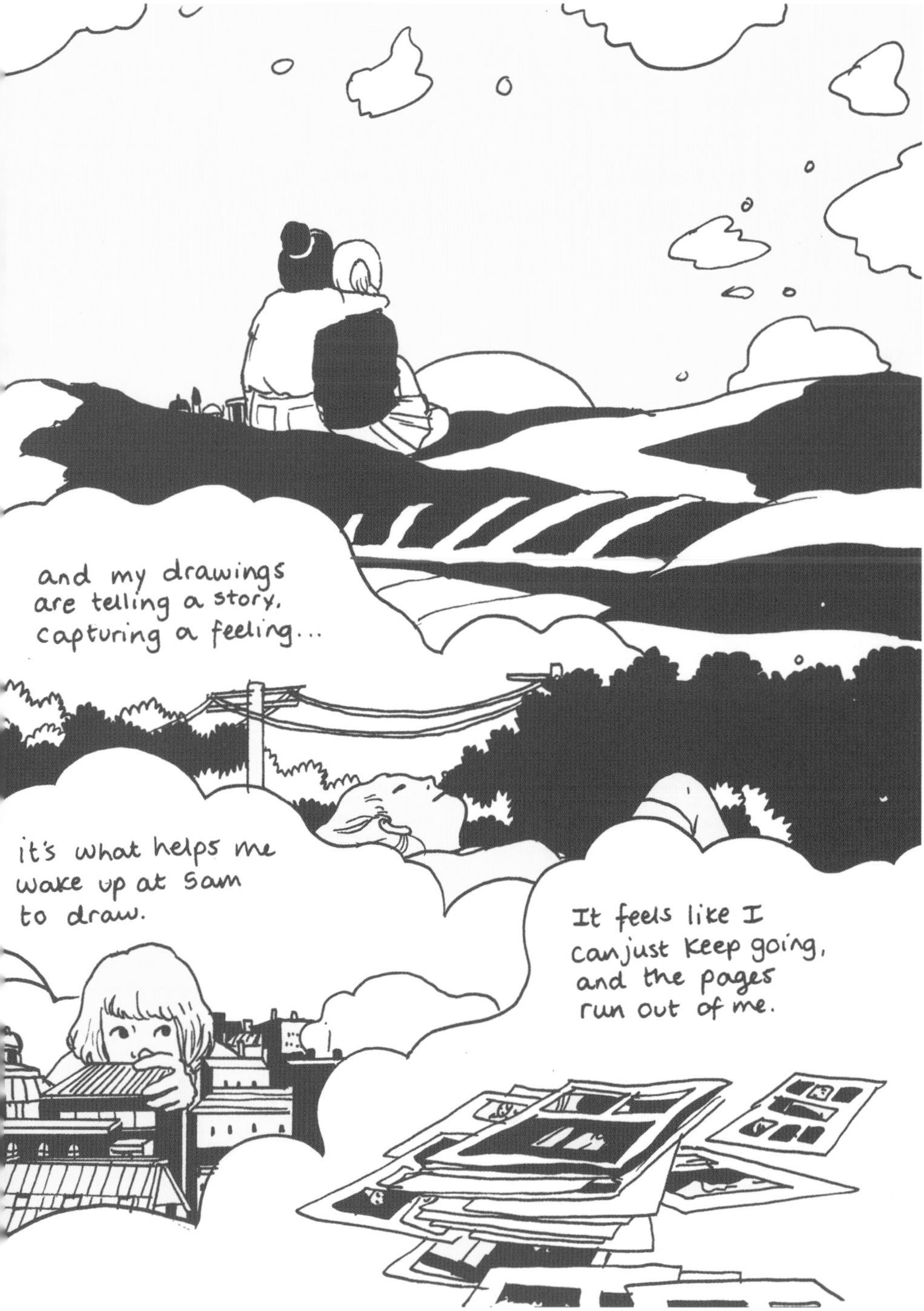
and my drawings are telling a story, capturing a feeling...
it's what helps me wake up at 5am to draw.
It feels like I can just keep going, and the pages run out of me.

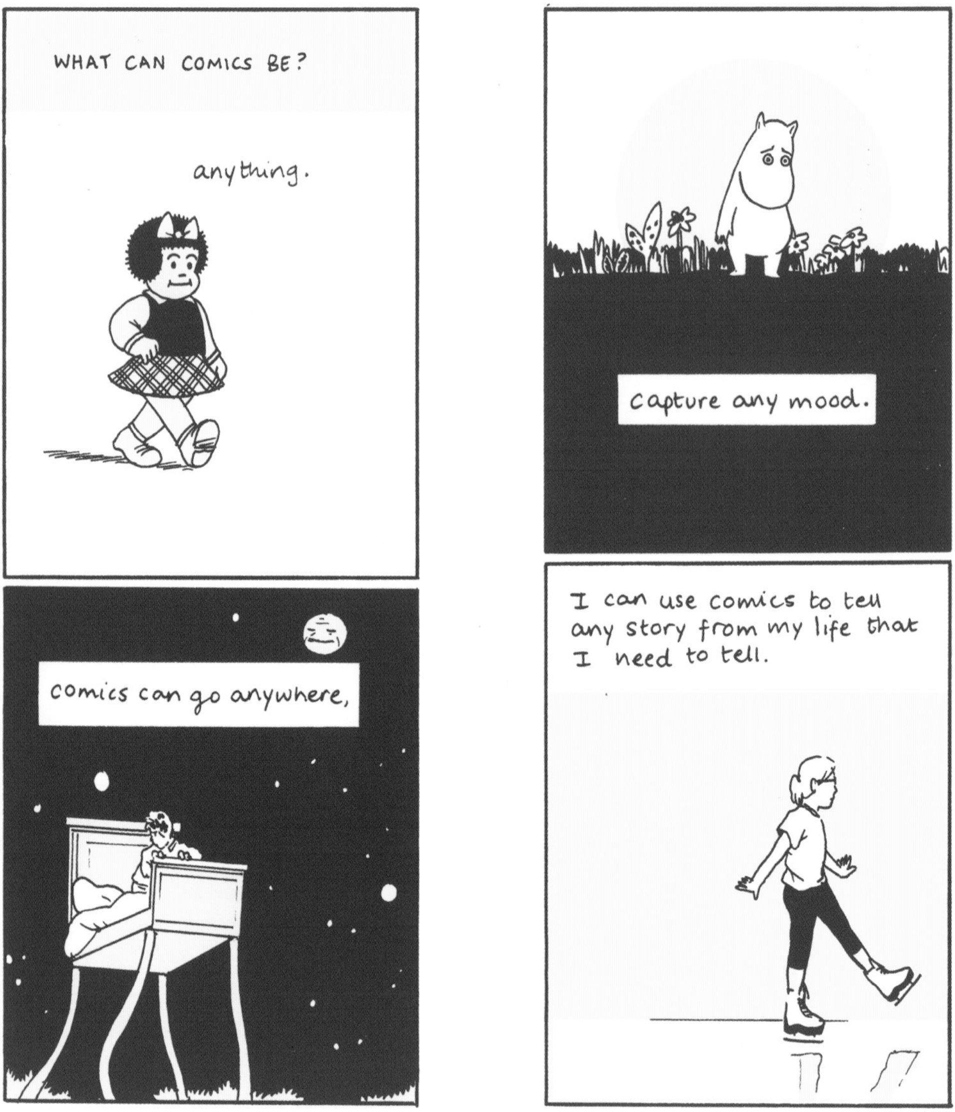
WHAT CAN COMICS BE?
anything.
capture any mood.
comics can go anywhere,
I can use comics to tell any story from my life that I need to tell.

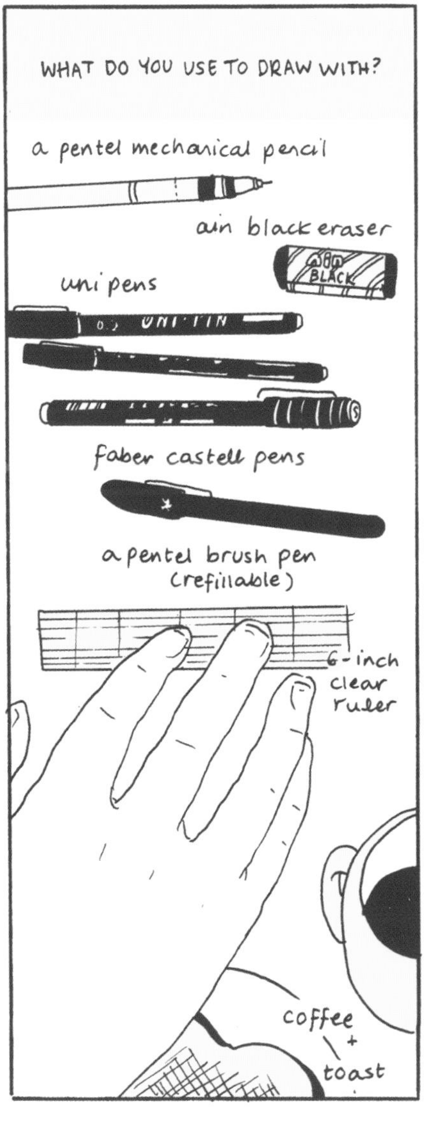
WHAT DO YOU USE TO DRAW WITH?
a pentel mechanical pencil
ain black eraser
uni pens
UNI-PIN
faber castell pens
a pentel brush pen (refillable)
6-inch clear ruler
coffee + toast

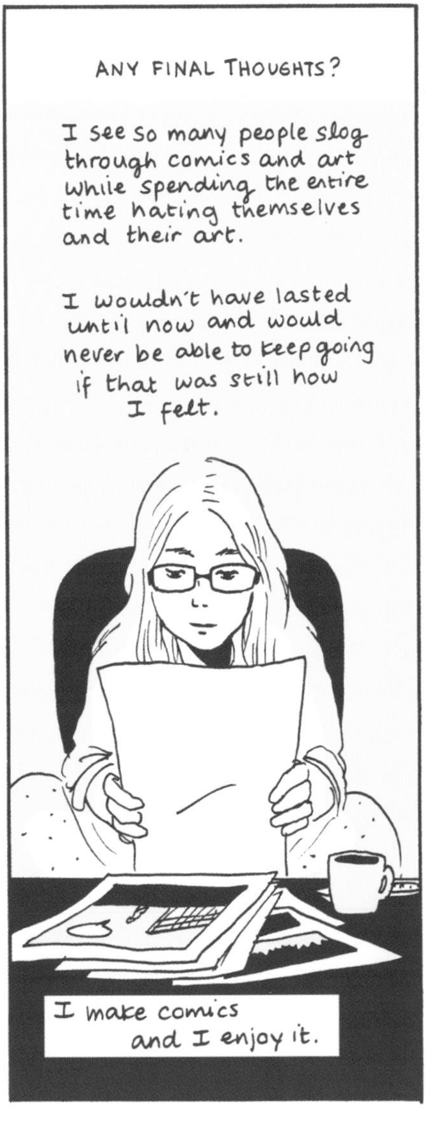
ANY FINAL THOUGHTS?
I see so many people slog through comics and art while spending the entire time hating themselves and their art.
I wouldn't have lasted until now and would never be able to keep going if that was still how I felt.
I make comics and I enjoy it.

The Fader (2018)

I made this for The Fader magazine. This was when I really figured out digital color. I also started using a ruler a lot less and began filling up spaces more abstractly.

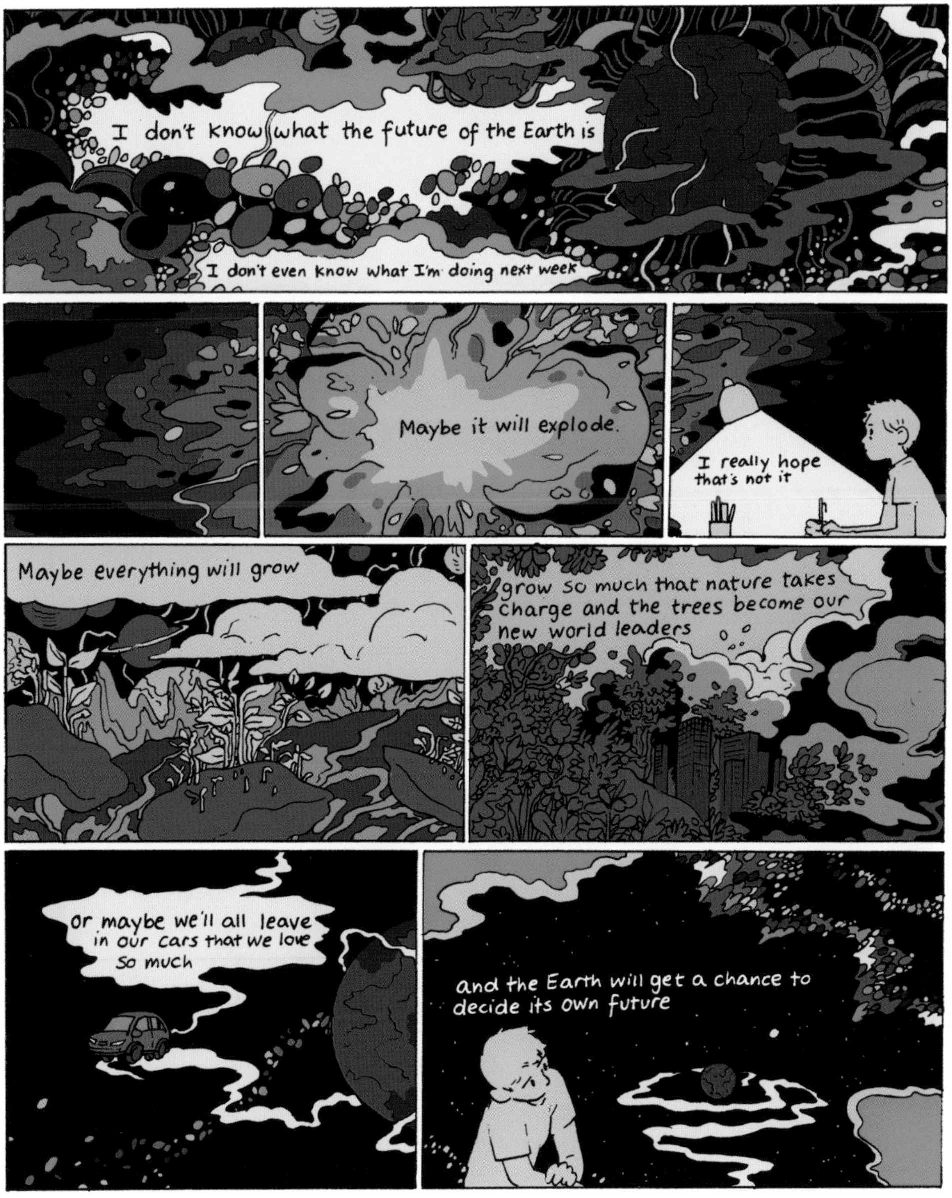
I don't know what the future of the Earth is
I don't even know what I'm doing next week
Maybe it will explode.
I really hope that's not it
Maybe everything will grow
grow so much that nature takes charge and the trees become our new world leaders
or maybe we'll all leave in our cars that we love so much
and the Earth will get a chance to decide its own future

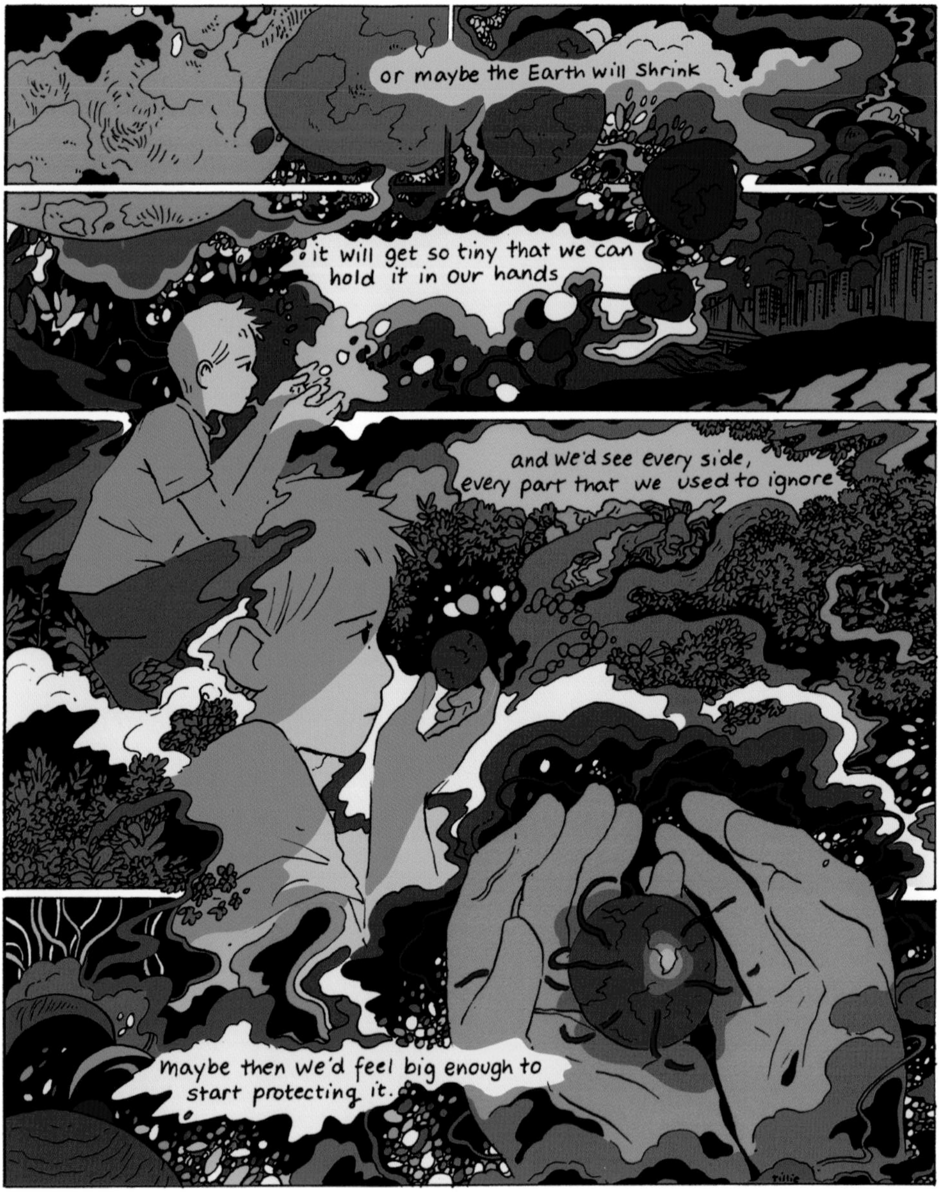
or maybe the Earth will Shrink
it will get so tiny that we can hold it in our hands
and we'd see every side, every part that we used to ignore
maybe then we'd feel big enough to start protecting it.

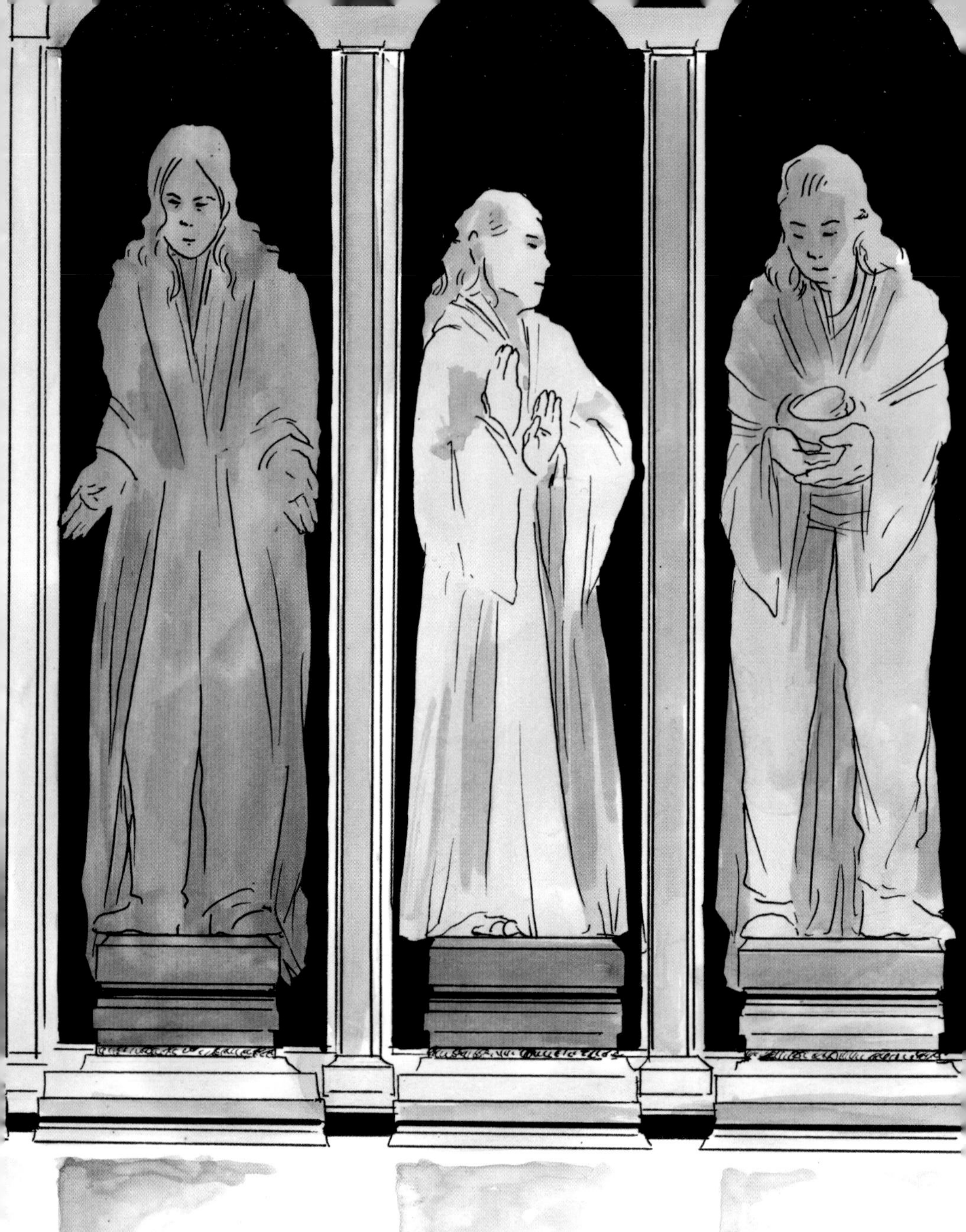

gallery

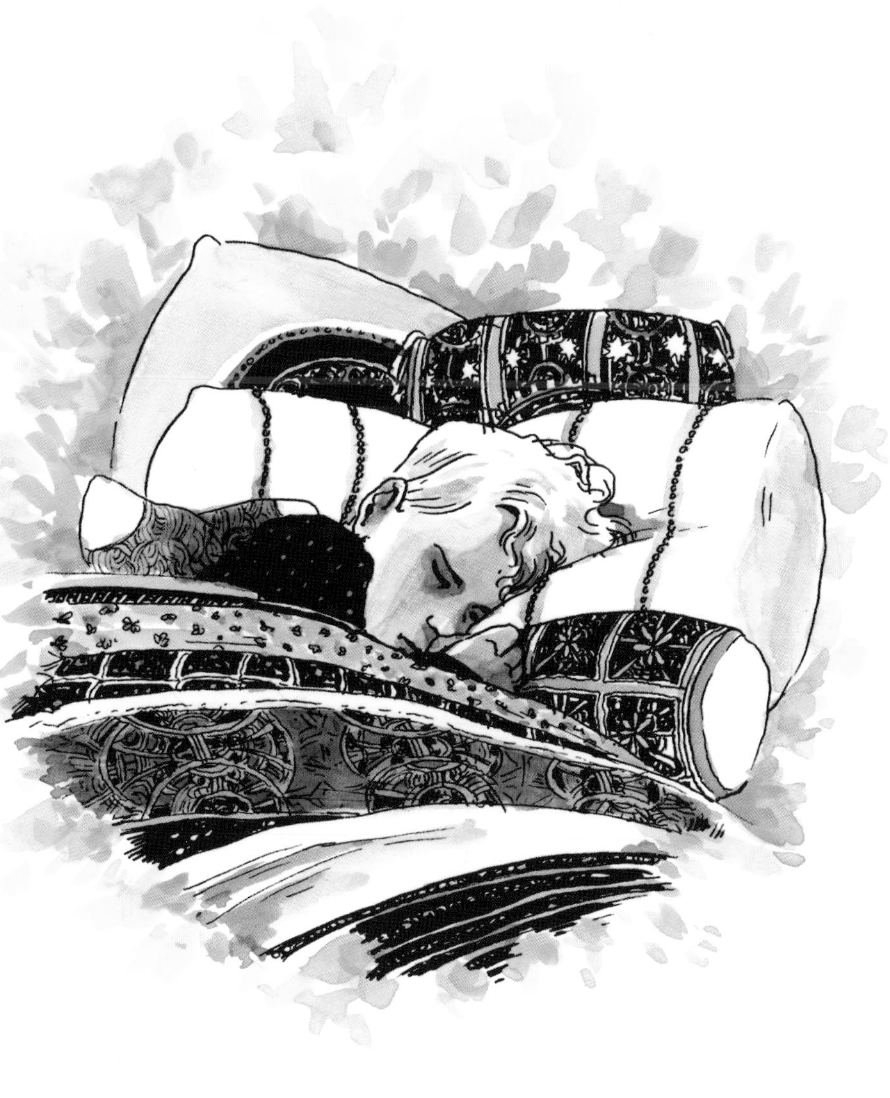

The End of Summer bookplate image for Gosh! Comics, London (2014)

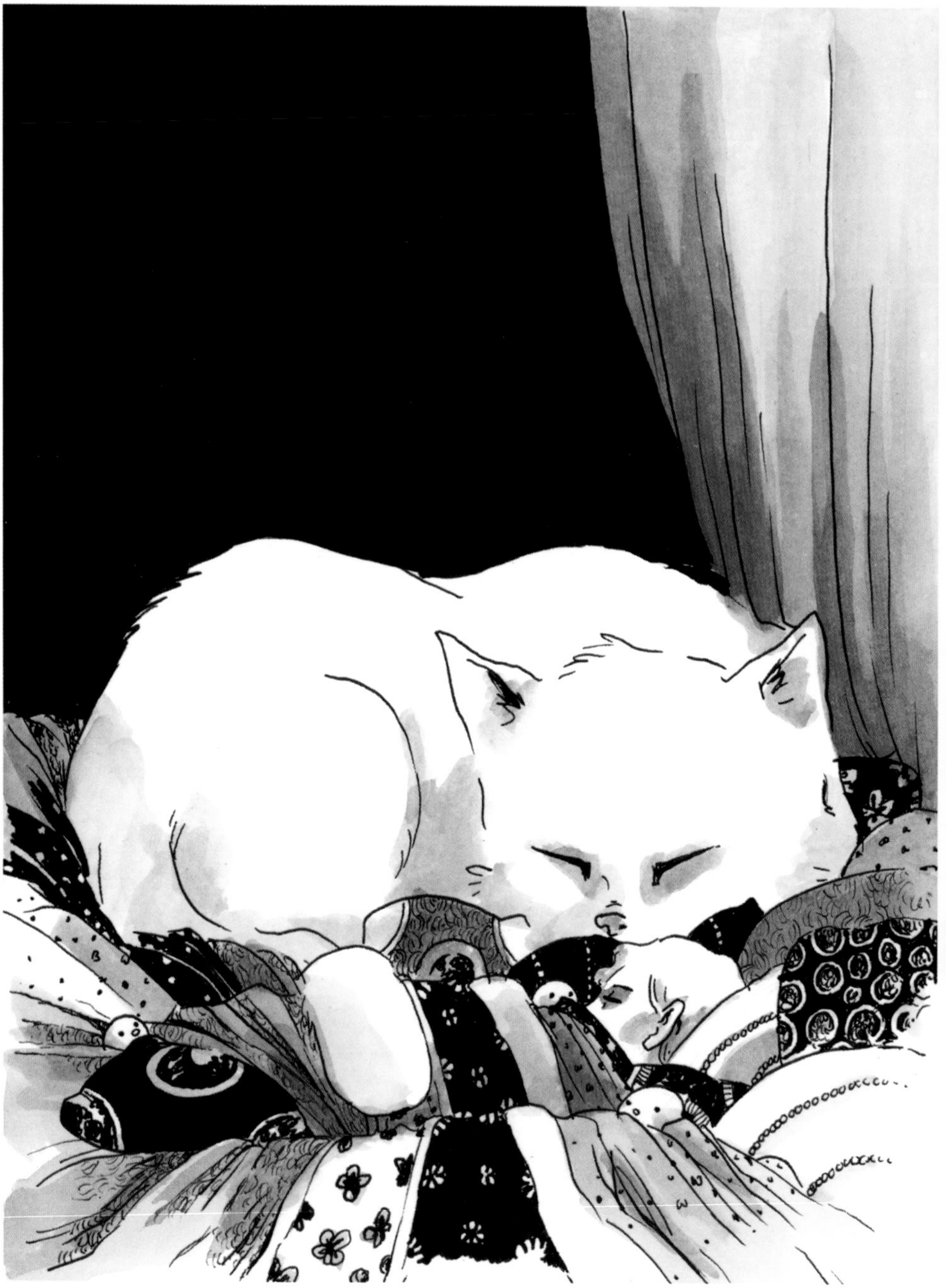

The End of Summer print (2015)

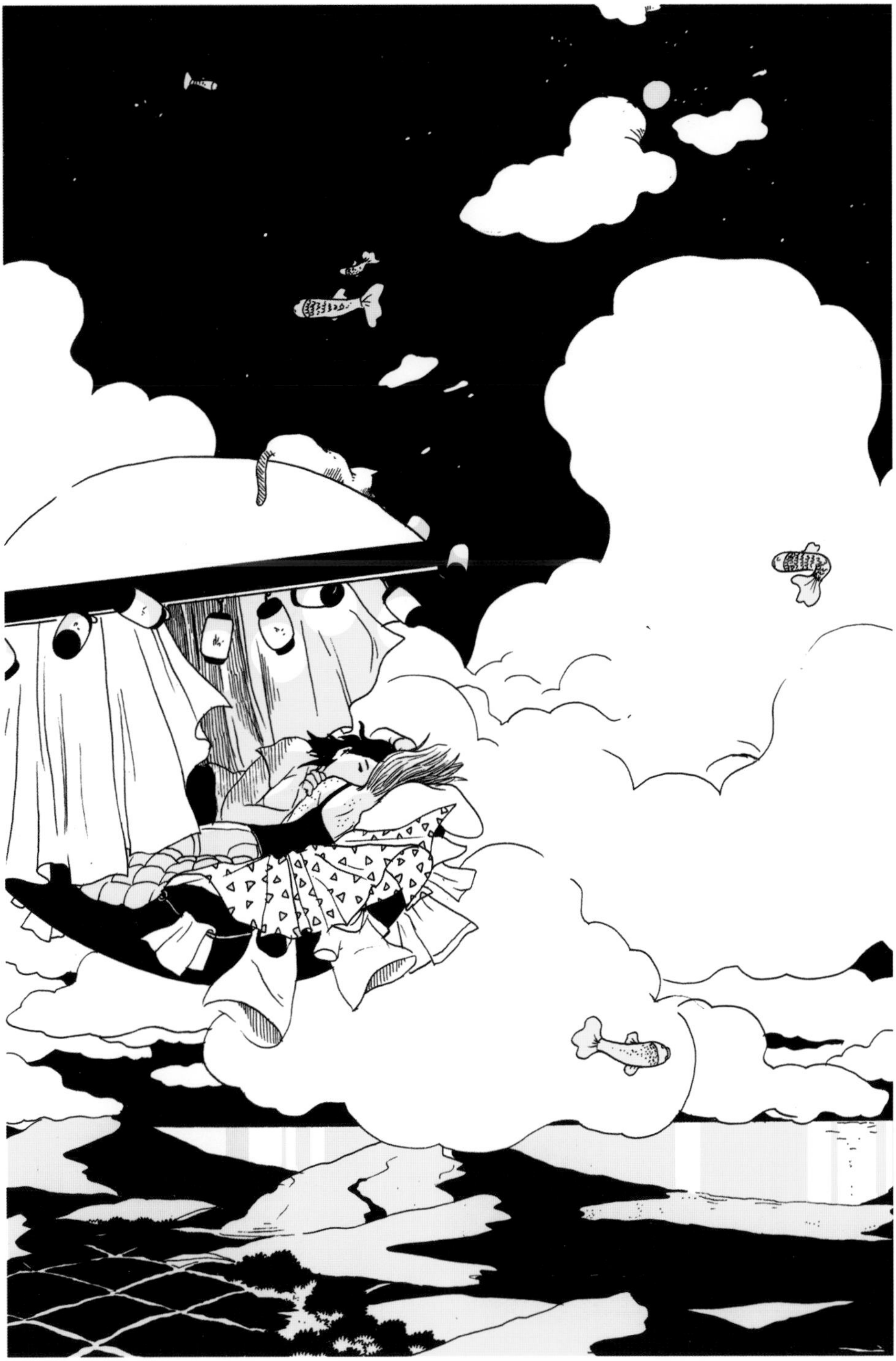

A City Inside print for Gosh! Comics, London (2016)

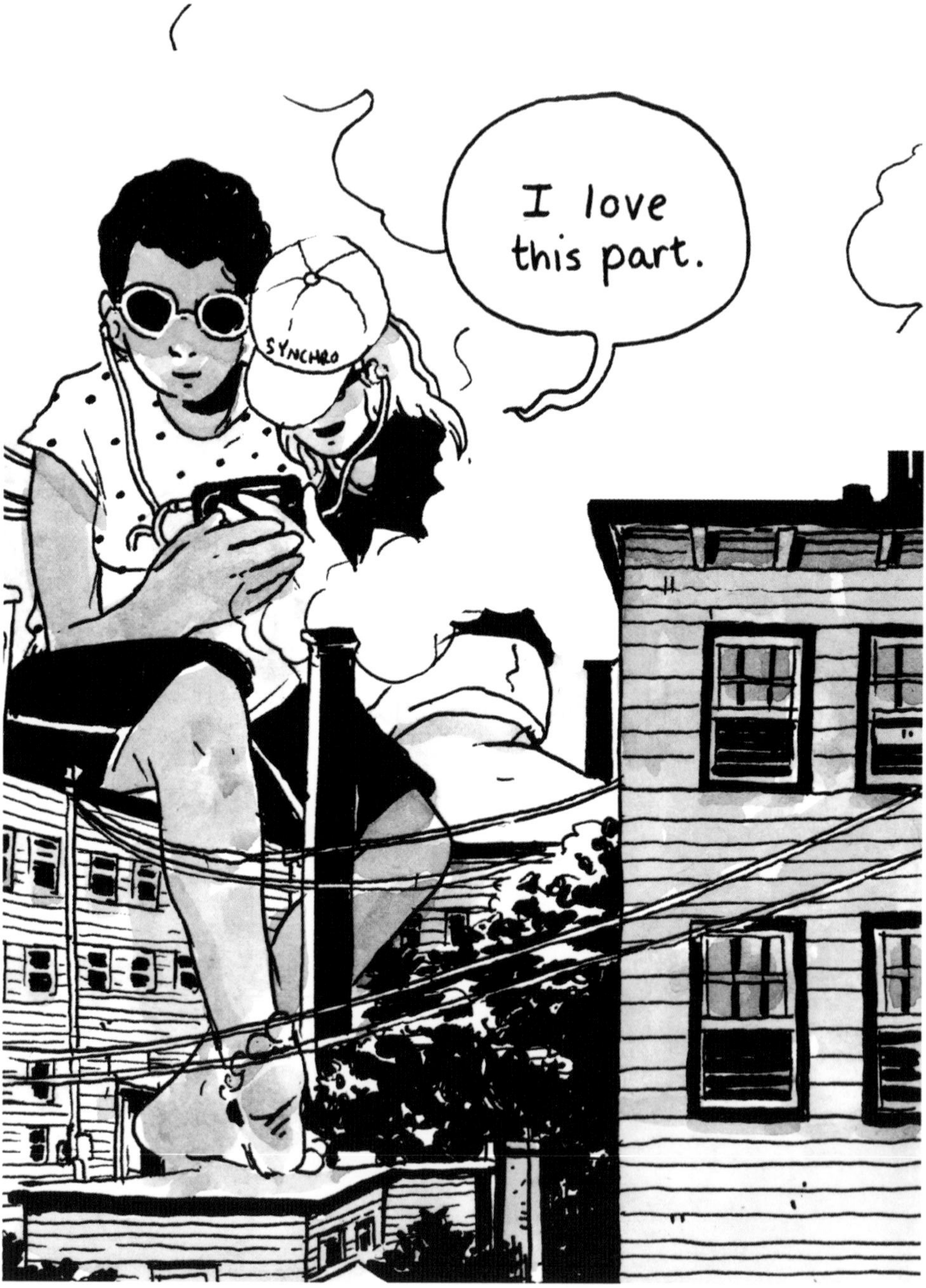
I love this part.
SYNCHRO

I Love This Part bookplate image (2015)

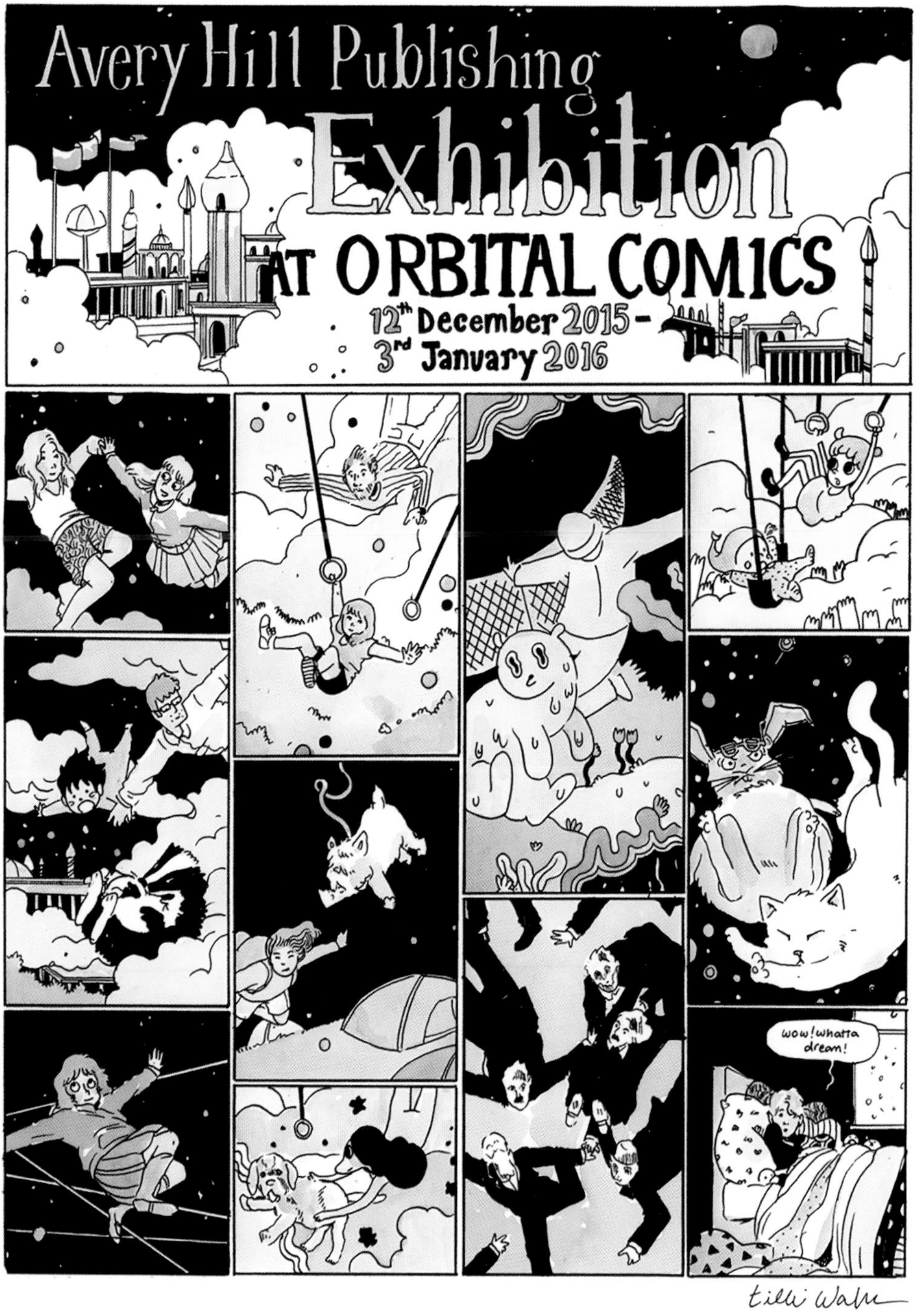
Avery Hill Publishing
Exhibition
AT ORBITAL COMICS
12th December 2015 -
3rd January 2016
wow! whatta dream!

Avery Hill Exhibition poster at Orbital Comics, London (2015)

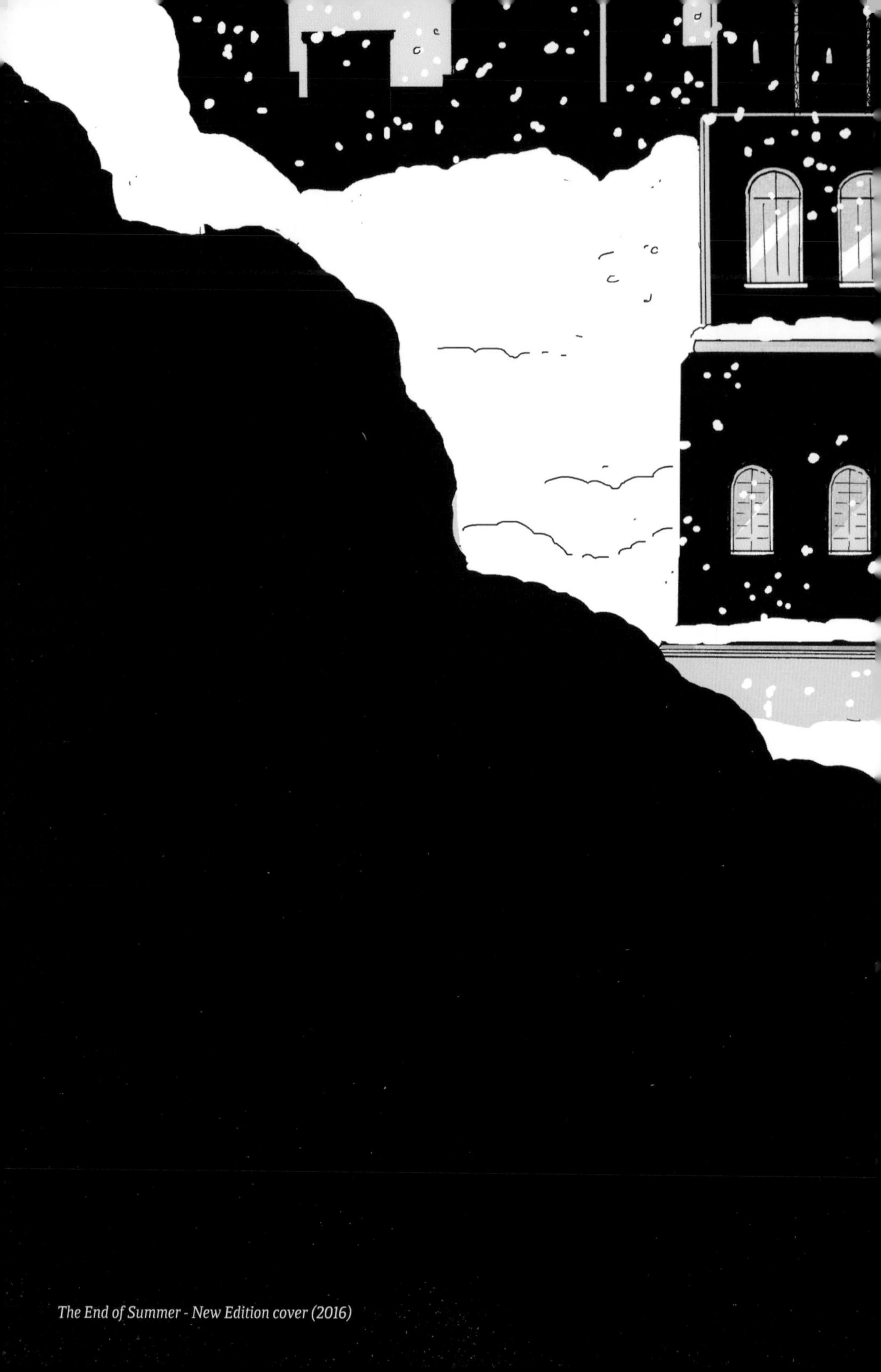

The End of Summer - New Edition cover (2016)

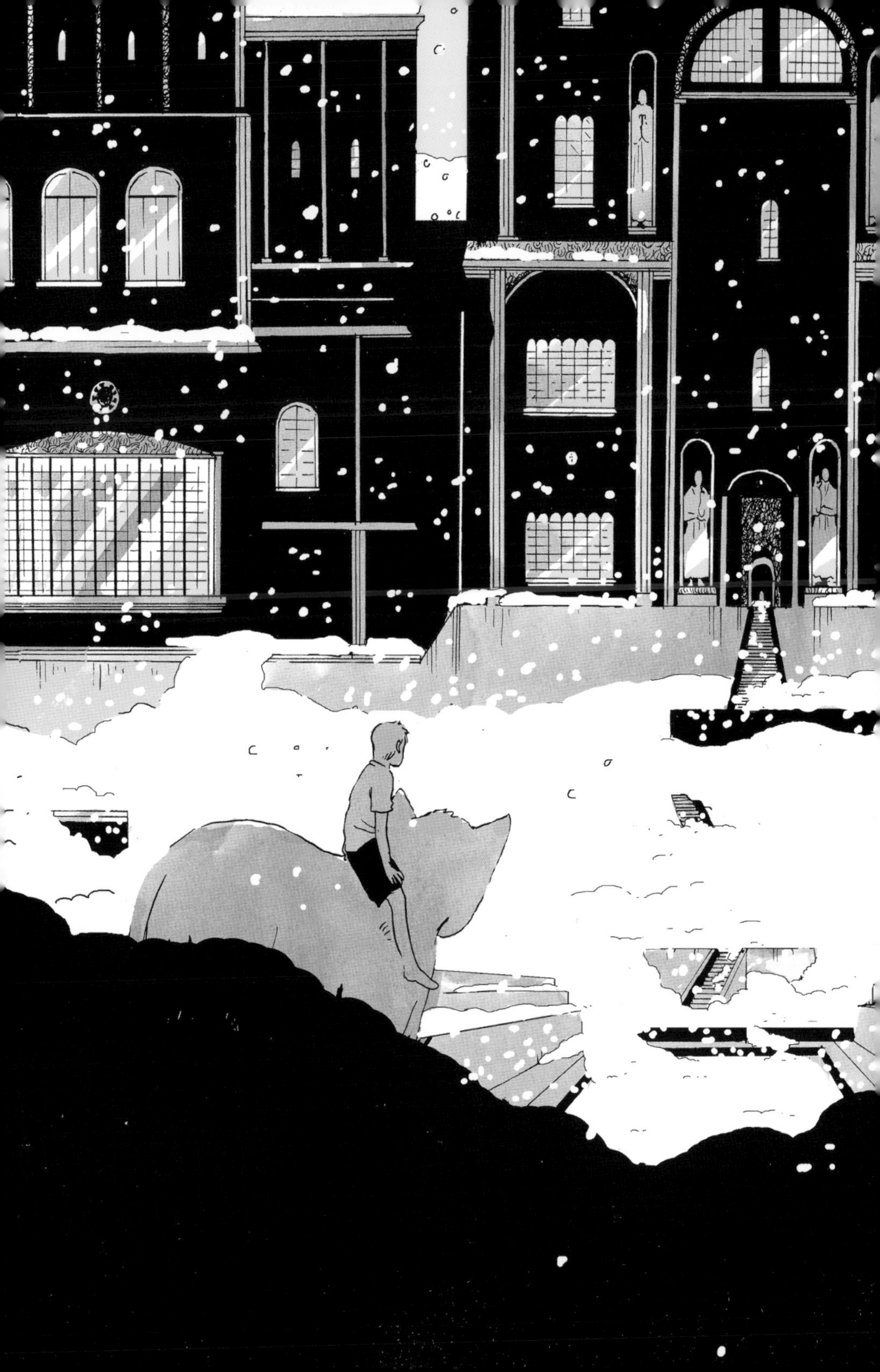

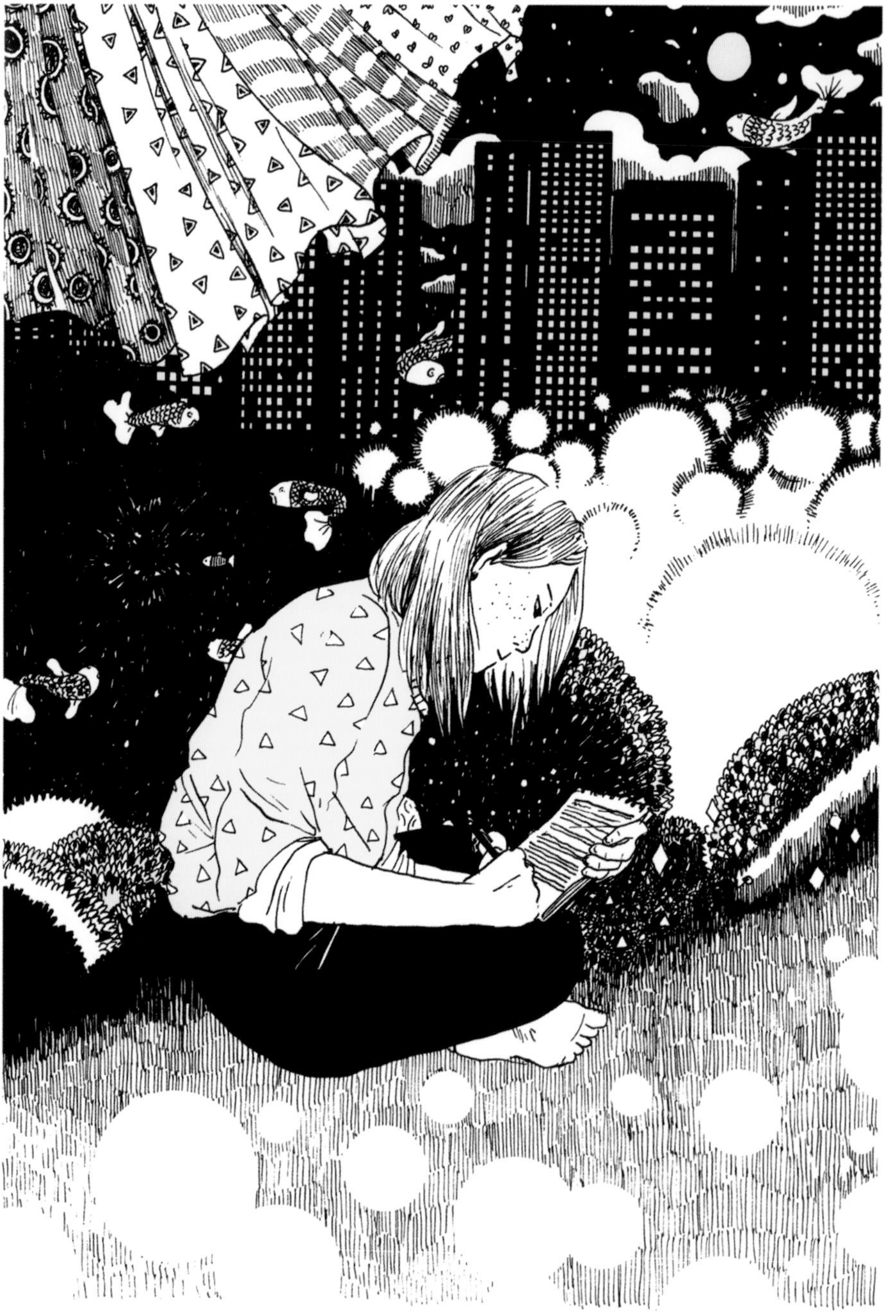

A City Inside bookplate image (2016)

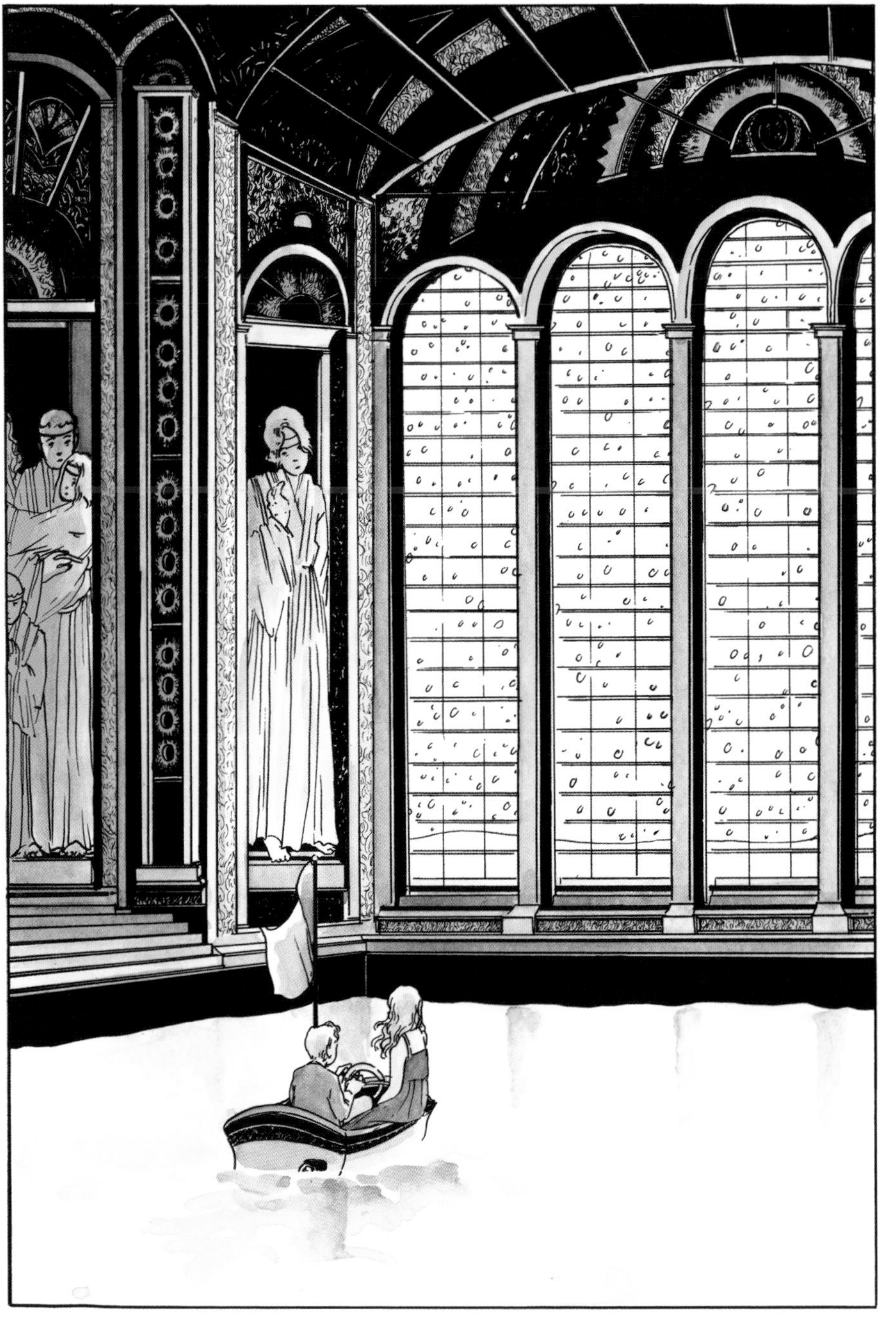

The End of Summer print for Gosh! Comics, London (2014)

tillie Walden is a cartoonist
and illustrator from Austin, Tx.
She first published 3 original graphic
novellas with Avery Hill Publishing
before going on to create her
Eisner Award winning graphic
memoir 'Spinning'. After 'Spinning' she
Created 'On a Sunbeam', which was
originally published as a webcomic
and is still available to read online
(for free.) Her latest graphic novel
'Are you Listening?' won the Eisner for
best graphic novel, and her first
picture book is due out in 2021.

She currently lives in Lebanon, New
Hampshire and teaches at the Center
for Cartoon Studies.

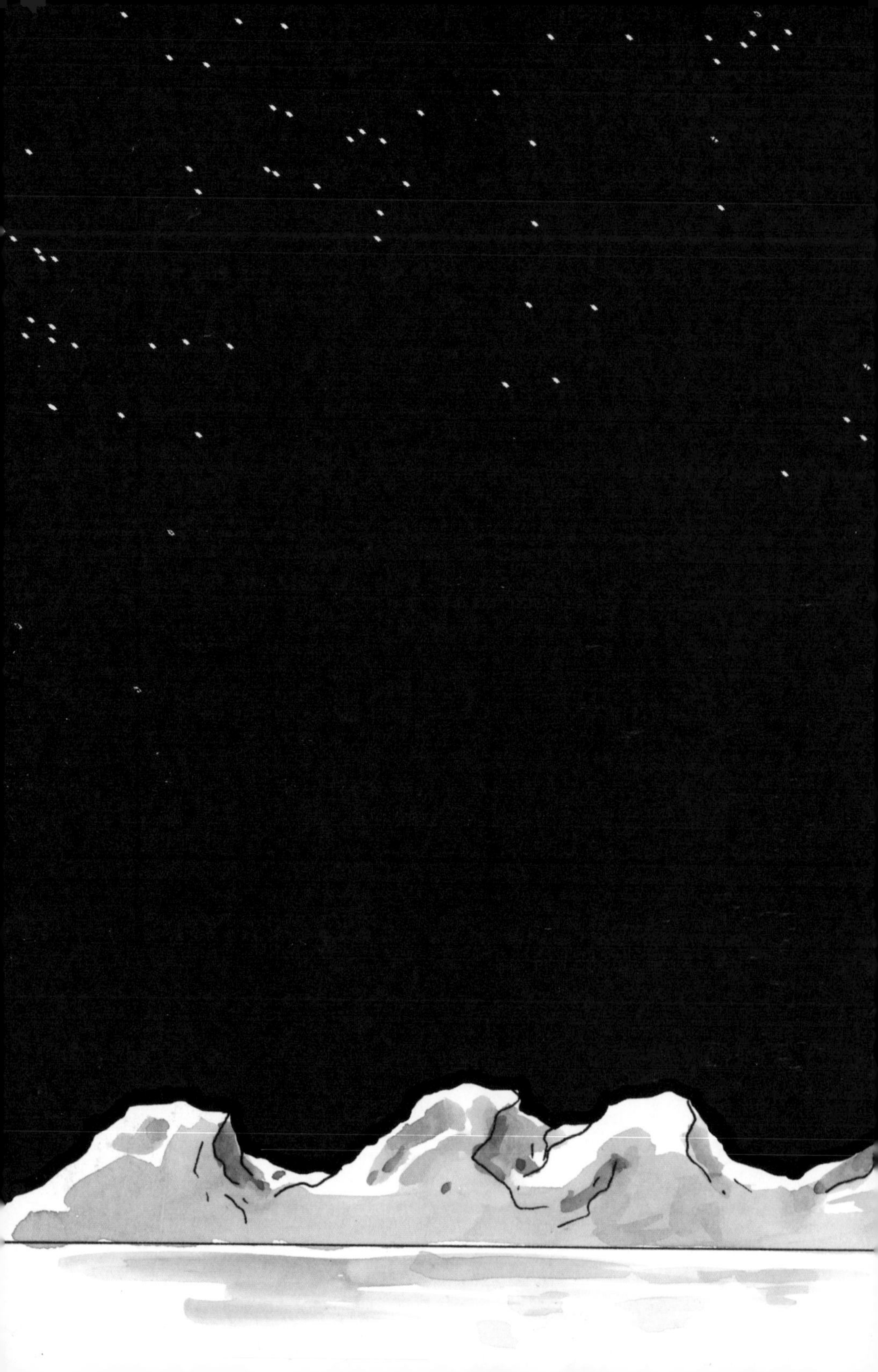